Praise for Works Performed at the Nuyorican

"I found *Hubba City** by Ishmael Reed fascina. . . . .
and the acting, strongly directed by Rome Neal, p   n-
viction."   *ost*

"Reed's technique is like Kurt Vonnegut's: taking f   to
their extreme logical conclusion."   —David Stewart, *Back Stage*

"*Hubba City* was phenomenal."   —Gina Kaufman, *The New York Beacon*

"Sometimes life seems to imitate art, and we can learn much from the comparison."
                                        —Playthell Benjamin (on *Hubba City*), *Daily News*

"History, legend and scandal are mingled provocatively by an effective cast. . . ."
    —Lawrence Van Gelder (on *The C Above High C* by Ishmael Reed), *The New York Times*

"I love this play [*The Preacher and the Rapper** by Ishmael Reed] and recommend any and all
who are concerned with our frazzled lines of communication to see it."
                                                —Reg E. Gaines, *Amsterdam News*

"*Life During Wartime** has the energy and intelligence of a crackling debate in which many su-
perimposed voices create a larger, more complex picture of strained social fabric. . . . Drives
into the heart of one of the most explosive issues a contemporary play could hope to confront."
                                                —Stephen Holden, *The New York Times*

"Wesley Brown's *Life During Wartime* is a work of sharp intelligence and bitter humor, cold re-
alism and warm compassion."   —Dan Hulbert, *The Atlanta Journal-Constitution*

"Alvin Eng's *The Goong Hay Kid** is a fine must-see play."
                                                —Yusef Salaam, *Amsterdam News*

"*Primitive World** leaps from its tiny stage singing, dancing, and glittering on a shoestring."
                                                —*The Village Voice*

"Director Rome Neal moves this fine ensemble around the small stage with amazing style and
creativity. . . . [*Primitive World* is] one of the best plays in two years."
                                —Quincy McCay, CD 101.9 (WQCD FM, New York City)

"Oh yes, there's a lot going on in this satirical play [*Primitive World*] and indeed through all of
'Theater at the End of the Millennium.' Baraka doesn't just tell stories. He offers his audience
themes, polemics, admonitions in the guise of stories."
                                                —Michael Sommers, *The Star-Ledger*

"*Meeting Lillie* is Baraka's reminder of [the] truth and an attempt at reintroducing the modern
audience conditioned by pop superficiality to the complications of heritage and the past. *Meeting Lillie* is a thesis play—with the stress on 'thesis'—an adversarial piece by a black writer
known for his maverick intransigence."   —Armand White, *City Sun*

"*General Hag's Skeezag* is Baraka at his best. . . . The acting is brisk and motivated, the script crackles with wit, sarcasm and astute, if cynical, observation . . . definitive Baraka."

—Abiola Sinclair, *Amsterdam News*

"You can go to the Nuyorican Poets Cafe and watch a piece of theatrical magic that probably cost no more than the price of your tickets—ten dollars. The production *Prism* by Alex McDonald . . . that's theatrical magic money can't buy." —Jack Temchin, *Our Town*

"*Shango de Ima* [by Pepe Carrill], described as a Yoruba mystery play being 'a ritual celebration of the seven African orishas,' [is] now being given a brilliantly orchestrated staging at the Nuyorican Poets Cafe." —Clive Barnes, *New York Post*

"The grand mythic sweep of *Shango de Ima* forces the realistic acting styles of [director Rome] Neal's company into a kind of fabulous mythic realm." —John Bell, *Theater Week*

"Under the title 'Theater at the End of the Millennium,' the Nuyorican Poets Cafe has started what promises to be one of the most rewarding seasons in its already important theatrical endeavors." —Alberto Mineiros, *Back Stage*

"Seguro que si Miguel Piñero y Joe Papp—cálidamente recordados en el espectáculo—pudieran dejar la eternidad por un segundo, se citarían en el Nuyorican Poets Cafe para *rapear* hasta el alba con la troupe de Miguel Algarín." —Alberto Mineiros, *El Diario/La Prensa*

"Nearly two years ago when I happened upon the Nuyorican Poets Cafe . . . I came away with the impression that this East Village cafe was arguably producing some of the best theater in New York." —Shannon Johnson, *The New York Beacon*

"In Manhattan's Lower East Side . . . there is an utterly brilliant diamond called the Nuyorican Poets Cafe." —Michael V. O'Neill, *Big Red News*

*Hubba City and *The Preacher and The Rapper* by Ishmael Reed, *Life During Wartime* by Wesley Brown, *The Goong Hay Kid* by Alvin Eng, and *Primitive World* by Amiri Baraka are all included in *Action: The Nuyorican Poets Cafe Theater Festival.*

Also from the Nuyorican Poets Cafe:

Aloud: The Nuyorican Poets Cafe Anthology

By Miguel Algarín:

Song of Protest
Body Bee Callin' from the 21st Century
Mongo Affair
Time's Now
On Call

By Lois Griffith

Among Others

Action

The Nuyorican Poets
Cafe Theater Festival

edited by
Miguel Algarín
and Lois Griffith

A Touchstone Book
Published by Simon & Schuster

TOUCHSTONE
Rockefeller Center
1230 Avenue of the Americas
New York, NY 10020

DESIGNED BY DEBORAH KERNER

Manufactured in the United States of America
10   9   8   7   6   5   4   3   2   1
Library of Congress Cataloging-in-Publication Data

Action : the Nuyorican Poets Cafe Theater Festival / edited by Miguel Algarín and Lois Griffith.
     p.   cm.
  "A Touchstone book."
  Anthology of plays performed at the Nuyorican Poets Cafe Theater Festival in New York City.
  1. American drama—Puerto Rican authors.   2. Puerto Ricans—New York (State)—New York—
Drama.   3. American Drama—New York (State)—New York.   4. American drama—20th century.
I. Algarín, Miguel.   II. Griffith, Lois.   III. Nuyorican Poets Cafe Theater Festival.
PS628.P84A28   1997
812'.5408097295—dc21   97-27602
                                                                                              CIP

ISBN 0-684-82611-9

Janis Astor del Valle, *Transplantations: Straight and Other Jackets Para Mí,* reprinted by permission of the author. Amiri Baraka, *Election Machine Warehouse* and *Primitive World: An Anti-Nuclear Jazz Musical,* reprinted by permission of the author. Wesley Brown, *Life During Wartime,* reprinted by permission of the author. Alvin Eng, *The Goong Hay Kid,* reprinted by permission of the author. Gloria Feliciano, *Between Blessings,* reprinted by permission of the author. Eva Gasteazora, *Amor de Mis Amores,* reprinted by permission of the author. Dennis Moritz, *Just the Boys,* reprinted by permission of the author. Frank Perez, *Special People of International Character,* reprinted by permission of the author. Pedro Pietri, *El Cabrón,* reprinted by permission of the author. Miguel Piñero, *Playland Blues,* reprinted by permission of the estate of Miguel Piñero. Ishmael Reed, *The Preacher and the Rapper, Hubba City,* and *Savage Wilds,* reprinted by permission of the author. Eugene Rodriguez, *Un Ghost,* reprinted by permission of the author. Carl Hancock Rux, *Chapter & Verse,* reprinted by permission of the author. Ntozake Shange, *I Live in Music,* reprinted by permission of the author. Peter Spiro, *Howya Doin' Franky Banana,* reprinted by permission of the author.

For Rome Neal
and Miguel Piñero

Many thanks to
the Nuyorican Poets Cafe
and to the actors, directors and staff
who bring the plays to life.

Contents

Foreword
Life Action

It's 1996 and I'm standing on East Third Street outside the Nuyorican Poets Cafe, observing the unfolding of some quintessential Nuyorican theater. It's a warm Friday night in May and the Cafe is crowded with people who have come to see the Poetry Slam, a mock competition among poets at which judges are chosen at random from the audience to rate the poems recited and to choose the best poet of the night.

Shut-Up Shelley is on stage with her cohost, Scott. They have been dressed by our resident costume designer Marcel Christian. Shelley is wearing the hat Madame Chairman wore in our production of Ishmael Reed's *The Preacher and the Rapper,* a wide brim straw hat, alive with every loud flower from a spring garden. Scott is a cross-dresser outfitted as a blue bunny with blue wig, blue ears, and blue feathered shift with boa. The poets on stage have aggressive styles of recitation, baiting the audience to be offended by provocative language. One poet recalls a 1960s riff by Gil Scott Heron about "The Revolution Will Not Be Televised." This updated version laments a revolutionary spirit with no revolution to engage him.

Outside the Cafe on the street, Julio's new wife catches him with Gladys, his ex-girlfriend. His wife goes off, claiming disrespect, demanding the keys to their apartment so that Julio will be locked out for the night. Simultaneously, some poetry lovers who have come from New Jersey are battling, accusing each other of flirtations each has carried on inside the room while listening to a lesbian poet's inflammatory verses about the power of pussy. The Jersey girlfriend tries to run away from her Jersey boyfriend. The boyfriend goes after her, captures her, picks her up, tosses her over his shoulder, and throws her into their Mercedes parked in front of the Cafe. He locks the car doors and she pounds her fists against the window because she is drunk and has to go to the bathroom. He lets her out of the car and wants to escort her to the bathroom and stand by to watch as she pees—to make sure that is all she's doing. They're out of control and there's not even a full moon.

It was 1973 when Miguel Piñero taught me about theater. Miky could stand on a street corner, gather a crowd around him, and spit out a poem that induced action from an audience—an audience completely unaware that their response was creating drama about the intensity of everyday life.

Standing outside the Cafe on that warm Friday night in May, I think I'm seeing a revival of some minor theater piece staged by Miguel Piñero. Drama, passion, love betrayed—broken trust and deception get played out on the night streets. Police arrive in a squad car, driving the wrong way down the one-way street, but they resist the impulse to intervene and take off. Then, the plain-clothes back-ups arrive in their unmarked Ford to watch the denouement. A bunch of backpackers from some other country, who have heard about the Cafe as a lively cultural spot, ignore the performance and negotiate a group entrance rate with our house manager. They just want to hear some good poetry.

All creative writing teachers hand their students the same tired line: "Write about what you know." I think that sometimes I don't know what I know. Real life shoves its ass in my face. I'm not always ready to embrace it. The journey from the street corner to the page is full of potholes. Images of purple sunsets, the abandon of palms dancing in the tradewinds are natural phenomena that color the stories of my Caribbean ancestors. My cityscape is painted in spit, blood, and curses that depict the devil as the uniformed accomplice in the murder of innocence. Theater captures life's intent from moments when we confront our motives for action.

The first theater production I was ever involved in was a piece written by Miguel Algarín, *The Murder of Pito.* The play was based on an incident that happened in the subway. A *congero* drumming in the subway was killed by a cop, whose rationale was that the youth was disturbing the peace. The account of the murder was related to Algarín by the poet Sandra Maria Estevez, who came to him in the middle of the night to spill the details of the confrontation she had witnessed. Algarín turned life into art to protest an injustice that law enforcement authorities considered just an episode in which an officer dealt with an unruly, young Latino who was a public nuisance.

In real life the police denied responsibility for the death of Tito Perez. The stories about the alleged suicide of the drummer in police custody were buried on the back pages of the New York dailies, along with the outcry of the city's Latino community.

At the Nuyorican Poets Cafe, our theater exists to document the history of our passions. For more than twenty-two years and in more than fifty productions, our theater has recorded the accumulated questions surrounding our understanding of events. To entertain and instruct becomes the mission of the dramatist. Somewhere between the artist's composition and the facts of the occurrence lies the truth. Respect for the social fabric compels us to find a nonviolent redress for our outrage. The repression of anger, pain, confusion, and bitterness can only restrict our evolution.

My part in creating *The Murder of Pito* was as one of the set designers. In 1974, before I had discovered writing, my creative expression took shape in the visual arts, painting and drawing. My task was to recreate the interior of Miguel Algarín's railroad flat for our small stage in the storefront space that was then the location of the Nuyorican Poets Cafe. To inspire my work, Miguel put into my hands some Mayan artifacts that he had brought back from a trip to Mexico. I fingered the small, carved stones. One was of Quetzalcoatl, the winged serpent. Another was of a figure that was both male and female.

These stones spoke to me in a way that ancient things speak to us—through their auras in which are infused the histories of lost times. If we are receptive, sometimes these ancient witnesses awaken our imaginations. For the set of the play we built a loft bed like the one Miguel had in his apartment. I painted a trompe l'oeil window with the view of the backyard from the apartment. I painted a mural that evoked images of the ancient Mayan mythologies—the plumed serpent, the hermaphrodite, the conception of the white man who would alter the landscape with his vision of progress.

Raul Santiago Sebazco, the other set designer, painted another mural of the interior of a subway car.

The play ran through the summer months of 1974 and was not reviewed in any major publication. Miguel "Lobo" Loperena was cast as Mitch, through whom we learn of the murder of Pito. Thea Martínez played Sandy, Pito's girlfriend, who comes to Mitch in the middle of the night with the account of the murder. Luis Guzman was Frenzy, the Cop, who appears at Mitch's door to menace him after learning that Sandy, a witness to the crime, has sought Mitch's counsel.

Seventeen years after presenting *The Murder of Pito,* we produced *Life During Wartime* by Wesley Brown, a piece based on the death of New York City graffiti artist Michael Stewart. This was another incident in which a young man of color met a questionable death while in police custody. The drama directed by Rome Neal, who has become our resident director, directing and staging almost all our theater pieces, received rave reviews in *The New York Times, Amsterdam News, The Village Voice,* the *Daily News,* and the *New York Post.* But, in many ways, this piece made us review our mission as theater producers. For many years we had worked to develop a style of theater that not only attempts to entertain audiences but also to address the controversial issues of our times. For many years we had worked without the endorsement of the powerful New York City critics who so often determine the financial success of productions. After so many years of doing what we always did, our efforts were being loudly acclaimed, and I felt confused by the attention.

Of course, part of the magic of theater is the communion between audiences and actors on stage. No two performances are ever the same. Each audience influences what transpires with a collective energy that affects the actors response to the lines guiding their actions. I have seen innumerable performances of our production of Pepe Carril's *Shango de Ima,* a play that brings to life the complex mythology of the Yoruba gods, whose religion was introduced to this hemisphere by African slaves. I have seen audiences view the play with the kind of seriousness attendant a Greek tragedy by Euripides. I have seen audiences transfixed by the humor and sportive nature of the piece, inspiring the actors to reveal more fully the depths of the play's message—that, ultimately, we create our gods in our own image.

A critic reviewing a play may see a performance on a night when, unfortunately, the audience is filled with deadbeats unable to respond to the presentation. Needless to say, the actors' performances and the subsequent review will reflect this.

In writing intelligently about theater, it seems to me that certain considerations should be taken into account, primarily that of the controlling vision of the producers, an aspect that is often overlooked and not questioned by critics. The obvious question often goes unasked: Why was this particular theater piece brought to the stage at this particular moment in history, given the enormous effort, the numerous manpower hours, and the economic factors involved in mounting any show?

A staff critic of *The New York Times* once described the style of theater presented by the Nuyorican Poets Cafe as "smart and snappy," which is as close as I've seen to a contemporary critic's addressing the issue of production vision.

Theater producers must have their fingers on the pulse of their times, if what they do is to have validity as an emblem of the culture out of which they have emerged, and if what they do is to reflect universal human concerns embodied in that cultural emblem. Choice is everything.

Miguel Algarín founded the Nuyorican Poets Cafe in 1973. He rented a storefront bar on East Sixth Street across from the railroad flat where he lived. His apartment had become overrun at all hours of the day by the poets, writers, actors, artists, and hangers-on who made up the community of creative movers and shakers that needed a central place to congregate, perform, develop, and exchange their energies. On Halloween, he opened the doors of the Cafe with the vision that he would nurture and display the talents of the best of those voices, especially of the underclass, dedicated to shaping American culture. He was aware that what is offbeat and cutting edge today is what becomes the substance of tomorrow's mainstream.

Miguel Piñero, Lucky Cienfuegos, Richard August, Willie Correa, Miguel Loperena, and myself worked with Algarín to make the Cafe a reality—a place that was open to the public three days a week, every week, year in and year out. When the Cafe was founded, Miguel Piñero was having an enormous success with his play *Short Eyes,* which was produced by Joseph Papp at the Public Theater and then at the Vivien Beaumont Theater at Lincoln Center. The play was a reflection of Miky's prison experiences where he had been introduced to theater by Marvin Felix Camillo. Marvin had created an ensemble of actors and writers, The Family. With him, The Family conducted workshops in prisons, making converts of people like Miky to the power of the arts.

The brilliance of Miky's poetic voice and his understanding of dramatic form brought us all international critical acclaim and attention. Never before had a Puerto Rican writer gained such recognition. Miky was a complicated man: an outlaw, a junkie, a notorious lover of both women and men, an artistic genius. When I first met him, I remember I was wearing a blouse that exposed my shoulders. He ran his hands over my bare skin, said something about *chula.* I took a step backward, smiled, and looked into his eyes, sensing that to be involved, body and soul, with this man might mean my death, or at least lead me to the edge of a nervous breakdown.

A year later I was to witness the breakdown of Sugar Saralegui, a young woman who had become involved with him, body and soul. He had written a theater piece called *Side Show* in which she had starred. She was sixteen at the time and crazy in love with Miky. Her father found out about the affair and she ran away from home. To put an end to the relationship, her father had her locked up in a mental ward in Bellevue Hospital for six months.

I remember the night the medics came to take her away. They had been chasing her through the streets of the Lower East Side when finally she ran into the Cafe as if it were a temple where she might find sanctuary. She must have been looking for Miky, but he was out of town at the time. I remember the medics coming into the Cafe on East Sixth Street, wrestling her into a straight jacket, and dragging her out to the waiting ambulance—a real-life drama etched in my psyche that has yet to be documented on the page.

This idea of the coincidence of life and art has been a hallmark of our theater productions at the Cafe. The reality of our circumstance—that we are located on the Lower East Side, a neighborhood that is an intersection point for Latino, Afro-

American, Asian, Italian, and Eastern European peoples—necessitates the making of our presentations relevant to these diverse communities. Yet, an underlying theme in all of our choices has been one in which, on some level, protagonists come into conflict with dominant power structures.

In Pete Spiro's play, *How Ya Doin' Frankie Banana?*, Italian Americans break trust with each other in a ruthless effort to maintain a brutal hold over the direction of their own lives. In Alvin Eng's *The Goong Hay Kid*, a Chinese American who is a product of contemporary rock 'n' roll culture attempts to define his unique identity in a world that denies his claim on the very culture that has spawned him. In Ishmael Reed's *Hubba City*, we follow the struggle of ordinary citizens combatting drug trafficking in their neighborhood. They are forced to take matters into their own hands when they discover that it is the very agents of the law who are responsible for the lawlessness that has communities under siege. In one of my own pieces, a choreopoem, *White Sirens*, I attempted to demonstrate the insidious affects of racism on the life of a Caribbean woman. Raul Santiago Sebazco's work *The Crime* is a piece that was developed in collaboration with the same disenfranchised youth whose story it documents, and heralds the emergence of hip-hop culture's rappers.

In 1982, two years after we bought the building at 236 East Third Street from Ellen Stewart of La Mama Theater and moved the Nuyorican Poets Cafe into its current home, Miky wrote the play *Nuyorican Nights*, which records the struggle of a group of people, tightly knit—almost like a family—and drawn together by the desire to create theater. He immortalized us by giving the characters our names—our personalities, our motivations. In seeing his image of me embodied on stage, I wondered at my own transparency—that the work that has occupied so much of my time on this planet has been a love affair with Miguel Algarín and his vision of art as the receptacle for the intensities of a passionate life.

—Lois Elaine Griffith
Brooklyn, New York
May 1996

Introduction by Miguel Algarín

IN 1990, I WAS STANDING AT THE EDGE OF THE BAR WHEN THE SECOND ACT BEGAN. IT had been an uneventful performance. Nothing new. The adaption of *Hedda Gabler* by Ibsen was going along as expected. It was then that I noticed a change in what we in the theater call blocking, that is, people onstage weren't standing where they were supposed to be standing. At first I thought some changes I hadn't been told about had been introduced into the scene. The audience seemed enthralled. Among these surprise changes, I noticed that Charlene Frederika Bletson, who was directing the piece, managing the stage, and simultaneously acting in a role, was not moving. As it turned out, seven minutes had elapsed, during which Madeline Barchevska, who'd been playing the role of Hedda Gabler, had been trying to resuscitate Charlene. This was indeed a change in plans, but it wasn't exactly what we'd thought. Madeline called for help and I immediately went to her. At the same moment the front door of the Cafe burst open to the sound of wailing sirens and flashing lights. Medics rushed in with all their EMS paraphanalia. I realized that Charlene Frederika Bletson was dead.

Charlene had walked onto the stage right on cue. She had raised her hand, pronounced her lines and then promptly swooned. She slumped to the floor looking completely at ease. We saw not a grotesque figure, face contorted, but a woman beautifully at rest. She didn't seem to have been in any agonizing pain. When the medical emergency unit began to apply electric shock, Charlene's body jolted and the audience seemed to emit a collective sigh of relief, thinking our tragic heroine had been revived. I then realized that in all the commotion, seemingly perfectly timed, as if it had been a planned scene, the audience had thought they were witnessing a choreographed theatrical moment. It took them a moment or two to digest that instead, what they had just witnessed was the death of Charlene Frederika Bletson.

From the stage, I looked up from Charlene's body and asked everyone in the audience to step into the backyard or to the front of the Cafe while we prepared the stage to continue. No one had officially pronounced Charlene dead, but judging from the looks being exchanged among the emergency personnel, I could tell that their attempts to revive her heart had failed. I think it was safe to say our performance of *Hedda Gabler* had ended, and we had reentered the real world, the world theater seeks to emulate.

After the emergency personnel had removed the body, I went into the backyard and brought people back to their seats, then I walked to the sidewalk in front of the Cafe and ushered that part of the audience back in. With everyone reseated, I announced that Charlene Frederika Bletson had passed. I told them that their money would be refunded at the door. I asked them to please be patient during this transaction, since it would no doubt go slowly. I asked them to show respect for the woman who had died onstage, before our very eyes.

What happened next was unexpected. Instead of lining up to ask for their money back, the audience sat very still. The two minutes that elapsed felt like an hour to me. A person in the audience stood up, took her hat, and suggested that everyone give a donation. The hat was circulated throughout the audience with the whole house still sitting; it had become a spontaneous collection for the burial of Charlene.

The Nuyorican Poets Cafe Theater Festival was started so that all actors of color could drop the bandanas wrapped around their heads, pull the razors out of their pockets and the knives from their jackets, and just act. At the Cafe they auditioned for roles that had substance, knowing they would not be stereotyped into the familiar urban guerilla war front image. We looked to portray the life characterized by urban decay, but after first locating the real pulse of the street. We looked for where the street drama was and who could write about it. Truth first, then theater. Actors benefitted from this process, because they were never asked to devalue their experience and backgrounds by playing *West Side Story* over and over. We looked for theatrical language that realistically portrayed life on Avenues D, C, B, and A, unlike the Hollywood versions epitomized by *Kojak* or *Baretta*. It worked as theater, but it also gave us the means to exorcise the pain of our lives. Theater as catharsis.

It was Mel Gussow, theater critic from *The New York Times,* who said to me that the most direct route out of the ghetto via the arts was to write a successful piece of theater. He said this to me in connection with the Miguel Piñero play *Short Eyes,* and while I was struck by his comment at the time, I rejected its validity. I know that only once in a very great while would a playwright break out into the commercial world. It was enough of a mission for us simply to commission works that came from the roots of the community surrounding the Nuyorican Poets Cafe, without concerning ourselves with whether each of us had a Broadway play in our veins. And for a time, we valued message over artistic value: it took time to integrate those two goals. Now, I can agree with him on one point: economically, the only way out of the urban ghettoes for 99.9 percent of our young people is a miracle, be it writing a major play, or the alternative, which is trafficking the contraband. Few of our young get a choice of destinies.

When a people are oppressed, the only way to hold their cultural space is to start talking. Language is inherently biased against people of color—I mean literally how the nouns, adjectives, and verbs work internally to show people their place in society. What language communicates to people who have already been put down is how society regards them; in their case, often with little respect. But a play provides a distance from which to view these sinister tricks of language. Plays can also bond people. That is why when I commission work from such writers as Frank Perez, Eugene Rodriguez, Amiri Baraka, and Ishmael Reed, I ask them for work that is written in words that do not feed these stereotypes. Rather, I ask them for plays that will open doors, showing audiences ways out of these debilitating linguistic traps.

At first the theatrical pieces that came from the community were naive and simple. We created productions out of the rawest material, plays that showed our collective victimization by the system. We knew that eventually, with enough exposure to the-

ater, the writers at the Cafe would grow. They would write good theater without aban-
doning the living source of the material, which is their lives and the lives of the people around them.

We saw how Ntozake Shange's poems, when read aloud, had the potential of becoming theater in the hands of the right director. We found that the lifting of poetry
to theater was not only possible but was a rich mine for our tapping. In the case of
Shange, her poems were structured into a significant story line and then these "choreo-
poems" traveled from the Cafe to a small bar nearby—the Del Monte on East Third
Street. The rest was history. Off-Broadway producer Woody King saw it and decided
to produce what was to become the Broadway-bound *for colored girls who have con-
templated suicide / when the rainbow is enuf.*

Ms. Shange's work was not the first to make that transition from the Nuyorican to
a more commercial venue. Miguel Piñero's *Short Eyes* had done it earlier when it
moved from the Riverside Church to the Public Theater and then to the Vivian Beaumont at Lincoln Center. This movement from nonprofit community theaters to
commercial Broadway productions is almost inevitably profitable, proving, not inci-
dentally, that nonprofit work originating from local communities can achieve commercial success. Not-for-profit theater as a rule is viewed as being fourth rate, but this
is far from always so. The last twenty years have proven that the not-for-profit sector
can produce rich and vastly innovative theater for the marquees of Broadway. Ntozake
Shange's and Miguel Piñero's successful moves to Broadway were followed by Rei
Provod's, whose first play *Cries and Shouts* was produced and directed by me at the
Nuyorican. It was also at the Cafe that Mr. Provod gave a reading of *Cuba and His
Teddy Bear* under his own direction. This work was later produced at the Public Theater by Joseph Papp and then moved to Broadway, with Robert DeNiro, Burt Young,
and Ralph Maccio in the starring roles. In fact, the work of the Nuyorican Poets Cafe
and other off-off-Broadway theater has proven that what succeeds on Broadway can
also be honest and "relevant."

These days, the selection of new work for every season for the Nuyorican depends
on Rome Neal and me. It is our joint responsibility to search for writers in our community whose plays feel real, both on the street level and in that mythological zone ex-
emplified by Pepe Carrill's *Shango de Ima,* which portrays the seven Yoruba saints in
their daily lives, arguing and competing with each other in an attempt to rule human
affection, politics, and feelings. In working with such new and exciting material,
Rome Neal and I find that it is better to have the season shape itself around a purpose,
an organic direction that is nevertheless constructed, that is instructive and entertaining at once. Rome has become a master at taking what is at first didactic work and
turning it around to squeeze the human and artistic juice out of the rhetoric. I have
worked with him now for at least two decades, and he is probably the most accomplished director I've ever worked with. Rome Neal demonstrates over and over again
his own willingness to travel into unknown territory and come out the other end with
a solid piece of theater. Whenever things seem to be falling apart, Mr. Neal steps in.
He has the talent to simultaneously design lighting and sets, and to direct. He is also
a gifted actor with the capacity to re-create a character on stage. Therefore, it isn't rare
to find Rome taking lighting, directing, and acting over whenever actors or techni-

cians have not been able to perform, or when the rules and regulations of Actors Equity make it impossible for an actor to continue performing in a popular run. He can step into any open hole and fill it with his presence and his complete command of theater. He makes sure that the action in the play is applicable to daily living and that it reflects the here and now of our audience. What Mr. Neal and I do, we hope, is to delight and challenge our audiences, while always keeping theater accessible.

I

Inner City Tragedy and Politics

Life During Wartime

Wesley Brown

CHARACTERS

Rhapsody: *A young black man of about twenty. He is brash and given to a great deal of self-dramatization.*

Eleanor Cummings: *A black woman in her mid to late forties. She has a biting wit and warms easily to any opportunities for conversation or argument.*

Avery Cummings: *A black man of about fifty. His personality is somewhat laid back but he is emotionally very high-strung.*

Cassandra Cummings: *An eighteen- or nineteen-year-old black woman. She is precocious and confused as is often the case with someone her age.*

Wanda Waples: *A black woman of about forty. She is an anchorwoman on a local television news program.*

Bernice Hightower: *A black woman of about forty who is a lawyer.*

1st Woman: *A black woman in her forties.*

2nd Woman: *A white woman in her thirties.*

Policeman: *A white man in his thirties.*

Time: *The end of the 1980s.*

Place: *A New York City subway station and the living room of the Cummings's home.*

Act 1: Scene 1

(Ella Fitzgerald's rendition of Harold Arlen's "Ill Wind" is heard as light comes up on stage that is a portion of a subway platform that leads into the living room of an apartment. Four people are on the platform: a black woman in her forties, a white woman in her thirties, a young black man in his early twenties holding a huge radio, and a white transit authority policeman. There are three people in the apartment: a black man and woman in their middle to late forties slouched down on a couch and a black teenaged girl at the periphery of the living room at stage right. Everyone on the subway platform is cautious and tentative in their movements. The needle sticks on a scratch in the record and everyone is still as in a freeze frame with expressions ranging from distress to grief. Light dims on the apartment and comes up on the young black man with the radio. The beat from the radio booms as the young man begins his rap over the sound.)

RHAPSODY: My name is Rhapsody/and if you ain't hip to me/
I'm an all-day tripper on the IRT./From Two Forty-deuce to South Ferry
I go back and forth/I'm in no hurry./To get the 411 on what the city's about/
you gotta be down with the subway where it all hangs out./So if you wanna get
the lowdown beyond skin deep/just listen to me for an exclusive peep. . . .

(He reacts as though someone has interrupted him.)

RHAPSODY: What's that? You want me to turn it down? Oh! *(Turns down volume of radio)* What do you wanna talk about? *(Looks at audience as though he is being questioned by someone)* Yeah, I knew him as Fly. He was a writer and used Fly as the tag on all his masterpieces. Oh? That's what you would call graffiti. We lived in the same part of Harlem near Morningside Park. He worked as a waiter at this club where I dee-jayed sometimes. That night we walked to the subway together . . . course we paid our fare. It's against the law to get on the subway without paying. I didn't really see when he put his tag on the wall . . . I don't know if he was drinking. I was the deejay not the bartender . . . yeah, he was pissed. But that's cause he was being harassed. . . . If you know what happened, then what are you talking to me for?

(Light goes down on RHAPSODY.*)*

Act 1: Scene 2

(A door slams. Light goes down on RHAPSODY *and comes up on apartment with young teenaged girl and her parents sitting in the living room. The man jumps up but is restrained by woman's voice.)*

ELEANOR: Let him go, Avery.

AVERY: Can you believe that? He just gets up and walks out.

ELEANOR: Well. You always told him that sometimes the best way to avoid trouble was to walk away.

AVERY: I'm not trouble! I'm his father!

ELEANOR: Lately, he seems to be confusing the two.

AVERY: You know, I can always tell when you're scared. You have an answer for everything.

ELEANOR: And you're not scared?

AVERY: I didn't say that. I just couldn't sit here and let him get away with the things he was saying.

ELEANOR: He's not getting away with anything, Avery. He's already gone.

AVERY: Spare me all the rope tricks with words, okay?

ELEANOR: I think I may be the next person to walk out of this house.

AVERY: What's wrong? I hurt your feelings too?

ELEANOR: No. But I'm about to hurt yours.

CASSANDRA: Why don't you two stop it!

ELEANOR: What's the matter with you?

CASSANDRA: I'm still here. Remember? But you're not interested in what happened to me! *(Gets up and stalks out of the room.)*

AVERY: Well, now that we've gotten rid of the children, where were we?

ELEANOR: About to hurt each other.

(Light goes down on AVERY *and* ELEANOR *looking at one another and communicating a wordless hostility.)*

Act 1: Scene 3

(Light comes up on BERNICE *and* CASSANDRA.)

BERNICE: I just called your folks. They're on their way. . . . Why did you have the police call me?

CASSANDRA: You're a friend of my parents and sometimes you even talk to me.

BERNICE: What's wrong, Cass? Trouble at home?

CASSANDRA: I guess you could say that.

BERNICE: Have you talked to your folks about it?

CASSANDRA: Yeah, but they can't hear me.

BERNICE: Cass. What were you doing in that train yard?

CASSANDRA: I was taking a walk.

BERNICE: I can take a walk right now, if that's what you want.

CASSANDRA: Okay! Okay! I was there to spray paint trains.

BERNICE: Were you alone?

CASSANDRA: *(Indignant)* I'm the only one the police arrested.

BERNICE: That's not what I asked you.

CASSANDRA: *(Beat)* I was alone. It was a real breakthrough for me. I finally did something without Darryl.

BERNICE: *(Angry)* This is no joke! You're being charged with criminal trespassing. Do you know what that means?

CASSANDRA: *(Distracted by another thought)* I guess I always knew it would happen eventually. But not this way.

BERNICE: I'm not following you, Cass.

CASSANDRA: What?

(Light goes down on BERNICE *and* CASSANDRA.)*

Act 1: Scene 4

(Light comes up on a black woman who is at an imaginary news desk. She is impeccably dressed and her makeup is flawless. She delivers the news in a dispassionate manner.)

VOICE: This is the evening edition of Newsbusters with Wanda Waples.

WANDA: Good evening. Today's top story is the opening of the grand jury investigation into the death of Darryl Cummings who was arrested last week for allegedly drawing graffiti on the wall of the West Twenty-third Street subway station. A controversy has raged over the cause of Darryl Cummings's death. The Cummings family and several prominent black leaders have charged that Darryl was beaten to death while in police custody. Police spokespersons have denied these charges, stating that Cummings collapsed after his arrest and was taken to a hospital where he died of an apparent heart attack. Bernice Hightower, director of Lawyers for Social Justice and the attorney for the Cummings family, held a news conference today to discuss the grand jury investigation.

(Light comes up on a black woman standing in front of several microphones.)

BERNICE: Since the preliminary report from the County Medical Examiner's Office found no evidence of physical injury to Darryl Cummings, we will be following the deliberations of the Grand Jury very closely. It is our contention that the murder of Darryl Cummings is part of a pattern that has resulted in over three hundred police-related killings of blacks since 1977. And in that time, not one police officer has ever been convicted of any wrongdoing. This shocking statistic should leave no doubt in anyone's mind that black life is not valued in this city.

(Light comes up again on WANDA.)

WANDA: Spokespersons for the Transit Authority police and the Medical Examiner refused to comment further on the case until the Grand Jury has completed its deliberations. And in another Newsbuster story, Indian summer continues to hold the city hostage with record-breaking temperatures. . . .

(Light goes down on WANDA.)

Act 1: Scene 5

(Light comes up on subway platform with RHAPSODY, the POLICEMAN, the FIRST WOMAN, and the SECOND WOMAN exhibiting a wariness of one another. Spotlight is on FIRST WOMAN as she and the others answer questions from an imaginary interrogator. RHAPSODY and the POLICEMAN go through a stylized re-enactment of what the women describe with lighting used for effect.)

1ST WOMAN: *(Wearing a nurse's uniform)* I come that way all the time when I get off from work.

2ND WOMAN: I'd had dinner with friends and was trying to get a cab home.

1ST WOMAN: He walked past me toward the end of the platform. I looked in his direction a few times so I'd know where he was. It had nothing to do with him, personally, except that he was a man. And I pay a lot more attention to what's going on around me when I'm alone.

2ND WOMAN: I didn't even see anything until I heard him screaming. He was surrounded by police but I could see him jerking his head with these very long dreadlocks whipping back and forth. It looked like the police were trying to restrain him. It was very upsetting to watch. I wish I hadn't seen it.

1ST WOMAN: The next thing I knew, he and the cop were in a shouting match. I kept asking myself: Why doesn't he keep quiet? Because the more he shouted, the angrier the cop got. But it was like he didn't care.

POLICEMAN: I arrived on the scene after a call came in that a black adult male had not paid his fare. As I walked toward the end of the platform, I saw a black male defacing a billboard with what looked like a magic marker. I called out to him and he immediately started shouting obscenities and creating a disturbance. When he refused to calm down, I placed him under arrest. I had him stand with his legs spread apart and his hands against the wall. I searched him and then handcuffed him. If he hadn't been so belligerent, I would've only given him a summons. But he wanted to be a tough guy.

RHAPSODY: I'd a been pissed too, if it was me. The cop moved on Fly when he saw him putting his tag on the wall. He started calling him all out of his name, using a lot of mf's and getting all up in his face. So when Fly dissed him right back, the cop busted him.

(Light goes down on RHAPSODY.*)*

Act 1: Scene 6

(Light comes up in living room. AVERY *and* ELEANOR *are looking at a family photo album, covering the various stages in the childhood of* DARRYL *and* CASSANDRA.*)*

ELEANOR: Look at him! Always so fearless.

AVERY: Yeah. Looking like he was supposed to be wherever his curiosity led him. . . . But it's gone to his head ever since he started growing those damn dreadlocks. I keep telling him he's not a teenager anymore. He's almost twenty-five years old! Nobody's ever going to take him seriously, looking like that.

ELEANOR: Nobody except Cassandra.

AVERY: She's not the only one. I don't remember you backing me up that strongly when I first argued against his running around the Bronx spray painting trains and spouting this nonsense about the artist as an outlaw who makes his own rules. Is that why we spent all that money for him to go to art school? So he could become a vandal?

ELEANOR: I'm not condoning what he's doing! I agree with you. He's much too talented to be running around with these kids who're dragging him down. And after what happened to Cassandra, I was hoping he would come to his senses.

(CASSANDRA has come into the room unnoticed by her parents.)

CASSANDRA: Hi, Mom. Dad.

ELEANOR AND AVERY: Hi.

(There is a physical discomfort in the room, suggesting a strain between CASSANDRA and her parents.)

CASSANDRA: What's all this? *(Referring to the photo album)*

ELEANOR: Recognize anybody?

(CASSANDRA flips the pages of the photo album.)

CASSANDRA: Almost all the pictures of me are with Darryl.

AVERY: You two were inseparable. There wasn't anything Darryl did that you didn't want to do.

CASSANDRA: I remember you saying once that photographs distort reality.

AVERY: But I thought this was the period when you're supposed to question everything we've ever told you?

CASSANDRA: Only if it serves my purpose.

AVERY: Oh? And what about that escapade in the train yard? What purpose did that serve?

CASSANDRA: *(Starts to say something but stops herself)* When I was arrested, you never asked me what I was doing there. All you wanted to know was if Darryl was with me or had put me up to it. I didn't even have your disapproval all to myself!

AVERY: If you wanted us all to yourself, then why did we have to find out what happened from Bernice?

CASSANDRA: I wanted to see how you liked being second in line.

ELEANOR: *(Makes a move to comfort CASSANDRA but she moves away)* Honey. It was wrong of us to do that.

CASSANDRA: You never do it to the children you teach.

ELEANOR: It's not as easy with your own children.

CASSANDRA: Why not? You either know what you're doing or you don't.

ELEANOR: *(Puts her arms around CASSANDRA from behind, giving AVERY a conspiratorial look)* Well, you know, Cass—your father and I didn't know YOU knew that we don't always KNOW what we're doing.

AVERY: *(Taking his cue from* ELEANOR*)* So now that WE know YOU knew, what should WE do?

(CASSANDRA *begins to soften a bit, almost joining her parents in laughter before catching herself and moving out of her mother's arms.*)

CASSANDRA: Well, whatever YOU do, I don't want it to be at my expense. *(She leaves the room.)*

(AVERY *moves over and puts his arms around Eleanor in much the same way as she had done with* CASSANDRA. ELEANOR *reacts with surprise.*)

ELEANOR: What's this about?

AVERY: Does there have to be a reason?

ELEANOR: *(Moves away irritated)* Yes! Especially when it's something we don't do that often.

AVERY: I haven't forgotten. Have you?

ELEANOR: No. Just out of practice.

AVERY: *(Rubs her thigh)* You want to do something about it?

ELEANOR: IT ain't the problem. WE are!

(AVERY *gets up and turns on the stereo. Frank Sinatra's rendition of "Last Night When We Were Young" is heard as* AVERY *reaches for* ELEANOR's *hand.)*

ELEANOR: What?

AVERY: Don't you remember?

ELEANOR: Not NOW, Avery.

(Expressing frustration, AVERY *sits down at the other end of the couch.)*

AVERY: NOW used to always be the right time.

ELEANOR: And you used to be a lot more persistent when you wanted to convince me of that.

AVERY: You're just full of insights, aren't you?

ELEANOR: I know you don't want me to tell you what you're full of.

AVERY: Why you want to get ugly?

ELEANOR: Because I'm fed up with your way of avoiding what I have to say when you don't want to hear it!

AVERY: Cassandra must be fed up too. Because that's what we just did to her.

(ELEANOR *pauses to consider what* AVERY *has just said.*)

ELEANOR: You're right . . . something's happening to us—to all of us. And it frightens me. Instead of turning TO each other, we're turning ON each other.

*(*AVERY *walks to stage right. Both he and* ELEANOR *direct their thoughts toward the audience.)*

AVERY: Until I met Eleanor, I believed having the strength of my convictions was enough to change the world. But it wasn't even enough to change the mind of the woman I loved. I've never fully recovered from that.

ELEANOR: I knew Avery was for me from the very beginning. I never felt I was being made up in his head. When we were in graduate school, we spent hours arguing about how to inspire children to learn. I couldn't have been happier during those first years after we were married. . . . But gradually, disappointment began to live inside Avery in a way that was different from its effect on me.

(Light goes down on living room.)

Act 1: Scene 7

(Light comes up on WANDA WAPLES.*)*

WANDA: Tonight begins part one of the Newsbusters' special reports on "Uncivil Liberties," which asks several New Yorkers how they treat and are treated by others who live in this city.

(Light goes down on WANDA *and comes up on the* POLICEMAN.*)*

POLICEMAN: People who aren't cops don't know what it's like to see so much personal tragedy and be exposed to the worst in people on a daily basis. I'm not complaining. I know it comes with the job. But I resent the fact that the same people who want us to protect them from the lowlifes keep their distance whether we're on or off duty. All my friends are cops because once I meet somebody and they find out I'm a cop, they don't want any part of me. It's rough on my kids cause I've got neighbors who won't let their children play with mine. It's the kind of thing that'll turn you sour on the human race. When I first became a cop, I thought I could make a difference. I remember at the police academy we were told a good cop has the wisdom of Solomon, the courage of David, the strength of Samson, the patience of Job, the leadership of Moses, the kindness of the Good Samaritan, the faith of Daniel, and the tolerance of Jesus. I can't say I ever believed that!

(Light goes down on POLICEMAN *and comes up on* FIRST WOMAN.*)*

1ST WOMAN: I can't believe what comes out of the mouths of these young people. It's loud and it's wrong. I listen to them on the subway. Every other word is a curse. When I was a girl, profanity was something I only heard people use in anger. But these young people today enjoy hearing those foul words coming out of their mouths. They think they've achieved something by talking that way. I don't know why they think they have to have so much to say. I think I was ten before I was even allowed to talk without permission.

(Light goes down on FIRST WOMAN *and comes up on* RHAPSODY. RHAPSODY *is very animated during his rap, which becomes a graphic illustration of what he is talking about.)*

RHAPSODY: There's always something to see in New York. So I always have to have something to say. You got to raise your voice in this city. Otherwise, folks don't believe you mean it. I'm loud but I'm not low. I don't take up no more room than I need. There're only two kinds of people in the world: those who're on the point and those who're beside the point! So when I cut out a big piece of city street for myself, that's my mobile home. I don't rent went I walk. I go condo!

(When he finishes talking, he sits down on a bench on the subway platform. His legs are spread-eagled and his arms straddle the length of the bench. Light dims on RHAPSODY *and comes up on the* SECOND WOMAN *who stands as though she is hemmed in by something.)*

2ND WOMAN: I feel bullied when I'm in the streets. I'm always yielding what little space I have, usually, to a man who sizes me up as someone who can be easily intimidated. I feel I have more room in my apartment than I do in the streets. At least in my apartment, as long as I pay my rent, no one hassles me. But there's no protection against being forced off the streets by these creeps who throw their bodies around like they're the only people in the world. They act like they want to control everything but themselves!

(Light goes down on SECOND WOMAN *and comes up on* WANDA WAPLES.*)*

WANDA: In the next installment in our special report on "New York: The City of Uncivil Liberties," we will focus on the role that attitude plays in coping with life in New York.

(Light goes down on WANDA.*)*

Act 1: Scene 8

(Light comes up on CASSANDRA *removing a photograph from her wall.* AVERY *comes to the entrance of her room and stops. When* CASSANDRA *realizes he's there, she stops what she's doing.)*

AVERY: Got a minute?

CASSANDRA: *(Unconvincingly)* Sure, Daddy.

AVERY: You know, I was thinking about what you were saying the other day. And you're right. It's difficult trying to figure out who you are. Even when you think you know. And sometimes when you look to people for help, they disappoint you.

CASSANDRA: Well, I don't plan on being disappointed anymore.

AVERY: That won't stop it from happening.

CASSANDRA: I don't believe that.

AVERY: Have your mother and I disappointed you that much?

CASSANDRA: Not really.

AVERY: How much is not really?

CASSANDRA: Just enough for me to notice and for you not to.

AVERY: Notice what?

(Before CASSANDRA *can answer,* AVERY *is distracted by something on the wall.)*

AVERY: What happened to that photograph of Darryl?

CASSANDRA: Oh! I guess that means the minute you wanted of MY time is over.

AVERY: *(Exasperated)* What's with you?

CASSANDRA: Myself.

AVERY: You're just like your . . .

CASSANDRA: No, Daddy. You're wrong. I've never been like Darryl. I used to want to be like him. But not anymore.

AVERY: I meant your mother, not Darryl.

(They begin talking more to themselves than each other.)

CASSANDRA: I've been playing hide-and-seek with myself inside Darryl.

AVERY: Whenever I warned you and Darryl of possible danger, your mother said something that made fear sound like just another opportunity to fly.

CASSANDRA: So maybe, all I can be for right now is . . .

AVERY: I admire that. . . . But you have to be careful.

(Light goes down on them.)

Act 1: Scene 9

(Light comes up on FIRST WOMAN.*)*

1ST WOMAN: It was that mouth of his that got him into trouble. I've got two grown sons. And the thing with these boys is always having to have so much to say. Every time the policeman said something, he had some remark to say back. The officer had him turn around, put handcuffs on him, and led him up the steps to the street. But he kept turning his head around to say something about being handcuffed. It must have made the policeman angry because he started poking him in the back with his nightstick. I remember wanting to take my hand and cover that mouth of his.

(Light goes down on FIRST WOMAN *and comes up on* SECOND WOMAN.*)*

2ND WOMAN: I was trying to hail a cab when I heard voices coming from across the street. I turned around and saw several policemen and a man who was handcuffed. The man was screaming: "What did I do? What did I do?" And when he tried to jerk away, he was surrounded. I really couldn't see what was happening after that. But I did see them put him in the police van. I assumed he was carried bodily into the van because he wouldn't get in voluntarily. . . . No. It didn't occur to me that he might be hurt.

(Light goes down on SECOND WOMAN *and comes up on* RHAPSODY.*)*

RHAPSODY: The cop wasn't provoked by anything Fly said. It was his tag. Fly's rep as a writer was made under the tag of FLY. So when the cop came up on him, Fly was tagging a wall advertisement. The transit cops know the tags of all the most well-known writers. And as soon as the cop see Fly's tag, he goes off. So instead of just giving him a summons, the cop busts him. So who's provoking who? That's why Fly was pissed and kept screaming: "I can't believe this! I can't believe this!" When the cop handcuffs him and leads him up to the street, he starts poking Fly with his nightstick and saying: "Do you believe it now?" By the time I get to the street, Fly's surrounded by all these cops and they won't let nobody get close enough to see what's happening.

(Light goes down on RHAPSODY *and comes up on* POLICEMAN.*)*

POLICEMAN: Handcuffing is standard procedure for any arrest. It's not only for the safety of the arresting officer, but for the perpetrator as well. You'd be surprised how many potentially dangerous situations are avoided when the person under arrest is restrained. But this guy was an exception to the rule. He became even more disorderly after he was handcuffed. And by the time I got him to the police van, he was like a man possessed. It took several of us to get him inside. It's not easy restraining someone without hurting him, especially when he's doing everything in his power to resist. I didn't see any transit officer use more than a reasonable amount of force. . . . By reasonable, I mean, given how much he provoked us, I think we handled the situation with unusual restraint. . . . I'm not a doctor, so I can't say anything about how he died. . . . I do know we found some drug paraphernalia on him. So he might've been so hopped up that he had a heart attack. But like I said, I'm not a doctor.

(Light goes down on the POLICEMAN.*)*

Act 1: Scene 10

(Light comes up on AVERY *and* ELEANOR *in living room reading the newspapers.* CASSANDRA *is in her room using mascara to paint a mask over her face. Suzanne Vega's "Small Blue Thing" is heard and* AVERY *and* ELEANOR *pay more attention to the song than to what they're reading.)*

ELEANOR: Cassandra! Cassandra!

CASSANDRA: Yes Mom!

ELEANOR: Could you turn that down?

*(*CASSANDRA *turns the music down without answering)*

ELEANOR: How many times is she going to play it? That record scares me.

AVERY: I had a talk with her earlier and she was telling me the same thing that the song is saying.

ELEANOR: What's it all about?

AVERY: It has something to do with Darryl. Have you been in Cass's room lately?

ELEANOR: No, why?

AVERY: She's taken his photograph down. Something's happened between them and I think it has to do with her arrest in that train yard. But when I asked, she didn't want to talk about it.

ELEANOR: Lately, we hardly see Darryl. Cassandra doesn't confide in us. And we don't talk to each other except when it's about the children.

AVERY: Well. Since we're not talking TO one another, maybe we can start talking ABOUT each other.

ELEANOR: To one another?

AVERY: Of course.

ELEANOR: I don't think I can be that civilized.

AVERY: Why not? We're two intelligent people.

ELEANOR: Intelligence has nothing to do with it.

AVERY: *(With mock realization)* Maybe . . . we need . . .

ELEANOR: No! You don't mean . . .

AVERY: Yes!

ELEANOR: Professional help!

(AVERY *nods his head.*)

ELEANOR: No! Please, not that! I'll talk!

AVERY: No! Let me! There's so much I've been wanting to say.

ELEANOR: I need to get it all out now. Otherwise, I'll explode.

AVERY: But there's so much I have to tell you. I can't wait another second.

ELEANOR: *(Serious)* All right. You first.

(AVERY *is stunned by the way* ELEANOR *has turned the tables on him. They sit quietly for a few seconds.*)

AVERY: *(Irritated)* You think you're slick, don't you?

ELEANOR: It's not good to keep so much bottled up inside you.

AVERY: I don't have any choice. You hardly let me get near you anymore.

ELEANOR: I feel the same way. But with me it's talk, not touch.

AVERY: *(Exasperated)* All right! What do you want to talk about?

ELEANOR: I want to talk about why we don't talk. Not just about the kids. But about our work. All the things that matter.

AVERY: *(A cynical half-suppressed laugh)* You're too busy in that funhouse you call a classroom to be bothered with the world I live in.

ELEANOR: Avery! We both live in the same world!

AVERY: If we do, how can you accept the fact that the schools we teach in are worse now than they were twenty-five years ago and that both our children are flirting with disaster?

ELEANOR: *(Angered)* What has your rage ever accomplished? Has it ever helped you to teach a child to read? Has it kept Darryl away from graffiti or stopped Cassandra from imitating him?

AVERY: *(Beat)* Maybe not. But like you said: "It's not good to keep things bottled up inside."

ELEANOR: Well, you've got your funhouse and I've got mine.

AVERY: I guess we don't live in the same world after all.

(Neither AVERY nor ELEANOR speaks. CASSANDRA charges into the living room. Her face is a painted mask of mascara.)

ELEANOR: *(Expressing shock)* Cassandra! What have you done to your face?

(Light goes down on living room.)

Act 1: Scene 11

(Light comes up on WANDA WAPLES.)

WANDA: This is part two in our special report on New York City and uncivil liberties. Tonight you will hear four New Yorkers talk about how their attitude goes a long way toward helping them keep their sanity.

(Light goes down on WANDA and comes up on FIRST WOMAN.)

1ST WOMAN: The thing about living in New York is: you don't want to look like a victim. That's difficult for women, since we're always prime suspects. In every movie I've ever seen about a sinking ship, women and children always receive first consideration for the lifeboats. Unfortunately, those who are chosen first to be saved are also the most likely to be victimized. So I asked myself: Was there anything, other than my sex, that gave me away as an obvious choice for a mugging? And it occurred to me that if you grow up believing in lifeboats, it'll always appear to others that you're waiting to be rescued. So when I'm coming home late at night from work, I don't act like I'm lost at sea. I walk like I know exactly where I'm going. *(She demonstrates and her movements are a mix of aerobics and martial arts)* That way, instead of waiting for a lifeboat, you can be one!

(Light goes down on FIRST WOMAN *and comes up on the* POLICEMAN.*)*

POLICEMAN: *(Holding up a .38 pistol and a nightstick)* This represents my authority to use deadly force, if necessary, to protect my own life and the lives of other citizens. And this *(opens coat to a bulletproof vest)* represents the possibility that someone may try to use deadly force against me. As you can see, this is not the kind of job that is likely to win you many friends. Since we usually deal with people at their worst, police work doesn't necessarily bring out our best either. We're made out of flesh and blood like everybody else. And sooner or later, no matter what we do, more of the street rubs off on us than we'd like to admit. So I've learned to keep my distance from people except other cops. And even some of them I don't get too close to. I know it sounds callous, but when you start to care too much about the people you come in contact with, you lose the edge. And that can be the difference between life and death.

(Light goes down on the POLICEMAN.*)*

Act 1: Scene 12

(Light comes up on WANDA WAPLES.*)*

WANDA: The top story at this hour is the death early this morning of a twenty-four-year-old black man who was arrested by Transit Authority police for allegedly scrawling graffiti on a wall of the West Twenty-third Street subway station. As of now there are conflicting accounts by both police and eyewitnesses as to what happened to Darryl Cummings while he was in police custody.

(Strobe lights are used to dramatize DARRYL's *altercation with the police.* RHAPSODY *and the* POLICEMAN *re-enact what happened when they are not giving short accounts of their version of things along with the* FIRST WOMAN *and the* SECOND WOMAN.*)*

POLICEMAN: He became disorderly, so I placed him under arrest.

RHAPSODY: You can't be jumping up in somebody's life like they ain't there! The cop started cursing Fly the moment he saw him tagging the subway wall.

1ST WOMAN: I knew there was going to be trouble when I heard them shouting at each other.

2ND WOMAN: All I could see were his dreadlocks whipping back and forth as he tried to twist away from two policemen who were trying to hold him.

POLICEMAN: We had to restrain him. He was out of control.

RHAPSODY: The cop kept jabbing him with his nightstick!

1ST WOMAN: The more he said, the angrier the cop got.

2ND WOMAN: Once the police surrounded him, I couldn't see what was going on.

POLICEMAN: He got himself so worked up, it took five of us to get him into the van.

RHAPSODY: When I got outside, he was surrounded. But he wasn't arguing no more. He was screaming for his life!

1ST WOMAN: I could still hear him yelling after he was taken to the street level.

2ND WOMAN: When they put him in the van, he was screaming his head off.

WANDA: The only undisputed fact is that Darryl Cummings was admitted to Bellevue Hospital at two-fifty A.M. and pronounced dead at ten-twenty this morning.

POLICEMAN: It's not what he said; it was his attitude.

(Light goes down on POLICEMAN, WANDA, FIRST WOMAN, SECOND WOMAN, *and* RHAPSODY *as the phone rings. Light comes up on* ELEANOR *picking up the phone and her face registers the horrifying news. She opens her mouth and stifles a scream with her hand. Light goes down on* ELEANOR *as Ella Fitzgerald's rendition of "Ill Wind" is heard again.)*

END OF ACT I

Act 2: Scene 1

("Life During Wartime" by Talking Heads is heard as lighting effects follow AVERY, ELEANOR, CASSANDRA, *and* BERNICE *through the motions of grief that include slow motion and freezes. The music dies down and* WANDA WAPLES*'s voice is heard.)*

WANDA: The funeral of Darryl Cummings, held this morning at the Greater Zion Hill Baptist Church in Harlem, was witnessed by an overflow crowd of mourners. Many of those outside the church who could not get in expressed anger over what they believe to be a pattern of police violence against blacks that has grown steadily over the last ten years.

(Light goes down on AVERY, ELEANOR, CASSANDRA, *and* BERNICE *and comes up on* WANDA *and* ELEANOR *facing the audience.* WANDA *is holding a microphone.)*

WANDA: Mrs. Cummings! What is your response to the police account of what happened to your son?

*(*ELEANOR *is grief-stricken and quite disoriented by the TV cameras and the questions she is being asked. When she does speak, it is in the manner of someone trying to convince herself that what she is saying is true.)*

ELEANOR: Is that what they call killing my son? An account?

WANDA: The coroner's report stated that your son died of a heart attack.

ELEANOR: *(Close to breaking down)* My—son's—heart—was—not—attacked. It—was stopped by the beating he took!

WANDA: Mrs. Cummings. I know this is difficult for you. But . . .

ELEANOR: This? What do you mean by "this"?

(BERNICE *and* AVERY *attempt to calm* ELEANOR *down, but she is too upset by what* WANDA *has said.* WANDA *signals the camera people to cut the videotape and walks away.*)

ELEANOR: She said "this" like she isn't part of all the wires, lights, and cameras trying to suck Darryl's life up into thirty seconds. He's not news! He's my son!

(*Light goes down on the scene and comes up again on* ELEANOR, *who moves around aimlessly on a subway platform.*)

ELEANOR: I've always fought THIS. (*Gesturing with her hands to encompass the subway*) Not the way Avery did. What I tried to do was help my children find a place inside themselves where they'd be safe.

(*Light goes down on* ELEANOR *and comes up on* AVERY.)

AVERY: I warned her! There's no safety. Not in a classroom. Nowhere! You can never come in from out of doors. Now we're all out in the open where we belong. And I'm going to bring those cops out of hiding where they killed Darryl and put them right back here in the subway, so everyone can see what they did.

(*Light goes down on* AVERY.)

Act 2: Scene 2

(*Light comes up on the Cummings's living room.* AVERY, ELEANOR, CASSANDRA, *and* BERNICE *are seated.*)

ELEANOR: Avery? Did you know there were moles on Darryl's neck? I didn't notice them until we went to identify him. I thought I knew every inch of him. . . . I wonder how many other things we didn't notice? When you don't even see the moles growing on your own son's neck. . . . No wonder we lost him.

BERNICE: Darryl's gone but he doesn't have to be forgotten.

AVERY: We're not going to forget him!

BERNICE: (*Sympathizing*) I know that, Avery. But it's the rest of the world I'm worried about.

ELEANOR: (*Incredulous*) Does the coroner really expect us to believe the police weren't responsible for Darryl's death?

AVERY: (*Bitterly*) Nobody cares what we believe as long as we don't do anything about it.

CASSANDRA: But what can we do if they say the police didn't do anything?

BERNICE: There's a lot you can do. But this may not be the best time to talk about it.

AVERY: (*Incredulous*) Whether it's tomorrow or next week, there's never going to be a GOOD time to talk about it!

BERNICE: Eleanor?

ELEANOR: *(Lost in her own thoughts)* They TOOK Darryl's life in less time than it TOOK ME to give him life! There's no way I'm ever going to get over that.

BERNICE: You may not realize it now, but your outrage is the most important advantage we've got. You don't want Darryl to become just another name on a long list of casualties. But that's what will happen unless we turn your outrage into a public outcry.

ELEANOR: The Grand Jury isn't going to indict those cops for murder? Is it?

BERNICE: It's possible. But there's no guarantee. That's why we have to do some other things to have a shot at getting them indicted.

ELEANOR: Like what?

BERNICE: Organizing public support, especially from blacks and our respected leadership. Then harness it through the media.

ELEANOR: *(Angered)* I won't have any more to do with those people! They're twisting everything to make it sound like Darryl was so wound up on drugs that his heart couldn't take it. Darryl wasn't like that. He never lost control of himself!

BERNICE: That's why we have to deal with the media. So they'll get the picture of Darryl we want them to have. One that brings out everything he represents.

ELEANOR: To whom?

BERNICE: *(Speaking to everyone)* I'm not minimizing what Darryl's death means to you. But if we're going to get the support we need, there's got to be a lot more at stake here than just Darryl.

ELEANOR: *(In disbelief)* More at stake than Darryl? What more is there?

BERNICE: I know how that sounds. But no matter how much people may empathize, your grief is not theirs. We need to find something for people to identify with or they won't care enough to see your fight as their own.

AVERY: See Eleanor! That's what I've been trying to tell you all along.

BERNICE: I can get Wanda Waples from Newsbusters to do a special report on Darryl—make him symbolic of an endangered species in American society: young, black males. Organize a vigil outside the courthouse that'll stay there until the Grand Jury hands down its decision. Before we're through, Darryl's name will be synonymous with a movement to stop these rogue cops from murdering us in the line of duty!

CASSANDRA: You really think using the media will get people to care about what happened to Darryl?

BERNICE: It'll get them to pay attention. That's a start.

(AVERY and ELEANOR exchange a look between them.)

BERNICE: Look . . . I understand. But up until now, everything that's happened has been concealed. Those cops beat Darryl to death in the back of that van. We haven't seen the autopsy report. And the deliberations of the Grand Jury are kept secret. You don't have that luxury. If you're going to fight, you're going to have to do it in public.

(Light goes down on the living room.)

Act 2: Scene 3

(Light comes up on WANDA WAPLES *whose face shows the strain of the pressure she works under. Something gets her attention and she snaps into her smooth on-air personality.)*

WANDA: Tonight, in our continuing coverage of the Darryl Cummings case, we focus on the vigil outside the criminal court building where the Grand Jury is still hearing testimony. Now in its second week, the vigil includes the parents, Avery and Eleanor Cummings, and approximately thirty of their supporters. Conspicuously absent from these daily demonstrations is Cassandra Cummings, the sister of Darryl Cummings. She has also refused several of our requests for an interview.

(Lights go down on WANDA.*)*

Act 2: Scene 4

(Light comes up on the Cummings's living room. AVERY *and* ELEANOR *are watching television in their coats. They both look tired.* AVERY *gets up from the couch and turns off the television.* ELEANOR *removes her coat and* AVERY *takes off his as well. The tone of their conversation ranges from mild irritation to open hostility.)*

AVERY: You need to talk to Cass.

ELEANOR: Why do I need to talk to her?

AVERY: She won't listen to me.

ELEANOR: What about?

AVERY: Coming to the vigil.

ELEANOR: I don't see how we can insist that she come if she doesn't want to.

AVERY: Didn't you hear what Bernice said? None of us are free agents in this! And Cassandra has to understand that!

ELEANOR: *(Without conviction)* I've already told her that.

AVERY: I can tell by your voice how persuasive you must have been.

ELEANOR: You can go to hell, Avery!

AVERY: It isn't enough that we've lost Darryl because you taught him it was all right to throw caution to the winds! Now you're willing to allow Cassandra to behave as though she doesn't care enough about her own brother to participate in a vigil on his behalf!

ELEANOR: Oh! So now the police didn't kill Darryl. I did! If anybody collaborated with his murderers, it was you! You never came into the house without bringing your twisted fear of the world in with you. You made Darryl and Cassandra afraid of everything that moved. Well, Darryl is dead. And you were right all along! Obviously, that's a consolation for you, but not for me!

AVERY: It's clear where Darryl got his talent for provocation. It's so typically female!

ELEANOR: At least I taught him how to dream! What's your excuse for not teaching him how to stay alive?

AVERY: *(Outraged, he advances toward her)* Shut the fuck up! Just shut the fuck up!

ELEANOR: *(Not moving)* What are you going to do if I don't? The same thing those cops did to Darryl?

(AVERY is stopped cold, stunned by ELEANOR's words).

ELEANOR: Come on then! Just a little further. We're almost back in the subway like Darryl and that cop! Out there where the world is low down, dirty, and wrong! Just the way you like it!

(CASSANDRA bursts into the room with a large leather portfolio.)

CASSANDRA: Hi, Mom! Dad! I've got something to show you.

(She starts to open the portfolio.)

AVERY: *(Accusingly)* Where were you today?

CASSANDRA: At school.

AVERY: *(Angry)* Don't you remember what you said yesterday?

CASSANDRA: *(With sudden recall)* Oh! The vigil! I'm sorry. I was in the darkroom developing these photographs and . . .

AVERY: You're not the only one who's busy. Your mother and I have lessons to prepare and papers to grade. But we're out there every day.

CASSANDRA: But I wanted to show you . . .

AVERY: *(Knocks portfolio out of her hands)* I don't think a few hours is asking too much. It's a sacrifice for all of us. But if we want to make sure those cops don't get away with killing Darryl, we have to stand together as a family. . . . People at the vigil have been wondering why you're never there. And now this evening on the news, Wanda Waples was asking the same question.

CASSANDRA: I don't care anything about that.

AVERY: You have to care! Otherwise, attention is going to be diverted away from Darryl onto you.

CASSANDRA: Right. And we wouldn't want that, would we?

AVERY: I didn't mean it the way it sounded.

CASSANDRA: Well, at least we agree on how it sounded.

AVERY: If you would stop thinking about yourself for a minute, you'd understand how important this is.

(CASSANDRA *picks up her portfolio case, starts to leave the room but stops.*)

CASSANDRA: You never complained when Darryl was in every breath I took. But now that I want to be full of myself instead of him, you have a problem.

AVERY: *(Barely able to control himself)* I have no problem with who you want to be. My problem is where you should've been!

CASSANDRA: I was where I should have been. It's not my problem if it wasn't where YOU wanted me to be.

(AVERY *moves threateningly, toward* CASSANDRA.)

AVERY: I've had just about enough of your mouth!

ELEANOR: Don't you dare!

(AVERY *is stopped by* ELEANOR'*s words.*)

ELEANOR: If you want to go after somebody, why don't you find those cops!

(CASSANDRA *looks from* ELEANOR *to* AVERY *and sees the hostility between them.*)

CASSANDRA: This really isn't about me, is it?

(CASSANDRA *eludes* ELEANOR'*s grasp and rushes out of the room. Light goes down on the living room.*)

Act 2: Scene 5

(*Light comes up on* WANDA WAPLES *holding a microphone.*)

WANDA: While the Grand Jury in the Darryl Cummings case continues to hear testimony, the rest of us can only speculate about what actually took place during the time he was in police custody. But with all the attention given to what happened to Darryl Cummings, not much has been said about who he was. . . .

(*Light comes up on* AVERY.)

AVERY: Whenever I talked to him, he always seemed on the verge of bursting from the mob scene of questions in his head. And even as he listened, I'd get the feeling he was making up his own version of everything I said. It was as though the answers I gave him were only of interest to him for as long as he could get questions out of them.

(*Light comes up on* ELEANOR.)

ELEANOR: I always knew exactly where he was in the house. It wasn't that he was particularly loud or liked to show off. It just never occurred to him that he shouldn't
make his presence felt. . . . I taught him to question authority but not to dis-
regard it.

(Light comes up on RHAPSODY. *As he talks about* DARRYL, *his mannerisms shift back
and forth between his own persona and* DARRYL*'s.)*

RHAPSODY: You could never tune in on Fly like a soap opera and find out what was
going on. At first, I didn't give him no RSVP 'cause if you gonna be real for me, you
gotta be regular. Even though the posse I hung with i-g'd him, he came around the
park anyway. And I have to say, he had more than a little bit a junk in his trunk
when it came to basketball. But he wasn't into dissing or dishing anybody—which
is all right if you down with detente. At the time, I was down with being low and
decided to see if I could get to what was hid under his lid . . . I caught him with an
elbow to the cheekbone on a drive to the basket and gave him my killer stare after
I scored. But he had this look on his face that was waiting for my murder on his eyes
when they got there . . . and it said: "What took you so long?" I still didn't dig
where he was coming from. But I knew where he was at. . . . He was the same way
with his masterpieces. He did 'em, put his tag on 'em, and split. But I could always
tell a masterpiece by Fly even without seeing his tag. His stuff was like a cross between the Smurfs and Nightmare on Elm Street. There wasn't nobody else doing
that. All these big-time downtown art dealers tried to get him to do stuff for their
galleries. But Fly i-g'd 'em. Subways and train stations were his gallery and his audience was anybody who was waiting on a train.

(Light goes down on RHAPSODY *and comes up on* WANDA, AVERY, *and* ELEANOR.*)*

WANDA: What about the stubs of marijuana cigarettes found in his pockets?

ELEANOR: What about them?

WANDA: They could have been the cause of what the police say was his erratic behavior.

ELEANOR: When the police took him to Bellevue Hospital, my son was in a coma. It
seems to me that the behavior of the police needs to be examined and not my son's.

WANDA: What about the fact that your daughter was arrested in the train yards a few
weeks before your son's death?

AVERY: That has nothing to do with the murder of our son.

WANDA: But maybe it has something to do with why she refuses to talk publicly and
her absence from the demonstrations at the courthouse.

AVERY: Our daughter was very close to her brother. And my wife and I respect her
wish not to make public appearances or to make herself available to the media.

(Light goes down on everyone except WANDA.*)*

WANDA: While Avery and Eleanor Cummings dismiss any connection made between their daughter's silence and the death of their son, the issue of Cassandra Cummings's silence is arousing as much speculation as the outcome of the Grand Jury deliberations.

(Light goes down on WANDA.*)*

Act 2: Scene 6

(Light comes up on CASSANDRA *and* BERNICE *in the Cummings's living room. They both are seated.* BERNICE *is looking admiringly at a batch of photographs.)*

BERNICE: These are great, Cass!

CASSANDRA: You really think so?

BERNICE: Of course! Don't you?

CASSANDRA: I don't know. I mean, I think they're too close to what I feel for me to know how I feel about them yet.

BERNICE: Why did you disguise yourself? In some of them you even resemble Darryl. If I didn't already know you, I couldn't recognize you from these.

CASSANDRA: Darryl would. . . . He used to tell me not to worry whenever anything went wrong; as long as I knew how to play in my head, everything would be all right. I watched him do it all the time. . . . I remember once when he was about twelve, he was doing something my mother told him not to do. Finally, she grabbed him by the shoulders and shook him! If you could've seen the expression on his face. It was like he'd just gotten what he wanted for Christmas. I didn't understand why he looked so happy until he explained to me that being scolded by adults wasn't so bad because once he did what they said, they left him alone. And then he could go on doing what he wanted.

BERNICE: But what's that got to do with making yourself up to look like Darryl? *(Gestures to photographs)*

CASSANDRA: Because I want to make myself up out of what's inside me . . . and Darryl makes up a lot of what's there.

BERNICE: But why can't you share that with the rest of us by joining the vigil?

CASSANDRA: That's not the way I want to do it.

BERNICE: Didn't Darryl say you could give people what they want without giving yourself away?

CASSANDRA: He's the main reason why I still can't do that.

BERNICE: *(Frustrated)* I don't understand you. Don't you want the cops who killed Darryl punished?

CASSANDRA: What kind of question is that?

BERNICE: If you do, you're going to have to start acting like it.

CASSANDRA: What do you mean?

BERNICE: Darryl's murder is now public domain. We have to keep it there. You can't continue to keep your feelings about Darryl to yourself. Because no one will care about what happened to him if it looks as though you don't.

CASSANDRA: *(Angrily)* I don't care what people think! They don't know me. They don't know what it was like for Darryl to find out those cops weren't going to leave him alone after he did what he was told. They don't know how terrified he must have been when he realized he wasn't safe in his own head anymore—that they were coming in after him. That's why Darryl wouldn't stop screaming. It was the only thing they couldn't touch no matter how much they hurt him. *(Near tears)* And when he stopped screaming, there was nothing for them to kill, because Darryl had already taken his life to a place where they couldn't get at him . . . You're just like everybody else. You don't understand what was between Darryl and me. You don't understand any of it!

BERNICE: Maybe I don't. But I do know what it means to be lost in someone else's life. I have a brother too. His name is Kevin. He's eight years older, which meant when we were growing up he was often saddled with me when he wanted to hang out with his friends. So he dragged me along. And it never ceased to amaze me how he could strong-arm any challenge to his will with a word or a gesture. I considered it an awesome display of power. . . . Then one day we were walking to the store and saw these cops beating a man with nightsticks. Kevin told me to wait for him at the corner and he walked over to them. I didn't hear what he said but one of the cops turned around and hit Kevin in the face. . . . I remember screaming and being frightened by the sound that came out of my mouth. I've never forgotten the thud of those nightsticks against his head. They beat him so bad that he never spoke again. . . . I saw those cops beat my brother into a vegetable. But everyone else seemed to want to forget what had happened. The cops denied it. The newspapers called it an allegation. And the Grand Jury was not convinced that what I saw had actually occurred. Even my own parents told me it wouldn't help to dwell on what had happened. . . . The loudest protest made over my brother's beating was when I screamed. . . . But it doesn't have to be that way with Darryl. You probably don't want to hear this, but we've got a much better chance of nailing those cops for killing Darryl than we would've if he'd ended up like Kevin. My brother lived! But the living don't make good symbols because they can always be broken. And no one wants to be reminded of that. . . . After all of our supporters and most of my family couldn't bear to look at Kevin anymore, I promised myself that people were going to pay attention to me no matter what I had to do. That's why I became a lawyer. But I've learned you can't only rely on a courtroom to be heard. You have to be willing to hold court in the street!

(Light goes down on the living room.)

Act 2: Scene 7

(Light comes up on the POLICEMAN.*)*

POLICEMAN: I don't know what you mean. We got a lot more to fear from the public than they do us. You forget. There's more of them than there are of us . . . I just resent the insinuation that there're all these cops running amok over the rights of innocent people. We got rights too, you know. And we have to take more abuse than anybody just for trying to do our job. I know that comes with the shield. But I get tired of listening to people who have a sewer for a mouth talking about their rights . . . No I'm not excusing cops who go over the line. I'm just saying that sometimes all the procedure in the world don't mean shit when you're in the streets.

(Light goes down on POLICEMAN *and comes up on* FIRST WOMAN.*)*

1ST WOMAN: I keep going back to all the hollering they were doing because that's what got my attention in the first place. . . . No. I don't like anybody raising their voice at me. I'm civil to everyone whether I like them or not. And I expect people to treat me the same. . . . Yes, I've been working the four-to-twelve shift for the last five years. . . . Yes. I have. About three months ago when I was coming home from work. Nothing like that had ever happened to me before. I'm very careful. But he came from out of nowhere. I didn't play around. I gave him my purse right way. I only had five dollars and when he found out that's all there was, he really got angry. He started screaming at me, calling me names I wouldn't dare repeat. Fortunately, some people heard him and when they told him to leave me alone, he ran off. I was lucky. But I still have these nightmares where men are screaming right into my face. . . . When I heard that young man getting loud with that cop, the first thing that came to my mind was the man who robbed me. I could tell he was working himself up to hurt me just like that young man was working those policemen up to hurt him; *(raising her voice to a shout)* I can't stand it when I hear someone raising their voice!

(Light goes down on FIRST WOMAN *and comes up on* SECOND WOMAN.*)*

2ND WOMAN: I think a healthy dose of paranoia is necessary to survive in this city. I can handle having my worst fears fulfilled. But the thing I fear most is the unexpected. . . . Once while I was walking in the rain to the supermarket, a man holding an umbrella approached me from the opposite direction. *(She begins to act out what she is describing)* He was about fifty feet away from me, and I watched him make shapes in the air with his free hand. It looked as though he was speaking some unspoken language. But as he moved closer, I realized his hand wasn't doing anything except pulling a nylon thread hanging from the edge of the umbrella . . . I have to say, I was disappointed. I've been in New York long enough so that I'm not easily shocked. Something has to be really outrageous to get my attention. But I couldn't believe what that man was actually doing was so different from what I saw.

(Light goes down on SECOND WOMAN.*)*

Act 2: Scene 8

(Light comes up on WANDA WAPLES.*)*

WANDA: Tonight on Newsbusters, we are still awaiting a decision from the Grand Jury on the charges of police misconduct in the death of Darryl Cummings. A decision from the County Court is expected by next Tuesday. . . . And in a related story, the police arrested ten black and Latino teenagers earlier today in the Bronx train yards. They are charged with criminal trespassing, defacing public property and assault on a transit worker. These arrests, according to police, are in connection with what has been termed "graffiti wars" by rival gangs over turf rights to certain train lines. Police spokespersons went on to say that the violence among these gangs has been going on for some time and that several MTA workers have also been assaulted in recent weeks. And in a stunning revelation, the police announced that two of the youths charged named Darryl Cummings as a former member of a graffiti gang known as the MAGIC MARKERS!

(Light goes down on WANDA WAPLES.*)*

Act 2: Scene 9

(Light comes up on Cummings's living room. AVERY *is seated, lost in thought and* BERNICE *is standing, in the middle of talking to him.)*

BERNICE: Okay. The Grand Jury will hand down its decision next Tuesday. We've got to mobilize as many people as possible to be at the court when the DA makes the announcement. So we're going to have to meet every night between now and Tuesday. *(Finally looks at* AVERY*)* Now what I have in mind . . . *(realizes* AVERY *is not listening)* Avery? Have you heard anything I've said?

AVERY: What's all this about Darryl being in a gang?

BERNICE: Don't worry about it. That's just chow time for the media. They need something to satisfy their appetite for headlines.

AVERY: Suppose it's true?

BERNICE: What if it is? Darryl isn't dead because he was a member of a gang or resisted arrest, or even because he wasn't getting along with you, Eleanor, and Cassandra. He's dead because those cops murdered him! That's the only thing we should be directing our attention to.

AVERY: Eleanor thinks I made him so frightened of the world that he went looking for danger to prove he could handle it.

BERNICE: Avery . . .

AVERY: *(Not listening)* I wanted him to enjoy the experience of being a boy: to give himself over completely to that boundless energy . . . to abandon himself to his body and find his own limits. But you can't do that in these cities. I had to set limits or he'd never have reached the corner. I found myself doing just what the schools did: badgering him to check himself as if any move he made could get him into trouble. No wonder he was confused. . . . I got him to the corner all right but somehow I failed to teach him the difference between avoiding trouble and running from life. And if Darryl didn't learn that about being black, then becoming a man was a death sentence.

BERNICE: Avery. You're not responsible for what happened.

AVERY: *(Almost crying out)* He was MY son!

BERNICE: You're doing the same thing Cassandra's doing. The only protection we have for ourselves is raising our voices loud enough to draw a crowd.

AVERY: *(Bitterly)* I thought that what we were doing would help me through all this. But it's not enough.

BERNICE: Nothing will ever be enough. But it's not just about Darryl anymore. I thought you understood that.

(AVERY looks at BERNICE, taking in what she's just said. ELEANOR enters the house. AVERY and ELEANOR avoid each others' eyes, which BERNICE can't help but notice.)

ELEANOR: Well, I guess you heard the news.

BERNICE: I was just telling Avery what we can do to counter the effect of the story.

ELEANOR: *(To no one in particular)* It wasn't enough that they killed Darryl. Now they're trying to kill my memory of him. . . . *(To* AVERY*)* Why don't they stop telling lies about my son?

(AVERY gets up and leaves the room.)

BERNICE: You can't let Darryl's death make you turn on each other.

ELEANOR: Those cops got up inside of Darryl and made something out of him that I never knew about. His life came out of me but I never got next to him the way they did.

BERNICE: Eleanor, I don't understand what you're talking about.

ELEANOR: Oh, it's even more profound than that. You don't KNOW what I'm talking about. . . . Loving and being loved by your children has nothing to do with making them happy. Anyone can do that. The real test of being a mother is knowing exactly what will hurt your children the most. If you know that, you can help them protect themselves against anyone, even yourself. . . . Those cops didn't know Darryl! But they touched something in him that hurt him in a way that Avery and I were completely unaware of. . . . All the pain I went through to give him life didn't help me know the pain those cops found before they took his life. . . . If I'd known how to hurt him like that, they would've never been able to touch him!

(Light goes down on BERNICE and ELEANOR.)

Act 2: Scene 10

(Light dims on WANDA *just enough for her to drop her on-air persona. She stretches, squeezes the bridge of her nose between her thumb and forefinger, and gets up as though preparing to leave. Light comes up on* BERNICE, *who is watching* WANDA. WANDA *is taken by surprise when she becomes aware of* BERNICE's *presence.)*

BERNICE: Do you know what they say is the biggest lie media people tell?

WANDA: I can't wait for you to tell me.

BERNICE: I'm sorry to bother you.

WANDA: What do lawyers say when they're about to fuck over someone?

*(*BERNICE *shakes her head.)*

WANDA: Trust me.

(They share a look.)

BERNICE: I guess that means we've become one of the boys.

WANDA: Speak for yourself.

BERNICE: Given your line of work, that's more your problem than mine.

WANDA: You watch too much TV.

BERNICE: You know that startled expression on your face when you saw me a minute ago? I never see that look on television—not even when you're reporting the most vicious crimes.

WANDA: Maybe that's because you're always much more of a surprise than the average serial killer.

BERNICE: Speaking of surprises, what's all this nonsense about Darryl being in a gang?

WANDA: Nonsense or not, two members of The Magic Markers told me the same story they told the police.

BERNICE: They probably cut a deal with the cops to say that.

WANDA: It's possible. If you get any real leads in that direction, I'll follow them up.

BERNICE: What about what I've already given you?

WANDA: By my calculations, we're even.

BERNICE: Not by mine.

WANDA: Haven't the demonstrations been covered?

BERNICE: Yeah, but stories about Cassandra and now this possible gang involvement have nothing to do with his murder.

WANDA: Look Bernice. It's not my job to raise issues. I report the news!

BERNICE: You mean create it, don't you?

WANDA: And what do you call this campaign to make Cummings into some kind of subway folk hero?

BERNICE: You don't think those cops killed him?

WANDA: It doesn't matter what I think. I'm not here to do public relations.

BERNICE: What are you here for?

WANDA: For the same reason you are: to do my job!

BERNICE: Reducing everything to making a living isn't as easy for me as it is for you.

WANDA: Oh? You don't seem to have that much trouble when it serves your purpose.

BERNICE: What do you mean?

WANDA: I've seen you on TV vilifying the courts for penalizing poorly educated blacks with criminal records—then turn around and use the very same methods to discredit the testimony of blacks against one of your "paying" clients.

BERNICE: *(Smugly)* It's legal.

WANDA: Which makes your corruption not all that different from most people, who, unfortunately, don't get as many opportunities to have the law on their side.

BERNICE: I do what a lawyer's supposed to do: I take sides! I use fair means or foul. But I know you're above all that. You don't take sides; the only thing you do is take notes.

WANDA: Objection!

BERNICE: What?

WANDA: Objection. That calls for a conclusion on the part of counsel. . . . Don't you remember? We used to say that in law school, when we had an argument that was reaching the point of no return.

BERNICE: Objection sustained . . . I never understood why you decided to stop practicing law.

WANDA: I didn't believe I could do anything with it.

BERNICE: So what have you done as a TV journalist that you couldn't do as a lawyer?

WANDA: It's what I DIDN'T want to do that made me decide not to practice law anymore. You always liked getting to the bottom of things. I never have. The smell of the truth has never appealed to me enough to want it in every breath I take. And if I learned anything from being a lawyer, it's that the truth will kill you a lot sooner than it'll set you free.

BERNICE: I rest your case.

WANDA: I'm what I've always been: someone who doesn't like to go too far below skin level. You're everything I'm not. Being around you is a way to stay close to that part of you I admire. You only get in touch with me when you want something. Which is fine, because if you ask a favor of me and I can do it, I will. But I don't do it for truth, justice or Amway. I do it for YOU. And I don't find it inexcusable that your reasons for friendship are different from mine. In all the years I've known you, I've never expected you to change your mind about anything you believed in. But I had hoped you'd learn to change the subject.

BERNICE: You look tired.

WANDA: I didn't know you still noticed things like that.

BERNICE: Well, you said I never change the subject.

(Light goes down on BERNICE *and* WANDA.)

Act 2: Scene 11

(Light comes up on Cummings's living room with ELEANOR, AVERY, *and* CASSANDRA *in the middle of a heated discussion.)*

CASSANDRA: I just told you! He never said anything to me about being in any gang!

ELEANOR: I'll never believe Darryl was involved with people like that.

AVERY: Cass? Do you think it's true?

CASSANDRA: *(Beat)* It's probably as true as anything else that's been said about him since he was killed.

ELEANOR: What's that supposed to mean?

CASSANDRA: Just that everybody's got their own version of who Darryl is. To the media, he's either the subway Picasso or a common criminal masquerading as an artist. To Bernice, he's an opportunity to continue her war against the cops who beat up her brother. And to you, he's the dutiful son and favored child.

*(*ELEANOR *walks over to* CASSANDRA *and slaps her hard across the face.)*

ELEANOR: *(Livid)* Stop it! You hear me! I've had it with the way you use thinking you're right as a weapon against your father and me. If there were some things you needed from us that you didn't get, I'm sorry. We did the best we could. And if that wasn't good enough, that still doesn't give you the right to be contemptuous. *(Grabs* CASSANDRA *by the shoulders)* We don't deserve that! And I'm not going to take it! *(She pulls* CASSANDRA *to her in a rough hug and then awkwardly releases her.)*

CASSANDRA: Well, I guess I finally got what I wanted. You always let Darryl get close enough to get on your nerves. You and Dad used to say it was the kids who gave you a lot of trouble that you wanted to reach. But no matter what I did to piss you off, you always seemed more interested in not losing control than in letting me know what you felt about what I'd done! It's like Darryl was your son. But I was some lesson you were trying to learn by heart.

ELEANOR: Cass! We never meant to favor Darryl.

CASSANDRA: I could accept it more from Daddy. But not from you. . . . It's like I was always waiting for you to tell me things you'd saved up just for me. I didn't care what it was. As long as it was from you.

ELEANOR: *(Grudgingly)* I guess I did let you stuff your life into Darryl's. Maybe I wasn't willing to give as much of myself to you as I had to him.

CASSANDRA: And it's still happening. Only now, Darryl's got millions of people paying attention to him. That's why I didn't get involved in the demonstrations and rallies. . . . You know, it wasn't until I got arrested that I finally understood why loving him as much as I did made me hate him sometimes.

AVERY: I can't believe you felt that way about your brother.

CASSANDRA: *(Beat)* The night I was arrested in the train yards, Darryl was WITH me.

(ELEANOR and AVERY exchange stunned looks and then turn back to CASSANDRA.)

ELEANOR: What!

AVERY: Why didn't you tell us?

CASSANDRA: Darryl told me not to.

AVERY: What do you mean? Where was he when you were arrested?

CASSANDRA: *(Beat)* He told me to wait by one of the trains while he went to get his stash of spray cans. While he was gone, some transit workers grabbed me before I could get away. He told me later they had spotted him before they saw me. He wanted to warn me but it was all he could do to keep from being caught himself. He said even though I was arrested, I was lucky that I wasn't caught with him. . . . I remember feeling glad that he'd finally given me a reason to admit to myself how much I disliked him when we were growing up. He'd always treated me like my life was in his way! He did all kinds of cruel things to me but that made me even more determined to get close to him. I didn't care what he did as long as I had his attention. He finally gave in and became the big brother I needed him to be. . . . When I cursed him for running off and leaving me, he seemed relieved to hear me say he was scared. And I couldn't believe I'd really gotten angry over what he'd done to me—like there was actually a "me" for him to hurt! We both looked at each other like we were brand new. . . . There's so much I wanted to say to him. But that's between Darryl and me. And I don't care what Bernice says! I'm not sharing it with anyone.

(Light goes down on living room with AVERY and ELEANOR looking directly at one another.)

Act 2: Scene 12

(Light comes up on WANDA WAPLES.*)*

WANDA: After almost two months the Grand Jury in the Darryl Cummings case has concluded its deliberations. At a press conference before a packed corridor in the criminal court building, Manhattan District Attorney Michael Scanlon announced the findings of the Grand Jury.

(Light goes down on WANDA *and comes up on* FIRST WOMAN.*)*

1ST WOMAN: That young man should've known that in an argument with the police he stood to lose a whole lot more than his temper.

(Light goes down on FIRST WOMAN *and comes up on* SECOND WOMAN.*)*

2ND WOMAN: You have to understand that most of the terrible things I hear about, I never see. And I prefer it that way. I've seen plenty of young men behave badly. But to see what the police did . . . I didn't want to believe it. So I told myself the police were preventing HIM from doing something far worse than what THEY were doing.

(Light goes down on SECOND WOMAN *and comes up on the* POLICEMAN.*)*

POLICEMAN: I know I'm the one who asked for counseling. It's just not easy for me to talk to people who aren't cops. I always feel like I'm put in the position of having to defend myself against the charge that all cops are thugs underneath this blue. I've gotten commendations for disarming assailants without using my revolver. In fact I've never had to use my gun in the ten years I've been a cop. And I hope to God I never do. I also have a little souvenir under here *(touches the area under his left arm)* that I got from this punk who was terrorizing people with a knife in the subway car. . . . I didn't know what was going on at first because nobody said a word until I was about to move to the next car. Then this woman screams and when I wheel around he's all over me with a knife. But that's the job I'm paid to do. I don't ask for any thanks for doing it. And I didn't get any from anyone in that subway car. But I didn't let that affect the way I do my job. I help people whenever I can and give respect when it's given to me. But what I can't understand is—if I could do all that without any public recognition, why do I have to take all the blame now for what happened to Cummings? *(Beat)* It was a legitimate bust! He broke the law and he had a big mouth! Like I said to him: "Who the fuck do you think you are?" I mean, it wasn't like he was physically imposing. In fact, he was kind of a delicate looking—which pissed some cops off even more because he didn't look the part of the wild man he was trying to play. I still could've handled him by myself. But once we got to the street, he wasn't my collar anymore. Everybody started teeing off on him; and he kept cursing and whipping those footlong dreadlocks around like he had all of Bedford-Stuyvesant in his head. But the worst of it didn't happen till he was put in the back of the van. I was in the front with the driver and I could hear him and what they were doing to him. And after a while, I stopped hearing him and only heard what they were doing. . . . I'm a cop, by training and experience. And this was the first time I didn't respond to a call for help. I wanted to but my experience as a cop overruled my training. The cops in the back of that van were family. And like any family, when something happens that you don't want to know about, you look the other way. That's right! For once I decided to do what I see people doing everyday. I didn't get involved! I know it was wrong. But tell me this? What about the ten years of answering the call for help? Doesn't that count for something? You know, it's funny. This guy Cummings couldn't keep his mouth shut. And he's being remembered for a lot more than that. I kept my mouth shut. But that's all anyone wants to know about me.

(Light goes down on POLICEMAN *and comes up on* RHAPSODY, *who goes into a rap.)*

RHAPSODY: New York is a city that takes all comers/from high and low rollers to different drummers./ And for those who come expecting kid gloves/they soon find out it's push and shove./I'm a walking motion picture/a thrill and a dream./I ain't all that mean./I just wanna be seen./But there are those who mistake every move I make./When they see me coming/they start to shake./The only MEAN in me is what I MEAN to be./To tell my story 'cause it's mandatory. . . . *(He stops as though listening to someone talk to him)* I told you before, I didn't jump no turnstile. When I got to the platform, he and the cop was already into it. . . . So what if I pumped up my friendship with him a little. There's nothing wrong with putting a little flavor into things that happen to you. People do it all the time. I just do it better. . . . What's the big deal. All that really matters is how close what I said is to what happened. . . . Hey! You don't need to tell me about perjury. I know what time it is. Cause the real deal is: everybody tells on somebody; but nobody tells on themselves. *(Laughs)* But I'm a do it—just this once—to show you I can do something even Presidents don't do. . . . We were never together at all . . . I hadn't done too well on tips that night and was in a kind of low-grade funk. When I got to the station I decided the MTA owed me one for all the times I paid my fare and didn't get no rapid transit in return. So I jump over the turnstile and walk toward the end of the platform. I didn't see Fly but he must a come through a few minutes later and walked to the other end of the station. When the cop shows, he looks down the other end of the platform and spots Fly using his Magic Marker on the wall. . . . If he'd a turned in my direction first, I'd a probably been busted instead of him. . . . Hey! I'm not the one who played the cop too close. . . . What could I do? We weren't that tight for me to get into what was going on and risk getting busted myself. He should a known better than to let that cop reflex him like that. That wasn't like Fly. I never met anybody who could chill quicker than he could. Sometimes we called him Mister Frosty. *(Without bravado)* It's kind a creepy when you think about it. The cop who was looking for me finds Fly; and the dude whose cool was ice-cubed, loses it along with his life. It could've been me; *(tries to sound as though he got away with something but his expression reveals that he's not so sure)* but it wasn't!

(Light goes down on RHAPSODY *and comes up on* WANDA.*)*

WANDA: Three New York City Transit Police officers, sergeants on the scene, have been arrested on an indictment charging them with either directly causing the death of Darryl Cummings or, by their inaction, permitting other police officers to assault him. After the indictments were read, they were denounced by protesters who had packed the corridors.

(Light goes down on WANDA *and comes up on* BERNICE.*)*

BERNICE: These indictments are an insult, not only to the Cummings family but to any civilized standard of justice. District Attorney Michael Scanlon would have us accept an indictment that doesn't charge any police officers for what they did to Darryl Cummings but for what they didn't do! This is unacceptable and we intend to do everything in our power to express our dissatisfaction with the State's handling of this case. And I'll guarantee you that if any of us are arrested today, the police will follow their usual practice of charging US with THEIR criminal behavior!

(Light goes down on BERNICE *and comes up on* WANDA.*)*

WANDA: When court security guards tried to clear the corridor, they were met with resistance by the demonstrators. It was an ugly scene as scores of arrests were made and many of the demonstrators were injured.

(Light goes down on WANDA.*)*

Act 2: Scene 13

(Light comes up on BERNICE, ELEANOR, *and* AVERY *in the Cummings's living room.)*

BERNICE: I would have expected this from Cassandra but not from you.

ELEANOR: People were seriously hurt! Aren't you concerned about that?

BERNICE: Of course I am.

ELEANOR: But you provoked the police!

BERNICE: They didn't need an excuse to beat up on people.

ELEANOR: Then why did you give them one?

BERNICE: Do you ask yourselves the same question about Darryl?

AVERY: *(Defensive)* What do you mean?

BERNICE: Do you believe Darryl provoked those cops—forced them to kill him?

AVERY: *(Beat)* It's not the same thing. What you did was planned.

BERNICE: Look. The likelihood is that those cops are going to walk. We have one last trump card we can play. Everything that happened in the corridor outside the courtroom was videotaped.

ELEANOR: So it was planned!

BERNICE: Not the way you mean. It's just that it's important to have the media around in case something like this happens.

ELEANOR: But what about all those people who've supported us? Didn't they deserve to know you were going to provoke a situation that would put them in jeopardy? They could have decided whether they wanted to be there. You didn't give them a choice.

BERNICE: A choice! You don't know what choice means! My brother didn't have a choice when those cops got a hold of him. And I didn't have a choice as I watched them beat his mind to mush! The people who were in that corridor chose to be there. Whatever I did to make our presence felt can't be compared to what those cops did to Darryl!

AVERY: No. It can't. But that doesn't make it right.

BERNICE: You can't always have it both ways. Winning and being right.

ELEANOR: Bernice. What did we win by those people getting beaten?

BERNICE: Only a few people saw Darryl beaten to death but millions watched the news as the police waded into that crowd of demonstrators swinging their billy clubs. The people who end up on that jury may not be convinced that the police killed Darryl. But after witnessing those beatings, I don't think anyone will doubt what they're capable of.

ELEANOR: That's no comfort to the people who got their heads beat in.

BERNICE: They'll be all right. Those cops taught them a valuable lesson. At least now they know police violence isn't something that always happens to someone else—which is what you believed until Darryl was killed.

AVERY: *(Defensive and irate)* That's not true! We know what goes on in the world!

BERNICE: No you don't. Not really. You UNDERSTAND. But you don't KNOW. Isn't that what you told me, Eleanor?

(ELEANOR stares at BERNICE but says nothing.)

BERNICE: It's the curse of middle-class comfort. We convince ourselves that we've made our own good fortune. And there's a part of us that believes there are people who make their own misfortune. That's what's tearing you apart about Darryl. You can't accept that he was treated like one of THEM.

ELEANOR: *(Softly and without conviction)* That's not fair.

BERNICE: I know. But it's true. Isn't it?

(Light goes down on living room.)

Act 2: Scene 14

(Light comes up on BERNICE and WANDA sitting at a restaurant table having a drink. They are both laughing.)

WANDA: Do you know why scientists are now using journalists instead of rats in their laboratory experiments?

BERNICE: No.

WANDA: It's because journalists will do things that even rats won't do.

(They both laugh.)

BERNICE: There's a story about a lawyer who goes on a camping trip with a friend who's not an attorney. They both have on their backpacks and suddenly they see a cougar about twenty yards away. The lawyer starts taking off his backpack and his friend says: "What are you doing?" And the lawyer says: "I'm going to run for it!" But his friend says: "You can't outrun a cougar." So the lawyer says: "I don't have to outrun the cougar. I just have to outrun you!"

(They both laugh hysterically and as they calm down they become more reflective.)

WANDA: You ought to tell that story to the Cummings family.

BERNICE: They wouldn't get it. They're too busy getting high in the friendly skies of a world that doesn't exist.

WANDA: *(Sarcastic)* But you of all people should be able to appreciate that.

BERNICE: They think I orchestrated that confrontation outside the courtroom to force the police to attack us in front of the TV cameras.

WANDA: What do you think you did?

BERNICE: *(Ignores her)* People think the courts are supposed to give them justice. That's not the way it is at all. You have to push and shove your way into a position to get justice! But it's like anything else that's good FOR you. It may not be good TO you. . . . I'm willing to take the blame. But if further down the road any of those cops do some time, I want the credit!

WANDA: Remember what Martin Luther King, Jr., said? "Be ye not conformed to this world. But be ye transformed by a renewal of your mind."

BERNICE: Well, in the meantime, if you can't get the law on your side, you have to put it in your mouth.

WANDA: Whose mouth? Just yours or everybody's?

BERNICE: A pox on your house, too!

WANDA: I'm already contaminated. My disease is adversarial and yours is advocacy. But we're both infected by whatever germ of truth we uncover. . . . You know what's black and brown and looks good on both a lawyer and a journalist, don't you?

BERNICE: What?

WANDA: A Doberman pinscher!

(They both burst into laughter as the light goes down on them.)

Act 2: Scene 15

(A recording of Ella Fitzgerald singing "Ill Wind" is heard as light comes up on ELEANOR *and* AVERY, *each sitting at the far end of the living room couch.)*

AVERY: Every day when we leave the court or a rally, there's something missing that doesn't return until everyone is gone.

ELEANOR: What's that?

AVERY: Darryl's life. We spend most of our time sharing his death but not his life. The only time we get to do that is when we're alone.

ELEANOR: I remember when school was out, I'd do whatever I had to do in the house near an open window so that I could keep track of him while he was outside playing with his friends. When they played "Hide-and-Seek" they'd get someone to agree to be "it." And when the person would start to count . . .

AVERY: Five, ten, fifteen, twenty . . .

ELEANOR: I could hear the soles of their sneakers beating against the pavement.

AVERY: Twenty-five, thirty, thirty-five, forty . . .

ELEANOR: There would always be arguments over who got to which hiding place first.

AVERY: Forty-five, fifty, fifty-five, sixty . . .

ELEANOR: But the arguments never lasted long because no one wanted to be caught without a place to hide when the person who was "it" stopped counting.

AVERY: Sixty-five, seventy, seventy-five, eighty . . .

ELEANOR: By the time they got to eighty, all I could hear was the counting.

AVERY: Eighty-five, ninety, ninety-five, one hundred. Anyone around my base is it!

ELEANOR: Those first few seconds after the counting stopped was as quiet as I ever remember it getting when children were outside playing. . . . But it wasn't quiet for long. Whoever was "it" would start finding kids immediately. But Darryl always seemed to be the one who couldn't be found. So as the person who was "it" began to venture out beyond the safety of the base to look for Darryl, the other kids yelled encouragement to him to get back to the base. I would stop what I was doing and listen. . . . And within a few minutes, screams would burst from the mouths of the children. Their screaming got louder and louder until Darryl's voice cut through all the cheering.

AVERY: Home! Free all!

ELEANOR: He was like that in everything. It didn't matter where he was or what he was doing. He always believed he was home free or not very far from being there. Maybe it was a mistake for me to teach him that?

AVERY: You think Bernice is right?

ELEANOR: About what?

AVERY: That we believe there're black people who deserve their misfortune but that Darryl was different.

ELEANOR: *(Beat)* I never believed that . . . but I felt it.

AVERY: So did I. *(There's a pause as they allow the full impact of what they've admitted to register)* You think she's right about how we have to fight so those cops don't get away with killing him?

ELEANOR: Maybe. . . . But I think we can do better than that.

AVERY: What about with Cassandra? *(Beat)* And us?

ELEANOR: *(Beat)* I don't know. But . . .

(Light comes up on POLICEMAN, RHAPSODY, FIRST WOMAN, *and* SECOND WOMAN, *who assume positions in the subway section of the stage. Each one speaks and then all at once. They are joined by* WANDA, BERNICE, ELEANOR, *and* AVERY. *This creates a clash of voices that degenerates into the noise that is so often a substitute for communication.)*

POLICEMAN: He had a sewer for a mouth.

RHAPSODY: He didn't lose his life all by himself.

1ST WOMAN: These young people talk too loud and too much.

2ND WOMAN: There're some things I don't want to know about.

WANDA: Before you can talk to some people, you have to get their attention.

BERNICE: The police deny that the injuries to the demonstrators were caused by an excessive use of force.

AVERY: I kept trying to tell her. *(Gesturing to* ELEANOR*)* You can never come in from out of doors.

ELEANOR: I thought I'd helped Darryl to find a place inside himself where he'd always be safe.

POLICEMAN: Who did he think he was dealing with?

RHAPSODY: I'm not bad. I'm better!

1ST WOMAN: If you have to shout to get someone to listen to you, you're better off not being bothered with them at all.

2ND WOMAN: I don't want to talk about it anymore!

BERNICE: The police riot outside the courtroom was just a continuation of the beating and murder of Darryl Cummings.

WANDA: District Attorney Scanlon praised the court security officers for their handling of the disturbance and promised to prosecute the demonstrators to the fullest extent of the law.

AVERY: I tried to keep him alive!

ELEANOR: I tried to keep him free!

(CASSANDRA *enters and takes up a position at the edge of the subway platform. She begins to sing, her voice moving in a wordless journey of sounds that encompass moans, wails, sighs, screams, laughter, and breathing. Gradually,* CASSANDRA's *singing silences all the other voices and commands everyone's attention. It's as though she has found a language that, for a brief moment, joins everyone together in such a way that each person can hear something of themselves reverberating in her voice. The light goes down on the scene with the sounds of* CASSANDRA's *voice lingering until they fade out, and the only sound remaining is the needle from the stereo turntable sticking on a scratch in the record, "Ill Wind," which opened the play.)*

THE END

HUBBA CITY

Ishmael Reed

Act I: Scene 1
Oakland, California. About Fall, 1989

(Home of the Warhaus's, a black couple living in the North Oakland section of Oakland, California. On the wall are pictures of a black Jesus Christ, Martin Luther King, Jr., JFK, and a younger SAM WARHAUS *in cowboy clothes. Also a young black man in Air Force outfit, goggles, etc.* SAM WARHAUS *is sitting in a wheelchair with a blanket over his knees. Coughs a lot. He is listening to the baseball game. Enter* MILDRED WARHAUS, MABEL *and* JAKE NELSON. *They're wearing yellow jumpsuits, and caps and carrying flashlights. They wear badges that read "Crime Watch." All of the characters are in their middle sixties.* SAM WARHAUS *is clearly annoyed by this interruption.)*

MILDRED: *(Wearily)* Ami, I tired. Some of the people in the Crime Watch are in their seventies. I don't know how they do it. Walking up and down these streets. Looking out for suspicious behavior.

JAKE: *(Sits down, removes his shoes and begins to massage his feet)* My feet hurt so bad that when I go home, I'm going to soak them in a pan of hot water.

MABEL: Do you think that "take back our streets program" is really worth it?

MILDRED: I don't know. We go to these Crime Watch meetings and hear the people from downtown and nothing changes.

MABEL: Soon as the hoodlums move out of one neighborhood, they show up in another.

JAKE NELSON: It's all coming from that apartment building on Forty-fifth and Market Street. That's the headquarters of Crackpot. You see those runners out there all day with their bicycles. They use that bus bench, pretending to be waitin' for the bus so's the police won't notice them.

MILDRED: I knew that his lawyers would get Crackpot out. He was suppose to do ten years for running down Mr. Johnson, our block captain.

JAKE NELSON: He only did two.

MILDRED: You want some tea or coffee?

JAKE: Coffee.

MABEL: Not me. My doctor told me to cut back on caffeine. It's making me a nervous wreck. And with these gunshots going off half the night. I'm sorry I left Texas. *(She disappears into the kitchen.* MABEL *and* JAKE *glare at* SAM)

JAKE: It's all over woman. You know what your sister said in her letter from Houston. It's down there, too. *(Turns to* SAM*)* Sam, we could use your help at the Crime Watch meetings.

SAM: I'm trying to listen to the ball game.

MABEL: If this drug war don't stop, you won't have a ball game. We'll all be dead.

JAKE: Crackpot and his gang are shooting up the neighborhoods and all you want to do is listen to the durn ball game.

SAM: That's my right, ain't it? Since when has it become against the law to listen to the ball game?

(Announcer says "Home Run!" SAM *leaves the conversation and returns to his radio. Enter* MILDRED *with two coffees and one tea.)*

MILDRED: You can forget about him. He ain't no help. *(*MILDRED *and* SAM *frown at each other.* SAM *waves her away contemptuously)*

MABEL: A lot of people are scared to come to the meetings, since Ms. Brown's house was burned down by them crack addicts. And that man down on Fortieth Street. They slashed his tires and killed his dog. They using these little boys to peddle their dope because they won't be prosecuted like the older boys.

MILDRED: Well, maybe the people are right not coming to the meetings. The police come out to talk to us. The district attorney comes and says that he's doing the best he can. But it don't change nothin'.

MABEL: Did you hear what that old crazy white woman said?

MILDRED: Which one?

MABEL: The one who tries to run the meetings every month and gets mad when she can't get her way. She said that we should go down to the council meetings and complain.

JAKE: The council meetings are televised. Every gang member in Oakland would know our faces. She must have been a fool to suggest such a thing.

MILDRED: White people live in a different world from us. They're free. They don't have to worry about these crack dealers. Yet they always complaining. Angry about the government. Angry about taxes. Angry about black people. Angry about who knows what else.

MABEL: I'll say, and that other white woman who represents us. The one who s'pose to be our councilwoman. We only get to see her once a year. She has a black man come in her place.

MILDRED: He's her liaison.

MABEL: Is that what he is? I was wondering what he was.

JAKE: Then what is she spending all of her time doing?

MILDRED: She's up at Rockridge where all of those young white professionals live. They worried about the ice-cream factory expanding.

(They all laugh, except SAM *who tries to silence them so that he might concentrate on the game.)*

MABEL: The ice-cream factory. We down here about to be driven out of Oakland by these thugs and she worried about ice cream. We have to drive ten miles to get ice cream. There ain't no stores or nothin'. We can't buy fresh vegetables.

JAKE: We have to go to the Arab stores.

MILDRED: You can go. I can't; Mabel can't. There are always these young people hanging out in front of those stores. Drinking whiskey.

JAKE: I thought that Arabs didn't drink liquor.

MABEL: They sellin' it all to us.

MILDRED: Next time Jesse Jackson goes to the Middle East and be hugging and kissing—what's the name of that man who be wearing that old nasty headrag and look like he ain't shaved or took a bath in thirty years?

JAKE: Arafat. Yassir Arafat.

MILDRED: Well maybe he ought to ask that Arafat to close down some of these Arab liquor stores. *(Pause)* We got more liquor stores in Oakland than churches and that's the problem. *(Pause)*

JAKE: Sam sure has changed since Port Arthur. Remember?

MABEL: Everybody respected him . . .

JAKE: Because they know they'd get a mouthful of bullets, that's why . . .

MILDRED: Texas white folks used to push black people off the sidewalk . . .

MABEL: But not Sam.

JAKE: Even the white folks respected Sam. *(Chuckling)* I remember when we were kids. The depression. Times was hard and Sam's family got back on their rent. His mother used to take in the wash of these rich folks, but some of them was broke too. Well, the landlord came to collect the rent and when Sam's mother said she didn't have it, the landlord slapped her. Then he started calling her all out of her name. Sam took a brick and hit the landlord on the head with it. Nobody did nothin' because everybody thought Sam was crazy.

MABEL: What happened to him?

MILDRED: He hasn't been acting right since his retirement. He says he's sick, but the doctor can't find anything.

(Shots are heard. Everybody scrambles for the floor except SAM. *Spotlight on* SAM *who's still listening to the ball game. After the shots stop they slowly rise to their feet.)*

JAKE: This is gettin' bad on my high blood pressure.

MABEL: A whole lot of our friends are moving out of North Oakland.

JAKE: Or turning their homes over to their kids. Some of their kids are setting up crack houses. We can put some pressure on some of the landlords, but what do we do when they the landlords?

MILDRED: It's gettin' bad. But I'm not going to move. Nothin' will make me move. We been living in this house for almost thirty years. My child grew up in this house until he went to war. We plan to stay here.

MABEL: Yes, but sometimes I get discouraged.

JAKE: So do I.

MILDRED: I know that it gets bleak sometimes. Looks like we have been abandoned. Looks like nobody cares anything about whether we live or die. But you know what Martin King said.

JAKE: What's that Mildred?

MILDRED: He said: "Walk together children, don't get weary." Whenever I get discouraged, I think of Martin. (*She glances up at his picture*)

MABEL: (*Spontaneously, begins to sing*) "We shall not, we shall not be moved." (JAKE *and* MILDRED *join in.* SAM *becomes really annoyed*) "We shall not, we shall not be moved. Just like a tree standing by the water, we shall not be moved. We shall not, we shall not be moved. . . . "

SAM: (*They sing over his lines*) Will you shut up and let me listen to my game?

Act I: Scene 2
The Warhaus Home

(MILDRED *and a* POLICEMAN *are arguing.*)

COP: What do you want me to do about it, lady? I'm telling you that the department is undermanned. Go to the city council and ask them for some more money. We've tried our best to drive these bastards from the streets and into rock houses.

MILDRED: You ain't trying hard enough. We go to these meetings every month and you hand out the same jive. About how you don't have no money and you're working double shifts, yet that situation on Market Street has been going on for years and now with Crackpot out of jail it's getting worse. And tell me this. Another thing I want to know is why do the police seem so cozy with these thugs? Carrying on conversations and acting all chummy.

COP: (*Nervously*) You people don't understand how the system works Ma'am. It's not just a matter of arresting these people. We have to have evidence—we have to be mindful of the law. The Constitution.

MILDRED: *(Angry)* You mean to tell me that the Constitution was some kind of suicide pact? That the men who wrote it went out and drank poisoned Kool-Aid afterwards. Crackpot sends these young people into our neighborhoods from that apartment building over on Forty-fifth Street. They talk nasty and look mean. They make filthy remarks to the women who walk by. They rob us. They mug us and break into our homes. The lady around the corner was raped and murdered and you talking about some durn system. Are you out of your mind?

SAM: *(Meekly)* No need to raise your voice at the man, dear. He's just doing his job.

MILDRED: *(To* SAM*)* You keep out of it. All you do is sit around, listening to the ball game all day. *(To* COP*)* If they spent the fifteen million dollars on this drug mess instead of puttin' all the money on that football team, there would be more money for the police.

SAM: Woman, what you got against the Oakland Raiders?

MILDRED: You shush. If you and the other men on the block would get together, you could get rid of these hooligans. Every time we have a Crime Watch meeting, a few more show up but it's mostly women and children show up. I wish that Mr. Johnson was still alive. He would do something. He would have chased these hooligans out of the neighborhood. They respected him. If James hadn't been shot down in Vietnam, he would have done something. He would have been right here with me. Standing up to these bums. Our son wasn't afraid of anything. Not like his father who is just a shell of his former self. You won't even get up from that chair so's we could take a trip to Washington to see the child's name on the Vietnam Veteran's Wall.

SAM: Aw Mildred, leave me alone. You know that I'm an invalid.

MILDRED: *(Ignores* SAM, *to* COP*)* It's been three months since I called you. You told me to organize a Crime Watch. So I went around and knocked on people's doors and got them to put those signs in the window saying that they would report any suspicious activities to the police. Next, we got everybody to make a phone tree. We call the police and call the police. We call that special number you gave us and a voice came on saying that the phone had been disconnected. We call all day and all night and they don't come. Sometimes we get a recorded voice and sometimes we don't even get that. It rings and rings. What will it take? One of us getting shot dead? Hell, I thought things would change after we formed our Crime Watch, but now that these boys see they can do anything and the police won't show up, they've gotten bolder. It's even worse now than it was before we organized.

COP: It takes time, lady.

MILDRED: Time? Time my foot. It's been a year. What are you going to do about Crackpot?

COP: *(Clearly uncomfortable with this question)* We haven't completed our investigation. Now if you'll just continue to write down license plate numbers and get the neighbors to call the police, it will be a big help and *(exasperated, looks at watch)*, I gotta go. *(Heads toward the door)* You have my card. If there's anymore trouble, let me know. *(She looks at him with disgust. He exits)*

SAM: You sure were hard on him. He's a nice young man. And I told you, you'd better leave those young people alone. You hear those automatic weapons going off half the night? They'll shoot you.

MILDRED: I wasn't raised to be no slave, and I didn't work thirty years of my life to spend my retirement in prison. *(Pause, then tenderly)* Why don't we get away for a while? You know they called up here last week and said I'd won that trip for two to Las Vegas.

SAM: But you know that I can't travel, the doctor said . . .

MILDRED: The doctor didn't say nothin'. You've been sent to twenty doctors and they can't find nothin' wrong with you, man.

SAM: It still hurts when I stand up.

(Shots are heard outside. SAM *cowers.* MILDRED *falls to the floor. Gets up slowly)*

MILDRED: That does it. *(She reaches for an overcoat and picks up a purse)*

SAM: Mildred. Where are you going? You have to fix me my lunch.

MILDRED: The lunch can wait. *(Puts on coat)* I'm going downtown to see the council lady who represents our district.

SAM: For what?

MILDRED: This neighborhood, that's for what. These people come into this neighborhood every first and fifteenth of the month to buy drugs. Soon as they get their checks from the county . . . everybody on the block knows about it, but nobody wants to do anything.

SAM: That's dangerous. Those young people don't respect nothin'. Why, one of these crack girls got into a fight with her own mother. You remember reading that? The child was selling drugs, and her mother wanted credit and she told her mother that she, her own mother, was just another customer.

MILDRED: We have to find some way to close down that apartment building. Get it condemned. The landlord don't care. He don't have to live around here. Probably live up there in the Oakland hills.

SAM: You just asking for trouble. You always was like that. Why can't you leave well enough alone? These are our retirement years.

MILDRED: And you want to spend it in that chair, listening to the baseball games, while I bring you lunch, dinner, and breakfast and rub your back. Wash your clothes. Everything for you, you. You and nothing for me. This is a time that we should be enjoying ourselves.

SAM: *(Puts hand on back as though he experienced a sharp pain)* Ohhhhhhh.

MILDRED: *(Concerned)* What's the matter?

SAM: My back. Please, Mildred. Rub it for me.

MILDRED: I can't right now. I have to catch the bus.

(She exits. He returns to the baseball game.)

Act I: Scene 3
Interior of the private club The Vassals of the Celestial Ocean

(Three club chairs, two facing the audience. A table with a pot of flowers on top. A framed portrait of Theodore Roosevelt in a safari outfit with bag, animal if possible. KRUD *is a realtor who owns properties in Oakland, including the apartment building used by* CRACK-POT. *He's in his late sixties. Dressed in an expensive suit, shirt, cuff links, has blow-dried white hair.)*

KRUD: *(To audience)* Sure am glad to be somewhere I don't have to run into a lot of blacks. My club, The Vassal of the Celestial Ocean, allows me to be around my own kind. Men who think the way I do.

*(*KRUD *tinkles a little bell. Black waiter appears, in white jacket, black bow tie, black trousers and shoes. Gray sideburns, mustache. He wears a black patch over one eye. Very dignified. About sixty-six. He carries glasses on tray.)*

MARTIN: Yessir, Mr. Krud.

KRUD: Fix me a manhattan, Martin.

MARTIN: Yessir. *(*KRUD *hands him five dollars.* MARTIN *looks at the five dollars disdainfully. Smiles. Puts it in his pocket)* Why thank you, Mr. Krud.

KRUD: Don't mention it, Martin. Sure wish we had more black people like you. They're down there in the inner city ruining the good name of the United States. Screwing like rabbits, and spending all of their welfare checks on crack and wine. You know, you can't blame the system or whitey anymore, Martin. You can't blame slavery or history either. Why, the Japanese are over here and you don't see them asking for any handouts. I'm trying to get Congressman Rapp to introduce a bill that would declare them honorary whites.

MARTIN: I lost an eye fighting the Japanese at Okinawa, Mr. Krud. We engaged the enemy in hand-to-hand combat.

KRUD: See? There you go. A prisoner of history. You and the other blacks ought to try to come into the twentieth century.

MARTIN: Yessir, Mr. Krud. *(With quiet anger. Looks contemptuously upon him when he's out of his view)*

(Banker KROCK *enters. Walks over to* KRUD *and gives him the secret handshake. Sits down in his chair, and begins to read* Baron's.*)*

KRUD: What's the latest?

KROCK: I feel great today. Deposits are up in the last two months, thanks to these black kids and their crack money. For a while there I thought we were going to have to get the Feds to rescue the company. I okayed so many bad loans to the club members and their friends. The Feds were about to audit our books.

KRUD: Those kids are getting all of us rich. I've rented out houses that I thought I'd never rent out. But I'm glad that we don't have to socialize with them as we do with the rest of our prime customers. It's a good thing that we have this club where we can get away from black people and our wives.

KROCK: You said it. I could make a helluva lot more money if I didn't have women in the way. A wife and mistress to support in that condo over near the lake. Only my daughter is making money.

KRUD: How is your daughter?

KROCK: Went to a stag the other night and they showed a dirty film. Guess who was the star?

KRUD: Who?

KROCK: *(Proud)* My twenty-year-old.

KRUD: What are you going to do?

KROCK: Buy half interest in the movie company. They've already drawn up the papers. You want in?

KRUD: No wonder you were able to build that chateau in the wine country. All of your investments. Your bank is holding the mortgage on half the property downstairs.

KROCK: These young ghetto kids are putting hundreds of thousands in the bank. Kid came in the other day and deposited ten thousand bucks in cash. The next day he deposited thirty thousand. They're making all of us rich. If anything happened to this cocaine traffic, the bottom of the economy would fall out. It's bigger than nuclear power and superconductivity. And the bio-tech industry—everybody thought this would be big in the late eighties? This crack stuff is bigger than that. And Jack Marsh, the gun dealer says he's making so much money he's talking about early retirement. Says these kids have bought so many weapons from him that they could supply three armies.

KRUD: We're getting ours, too. Crackpot, remember him?

KROCK: Do I remember him? He's one of the bank's best customers.

KRUD: He's renting that apartment building of mine over on Market and Forty-fifth Street. Now he wants me to buy him a home in the country. Those bastards down there can all die if it were up to me. This crack stuff is merely hastening the day, but while the cash is coming in I'm going to get all that I can lay my hands on. *(KROCK looks at watch)*

KROCK: I'll be right back, I have to call the bank. *(Exits)*

KRUD: *(Rings the bell)* Where's that Martin?

(MILDRED enters in her Crime Watch jumpsuit. MARTIN walks sheepishly behind her. Sets down KRUD's drink.)

KRUD: What do you . . .

MARTIN: We tried to stop her Mr. Krud. *(Out of KRUD's view, he grins)*

MILDRED: You the man who owns that apartment building on Forty-fifth Street? *(She hands him the address)* That's what they told me at the City Assessor's office.

KRUD: What's it to you?

MILDRED: You ought to be ashamed of yourself. We poor colored people work all of our lives to live in a quiet neighborhood and you come in with this apartment building. They got a rock operation going on. Some of our neighbors haven't had sleep in eight months. They leave these little packages all over the street *(flings a cellophane package at him; he recoils),* and that ain't the worst.

KRUD: *(Rises from his chair. She begins to back him up)* So what do you want me to do about it?

MILDRED: I want you to evict them.

KRUD: Evict them? Look, I have to rent to whomever can come up with first and last month's security. Hell, you people have been fighting for fair housing all of these years and you're asking me to evict some coloreds. *(Laughs)*

MILDRED: You can evict them if you wanted to. You know you can. Besides, I'll bet you wouldn't tolerate any rock houses in your neighborhood. Where do you live?

KRUD: *(Weakly)* Hillsborough.

MILDRED: That's where Bing Crosby used to live, ain't it? If some of these kids come to your neighborhood selling rock, they'd call in the army.

KRUD: I'm sorry lady. My hands are tied. Why don't you go see the council person. Don't bother me with your problems.

MILDRED: I called the police, and the police don't answer. They asked me to start a Crime Watch program and they still don't answer. I go to the councilperson and her assistant tells me to go to the vice mayor, and then I go to the vice mayor and he tells me to go to the mayor. The mayor is never in town. So I decided that since you own that place, I should come and see you about it. I don't blame some of these people saying that they want to take the law into their own hands.

KRUD: I'm sorry I can't help you. I know that you'd like to blame it all on the landlord, blame it on the system, blame it on anything but where the blame belongs.

Your own self-destructive behavior. These are the nineties. We don't cater to special interest anymore.

MILDRED: Some landlord. That building is the worst one in the neighborhood. It should be condemned. You could at least cut the lawn from time to time. They use our sidewalks for a bathroom

KRUD: Look. Here's my card. If you can think of something that I can do legally, within the law, I'll do what I can. You people ought to band together like the Asians. You don't see them whining and complaining all of the time. You don't see them asking for affirmative action and welfare, or begging to be compensated for past acts of discrimination.

(Glares at him while approaching him. Puts her finger on his chest. He recoils)

MILDRED: Now you look here. I never asked for no welfare or anything else from you. Me and my husband worked all of our lives. I worked ten years on the night shift at Highland Hospital. Working with sick people. Praying with them, emptying their bedpans and changing their sheets. Bathing them and entertaining them. I was the one who cleaned them when they were dead and got them ready for the morgue.

KRUD: Now don't get violent.

MILDRED: My husband worked in the aluminum plant ever since we came up from Texas in 1943. We pay our taxes, and our only son was killed in Vietnam. So don't you ever accuse us of taking things from this country. We're the ones who are being bled. We do all of your dirty work and get treated like dogs. *(MARTIN comes in and takes her elbow. She yanks it from his grip and gives him a contemptuous look)* And all we're asking is that we have a little peace and quiet in our last years. Well, you're not going to help us, but I tell you one thing. That rock house will be closed if it's the last thing I do on earth, and as far as I'm concerned you're worse than those damned kids. You got them packed in schools like sardines and they don't learn nothin', you cut the money you was giving them for college, and you call them all kinds of dirty names, the TV, the politicians, and the newspapers, so what do you expect?

(She exits. His son, BOBBIE KRUD, enters. He is dressed casually. He is accompanied by JAKE HANDSOME, and a man with an aviator's cap, knickers, boots, white scarf, dark glasses, and black gloves.)

KRUD: Bobbie, my boy.

BOBBIE: What was that all about, Dad?

KRUD: One of these black malcontents. Blaming everything on the white male power structure. Demanding things. Some kids I rented an apartment to are operating a rock house. She wants me to evict them. *(BOBBIE looks to his companion, JOE HAND-SOME, with anxiety)* Anyway, what brings you boys to the club?

BOBBIE: Thought I'd come over and take a swim. Meet my guest, Joe Handsome. *(KRUD shakes his hand)*

HANDSOME: Ciao.

BOBBIE: Joe's a pilot.

KRUD: Pilot? How exciting. You know, I always wanted to fly. Took a few lessons even.

HANDSOME: It's an exhilarating experience. I'd rather fly than eat, or be with a woman. Being up there with all of that mystery. What Swinburne calls "The Flowerless fields of heaven." A man is really alone with his thoughts. Sometimes when I'm flying late at night I turn on my tape deck and play Richard Strauss's "Also Sprach Zarathustra." *(Music comes up in the background.* KRUD *looks to his son quizzically. His son shrugs his shoulders)* And contemplate the moon. I think of the new man. The new god. I think of how we can transcend this puny shell in which we find our souls, or sometimes I put the ship on automatic pilot and read poetry. "When the bounds of spring are on winter's traces / The mother of months in meadow or plain / Fills the shadows and windy places. With lisp of leaves and ripple of rain."

*(*KRUD *gives* BOBBIE *a puzzled look.)*

BOBBIE: *(Nervous. Trying to change the subject)* Joe's just made a trip up from Mexico. He's staying with me for a couple of days.

KRUD: That's nice. You must be really tired, Mr. Handsome. How do you like Oakland Airport?

HANDSOME: I didn't land at the airport, I . . . *(*BOBBIE *takes his arm, eager to get him out of the room)*

BOBBIE: Dad, Joe and I should take our swim now.

KRUD: You boys come over for dinner tomorrow night. We'll barbeque in the backyard and have a round of Old Fashioneds. *(They exit, and the banker* KROCK *enters)*

KROCK: Remember Richard Cummings, used to play golf up here with the boys?

KRUD: Yeah, what about him?

KROCK: Just called to ask for another loan. He's defaulted on three and he's two years behind in his mortgage payments.

KRUD: So what are you going to do?

KROCK: What the hell, I decided to go him another million. Anything to help a brother of the Vassals of the Celestial Ocean. Besides, at the peak of the Vietnam War he got my kid a cushy job in the National Guard. Cummings was a commander. He had influence.

KRUD: Can't let a lodge brother down. Say, you just missed my son. He's here to do the pool with a friend of his, a pilot.

KROCK: That son of yours is a comer. He's going to carry on the tradition. I wish . . .

KRUD: Look, Krock. It wasn't your fault. Your oldest was just depressed. A lot of people suffer from depression.

KROCK: But when he jumped out of that window he took a part of me with him. I was such a hero to him, but when the Grand Jury indicated me for embezzlement, he took it real hard. Good thing the DA was a brother. He got the whole thing squashed, and fired the young zealot in his office who brought me up on charges. I don't know what I'd do if I didn't have the club, and my friends. Oh, did you hear? They're lettin' in a minority.

KRUD: They what? *(Shaken)*

KROCK: Aw you know the NAACP was raising such a fuss about our being on city land and being an all-white club. The board of directors decided to let one in.

KRUD: Are they out of their minds? Besides, it costs twelve thousand dollars per year to belong to this club. What minority can afford that? They must be crazy.

KROCK: That's what I thought, but they said that if we didn't do it, the city might scrutinize the operation and we don't want to have them up here. Suppose they find out that we're using up all the water keeping the golf club lawns green, while the people in the flats have to go without because of the drought, or that we're bringing prostitutes to our parties. The board decided that if we let one in, they'd call off the dogs.

KRUD: I don't like it at all. Have you met him?

KROCK: No, but I hear that he's an auto dealer.

(ROBERT HAMAMOTO enters, snappily dressed, well-groomed.)

HAMAMOTO: *(Bows)* Gentlemen. My name is Robert Hamamoto of Hamamoto Motors. I'm the new club member.

(KRUD's jaw drops. KROCK rises and gives him the secret handshake. They both look at KRUD. KRUD glares at both of them. Angrily, returns to his newspaper rattling it in anger.)

Act II: Scene 1
The Warhaus's Home

(SAM is sitting in the wheelchair. He's frightened. Cowering. Gunshots are heard off stage. MILDRED is on the telephone.)

MILDRED: You can't send nobody right now? But they're out there shooting up the neighborhood. . . . What do you mean maybe an officer will be available in an hour? Somebody might be dead in an hour . . . some neighborhoods are worse? *(To SAM)* It sounds like Vietnam outside and she talking about some neighborhoods are worse. *(MILDRED slams down the phone. She starts out of the door)*

SAM: Dear, where are you going?

(She doesn't answer, but exits. Momentarily, the gunfire stops. She comes back in. She throws the Uzi to the floor.)

SAM: *(Petrified)* Where did you get that thing?

MILDRED: I took it from one of those snotty-nosed punks. The rest of them ran away. He gave me some lip, but I aimed this thing right at his privates. He ran too.

SAM: Are you out of your mind? You took that gun out of that boy's hand? You could have been shot.

MILDRED: The way we livin', we better off dead.

SAM: But . . . but they might come back. I'm scared. You know that I'm disabled. They might blame me for snitching on them or something.

MILDRED: Don't worry. I'll save you *(sarcastically)*.

SAM: Mildred. You done gone too far with this. You becoming one of those vigilantes. Take the law into your own hands. Why, it's unchristian.

MILDRED: I'm like Charles Bronson in *Death Wish*.

SAM: Like what?

MILDRED: Charles Bronson. You know that movie we saw on TV last week where the man's wife and daughter are killed and he goes out and shoots him up a bunch of punks?

SAM: This ain't no movie. This is life. These punks will come back and blow us away.

MILDRED: We have to take a stand. I organized the Crime Watch in our neighborhood as they told us and that didn't work. I called 911 and nobody showed up. I went to the councilwoman's office and she made me wait. I think that she must have sneaked out the back after she heard the fuss I made in the reception area. I went to the vice mayor's office and they said he was in Chicago. It was impossible to reach the mayor. I went to the landlord and he laughed at me. What are we supposed to do? Nobody will help us. We have to do it ourselves. *(Knock on the door)*

SAM: *(Frightened, hiding under a blanket)* There they are now! (MILDRED *goes to the door. A black middle-class woman, well-groomed,* MARTHA WINGATE, *and a cameraman)*

WINGATE: Mildred Warhaus?

MILDRED: Yes.

WINGATE: We were in a neighborhood a few blocks from here, filming a crack bust when the call came on the radio about the shoot-out over here and when we arrived the people in the crowd told us that you'd disarmed one of the lookouts and chased him and his gang out of the neighborhood. The phones all over the city are ringing. We'd love to interview you for a few minutes. May we come in?

MILDRED: Word travels fast. Come on in. *(They set up for the interview.* MILDRED *sits next to* MARTHA WINGATE *on the couch. Smooths her dress, touches her hair)* Won't you give me a chance to change into some decent clothes?

WINGATE: You look fine. Don't worry.

CAMERAMAN: *(CAMERAMAN counts)* 10, 9, 8, 7, 6, 5, 4, 3, 2, 1 *(Points to* WINGATE*)*

WINGATE: This is Martha Wingate, Channel 8 News, in the home of Mildred Warhaus. Ms. Warhaus has become a celebrity within a half hour, and crowds are gathered in front of her house. This woman dared to disarm one of the members of the notorious Runners, an Oakland gang that's said to be responsible for the high homicide rate that has made Oakland the Miami of California. Many have begun calling it "Hubba City," Hubba being a nickname for crack. Ms. Warhaus, why would you risk your life by taking a gun from a dangerous drug runner?

MILDRED: It's about time somebody did something about these kids. This used to be a good neighborhood, but since Crackpot took over that apartment building on Forty-fifth and Market, life in our district has become a living hell. We have these hoodlums milling about on the street, and the children are scared to go out to play. Our elders are trapped in their homes. I just had enough of it. Just like that lady down in Montgomery who's feet was tired and she didn't give her seat to the white man because she had enough . . . .

WINGATE: Rosa Parks.

MILDRED: Yes. I believe that's the lady's name. Just like Jesus when he chased the money changers out of the temple. He too had had enough.

WINGATE: Why didn't you call the police?

MILDRED: We been callin' and callin' the police. They told us to organize a Crime Watch. We did that. I called the city councilwoman. I went to the vice mayor. I tried to reach the mayor, the city manager. I even went to the landlord. He laughed at me. We patrolled the streets. We had a block party. Nothin' worked.

WINGATE: You certainly are a brave woman. *(Turning to* SAM WARHAUS*)* Mr. Warhaus, you must be proud of your wife?

SAM: *(Throws a blanket over his head)* Get those cameras away from me. Get them away. Those hoodlums might see me. Might blame me. You see what they do to snitches. You saw them burn up that woman's house. Besides, what she did was unchristian. You're supposed to forgive. There's no sin that can't be forgiven. It's in the Bible.

MILDRED: The Bible also says: "Wherefore lookest Thou upon them that deal treacherously, and holdest thy tongue when the wicked devoureth the man that is more righteous than he?" Habakkuk, first chapter, verse thirteen.

SAM: *(Waves her off)* Aw woman. Nobody can win an argument with you.

WINGATE: This is terrific footage. You getting it all?

CAMERAMAN: Got it.

WINGATE: Thank you very much, Ms. Warhaus.

MILDRED: Thank you. *(They exit.* JAKE *and* MABEL *enter)*

MABEL: Mildred. We just heard the news. You took that boy's weapon?

JAKE: Weren't you scared?

MILDRED: Something just came over me.

SAM: She puttin' all of our lives in danger.

JAKE: *(Ignores him)* It's all over town. People are calling up asking about Crime Watch. They asking Mabel and me where to sign up.

MABEL: All because of you, Mildred. *(They embrace)*

SAM: I don't like it. Strange people comin' in my house all day. The TV people will be parked out in the street all day. People will be calling up here. That ain't right. I can't concentrate on my baseball and, and . . . Mildred this rock house mess is coming between us. I'll bet you going to be going out on these speaking engagements. Talking to club women. Doing interviews.

JAKE: Sam, she's done in an hour what the police and City Hall haven't been able to accomplish in years. Put heat on Crackpot.

MABEL: Seem to me you would be proud, Sam. What's come over you? You used to break all of the horses and kiss all of the women when we were young.

JAKE: You could zydeco better than anyone.

MILDRED: Remember his barbecue ribs? His standing up for people who couldn't take care of themselves? Back in Texas you wouldn't let nobody step on you. That was the man that I loved, and that was the man that I married. Then when we moved here we had our child and you had a good job, working at the aluminum plant. Got your head busted when you led that strike back in fifty-three and then they gave you that foreman's job.

SAM: I was the first black foreman.

MILDRED: It all began to change, you got quiet.

SAM: It was different from the inside. You can't go through your life yelling and screaming.

MILDRED: Then they brought you down to the front office.

SAM: I earned it.

MILDRED: And as soon as you retired you got sick. I think that you're okay. You just sat at that desk for so many years you can't get up. They used you to keep out the other blacks, anyway.

SAM: I was qualified.

MILDRED: There were plenty others who were qualified. Every time they asked for a promotion the front office said they had you.

SAM: *(Sadly)* Why do you stay with me? A poor broken-down patient.

MILDRED: I stay with you because I love you and because one day you will stand up. One day you will be the man I married again.

MABEL: Come on Mildred, we have to go on patrol.

JAKE: It used to only be a few people walking out on crime patrol. But now, thanks to Mildred, we will have to turn people away. *(They exit.* SAM *returns to the baseball game)*

Act II: Scene 2

*(*CRACKPOT's *apartment is filthy. Littered with empty fast-food boxes, empty bottles of Hi Life beer. Pairs of running shoes and clothes strewn around the room. Big sound system.* CRACKPOT, *about thirty years old, wears jeans and sweater, gold chains, sneakers, do rag on his head. Lying on a dirty mattress on the floor.* VEILED LADY IN THE RED DRESS *does her tape dance to the song, "Lady in Red."* CRACKPOT *is asleep on the sofa with a smile on his face. Toward the conclusion of the dance she kneels down and begins to take* CRACKPOT's *measurements with the tape.* SAM WARHAUS *comes on. He is smoking a cigar. He is dressed in white shirt, pants, and shoes. He glares at her. She sees him and recoils from* CRACKPOT. *She is frightened. She flees.* CRACKPOT *frowns and begins to toss and turn in his sleep.)*

SAM: Whatever you're doing son, you'd better quit. She's a bad one and she's got her eye on you. She wants to add you to her harem of lovers. The only catch is that you have to die to get the honor. She was taking your measurements for your coffin is what she was doing. *(*CRACKPOT *begins to thrash around and moan)* You'd better straighten up and get yourself together or you're going to find yourself somewhere where you don't want to be.

*(*CRACKPOT *wakes up screaming. Sits up. Two figures vanish. His bodyguard,* BUMP, *rushes in.)*

BUMP: Crackpot, what's the matter?

CRACKPOT: That dream. I had that dream again. This woman. There was this beautiful woman dressed all in red. And she was doing this dance. And when she finished she started to take my measurements. Then, a man dressed in white came on. He warned me that this woman wanted to take me as a lover, but I would have to die to get the honor. It was horrible. Must have been the Mama Rosa's pizza I ate last night. I ate two large sizes. Everything on them. *(Clutches his stomach)*

BUMP: Damn, Crackpot, I'm sorry.

*(*MOTHER *enters. She has a frantic look. She's ragged. Her hair is uncombed. She's a mess. No shoes. Hasn't had any sleep for days.* BUMP *and* CRACKPOT *are startled at first.)*

BUMP: Ms. Jenkins. *(Shocked)*

CRACKPOT: *(Contemptuously)* What do you want?

MOTHER: *(Drowsily, weakly)* Crackpot, I haven't had any sleep in five days, please Crackpot. *(She moves toward him)*

CRACKPOT: I told you to stay away from here. Besides, I'm busy.

(She approaches him with arms outstretched.)

MOTHER: Just a bag, Crackpot. I'll pay you back. Honest I will. I won't bother you no more.

CRACKPOT: Yeah, that's what you said the last time.

BUMP: Crackpot. *(in sympathy with* MOTHER*)*

CRACKPOT: *(Shouts)* You keep out of this. *(To* MOTHER, *who is now trembling)* You owe me already. You'd better be glad that we have a special relationship. If you were anybody else, you'd be dead.

MOTHER: *(Drops to her knees. Clasps her hands. Begs.* BUMP *turns his head, arrogantly folds his arms)* I need just a little bit to get me through to the first. My check . . .

CRACKPOT: Your check. That's what you said the last time. And the time before that. Bump. Get her out of here.

*(*BUMP *moves to where* MOTHER *is kneeling. He takes her arm gently and she rises.* CRACKPOT *turns his back on them and folds his arms. She continues weeping. When they reach the exit,* BUMP *gives her a bag. She looks at* BUMP, *with gratitude, and begins to thank him but he moves her off the stage.)*

BUMP: Damn, Crackpot. Your own mother!

CRACKPOT: *(Calmly)* She got to pay like everybody else. Ain't no exceptions. Once you start extending credit, people start taking you as a chump. You get a reputation for being easy. I can't afford to give her any more credit. I'd be out of business if word got around that I was easy.

BUMP: But Crackpot, you're supposed to love your mother.

CRACKPOT: Love. Don't be givin' me that love shit. I'll tell you what I think about love. I agree with O. O. Gabugah.

BUMP: O. O. Ga-what?

CRACKPOT: O. O. Gabugah. He's this militant poet we used to read in that community college I went to for a semester. He said that: "Love is a white man's snot rag." That's the way I feel. Love is whitey's trick to keep the blacks soft so that he can mold them, and mess over them. The only one that I love is myself. There's no room in my heart for anyone but me. *(Pause)* Look, did they find that kid? The one who let the old biddy take his gun from him?

BUMP: Yeah. He was hiding at his mother's house. We had to waste his mother. While we were doing that he jumped out of the window. We had two of the runners outside waiting for him. They left his intestines in the middle of the street. It was a mess. Damn, Crackpot. The kid was only twelve. Couldn't you have given him a break? When that old woman took the gun from him he lost his cool.

CRACKPOT: We have to make an example. These kids don't know nothin' about discipline. Now we got people all over the city messing with our people. All because some punk let an old woman take his gun. They having neighborhood rallies and who knows what else. Block parties. This Mildred Warhaus is on TV all day. She's messin' with our credibility. All we have is fear. We keep those people afraid of us, but now that they've lost their fear, we've lost our greatest weapon. Now get back to guarding the front door.

(BUMP *exits. During the following monologue,* CRACKPOT *paces up and down the stage, haranguing the audience, smoking a cigarette.*)

CRACKPOT: I have to do all of the thinkin' for this group. That Bump is gettin' soft. We have to enforce our way or people don't have respect. I don't care if the bitch is my own mother. If I find her snitching she would have to go, too. As far as the kid being twelve, you got to go sometime. We all got to go. You might be walking across the street and get hit by a car. I'm ready. I know that if I'm in the wrong neighborhood, somebody from another gang might get to me. But while I'm here I'm going to have all of the money, cars, and clothes I can buy. Homes, too. Never had no home. Lived with my mother in these shelters. In the street. Living room was a shopping cart and sometimes I was so hungry I cried myself to sleep. Now I got plenty of food and money. Boss hootchies. Respect. Ain't nothin' wrong with me gettin' mine. The way I see it, I'm supplying a need. A dirty need, but what I've found in my business is that in America, few people are clean. You either pimpin' or you ho'in. (*Beeper. Dials the telephone number*) Yeah. I told you that I can't give you no credit so don't be callin' up here. There's nothin' you have that I want. (*Hangs up*) You know who that was? Bitch's picture be on the society page every week. Always at some charity ball. She was down her yesterday crawling on that floor right there (*points*) naked, begging me for credit. Asking me whether I wanted her to do nasty things to me. She scared her husband will find out. Dude is a big stockbroker. She don't know that he's a customer, too. She don't want him to know, he don't want her to know. Meantime, I have all their money and their jewelry. She spends her whole day chasing the bag, and trying to get credit. You know these people you see who supposed to be so high and mighty? Be talking about family values and running down welfare mothers on TV? I know a lot of them. Lawyers, priests, accountants. You know that congressman that always be saying: "Just Say No." My best customer. Sucker be tweaked out all the time. Police, too. So the way I look at it, everybody in America is high on something. I'm performing a service. Some people are high on crack, some people are high on smack, and other people are high on things that you don't put in your mouth or up your nose or in your arm. They high on religion, or love. Or some other spacey thing. All these politicians who be passing these get-tough-on-drug laws? They drunk all the time. They just arrested the head of the vice squad last week for driving under the influence. Besides, what about all of the hubba they pushing? So why is everybody coming down on me? I read where one of these men who was running for President, Du Pont I think the fellow's name, ran a company that's responsible for the warming of the earth. Some chemical that you get out of an aerosol spray can and when it get into the space it makes a huge hole in the sky so that in five hundred years mankind will be dead. At least I ain't responsible for something like that—yet the people are mad at *me*. But this man who could be responsible for the oceans rising and skin cancer is allowed to run for President? And what about the government? They peddling dope, too. They sell cocaine and heroin in order to buy arms for the people down in South America who are killing babies and burning down people's houses, yet they talking about the penalty for drug kingpins. So I don't see any difference between what I'm doing and what everybody else is doing. The way I look at it, the White House is the biggest crack house there is. *(Pause)* I don't be planning to be on the street all that long. I'm working with this partner of mine to go wholesale, so that all of these chumps will have to buy from me. I'll be one of the first brothers to be in on this. I can do what the whiteys do. Operate my business from home, with a fax, two computers and a Xerox machine. Get off the streets. You don't see whitey in the streets. He be operatin' from legitimate business fronts. You never see his name in the paper. *(Muses)* You never see him being dragged away in handcuffs, placed in leg chains, and strip-searched. That's only for the brothers.

When they put me out of school for stabbing the teacher, they said that my ass was going to end up dead. Now I'm making more money than all of the teachers in school put together. I'm making more money than the President. I'm a new breed. And one day—I may not do it myself—but somebody is going to take over this whole operation for the brothers who spend all of their money buying the very products that they're selling and getting us strung out as their customers. We'll put it in stocks and bonds and real estate. We'll start businesses in the community and hire people like Al Capone, Legs Diamond, Dutch Shultz, and Arnold Rothstein used to do. That time ain't here yet. But it's comin'.

*(*BUMP *enters with* MR. KRUD.*)*

KRUD: Crackpot, my boy. I have good news. Good news.

CRACKPOT: Yeah? What's the good news?

KRUD: That house you wanted to buy near Mount Diablo? It's all yours.

CRACKPOT: How much is it?

KRUD: Three hundred thousand dollars. I'll have to draw up the papers. There's usually a ten percent down payment, but I can get you in for five.

CRACKPOT: That won't be necessary. Bump, go over and get that bag.

*(*BUMP *goes over and fetches a bulky mailbag that rests in a corner of the room.* CRACKPOT *reaches in and removes some cash. He pays* MR. KRUD. KRUD *is shocked and his facial expression shows it.)*

CRACKPOT: Anything wrong, Mr. Krud?

KRUD: No, I just—do you mind if one of the boys help me carry it to the bank? I just don't want to walk around the streets with this kind of money.

CRACKPOT: Sure. Bump, get one of the fellas to take the money back with Mr. Krud.

KRUD: Nice doing business with you Crackpot.

CRACKPOT: Sure. And get the place ready. I want to drive up with my girls this weekend.

KRUD: I'll send the keys and the directions back with the boy.

(They exit. CRACKPOT *puts on a hip-hop cap, backwards.)*

BUMP: Where you going, Crackpot?

CRACKPOT: *(He picks up a pistol and puts it into his waist pocket)* Get the car. We're going to make a visit on this Mildred Warhaus. We have to teach these people to respect us. *(They put on ski masks)*

BUMP: But . . . but, Crackpot. She's a sixty-eight-year-old woman. She . . .

CRACKPOT: Did you hear what I said? *(*BUMP *looks at him for a moment. His fear is obvious)*

BUMP: But she was on television. She's all in the news. Aren't you taking a chance?

CRACKPOT: I know what I'm doing. One thing I learned in prison. You let one person walk over you, soon your body will be a highway. Bump, you actin' like a regular little ho these days. *(Mocks him in an effeminate manner)* "She's all in the news. Aren't you taking a chance?" Bump, I chose you to be second in command. Now if you becomin' some kind of pussy then maybe I should get somebody else. That means we'll have to burn yo black ass. You know too much.

BUMP: *(Trembling, excitedly)* No Crackpot. I'm . . . I'm the same Bump. I just don't think we should be takin' chances. I'm lookin' out for you, Crackpot. *(*BUMP *glares at him with hostility for a moment)*

CRACKPOT: Okay. Let's go. *(They exit)*

Act II: Scene 3
The Warhaus Home

SAM: *(Whining)* You hardly spend any time with me anymore. I have to go to the bathroom by myself. I have to shave myself. You always at meetin's or answering mail. Now you talkin' about running for city council.

MILDRED: I haven't made up my mind.

SAM: The phone rings all day. I can't hardly concentrate on the ball game. And now you want to travel to Washington to make a speech. Who is going to take care of me? Wash my clothes? Turn on the TV?

MILDRED: I'm taking you with me. With the contributions people have sent me, we'll be able to hire an assistant for you. While we're down there we can see our son's name on the Vietnam Veteran's wall.

SAM: I don't know about flying. Them planes ain't safe.

MILDRED: Sam, I'm worried about you. You haven't been out of the house in two years now. I'm thinking about getting a head doctor to come and look at you. You haven't been acting right ever since you retired.

(Doorbell. She goes off to answer offstage. SAM *hears* CRACKPOT *ask: "Are you Mrs. Warhaus? Mrs. Mildred Warhaus?" Shots are fired. Sam is shocked. Wearing an expression of great agony,* MILDRED *staggers onto the stage, holding her chest. Her blouse is bloody as she collapses.)*

SAM: *(Screaming)* Mildred!!!! Mildred!!! *(He slowly rises from the chair. With much effort he walks over to where she lies. He lifts her head.* SAM *looks at his legs. Goes to phone.)* Hello. 911. My wife has been shot. Please send an ambulance. . . . A half hour? What do you mean a half hour? I . . . *(He goes to* MILDRED. *Struggling, picks her up and carries her off stage. Dark)*

(Spotlight on MARTHA WINGATE, *reporter.)*

WINGATE: Hundreds of people have gathered outside of Highland Hospital waiting for news about the condition of Mildred Warhaus who was shot earlier today by unknown assassins at her residence in North Oakland. Ms. Warhaus received national attention when she disarmed a crack dealer, one of many who had been terrorizing her neighborhood for over a year. For her heroism she has been called the Rosa Parks of the anti-drug movement. Ms. Warhaus has been in surgery for five hours, and according to attending physicians, the prognosis is not good. The police have no suspects in the shooting, but word has it that the shooting may have been a reprisal by the notorious Runners led by Crackpot Jenkins, a notorious drug kingpin who served two years as part of a plea bargaining deal struck with the District Attorney. The gang leader was charged with the murder of Ezekiel Johnson, a leader in the North Oakland community.

(Spotlight out. Lights on Warhaus home. JAKE *and* MABEL *are sitting at a table having coffee. They are glum.* SAM*'s wheelchair is empty. The phone rings.)*

SAM: *(From offstage)* Will you get that?

MABEL: *(On phone, excitedly)* Hello. . . . She's out of surgery? . . . She's going to have full recovery? Well, thank the Lord for that. *(She puts down the phone)*

JAKE: That woman is made of lead. I knew that she would recover.

*(SAM *enters. He is dressed in cowboy clothes. Campy, like in the movies. With sequins and other glitter.)*

MABEL: Sam, Mildred's going to be okay—what . . . *(The sight of him shocks her)*

JAKE: Sam, what's the matter with you?

SAM: I'm going to take care of that punk who shot my wife.

MABEL: You don't have to be no hero, Sam. (JAKE *tries to block his way*)

SAM: Get out of my way, Jake.

JAKE: The police will take care of Crackpot. (SAM *laughs.* JAKE *realizing what he's said, backs away dejectedly. To* MABEL) You try to talk some sense into him, Mabel.

MABEL: Sam, what's the use of Mildred coming home to a dead husband? You don't have a chance against those boys. They'll kill you as soon as smash a bug. You know they don't care about life.

SAM: I have to do what I have to do.

JAKE: Sam, you ain't in Texas no more.

SAM: The hell I ain't. Texas is anywhere hell is. Now move out of the way and let me do my business.

(*Lights*)

Act II: Scene IV
Crackpot's Apartment

(MARTHA WINGATE *is on TV. Picture of* MILDRED *flashes on. Then picture of* CRACKPOT.)

BUMP: Damn, Crackpot. They trying to trace it to you.

CRACKPOT: Change the channel.

(BUMP *changes the channel to a cowboy movie. They watch it for a few minutes.*)

BUMP: Crackpot, you don't seem worried? The public wants to ice you for what you did to Mildred.

CRACKPOT: Don't worry about it. Just like the other times, they'll pick me up, and my lawyers will have me out the next day.

(*Same* COP *whom we've seen in the scene with* MILDRED WARHAUS *enters.* CRACKPOT *nods his head to* BUMP *and* BUMP *goes to the bag and takes out some bills and hands them to the* COP.)

COP: No, I didn't come for that this time, Crackpot.

CRACKPOT: What are you talking about? You know the arrangement.

COP: (*Nervously*) That Warhaus woman, Crackpot. There's a lot of pressure downtown to take you out, Crackpot. Why the hell did you have to go ahead and do it?

CRACKPOT: How and I going to maintain authority if I let a sixty-eight-year-old woman call my bluff? Everybody will be on my case. I won't be able to go nowhere without risking a drive-by by these people who think I'm weak.

COP: It was a big mistake.

CRACKPOT: What the fuck do you know about it? You livin' out there in the suburbs with your family. I clothed your wife and I sent your children to college. Every additional room you built on your house, I paid for. When your mother was sick, I paid for her bills. And now, with the first sign of trouble, you cut and run—why, you little cunt?! *(Grabs him by the collar)*

COP: I'm sorry, Crackpot. I won't be coming around anymore.

CRACKPOT: *(Shouting)* Well, run then, and I tell you what. If I go down, a whole lot of these high and mighty people downtown will go down with me. All of these people who drive in here in their Mercedes and BMW's will go down. I will name names and tell everybody where the dogs are buried. *(To* COP*)* Do you hear me?

(Enter HAMAMOTO, *the auto dealer)*

CRACKPOT: Hey! You get that order?

HAMAMOTO: Came in three days ago. It's in your garage next to the Mercedes and the Porsche. You have quite a collection.

CRACKPOT: Yeah. Well I don't like to drive the same car every day.

HAMAMOTO: I need eighty thousand dollars. *(*CRACKPOT *goes over to the bag and shoves some money into a bag)*

HAMAMOTO: Nice doing business with you.

CRACKPOT: Hey, didn't I see you in the paper last week?

HAMAMOTO: Yeah. Everybody in town must have seen it.

CRACKPOT: You got into some club?

HAMAMOTO: Yeah. They made me a Vassal. The club's name is the Vassals of the Celestial Ocean. I'm getting a lot of orders up there. Some of the big shots in Oakland belong to the club. We Vassals look out for each other and are always passing each other tips on the stock market and helping some of the brothers who suffer setbacks. We play tennis, golf, get massages, and have Christmas dinner together. It's a real fraternity. There are great opportunities for networking.

CRACKPOT: Maybe you can get me in. I have a lot of money. I have cars and houses.

HAMAMOTO: Takes more than that, Crackpot.

CRACKPOT: What do you mean it takes more?

HAMAMOTO: Look at it this way. You're black. They know that the kind of wealth you have is transitory. Guys like you are a dime a dozen. As soon as somebody takes you off the scene, somebody else will take your place. Mr. Krud will sell him houses. I'll sell him these Suzuki Samurai Hubba jeeps. And the Banker Krock will keep his money under lock and key. Every time they look at you they see a loser. Every time they look at me they see Japanese power, because even though my family has lived here for a few generations, I'm still an alien to them. But the biggest banks in the world are in Tokyo. That backs me up. You don't have any insurance. Suppose they legalize the stuff or somebody concocts a synthetic version and corners the market? You'd be back in some corner lot playing basketball.

(He starts to exit, laughing. BUMP *comes in the room with* BOBBIE KRUD *and* JOE HAND-SOME. KRUD *and* HANDSOME *see* HAMAMOTO. BOBBIE *and* HAMAMOTO *exchange hand-shakes.)*

CRACKPOT: What was that all about, Bobbie?

BOBBIE: Oh, that was one of the brothers from the lodge. Every time we see each other we exchange the secret handshake. Look, I got some news.

CRACKPOT: What news?

BOBBIE: The guys in Colombia have come up with a new hit. Smokeable heroin. It should be on the market in the fall. And get this. It'll be five k's per kilo.

CRACKPOT: Man, can you imagine the profits? Joe, they're going to have you flying in day and night. Think you can handle it?

HANDSOME: Can I handle it? As long as they pay me the money I can handle it.

BOBBIE: All of mine goes to the stocks and bonds. When you come back from Rio next year, the operation will be in full swing.

CRACKPOT: *(Pause. Studies* BOBBIE KRUD*)* Rio. What are you talking about?

BOBBIE: We've decided that it might be a good idea for you to disappear for a while until the heat's off.

CRACKPOT: I don't understand?

BOBBIE: That woman. Look, I understand that you might have been under a little stress. I mean, hypertension is hereditary among black people, but you went too far when you shot that Mildred Warhaus. It's all in the papers and on television. I've decided that Bump should take over for a while. (CRACKPOT *looks shocked at* BUMP. BUMP *lowers his head. Shrugs his shoulders)* You're excitable. You need to rest your nerves on the beach for a while. If that woman dies, it'll be Murder One.

CRACKPOT: I'll be out on the street in an hour. You get that lawyer who's always defending me.

BOBBIE: He says you're at the end of your rope. He got you a light sentence for running down that old man, but now they have to give you some hard time. The cops say that they can't cover for you anymore.

CRACKPOT: They're gettin' their cut. Anyway, Bump does what I say. Right, Bump? Bump, home? (BUMP *looks at his shoes)* Hey, wait a minute, man. Bump. What's going on man? Don't let this white boy come between me and you just because of some bread. Man, you and me, all the ass we used to chase, the way we used to get high together, remember when we took the principal and had him hanging out of a window, man? Remember when we stabbed that teacher? *(BOBBIE goes for his gun)*

CRACKPOT: Hey, Bobbie, what are you doing?

BOBBIE: Look, Crackpot, nothing personal, but the Cartel has decided that you're just too flighty to be of any use to us any longer. The days of wild men are over. We need a clean, efficient operation. We want this thing to be operated like IBM.

CRACKPOT: *(To* BUMP*)* Bump, help me, Bump. I'll give you all of my cars. My women, you can have them. Look, Bump there's all the money in the sack, you can have . . . *(BUMP draws a gun. But before he can fire,* HANDSOME *shoots him)*

BOBBIE: *(Shocked)* Joe, what—what's going on?

HANDSOME: Drop it, Bobbie.

BOBBIE: Joe, I don't understand. *(Drops his gun and raises his hands)*

HANDSOME: I've decided to make it a two-man operation. Crackpot and me. *(CRACKPOT is relieved)*

BOBBIE: You, you siding with this . . . this spade against me? Why, we were room-mates together at Harvard and pledged for the same fraternities, double-dated at Yale Winterfest; I was the one who recommended you for the Elite club. We had that apartment in Greenwich Village.

HANDSOME: We've decided that we don't need you anymore. Cut out the middle man and I can deal directly with Crackpot. *(CRACKPOT laughs)*

BOBBIE: But, but . . . *(JOE shoots him. He falls and begins to squirm in agony until he is dead)*

HANDSOME: Two less to share with. From now on when I fly in you meet me and I'll deliver the goods to you directly. Deal?

CRACKPOT: Look. You drop it, I'll distribute it. That Bobbie was slick but he wasn't as slick as you and me, huh, Joe? And Bump. How could he have ever thought that Bump could replace me?

HANDSOME: This is a big operation, Crackpot. Bigger than you ever thought. My orders come directly from the White House basement.

CRACKPOT: The White House basement? It must be big then.

HANDSOME: *(With a glazed look, begins to paint his vision with gestures. First few strains of Zarathustra music again)* I'll explain, Crackpot. You see, billions of dollars are going back and forth across the border. Some of it is making a lot of people rich. But some of it is making our country stronger, Crackpot. We're helping freedom fighters all over the world, Crackpot. From the jungles of Angola to the mountains in Afghanistan. Crackpot, you and I are patriots. Do you follow me, Crackpot?

CRACKPOT: *(Bewildered)* I guess so.

HANDSOME: Crackpot, there are people, bad people all over the world who are aligned with the traitors in this country to undermine our traditional values. Some of the profits from this operation are going to men and women who are keeping our liberties alive. Bobbie didn't understand that, Crackpot. He always felt that these sentiments were corny, Crackpot. He used to mock the small band of patriots who were outcasts at Harvard, Crackpot. There's plenty of red in that *Harvard Crimson,* Crackpot. He always had the fast cars and the women, Crackpot. He didn't understand what was at stake, and so when we got into this business after graduation, all he saw was an opportunity to make quick money. I saw it as a way to achieve a higher and nobler purpose. And I found plenty of brave and selfless men in the government who agreed with me, Crackpot. Crackpot, with the profits we're making from crack, we're stockpiling weapons in three western states and as soon as we get the signal that Armageddon is on—the final battle between the forces of good and evil—our patriots will heed Gabriel's call.

CRACKPOT: What call?

HANDSOME: For the day when we take back our government and restore justice to the American people. *(SAM WARHAUS has entered. He's dressed up like Gene Autry. Has two guns drawn. He looks comical. Both men laugh)*

SAM: I got your justice. Stick 'em up. *(His hand trembles as he holds the guns. They continue to laugh. They're in stitches. SAM tries to whirl the gun around his thumb, like in the movies. The gun falls to the floor. They really laugh then)*

HANDSOME: *(Laughing)* Who's this clown?

CRACKPOT: *(Laughing)* He's the husband of that woman we hit. Think we don't know that he's carrying a toy gun.

(As SAM picks up the gun, the gun goes off accidentally. This startles SAM, even. CRACKPOT and JOE are shaken up. SAM holds the gun again.)

HANDSOME: *(Panicky)* Look pal, I didn't have anything to do with it. It was this lunatic, Crackpot. He shot your wife. We can do without him. You and me. That's it. We can split the cash. Cut him out. I'll deliver directly to you.

(SAM waves JOE away gesturing with the gun toward the exit. JOE flees. CRACKPOT gets on his hands and knees.)

CRACKPOT: *(Sobbing)* Hey man. Let's talk this over. It was Bump's idea. I didn't want anything to do with it.

SAM: Bump. Who is Bump?

CRACKPOT: My partner. It was his idea to hit Mrs. Warhaus. He ordered me to run down that Mr. Johnson, too. He drove the car.

SAM: I don't believe a word you say. Now get ready to meet Satan. I'm going to give you the same chance you gave my wife.

CRACKPOT: Man you don't have to do it. Please *(sobbing)* don't kill me. Look, I got some cash. There's over a hundred thousand dollars in that bag over there. You can have it.

(SAM walks over to the bag, and removes some cash. Examines it. While he is doing that, CRACKPOT reaches for a small pistol that he has in his shoe. He shoots SAM in the arm. SAM grabs his arm. He prepares to shoot again. Shots are fired from offstage, mortally wounding CRACKPOT. SAM turns to the entrance. This dramatic pause should be milked. Momentarily, JAKE enters. He is dressed in corny cowboy clothes.)

SAM: Thanks, partner. *(They embrace. SAM then goes over and picks up the bag)*

JAKE: *(Gazing upon CRACKPOT's corpse)* What a waste. Bright kid like that. No telling what he could have done with his life if somebody had given him a break. What's that? *(SAM removes some stacks of bills from the bag. Shows it to JAKE. SAM has a broad grin)* What are you going to do? Turn that over to the police?

SAM: That's not exactly what I had in mind, Jake. Seems to me that if we don't take it, these police will take it and spend it in the suburbs. If we take it, it goes back into the community.

JAKE: Put it back.

SAM: Are you crazy?

JAKE: I said put it back, Sam. *(Insistent. Growing angry. As SAM returns the bag, JAKE turns his back to SAM and faces audience. He folds his arms in a manner of moral superiority. He doesn't see SAM take a few stacks of bills and put this in his pocket, but the audience sees)* We have to be better than these people. We're Christian people. The Bible says: "Woe to him that increaseth that which is not his."

SAM: Yeah. Uh, thanks Jake. Thanks for reminding me.

(They exit. Dark. Then, spotlight on MARTHA WINGATE.)

WINGATE: We interrupt this program to bring you further news on the bizarre murders that were discovered this morning in an apartment building located in North Oakland. The bodies of three men, Crackpot Jenkins, Bump Disney his sidekick, and Bobbie Krud, son of the well-known realtor and community leader, Jack Krud. Neighbors said that they heard a number of shots and called the police. When the police arrived an hour later, they were too late to catch the assassin or assassins who escaped without being noticed by the drug kingpin's neighbors. The police had no explanation for how the three came to be found in the apartment together, but surmised that Bobbie Krud had been kidnapped by Crackpot and members of his notorious gang, the Runners, in an attempt to collect ransom from Mr. Krud's father. The young Mr. Krud's red Porsche was found parked outside the building, a clear indication, the police say, that he was a victim of a carjacking. Jack Krud, the civic leader and philanthropist, was in tears after identifying his son at the morgue. He said that the young man was doing well in his investment firm and was presently expanding his business to foreign markets. Mr. Krud offered a fifty thousand dollar reward for anyone who has information leading to the perpetrator or perpetrators of his son's killer or killers.

Act II: Scene 5

(SAM enters carrying some luggage. He is dressed in a suit and wears a Stetson hat. He's smoking a cigar. JAKE and MABEL enter. They are also dressed well. MABEL wears a corsage.)

JAKE: The car is ready. Where is Mildred?

SAM: Oh, you know that woman. Take her hours to get ready.

JAKE: *(Looks at watch)* Well, we'd better get going. The plane leaves in an hour.

SAM: What's the weather in Washington?

MABEL: Say it's going to be seventy.

(MILDRED enters. Looks great. Hair done. Corsage. Mink. Walks with a cane. SAM's eyes widen.)

MABEL: Mildred. Now don't you look nice.

JAKE: Like a million dollars.

SAM: She do now don't she? I knew what I was doing when I married the most pretty girl in Port Arthur.

MILDRED: *(Flattered)* Sam, you still know how to talk that trash, and it was awfully nice of you to arrange for all of us to fly to Washington. Then to New York. Puttin' us up in the Mayflower Hotel in Washington and this fancy New York hotel called the Plaza. Hiring that limousine driver . . . we can see our son's name on the Veteran's Wall of Respect before we die. Thank the Lord.

MABEL: How are you able to afford all of this, Sam?

SAM: Oh, been saving a little on the side for all these years. *(JAKE and SAM have eye contact. JAKE frowns)*

MABEL: Well, I appreciate it, Sam. Jake and I never go nowhere.

JAKE: That ain't true, woman. I took you to Reno on that gamblin' special bus once.

MILDRED: When we go up to New York, I want to see Radio City Music Hall. The Statue of Liberty. The Empire State Building.

SAM: Maybe me and Jake can check out one of those fights at Madison Square Garden. Or even go to one of them OTB establishments.

JAKE: Harlem. I want to see Harlem.

MILDRED: And Abyssinian Baptist Church where Adam Clayton Powell used to preach. That man was a fighter. He took on the whole Congress and beat them. He's the kind of fighter that I want to be when I run for city council.

SAM: Now Mildred, you get that foolishness right out of your mind. *(All three of them glare at him. He backs down, sheepishly)* But on the other hand, I think that you will make a fine council . . . person.

(They exit, carrying bags. Turning down the lights.)

THE END

Howya Doin' Franky Banana?

Peter Spiro

CHARACTERS

Victor: *Mid to late twenties.*

Bobby: *Mid to late twenties.*

Gus: *Mid to late twenties.*

Mister K: *A man about fifty years old.*

Vita Carla Marie: *Victor's mother. Early forties.*

Setting: *Brooklyn, New York: The back room of a bar.*

Time: *The present.*

Act 1: Scene 1

(The back room of a bar. There is a desk, a few chairs, and a telephone. At rise, BOBBY *and* GUS *are in conversation.)*

BOBBY: So what'd you do then?

GUS: I get behind him.

BOBBY: In back?

GUS: Behind the guy.

BOBBY: You didn't front him?

GUS: I'm tellin' you . . .

BOBBY: You Japped him?

GUS: I'm tryin' to tell you . . .

BOBBY: You're supposed to front the creep.

GUS: That was after.

BOBBY: First you Japped him.

GUS: Then I front him.

(Pause.)

BOBBY: Okay. You front him.

GUS: I walk up, I say . . .

BOBBY: After you front him.

GUS: I tell him: "Mister K says hello." I flick my cigarette in his face.

BOBBY: Oh shit!

GUS: Bounces off his nose.

BOBBY: It was lit?

GUS: His eyes go . . . like oh man, he's thinkin . . .

BOBBY: Lit or not lit?

GUS: Bounced off his big nose . . .

BOBBY: While it was lit?

GUS: It was lit. I said it was lit. IT WAS LIT!

BOBBY: Don't work yourself up into an uproar.

GUS: It was lit.

BOBBY: You threw the lit cigarette in his face and . . .

GUS: He tries to run.

BOBBY: Where?

GUS: Away!

BOBBY: I thought you fronted him?

GUS: Backwards.

BOBBY: He runs backwards?

GUS: I had him fronted. How else could he run.

BOBBY: I can see this.

GUS: He trips. I stand over him like this, I straddle the creep. I pull out my pecker. I start to piss on him. Out of the neighborhood, faggot. Like that I says. He goes: "Why?" I shake it off. I go: "Because."

BOBBY: Because?

GUS: And then I walked away.

BOBBY: You were supposed to stab the guy.

GUS: I was supposed to scare the guy.

BOBBY: Mister K said stab the guy.

GUS: I was right here. He said: "Scare."

BOBBY: Which guy?

GUS: The guy I was supposed to scare.

BOBBY: There are many guys, Gus.

GUS: The faggot with the leather coat.

BOBBY: The guy with the green Chevy you're supposed to scare. The faggot with the leather coat you're supposed to stab. The guy with the blue do, you're supposed to steal his dog.

GUS: I'm supposed to stab the green Chevy, scare the fag.

BOBBY: Scare the green Chevy, stab the fag.

GUS: Stab the green Chevy, scare the fag.

(Pause.)

BOBBY: All right.

GUS: I know it's all right. (Pause) What did you mean by "all right?"

BOBBY: I said all right. Squash it.

GUS: You said all right. But you didn't mean all right.

BOBBY: All right! (Pause) All right?

GUS: All right, what?

BOBBY: Stab the green Chevy, scare the fag.

GUS: All right.

(Pause.)

BOBBY: And the guy with the blue dog?

GUS: Steal his dog.

BOBBY: Beagle or poodle?

GUS: The blue one.

BOBBY: Was it a collie?

GUS: A little blue dog.

BOBBY: I grew up watching Lassie.

GUS: You know what I did?

BOBBY: After you stole it?

GUS: I killed it.

BOBBY: Were you supposed to kill it?

GUS: And then I sold it.

BOBBY: You sold a dead dog?

GUS: To the Chinese restaurant.

BOBBY: They bought a dead dog?

GUS: They put it in the chow mein.

BOBBY: They don't put it in the chow mein.

GUS: You think I'm making this up?

BOBBY: I buy their chow mein all the time. I never tasted no blue dog.

GUS: You sayin' I'm lying?

BOBBY: I'm sayin' maybe you were lied to.

GUS: Who lied to me? *(Pause)* Put your arm out.

(They put their arms out on the desk, roll up their sleeves, and place a lighted cigarette between their arms.)

GUS: Someone lied to me? *(Pause)* No one lied to me. *(The cigarette continues to burn. Pause)* I had a dream last night. My mother was in the dream. In the dream my mother wanted to fuck me. *(Pause)* Did you hear me?

BOBBY: I heard you. Your mother wanted to fuck you.

GUS: In the dream she was a beekeeper. I said, Ma, no. What about Dad? She let a bee loose that landed on my eyelid. Fuck me or I let it eat your eye, she says.

BOBBY: So what'd you do?

GUS: The bee had a stinger this long!

BOBBY: So you fucked your mother.

GUS: She gave me no choice.

BOBBY: I wanna fuck Victor's mother.

GUS: I think that's strange.

BOBBY: Every time I see her my balls swell up with love.

GUS: If it was his girlfriend I could understand.

BOBBY: They get this big! *(Pause)* She ain't married no more.

GUS: It's the guy's mother for chrissakes.

BOBBY: You fucked your mother.

GUS: That was inside a dream.

BOBBY: You still fucked her.

GUS: In a dream you can do anything and get away with it: fly, run through walls, eat a whole tub of rainbow ice and four dozen zepoles . . .

BOBBY: And fuck your mother.

GUS: If you wanna get technical, yeah.

BOBBY: Did you like it?

GUS: Humpin my mom?

BOBBY: Was she good?

GUS: This was the funny part. She tells the bee to get offa my eyelid. The bee does this and jumps back in the jar. She turns on a black light, puts on a Tony Bennett record, and starts doin' this dance. She jumps on top of the dresser with her legs all up in the air going: "I'm ready for you Carl." I'm goin: "Who the fuck is this guy Carl?" I tell her: "This is your son Gussie." She goes: "Carl. Carl." I whip off my belt and tell her: "Call me Carl again I hit you with the buckle." She goes: "Carl." So I threw her on the bed and fucked her. We screw about four more times and we go to sleep.

BOBBY: You go to sleep in your dream?

GUS: I'm dreaming that I'm sleeping and having a dream that I'm doin' all this. And when I wake up . . .

BOBBY: In the dream?

GUS: When I wake up in the dream my mother's gone. Next to me on the bed is a jar of dead bees.

BOBBY: Where did your mother go?

GUS: The fuck do I know.

BOBBY: She left you dead bees?

BUS: She didn't leave them.

BOBBY: Where did they come from?

GUS: Mama and daddy bees.

BOBBY: Why were they dead?

GUS: Maybe they were just sleepin'.

BOBBY: Don't change nothin'. I still want to fuck Victor's mother.

GUS: He catches you with his mother, he won't like it.

BOBBY: He'll get over it.

GUS: Victor is Victor.

BOBBY: You think I'm scared of Victor?

GUS: He's the guy sits at the desk.

BOBBY: Now he's the guy sits at the desk. But tomorrow? Or the next day?

GUS: You're gonna overthrow Victor?

BOBBY: Things change.

GUS: I never seen anyone could take Victor.

BOBBY: Franky D'Banano could take Victor.

GUS: Franky D'Banano was the toughest guy in Brooklyn.

BOBBY: *(Goes to the desk, pulls out an urn)* Franky D!

GUS: Franky D.

BOBBY: I'm surprised they fit all of him in here.

GUS: He had huge arms.

BOBBY: Franky D. used to sit behind the desk.

GUS: Franky D. was a stand-up guy.

BOBBY: They say he ripped a sink off the wall when he was at Riker's.

GUS: They say it took six CO's to bring him down.

BOBBY: This is what I'm talkin' about Gus. Franky D. could do things most of us only dream of. What, he lead a charmed life? He was blessed by the angels? He ate right?

GUS: I seen him eat a bottle of beer.

BOBBY: To look at him now you'd never know it. *(He pours the ashes on the desk)* This guy used to be greatness. He was admired by all his friends and relatives. You don't get that way by eatin' beer bottles alone. You get that way with balls. Balls the size of watermelons. You don't show your balls by going: "Victor is Victor." You throw yourself into danger and then you figure a way out of it. You go up on cops. You rob a store, the guy behind the counter gives you the money, you don't just walk out. You slam the gun on the counter and fire off a round into the ceiling before you go. You don't walk no place with a .22 special. You tote a biiiig fuckin' gun. *(Pulls out a .357 magnum)* This was Franky D.'s. He give it to me as a gift.

GUS: You stole it off him?

BOBBY: Did I just now say he give it to me as a gift or not?

GUS: You stole it off him.

BOBBY: I can see you're only interested in jokes, Gus. To you life is a cruise on the Day-Line up to Bear Mountain. To me it is a meatball hero. I take large bites and I'm always hungry.

GUS: Put him back in the jar.

BOBBY: You remember this Gus. *(Picks up a handful of ash)* This guy had a rep you couldn't touch. I used to love this guy. He was my idol.

GUS: You're spillin him all over the place.

BOBBY: Franky D. coulda lived forever. The thing that killed him was his twelve-inch schlong. He couldn't keep it outta other guys' wives. He used to be the guy sits at the desk. Franky Banana's a fuckin' douche bag. *(He blows out the ashes in his hand)* I always wanted to tell him that. Soon I'll be sittin' at the desk.

GUS: He's all over the floor.

BOBBY: Ever since he kicked my brother in the balls I wanted to tell him that.

GUS: Put him back in the jar.

BOBBY: *(Puts the remaining ashes back in the urn. Puts the urn on the desk. Sits behind the desk)* I was born to sit behind the desk.

GUS: You know what Victor said: "Sit on the desk, you sit on me."

BOBBY: Shit like that don't scare me. *(Pause)* Fuck scared! I piss on scared! *(Takes out a pistol, empties it, puts one bullet back in)*

GUS: You're gonna play Russian Roulette?

BOBBY: You think I'm scared? *(He fires the gun at GUS's head)* You still think I'm scared?

GUS: Don't fuck around, Bobby.

BOBBY: *(Fires another round at GUS)* I can take Victor and Victor's mother whenever I feel like it.

GUS: Don't shoot that gun again.

BOBBY: YOU THINK I'M SCARED? *(VICTOR comes in)*

VICTOR: Whoa! Whoa! What the fuck is goin' on in here?

GUS: This guy is playin' Russian Roulette.

VICTOR: Get offa my desk.

GUS: With my head.

VICTOR: You're playing Russian Roulette with Gus's head? I told you: get offa my desk! *(BOBBY gets off the desk)* Gimme that gun. *(Takes the gun)* You think you're bad? You wanna see bad? *(He takes the bullet out, puts it back in and spins it)* This is bad. *(He fires the gun at GUS's head)* This is badder. *(He fires the gun at BOBBY's head)* I ain't scared of any sonofabitch on two feet. *(He points the gun barrel at himself)* Not even you motherfucker. *(He puts the gun in his mouth and fires)* That was the baddest. Don't sit at my desk again. *(Sits at the desk)* When I was six I had a brown and white cat. I put the cat inside a dryer and watched it spin. Do you know why I did that?

GUS: You didn't like the cat?

VICTOR: Can you guess, Bobby?

BOBBY: Because the cat was wet.

VICTOR: Exactly! I put it in the dryer because it was wet.

BOBBY: So what does that prove?

VICTOR: Violence always has to have a motive.

BOBBY: Gussie fucked up.

GUS: I didn't fuck up.

BOBBY: He fucked up.

VICTOR: Was there a fuckup or was there not a fuckup?

BOBBY: He fucked up.

GUS: *(Same time)* I didn't fuck up.

VICTOR: Well something's fucked up.

BOBBY: He was supposed to scare the green Chevy, stab the fag.

GUS: Stab the green Chevy, scare the fag.

BOBBY: Instead he stabbed the green Chevy, scared the fag.

VICTOR: What about the blue dog?

BOBBY: He killed it.

GUS: And I sold it to the Chinese restaurant.

VICTOR: You stabbed somebody, Gus?

GUS: No.

BOBBY: You said you stabbed him?

GUS: I said I'm supposed to stab him.

BOBBY: I lose all respect for you.

GUS: Tomorrow I'm going to stab him.

BOBBY: Even if you stabbed the wrong guy. But to not stab the wrong guy even . . . no respect.

VICTOR: Who're you gonna stab, Gus?

GUS: The green Chevy.

VICTOR: Tomorrow you're gonna stab the green Chevy?

GUS: Yes.

VICTOR: Why tomorrow are you gonna stab the green Chevy?

GUS: I'm supposed to.

VICTOR: Why tomorrow are you gonna stab the green Chevy, supposed to?

GUS: Mister K!

VICTOR: I cannot believe that, Gus.

GUS: I was right here. He goes: "Gus, stab the green Chevy, scare the fag." I go: "Which fag?" He goes: "The fag with the leather coat."

VICTOR: Tomorrow, when you're gonna stab the green Chevy supposed to, you're wrong.

BOBBY: You blew it and you didn't even do it yet.

VICTOR: You don't stab people, Gus.

BOBBY: You stab them.

VICTOR: For business I do stab them.

BOBBY: What about me and Gussie?

VICTOR: You know the rules.

BOBBY: Those rules suck.

VICTOR: You ain't got rules, you're like a branch without a tree.

BOBBY: I piss on the rules.

VICTOR: You piss on the rules? *(Pause)* You said you piss on the rules? *(Pause)* Now you see: This is what I'm talkin' about.

BOBBY: I don't agree with those rules.

VICTOR: You don't have to agree with the rules.

BOBBY: Well this is what I'm talkin' about.

VICTOR: But you do gotta follow them.

BOBBY: I got no use for rules.

VICTOR: You take that up with Mister K.

BOBBY: How much you make per?

VICTOR: Stab goes for a note.

BOBBY: Now you see why I don't like those rules.

VICTOR: Put in your time, you'll get the stabs.

BOBBY: Whata we have here, a union for chrissakes?

VICTOR: You understand me, Gus?

GUS: No stabs and no I'm gonna stabs.

VICTOR: I don't wanna do what I gotta do but I gotta do it.

GUS: Whataya gonna do?

VICTOR: And you know if it was up to me I'd let you go on this one.

GUS: You're gonna do it?

VICTOR: You know I'm gonna do it and you know why.

GUS: Rules.

VICTOR: *(Pulls a chart from the wall, marks an "X" next to* GUS's *name)* It's only your first. One demerit never killed anyone.

BOBBY: How come I got six?

VICTOR: Because you earned six.

BOBBY: Yesterday I had five.

VICTOR: Yesterday was yesterday.

BOBBY: Where did I fuck up between yesterday and today?

VICTOR: One more and you're at the limit.

BOBBY: There isn't time to fuck up between yesterday and today.

VICTOR: When you reach the lucky seven you run outta luck.

BOBBY: Franky Banana had twelve demerits.

VICTOR: Franky Banana is in the jar.

BOBBY: The only thing between yesterday and today is night. And last night I was sleepin'.

VICTOR: That's when you earned the sixth demerit.

BOBBY: In my sleep?

VICTOR: The Mexican with the tan raincoat.

BOBBY: That's tomorrow night.

VICTOR: Last night, the Mexican with the tan raincoat, you were supposed to break his window.

BOBBY: Last night, the bus driver with the striped hat, I was supposed to flat his tires.

VICTOR: Bus driver with striped hat to flatten tires is tomorrow night. Mexican with tan raincoat to break window was last night.

BOBBY: I think you got it wrong.

VICTOR: The sixth demerit.

BOBBY: It's not right.

VICTOR: It's the way it is.

BOBBY: The way it is wrong.

VICTOR: You callin' me a liar?

BOBBY: I'm sayin' there's a mistake.

VICTOR: You sayin' there's definitely a mistake or there might be a mistake?

BOBBY: Definite, might, what's the difference?

VICTOR: A might mistake means someone got it wrong. A definite mistake means I got it wrong.

BOBBY: Might mistake.

VICTOR: That's what I thought. You're wrong.

BOBBY: I ain't wrong.

VICTOR: Might you, definite, me.

BOBBY: Convicted on the might.

VICTOR: That's right.

GUS: What about me?

VICTOR: What about you?

GUS: I was convicted on a definite.

VICTOR: Yours was a might, me, definite, you.

GUS: I hate demerits.

VICTOR: Don't fuck up again.

GUS: I got my first demerit when I ran into Pi.

VICTOR: What Pi?

GUS: Two lines with the squiggly thing on top.

VICTOR: I don't get it. You get it Bobby?

BOBBY: I don't get nothin' he says.

GUS: *(Draws the symbol Pi on the wall chart)* That's Pi.

VICTOR: What's that?

GUS: That's Pi.

BOBBY: Don't look like no pie to me.

GUS: Mathematics.

VICTOR: That's math?

GUS: That's math.

BOBBY: That's not math.

GUS: It is too math.

BOBBY: You wanna see math?

GUS: It's math.

BOBBY: I'll show you math. *(Draws on wall chart)* Plus is math. Take-away is math. Multiply and divide is math. *(Pointing to Pi)* This is not math.

GUS: It's math.

BOBBY: If this is math then I don't wanna know math.

GUS: I don't know math because of the Pi.

BOBBY: It is an ugly little fucker.

GUS: I hate it.

VICTOR: Someone oughta kill it.

GUS: It tried killin' me.

BOBBY: Hey, Pi, we hate your fuckin' guts.

GUS: Dirty little cocksucker.

BOBBY: I hear your sister takes it up the ass, Pi.

GUS: I wasn't ready for a thing like that. Where do they get a thing like that?

BOBBY: I'll tell you where they get them . . .

GUS: Right after division they give it to me. It hits me like . . . whoa, I'm not ready for this.

BOBBY: They make them up? Am I right, Vic?

VICTOR: You may be right on this one.

BOBBY: This is no might.

VICTOR: You're right.

BOBBY: This is a definite. They pull this kinda crap outta their hats like, now I'm really gonna screw you up.

GUS: It's got something to do with a circle.

BOBBY: No way! Circle's a good lookin' thing, nice and round. You look at a circle you know it's a circle because it's always round. If you unround it it's not a circle anymore. This much I do know.

GUS: I like a good circle.

BOBBY: We all like a good circle.

GUS: Pi is related to a circle.

BOBBY: A distant fucking cousin.

VICTOR: Someone kill the Pi. *(BOBBY erases the Pi)* I'm removing one of your demerits, Bob.

GUS: Because he killed Pi?

VICTOR: You deserve to lose one because you earned it.

GUS: What about me?

VICTOR: What about you?

GUS: Remove my demerit.

VICTOR: I can't do that Gus . . .

GUS: You removed his.

VICTOR: Because you didn't earn it.

GUS: It was my Pi.

VICTOR: But you let Bobby kill it for you. Never let someone do what you should do yourself. Responsibilities lost are like little toes looking for a foot.

GUS: I was gonna do it.

VICTOR: Gonna do it only counts when today becomes tomorrow. But when what shoulda been today remains tomorrow, gonna do it just stinks up the joint.

GUS: You're gonna do something?

VICTOR: I hate to do this, Gussie, but you force me to give you another demerit.

BOBBY: He's catchin' up to me.

VICTOR: Two in one day is not a good thing.

BOBBY: I'm down to five.

VICTOR: You do not look well, Gus. I'll tell you what your problem is. You don't eat enough peppers.

GUS: I eat plenty.

VICTOR: Franky D. did not eat enough peppers either. *(Pulls out the urn)* Howya doin' Franky Banana? *(Looks at the urn)* Somebody been fuckin' with Franky? There used to be more of him in here.

GUS: He took him out and blew him on the floor.

VICTOR: Don't fuck with Franky D.

BOBBY: I put him back.

VICTOR: Franky D. coulda lived forever. You know what killed him?

BOBBY: His fourteen-inch schlong.

VICTOR: All he ever ate was beer bottles and cigarettes. He'd never even think of tak-ing a vitamin pill. You overload your system with junk, something's gonna give. You eat a hamburger, put some lettuce and tomato on it. This guy had arms as big as eggplants. But he never fuckin' ate one. Yo Franky, how many peppers did you eat? Franky says none.

GUS: I eat three.

VICTOR: A day or week?

GUS: Three a week.

VICTOR: Well there it is. You should be eatin' at least two a day. I'm surprised at you, Gus. This is basic. Now I want you to run down to the vegetable place and get some peppers. On me. You know why?

GUS: You like me.

VICTOR: I do like you, Gus. But that's not why I'm payin' for the peppers. I do this because I need you to be strong. Fit bodies, chip, chip, you know the rest.

GUS: Fit bodies lead to fit minds.

VICTOR: Excellent, Gus. You shoulda gave up the math for philosophy.

GUS: They don't give you that choice.

VICTOR: *(Peels off some bills)* Get two for yourself. You want any, Bob?

BOBBY: Get two for me.

VICTOR: Get two for me, too.

BOBBY: Make that three for me.

VICTOR: I told you Bobby eats them. Get two for yourself, three for Bob, and four for me. What are they now? Dollar ninety a pound?

BOBBY: Red are dollar ninety-nine. Green are ninety-nine cents.

VICTOR: How many in a pound? You know how many in a pound? All right, looky here. Two pounds green, half pound red. Ninety-nine and ninety-nine plus dollar ninety-nine, what's that, four dollars, some change?

GUS: Three dollars ninety-seven cents.

VICTOR: And this is the guy flunked math?

GUS: I can do plus no problem.

VICTOR: Plus eight percent sales tax on the dollar . . . here's a ten, bring back the change.

GUS: Do I get to buy a Pepsi with the change for flyin'?

VICTOR: You wanna buy a Pepsi, buy a Pepsi. (GUS *begins to go*) Hey Gus, a can of Pepsi, not one of those fuckin' ten liter drums. And Gus, don't get the Pepsi at Big Five. Go to Superette. That's where my mother shops.

(GUS *leaves.*)

BOBBY: So how's your mother doin'?

VICTOR: She's workin'.

BOBBY: She's workin' now?

VICTOR: She's runnin' two shifts.

BOBBY: She's here now?

VICTOR: She's inside the bar. *(Pause)* Bobby, Bobby . . .

BOBBY: Victor, Victor.

VICTOR: Bobby.

BOBBY: Victor.

VICTOR: I get no sleep, Bob.

BOBBY: Sleep is a waste of time.

VICTOR: Bad dreams . . .

BOBBY: This is why sleep is a waste of time.

VICTOR: They keep me up all night.

BOBBY: Late night TV is better than most dreams. You take that show, whataya call it, with the one guy and the other guy, what's his name . . .

VICTOR: I have this same dream every night . . .

BOBBY: They repeat the reruns over and over again all the time.

VICTOR: Someone breaks into my house when I'm sitting on the toilet takin' a dump.

BOBBY: I think I seen that dream before.

VICTOR: I hear them break in the front door but I'm too embarrassed to jump up and go see who it is.

BOBBY: You know it ain't me, Vic.

VICTOR: I run out anyway with my pants down and who do you think it is?

BOBBY: This is what we wanna know.

VICTOR: Who do you think it is?

BOBBY: I know who it's not.

VICTOR: You believe me if I tell you it's my father?

BOBBY: This is what I was gonna suggest.

VICTOR: There he is with his hands around the silverware.

BOBBY: Fuckin' figures.

VICTOR: I start smackin' him around but my hands go through him like he's a ghost.

BOBBY: Is he dead?

VICTOR: He starts laughin' hysterical mad . . .

BOBBY: He died a while back, am I right?

VICTOR: I go to pull up my drawers and my dick is gone.

BOBBY: Didn't we go to the funeral together?

VICTOR: My old man pulls my dick out his shirt pocket, put the dick on a bun and eats it.

BOBBY: He was uh . . . whataya call it . . . in the box, wasn't he?

VICTOR: He leaves. I go back to takin' a crap. My dick grows back but it grows back black.

BOBBY: You grow a Yom dick.

VICTOR: With the fuckin skin on it. *(Pause)*

BOBBY: If I told you somethin' would you get mad at me?

VICTOR: Depends on what you told me.

BOBBY: Something about a mother.

VICTOR: You mean mothers in general or a particular mother?

BOBBY: Particular mother.

VICTOR: Depends on which particular mother we're talkin' about.

BOBBY: Did you ever think: "Look, what is a mother?"

VICTOR: A mother's where you come from.

BOBBY: To the guy who comes from her. But to another guy?

VICTOR: To another guy it's where another guy comes from.

BOBBY: To the other guy it's not a mother.

VICTOR: What is it then if it's not a mother?

BOBBY: A regular woman.

VICTOR: To the guy or the other guy?

BOBBY: To the guy whose mother it isn't.

VICTOR: If it isn't his mother then it's someone else's mother.

BOBBY: It's always someone's mother.

VICTOR: So whata we talkin' about?

BOBBY: His mother is not your mother.

VICTOR: Goes without saying.

BOBBY: And if it's not your mother then it doesn't have to be a mother.

VICTOR: Only if it isn't.

BOBBY: I'm only sayin' it could not be a mother.

VICTOR: It could but I doubt it.

BOBBY: It's possible though.

VICTOR: Possible but unlikely.

BOBBY: Not unlikely to the other guy.

VICTOR: It's somebody's mother?

BOBBY: They don't get born mothers.

VICTOR: But they come from them.

BOBBY: Before they become them, what are they?

VICTOR: Potential mothers.

BOBBY: Before your mother had you, what was she?

VICTOR: My father's wife.

BOBBY: Before she married your father.

VICTOR: His girlfriend.

BOBBY: Before that.

VICTOR: A little girl.

BOBBY: So you admit that your mother was once a little girl?

VICTOR: Well, she wasn't a little boy.

BOBBY: When little boys grow up they become? *(Pause)* I say, when little boys grow up what do they become?

VICTOR: You think I don't know the answer?

BOBBY: What do they become?

VICTOR: Is this a test?

BOBBY: When little girls grow up they become—A: Men. B: Taller. C: Regular women.

VICTOR: B is sometimes correct but not always. C is always correct. A is always wrong.

BOBBY: When little girls grow up they become regular women. Always!

VICTOR: Absolutely.

BOBBY: Thank you.

VICTOR: It's good when we talk this way, Bob. I feel I understand you more as a person.

BOBBY: I like your mother even though she is your mother because to me she is a regular woman.

VICTOR: See what I mean, this is good. We're talkin'. Person-to-person like.

BOBBY: That's all you got to say?

VICTOR: What should I say? Rotate on my middle finger? Go fuck a duck? What?

BOBBY: Can I tell your mother that I like her?

VICTOR: *(Opens door leading into the bar)* Hey ma! Could you come in here when you get a chance. I don't tell her why I don't sleep. She thinks I don't eat right. She tries to feed me liver. If she comes out with liver I'm leaving.

BOBBY: We'll be alone.

VICTOR: You, my mom, and the liver.

BOBBY: I like liver.

VICTOR: You shouldn't eat it. They found out it has a shitload of cholesterol.

BOBBY: I like to eat the things I hate to eat. It builds character.

VICTOR: You like it with onions only or plain also?

BOBBY: I like it both ways.

VICTOR: Tell me if you see her coming.

BOBBY: *(Looks through the door)* Here she comes. With the liver.

VICTOR: *(On his way out)* Anyone wants to know, I'm on my way to the doctor. Stomach virus. Eight hour thing. *(He leaves.* VICTOR's *mother enters with a plate of food)*

VCM: Where's Victor?

BOBBY: He took outta here.

VCM: He asked me to come in.

BOBBY: I told him it was liver.

VCM: You told him what was liver?

BOBBY: The chicken.

VCM: So why did you tell him liver?

BOBBY: Mrs. Vanilla . . .

VCM: Villanella.

BOBBY: Can I call you by your first name?

VCM: How old are you?

BOBBY: Twenty-seven and a half.

VCM: Just this once.

BOBBY: Mrs. Vanilla . . .

VCM: I thought you were gonna call me by my first name.

BOBBY: I don't know your first name.

VCM: Vita Carla Marie.

BOBBY: Mrs. Vanilla . . .

VCM: Just call me V.

BOBBY: You can call me Carl.

VCM: I thought your name was Robert.

BOBBY: Carl is my, whataya call it, they make the sign of the cross on your head with the water name. *(Pause)* V, I gotta whole collection of Tony Bennett records at home.

VCM: That's nice. Where did Victor go?

BOBBY: He's on his way to the doctor.

VCM: He doesn't get enough sleep.

BOBBY: He said stomach virus, eight hour thing.

VCM: Then he shouldn't eat the chicken.

BOBBY: He thinks it's liver anyway.

VCM: Why does he think the chicken is liver?

BOBBY: I told him the chicken is liver.

VCM: And he believed you?

BOBBY: He didn't know what it looked like.

VCM: He knows the difference between chicken and liver.

BOBBY: If he woulda saw it like . . . skin, drumstick, wing, then he woulda known, yeah, that's chicken. Liver does not have those things on it.

VCM: So he never actually saw the chicken.

BOBBY: Because I told him it was liver.

VCM: You eat the chicken then.

BOBBY: I'm the guy who likes liver.

VCM: I'm not going to throw away good chicken. Somebody's going to eat it. There are children starving in Poland.

BOBBY: They used to be in India. What'd they do, move all of a sudden?

VCM: You eat the chicken. When Victor comes back tell him to poke his head in.

BOBBY: V . . .

VCM: I change my mind. You're too young to call me V.

BOBBY: Mrs. Vanilla. I ask you: What is a mother?

VCM: What is this, a quiz?

BOBBY: You like Tony Bennett?

VCM: He's okay.

BOBBY: A mother is?

VCM: A good thing to have.

BOBBY: To the guy whose mother it is. But to the guy whose mother it isn't, she's just a regular woman.

VCM: I'm on my break.

BOBBY: The thing of it is . . .

VCM: You have three minutes.

BOBBY: I . . . uh, whataya call it, have warm feelings for you.

VCM: I'm too old for you.

BOBBY: How old are you?

VCM: Uh, uh.

BOBBY: You're the most beautiful woman in all of Brooklyn.

VCM: I can accept that.

BOBBY: You're not mad at me?

VCM: Compliments are fine.

BOBBY: If I told you . . .

VCM: No.

BOBBY: How come?

VCM: Get a girlfriend, take her to the movies.

BOBBY: I already got a girlfriend.

VCM: Tell her these things. *(Pause)* Look sugar . . .

BOBBY: I have these dreams about you.

VCM: You have a crush. I can understand that.

BOBBY: You're laying down in a field of roses . . .

VCM: That's natural for boys your age.

BOBBY: The trees are gently swaying . . .

VCM: But a crush is something you don't act on. You just sit back and endure the pain.

BOBBY: And the birds are folding your clothes.

VCM: Why are the birds folding my clothes?

BOBBY: Chinese birds.

VCM: Where are my clothes?

BOBBY: All over the grass.

VCM: I have nothing on?

BOBBY: Just a small pearl necklace.

VCM: That's enough!

BOBBY: . . . and an ankle chain.

VCM: You're moving from crush to disrespect real fast . . .

BOBBY: I'm in the dream, too.

VCM: . . . and I will not allow that.

BOBBY: I'm dressed in this clown suit with size sixteen shoes. The birds are singing my name. They're goin: "Bobby-Loo. Bobby-Loo." Then a mob of dead bees comes along and go to sleep in a jar and one hundred and forty million of those fishy things start growing until my balls swell up . . .

VCM: What swells up?

BOBBY: My balls swell up to the size of watermelons with love for you.

VCM: I want an apology this instant!

BOBBY: You got the sweetest ass I ever seen! *(She knocks him to the floor)* You're mad at me?

VCM: You don't know my mad.

BOBBY: I apologize.

VCM: If I was mad you'd know it.

BOBBY: I lost control of my head.

VCM: Learn to control your emotions.

BOBBY: I will.

VCM: Don't let them control you.

BOBBY: I won't.

VCM: Learn to take the pain before it's too late. *(Pause)* Now eat the chicken before it gets cold.

   (She leaves. MISTER K *enters.)*

K: I don't pay you to lie around, Bob.

BOBBY: *(Getting up quickly)* Mister K!

K: Where's Victor?

BOBBY: Doctor's office.

K: Is he ill?

BOBBY: He didn't want to eat his liver.

K: *(Looks at plate)* It's chicken.

BOBBY: He thought it was liver.

K: He must know the difference between chicken and liver.

BOBBY: I told him it was liver.

K: And he believed you?

BOBBY: He hadn't seen it yet. *(GUS enters with the peppers)*

GUS: Mister K!

K: Hello, Gus.

GUS: Where's Victor?

BOBBY: Doctor's office.

GUS: He got sick?

BOBBY: He didn't wanna eat the liver.

GUS: What liver?

BOBBY: *(Holding the plate)* This liver!

GUS: But this is chicken.

BOBBY: I HAD ENOUGH OF THIS SHIT!

K: Calm down boys. *(Pause)* What do you have there, Gus?

GUS: Two pounds green peppers, half pound red.

K: Are they like the liver or are they real peppers?

GUS: *(Spreads the peppers out on the desk)* Peppers!

K: Fine. *(To* BOBBY*)* Will you tell Mrs. Villanella that I'm here.

BOBBY: She mad at me.

K: *(To* GUS*)* Will you tell Mrs. Villanella that I'm here.

GUS: *(On his way inside)* What'd you do to get her mad at you?

BOBBY: Nothin'.

GUS: I know what you did.

BOBBY: I DIDN'T DO NUTTIN!

K: Boys. Boys. Please. Go ahead, Gus. *(Pause)* Eat your chicken, Bob, before it gets cold. *(*VCM *enters)* V!

VCM: K!

K: Say hello, boys.

BOBBY AND GUS: Hello, Mrs. Vanilla.

VCM: Hello, boys.

K: I stopped by to see Victor.

VCM: He's at the doctor's office.

K: Is he ill?

VCM: Stomach virus. Eight hour thing.

K: He's a good boy. They're all good boys.

VCM: When they want to be.

K: I give them jobs. Pay them well. Set their minds to work.

VCM: This is what Victor tells me.

K: It's demanding work. But satisfying.

VCM: He says he enjoys working for you.

K: It's also a great opportunity for someone who is career-minded.

VCM: He says he wants a suit like yours.

K: Turn your back boys. *(They turn around. He puts money in* VCM's *hand)* I want you to take this, V. Buy him a nice suit. And buy yourself something nice. *(She takes the money)* Okay, you can turn around boys. *(*VICTOR *enters)* Were your ears burning, young man?

VICTOR: No. It was a stomach virus. Eight hour thing. Went away in twenty minutes.

VCM: I'll leave you guys to your work.

K: You're looking wonderful, V.

VCM: *(To* VICTOR*)* Drink some tea and have a piece of toast. It'll calm your stomach.

K: I'll see that he does.

VCM: So long boys.

(Pause.)

K: Boys!

BOBBY AND GUS: So long, Mrs. Vanilla.

VICTOR: Villanella!

(Pause.)

K: *(To* VICTOR*)* Bring the urn over here. *(*VICTOR *gets the urn and hands it to* K*)* Boys!

ALL: Howya doin' Franky Banana?

K: This is all that's left of Frank D'Banano. He used to be a good-looking young man. And strong. They say he ripped a sink from the wall in his cell at Riker's Island. They also say it took four corrections officers to subdue him.

BOBBY: It was six.

K: I want you all to take a good look at him. This young man could have lived forever. He died as a result of carelessness. He got sloppy. He placed his own feelings above the needs of the moment. *(He passes the urn around. They all take a look)* Put the urn back, Victor. *(*VICTOR *puts the urn back in the desk)* You boys know Mister Scarpacci? Sicilian man, fiftyish, well tanned, curly hair?

VICTOR: He owns the little brown building on the corner of Eighteenth Avenue.

K: Have you ever heard of anything called fair housing?

VICTOR: Housing which is fair.

K: Or open housing?

VICTOR: Housing which is open.

K: Take a Puerto Rican fellow or a Black man. He wants to live in a decent home. We don't deny him that. We only ask that he finds a decent home in his own neighborhood. *(Pause)* But how many decent homes are there in his neighborhood? So what does he do? He gets a court order and tries to force himself into your neighborhood. And what is that?

VICTOR: Bogarting.

K: We don't want to deny this man health and happiness. We just don't want him being healthy and happy around here. He may even be a very nice man. But what about his relatives? What about property values? And if we allow him here, who knows how many will follow? Before you know it your neighborhood will go the route of the South Bronx. *(Pause)* Mister Scarpacci came to me the other day with tears in his eyes. Poor man, he speaks so little English. But desperation is a universal language. *(Pause)* Very plainly, he wants the man out.

BOBBY: You want us to stab the guy?

K: I want you to scare him away.

BOBBY: Why scare when you can stab?

K: No stabbings! Is that understood? When you get carried away you get sloppy. What happens when you get carried away and stab the wrong person?

BOBBY: He goes: "Ouch."

K: Get the urn, Victor. *(Victor gets the urn and hands it to K)* Boys.

ALL: Howya doin' Franky Banana?

K: *(Gives* VICTOR *the urn.* VICTOR *puts it away)* Unnecessary violence upsets me. All I want you to do is frighten him. I want him frightened tonight and out of the building by week's end. *(Pause)* Remember boys, what are we doing?

ALL: Keeping our neighborhood decent.

K: And how do we do that?

ALL: Keep out the undesirables.

K: Who are they?

ALL: Yoms and Spics.

K: And?

ALL: Communists.

K: And?

ALL: Men that sleep and do things with other men.

K: And finally?

ALL: All other miscellaneous undesirables not mentioned.

K: *(Writes down in a pad)* The man in question arrives home around six, six-thirty. You get there around sevenish. He lives in apartment 3G. You ring the bell and do the thing we've done before. You do it as practiced. And no unnecessary violence. Do you understand? *(Gives the paper to* VICTOR*)* See you later, boys. *(K leaves)*

ALL: So long, Mister K.

VICTOR: *(Sees the chicken)* I thought you said liver.

BOBBY: I thought it was liver.

VICTOR: It's chicken.

BOBBY: Before I thought it was liver. Now I think it is chicken.

VICTOR: The first thing we do, call the guy up.

BOBBY: He don't get home till six, six-thirty.

VICTOR: He called in sick today. Or his wife is home. Or he's got a live-in maid. We find out, does anybody else live there? Bob, this is basic.

BOBBY: I got to make a personal call first.

VICTOR: Who you got to call?

BOBBY: 1-800-Loan Yes. They send me this notice: "You're behind on the blue Camaro." This is not what my coupon book tells me.

VICTOR: You do this on your own time, Bob. This is a business phone. Here's the number, Gus. *(Gives him the slip of paper)*

GUS: What do I say if someone answers?

VICTOR: You're the dry cleaners. You have his shirts, the ticket's over thirty days' old. You're going to throw them out if he don't come get them by Saturday.

GUS: What if no one answers?

VICTOR: Then you hang the fuckin' phone up.

GUS: All right. I'm gonna call. *(Goes to the phone)* I'm dialin'. *(He dials)* I finished dialin'. *(Pause)* It's ringin'. *(Pause)* Sorry, wrong number. *(He hangs up)*

VICTOR: The fuck you do that for?

GUS: I called the dry cleaners.

VICTOR: Gimme the fuckin' phone. Watch what I do and learn from it. *(He dials)* I'm dialin'. *(Pause)* I'm finished dialin'. *(Pause)* It's ringin'.

GUS: What if another guy answers?

VICTOR: *(Holds the phone in his hands)* What other guy?

GUS: He lives with another guy.

VICTOR: Can't you see I'm fuckin' busy? *(Phone still in his hand)* You mean like a friend is visiting or he lives with another guy?

GUS: Lives with another guy.

VICTOR: A guy he does things with?

GUS: Yeah.

VICTOR: Then I give the phone to you and you talk to him.

GUS: I ain't talkin' to one of those guys.

VICTOR: Then Bobby talks to him.

BOBBY: Not me.

VICTOR: *(Puts his ear to the phone)* Musta got a crossed wire. *(Hangs up, dials)* All right. I'm dialin'. *(Pause)* It's ringin'. *(Pause)* Elliot's Dry Cleaners for Mister J. Ramirez. *(To* BOBBY *and* GUS) It's a broad. *(Pause)* Do you expect him home, say six, six-thirty? Fine. Have a nice day. *(Hangs up)* We know something. He's got a broad. She's home during the day. That tells me he's married, probably drives a station wagon. *(Picks up a pepper from the desk)* You brought change from the peppers, Gus?

GUS: On the desk.

VICTOR: Gus takes the sock with the chalk in it. Bobby you take the bag with the shit inside. I'll take the eggs.

GUS: What about the spray paint and the glue?

VICTOR: The last time you glued the guy's fuckin' eyelids shut! *(Pause)* All right. Take the paint but no glue. Who wants to leak on the guy?

GUS: I'll leak on him.

VICTOR: All right. We leave at five, get there by five-fifteen. Take a look down the cellar. Stand around the front, play a few games of Chinese handball. You two eat some peppers. I'm gonna get some tea and toast to calm my stomach before we go out.

BOBBY: There's nothin' wrong with your stomach.

VICTOR: Not now. But there could be later. You gotta be prepared for anything, Bob. *(*VICTOR *goes inside the bar)*

GUS: I always get a little nervous before a job. You?

BOBBY: I take no chances. *(Takes a pistol, loads it)*

GUS: Mister K said none of that.

BOBBY: He said no stabbings.

GUS: No shootings is included in no stabbings.

BOBBY: Where do you get your information from?

GUS: Unnecessary violence upsets him.

BOBBY: It's for just in case.

GUS: Franky D. used to walk outta here with shit strapped all over hisself.

BOBBY: Franky D. could walk into any town and own it in two days.

GUS: I seen him once, he went into this club with a sausage strapped onto his leg.

BOBBY: Franky D.?

GUS: I seen him do it.

BOBBY: Franky D. didn't need no sausage strapped to his leg. His schlong was sixteen inches long.

GUS: How do you know?

BOBBY: You tryin' to say somethin'?

GUS: How do you know how big a schlong he had?

BOBBY: I seen him in the showers after gym class. I tell you this, and I am not shit-tin', he had a tattoo on his dick. When it was soft it said: "Mom." When it got hard it said: "Mom and Pop forever."

GUS: You seen his dick get hard?

BOBBY: He used to get it hard to show people the tattoo. Eat your peppers and shut up.

(Pause.)

GUS: You came on to Victor's mother.

BOBBY: Who told you that?

GUS: She busted you in the eye.

BOBBY: No she didn't.

GUS: Your eye's all swelled up.

BOBBY: I punched myself in the eye.

GUS: I don't believe it.

BOBBY: I do it because it builds character.

GUS: You punch yourself?

BOBBY: Yeah. *(Punches himself in the eye)* Like that.

GUS: Does it hurt?

BOBBY: It feels all right.

GUS: Lemme see you do that again. *(BOBBY does it again).* Good. Very good.

(BOBBY *and* GUS *eat peppers and the lights fade to black.)*

Act Two: Scene One

(The same place. A few hours later. VICTOR *is at the desk looking through a phone book.* GUS *is in the room.)*

VICTOR: Nothin'.

GUS: Huh?

VICTOR: Not a thing.

GUS: You started with K?

VICTOR: First things is K and A Laundromat.

GUS: No plain K's?

VICTOR: No.

GUS: You should have his number.

VICTOR: I know I should have his number.

GUS: What about K-A?

VICTOR: That's Ca not K.

GUS: K-A-E?

VICTOR: First thing is Kaelin, Fred, 430 Fulton Street. I don't think he lives around there.

GUS: K-A-I?

VICTOR: That ain't no name.

GUS: Chinese name.

VICTOR: Does he look like a fuckin' Chinaman to you?

GUS: K-A-Y.

VICTOR: I checked those too.

GUS: Well the last thing I could think of is K-A-Y-E.

VICTOR: *(Looks through the book, counts the names)* We'll be here all night with this.

GUS: Maybe it's not his real name. Like a stage name. You know, like Marlon Brando's name is really Mervin Dishbuckfuckslut. Like that.

VICTOR: No one's name is Dishbuckfuckslut.

GUS: I'm sayin like a made-up name.

VICTOR: Special K.

GUS: Anything.

VICTOR: It's a cereal.

GUS: There it is.

VICTOR: Maybe it stands for something.

GUS: Cocksucker.

VICTOR: Cocksucker starts with a C.

GUS: Cunt.

VICTOR: Would you name your son Cunt?

GUS: He didn't get named that. He chose it.

VICTOR: Who would choose Cunt?

GUS: It's a code of some kind.

VICTOR: First initial.

GUS: Kill. Creep. Candy. Kick. Kansas . . .

VICTOR: Shut up. I can't think.

GUS: Cockadoodle-fuckin'do!

VICTOR: K, somethin', somethin' . . .

GUS: Ask you mother.

VICTOR: Why should I ask my mother?

GUS: Maybe she knows.

VICTOR: Whataya tryin' to say? She knows him?

GUS: Not knows him "knows him." But maybe she knows him. *(*VICTOR *goes inside the bar.* GUS *pulls down the wall chart and erases a few of his demerits.* VICTOR *returns)*

VICTOR: Put those back.

GUS: What?

VICTOR: I saw what you did.

GUS: What'd I do?

VICTOR: Put them back! *(*GUS *puts back the demerits)* Now give yourself another one.

GUS: You want me to give myself another demerit?

VICTOR: Mark the "X" by your name. *(Pause)* Give yourself one or I'll give you two. *(He marks the "X")* Put two more by Bobby's name.

GUS: That makes seven for Bob.

VICTOR: He's over the limit.

GUS: Whataya gonna do?

VICTOR: The only reasonable thing to do. *(Pause)*

GUS: You got the number?

VICTOR: You'll never believe this.

GUS: She gave it to you?

VICTOR: You know what K stands for?

GUS: No.

VICTOR: Take a guess.

GUS: Klondike. Kickstand. Cherrybomb.

VICTOR: K-L-E-E-N-E. Huh?

GUS: Yeah.

VICTOR: You know what that spells?

GUS: Kleene.

VICTOR: And what does that make him?

GUS: Mister Kleene.

VICTOR: Eh?

GUS: Mister Kleene.

VICTOR: You tell me this ain't a strange world.

GUS: Mister Kleene.

VICTOR: Mister-fucking-Kleene.

GUS: You gonna call him? *(VICTOR goes to call)* When he answers ask for Mister Kleene and hang up.

VICTOR: It's ringin'.

GUS: What if his wife answers?

VICTOR: *(Into phone)* Victor Villanella calling for Mister K please.

GUS: Maybe he's not even married.

VICTOR: Of course.

GUS: That's him?

VICTOR: I understand.

GUS: He's on the phone?

VICTOR: I agree.

GUS: Mister Fucking Kleene!

VICTOR: *(Cups the phone)* Will you shut up! *(Pause)* Yeah. Yeah, yeah, yeah. Yes. Have a nice day. *(He hangs up)*

GUS: What'd he say?

VICTOR: You almost blew it. "Mister Fucking Kleene." He's right there!

GUS: You think he heard?

VICTOR: I don't know. *(Pause)*

GUS: It's his name.

VICTOR: How would you feel if your name was Mister Kleene?

GUS: If it's my name . . .

VICTOR: Bullshit.

GUS: How do you know?

VICTOR: Just wait for a horse's minute. Think about it.

GUS: A horse minute.

VICTOR: If you had a fucked-up name like him you'd do what he does.

GUS: Pick a letter.

VICTOR: You'd get laughed at if you didn't.

GUS: You think they laugh at Mister K?

VICTOR: Not now. But when he was young.

GUS: But when he was young they didn't call him mister.

VICTOR: They called him something.

GUS: Franky Kleene, Johnny Kleene, Richard Kleene, Dick Kleene is hysterical funny.

VICTOR: His father.

GUS: Huh?

VICTOR: I'm sayin' they probably laughed at his father.

GUS: Who?

VICTOR: People.

GUS: Which people?

VICTOR: Sometimes I think you were born mental, Gus. *(Pause)*

GUS: What is a horse's minute? *(BOBBY comes in)*

VICTOR: Where the fuck you been?

BOBBY: Dick shitting fuckhead.

VICTOR: Where'd you go?

BOBBY: Nickel and dime shit.

VICTOR: You got the gun?

BOBBY: I shoulda joined the Mafia. Or the Marine Corps.

VICTOR: Gimme the gun, Bob.

BOBBY: They, at least, don't dick around like we do with shit inside a paper bag.

VICTOR: You're gonna gimme the gun?

BOBBY: You want the gun?

VICTOR: What did I just say? Am I talkin' to myself?

BOBBY: I don't have it.

VICTOR: You don't have it. *(To GUS)* He doesn't have the gun. *(To BOBBY)* Where'd you go?

BOBBY: Overpass.

VICTOR: You went to the overpass?

BOBBY: You want me to say it again in Chinese? Overpass.

VICTOR: What were you doin' up on the overpass?

BOBBY: To throw away the gun.

VICTOR: You threw it off the overpass?

BOBBY: Nobody talks the same language around here.

VICTOR: Onto the highway?

BOBBY: Into the ocean. *(Pause)*

VICTOR: Which ocean?

BOBBY: I'm the fuckin' duck. You're the fuckin' mouse. And this is Disneyland.

VICTOR: The ocean by the flea market or the ocean by Fourteenth Avenue?

BOBBY: Fourteenth Avenue.

VICTOR: All right. *(Pause)* It's all right.

BOBBY: You told Mister K?

VICTOR: If you was me, would you tell Mister K?

BOBBY: I think I'd wait to see.

VICTOR: Waitin' plays no part in this.

BOBBY: I'd wait to see how it all turns out. *(Pause)*

VICTOR: Do you know what happened?

BOBBY: I know.

VICTOR: Did you see who it was?

BOBBY: I saw.

VICTOR: And you still say: "Wait to see how it turns out?"

BOBBY: Nobody's a hundred percent without mistakes.

VICTOR: Mistakes? *(Pause)* Mistakes, sure.

BOBBY: Well this is what I'm talkin' about Vic.

VICTOR: Takin' a dump in your drawers is a mistake. This was no mistake.

BOBBY: I didn't mean to kill him.

VICTOR: You meant to kill somebody.

BOBBY: It shouldn't have happened.

VICTOR: You point a loaded gun at someone's head and pull the trigger somethin's bound to happen. Someone's gonna die, you do a thing like that.

BOBBY: It was dark down in the basement.

VICTOR: It was dark but it wasn't that dark. We had the light from the milk machine. Was it that dark to you Gus?

GUS: Dark but not that dark.

BOBBY: Dark enough.

VICTOR: Dark enough to see the fucker's head explode.

BOBBY: The fuck was I supposed to know. This bozo's got a sock tied around his head shootin' spray paint everywhere. It's like a red fog down there him goin' pssssst, pssssst.

VICTOR: You can't tell the difference between a spic and a Sicilian?

BOBBY: Can you?

VICTOR: You can tell them by the smell.

BOBBY: He couldn't tell. I seen him hit Scarpacci on the head with the sock. *(Pause)*

VICTOR: Give yourself another demerit, Gus.

GUS: What for?

VICTOR: For hittin' Scarpacci on the head with a sock.

GUS: I ain't doin' it.

VICTOR: Give yourself a demerit or I'll give you two.

GUS: They was all mixed up on the floor like a spic and Sicilian salad.

VICTOR: Give yourself two or I'll give you three. *(*GUS *gives himself two demerits)* He hit him with a sock, Bob, but he didn't shoot him.

BOBBY: He didn't have a gun.

VICTOR: Well this is what I'm talkin' about.

BOBBY: Fucking clown's college.

VICTOR: You just flunked.

BOBBY: I got seven now.

VICTOR: You got more than seven but they don't fit.

BOBBY: I quit.

VICTOR: What is this: "I quit?"

BOBBY: I resign.

VICTOR: You don't quit.

BOBBY: I've never liked this job.

VICTOR: You're history. *(Pause)*

BOBBY: You're gonna do somethin'? *(Pause)* Whataya gonna do? *(Pause)* I want you to know this now: I never like that desk. That desk sucks. Who the fuck ever heard of a green desk. That desk is cheap. *(Pause)* Cocksucking fuckhead. *(Pause.* MISTER K *comes to the back door. He whispers something to men he has outside. He comes in)*

ALL: Mister K.

K: Boys.

BOBBY: I swear to God it was dark. He came at me. Everybody was swingin'. They looked the same down there.

K: Did you smell him?

BOBBY: Who had time to smell him?

K: You should have taken the time. They smell different you know.

BOBBY: It was dark. My nose is all stuffed. *(Pause)* You don't believe me? *(Takes out bottle of nose spray)* What is this, huh? What is this for?

K: But you had the gun.

BOBBY: "But I had the gun." This is a statement of fact like: "A chicken is not a duck," which seems obvious. I know a chicken from a duck. A duck goes: "Quack," a chicken goes, "Cocka-doodle-do." From the outside they do look different. But once you put them on a plate you could hardly tell which one goes, "Quack" and which one . . .

K: I told you: "No guns."

BOBBY: You told me: "No stabbings."

K: "No guns" is implied in "No stabbings."

BOBBY: Implied! Jesus, whataya call him, Christ. I don't even know if I know what that really means, "Implied."

K: We're in a crisis, boys.

BOBBY: You're gonna kill me, Mister K?

K: I can see I've been too lenient with you boys.

BOBBY: You're gonna kill me?

K: I take partial responsibility.

BOBBY: This is what I'm talkin' about.

K: I should have asserted more control.

OBBY: So you're not gonna kill me?

K: I'm not going to kill you, Bob. But I want your word you will never carry a gun again.

BOBBY: I swear.

K: Where is it?

BOBBY: I threw it away.

K: Where?

BOBBY: Into the ocean by Fourteenth Avenue.

K: Okay, boys. Leave me alone with Victor for a few minutes.

BOBBY: You want us to go home?

K: Wait outside. (BOBBY *and* GUS *leave out back*) Victor. Victor. Victor. Do you understand me when I say to do things as practiced? We've gone over this, haven't we? *(Pause)* Answer me, Victor.

VICTOR: Yes. My answer to you is yes. Yes.

K: You're my link with the other two. You're my buffer. Do you understand the need for discipline? To follow orders? To do what's said to do and what goes without saying?

VICTOR: What's implied.

K: What happened tonight is very embarrassing. Not to mention disheartening. There's a widow to take care of.

VICTOR: Mrs. Scarpacci.

K: Three young children in school. *(Pause)* Do you understand the implications? The cost involved?

VICTOR: What's implied and what's not implied.

K: Do you believe in karma?

VICTOR: When I was a small little young kid I did.

K: For every action there is a reaction. Like when the doctor taps you on the knee with a hammer it jumps. Do you follow?

VICTOR: Reflexes.

K: When you remove an object from space the space becomes vacant. And if you're responsible for removing that object, then you are also responsible for filling that space. Do you follow?

VICTOR: "Vacancy. No Vacancy." I follow this.

K: A space is now vacant. This space cannot go on unfilled. *(Pause)* The universe functions on sound principles. It's an ordered place we live in. The principle on which all other principles are grounded in justice. Justice will not be disregarded. We follow some simple laws. We obey certain rules. We are not savages sitting around a pile of animal bones. Do you understand?

VICTOR: No animal bones.

K: I want you to take this. *(Gives* VICTOR *a syringe and a bag of heroin)* There's enough dope here to kill an elephant. *(Pause)* Do we understand one another?

VICTOR: Enough to kill an elephant.

K: You take this and do what must be done.

VICTOR: Fill that space.

K: This is what I'm saying.

VICTOR: No vacancy.

K: I want justice carried out.

VICTOR: I saw on the TV they make pianos outta elephants.

K: A decent man has been wrongly killed tonight.

VICTOR: Is this a strange world or what?

K: Justice should be neat. No telltale signs.

VICTOR: Stick the needle in. Shoot him up and watch him drop.

K: I'll be in the Chinese restaurant around the corner. You come and get me. *(Pause)* You're a good man, Victor. I'm depending on you. It goes smooth, there's a big bonus in it for you. How about one thousand?

VICTOR: Wow.

K: Eh?

VICTOR: I said wow.

K: You know what to do. It's in your power to do the right thing and do it right. *(On his way out)*

VICTOR: Don't eat the chow mein, Mister K.

K: Some problem with the food over there?

VICTOR: They put dead dogs inside of it.

K: Nonsense.

VICTOR: I only tell you what I hear. Gussie sold them the blue dog.

K: What did Gussie do?

VICTOR: Have a good meal, Mister K. Enjoy. *(K leaves.* GUS *helps* BOBBY *in.* BOBBY *is bound and gagged)*

VICTOR: Boys. Boys. Boys.

GUS: Leave me outta this.

VICTOR: Bobby. Bobby. Bobby. *(*BOBBY *mumbles under the gag)* What'd he say?

GUS: How should I know?

VICTOR: Take the gag off.

GUS: They told me don't take the gag offa him.

VICTOR: I'm tellin' you take the gag off. *(*GUS *takes the gag off)* Bobby.

BOBBY: This is horseshit.

VICTOR: You're upset.

BOBBY: This is bullshit.

VICTOR: You have a right to be upset.

BOBBY: Dick shitting fuckheads.

VICTOR: But we're upset too.

BOBBY: I'm not upset.

VICTOR: "Dick shitting fuckheads" sounds to me like upset.

BOBBY: You're gonna kill me?

VICTOR: Calm down.

BOBBY: I'm gonna be killed?

VICTOR: Did I say that?

BOBBY: It was dark down there! I couldn't see shit! I don't deserve this treatment. What about all the jobs I did right?

VICTOR: You're gonna catch a case of high blood pressure you keep this up.

BOBBY: Are you gonna kill me or what?

VICTOR: Questions. Questions.

BOBBY: Tell me now.

VICTOR: You'll find out.

BOBBY: When I'm dead?

VICTOR: I work at my own pace, Bobby m'man.

BOBBY: Ask your mother in here for a minute.

VICTOR: You're bringing mothers into this now?

BOBBY: I wanna tell her something.

VICTOR: What you got to say to my mother?

BOBBY: We have an understanding. *(Pause)*

VICTOR: You have an understanding? *(Pause)* You have an understanding with my mother?

BOBBY: Call her in here.

VICTOR: I know what you did, Bob.

BOBBY: What'd I do?

VICTOR: Telling her how big your balls are.

BOBBY: I never said that.

VICTOR: That she's got a real sweet ass? *(Pause)* You never said that?

BOBBY: Would I say that to your mother?

VICTOR: I gotta tell you, Bobby, she told me these things.

BOBBY: Call her in here.

VICTOR: So you can tell her more?

BOBBY: So I can tell her she misunderstood me.

VICTOR: You fuckin' lowlife!

BOBBY: I'm a dead man.

VICTOR: You'll be lucky to be a dead man. You scum! You weasel! You prick! So you wanna hump my fuckin' mother, huh?

BOBBY: I never said I wanted to hump her.

VICTOR: Tellin' her the size of your balls sounds like somethin' to me, Bob.

BOBBY: I told her I had warm feelings for her.

VICTOR: What kind of warm feelings?

BOBBY: Warm feelings. Feelings which are warm.

VICTOR: How warm?

BOBBY: "How warm is a feeling?" Is this your question?

VICTOR: This is my mother we're talking about, Bob.

BOBBY: Warm is the middle between hot and cold. And this is what any good dictionary will tell you.

VICTOR: Get your own fuckin' mother for chrissakes.

BOBBY: I got my own mother.

VICTOR: Then give her your warm feelings.

BOBBY: I do give her my warm feelings.

VICTOR: I'm very glad to hear that.

BOBBY: I love my mother like a mother.

VICTOR: That's fine, Bob. That's beautiful. We all should love our fuckin' mothers. How would you feel if I told your mother I had warm feelings?

BOBBY: If you mean it sincerely I see no earthly reason in the world you shouldn't tell her.

VICTOR: If I told her how big my balls were? If I told her she's got a sweet ass? If I told her I wanted to lick her cunt?

BOBBY: I don't wanna lick your mother's cunt.

VICTOR: But you do wanna fuck her?

BOBBY: I never told her that to her face.

VICTOR: Where did you tell her that to?

BOBBY: I told her that in my mind. To her face I told her I dreamed she was lyin' in a field of flowers naked.

VICTOR: This is my mother, Bob.

BOBBY: That the birds were folding her clothes . . .

VICTOR: Do you understand who you're talkin' about?

BOBBY: And the trees were gently swaying . . .

VICTOR: What's my mother doin' naked in your dreams with no clothes on? *(Pause)* You saw her tits in your dream?

BOBBY: She was naked.

VICTOR: You saw the nipples on her tits? *(Pause)* And you did tell her the size of your balls?

BOBBY: I told her my things swelled up with love.

VICTOR: You told her she's got a sweet ass? *(Pause)* Did you or did you not tell my mother she's got a sweet ass?

BOBBY: She's uh, what I keep tellin you is my warm feelings extend, they go out to her, whataya call it—did you say, "ass?"

VICTOR: And you told her that? *(Pause)* Talk to me, Bob.

BOBBY: I told her something like her ass is, you know, is like round sorta like soft.

VICTOR: You used the word "ass"? You disgust me! You cocksucking fuckhead. You're dirt. You're shit. *(He gets the urn, pours ashes on* BOBBY's *head)* Say hello to Franky Banana. Gussie, watch him, I'm gonna go wash my face. This fuck, my blood pressure's way up to here. *(On his way into the bar)* I gotta tell you, Bobby, my mother does not have a sweet ass. Mother's don't have asses. They got behinds! *(*VICTOR *leaves)*

BOBBY: Untie me, Gus.

GUS: No.

BOBBY: I'll give you something.

GUS: What?

BOBBY: Something good.

GUS: How good?

BOBBY: Very good.

GUS: Nahhhh.

BOBBY: You'll like it.

GUS: I can't.

BOBBY: Don't say you can't. You don't want to. *(Pause)* He's gonna kill me.

GUS: You don't know that for sure.

BOBBY: It's pretty obvious.

GUS: Don't count your chickens unless you know damn sure they're your chickens.

BOBBY: It's the proof of the pudding, Gus.

GUS: But the pudding has skin on it.

BOBBY: You wanna see me die? *(Pause)* We go back, am I lyin'? Way back together.

GUS: I know you since I moved here from Ninth Street.

BOBBY: That's a long time, Gus.

GUS: It ain't that long.

BOBBY: Gussie! You were a little fuckin' kid when you moved here from Ninth Street. I remember the day you moved here. We kicked you off your Schwinn.

GUS: I know you long but I know someone else longer.

BOBBY: Who? Your mother? Who?

GUS: This guy named Paul.

BOBBY: Where is he?

GUS: Probably out workin'.

BOBBY: Who's here now? Who's here, me or Paul? Lookit, you're walking down the street with your grandmother, somebody, maybe your aunt. I come up. We talk: "Howya doin' howya doin' howya doin'? Ba-bing, ba-boom, see you later good-bye say hello to what's his name for me." I go down the street. They say to you: "Who was that nice boy, Gus?" What do you say?

GUS: I say Bobby.

BOBBY: You say: "That was my close friend Bobby." Do you see what I mean? Without a close friend, where are you? Things amount to a hill of fried shit you got no close friends. Without a close friend you're friendless. You walk by your lonesome.

GUS: I can't untie you Bob.

BOBBY: Friendship is a fuckin' myth.

GUS: I'd be in biiiiig fuckin' trouble I cut you loose.

BOBBY: We walk out of here together.

GUS: They come looking for us.

BOBBY: We hide out.

GUS: You can't hide from these guys. They got eyes.

BOBBY: I know a place. Way up in the fucking Ozarks. Nobody ever find us there.

GUS: I ain't going to no fuckin' Ozarks.

BOBBY: It's beautiful there.

GUS: They got country clubs? They got horse and pony shows? They got jai alai?

BOBBY: They got llamas, Gus.

GUS: What's a llama?

BOBBY: Animal with two heads.

GUS: Get the fuck . . .

BOBBY: One American dollar is worth fifteen of theirs. Gus we leave here we go straight to the airport. TW motherfucking A us out of here. We sit up in first class where they give you those little bottles of Scotch. Gussie!

GUS: I can't do it.

BOBBY: You don't wanna do it.

GUS: I never been in a plane before.

BOBBY: So what! So what! You walk in, you sit down. They buckle your seat, off you go. Before you were born you were never born before. So what! Did that stop you?

GUS: Sorry, Bob.

BOBBY: You're telling me "sorry"?

GUS: This is what I'm telling you.

BOBBY: You're sorry. He's gonna kill me and you're sorry.

GUS: That's the way it is this time.

BOBBY: It's the way you let it be. It rests on your head. God knows about these things. *(Pause)* You got nose hair, Gus?

GUS: Why do you wanna know?

BOBBY: I got ass hair.

GUS: So what?

BOBBY: Why don't we knit a sweater?

GUS: What does that mean?

BOBBY: It means what it means.

GUS: It don't mean nothin'. And I'm not surprised. Sometimes I think you were born mental. I hate you, Bobby. *(Pause)* Not only that but I think you smell bad. You're uglier than Pi. You're the south end of a northbound frankfurter dog.

BOBBY: I fucked your mother.

GUS: That's bullshit.

BOBBY: And your mother sucked my dick.

GUS: Fuck you.

BOBBY: The truth hurts, don't it? *(GUS puts the gag back on BOBBY, VICTOR enters)*

VICTOR: Whataya doin', Gus?

GUS: He started sayin' shit.

VICTOR: He's allowed.

GUS: Said he fucked my mother.

VICTOR: You can't stay offa people's mothers, can you?

GUS: Said she sucked his dick.

VICTOR: That's a low blow. A very low blow. *(Pause)* Take the gag off, Gus.

GUS: He's gonna start sayin' shit again.

VICTOR: He's gonna say sorry. *(GUS takes off the gag)* Say sorry to Gus.

BOBBY: Sorry, Gus.

GUS: I don't accept it.

BOBBY: I said: "Sorry!"

VICTOR: He don't have to accept, he don't wanna.

BOBBY: Whataya gonna do?

VICTOR: What happened tonight is very embarrassing. Not to mention disheartening. There is a widow to take care of. Three young children in school. Do you believe in karma?

BOBBY: The fuck should I know?

VICTOR: For every action there is a reaction. Empty holes have no objects in them. You take the object out, you put the object right back in or you're fucked. Someone may fall in the hole. A hole is not a good thing.

BOBBY: You're still mad at me.

VICTOR: Simple fucking laws. Rules! We obey these rules because if we don't we're like fiendish fucking cocksuckers sitting around a pile of dead animal bones going: *(Makes a face)*. I smack you on the knee with a hammer and what happens?

BOBBY: I go ouch.

VICTOR: Your knee pops out. And that's how justice works my friend. You hit it, it pops right back out at you. You cannot escape justice. Because in the end justice will find you and fuck you dead in the ass. You follow?

BOBBY: My ass is bleedin'.

VICTOR: So whata we do about it?

BOBBY: I don't know.

VICTOR: Whataya think we do about it?

BOBBY: Forget the whole thing, shake hands.

VICTOR: If you were me what would you do about it?

BOBBY: If I were you I'd let me go.

VICTOR: Why is that?

BOBBY: Because I'm me.

VICTOR: I'm not doing this because I hate you, Bobby. There's nothing personal here. You think this is personal?

BOBBY: You're mad about your mother.

VICTOR: This has nothing to do with that.

BOBBY: What does this have to do with?

VICTOR: This has to do with justice does not wear a blindfold or smoke cigarettes. Justice knows. And when justice calls you can't say: "No, I'm busy now, call me back later."

BOBBY: So you're gonna kill me.

VICTOR: I am not gonna kill you. Whataya think of that?

BOBBY: I think that's okay.

VICTOR: Does that make you happy?

BOBBY: It makes me feel a whole lot better.

VICTOR: Good. *(Pause)* Gus is going to kill you.

GUS: I never done a thing like that before.

BOBBY: This guy, he ain't never done nothing before. I'm surprised you managed to get born.

GUS: I don't wanna kill him, Victor.

VICTOR: I know you don't.

GUS: You're gonna make me?

VICTOR: I can't make you do a thing like that. But I can suggest. And it is my recommendation that you do it. If you pick up and it's justice on the other end you tell her what she wants to hear. *(Pause)* Ring, ring. He picks up. Hello. Who's this? This is Gus. Who are you? This is Justice. I want you to kill Bobby. Gus says . . . she's waitin' Gus.

GUS: All right.

BOBBY: You little fuckin' twerp!

GUS: You fucked my mother, huh?

BOBBY: I was only kiddin'.

GUS: She sucked your dick.

BOBBY: I sucked my own dick.

GUS: Cocksucking fuckhead. Shitburger on a bun. You disgust me.

BOBBY: I take it all back. We'll pretend like I never said it.

GUS: Because it never really happened did it?

BOBBY: You think I'd actually try to fuck your mother, Gus? Who you kiddin'? C'mon. She walks with a cane for chrissakes. *(GUS goes to put the gag back on* BOBBY*)* Whataya doin', Gus? I said I take it all back.

GUS: Justice called, Bob. Sorry.

BOBBY: You fuck. You shit. I did too fuck your mother. She called me Carl. I fucked her all night long. *(GUS gags him)*

VICTOR: You're really startin' to get on my nerves, Bob. When do you ever learn to stay away from other people's mothers?

GUS: Tell me what to do.

VICTOR: Shoot him up.

GUS: Get him high?

VICTOR: O.D. the cocksucker. *(GUS prepares the heroin)* I want you to know, Bobby, this is not for telling my mother the size of your balls. I wanna set the record straight on this. I don't harbor any ill feelings for what you done. This is strictly business. This is justice. *(Pause)* The thing with my mom I'd just be mad at you. Probably smack you on the head with a hard object some day. But not this. Okay, Bob? *(Pause)* Okay, Bobby?

GUS: It's ready.

VICTOR: Say good-bye to Bob.

GUS: Bye, Bob.

VICTOR: Bye, Bob. *(Pause)* Okay, Gus.

GUS: *(To* BOBBY*)* You mad at me? *(*BOBBY *struggles)* You're not mad? Shit, I'd be mad as hell. *(Pause)* Okay, Bobby I'm gonna do it. I don't wanna but I gotta. Okay? *(Pause)* Okay here goes. *(He shoots* BOBBY *with the heroin.* BOBBY *falls)* You think he's dead already?

VICTOR: Put your ear on his heart.

GUS: *(Listening to* BOBBY*'s heart)* He's still going. *(Pause)* Getting smaller. *(Pause)* I can hardly hear it now. *(Pause)* So long, Bob. *(Pause)* It stopped.

VICTOR: Let's go.

GUS: Where we goin'?

VICTOR: Let's go.

GUS: Where we goin'?

VICTOR: Take him outta here.

GUS: Where?

VICTOR: Out back behind the Chinese restaurant.

GUS: They'll put him in the chow mein.

VICTOR: We'll throw him in the dumpster then. *(They carry* BOBBY*'s body out as the lights fade to black)*

Act 2: Scene 2

(The same. A few minutes later. VICTOR *is sitting at the desk, making a phone call.)*

VICTOR: Bobby Smith with one "I." *(Pause)* Yes, on the blue Camaro. *(Pause)* Larry Vanilla. *(Pause)* Home or office? *(Pause)* 976-2828 *(Pause)* I'm positive. *(Pause)* Forget about it. I was callin' a wrong number. *(Hangs up. Sings softly to himself)* "Yankee doodle went to town riding on his pony . . ." *(*GUS *enters)* You got him?

GUS: Yeah.

VICTOR: He's on the way?

GUS: He was eatin'.

VICTOR: What was he eatin'?

GUS: I wasn't gonna say nothin'.

VICTOR: Whataya gonna do?

GUS: I don't know.

VICTOR: I say, whataya gonna do?

GUS: There's nothin' you can do.

VICTOR: Well there it is. *(VCM enters)*

GUS: Mrs. Vanilla.

VCM: What are you boys still doing here?

VICTOR: Workin' late.

VCM: You come on home.

VICTOR: We gotta wait for Mister K.

VCM: Well, you come on home right after you see him. *(Pause)* How's your stomach feel?

VICTOR: *(Feels his stomach)* Hard and smooth.

VCM: How does the inside of your stomach feel?

VICTOR: I ate toast and drank the tea. *(She walks into the bar)*

GUS: She left.

VICTOR: I can see that.

GUS: She didn't say: "Good-bye. I love you be a good boy."

VICTOR: That's how I know she's comin' back. *(Sings softly to himself)* "I ate the toast and drank the tea. I'm Barnacle Bill the sailor."

GUS: Whata you doin'?

VICTOR: What does it look like I'm doin'?

GUS: Singin'.

VICTOR: Well, that's what I'm doin'. *(VCM enters with a plate of food)*

VCM: Eat this.

VICTOR: Ma!

VCM: It's good for you.

VICTOR: They got a ton of cholesterol in there.

VCM: Eat it anyway.

VICTOR: It's ugly.

VCM: Give some to your friend.

VICTOR: *(Gives plate to Gus)* Eat it.

VCM: I said some, not all. *(He takes some back)* Don't come home too late.

VICTOR: I won't.

VCM: Lock the door behind you when you come in.

VICTOR: I will.

VCM: Be good boy.

VICTOR: I am.

VCM: I love you.

VICTOR: Okay, ma.

  (VCM *leaves*)

GUS: So long, Mrs. V.

VICTOR: Villa-fuckin'-nella!

GUS: You got a nice mother.

VICTOR: What does that mean?

GUS: It means what it means.

VICTOR: Well let's keep it that way. (K *enters*)

VICTOR AND GUS: Mister K.

K: Boys.

VICTOR: We threw him in the dumpster.

K: I told you to come get me when you're finished.

VICTOR: I thought you meant after.

K: You put him in the dumpster out back?

VICTOR: In the dumpster behind the Chinese restaurant.

GUS: Don't worry, Mister K. He's probably in a big pot right now.

K: I worry boys because you don't do exactly what I tell you to do.

GUS: You're mad at us, Mister K?

K: I'm not mad at you. I want you to learn to do the right thing. (*Pause*) Okay, now go home. Get some sleep and I'll see you in the morning.

VICTOR AND GUS: Goodnight, Mister K.

K: Goodnight, boys. (*Leaves*)

GUS: Mister fuckin' Kleene!

VICTOR: Shut up! He might hear you.

GUS: He's gone.

VICTOR: He's got ears everywhere. He could be listenin' by the keyhole.

GUS: Why would he do that?

VICTOR: To hear things.

GUS: What things he wants to hear?

VICTOR: Things, things. Guys like him like to hear what guys like me and you got to say about him. *(Pause)* You got a cousin needs a job?

GUS: My cousin John maybe.

VICTOR: You call him on the phone tomorrow, ask him does he want to work with us.

GUS: He lives long distance.

VICTOR: Where long distance?

GUS: Los Angeles.

VICTOR: You ain't got nothing closer?

GUS: My cousin Denise who lives on Bay Thirty-first Street but I ain't callin' her.

VICTOR: You give her a call, send her down, we take a look at her.

GUS: I ain't workin' with no girl.

VICTOR: Things are changin' all over. They even give them guns now and send them to the moon so they can blow up inside a space shuttle. *(Pause)* It's a democracy, Gus. Make sure you never forget about the guy with the drum.

GUS: What guy with the drum?

VICTOR: The guy with the drum who's next to the guy with the flute.

GUS: What guy with the flute?

VICTOR: Next to the guy with the flag.

GUS: Where you get these three guys from?

VICTOR: The guy with the drum. The guy with the flute. The guy with the flag. They got bandages on their heads. The guy with the flute walks with a limp. They're singin' the song: "Yankee Doodle went to town riding on his pony. Stuck a feather in his cap and called it macaroni."

GUS: Oh! That guy with the drum!

VICTOR: I wonder why he called that feather macaroni?

GUS: He got a head wound.

VICTOR: It's a strange world we live in, Gus. Let's go home. It's been a busy but exciting day.

GUS: You never told me what's a horse's minute?

VICTOR: It's a horse's ass with time involved.

K: *(Pokes his head back inside)* Have a seat boys. I'll be back in a second. *(Pokes his head back out)*

VICTOR: I told you he listens through the keyhole.

GUS: We're in biiiiiig trouble now.

(K points a sawed-off shotgun inside and fires off two rounds that hit VICTOR *and* GUS. *He carries in a gym bag. From the bag he takes out drug paraphernalia and spreads it around the room. He puts a pistol by* VICTOR *and* GUS. *He goes behind the desk, makes a phone call).*

K: John? Bill. Sure, sure. Listen. I got the three on the Scarpacci thing. Sure I'm sure. John, you should see this place. Vials, syringes, bottles of cheap wine. It's like a regular shooting gallery. Sure. I got two. The other's out back with an overdose. You tell them, John, probably drug related but we don't know for sure yet. Sure. So what's up? You going bowling tomorrow night? I know, I know. But John, switch to the soft rubber ball. I know. They grease the alleys too damn much. John. You think I don't know that?

(Lights out)

The Election Machine Warehouse

Amiri Baraka

Scene 1

(The long gray-brown metal shadows. The long aisles of gray-brown quilted election machines. A full square block of them. Orderly parallel rows of sleeping beings. A maze of walled paths. The shadowy factory almost seems to be breathing, as if full of softly breathing sleeping life.

A door opens and a few moments later a bald, gray, brown, dignified-looking black man, adjusting a soft brown homburg upon his head, pulls watchman's round, strapped clock upon his shoulder.

He looks around, lights his cigar, and trudges down the halls of the interior humming "This Is My Story, This Is My Song/Blessed Redeemer." As he walks down the long, shadowy outer aisle, the low breathing drops into muttered phrases, melodies, thumping momentary heartbeats.

A light chord of changing tint touches each passed machine, like the notes of an infinite piano. A man on stilts looms with long strides blending and re-emerging from the shadows—a sudden shudder of talking drums. As the drums play softly, a Voice brushes through the otherwise silent place as if translating the drum.)

VOICE: "Ah, the people of the sun . . . the people of the sun . . . where will you be as West your soul is drawn."

(WATCHMAN stops to put in key and turn it in time box. It is obvious WATCHMAN hears the song, but he turns unalarmed, though slightly piqued by the mood, to a vague, half-shrug "acknowledgment."

He turns slightly, but then resumes his tour. The sealike sounds gradually increase as he moves somewhat stiffly past the next machines. The same Voice is heard again, just above a whisper, as if in someone's mind.)

VOICE: The slave trade thus begun by the Portuguese enlarged by the Dutch and carried to its culmination by the English centered on the West Coast.

(We hear the old man humming going to the next machine.)

VOICE: The full significance of the battle of Tenkadibou, which overthrew the Askias was now clear. Hereafter, Africa for centuries was to appear before the world not as the land of god and ivory, of Mansa Musa and Meroe, but as a bound and captive slave . . . *(as if hurt)* dumb and degraded.

(Lights on radio come on in the room, a station change even though no one is in the room. We can hear Jack Benny and Rochester's gravelly voice.)

ROCHESTER V.O.:   Well, I don't know, Mr. Benny, I left the car out front now it ain't there no more.

BENNY V.O.:   Whhhhhaaat? My caaar? Rochester, how do you do these things all the time?

ROCHESTER V.O.:   Wait a minute, Mr. Benny. I didn't do nothing but what I usually do, park the car right out there in the driveway.

BENNY V.O.:   Rochester, Rochester, are you sure . . . did you look everywhere? Rochester, I need my car . . . *(shrieks answered by peals of audience laughter).*

(Doorbell rings, radio is turned off. WATCHMAN *turns and crosses the raised aisle. Begins humming low, then more distinct "Wade In The Water." The rush of waves of the sea can barely be heard. He stops again to put the watch key in the time box. Faint cries waver and barely reach us, a musical rhythmic keening of cries like a wet, relentless spray of millions in pain.)*

VOICE: The American slave trade, therefore, meant the elimination of at least sixty million Negroes from their motherland. The Muhammadan slave trade meant the forcible migration of nearly as many more. . . . It would be conservative, then, to say that the slave trade cost Negro Africa one hundred million souls. . . .

*(*WATCHMAN *pauses, as if listening, but not so one could be embarrassed if there was actually no real sound! Lights change, then as they slowly fade, we see* WATCHMAN *in silhouette.)*

VOICE: Whole regions were depopulated, whole tribes disappeared . . . the dark irresistible grasp of fetish took firmer hold on men's minds. . . .

(Humming of WATCHMAN *gets louder. He has not heard the doorbell yet. It is still ringing.* WATCHMAN *begins to sing "Nobody Knows The Trouble I Seen.")*

VOICE: They told us we were not to be eaten, but to work, and were soon to go on land, where we should see many of our people. This report eased us much.

(Figure of a boy moving quickly, almost unseen through machines like forest, a runaway. We hear his panting breath and dogs barking in the distance.
WATCHMAN *moves still humming, occasionally fragments of lyrics. At the next station he puts in the key and turns it as before, pretending not to listen to the Voice.*
WATCHMAN *puts a key in the next box. At the same time, the phone rings in the office. There is banging on the door and bell.* WATCHMAN *stops to register. Also at the same time, a ghost sweeps among the machines while making a moaning sound. A boy pursues stealthily. They disappear.)*

Scene 2

(Outside the door a man and woman [MOTHER *and* FATHER] *are just arriving in a car. An older woman* [GRANDMOTHER] *and two young children* [BOY *and* GIRL] *are ringing the*

bell and banging on the door. The BOY *and* GIRL *jostle each other and alternate kicking the door.)*

GRANDMOTHER: My land, will you children stop acting like heathens!

(The GIRL *is trying to smack the* BOY *for pushing and annoying her.)*

BOY: *(Taunting little* GIRL*)* Mad Dog Moments, Mad Dog Moments . . .

(Little GIRL *is swinging. Their* MOTHER *is standing by the car talking to their* FATHER.*)*

MOTHER: I'm gonna give Papa this Roosevelt button!

FATHER: Elise, you know Mr. Rays won't like that. A lotta black people still think the Republicans freed them.

MOTHER: Old-time colored thinking. *(Calls, joking)* Mama, tell Papa I got a Roosevelt button for him.

GRANDMOTHER: *(Half turning, half dealing with children)* Ray's for Wilkie. You know that. I heard him tell you more than once.

GIRL: We got a Wilkie button!

BOY: He got a smooth shiny forehead.

MOTHER: *(Still by the car)* Mama, tell Papa to stop giving them children Wilkie buttons.

GRANDMOTHER: Ray must not hear us.

(Still banging and ringing. The radio pops on inside. The marching feet of criminals is heard, the prologue soundtrack to the radio program Gangbusters!*)*

RADIO 1:   This is Warden Warren B. Schwartzkoft. *(Quiet)*

RADIO 2:   You think I'm a killer, wait till you get ahold of my son. He's the real gangbuster!

(The night WATCHMAN *is walking toward the office and the bell.)*

GRANDMOTHER: *(Finally)* Oh, my land, I got a key. Ray give me a key last time.

MOTHER: Mama, Papa probably in there sleeping. Why don't you just use your key?

GRANDMOTHER: I'm looking for it. *(Searches through bag)*

(In the interior of the warehouse, while WATCHMAN *is moving toward the door the Voice is heard again. This time he pauses slightly, as if to listen.)*

VOICE: . . . and I looked and saw the forms of men in different attitudes. And there were lights in the sky to which the children of darkness gave other names than what they really were. For they were the lights of the Savior's hands, stretched forth from east to west, even as they were extended on the cross on Calvary.

*(*WATCHMAN *starts to walk.)*

VOICE: And shortly afterwards while laboring in the field, I discovered drops of blood on the corn as though it were dew from heaven . . . and I then found on the leaves in the woods hieroglyphic characters and numbers.

(WATCHMAN *stands till the Voice has stopped. Then without reaction he trudges toward the front office. As he reaches the office, the door swings open and his wife,* NAN, *and the* BOY *and* GIRL *come in. His daughter is still at the car talking to her husband. They now have a more animated conversation, which can barely be heard.*)

MOTHER: You going bowling tonight?

FATHER: I told you that last week . . .

MOTHER: But we are having the Greens and the Strutters over tonight. You know that.

FATHER: We got a tournament beginning tonight.

GRANDMOTHER: Ray, we've been out here knocking for quite a spell.

WATCHMAN: That's why I gave you the key, Nan. You know I can't hear you back inside that place.

GRANDMOTHER: Here's your dinner (*laying bag down on the desk*).

WATCHMAN: (*Kisses her on the forehead*) Thank you, mam, but I got to turnkey three or four more boxes. It ain't gonna get cold is it?

GRANDMOTHER: No, you know I got it wrapped so it'll stay hot.

WATCHMAN: (*Begins to look in bag*) What you brought?

GRANDMOTHER: Ray you gonna go in the bag and it's gonna be cold. Chicken and dumplins and biscuits and greens.

WATCHMAN: Well, let me get out there and finish turning those keys.

BOY: (*Still pushing and pulling with* GIRL, *but anxious to get inside the warehouse*) I'll go with you, Granddaddy. I want to turn the keys too.

GIRL: I wanna go too.

BOY: Aw, you always wanna do everything I do . . .

GIRL: So what? No, I don't anyway.

GRANDMOTHER: You all gonna get me vexed.

GIRL: Okay, come on. (*To* GRANDMOTHER) We'll be back in a minute.

GRANDMOTHER: Now Ray, don't take too long or the food will get cold.

(GRANDMOTHER, BOY, *and* GIRL *move through the door with* WATCHMAN *leading and the children jumping up and down bringing up the rear.* GRANDMOTHER *sits in the chair and turns on radio. A religious program comes on.*)

RADIO SINGERS: What a friend we have in Jesus, daily slavery he makes you bear. What a friend we have in Jesus. Brought you in the slave ship here.

(GRANDMOTHER *is looking through a Bible, half listening at first, then something makes her look up.*)

RADIO SINGERS: What a friend we have in Jesus, daily slavery he makes you bear. Brought you on a slave ship to us. Brought you on a slave ship here.

GRANDMOTHER: *(Can't believe her ears)* What is this? *(Still hasn't heard it clearly. Applause from congregation)* What they sayin'? *(Looks at radio closely)* What kind of heathen?

RADIO PREACHER: Good evening, my good colored friends. This is the Disholiness Hour, brought to you by Unheavenly Rest. Where you can spend your not life like you spent your life, on ice.

(GRANDMOTHER *is now seriously confused and a little frightened. She looks at the radio and then, at the next outburst takes a visible step back.*)

GRANDMOTHER: What in God's name? Maybe I'm not hearing so well, but—

RADIO PREACHER: Yes, my good colored friends. Have you ever considered that there might not be a Heaven? Just a Hell. Suppose I was to tell you that can't no colored person get in Heaven in the first place, even if there was one. That's why Heavenly Rest is your best bet. We sell coffins *(gets religious cant and tone and rhythm like prayer).* We sell coffins that will seal you off forever, where nothing can get to you. So even if there ain't a Jesus or a God and there's only the Devil, can't no Devil get to you because in our boxes you can be touched by nothing. Even if there was a God for the colored, he'd have to knock on the box to get in. This box—

(GRANDMOTHER *reaches over suddenly and shuts radio off, but it pops on again.*)

RADIO PREACHER: Don't do that! I was talking to you, lady.

GRANDMOTHER: *(Steps back)* Ray . . . Ray *(she turns and goes through the door into the warehouse interior).* Ray . . . Ray . . . where are you?

Scene 3

(MOTHER [ELISE] *comes into office.*)

MOTHER: *(Calling back over her shoulder to her husband)* I'll be right out. You gotta take me to Gloria's house. *(As she enters the room, radio pops on. Kate Smith is singing: "God Bless America." MOTHER stops as the song ends and Kate Smith begins to talk to her.)*

KATE SMITH: You love America, don't you?

MOTHER: What?

KATE SMITH: You, lady. You, colored woman standing there wondering where your mother and father and two children are.

MOTHER: What? *(Looks sharply at radio. Begins to approach it)* Pop?

KATE SMITH: Just listen *(exasperated, but still "cheerful")*. If you love America, you'll get in it!

MOTHER: Hmmmmm *(looking around)* Pop, Mama, Elroy, Sandi . . . *(to outside door)* Curtis.

KATE SMITH: Now listen, you're a citizen. A modern American woman. Don't let anyone hold you back. The old nigger slaves. Your uneducated insensitive husband. Not even your children.

MOTHER: What? *(She is fully awake now)* What did you say . . . radio? The radio? *(Moves closer)*

KATE SMITH: *(Laughing lightly begins to sing "God Bless America" again.)*

MOTHER: *(She reaches and switches radio off and turns and goes into the warehouse interior)* Papa, Mama, Sandi, Elroy—

(The radio pops back on.)

RADIO: *(Singing)* On the Prairies, In the Mountains, on the ocean . . . white with foooooooammmmmmmmmmmm. Gaaaaaaaaaaahhhhhhd Blessssssssss Americaaaaaaa.

(The stage is half lit as the song goes on. The interior of the warehouse is now seen. The song faded somewhat in the background. The old man is going to the various key stations. As he moves, Klansmen duck out of sight behind the machines. They have a black man in a Union uniform, with a noose around his neck, torturing him as they move. The two children have climbed on top of an election machine in its quilted cover and are squatting on top of the machine talking.)

BOY: These machines are how you vote.

GIRL: I know that. Granddaddy told both of us.

BOY: So what. Bet you didn't even know what voting means.

GIRL: Do so. When you vote you vote for Roosevelt.

BOY: Granddaddy didn't vote for Roosevelt.

GIRL: He did so.

BOY: He did not.

GIRL: Did so.

BOY: He voted for Wilkie. See, you don't know nothin'.

GIRL: Wilkie? Did not.

BOY: Did so. You didn't see him with a Wilkie button on?

GIRL: So what, he still voted for Roosevelt. That's why Roosevelt won. You so dumb.

(ELISE, their MOTHER, has stopped now and questioning her "running away," she retraces her steps and goes back in the office. As she enters, the radio begins speaking to her.)

KATE SMITH: Now you know America is a greaaat country. You know that. And you're . . . well, an American. . . . Equal opportunity.

MOTHER: *(Approaching radio slowly, sensing the bizarre, draws herself up)* Are you speaking to me?

KATE SMITH: Of course! No one else is here. No one else could understand. Our America—The Red, The White and The Blues. America the Beautiful! And even though your father can be threatened by those still developing an understanding of modern America—where everybody is equal and free.

MOTHER: *(Turns and looks at door to interior at mention of her father. Tries to go with the situation as best she can)* Oh yeah. *(Getting in it despite herself)* You must be talking to somebody else. Equal? Free? Colored people ain't. Free, my foot!

KATE SMITH: Your husband didn't go to college did he? *(Pause)* I know all about it! A young wild buck. A barber *(laughs almost unwillingly)*. Those are their fathers shouting at your father!

MOTHER: *(Looking)* Wow! Here by myself, I think Kate Smith is talking to me.

KATE SMITH: I am!

MOTHER: *(Steps close again)* Hmmmmmm.

KATE SMITH: Because you are educated. You should have waited and married a college colored. But you let your niggerness get the best of you.

MOTHER: *(Backing away, uncertain)* Pop, Mama where are you?

KATE SMITH: But you to your husband are your father to your mother.

MOTHER: What? Pop. . . .

KATE SMITH: No, you cannot be a modern woman with equal rights if your man *(happy at pun)* di-capped with a barber.

MOTHER: What's going on, a joke? Some kind of microphone. *(Begins to look behind radio, but not getting too close. Calls)* Elroy, Sandi! *(She is staring at the door to the warehouse)*

KATE SMITH: Ignorance is not to be tolerated, unless you are ignorant or like it as an exchange for a charm representing, well, love!

MOTHER: Will somebody come out here! And what's with this radio?

KATE SMITH: You should have held fast until your real class partner came along—instead of niggerizing into this lamentable social downgrading. Your . . . ah . . . mate . . . is not even a churchgoing person. No money. No ambition. You should have waited like me. That's why I'm still chaste.

MOTHER: Oh boy! *(Looking)* Hey, somebody! Where is everybody?

KATE SMITH: My closest associates are women of like mind. My speech writer, Gertrude, our secretary, Alice B.

(MOTHER finally exits, shaking her head and lurching through the door into the warehouse interior. When she leaves the radio opens up, a fat female midget with a US flag climbs out of the interior. The inside of the radio is like a huge flag and the midget is one of the stars that climbs out, so that the star on the flag is visibly missing. She begins to follow the MOTHER on tiptoe exaggeratedly.)

Scene 4

(The front door is pushed open hard. The FATHER comes in looking around.)

FATHER: Elise! Elise! Wha . . . Where the . . . *(checks that he can't be heard)* hell did they go? I gotta get outta here. *(He starts toward warehouse door. Radio comes on again. This time it is a baseball game. Mel Allen is doing the game.)*

MEL ALLEN: It's a long drive into right field. *(Crowd)* Doby rounds first as Lindell runs the ball down.

FATHER: *(Stops and begins to listen. Voice changes from doing game)*

MEL ALLEN: Why can't you do what you wanna do? You can do what you wanna do, but can you feel what you're doing? *(Crowd)*

FATHER: *(Forgets quest)* Hey! What's up radio? Where's the game?

MEL ALLEN: The interior and superior are the posterior and the anterior. Like the head is to the derriere. How they talk. You need a better job. How they talk and talk. That Curtis, they say. Why don't he get a better job? Why does he drink so much? And even we loyal fans must admit you were exposed with no clothes with a slut or two . . . in the gutter too.

FATHER: *(Rises and listens closely now, turning his head to see if anyone else is in the room)*

MEL ALLEN: You can be all everybody wants if you give up what you is and be what you ain't.

FATHER: *(Defensively, still not quite admitting something is very wrong)* Where's the game?

MEL ALLEN: Leave those girlfriends of yours alone. Stop drinking. Get a better job. Be more intelligent! Be interested in the world! In education! In history! In helping people! Don't just bowl in the alley and be in the alley bowling. Be somebody that can wear suits to work.

FATHER: Elise! Ellll . . . iiiiiise! *(He rushes through the warehouse door looking over his shoulder)*

Scene 5

(Inside lights up on WATCHMAN *turning key.* GRANDMOTHER *catches up with him as he stops and turns when he hears her calling. All movement, moving in and out of the aisles and around the machines, is performed in silhouette.)*

MOTHER: *(Enters and is walking exasperated behind them. They turn and greet her. There is some laughter.* MOTHER *points back and* GRANDMOTHER *is shaking her head. They are talking about the radio)* Oh, Mama hush! *(Laughing and joking)* What you mean the radio don't believe in God? *(Turns)* Where's them two children?

(Then a flash of lights on an empty Klan hood hanging from an artificial tree. We hear voiceover of a Southern white merchant.)

MERCHANT: Now you know you taking business I should have. My papa was your goddam overseers! No, sir. Either you gonna work for me or your luck's gonna change, Mis . . . ter Rays. Yeh, I hear folk, even some white fools call you Mis . . . ter. It's stupid.

(The whole scene changes in mood and intensity. We are apparently somewhere else in some other time. GRANDFATHER, GRANDMOTHER, *and* MOTHER *stand fixed by the scene.)*

GRANDFATHER: I worked to build what I have, sir. I don't owe anyone money or anything else. Why do you want my store? You have two already.

MERCHANT: Niggers don't need no stores. It makes 'em sour and hard to get along with. Everybody with sense knows that.

GRANDFATHER: I thought all that was changed. I thought the Union won the war!

(The hood catches fire and now there are lynch mob sounds, which seem to come out of it like electronic music. It is "This is My Story" and "Dixie" at varying speeds and pitches. The three, as if in another time and place, suddenly grab everything they have, screaming and crying. They rush around the election machine to a ramp that brings them higher off the ground, as if they were entering a coach so that one of the election machines becomes a train chugging up to the north. A map, like a weather map, lights up and shows their route.)

FATHER: *(Rushes in. He is calling them. He is also running)* Where is everybody?

(He begins to wander among the machines shouting and calling.)

Scene 6

(Lights go up and WATCHMAN *and* GRANDMOTHER *are building some kind of structure with boxes, groceries, bills, bibles, coins, and newspapers, in a small space among the machines. Radios are playing Gabriel Heater, Jimmie Fiddler, Drew Pearson, The Southernaires.* MOTHER *has moved a little away and sits on a box in a college sweater [Fisk] reading a newspaper.)*

MOTHER: It's not right! It's not right! *(She is reading)* Pop, did you see this? Keenan is messing up again.

WATCHMAN: He thinks he's always right. They all always think that. *(The three give a little knowing laugh)* But Keenan will admit he's wrong later, in private.

MOTHER: But none of those people ever want to give us anything really, do they, Papa? You know, Papa, the Democrats are really trying to work with black people it seems to me.

WATCHMAN: They got a trick for you just like the others. I'm staying with the Elephants.

MOTHER: *(Haughty)* I know because they are the part of Lincoln! Because they freed us.

GRANDMOTHER: The Lord freed us, Chile, please don't forget that.

WATCHMAN: The Lord and them guns *(small laugh)*. No. I'm with ol' Elephant because of what they promised and because I know them. I don't have no illusions they're anything but who they are.

GRANDMOTHER: And besides, the Lord freed us, not no jealous crackers.

(They chuckle at the statement and at GRANDMOTHER *who usually doesn't say much. Light flashes and the "vehicle" they were riding falls in on the structure they are building.* MOTHER *leaps to her feet and runs into* FATHER, *who is half wandering, half rushing up the aisle. There is a contradiction in time where some of what is happening has already happened, some is happening "now".)*

FATHER: Hey, hey! Where's everybody?

*(*MOTHER *and* FATHER *collide, look at each other, embrace and disappear around the corner of a machine. A Voice calls to* GRANDMOTHER *and* WATCHMAN, *still fixed in the light, contemplating the crash.)*

MERCHANT: You owe me money!

GRANDFATHER: If I could get a loan. The Depression.

(He's now raised himself from the small merchant he was in the South. He is now a banker.)

BANKER: A loan? You're beside yourself, Rays! Those colored customers of yours ain't payin' you. You can't run a business and be friends with colored people. That's why you people fail in business, too soft. Don't know how to crack the whip. You can't be rich unless you can get high off it. Unless you can pray to it. Worship it. Money is Heaven and God and whiskey and women! And the colored don't understand. But wait a few years. A few will. Just wait. I predict that. You know I like you people.

WATCHMAN: Aren't you a Christian?

BANKER: No. Religion is all right with me. It has its place. But I don't let it interfere with my business.

WATCHMAN: You do worship God?

BANKER: Money. That's why you have nothing now. I'm taking it.

GRANDMOTHER: *(Crying)* He's just trying to help people. To be a Christian.

BANKER: Good for him! *(Pause)* Now you got to get out.

(MOTHER *and* FATHER *rush into the scene at this point and stand watching. The* BANKER *moves into the center of the scene now. He is seated on a* Negro Donkey *[ears and tail fastened on like Dems. The* Negro Donkey *is singing like Cab Callaway.)*

DONKEY: Hidee Hideee Ho! It's a new deal, McNeil! Your old line don't rhyme with the new time . . . *(snorts)*

WATCHMAN: If we had the same way to get loans and insurance and stock and advertising and larger lots of merchandise, we'd have strong business and money—just like you. Just like everybody else. Colored people can run a business if you make the politics agree.

DONKEY: Oh, Elephant doo doo. Hee Haw. Elephant doo doooo. Elephant doo dooed all over you so you was his fertilizer. You thought it was love! And now they gone! *(Shouts)* New deal!

(MOTHER *and* FATHER *are watching, holding each other.)*

DONKEY: And now you ain't even got much doo doo!

BANKER: New owners. New crowd. New Jack. New Asses!

DONKEY: Hidee Hideee Hooo. And when Elephant split the mule arrive new as gold.

BANKER: Give and get!

DONKEY: Come and go!

WATCHMAN: We are not less than anyone. Politics is what will lift us. Politics and Business and God.

(The Donkey is moving with the BANKER *riding him doing a stately "Money getting/Me get, You don't dance."*)

WATCHMAN: But the power of The Lord is mighty. A mighty fortress is our God. But it is politics which allows progress, that allows movement. So we must be able to go to the ballot box. We must support each other. We must support colored business and the colored church. We must get in politics and join together and finally take office. Join together so the whole race can go forward.

(MOTHER *and* FATHER *advance.* MOTHER *pointing at* WATCHMAN, *at his example, his heroism, as example. A freeze. The Donkey and* BANKER, *riding the donkey, begin a gyrating dance and song. The* BANKER *seems to be changing clothes, changing into more sophisticated garb. He begins to look almost like a movie star.)*

BANKER: *(Singing)* Don't be afraid. Get out of the dark. Be partners.

DONKEY: *(Singing. Underscoring and yea-saying chorus)* Be partners. Partners. *(Sings)* Change partners and dance.

BANKER: How wonderful. One half riding the other half on all fours.

DONKEY: *(Lurches forward, snarling)*

MOTHER: *(Chastising Donkey)* He won't break. Not my pop. Watch him hold. Watch him hold up the whole world.

DONKEY: *(Still singing)* The New Deal/A New Deal/Woof Woof/Hee Haw.

BANKER: *(Singing)* Don't be afraid. You don't have to be afraid.

DONKEY: *(Now the* Negro Donkey *"hee haws" in a violent way. Twisting his head, terrorizing* GRANDMOTHER *and* WATCHMAN, *like he will bite them or trample them. His "hee haws" change easily into a police car's "hee haw hee haw hee haw" of sirens.)*

WATCHMAN: The Lord is my Shepherd I shall not want. . . .

*(*FATHER *and* MOTHER *watching.)*

MOTHER: *(Shaken)* Pop, pop, what's happening?

(A streetlight appears with a bulb held to it in the circle of a noose.)

BANKER: You have no fraids except being fraid.

DONKEY: It's a new deal. You gonna march in the phantom negro salute? We're gonna strut and kick and jump to D.C.

WATCHMAN: The Lord is my Shepherd . . . *(A blinding flash)* We must have something for ourselves *(gasps)*.

(A blinding flash. The bulb suddenly plummets down and explodes on WATCHMAN*'s head.)*

DONKEY: What happened to your father? Am I still gonna get a better job? He can't pay me! How can I work for him. That's all right for your brother. But he don't have these mouths to feed. Am I gonna get another job? What kind of job? . . .

*(*WATCHMAN *is hoisted slowly up the "light pole" like a flagpole with the flag being him. The noose around his neck as he is drawn up makes his arms slap back and forth like Ahab, killed by Moby Dick, as if he is beckoning. The Donkey/Dog salutes. The* BANKER*/Rider salutes).*

MOTHER: Papa.

GRANDMOTHER: Ah, Rays . . . ah, Rays. . . . *(Weeping)* It was always this way. God let the Devil rule earth.

FATHER: Now he can't give or get me a job. Now I gotta get something else.

GRANDMOTHER: *(As body is lowered to half-mast she begins to sing)* Leaning . . . leaning. Safe and secure from all around. Leaning. Leaning. Leaning on the everlasting light!

WATCHMAN: Light! *(Like dead, all look up)* Light! *(His body is slowly lowered)*

BANKER: You see he made a mistake *(half light)*. Real God and real religion ain't for the colored. Imagine, he wanted an office.

WATCHMAN: *(Moaning)* Wilkie . . . Wilkie . . . Wilkie . . . Wilkie.

FATHER: I need a job. She says I need a job. He says I need a job. Do you all think I need . . .

BANKER: He wanted an office. He's gone now *(mock)* so *(like trumpets)* I am giving you the Post Office.

MOTHER: Pop! Pop!

FATHER: Hoo Ray! Hoo Ray! *(A cheer and a question.* WATCHMAN *is slowly lowered into a wheelchair)* No turndown can diminish me. Can diminish all. No turndown can diminish Jackie Rawbeenson!

MOTHER: Pop!

GRANDMOTHER: Leaning, leaning.

MOTHER: *(Begins to do a Pavanna, inadvertently to* GRANDMOTHER*'s singing. All are transfixed)*

FATHER: Now I can be head of the house!

MOTHER: Pop.

GRANDMOTHER: Rays!

(The midget flag woman comes in holding the Donkey's tail. She has gigantic feet painted like Paul Klee. She does a sidestep "Stop-Look-Slide-Wink" dance).

KATE SMITH: *(Sings)* Oh, say can you see . . . *(then)* Mairzy Doats and Dozie Doats and Little Lambs eat Ivy . . . A kid'll eat Ivy too, wouldn't you . . . *(Speaks like lecturer)* We will be more equal if equal be more us. *(She twists her flag dress costume into a rope ladder, a stair step)*

DONKEY: A new deal, it . . . can't you feel it? Heeee Haw . . .

FATHER: Now I can be head of the house!

KATE SMITH: *(Beckoning to* MOTHER*)* Come up. Come up. It's modern times. For modern ladies. Like you and me. *(Offering her hand to* MOTHER *they both ascend the Donkey/Dog's back).*

DONKEY: Hee Haw . . . heee haw.

KATE SMITH: *(Twists to "scoop up" the old woman's song, which clatters after her gesture like coins in a brass bucket, like a thousand cash registers. We hear the children's voices, their calling and crying as lights.)*

BOY AND GIRL: *(Together)* Maaaaaaamaaaa . . . Dadddy. . . .

(As the Midget helps MOTHER *step up on the Donkey, the Midget looks like Eleanor Roosevelt. She's cheering* MOTHER*'s rise to Donkey's back and grabbing notes of* GRAND-MOTHER*'s out of the air throws them clanging in a bucket. Now she does a ritual show-and-tell, miming that she is the one on the Donkey for real. Lights fade.* MOTHER, *her face more fixed and made-up, sings like Marion Anderson and does a symphonic version of "Leaning." While soaring up, the Midget is talking between each phrase in a running commentary of what the song means.)*

KATE SMITH: The United Nations.

DONKEY: The New Deal.

KATE SMITH: Have lunch at the UN, don't you see? Now that's dignified. The new dignity! *(Pointing at* FATHER*)* And we even get the albatross! *(They laugh)* A reg-u-lar job, a miracle!

WATCHMAN: *(In wheelchair, being rolled into fade by* GRANDMOTHER, *singing)* I had an office. I ran my affairs. I ran for office. I planned to run for higher office. I had a good business.

DONKEY, KATE SMITH AND BANKER: But Niggers killed it!

WATCHMAN: No! *(his strength is waning)* No . . . it was . . . you *(points to* BANKER, *who is now reciting* The Gettysburg Address, *then Roosevelt's speech after Japan bombed Pearl Harbor)*

Scene 7

*(*BOY *and* GIRL *enter inner office, one at a time. The* BOY *enters first.)*

BOY: Mama . . . Daddy . . . where'd they go? *(Turns)*

(Radio comes on with laughter.)

RADIO: Heh, heh, heh, heh . . . many years ago in the orient, Lamont Cranston, a wealthy young man about town, discovered the power to cloud men's minds so they could not see him.

*(*GIRL *enters.)*

RADIO: Together with his companion, Lorelei Kilborne, who is the only person who knows Cranston's powerful secret—or The Shadow's real identity!

GIRL: Boy, where did everybody go? *(Brightens at LK mention)*

BOY: Hey, shut up. I'm listening to *The Shadow!*

GIRL: You the shadow. I'm Lorelei Kilborne.

BOY: Ah, okay.

RADIO: Heh, heh, heh, heh, the weed of crime bears bitter fruit. Crime does not pay! "The Shadow" knows! Heh, heh, heh, heh . . .

(At this point the Midget tips, climbs into the office, making a whisper sign to the audience.)

BOY: *(Turns to talk to his sister who is standing frozen, her hands in the air)* Hey, ain't that great! *(Stunned)* Hey, where this midget come from?

GIRL: *(Tense)* I donno . . . off the radio . . . outta that *Shadow* program.

(Kate Smith advancing toward BOY. GIRL *runs into him so that they are clutching each other.)*

BOY: Mama, Daddy, Grandma! A midget. . . .

GIRL: *(Frightened but defiant)* Old ugly thing with funny feet!

KATE SMITH: *(Laughing like The Shadow)* Heh, heh, heh. Who knows . . . huh? One never knows do one? *(Her voice changes to The Shadow's companion, Lorelei Kilborne)* Don't be afraid. There's a whole world I live in where there's almost nothing but me!

BOY: Mama . . . Daddy.

GIRL: You better get outta here ya little ugly midget.

KATE SMITH: Not talking to you, *(affected)* Dah . . . ling.

BOY: Get away from me!

KATE SMITH: Look, I just want to send you a gift, a present. *(Midget slinks toward door)* Okay, I'll see you. Wait till you get my gift. *(Turns)* All, all, all. Gifts for all!

(Like maniac spider boogalooing, Midget leaves, trying to laugh, forgets it and is gone. The two children embrace each other shivering.)

BOY: Mama!

GIRL: Daddy!

(Suddenly outside door bursts open and the Kate Smith Midget leaps back into the room, runs past the children to the interior door, and begins calling.)

KATE SMITH: Will the other guys please come in! We've got lots of other stops.

(While she's holding the door she does little freezes, model steps; the children shrink from her. The door opens and the BANKER *with overcoat draped over his shoulders smoking a cigarette in a long holder. His hat tilts to one side. He is a caricature of continental suave. When he appears he does a knightly pivot and in perfect smoothness offers to kiss the* GIRL's *hand. But she, stunned as he touches it with his lips, pulls her hand back and starts crying.)*

GIRL: Mama! *(Shrinks back to* BOY*)*

BOY: Daddy!

KATE SMITH: *(To* BANKER*)* She's not ready yet. Or maybe *(laughs)* never.

BANKER: My dear, never fear. There is nothing to be afraid of but . . .

(The door slams open and the NEGRO DONKEY/*Dog enters.)*

DONKEY: A New Deal. Camille. It's real. You don't have to steal or kneel. A new deal. *(Slobbers on himself. When he sees* GIRL, *he stops. With great effort he pulls himself up on two legs and staggers uneasily toward the* GIRL. *He has something horrible in his mind, which even he does not quite understand)* Hee Haw, hee haw—

GIRL: *(Screams)* Maaaaaaa!

BOY: Maaaaaaa!

KATE SMITH: All right gents, let's go then. You and I—

BANKER: Yes, I've miles to go before I sleep.

DONKEY: Beep, Beep. Hee Haw. Hee Haw. New Deal.

(The three leave together like a chorus line of Frankensteins.)

KS, B AND D: *(Together)* Tee hee. Okay! Tee hee we'll see. You will see. You tee hee. You'll see. All three.

(Kate Smith, BANKER *and Donkey exit.)*

Scene 8

*(*BOY *and* GIRL *stand staring at each other crying.)*

BOY: Ma. . . . Let's go look for them.

(As they move to the door it swings open. GRANDMOTHER *and* WATCHMAN *come in.* GRANDMOTHER *is wheeling* WATCHMAN *in wheelchair. She is still singing "Leaning On The Everlasting Light." He is repeating over and over, in some disconnected sequence.)*

WATCHMAN: Light! Light!

BOY AND GIRL: *(Together)* What happened to Granddaddy?

GRANDMOTHER: *(Sings while looking at him a long time without speaking. Finally she speaks)* They say a streetlight hit him in the head.

BOY AND GIRL: A streetlight?

GRANDMOTHER: On the corner where South Orange Avenue and Springfield Avenue meet.

BOY AND GIRL: A streetlight?

GRANDMOTHER: He was coming home from a meeting with them politicians. They brought him in on a stretcher. He was moaning just like you hear him now.

BOY AND GIRL: Where's Mama and Daddy?

GRANDMOTHER: *(Stands looking at* WATCHMAN*)* They hurt him before. A long time ago. But this time they hurt him bad . . . real bad. *(She is trying to weep and can't,* *trying to sing and can't. Barely begins humming, trying to comfort* WATCHMAN *and herself, but she cannot. Stands, staring. Again she begins humming to comfort her husband)*

BOY AND GIRL: Where's Mama and Daddy?

BOY: Mama! *(Sticks his head inside the warehouse interior door)* Mama!

GIRL: *(Looking at* WATCHMAN *in the wheelchair, she backs away terrified and moves toward her brother)* Daddy!

(We hear singing inside. A shrill Marion Anderson voice.)

MOTHER: *(Singing)* This is My Story, This is My Song. *(Mother enters adorned in full makeup and evening dress with a corsage, which she smells from time to time to accent something. Continues singing)* This is My Story, This is My Song.

*(*BOY *and* GIRL *rush to Mother oblivious of the change in her.)*

MOTHER: *(Singing)* Working for Jesus All The Day Long.

(The BOY *and* GIRL *stand clasped together.* WATCHMAN *spits.* GRANDMOTHER *begins singing "What A Friend We Have In Jesus." They are singing in a duet. The children sway yet are repulsed by* WATCHMAN *in the chair who keeps spitting and occasionally raises his head and tries to raise his arm to point.)*

WATCHMAN: Light! Light!

(We hear a rush of hoof beats and the William Tell Overture. *The* FATHER *rushes in.)*

FATHER: I got a job. A good job. I'm in the Post Office!

MOTHER: *(Turns and with great dignity)* Who? Ray!

(The BOY *and* GIRL, FATHER *and* MOTHER *raise hands and cheer.* GRANDMOTHER *nods and puts her head close to* WATCHMAN. *She is still singing "What A Friend We Have in Jesus." Suddenly we hear the music of the Lone Ranger and horses rushing off into the distance. The three radio characters laugh and shout profanity at the family from all sides of the stage.)*

WATCHMAN: *(Raises his head)* Light?

GRANDMOTHER: *(Weeping uncontrollably, singing and humming)* What a friend we have in Jesus.

FATHER: Oh! Wait a minute!! First day on the job and I've got mail for everybody. There are presents for everybody!

*(*MOTHER, BOY, *and* GIRL *cheer and gather.* GRANDMOTHER *just looks and hums.)*

FATHER: For Elroy *(a white box with pink ribbon)*. For Elise *(a flat envelope with powder blue and white wrapping. It says "Official Business: United Nations.")* For Sandi! *(a gold box with a little American flag)*. A gold box with a little American flag! I even got one myself *(a small jewelry box with silver paper)*.

(All begin opening packages with much gaiety. WATCHMAN, *with his head down, spits from time to time.* GRANDMOTHER *is still weeping, singing, humming the same song.)*

GRANDMOTHER: *(Head up, holding wheelchair)* I guess this is your present, Rays.

BOY: Wow. What's this? All that box! Ain't nuthin' in it but a coin. And some note.

MOTHER: A coin? Let me see. *(*BOY *gives it to her)* This is not a coin. It's a brand, new token—they call 'em—for the New York City subway.

BOY: Subway? Yeh, I rode on that when we went to the Bronx Zoo with Miss Powell's class. That's when that white man in the elephant house told me that he was used to the stink . . . because he lived in Harlem!

(This changes MOTHER*'s mood as she recalls and then tries to associate it all. She stares at the* BOY, *who stares back at her.)*

BOY: I know what he meant. *(Looks up into* MOTHER*'s face)* He meant colored people stink, didn't he, Ma?

MOTHER: A stupid little dirty man. *(Fazed)*

BOY: What I need with that, Mama?

MOTHER: Well, somebody . . . *(associating, but not quite)* thinks you'll use it one day!

BOY: Hey, Ma, there's an apple in it too.

MOTHER: An apple? What's that note say? Can you read it?

BOY: Mama, you know I can read . . . good too.

MOTHER: Okay, well . . .

BOY: It says: "See you later, Alligator, when your head get straighter." *(All laugh)* And why I get the apple?

MOTHER: An apple a day keeps the doctor away. Also, that's what jazz musicians call New York City. Or what you learned about in Sunday School.

GRANDMOTHER: *(Like an undercurrent)* Eve and Adam! Bible older than New York City—

BOY: I dunno why I get this stuff.

GIRL: That midget say she'll see you later. She said you was gonna get a present too.

MOTHER: Midget?

BOY: Yeh, Mama. Some crazy people was in here. Look like out the horror movies.

MOTHER: Crazy people? *(Her face changes as if she is trying to remember and becomes frightened)* Did they sound like they was on the radio? *(Turning and looking for it, but her concentration is broken by the* FATHER*)*

FATHER: Come on! Come on, open up the rest!

GIRL: *(Unwrapping)* Hey, it's a little black Raggedy Ann doll! *(Screams)*

MOTHER: What?

GIRL: But this is a boy doll, Mama! And he got a knife! *(She throws it down on the floor and begins crying)*

BOY: *(Picks up the doll and cuts his finger as well)* Oh! Dog! Who sent this crazy thing? *(Pushes it at his sister who whines, backs up, and cries)*

GIRL: I don't want that ugly thing.

MOTHER: Yeh . . . who sent these crazy things? That knife is dangerous.

BOY: I already cut myself on this stupid doll. A boy doll! Whoever heard a that? *(Begins laughing)* See, see Sandi? I told you you was a tomboy!

GIRL: *(She strikes out at him for bothering her)* Stop! Stop! *(Cries, hugs MOTHER)*

(BOY *picks up doll and taunts* GIRL *with it.*)

MOTHER: Will you stop bothering your sister! *(Snatches doll, cuts her finger, too)* Ow! Curtis, take this thing and throw it away!

FATHER: *(Takes doll and cuts himself)* Good Night! *(He tosses it into wastebasket.* GIRL *watches with regret)*

FATHER: What about your present, Elise?

(MOTHER *unwraps her present, a large photo of the real Kate Smith pictured with the* BOY *and the* GIRL *at a younger age on either side of her.* BOY *and* GIRL *wear Buck Rogersesque space suits.*)

MOTHER: What? When did this photo get taken? I don't remember this. We never took the kids to see no Kate Smith.

ALL: *(Together)* What?

MOTHER: Curtis, look at this. It's Kate Smith with the children.

FATHER: Children? *(Takes photo)*

MOTHER: These children. Our children.

FATHER: What? In these weird getups, like they was in the future or outer space somewhere. How in the world? *(To* MOTHER*).* You didn't take 'em? I know I didn't. Wasn't no Kate Smith at the World's Fair.

BOY AND GIRL: Let me see. Let me see!

FATHER: Aw . . . Elise, it's probably a trick photo. You know, like at Coney Island or somewhere, where you stick your head in a hole and there's a picture painted on the front. Like that picture we took riding in that make-believe car.

MOTHER: *(She takes photo and looks at it deeply)* Good God!! This really is something. How real it looks! But I still don't know when and where it got made! It looks like Kate Smith is their mother or something.

GIRL: *(Tries to fish doll out of garbage can cautiously so that it doesn't cut her)* Nasty thing!

BOY: Crazy black ragman doll. Tomboy doll.

GIRL: Oh, shut up!

MOTHER: Well, we all got a present today. *(To* FATHER*)* Open yours!

FATHER: Oh! I forgot. But my new job is my real present. The Post Office! *(He opens package)* It's a button. I guess like they have in church. It says: "Deacon."

MOTHER: Deacon, huh? I know that's a joke. I can't even get you to go to church.

FATHER: Some practical joker all right.

· BOY: Well, that's what Louie Gordan be singing: "Who threw the whiskey in the dell?" The song say it was you, daddy. *(All laugh, expect* GRANDMOTHER *and the* WATCHMAN*)* Deacon Bell! He threw the whiskey in the well!

(Now sensing GRANDMOTHER *and* WATCHMAN*'s silence. They all turn and* MOTHER *starts to speak to* GRANDMOTHER*.)*

GRANDMOTHER: *(Raising her head, she puts her fingers to her lips to say that* WATCHMAN *is asleep. She begins to sing, like she is putting a child to sleep, rocking him)* What a friend we have in Jesus. . . .

(Lights begin to fade, as black deepens. We hear the radio from inside the interior of the warehouse. Sound of three piano notes, indicating change of station. As the lights fade we hear announcer's voice.)

ANNOUNCER: W.H.Y. New York.

*(*GRANDMOTHER *still singing softly, then there is a silence. Then a pause and we hear the faint horrible laughter of the radio trio, quick and deadly. Blackout.)*

Playland Blues

Miguel Piñero

CHARACTERS

Fat Belly Nelly   *A fat, white fifteen-year-old girl*

Louie   *A young fifteen-year-old hustler*

Hector   *A young fourteen-year-old hustler*

Bill   *A Trick*

China   *A sixteen-year-old girl*

Comixbook   *A fifteen-year-old hustler*

Breakaleg   *A fifteen-year-old girl*

Pepper   *A twenty-year-old hustler*

Monkey Three   *A pusher in his late twenties*

Cabeza   *A junkie in his early twenties*

Cuchara   *A junkie in his late twenties*

Mike   *A man in his middle twenties*

Electric   *A young fifteen-year-old hustler*

Wrecker   *A man in his late thirties*

Crip   *A man in his late thirties*

Rubberband   *A sixteen-year-old hustler*

Just Begun   *A fourteen-year old hustler*

TO EXIST
The sky without cloud
the sea without sail
meet in a line.

Against my eye
they draw me in.

But between sea
and sky
no room.

Act 1

The Playland Amusement Center on Forty-second Street

(Late in the evening, a young man is shooting a rifle on a machine. There are many other people about. Cops walk the beat ignoring the obvious. There are whores and pimps, junkies nodding, some sick. Rehab dope fiends rappin' about their program. Muslims hocking their paper. Jesus freaks saving the world of sin. Hare Krishna music and chants. Some are on stage dancing, praising Krishna. There are people going somewhere and people going nowhere. Some are taking pictures. Siren screams. Neon lights blaze. Cripples are begging. Blind men singing, playing an instrument. Cops are dragging a man off—a young man. LOUIE *is arguing with* NELLY, *a fat girl. Both are about 15 or so.)*

LOUIE: Why the hell do you always follow me around, man? 'Cause I did it with you once doesn't mean that we are going steady, baby. Can't you get that through your head, or is it that all that fat on your belly is also on your head? You want me to say it in Spanish, bitch? Porque te chiche no quiere decir que te quiero, capiche . . .

NELLY: But, what if I have your baby?

LOUIE: That's your problem, not mine.

NELLY: It'll be your baby.

LOUIE: It'll be *your* baby.

NELLY: It'll be our baby.

LOUIE: Fuck you.

NELLY: Louie, please . . .

LOUIE: Look here, bitch . . . I told you to take the pill, right? You refuse right? Right?

NELLY: But Louie, you know I'm against the pill.

LOUIE: I don't wanna hear all that shit. I told you to take the pill, right? You refused, didn't you? Then if anything pops up, it's your problem. You deal with it like you deal with your food. Now leave me the fuck alone.

NELLY: Louie, you told me you love me.

LOUIE: Man, that's a lot of bullshit. I ain't never told you anything like that. I told you I'd like to get between your legs, 'cause I never did it to a fat girl before. That's just what I told you. I sure love to get between those thighs of yours.

NELLY: You said you loved me when we were in bed. You said you loved me.

LOUIE: Man, I was comin'! When you is comin' you is comin'. And when a man is comin', he say all kinds of shit like that. It has nothing to do with the person he is with. It's just that the thrill is so great you go crazy with words like that.

NELLY: Like what?

LOUIE: Like LOVE. Like MARRIAGE. Man, it don't mean nothing at all. Nothing. Can't you get it through that fat head of yours?

NELLY: But Louie, I told all my friends that we were going steady.

LOUIE: Then go back to your friends and untell it.

HECTOR: Man, about time I got this extra free game. Got it now, shitttt. . . .

LOUIE: Wacha got man?

HECTOR: Aww, man. Don't bother me now, bro . . . I'm on my freebee. Check out the store.

LOUIE: Aww, man. That ain't nothing. My baby sister can top that blindfolded.

HECTOR: Fuck you and your baby sister. Let's see you top it. You talk a lotta shit.

LOUIE: You wanna bet.

HECTOR: Yeah. You put the money in the machine, 'cause I'm broke. All I got is some pills. You wanna cop?

LOUIE: You must be crazy. You know I don't fuck with that shit, man. You wanna bet?

HECTOR: You, the ones that talkin', bro. You put in the silver.

LOUIE: I'm broke too.

HECTOR: Hustle some bread.

LOUIE: Today is Monday, you know? Ain't that many of them on Mondays.

HECTOR: Over there by the cowboy machine. See him? See him?

LOUIE: Yeah. Yeah. Eyes dead center on my zipper.

HECTOR: Go on, man. Do your thing. Git the MONEY.

LOUIE: What if he's a cop?

HECTOR: Aw, come on, man. The cops don't look so hard at someone's dick.

LOUIE: Oh, yeah! That's what you think. Wait till Pepper gets here and ask him what happen to us last night out in Brooklyn.

HECTOR: What happened?

LOUIE: Just wait till Pepper shows, ask him.

HECTOR: Come on, what happen?

LOUIE: Wait till Pepper shows. You won't believe me if I told you anyway.

HECTOR: Come on, I'll believe you, really. I swear.

LOUIE: No you won't. When Pepper shows he can tell you.

HECTOR: Okay.

CHINA: Hey Hector.

HECTOR: Hey China.

CHINA: Hey Louie.

LOUIE: Hey China.

CHINA: Whacha doing?

LOUIS: Nothing.

HECTOR: Just hanging out.

LOUIE: Whacha doing?

CHINA: Nothing.

HECTOR: Whacha gonna do?

CHINA: Nothing.

LOUIE: Where you gonna do it at?

CHINA: Here.

HECTOR: Why don't you do it over there?

CHINA: Why?

HECTOR: Because.

CHINA: Why because?

LOUIS: Because.

CHINA: Who's over there?

HECTOR: Everybody.

CHINA: Everybody? I don't see everybody there.

LOUIE: 'Cause you ain't looking hard enough.

CHINA: I don't wear glasses.

HECTOR: Could've fooled me.

CHINA: Fuck you.

LOUIS: I sure would like to.

CHINA: It ain't big enough.

LOUIE: That wasn't what you said at Orlando's house.

CHINA: I was drunk.

LOUIE: So is your father.

CHINA: For your information, my father hasn't had a drink in three years.

LOUIE: No shit.

CHINA: He's in Attica doing ten years. See you later.

HECTOR: Later.

LOUIE: Later.

HECTOR: Why don't you just tell her you like her?

LOUIE: She knows it.

HECTOR: Go get the quarter, he's still there.

LOUIE: Still looking?

HECTOR: Harder than ever.

LOUIE: Same place?

HECTOR: I think he's glued to the floor.

LOUIE: Mister, can you spare a quarter?

BILL: What you want a quarter for?

LOUIE: Play some games over there with my friend.

BILL: What are you playing?

LOUIE: Just shooting a rifle.

BILL: You shoot?

LOUIE: Since I was thirteen.

BILL: Him too?

LOUIE: I guess so.

BILL: My, you two are young.

LOUIE: Who wants to be old?

BILL: You have a point there, young man.

LOUIE: Yeah, I guess so.

BILL: Maybe.

LOUIE: What about the quarter?

BILL: You will have to get change. Here's a dollar.

LOUIE: What about my friend. Can he have one, too?

BILL: Well, I don't know. You see, I don't know your friend.

LOUIE: Come on. I'll introduce you.

BILL: Why, thank you.

LOUIE: Don't worry about it.

BILL: By the way, what is your name?

(LOUIE *mumbles.*)

LOUIE: Tommy, this is . . . what's your name, mister?

BILL: Bill.

LOUIS: Tommy, this is Bill—

HECTOR: Hey, Bill.

BILL: How do you do, Tommy?

HECTOR: Shit, I do all right. Dig that score. Right, Louis?

LOUIE: Right on, but I'm gonna top it.

BILL: Are you Louie?

LOUIE: My name ain't Louie, it's Angel.

BILL: But I thought he called you Louis.

LOUIE: He did. That's my middle name. He's my brother.

HECTOR: Yeah. I always call him by his middle name.

BILL: Why?

HECTOR: Er . . . er. 'Cause I like it better than Angel.

LOUIS: Let me go get change.

CHINA: Hey, mister! Can I get a quarter, too?

COMIXBOOK: Me too?

BREAKALEG: Can you spare me a quarter, sister?

BILL: Good night, Tommy. Angel. Nice to have met you both. See you sometime around I hope.

LOUIE: Aw, man. What the fuck is it with you people?

HECTOR: Shit, do we bother you when you got a fish on the hook?

CHINA: Ah, that breaks my heart.

LOUIE: Something else is gonna break in a few minutes.

CHINA: Oh yeah? What?

LOUIE: Your ass.

CHINA: Kiss it.

COMIXBOOK: Lick it.

BREAKALEG: Stick it.

HECTOR: Trick it, baby, trick it.

CHINA: That's right, honey. Why give away for free?

LOUIE: I wouldn't pay you a dime.

CHINA: You paid more than that last night at Orlando's house.

LOUIE: That's bullshit.

COMIXBOOK: You bought me two hamburgers and a malted milkshake. You paid my way into the subway, even though you snuck in and you gave me wine and some smoke.

LOUIE: So what that mean?

CHINA: So, honey, add it up.

HECTOR: The price of pussy has gone up.

BREAKALEG: What does that have to do with the energy crisis?

HECTOR: Woo! Big words from a big mouth.

BREAKALEG: Bet you wish you had this big mouth.

HECTOR: Yeah, around my you know what.

BREAKALEG: Funny.

HECTOR: My father is, but not me, baby.

BREAKALEG: Got any pills, Hector?

HECTOR: The price of pills has gone up, too!

BREAKALEG: For me, too?

LOUIE: What you want, a discount?

COMIXBOOK: Naw, she looking for a penny sale.

CHINA: Hi, Pepper.

PEPPER: Fuck you very much. *(Greeting all around by* PEPPER*)*

LOUIE: Oh yeah, tell this motherfucker here what happen to us last night with the cops.

PEPPER: Yeah, man. That was really a trip. I wish I had been high on acid, my man. Check this shit out. Me and Louis are coming from this trick's house.

CHINA: Trick?

LOUIE: A faggot.

CHINA: You go out and fuck a faggot, then you come and fuck me?

LOUIE: Come on, China. I didn't fuck em. . . .

PEPPER: Yes you did, motherfucker.

CHINA: You got a lotta nerves.

LOUIE: China, baby! Don't act that way with me.

CHINA: How much did he give you?

LOUIE: Twenty-five dollars.

CHINA: Twenty-five dollars? Wow! That's more money than my sister makes on the avenue.

HECTOR: Your sister is a two dollar ho', anyway.

CHINA: For your information, my sister is a top money-making lady of the streets.

COMIXBOOK: She's a whore.

CHINA: So's your mother.

BREAKALEG: Git 'em China.

CHINA: My sister makes over two hundred dollars a night.

PEPPER: Ten for the head and twenty for the bed.

LOUIE: Yeah, but your sister works all night.

COMIXBOOK: Man, sometimes in the winter I come down here and see them whores stand ass deep in snow, freezing their tits off, talking about you wanna lay. Wanna nice time? For the price of a cup of coffee.

CHINA: That's bullshit, man. No girl does it for that low.

COMIXBOOK: Your mama does.

BREAKALEG: Payback is a bitch.

COMIXBOOK: You girls stick together.

BREAKALEG: So do you guys.

CHINA: Sometimes you guys stick so much and so close together it makes me wonder about you.

BREAKALEG: Makes you think, don't it.

CHINA: Sure it does.

PEPPER: I didn't think you girls could think.

CHINA: Oh, that's nothing. My mother even votes.

BREAKALEG: Mines is a numbers runner.

CHINA: What does your mother do, clean house?

PEPPER: She takes welfare.

COMIXBOOK: With fifty hundred eleven kids, what else can she do?

LOUIE: She can git on the corner like yours.

COMIXBOOK: My mother never been on the corner.

PEPPER: No, she's in the middle of the block.

LOUIE: Near the Chinese laundry. Fucky, fucky, two dollars . . . fucky, fucky.

COMIXBOOK: Later for you guys.

LOUIE: What's the matter? You can't take it?

HECTOR: What happen to you last night?

PEPPER: Oh yeah. Dig this. It is real late, right? And we are just walking, minding our own business, smoking a jay the faggot had given us, right? Okay, Louis got his radio on blasting real fucking loud. All of a sudden this cop car, as we hit the corner, shoots right out in front of us. Sirens screaming, yelling and shouting at us. "All right, you spics, get against the wall. Don't move or I'll blow your heads off." You know the routine. Spread 'em. Louie started yelling at them: "Don't shoot. Don't shoot. I'm only fifteen. I'm only fifteen. Don't shoot!"

LOUIE: Oh that's bullshit.

HECTOR: If I know you, it ain't.

BREAKALEG: Oh you know that it's true. Pepper don't lie.

LOUIE: That's the biggest motherfucking liar in the world.

PEPPER: I'm telling the truth. I'll swear to that on a stack of Bibles.

LOUIE: Yeah, 'cause you don't believe in God anyway.

CHINA: God is dead.

PEPPER: God ain't dead, he's just unemployed.

LOUIS: And Jesus Christ is on methadone.

HECTOR: You guys shouldn't talk about God like that—

PEPPER: I'm sorry, Father Hector. Blessed Father forgive us our sins and hear our confessions.

HECTOR: You shouldn't do that—well, anyway, not around me.

LOUIE: You scared the boggie man gonna eat you, babbbyyyyy?

BREAKALEG: Hector's right, you guys shouldn't do that. Laugh if you want, but I'm being serious.

CHINA: It's bad luck, man.

HECTOR: You guys are too much, man. You don't believe in God. I mean like I ain't scared of no boggie man. Shit like that ain't true. I mean talk about anything you want, man. But don't talk about God that way. It ain't too cool.

PEPPER: Can I talk about your mama that way? Man, she's your mother? Like where's that at, man.

LOUIE: Be cool, Pepper. You coming out of line.

BREAKALEG: That's the devil pushing you.

PEPPER: That's your mama pushing me.

CHINA: What happen after all the girl came out of Louie?

LOUIE: Better watch your mouth, bitch.

CHINA: Wow! All the man is coming out of him, now—

BREAKALEG: Shoulda used it last night with Pepper, right?

PEPPER: He ain't shit.

LOUIE: You see, Pepper? You shouldn't lie like that 'cause they believe your lying ass.

PEPPER: Who's lying?

LOUIE: Oh, fuck you, man.

PEPPER: Thank you. Thank you kind sir for those encouraging words of wisdom. Seriously, the man pulls the gun right into my fucking ear like he gonna clean out all the wax in it. Now all these people are looking out of their windows like if some big-time gangster got busted.

LOUIE: He did. Me. How big can you get? Shit, I'm a gangster.

BREAKALEG: So is your mama.

PEPPER: So the cop yelled right in my face, spit flying out his ugly mouth giving me a shower.

CHINA: And it ain't even Saturday.

PEPPER: No more comments from the peanut gallery please.

CHINA: I'm paying dues, baby.

PEPPER: So is everybody else. The cop's jumping up and down like a monkey man, screaming and shouting and carrying on, dig? So I figure they gonna pull the mutt and jeff routine. And I'm thinking: What the fuck is all this about? You know? Louis is still screaming: "Don't shoot, I'm only twelve" every five minutes he got a year younger. You know, I'm the oldest of the two.

LOUIE: Big fucking deal. You're seventeen.

PEPPER: Big fucking deal, right. Shit if they take us in. You go to the Youth House. Shit, I go to Riker's Island.

HECTOR: You scared they gonna eat your bootty?

PEPPER: Ain't nobody gonna do anything to Pepper, little brother. 'Cause Pepper could fight.

BREAKALEG: My brother told me it's fuck or fight.

LOUIE: Blood on my knife or shit on my dick.

CHINA: Pepper goes in with a dime and comes out with a quarter.

PEPPER: Dig this, man. This is the best part. The cops drag us in the hallway, right? I mean drag us in. We get inside and the man said: "Okay, punks, we know you dealing stuff. Where's the shit at?" All I got is a joint in my pocket—one fucking jay. That's all. This sucker rips my coat pocket, pulls out the joint and yells: "Hey, this guy got shit on him. I think he's got shit all over him." I told him I ain't got no shit. Smack! "Give me the shit, kid." "I ain't got no shit." Smack! Smack! "Drop the shit on the floor, kid, or we'll kick the shit out of you." Smack! "Give me your shit, kid." Smack! Smack! "I want your fucking shit." "I ain't got no shit."

BREAKALEG: Did you give him your shit?

PEPPER: No! I had no shit to give. So he said: "Strip." I said: "Strip? Here in the hall-way? Naked? Man, it's cold." He said: "Shut up punk, I'm gonna get your shit one way or another." So I take off my clothes, right. Now, I'm standing naked in the freezing ass hallway.

CHINA: What about Louie?

LOUIE: I had to take mines off, too. Both of us.

PEPPER: That's right, both of us naked to the world. "Okay, kid, turn around. Bend over and spread them." I said: "What?" Boom. Boom. Zap kapow. "You heard what I said. Bend over and smile."

HECTOR: What you do?

PEPPER: Shit, I bent over and spread them, what the hell am I supposed to do? They got a gun and my name ain't Bruce Lee. The cop shoves his finger in my ass. And I jumps up: "Hey, what the fuck are you doing? I ain't no faggot motherfucker." Then the motherfucker rains on me. Bim, bam, bang. "I'm looking for the shit, kid." In my fucking ass!

HECTOR: Where else?

PEPPER: Funny, funny. "Pull up your ding dong, kid." I said: "What?" "Your ding dong." So I pulls up my ding dong.

LOUIE: Yeah, the other cop didn't make me go through that. He just kept his flashlight on my dick all the time.

PEPPER: The cop grabs my dick and pulls it hard. Now we just standing there, naked, right. I'm trying to keep all this sex shit out of my head, but it was like if I was a horny thirteen-year-old kid who just found out he could come. And my dick starts getting hard. The cop looks at me, then looks at his partner and they both start laughing. And Louie is throwing farts, stink bombs, the hallway smells like a piss-stained mattress. The cops put the gun on my dick and said: "If you want to be able to fuck tomorrow, your ding dong better stop dinging." Them words were like a cold shower, baby. So he tells his partner to get Louie out of there.

LOUIE: Man, I dressed faster than flash. Superman ain't had nothing on me.

HECTOR: Right on.

PEPPER: Now I'm alone in the hallway with this freak of a cop. I think: "Oh shit, the motherfucker is either gonna suck me off or dick me up. Man, I was scared. Man, I was so scared the motherfucker almost found the shit he was looking for. The cop says to me: "Punk, I don't ever wanna see you up in Tony's house again." I said: "Who the fuck is Tony?" You know who Tony turns out to be? The trick we just took off. He told me: "Better tell your two-bit hustling friends on Forty-second Street to stay away from Tony." You see, Tony is the desk sarge at their station house and he goes out with these two cops.

BREAKALEG: They're smart. They get easy assignments.

PEPPER: They must be getting something.

BREAKALEG: Hey! Let's go to a club. There's nothing to do around here today.

HECTOR: Monday, most of them are closed.

LOUIE: At least up to eleven o'clock. Let's hang out.

BREAKALEG: There's a new spot that just opened up and it's open now. They're trying to get customers. Three dollars at the door and free drinks.

HECTOR: What is it?

BREAKALEG: Gays and straights. Gotta be eighteen to get in.

HECTOR: Aw, fuck it. I ain't got my phony I.D.

LOUIE: That's cool.

PEPPER: That's cool. That's everywhere.

MONKEY 3: Yerba. Yerba. Coca. Methadone-tengo tabaco suelto y en saco.

LOUIE: Esa coca no estaba en na'.

MONKEY 3: Qué tu sabe te coca muchacho si tu eres un nene.

LOUIE: I'm a kid, Monkey 3. But I wasn't a kid when I put ten dollars in your hand for a spoon, right?

MONKEY 3:   What the fuck you doing, man. You call my name out like that. You wanna get me busted?

PEPPER: Yeah, why don't you use a loudspeaker, Louie. Monkey 3 got some.

MONKEY 3:   Tube you. You todavía eres un nene. A baby still.

LOUIE: I don't give a shit about that dude, Pepper. Not a fucking shit. Not a fucking shit 'cause that motherfucker is nothing.

MONKEY 3:   What you say, punk? You talking to me?

LOUIE: Yeah, that's right, motherfucker. I'm talking to you. About you and I'm standing right here, sucker. I ain't moved an inch—so what you got to say, sucker?

MONKEY 3:   You pull a knife on me, punk?

LOUIE: Come on, brother. I ain't nothing but a kid, right? Well, come on, you a man, ain't you?

MONKEY 3:   Maricón pendejo. I cut your fucking heart out.

LOUIE: You put my left ball in your mouth, faggot.

PEPPER: Come on, be cool.

LOUIE: Stand out the way, Pepper.

HECTOR: Get out the way, Pepper.

PEPPER: What the fuck you doing, Hector? Put that shit away. What is it with you dudes? You gonna get us all busted.

MONKEY 3:   You better tell your friends to be cool, kid.

PEPPER: Who the fuck you calling a kid, motherfucker?

MONKEY 3:   Oye, qué pasa.

PEPPER: Qué pasa. I'm gonna cut your pasa, that's what, pasa sucker.

HECTOR: Git him on that side, Louie.

LOUIE: Come on, sucker. I'm gonna show you what a kid can do.

MONKEY 3:   Hey man, be cool! Fellas. Hey man, sorry. Brodel.

HECTOR: Oh, he's sorry, ain't that nothing?

PEPPER: Sure ain't.

LOUIE: Say, Mr. Louie. Say, come on, man. You wanna make the next sale. You better say, Mister.

PEPPER: And say it like you proud to say it.

MONKEY 3:   Okay. Okay, man. Mister Louie. Mister Louie.

PEPPER: Git on out of here, punk.

MONKEY 3:   You gonna die, kid.

PEPPER: Fuck you, you ugly motherfucking monkey. No wonder they call you Monkey 3.

HECTOR: Come on back, suckerball.

LOUIE: Why didn't you say that before, maricón?

PEPPER: Silly ass chump-change pusher.

LOUIE: Cabrón hijo la gran puta.

MONKEY 3:   You gonna die kid. You gonna die, dead.

LOUIE: Tell that to your mother, creep.

PEPPER: Motherfucking faggot.

HECTOR: Let the motherfucker rap. It ain't nothing but baba.

PEPPER: Baby shit coming out his mouth.

BREAKALEG: Now you guys better be cool. That dude is sneaky. Why you think they call him Monkey? He's sneaky.

PEPPER: Like a rat?

HECTOR: We shoulda taken the sap's shit.

LOUIE: Bet he had a lot of bread on him, too.

PEPPER: Fighting is one thing, but taking his money is another.

BREAKALEG: It's all the same thing. You guys made him look bad. That's what counts.

LOUIE: You worry too much. We can take care of ourselves.

HECTOR: Fuck that dude. He's not worth rapping about, anyway.

LOUIE: Hey, what the hell is that punk doing?

HECTOR: Ain't that your score over there?

LOUIE: It sure is. Oye, man, come here. Come here?

COMIXBOOK: What's the matter?

LOUIE: What you mean, what's the matter, motherfucker? I'll bust your fucking ass, sucker. What you doing cutting into my shit, man?

COMIXBOOK: Man, I ain't cutting into anything of your shit. I don't know who's what around here.

LOUIE: Man, don't run that bullshit on me. I'll kick your fuckkkkkkking asssssss. . . .

COMIXBOOK: Man, you ain't doing anything to me, punk. I don't mind you talking to me, but don't think you gonna beat on me and I'm supposed to stand there like a punching bag. My mother don't hit me. I'm gonna let a creep from Forty-second Street put his hands on me? Shit, you must think you're Muhammad Ali or something.

LOUIE: No, Smoky Joe.

COMIXBOOK: Well, smoke my dick.

LOUIE: I'm gonna smoke your ass. Shit, you run on a score of mines again and there's gonna be more than smoke coming from your ass. I'm gonna set your ass on fire.

COMIXBOOK: You think you own Forty-second Street?

LOUIE: No, but my fist in your mouth gonna let you know that I rent a part of it.

COMIXBOOK: I told you before you ain't gonna do nothing to me.

LOUIS: You better shut the fuck up and git out of my face. 'Cause you said your mother don't hit you? Shit, I ain't your mother and I beat you like I own you.

HECTOR: Oye, man. Why don't you guys stop being so stupid fighting over a fucking faggot. You guys are acting like *two* faggots.

LOUIE: Who are you talking to?

HECTOR: You, Louie. And you, too, Comixbook: You guys shouldn't fight, man. Like we supposed to be together. Supposed to be brothers. Man, you guys are acting like sisters in love with the same man. That's because you guys are greedy.

LOUIE: Okay, okay. But dig this. This is the last time I'm telling you about cutting into one of my scores.

COMIXBOOK: You must think you're really mean, don't you?

LOUIE: Man, can you stop a .38?

HECTOR: You ain't got no gun, Louie.

LOUIE: No, I ain't got no gun, man. But if he can't stop a .38, what makes him think he could stop my fist?

HECTOR: *(Laughing)* You stupid ass motherfuckers.

LOUIE: What you laughing at?

HECTOR: While you guys were fighting over the trick, green eyes walked away with the money.

LOUIE: *(Laughing)* Well, that's the way it goes.

COMIXBOOK: Sorry, Louie.

LOUIE: That's okay.

COMIXBOOK: Just that I'm broke.

LOUIE: Well, why don't you just come and tell me. And I would lend you a trick. What are friends for?

COMIXBOOK: No Puerto Ricans. They're mean.

LOUIE: Would I do that to you? For that, I give you nothing.

HECTOR: Oooooooohhhhh, they're cheap. Fucking jíbaros, they want to give you six dollars and then they want to do what they feel. Shit, if a spic can't split with fifty he can split cause it's fifty just to look at it.

COMIXBOOK: I don't really trust young spics. Most of them are bugarones.

LOUIE: Let me look in my book.

COMIXBOOK: One time I was standing on the corner. It was hot like a motherfucker. I had on a pair of shorts and a T-shirt, right? I'm holding a basketball, just playing with it, shooting a couple of shots, and this Puerto Rican dude, a young guy and the man gives me twenty dollars.

LOUIE: For what, man?

COMIXBOOK: For looking so good to him. Wow! Is that sick?

BREAKALEG: Oh, there's that old hag again. She just left with flaca.

CHINA: What is it with a bitch like that?

BREAKALEG: Who cares? She pays well and she doesn't expect too much.

CHINA: In that case, get on the case. See you later, girl.

BREAKALEG: In about half an hour.

LOUIE: Let's see if any doors are open.

HECTOR: Man, I seen every movie on the square.

LOUIE: So see them again.

CHINA: Come on, man. I'll pay your way and you open the door for the rest.

HECTOR: Nawww, forgit it.

LOUIE: Aw, man. You's a dud.

HECTOR: So's your mama.

LOUIS: I don't play that shit.

HECTOR: Who's playing?

LOUIE: Oh, here's a nice trick for you, Comixbook. Twenty-five dollars. But don't let him run no game under your belt.

COMIXBOOK: What he do, man?

LOUIE: He takes gold baths.

COMIXBOOK: Gold what?

CHINA: That means that you gotta pee on him.

COMIXBOOK: Yeah? Well, let me see if I can git one of these dope fiends to buy me a beer.

HECTOR: Later . . . *(the rest of the crowd bid him good-bye)*. Where's the trick at?

LOUIE: In Queens.

HECTOR: In Queens? For twenty-five dollars? Shit.

LOUIE: Just part of a payback.

CHINA: Ain't it all part of the payback?

LOUIE: I don't know, some of it comes up front.

CABEZA: Man, you down that color TV off for seven lousy bags.

CUCHARA: I'm not the French Connection, my man.

CABEZA: You ain't no connection at all, motherfucker.

CUCHARA: You didn't have to shoot the stuff. I didn't put a gun to your head.

CABEZA: No, but you put the bags in the cooker.

CUCHARA: What can I tell you, man?

CABEZA: Shit man. Just that that weren't nothing for a color TV. Almost brand new, too. I mean, seven lousy bags of shit that was into shit.

CUCHARA: Yeah, but dig this man, you act like you got an attitude with me over that. Man, it wasn't my fault. No man, listen to me. I tried to warn you that Flaco shit was into nothing, I mean, didn't I?

CABEZA: Yeah, man, okay, baby.

CUCHARA: No, man. Listen up. Dig where I'm coming from.

CABEZA: Man, I don't have to look at you to listen.

CUCHARA: Okay, check this out. I told you about the stuff. But you came out your face talking about everybody else saying that Flaco got a dynamite bag. Man, like you should know that everybody has a dynamite bag.

CABEZA: Yeah, dynamite baking power. Shit, the way things are today, you go to cook your stuff and end up with a birthday cake.

CUCHARA: It ain't your fault, my man. I know.

CABEZA: Let's make a sting.

CUCHARA: Bet.

CABEZA: Why don't we try to down this watch, man? Before we go we can git off.

CUCHARA: That takes too long, man. I'm gonna be sick in a little while.

CABEZA: What we gonna do???? Rip somebody off??

CUCHARA: Yeah, but somebody safe.

CABEZA: What you talking about?

CUCHARA: Wait a second will you? I got an idea. Oye, little brother, come here for a second.

LOUIE: Yeah, what is it, man?

CUCHARA: Just wanna rap to ya brotherman.

LOUIE: Whatcha wanna rap about?

CABEZA: Look man, we ain't aiming to take you off.

LOUIE: Shit, I know that both of yous couldn't do that riding inside a tank.

CUCHARA: Oh, big man!

LOUIE: Faith, baby, faith in Louie cool.

CUCHARA: Really?

LOUIS: Really. Look man, you guys call me over to rap, right? Rap. I mean if you ain't got nothing to say or do, then I may as well do it with my boys.

CUCHARA: Well, you see? That's what we wanna talk to you about. Your boys.

LOUIE: Static?

CUCHARA: No, no static at all.

CABEZA: Ain't nothing like that hermanito.

LOUIE: What is it?

CABEZA: Be cool and he'll run it down to you.

CUCHARA: Okay, dig this. This is the deal. You know a lot of tricks.

LOUIE: A lot of whats?

CABEZA: Tricks. Johns. Scores. Suckers.

LOUIE: Man, I don't know what you talking about, brotherman.

CUCHARA: Come on, man. Don't be like that. We ain't the man.

LOUIE: NO SHIT!!!

CABAZA: Look man, you know we ain't the man, so why the big put on?

LOUIE: This ain't no put on.

CUCHARA: No? What do you call it?

LOUIE: Okay, so I know OF some fags. So what about it?

CUCHARA: So this about it. Look, you give us the name and address of one that you don't really like, right? Check this out. Me and the brother will rip him off.

LOUIE: Oh. Wow! Gee willikers, shucks man, I could have never thought of doing something as dishonest as that.

CABEZA: Wise guy.

LOUIE: Look, are you guys trying to make a point or something?

CABEZA: Or something.

LOUIE: Okay, what is it? Bring it out. Let's deal with it.

CUCHARA: Look, man, like I said. You give us the name and address of a trick that you really don't like, right? Then you call him up on the phone and tell him you got some friends he should make it his business to meet, right? And what we rip off we share with you.

CABEZA: After our jones are taken care of first. You know, first things first.

LOUIE: Oh yeah, that's real nice of you.

CABEZA: Look, man. We are taking the risk, not you.

LOUIE: Oh, I ain't even gonna be there for the liberation of cash.

CUCHARA: Man, we ain't gonna beat you.

LOUIE: I told you, I already knew that. Now, tell me something I don't know.

CABEZA: That's hard, since you think you know everything.

PEPPER: What's happening, Louie?

CUCHARA: Ain't nothing happening. We just rapping business, my man.

PEPPER: Sounds personal.

LOUIE: Not that personal that my boy couldn't hear.

PEPPER: Let's hear it then.

CABEZA: Well, what you say, man. Think it over.

LOUIE: Wait a second. Don't rush me.

PEPPER: What he mean, think it over. Think what over?

LOUIE: They want me to give them a score so that they could rip him off. Give me a share of the take, but I don't know.

PEPPER: You don't know, but I do.

LOUIE: Do what?

PEPPER: Said I know what to do.

LOUIE: I know you said you know what to do, but what is it that you know what to do?

PEPPER: Man, just play it with me, that's all.

CABEZA: Man, what you guys gonna do?

CUCHARA: Wait a second, brotherman. Where do you come in?

PEPPER: I come in from the streets.

CUCHARA: Well, that's where you gonna go.

LOUIE: Okay, see you guys later.

CUCHARA: Man, wait a second. What's all this about?

CABEZA: You gonna look out or what?

LOUIE: Yeah. I'm gonna look out for my partner and me.

CABEZA: He's your crimey?

LOUIE: He's my partner, man.

CABEZA: He's his crime partner.

LOUIE: He's partner all the way.

PEPPER: He's heart all the way.

CABEZA: Okay, okay, so he's your heart.

CUCHARA: Look man, all we want is an address, man. We'll do the work, you make the money. Well, some of it.

PEPPER: Man, what we think is that if we give you a score to hit, you might end up hurting the dude and then get busted. And if they find out that we gave you the number, well, you know what I mean, don't you?

CABEZA: Look man. We don't give out guarantees.

CUCHARA: Shit man. If we get busted, then we git busted, that's all to it.

CABEZA: Check it out.

PEPPER: That's what we're doing.

CABEZA: Doing what, my man?

PEPPER: Checking it all out my man.

CUCHARA: Vaya, then let's get down.

LOUIE: It's time to get down.

PEPPER: Wait a second, Louie. If we give this up to these dudes and they run, like we left out. All the way around.

LOUIE: Yeah, that's right.

CABEZA: Look, my man. We'll let you hold the watch my partner got on. Is that cool? Well, is it?

PEPPER: Yeah, I guess so. What the fuck, it ain't our money. Either way, it goes.

LOUIE: Yeah, right?

CABEZA: See, I knew you get hip sooner or later.

PEPPER: Go on, Louie, give them one of the cheaper scores.

LOUIS: Let me see what I got here.

PEPPER: Man, all your scores are cheap anyway, so just pick one.

CABEZA: Look, my man, the dude don't have to be Rockefeller.

LOUIE: Man, lay on simmer. Here. Here's one, man. This dude was the cheapest motherfucker that ever picked up a kid on the duce. Wow! Cheap!

CABEZA: Where he live at?

LOUIE: Forth-sixth and Ninth Avenue. Here's the address.

CUCHARA: Who's gonna call 'em?

LOUIE: I will. He don't know him that tough. Got a dime?

PEPPER: Broke.

CUCHARA: Okay, here man. I got to stop this shit.

CABEZA: What are you talking about, bro?

CUCHARA: Kicking this bad motherfucker off my back.

CABEZA: You ain't got the heart.

CUCHARA: Get out of my face with that, man. I kicked plenty of times. Go make that call, kid.

LOUIE: The name's Louie.

CUCHARA: Sorry, Louie.

LOUIE: Sorry didn't say it. Be back.

PEPPER: I'll be here.

CUCHARA: Yeah, man. I kicked this shit off my back a number of times, but every time I comes out the joint or a hospital, I always seem to run into someone that has some dynamite tres or duces. I mean, you know, like you spent half the time in the streets looking for those tres and duces that seem to disappear the minute you strung out. Like, sometimes I wonder if some pusher from the unknown is out there keeping us in check, you know what I mean? How does the connection know that I'm stepping into the street? These dudes must have radar or are with the CIA or the FBI . . . or . . .

CABEZA: Working with your mother.

CUCHARA: Man, leave my mother out of this shit.

CABEZA: Shit, your mother knows everything that's going on in the block.

CUCHARA: Come off it, man.

CABEZA: Shit, your mother knows what happened. What's happening. And what's about to happen. Local news reporter.

CUCHARA: Come on, man. I said be cool about my moms, man. I mean it.

CABEZA: Man, I'm just jiving you know that.

CUCHARA: Yeah, but he don't. And he might start coming out his face all wrong and what not about moms and he don't know me that well.

PEPPER: Don't know you that well and don't want to know you that well.

CUCHARA: Solid on that.

PEPPER: Solid on the solid. Excuse me, here comes Louie. Qué pasó?

LOUIE: Oye, el maricón no estaba. What we gonna do?

PEPPER: Give them Caesar's number.

LOUIE: Caesar the faggot?

PEPPER: Yeah, man.

LOUIE: Yeah, man, but Caesar the faggot. Like, wow, man, that's too strong.

PEPPER   Not strong enough for them suckers.

LOUIE: Okay.

CUCHARA: Hey, and what's going down?

CABEZA: Yeah, like what's happening?

PEPPER: Here's what's happening. The man we called was not in, so we gonna give you another dude.

CABEZA: How's this dude?

PEPPER: He's cool. A real punk. You know, he likes to get beat on.

CABEZA: Shit, I'll beat the shit out of him.

CUCHARA: Sure will.

PEPPER: Well, was he in?

LOUIE: Yeah, told him that I was sending my cousin over to see him.

PEPPER: Okay, it's set. Wait a second. The watch, my man. The watch.

CABEZA: Man, you don't have to sound like that. I just forgot, that's all.

LOUIE: Yeah, that's all.

PEPPER: Which is enough. See you guys later. At the park.

CUCHARA: Right on.

CABEZA: Later. At the park, late, my man, late.

LOUIE: Why you give 'em Caesar's number? That's one of those liberated faggots.

PEPPER: Yeah. Ah ha. He gonna sure enough liberate them suckers.

LOUIE: Yeah, but you know that Caesar is . . .

PEPPER: A third degree black belt in karate?

LOUIE: He gonna beat them guys bad.

PEPPER: He gonna beat them like he owns them.

LOUIE: That's dirty.

PEPPER: Yeah, ain't it?

HECTOR: Hey, what's so funny, man?

LOUIE: Them two dudes that were rapping with us?

HECTOR: Yeah, I know them, they hang out on the corner.

LOUIE: Well, they may be hanging out in the hospital tomorrow, man. They went to rip off Caesar, the faggot.

HECTOR: Holy shit! *(They go through karate sparring)*

(Man enters. He watches the kids playing for a while. At the same time checking the machines and getting closer to where the kids are.)

MIKE: Hey there, watch yourself. Haha . . . hahahahahah. Think you're Bruce Lee, hahaha . . .

HECTOR: Man, if you weren't standing there, I wouldn't have run into you.

MIKE: I'm just teasing you, fella.

HECTOR: You don't know me to be teasing me.

MIKE: Look, I'm sorry. You wanna play some game with me?

HECTOR: I'm broke, man. Can't afford to lose.

MIKE: Who said anything about losing or winning?

HECTOR: Nobody plays for fun, at least almost nobody. Play either to win or lose.

MIKE: Even with friends?

HECTOR: Friends fight, don't they?

MIKE: Not close friends. Real friends don't fight.

HECTOR: Shit, if you can't fight with your friend, then you ain't got a friend.

MIKE: I guess you got a point there.

HECTOR: I got many points.

MIKE: Let's see how many points you can make.

(They begin playing a game.)

HECTOR: You come around here a lot?

MIKE: You come around here a lot?

HECTOR: I asked you first.

MIKE: I asked you second.

HECTOR: First is first. Second is nobody.

MIKE: You win. Yeah, once or twice a month.

HECTOR: Is this the once or the twice?

HECTOR: Hey, man, you're not watching the game.

MIKE: Phoooooyyyyy.

HECTOR: Phoooyyyyy? Phoooy, hahahahaha, phooy.

MIKE: Ah, come on, man, don't make fun of me.

HECTOR: Why not?

MIKE: 'Cause I asked you not to?

HECTOR: Man, I see you later.

MIKE: Wait a second, I don't mean it that way. What I mean is, that if you don't make fun of me, I won't make fun of you.

HECTOR: Shit. You can make all the fun of me that you wanna. Man, that don't bother me none at all. 'Cause I may be young, but I know where I'm at, my man.

MIKE: Hey, look now who ain't watching the game.

HECTOR: Is this your game?

MIKE: No, not really.

HECTOR: So you only come around once in a while, huh?

MIKE: Yeah, mostly on my payday. You know, like I paid up all my bills and rent.

HECTOR: Take care of business.

MIKE: Yeah, and since I live by myself I got all this money left over and no one to spend it on, you know?

HECTOR: No, I don't know.

MIKE: Well, what I mean you know in is . . .

HECTOR: Man, I'm just goofing.

MIKE: I know that. And I'm just letting you know that it's okay.

HECTOR: Shit, I know that you know.

MIKE: I don't know.

HECTOR: Fuck you, man. You ain't getting me with my own shit. What you do, man? You a shipping clerk?

MIKE: No. I . . . I work for the city.

HECTOR: COP???

MIKE: Hell, no.

HECTOR: Garbage man.

MIKE: The money they make, I wish I were.

HECTOR: Why don't you become one?

MIKE: Because I hate hard work. My father worked hard all his life and he ended up with the same thing I'm gonna end up with, except that I'll have a little more of it.

HECTOR: MONEY???

MIKE: Time.

HECTOR: Shit, who needs time?

MIKE: Everybody needs time. Me, you, everybody needs it.

HECTOR: Bullshit. You can keep the time, just give me the bread.

MIKE: You need the time to spend it.

HECTOR: I don't need nothing to spend money except money.

MIKE: You like money?

HECTOR: Don't you???

MIKE: Not really.

HECTOR: Then why do you work?

MIKE: To live.

HECTOR: But you need money to live and you work to make money, right? So don't hand me that shit about not really caring about money. 'Cause like I told you, I may be young, but I'm not stupid.

MIKE: Nobody said that you were stupid.

HECTOR: You don't need to say it. When you say things like that and expect me to go for it, too.

MIKE: You hungry?

HECTOR: You treating?

MIKE: Yeah, I'm treating.

HECTOR: Then I'm hungry.

MIKE: Would you like to go to a movie? After we eat, of course.

HECTOR: No, I don't feel like going to a movie.

MIKE: Oh, by the way? What's your name?

HECTOR: Hector.

MIKE: Mine's Mike. Mike.

HECTOR: Hi, Mike.

MIKE: Hi, Hector.

HECTOR: You wanna go to go a movie, huh?

MIKE: Yeah, why? Anything wrong with going to go a movie?

HECTOR: No, if that's your thing. It's okay. Is that the only reason that you come around here? To go a movie?

MIKE: No, to go play the games here, too. You see, I'm also a musician.

HECTOR: So . . .

MIKE: Well, I come here to go get inspiration to go write music.

HECTOR: What kind of music? Latin? Rock? Soul?

MIKE: Jazz.

HECTOR: Jazz, what's that?

MIKE: It's music, that's what it is.

HECTOR: That's your opinion.

MIKE: Someday, I'll take you up to my pad and play you something I wrote about this place.

HECTOR: Really? What you call it? Forty-second Street Rock.

MIKE: No. Playland Blues.

HECTOR: Playland? Sounds like a kindergarten song.

MIKE: What you gonna be when you grow up, Hector?

HECTOR: What you mean, when I grow up? I am grown up.

MIKE: Excuse me. I mean, like when you get older.

HECTOR: I don't know. Maybe a cop.

MIKE: A cop? The way you acted before when I told you I worked for the city? I thought you hated cops?

HECTOR: I do hate them. All them motherfuckers ain't shit.

MIKE: Then why you wanna be a cop if you hate them so much? That means that there are gonna be people your age who are going to go hate you. You know that, right?

HECTOR: No, 'cause you see, I'm gonna be a good cop. Like Serpico.

MIKE: What makes you think Serpico was a good cop? Just because he was in a movie?

HECTOR: You mean Serpico wasn't a good cop?

MIKE: I don't know.

HECTOR: Then you shouldn't talk.

MIKE: Just curious.

HECTOR: You gotta lot of records in your house.

MIKE: Yeah, I guess so.

HECTOR: All kinds of sounds.

MIKE: All kinds of sounds.

HECTOR: Hey, can we go up to your house and party?

MIKE: Who is we? Me and you?

HECTOR: Yeah, and them, too.

MIKE: Them, too? I don't know them.

HECTOR: Oye, fellas! This here is Mike.

(Greetings around.)

MIKE: Hector, I don't know about . . .

HECTOR: Mike is cool, people. He said that we can go up his house and listen to music and dance.

MIKE: Wait a second, man. I said nothing like that.

(Walks away.)

LOUIE: Is he a score?

PEPPER: Shit. Sure he is, can't you tell?

LOUIE: Is he a score?

HECTOR: I don't know, man.

LOUIE: What you mean you don't know?

PEPPER: Why didn't you find out, already?

CHINA: Shit. With all the signs these motherfuckers were making at you.

LOUIE: Yeah, that's another thing. Why didn't you answer us?

HECTOR: What you mean? Why didn't I answer you?

PEPPER: You goddamn well know what Louie means.

LOUIE: Man, what the hell I got to go do? Yell at you: "Is he a faggot?"

CHINA: I don't know about you, Hector. You come off very funny sometimes.

HECTOR: What you mean by that, bitch?

PEPPER: You don't have to go treat her like that, Hector.

HECTOR: What did she mean by that, man? What did you mean by that, China? You trying to go say something about me, motherfucker?

CHINA: If I had something to say to you, I would.

LOUIE: Forget about it, man. Just tell me, is he a score or not?

HECTOR: Man, I don't know. I don't go asking them if they are faggots.

PEPPER: Bullshit! 'Cause you always do that.

HECTOR: I do not.

LOUIE: You do too. I heard you say many times: "Ask faggots if he is looking for someone to go take home."

CHINA: Yeah, you see? You acting funny, man.

HECTOR: Man, you better stop saying that I'm funny. Sounds to me you saying that I'm a faggot.

CHINA: I didn't say it. You did.

(HECTOR smacks her. LOUIE punches HECTOR. They begin to fight. The man who works there comes over and breaks up the fight.)

WRECKER: Okay, you kids get out and stay out!

PEPPER: What you mean, stay out? This is a public place.

WRECKER: Well, I just made it private for the rest of the day.

PEPPER: You's a dirty motherfucker.

WRECKER: Now, you see? I wasn't talking to you before, but to these three. Since you open your big mouth, you can stay out of here for good.

PEPPER: You can take this place and shove it up your ass, Wrecker.

WRECKER: What did you say you little punk?

PEPPER: Your mother's a punk.

HECTOR: Go on, Pepper, stab the motherfucker.

WRECKER: Go on, stab me, punk. Go on, see if you got the heart.

LOUIE: No, don't, Pepper! Forget it, man.

CHINA: Come on, Pepper. What's the matter with you lately? You been jumping in people's faces for nothing.

WRECKER: You better not come back in here that's all I say.

PEPPER: Fuck you.

WRECKER: Fuck you, too.

HECTOR: Fuck you, back. And fuck your mama.

MIKE: Come, Hector. What is it with you? You want to go get in trouble, is that it?

LOUIE: Come, Pepper. Let's take a walk up the block.

CHINA: Coming Hector. . . .

HECTOR: Fuck you, bitch.

WRECKER: And you, you little squirt. I treat you better than any of the other kids that come around here and you trying to go get that other jerk to go use that knife on me. You ungrateful little bastard. I ought to go break your fucking little ass.

MIKE: Listen, mister, all he was doing was trying to go protect his friend.

WRECKER: Who the hell are you?

MIKE: A friend of his.

WRECKER: You're kind of old to be his friend, ain't you?

MIKE: Friendship has nothing to do with age.

WRECKER: It has everything to do with your type.

MIKE: What do you mean by that?

WRECKER: Listen, sucker, I've been working here too long to know a pick up when I see one.

MIKE: You're making insinuations that can cause you a lot of trouble.

WRECKER: Then why don't you jump, stink.

MIKE: I don't stink. I take baths. And showers.

WRECKER: With little boys, I bet.

MIKE: Look, Mister, this is all . . .

WRECKER: What, you don't like it? Call the cops or come on and fight, come on. . . .

MIKE: I don't fight in the streets—like a bum.

WRECKER: You don't fight, period, 'cause you's a faggot.

NELLY: Where's Louie, Hector?

HECTOR: He's up the block . . . he'll be back.

NELLY: Is he all right?

HECTOR: Yeah, don't worry about him.

NELLY: Oh, ain't worried. Just asking, that's all.

HECTOR: Sure, sure.

MIKE: Coming, Hector?

HECTOR: Yeah, wait a second. Go on, I'll catch up to you . . . LATER.

MIKE: Okay, don't take long. . . .

HECTOR: Hey, listen, Nelly! Give this address to Louie when he gets back. Tell him I went with the dude, Mike. Okay? Later.

MONKEY 3: Come here, punk. Ven aca . . . si corre te mato como un perro cabroncito.

HECTOR: Man, what the fuck you want?

MONKEY 3: Oye, tengo un revolve conmigo so be cool, kid.

HECTOR: You gonna shoot me? Man, I didn't fight with you.

MONKEY 3: You ain't the one I want. I want Mr. Louie and his partner.

HECTOR: Look, man, I don't know where they are, so let me go. I got some business to go take care of.

MONKEY 3: You're not such a big boy now, huh? Qué pasó, you become a baby all of a sudden?

HECTOR: Man, I ain't no baby. Just that I don't wanna get hurt, that's all. Not for something I had nothing to do with. You know, like, if I was in it with them for real I wouldn't care 'cause payback always comes around.

MONKEY 3:   Look, I don't know what the fuck you talking about. Vete, you faggot hustler. Eso se paga. Tu vas a hacer maricón. One day you'll see . . . tu vas a hacer maricón.

NELLY: Please let him alone . . . please.

MONKEY 3:   Vete gorda. Get out of my face, fat girl. Get out of here. And take him with you. You lucky kid. Qué suerte tienes, papi.

HECTOR: Come on, Nelly.

NELLY: You go. I'm going this way.

MONKEY 3:   Hey, mister! Give me some change. Plenty change.

COMIXBOOK: Hey, fat girl! What's happening.

NELLY: Look, there's a guy waiting to go hurt Louie. Please, if you see him, give him this address. Tell him Hector went there—with the dude named Mike.

COMIXBOOK: Yeah, sure. Okay, is he a score?

NELLY: I don't know.

COMIXBOOK: Where you going?

NELLY: To go look for Louie.

COMIXBOOK: But he's . . . ah, fuck you.

ELECTRIC: Vaya Comixbook, what's happening?

COMIXBOOK: Ain't nothing much. Hey, you seen Louie or Pepper?

ELECTRIC: Yeah, man. Pepper and Louie are on Forty-third.

COMIXBOOK: Trying to go open a door?

ELECTRIC: No, man. They are having a meeting with all the hustlers on Forty-second Street.

COMIXBOOK: What about?

ELECTRIC: About us all chipping in our books. Our scores, you know, like a big-time corporation. Sharing in on the profits and so on.

COMIXBOOK: That sounds like a Pepper beat to me.

ELECTRIC: No, man. It sounds real cool to me. Like, I can't explain it like Pepper does, but it sounded real cool to me. Shit, I gave mines up.

WRECKER: I told you guys I didn't want you around here today and . . .

COMIXBOOK: Man, what are you doing?

ELECTRIC: Hey, man, be cool.

WRECKER: Oh, it's you. I thought it was them other friends of yours.

COMIXBOOK: He got hand trouble.

ELECTRIC: Sure does. Big punk motherfucker.

COMIXBOOK: Bet he talking about Pepper and Louie. Them guys make things hot around here. Like lately they be jumping in people's faces over nothing, petty little shit.

ELECTRIC: Man Pepper uptight! You should know that.

COMIXBOOK: Yeah, but still, man.

CHINA: Hey Comixbook! You seen Pepper? He's looking for you.

COMIXBOOK: No, what he want me for?

CHINA: So you could join Hustlers Incorporated.

COMIXBOOK: Hustlers in what? Man, are you serious?

CHINA: As serious as cancer in the third stage.

COMIXBOOK: Well, I don't believe you're serious. You got to be kiddin' man, 'cause I ain't going for no dumb shit like that. El hijo de Doña Ana is not a fool.

CHINA: Why you gotta be a fool, man?

COMIXBOOK: 'Cause I think anybody that goes for that is a fool or a nonhustler.

BREAKALEG: Look, if we all put our thing together, things could be safer. The hustle wouldn't be so dangerous, man.

COMIXBOOK: That's bullshit. If something is going to go happen, something is going to go happen and you can't stop it.

BREAKALEG: Yeah, but you could prevent things from happening if you watch your back.

COMIXBOOK: I watch my own back.

BREAKALEG: Comixbook, that's a real good name Pepper gave you, Comixbook. 'Cause that's you, always coming out of a fucking Comixbook!

CHINA: Man, I was right here when Louie gave you a score.

COMIXBOOK: I've given Louie scores too.

ELECTRIC: What you mean, man? Express yourself. Make yourself clear, bro.

COMIXBOOK: That Pepper is getting old and big for the hustle and the tricks don't want anybody that scares them.

CHINA: Pepper's gonna kick your ass.

COMIXBOOK: He ain't going to go do shit.

ELECTRIC: Okay, you do your thing. We do our thing and let's see what happens.

CHINA: Okay, let's forget it for a week and see who makes the bread.

COMIXBOOK: Hey, listen. That fat girl that likes Louie gave me this address to go give to Louie. She said Hector will be in a guy named Mike's house.

CHINA: Oh, yeah! There's going to be a dance there tonight.

ELECTRIC: At a faggot's house?

CHINA: I don't know the dude's a faggot.

ELECTRIC: Why not?

CHINA: Well, cause the dude is a Puerto Rican and Hector don't go with P.R.'s

COMIXBOOK: A party, huh?

ELECTRIC: Food.

CHINA: Shit! I don't know! But I sure am going to go check out the refrig.

COMIXBOOK: Come, let's go. You wait for them.

BREAKALEG: Oh, holy shit!

CHINA: What's the matter? There's something wrong, Breakaleg?

BREAKALEG: There's the dude, Pepper, Louie, and Hector had some static with today.

ELECTRIC: Were you there?

BREAKALEG: Yeah, man.

ELECTRIC: Come, let's tip before he sees you two.

COMIXBOOK: Yeah, I don't feel like rumbling.

BREAKALEG: That dude doesn't rumble, he's sneaky.

ELECTRIC: Backstabber.

CHINA: You got the address?

COMIXBOOK: Yeah, I copied it.

CHINA: Well, I see you people later.

ELECTRIC: Come on, man, let's go.

CHINA: I'm going this way to go see if I find Pepper or Louie.

COMIXBOOK: Give it to Crip, he knows Louie.

ELECTRIC: Yeah, 'cause . . .

BREAKALEG: Yo, Crip.

CRIP: Hey, kids! You want your picture taken? Got me a new camera.

COMIXBOOK: Man, fuck that.

BREAKALEG: Hey man, that's no way to come out on Crip.

COMIXBOOK: Man, I don't feel sorry 'cause he's a cripple bitch.

ELECTRIC: Comixbook, right. You shouldn't feel sorry for nobody if you don't like people feeling sorry for you.

CRIP: Electric, someday you'll be a philosopher of the highest caliber.

COMIXBOOK: Yeah, forty-five.

CHINA: Funny.

COMIXBOOK: Listen, Crip, if you see Louie, give him this.

CRIP: Okay. Sure you don't wanna take a picture? New camera?

ELECTRIC: Later, man. Later, man. Bye.

CRIP: Byeeeeee. . . .

CHINA: What if Crip doesn't see Louie or Pepper before that dude does?

COMIXBOOK: They got sneakers, they could run.

ELECTRIC: Man, I'm hungry.

BREAKALEG: Stop worrying so much! You cause things to go happen.

CHINA: Okay, okay. You don't have to go drag me.

BREAKALEG: Then come on.

PEPPER: You know something, Louie?

CRIP: Hey, Louie here. China and Electric gave me this for you. You take a picture. Got me a new camera. Better colors than before.

LOUIE: No thanks, Crip. Thanks for the note, later.

CRIP: Later, boys.

PEPPER: You know Louie, that's how I feel, like a cripple, man.

LOUIE: Yeah, but that's one cripple that on his own making things happen.

PEPPER: Yeah, but how long did that take, man? We used to go goof on him every day when he was begging, remember? Like if we hadn't done that he wouldn't have never gotten himself together. That what I mean like I feel like a cripple because I can't get things together in my head. You know I didn't give any scores away.

LOUIE: Man, I got a whole list you gave out.

PEPPER: Oh yeah! Sure! They were scores of mine at one time.

LOUIE: What you talking about, my man?

PEPPER: At one time they were scores of mine, but man, I made one of them in weeks. I just been hanging out on the square bullshitting about the money I'm making and about all the scores that I have. Like I have nothing going for me anymore. Remember the time I didn't show for a while? Well, what happened was I got busted. Yeah, busted for smoke. Cop me an o.z. and try downing it but the first one was a beat, the second time was a bust so I gave up trying to go deal, man. I'm on probation now. If I get busted with a joint—in I go! Fuck that shit, I ain't a burglar, you know that. Mugging ain't my shot. Look man, I'm not seventeen. I'm nineteen. I'm tall. And I'm black, and I look mean. My face ain't as sweet-looking as Electric's or Comixbook. All the tricks are scared of me. And I wouldn't know how to go pimp off a broad if I had one to go pimp off. Man, Louie and I don't even have a girl—Louie—not a girl.

LOUIE: Aw, come on man, what about that broad we fuck . . .

PEPPER: That was a ho' I pay . . . yeah, man I paid for some pussy. Man, that was it. Like you was in the room with the broad having fun smoking. I was in the bathroom crying. Louie . . . I . . . I . . . I . . . felt that I had lost my manhood that day. Man, you know something? Louie, I can't read. I never told that to anybody before, but that's the truth. Man, like man, I sat in that cell . . . and I could get in touch with no one 'cause I can't read, man. Man, I almost hung it up. For good, Louie. It was boring.

LOUIE: Go back to go school, man. Shit, I still go to school. I go to school in the day and hustle at night. You could do the same thing.

PEPPER: Man, I'd be ashamed to go to school not knowing how to read.

LOUIE: So, what you gonna do, man?

PEPPER: Listen, Louie. When I was in there I heard a lot of old-timers rap about organizing. This is the thing to go do. Get together.

LOUIE: Man, you don't have to go sell me, bro. You my man.

PEPPER: I'm not trying to go sell you anything, Louie. Don't you think I know we is tight. That's why I pulled you in as vice pres of Hustlers Incorporated, man. Listen, we going to go start shaking them down. Crip could take pictures for us. Develop the ones we take. Beat the ones that don't pay nothing. Rip off other hustlers' scores. Man, we can make money. Money, Louie: M-O-N-E-Y. Look, Louie, check this out. After we save some bread we get all the other dudes up here who are stealing and take a cut of the shit. Guys our age who are dealing we can offer them protection.

LOUIE: From what?

PEPPER: From us. Either they pay or they blow. Man we can make some bread mucho cash. Then . . . then . . . hey, dig this, Louie. After we save enough cash, we open a disco. Get me a car. A baddddassss apartment. Some baddddasss clothes. Man, we be kings, Louie! Kings! We call the place Pepper and Salt.

LOUIE: Salt and Pepper.

PEPPER: That's too common. Pepper and Salt is cool. Man, we be walking in, the music blasting, the walls down. People sweating up a storm. Girls wiggling their asses for us to go feel. Get down with whenever we want. The other hustlers will be turning us on for free just so that people can see them with us. Man, me and you are going to go be so baaaadd they gonna have to go invent another word for baaaadddd. Shit, Louie, I was born to go my own way in this bad motherfucker. I'm gonna be badder than Bubba Johnson, than Big Boy. I'm going to go be a baaaad-dddassss nigger.

LOUIE: I'm going in here to go take a leak.

PEPPER: Yeah, all right. Man, I'm gonna have this big bad motherfucker pay me some dues. I got them coming. People gonna have to go start calling me Mister from now on. Mister with a capital M. Shit, that's the way it was meant to be . . . 'cause it's the only dream I ever had.

(LOUIE *comes out running, shouting to* PEPPER. *A shot is heard.*)

LOUIE: Run, Pepper, he got a gun. Run!

(PEPPER *turns, the pusher faces him and shoots him.* PEPPER *falls.*)

MONKEY 3:   Cabrón . . . I told you I was going to go shoot you. Maricón, I am un hombre. I kill you dead.

PEPPER: Please, no! Don't kill me, bro. My dream, my dues. I got to go collect my dues. My dream.

(*Shoots him until gun is empty. He then begins to go kick him, cursing, spitting.*)

[Act II of *Playland Blues* by Miguel Piñero does not appear because of the constraints of space. Anyone needing Act II in case of a production can contact the editors through the publisher.]

Act III
Playland on Forty-second Street

(*A couple of weeks later, Saturday night. The street is alive with people: hustlers and suckers, faggots and freaks, straights and gays, cops and robbers, beggars, hawkers. Music is blasting, winos patrol the streets. Junkies prowl. Whores stalk their prey.*
JUST BEGUN *is talking with a trick.* RUBBERBAND *is dancing with* BREAKALEG *to a radio. Cops walk down the block. Everybody finds somewhere to go. It's like the parting of the sea. Cops stand there for a while by themselves. They depart and the ground in front of Playland is crowded again.*)

COMIXBOOK: Boy, what's happening people? What you guys staring at me like that? What's happening?

BREAKALEG: You already asked that question.

COMIXBOOK: What's your question, Breakaleg?

BREAKALEG: Same as everybody else's, I think.

JUST BEGUN: You usually don't stop cops on the street to go talk with.

RUBBERBAND: Don't look at me, brotherman.

COMIXBOOK: Eh, him. Man, I met him at Fifty-third and Third, about a couple of days after what's-his-name got killed.

JUST BEGUN: Pepper was what's-his-name.

COMIXBOOK: Yeah, Pepper. Look man, what can I tell you?

RUBBERBAND: Nothing you can say, brotherman.

JUST BEGUN: That's where you been hanging out.

COMIXBOOK: Yeah, man. That's the place to go if you gonna take this hustle serious and you wanna make some money.

RUBBERBAND: Yeah, man. There's plenty of bread over there, but like, that's white boy territory.

COMIXBOOK: This territory—like any other hustling place—belongs to those that are willing to go make the hustle.

JUST BEGUN: Yeah, man. But like, you know, what's that over there?

COMIXBOOK: All I know is that the tricks pay better and don't give up no hassles whatever.

BREAKALEG: What brings you up here if there's so much cars to go make on Fifty-third and Third?

COMIXBOOK: I get lonely for you, Breakaleg.

RUBBERBAND: You might laugh, but I believe you.

COMIXBOOK: What makes you think I'll laugh? I'm telling the truth.

JUST BEGUN: Better shut up already 'cause the next thing you know, you're gonna have me believing you about that.

BREAKALEG: Yeah, you don't want us to go think you are human, do you?

CRIP: What's happening, fellas?

COMIXBOOK: What's happening, Crip? Sitting down on the job, heh?

RUBBERBAND: You got some sense of humor, baby. Hey! Crip!

CRIP: Take your picture, fellas?

COMIXBOOK: Later, man, later.

BREAKALEG: No thanks, Crip.

COMIXBOOK: Got any wine?

CRIP: Someday, sonny, life is gonna pass you up so fast that you'll be standing on the duce picking up young boys for a conversation. Life can be very boring, dull and lonely sometimes. You think you're . . . you're . . .

COMIXBOOK: I'm what? What? What do you think I am that you think I think I am what I think I am but I ain't?

CRIP: Everything that you ain't. Because with you everything ain't everything. You're not even a part of a fraction of what is.

COMIXBOOK: But I can run from a cop. What do you do?

CRIP: I never put myself in the position to go run from anyone.

COMIXBOOK: That's because you're a cripple.

CRIP: Only in my legs, sonny. Only in my legs.

COMIXBOOK: And in your hands, motherfucker, you can't even get the wine bottle out of the sack.

CRIP: Here you are.

COMIXBOOK: That's good. Later Crip.

CRIP: Thanks for the wine, Comixbook.

COMIXBOOK: Anytime, Crip. Anytime.

CRIP: Be back to go take your picture.

COMIXBOOK: Be waiting. Yeah, that's my boy, Crip. Good people all the way.

BREAKALEG: Sure don't sound that way, the way you guys were rappin'.

COMIXBOOK: Yeah, that's because he's been my friend a long time, boy. A long time.

CABEZA: Hey! What you guys did was out of line, my man.

JUST BEGUN: Like, what we done, man? I ain't never done anything to you.

BREAKALEG: He's high.

CABEZA: I may be high, but I know what I'm saying, baby.

COMIXBOOK: What are you saying, my man?

CABEZA: Sending me and my man to go that faggot's house. Man, that dude was a karate freak. Besides other things than that.

RUBBERBAND: Man, I didn't send you to no faggot's house.

CABEZA: Not you, man. Not you. Wait! In fact, it was none of youse, right?

JUST BEGUN: Rigggggghhhhht. . . .

BREAKALEG: This guy should go on them TV quiz shows.

RUBBERBAND: Dude, you are very smart.

CABEZA: Yeah, a lot of people tell me I'm not, but I know that I am.

BREAKALEG: I can't believe that, man. People really say shit like that?

JUST BEGUN: What's that? He's smart? That he is or he isn't?

BREAKALEG: Only his homeroom teacher knows for sure.

CABEZA: Man, my boy's in the hospital.

RUBBERBAND: Beaten bad, brotherman.

JUST BEGUN: Broken bones.

CABEZA: Broken ass. That faggot dug Cuchara so much, Cuchara got six stitches in his ass.

JUST BEGUN: Man, I don't want nobody to go dig me THAT much!

RUBBERBAND: He could hate me all he wants and I'll dig him for it.

CABEZA: Any of you guys got a dollar to go lend me?

COMIXBOOK: Whatever happened to good old panhandling? Where people would give you a nice story before they hit you with the lend, spare, give me a dime routine.

BREAKALEG: Yeah, and the most they ever panhandled was a quarter.

CABEZA: Man, I ain't panhandling you guys. I'm just asking you to go do me a solid.

RUBBERBAND: . . . and lay some money in your hand.

BREAKALEG: PAN for bread, HANDLING for hand.

JUST BEGUN: I didn't know that!

CABEZA: Know what? Man, you guys fucking with my head. I don't like nobody fucking with my head, man. Like I don't fuck with nobody's head, so nobody should fuck with my head. Can you dig it?

JUST BEGUN: I can dig it.

COMIXBOOK: I can dig . . . dig . . . dig it. . . .

RUBBERBAND: I can dig it . . . she can dig it . . . he can dig it . . . they can dig it . . . dig it . . . dig it . . . dig it . . . dig it! Oh! Let's dig it!

(They begin to go sing the phrase like the song.)

CABEZA: Let's see what I got *(pulls out a roll of dollars)* shit! I don't have any change . . . ain't that a shame.

BREAKALEG: Oh! How can you walk out of the estate without change? Really, redneck, whatever am I to go do?

JUST BEGUN: For me to give you a dollar I'll tell you what you got to go do. You got to go walk backwards on water like you do on land. Roll your eyes in burning sand. Jump off the Empire State Building on your head. Jump back up to the top. Do the boogaloo! Jerk off to prove to me you're still alive and then I might recommend you to somebody that may, if he has time, give you a loan on a dime.

CABEZA: Fuck you guys! You think everything's a joke, man. I wish to go see one of you guys strung out, man, then you'll know. 'Cause I . . . man, you see? I hope to go see one of you people strung out on scag and not on faggots.

BREAKALEG: Man, here's a dollar.

COMIXBOOK: Here, I'll give it to the dude.

CABEZA: Rub it on your chest. I don't want nothing from any of you people. Nothing. I just hope I see one of you guys strung out 'cause I'm gonna do like you did me.

COMIXBOOK: He don't want it? Fuck him then.

RUBBERBAND: Man, I guess if I had some pride left in me I wouldn't take it either.

JUST BEGUN: Yeah, me neither.

COMIXBOOK: I would . . . that don't mean shit to me.

BREAKALEG: That's 'cause you don't give a fuck about anyone but you.

COMIXBOOK: Man, I was willing to go give it to him, but he didn't want it.

RUBBERBAND: After all that shit, who would?

COMIXBOOK: I would, that's who would.

BREAKALEG: Yeah, you would.

COMIXBOOK: That's right, bitch. I would. What of it?

ELECTRIC: What's happening people?

COMIXBOOK: Nothing but an old movie story about sentimental fools.

ELECTRIC: That's cool, I guess.

RUBBERBAND: Yeah, I guess so, too!

ELECTRIC: Hey, did you go to Pepper's funeral, Comixbook?

COMIXBOOK: Were you there?

ELECTRIC: No, I didn't.

COMIXBOOK: Well, there you have it. No, I didn't go to Pepper's funeral, so what?

ELECTRIC: Just asking man. Just asking, you don't have to go catch an attitude, man.

COMIXBOOK: Well, I caught one. So what?

ELECTRIC: Rubberband, what's with him?

COMIXBOOK: Ask me, not him. He's not me nor my father.

ELECTRIC: Man, squash it, okay? Sorry I asked.

COMIXBOOK: I bet you are.

ELECTRIC: Later. I'll see you guys much later.

JUST BEGUN: Hey, bro'. That dude with the white hair was here looking for you earlier in the day.

ELECTRIC: What dude with the white hair?

JUST BEGUN: You know what dude I'm talking about, man. The twenty-five dollar trick that takes you to go see them dirty pictures, you know.

ELECTRIC: Oh, yeah. Louie the cab driver.

BREAKALEG: Hey! Where is Louie? I ain't seen him in a long time.

JUST BEGUN: After Pepper was killed, one of the dudes that works here saw Louie run while the dude was shooting Pepper.

BREAKALEG: So what?

JUST BEGUN: Well, Louie came back up here to go pick up this here trick and the dude told the cop that he was the kid who ran. Well, the cops picked up Louie as a witness, so . . .

BREAKALEG: Material witness.

RUBBERBAND: You mean he had something on him?

BREAKALEG: No, stupid.

RUBBERBAND: I know what it means, man. I was just goofing, that's all.

BREAKALEG: Oh, okay! Here's a laugh—ha ha.

RUBBERBAND: Thanks.

JUST BEGUN: Well, the cop takes Louie in. So Louie decides to go squeal.

BREAKALEG: Man, that's not squealing. That was Louie's main man, shit!

JUST BEGUN: You know what I mean, man. Anyway, he went to court and the dude got off.

RUBBERBAND: He did?

JUST BEGUN: Yeah. After the dude got off he told Louie he was gonna jailhouse him, too.

BREAKALEG: And what did Louie do?

JUST BEGUN: He did the best thing to do. He disappeared.

COMIXBOOK: That's hip. Very hip. I give more credit to Louie.

BREAKALEG: Oh, he'll be thrilled to know that, simply thrilled.

WRECKER: You guys gonna have to go move along.

BREAKALEG: Okay . . . shit man, like what's the . . .

WRECKER: The boss is here today, man. Like these TV people came around yesterday shooting the place over.

COMIXBOOK: Yeah, they did? What about?

WRECKER: They're doing a story about you kids who hustle on the Square.

JUST BEGUN: You got to go be kidding!

WRECKER: If I'm kidding, I'm shitting.

RUBBERBAND: You are shitty anyway, so that don't count.

WRECKER: Fuck around and they'll have a real reason to call you Rubberband. Boy, I'll whip you like I own you.

RUBBERBAND: You can whip me after you lend me a quarter, man.

WRECKER: Man, what you think I am? Your father? Come on, fellas. Just move away from the front of the door for a while until the creep leaves you, okay?

RUBBERBAND: Later. . . .

ELECTRIC: What time did you say that dude was around?

JUST BEGUN: I don't know. I didn't notice the time. You know, like, I ain't . . .

ELECTRIC: Everybody's coming out the side of their neck today.

BREAKALEG: Just ain't your day, Electric.

ELECTRIC: Shit, I guess not.

COMIXBOOK: Motherfucker is always guessing. Don't you ever know anything?

ELECTRIC: Yeah, I know that if I stay here listening to your rap I'll end up getting my ass kicked by you 'cause I'm gonna deck you in the mouth. Later, Just Begun. Hey! You wanna come?

JUST BEGUN: Where to go?

ELECTRIC: That trick's house. I got the phone number. Call him now. Yeah, wanna come, he pays real good, share the thing with you.

JUST BEGUN: Yeah, why not? Later people.

RUBBERBAND: Later. . . . Hey! There's that dude, Mike. Oye! Mike! Mike! Over here, man.

ELECTRIC: Coming bro'?

JUST BEGUN: Wait up, man. Wait up.

ELECTRIC: Come on, man. That dude don't pay nothing at all.

RUBBERBAND: He's not a trick, man. He's good people.

COMIXBOOK: He's all right.

ELECTRIC: Come on, man. Let's go.

BREAKALEG: What's happening? You going with him?

COMIXBOOK: Later, bro'. I'm going in to go play some games.

ELECTRIC: Come on, bro'. Man, listen, I'm leaving bro'.

JUST BEGUN: Later. You go. I think I'll stay and see this dude.

ELECTRIC: He ain't got no money bro'.

JUST BEGUN: I know, later bro'. See you later.

ELECTRIC: Later then. Later Rubberband. Breakaleg.

BREAKALEG: Later. Let me get a cigarette, bro'. Thanks. Later. Hi, Mike! Let me get a match?

MIKE: What's happening people?

JUST BEGUN: Not much.

RUBBERBAND: Everything. . . .

MIKE: Well, which is it? Not much or everything?

RUBBERBAND: A little of both.

JUST BEGUN: Yeah, not much of everything is happening today.

MIKE: What happened to that guy, Louie?

RUBBERBAND: I don't know. Like I ain't seen him since that day up in your crib.

MIKE: He was really messed up over his friend getting killed.

JUST BEGUN: He sure was, man. He and that dude were this close, man.

BREAKALEG: Like brothers, man. Just like brothers.

MIKE: He left with that fat girl.

JUST BEGUN: Fat Belly Nelly.

MIKE: Yeah! Fat Belly Nelly. Didn't say anything at all. He just got up the next morning and left.

BREAKALEG: You mean he stood over your place?

MIKE: Yeah, him and that fat girl both.

JUST BEGUN: . . . and you let him?

MIKE: Why not? They didn't steal anything.

RUBBERBAND: They stood together.

MIKE: Yeah, man. You guys act like that's a crime.

JUST BEGUN: No, it's no crime, man. Just that, you know most people . . .

MIKE: I ain't most people.

JUST BEGUN: I can see that. Man, you all right.

RUBBERBAND: Yeah, you are.

MIKE: Thanks a lot.

JUST BEGUN: Well you are, man.

RUBBERBAND: Yeah, you are.

MIKE: Thanks . . . I feel that any second now you guys are gonna pull out a gold medal and the TV cameras are going to go appear.

BREAKALEG: Nothing that hip, baby.

JUST BEGUN: Ain't nothing hip about that. He's cool people, man.

RUBBERBAND: There's a lot of cool people in the world, man. Black, white, red, you name the colors.

JUST BEGUN: Yeah, but how many of them do we know?

RUBBERBAND: Like, none.

MIKE: Wasn't that guy what's-his-name the guy who had the fight with Hector here a little while ago?

RUBBERBAND: He's inside.

BREAKALEG: Yeah, he's hustling up on Fifty-third now.

MIKE: Fifty-third and what?

JUST BEGUN: Fifty-third Street and Third Avenue, my man.

RUBBERBAND: That's where the big hustling money is.

MIKE: I thought you guys are out to make some money? What you doing here if the money is there?

JUST BEGUN: Yeah, but so are a lot of other things, too. Like they expect you to go give up your bunkie up there.

MIKE: They do?

RUBBERBAND: No man, he's serious. Them motherfucking tricks expect too much from a kid up there.

BREAKALEG: Like getting fucked?

MIKE: Is that why you guys are not up there?

RUBBERBAND: Yeah, that's why.

MIKE: You think what's-his-name gives it up there?

JUST BEGUN: Comixbook? Shit, man, he gives it up down here. I went with one of his tricks once and the dude tells me he gonna give me seventy dollars, man. Shit! That's a lot of bread, right? I tell him: "What you do?" He says: "The regular thing I do with your friend." I say: "What's the regular thing you do with my friend?" He says: "Well, I do it to him and blow him later." I told him, man, you keep your regular thing for your regular customer. Shit, that's a weird dude.

RUBBERBAND: Don't say that! He ain't weird, man. He's just, you know.

BREAKALEG: A closet case.

MIKE: You mean he's gay?

BREAKALEG: Bingo!

MIKE: Fifty-third and Third, huh?

JUST BEGUN: You thinking of going up there?

MIKE: No, just thinking that's all . . . you don't mind if I think?

JUST BEGUN: No, go ahead. It's free.

RUBBERBAND: Also like that place is for, you know, white people. Like most of them are already in their late twenties and shit. Yeah, man, and like most of their shit is like, you know what I mean.

MIKE: I don't.

JUST BEGUN: You don't . . .

MIKE: I mean I do and I don't. Like I could dig that they're old, late twenties. Wow! Like that's real old. Ready for the old folks home. . . .

BREAKALEG: Come on, man, be serious.

MIKE: Oh! But I am. . . .

BREAKALEG: No, you ain't. You're making fun of us.

RUBBERBAND: Yeah, you are man. We're being serious with you.

MIKE: Like I'm sorry, man. I was just kidding around. Tell me more about Fifty-third and Third.

RUBBERBAND: Some other time.

JUST BEGUN: Yeah. Like later, man.

BREAKALEG: See you around sometime.

MIKE: Hey, come on, man. I said I was sorry. What more you guys want me to go do?

JUST BEGUN: Man, like we tell you you cool. Then you go fuck with our heads, man, like that ain't together at all.

RUBBERBAND: Not at all.

MIKE: Okay. Okay. I already apologized, man.

JUST BEGUN: Right on.

MIKE: Tell me about . . .

RUBBERBAND: Man, like that's not the only place to go hustle money off tricks, man.

MIKE: No? Where else?

JUST BEGUN: There's lots of places. Only thing is that these are the two most famous places to go make money and there's no real money to go be made in either of these places.

RUBBERBAND: Yeah, forty duce because of the movies and Fifty-third because of the bread.

MIKE: Yeah, but I thought . . .

JUST BEGUN: Yeah, yeah, yeah.

RUBBERBAND: Look man, we find people to go be sometimes just a little overbearing with their dumb fucking attitudes about the way we make our money and really, like, we're the ones that chose to go hustle our bread this way. And if we choose to go hustle our bread this way, then that's the way it's gonna be, man. Like so fucking what. Like, it's the way these suckers come up on you around here. Selling you some type of revolutionary packages, you know? Free this guy and free that broad here and shit like that, man. But like when I was in the joint, none of them came up with a bail for me, and none of them were parading in front of the court building with signs or yelling: "Free Rubberband." Shit, all the shit is played out as far as I'm concerned. Can you dig it?

MIKE: Yeah, I can dig it.

JUST BEGUN: That's what they all say.

MIKE: Look, man. I said I can dig it. Can you dig that?

RUBBERBAND: Motherfucker, of course we can. Hey, Hector, what's happening.

COMIXBOOK: Well, if it ain't the big-time lover.

BREAKALEG: Come here, man. Hey! Come here.

WRECKER: They calling over there, Hector.

HECTOR: Mind your own business.

WRECKER: Okay! If that's the way you feel about it.

ELECTRIC: Hey, Hector! Qué pasa?

JUST BEGUN: Hey! I thought you left to go see that dude?

ELECTRIC: Yeah, man. But I kinda changed my mind on the way over.

COMIXBOOK: Hey Hector! Your lover is here. Ain't you gonna talk to him?

HECTOR: Fuck you.

COMIXBOOK: Fuck you too, punk! You wanna start something with me, mother-fucker?

MIKE: Man, shut the fuck up, punk.

COMIXBOOK: Man, get the hell off me, motherfucker. You ain't nothing to me.

MIKE: That's why you better dig yourself, punk. Now get the fuck out of here before I bust up your little tight ass.

COMIXBOOK: Man, get the hell off me.

MIKE: Get the fuck out of here, now.

COMIXBOOK: See you later, Hector.

MIKE: You can see him now. If you see him later, you better just keep on walking or you gonna be crawling after I get through with you.

COMIXBOOK: Fuck you. If I see you on the street next time, you better be carrying something.

MIKE: See a kid like that making statements like that can get him all beat up or killed.

BREAKALEG: Sure it can, but he ain't got no sense anyway.

MIKE: Well, for his own good he better find some.

JUST BEGUN: They sell it right here in Playland for a dollar.

HECTOR: Hi, Mike.

MIKE: About time you noticed I was here.

HECTOR: I knew that you were there all the time.

MIKE: Why didn't you say hello?

HECTOR: Because I didn't feel like it.

MIKE: It's as simple as that, is it?

HECTOR: I guess so.

MIKE: Don't you know?

HECTOR: Yeah, I know.

MIKE: Why did you tell Comixbook the things you told him?

HECTOR: What did I tell him?

MIKE: You told him that I was your lover and that you were living with me and if I were your lover it's the first time I heard about it.

HECTOR: I . . . I . . . I . . . don't know.

MIKE: Yes you do.

HECTOR: I didn't say anything to him.

MIKE: You want me to go call some of your friends to be witnesses?

HECTOR: I don't care.

MIKE: Okay. Hey! Rubberband! Come 'ere, please.

RUBBERBAND: Yeah, what is it, Mike?

HECTOR: No.

MIKE: You got a match?

RUBBERBAND: Here! Keep them . . . later. What's happening, Hector?

HECTOR: Nothing, man. Nothing at all.

MIKE: See why you wanna play these dumb games for? I have nothing to go lose, so I can play any dumb game you want to go play.

HECTOR: He was supposed to go be my boy, right? And everything I did was cool with him, just like everything he did was cool with me. Then, like one night—

MIKE: Like one night, what? The night you were up at my house?

HECTOR: No, the night I was up at his house. The night before we was up at your house.

MIKE: What happened?

HECTOR: I was living with him and his mother, right? Well, he told me that if I wanted to go stay living with him and having a place to go sleep for the winter I'd better get down with him.

MIKE: Did you?

HECTOR: Well, I would have done it, but my way.

MIKE: What you mean by that?

HECTOR: Like we're almost the same age and shit like that, you know? You know, like it seemed stupid for him to go be wanting to go do something with someone his own age and a guy at that, with so many broads out here that dig him so much, you know?

MIKE: Well, some people, that's their thing.

HECTOR: They should keep it their thing and, you know? Like the dude told this and I thought well, what the fuck? Ain't nothing if I let a faggot do it for money, I guess I can let my own boy jump on it for free. So I told him that's cool with me and that night, man, that night, he wanna to go bunkin' me. He wanna bunkin' me. Man, that's out.

MIKE: That's out?

HECTOR: Yeah, it's out with me. I don't play that shit at all.

MIKE: You don't, huh?

HECTOR: No, I don't. So I told him I was leaving.

MIKE: You told him that night?

HECTOR: No, that night after he tried doing it to me I slept on the kitchen table. And well, you know that shit jumped off at your house with me and him. Do you believe all the shit he said about my mother?

MIKE: Is it true?

HECTOR: Some of it, I guess. Some of it is true. I don't know.

MIKE: Would you like to go live with me?

HECTOR: What?

MIKE: Would you like to go live with me for real and really be what you told Comix-book you were to me?

HECTOR: Are you crazy, man?

MIKE: No, I'm asking you a very straight question. If you wanna, that's cool. If you don't, that's cool, too. Ain't nothing lost. On my part, I got a place to go.

HECTOR: What would it be like? You know? Me and you?

MIKE: It'll be like you make it, Hector.

HECTOR: What if I don't wanna do it with you?

MIKE: That's up to you, too. Ain't no one forcing you to go do anything you don't want to go do.

HECTOR: I got to go think it over.

MIKE: Don't take too long.

HECTOR: You mean there's a time limit on the offer? Why?

MIKE: 'Cause you would have to go say good-bye to all this out here, baby. You see? I'm moving to Philadelphia this week.

HECTOR: What about me?

MIKE: You would come with me. I'll take care of you forever.

HECTOR: Forever. That's a long time, Mister.

MIKE: It sure is, ain't it? I'm going to go Tad's for dinner. Wanna come?

HECTOR: No, thanks. I already ate.

ELECTRIC: Hey, Mike. Whatcha gonna do? Take me to go eat? I'm hungry.

MIKE: Sure, come on.

JUST BEGUN: You treating everybody?

MIKE: Only some.

JUST BEGUN: Am I part of that some?

MIKE: If you feel part of it, I guess that you are.

   (*They exit with* MIKE.)

WRECKER: What's the matter, Hector? You look out of place today.

HECTOR: You're okay, you know that?

WRECKER: Why, thanks a lot. That's the first time you said anything nice about me since I first met you.

HECTOR: Remember it 'cause it'll be the last time you'll hear it.

WRECKER: You feel like playing a free game?

HECTOR: Naw. Yeah, okay. Thanks!

WRECKER: Anytime, Hector.

CRIP: Where did all the fellas went?

WRECKER: How should I know?

CRIP: Well, they were here, right?

WRECKER: What fellas are you talking about?

CRIP: The fellas that hang out here at night. Oh, you know who.

WRECKER: They went into Tad's with this freak.

HECTOR: He's not a freak. He's no faggot and you shouldn't be saying things about people unless you know it's true. And anyway, it's none of your business if he were. Here's your money. I don't need to go play anything in here. In fact, I don't even need to go be here.

WRECKER: Calm down, son. All I was saying is what I thought.

HECTOR: Well, your thoughts are shitty and they stink.

CRIP: What's with him?

WRECKER: Who the fuck cares? Listen, you got to go move out of here with that camera. You know the boss doesn't like pictures being taken here.

CRIP: Hector, if your friends come back, tell them that Crip is gonna take their picture for them, okay?

HECTOR: Yeah, yeah, later.

WRECKER: Listen, Hector, I didn't mean any harm.

HECTOR: Leave me alone, please.

WRECKER: Okay. But don't hang out here too long. The boss is around tonight.

(HECTOR *remains by himself. A trick approaches him. He turns him off. He doesn't seem to be paying any attention to where he is—he is in his thoughts.*)

LOUIE: Hey, Hector! Hector! Hey, man. You don't wanna talk with anybody?

NELLY: Maybe he thinks he's special. Now that you ain't hanging out.

HECTOR: Oh shit, Louie. Fat Belly Nelly.

LOUIE: Don't call her that. That's my woman. She's gonna have my kid, man. I'm gonna be a father, can you dig that? Check it out! Me, a daddy!

HECTOR: Yeah, I guess that sounds cool. Sorry, Nelly.

NELLY: That's okay. Just don't do it again.

HECTOR: Yeah, right.

LOUIE: Wow! You must be really out there, man. If she had said that last time I saw you, you'd be all on her case.

HECTOR: Said what?

LOUIE: Nothing, man, nothing. Where is everybody at?

HECTOR: I think they're in Tad's eating with that dude Mike.

LOUIE: Oh yeah, that dude I ran up that night.

HECTOR: Yeah, him, he's been around a few times.

LOUIE: What you doing now?

HECTOR: Trying to go make it happen.

LOUIE: Me and Nelly, we living up my mother's place. You know? Like it kinda gets to you having a baby, you know?

HECTOR: Yeah, I don't know, man. I ain't even fucked a broad yet.

LOUIE: What? You kidding me? I thought you and that broad what's-her-name?

HECTOR: Me and no broad.

NELLY: Oh, shit! A hustler who's a virgin.

LOUIE: Excuse me, Nelly. Let me rap with Hector alone, please.

NELLY: Oh, shit. Look, I'm sorry. Man, I meant nothing. Just goofing, you know?

LOUIE: Yeah, she kinda gets out there now to go goof with people, not like before, you know what I mean?

HECTOR: That's cool. Man, that's cool.

LOUIE: Yeah. That may be cool, but I like to go know why you ain't?

HECTOR: What you mean by that, man?

LOUIE: Come on, Hector. You know me better than that, man. To go be pulling that on me.

HECTOR: Man, you better be cool. You know that dude is still looking for you.

LOUIE: Man, I don't care about that. Me and Nelly came up here to go to a movie. If the dude runs up on me, I guess we just gonna have to go play Dodge City.

HECTOR: Check it out.

LOUIE: I already did, man. Like, you can't live running from anything, dig it?

HECTOR: But you gonna have a kid and shit like that, man.

LOUIE: Like I put myself here. I get myself out some way, but it's got to go be clean and clear of fear for me and Nelly. Like, I really don't know if me and her gonna make it together, you dig? But while we're trying I can't be dealing with a shit like that on my mind.

WRECKER: Hey, Louie. Long time no see! How you doing?

LOUIE: How you been, Wrecker?

WRECKER: So, so. You know, fair to middling. See you later. Take care now.

LOUIE: You too, man.

HECTOR: You know something, Louie, I can't even read.

LOUIE: So what? Learn like everybody else does.

HECTOR: Who's gonna take time out to go teach me?

LOUIE: Find someone.

HECTOR: Yeah, that's easy to go say.

LOUIE: And easy to go do. Man, with all the tricks that you know, you mean to go tell me that you can't con one of them with your fine looks to go teach you some things, man?

HECTOR: That's what's fucking me up right now.

LOUIE: Not knowing how to go read?

HECTOR: No man. Having someone.

LOUIE: Who?

HECTOR: That dude, Mike.

LOUIE: He's gay?

HECTOR: That's what I really don't know, man. Like he asked me to go away with him. And like, I don't know what to go do.

LOUIE: Why not? Man, you do what you think is best for you.

HECTOR: Yeah, man, but like you know I'm only fourteen years old, man.

LOUIE: So what, man? You got nobody out here, right, that's looking out for you, right? And if you go to go the man you know that he's gonna put you in a home.

HECTOR: Yeah. Like I don't wanna be put away, man. That's not my thing, being locked up. Some people dig that scene. Not me, man, not me.

LOUIE: So what you gonna do, man?

HECTOR: Like, he just asked me to go away with him. Like, I don't know, man. But I ain't got nowhere to go but to go my sister's house and you. I can't make it there with her, she's too fucking much, man. See, like he didn't ask me to go do anything with him.

LOUIE: What if he does?

HECTOR: What would you do? Like if you had nobody checking you out nowhere to go check into—and be free about it—what would you do, Louie, if a man like him came up to you and told you that he wanted to go take care of you, but that you would have to go have sex with him. Would you go with him? Would you live with him? Would you have sex with him?

LOUIE: Yeah. I would go with him. Yeah, I would live with him and yeah, if he wanted to go have sex with me I would have sex with him.

HECTOR: No matter if he's doing it to you, Louie?

LOUIE: No matter if he's doing it to me. But, you see? I would check him out, like, if the next day he treats me cool, I guess I would stay with him. If he don't, well, I rip him off and look for someone else 'cause you know, Hector, there ain't no guarantees in hustling. If they really mean it or if it's just part of their thing, dig it. But like this dude asked you to go get down with him?

HECTOR: No, man, he just said come live with me, that's all.

LOUIE: So maybe the dude is for real. Maybe he wants you to go be with him. There's some people like that, you know? That are lonely, dig it?

HECTOR: Yeah, but he don't look like that type that is lonely for anything.

LOUIE: You don't know, man. You don't know. You ain't inside his head. You don't know what he's thinking.

HECTOR: That's what I'm scared about, man. He might be one of those dudes that kill little kids. You know? Like that dude in the Lower East Side that killed all those kids, remember?

LOUIE: Yeah, I remember. I stopped hustling until he got busted. But look, man. You got to go do something. Nobody can tell you what to go do, man. You got to go do your own thing. I told you what I would do, but then I ain't you. And what I need is not the same thing you get to go get over. Me, Hector? Whatever you do, you be all right with me all the time. I got to go cut you loose, man, 'cause I got to go get up early to go to school tomorrow. Yeah, that broad got me going to school and besides, I get paid for it, too. Hey, man. I moved to the building across the street from where I used to go live at. Apartment twelve. Drop by sometime. And I got some good smoke if you wanna cop anything over an o.z. Later, Hector.

NELLY: Bye, Hector.

ELECTRIC: Hey, man. That dude Mike is a funny dude, man. He had everybody cracking up in there. You should have gone to go eat. He's got break, too. Man is all right.

NELLY: Bye, Hector.

BREAKALEG: I see you guys later, man. I got to go get home. Going to go the Peel tonight. China called me and told me she gonna be there tonight. Later, fellas.

JUST BEGUN: Later . . . that broad is dizzy.

MIKE: Sure is, ain't she?

JUST BEGUN: Hey listen, Mike. You know last time we were at your place I ran down a poem.

MIKE: Yeah, but I heard that before.

JUST BEGUN: Yeah, yeah. I know 'cause that was a thing my brother taught me. He learned it in the joint, I think.

RUBBERBAND: Now you gonna run down one your mother taught you?

ELECTRIC: That she learned in the crazy house?

JUST BEGUN: Fuck you guys. I wrote this one my motherfucking self.

MIKE: What's it about?

ELECTRIC: Just Begun's eyeballs are dusted. His underarms rusted and his asshole busted and now he's feeling disgusted.

JUST BEGUN: Hold it everybody! Silence please! And that means everybody out there too.

RUBBERBAND: Okay, all you cars out there stop making so much noise.

JUST BEGUN: Okay, okay. Here goes. Is everybody ready? You all sure now? Is all the wax out of everybody's ears? I ain't gonna say my poem until everybody is dead silent.

MIKE: You know the city of New York says to poets like you: "Fuck You."

JUST BEGUN: That's the same thing I say to the rest of the city of New York 'cause this is about the Lower East Side, where everything is jumping . . . humping and you got to go be thumping if you wanna make it through one day to go the next.

MIKE: That's a nice poem.

RUBBERBAND: Great. A little longer and I'll be sleeping.

JUST BEGUN: But that ain't it.

ELECTRIC: That ain't it? No shit? Now we're in for it.

JUST BEGUN: Here goes. . . . It's called: Meeeeeee meeee aahhhhh *(clears his throat)* A Lower East Side poem:

Just once before I die
I wanna climb up on a
tenement sky
to go dream my lungs out till
I cry
then scatter my ashes through
the Lower East Side.

So let me sing my song tonight
Let me feel out of sight
and let all eyes be dry
when they scatter my ashes through
the Lower East Side.

From Houston to Fourteenth Street
from Second Avenue to the Mighty D

Here the hustlers and suckers meet
the faggots and freaks will all get high
on the ashes that have been scattered
through the Lower East Side

There's no other place for me to go be
There's no other place that I can see
There's no other town around that
Brings you up or keeps you down
No food—little heat sweeps by
fancy cars and pimps, bars and juke sloon
and greasy spoons make my spirit fly
with my ashes scattered
through the Lower East Side.

A thief, a junkie I've been
Committed every known sin
Jews and gentiles, bums and men
of style . . . run away childs
police shooting wild
mother's futile wails . . . pushers
making sales . . . dope wheelers
and cocaine dealers . . . smoking pot

Streets are hot and feed off those who
bleed to death
All that's true
All that's true
All that is true
but this ain't no lie
When I ask that my ashes be scattered through
the Lower East Side.

So here I am, look at me
I stand proud as you can see
Please to go be from the Lower East
a street-fighting man
a problem of this land
I am the Philosopher of the criminal mind
a dweller of prison time
a cancer of Rockefellers ghettocide
this concrete tomb is my home
to be long to survive you gotta be strong
you can't be shy less without request
someone will scatter your ashes through
the Lower East Side.

I don't wanna be buried in Puerto Rico
I don't wanna rest in Long Island cemetery
I wanna be near the stabbing, shooting,
gambling, fighting, and unnatural dying
and new birth crying
So please when I die
Don't take me far away—
Keep me nearby.
Take my ashes and scatter them throughout
the Lower East Side.

MIKE: Hey! That was nice.

RUBBERBAND: Not bad. Not bad. I couldn't do better myself.

MIKE: You write, too?

RUBBERBAND: Only on the subways, my man. Only on the subways.

ELECTRIC: Hey, Mike, Hector's calling you.

MIKE: Yeah, Hector.

HECTOR: I thought it over.

MIKE: And what did you decide?

HECTOR: I'll go with you.

MIKE: Are you sure?

HECTOR: I'm sure that if I don't I have to go somewhere else that I don't want to go.

MIKE: Okay, let's go. This is forever, Hector.

HECTOR: It's as far as the word goes.

MIKE: You really fourteen, huh?

HECTOR: Yeah, you scared of it?

MIKE: A little. Just a little. Say good-bye to go your friends, Hector.

ELECTRIC: Look, man. I got to go make me some money. You gonna come, J. B.?

JUST BEGUN: Yeah, let me say good-bye to go Mike.

ELECTRIC: Man, later for that dude. Man, he ain't upping no money except maybe to go Hector.

JUST BEGUN: Okay, later Rubberband.

RUBBERBAND: Later, fellas. Gonna cop me some wine. Later, Mike. See you, Hector.

JUST BEGUN: But that's a cool dude, that dude Mike.

ELECTRIC: Yeah, I know that I like him too, but cool people don't get you money, check it out.

JUST BEGUN: You got to go make that money.

ELECTRIC: Anyway you can, man. Anyway you can make it. If it's there, grab it.

JUST BEGUN: You got this dude's number.

ELECTRIC: He likes to go take pictures of young people and put his head on top of the body of the young guy in the picture. Weird motherfuckers in this world.

HECTOR: Good-bye!

Estorias del Barrio: Un Ghost

Eugene Rodríguez

CHARACTERS

Frank Pérez: *Son of the Ghost*

Gloria Pérez: *Wife of the son of the Ghost*

Ghost: *Ghost of the father of the son of the Ghost*

Time: *July 1990.*

Place: *A Brownstone House in El Barrio*

Act 1: Scene 1

(Lights up on table and two chairs. FRANK *sits checking his lotto numbers in the newspaper. There's a phone stage right. A hat stage left.)*

FRANK: Let's see now. Daily number . . . nothing. Win four . . . nothing. Pick ten . . . nothing. Lotto . . . twenty-four, thirty-six . . . damn! Not even one number this time. Jesus, I can't hit a horse, can't hit a number, forget about Lotto. Yo estoy bien salau, and I need some big money right away. Gotta pay that bill and my man St. Jude ain't workin'. Papi . . . hold it. *(He walks over to the hat and puts his hand on it reverently)* Papi, you know I never asked you for nothin'. When you died, all I took was your hat. Your favorite hat. I took it cause if your spirit is anywhere, I know it's here in this hat. Now, Papi, you know I'm not one to bitch or cry for help. When you died and didn't leave me no money, did I bitch? No. And when my slut sister, Carmen, found that bank account with four thousand dollars for her, did I ask for mine? No! And even when my no-good, pot-smoking junkie no-good brother, Louie Palangana, got that four thousand dollars, I still didn't ask for nothin', did I? But Papi, I need your help now. Please send me a horse. A number. No wait, six numbers. You know, the Lotto numbers. I don't have to hit it big. A million is good. Please, Papi. Please, please, please. Just six little numbers.

*(*GLORIA *enters interrupting his prayer. She has the mail.)*

GLORIA: Hi, Nene. *(Pause)* What are you doing?

FRANK: *(Embarrassed)* Oh, nothing. Nothing.

GLORIA: Are you talking to your father's hat again? No te pongas loco, Nene.

FRANK: *(Returning to his paper)* Tu eres la loca! What do you think I was doing anyway?

GLORIA: I think you were trying to ask your father's ghost to give you a horse to play.

FRANK: Come on, Gloria. You know I don't believe in Ghosteses. *(He crosses himself)*

GLORIA: I know you like to gamble.

FRANK: Come on, Sweetie. You know I don't gamble anymore. That was the old me. This is the new and improved me.

GLORIA: Right . . . right. I knew that. *(She kisses him, then slaps him)*

FRANK: Owww! What was that for?

GLORIA: Just in por si acaso. Remember our serucho? You gamble, I'm gone. No money, no honey!

FRANK: Yeah, yeah, yeah. I remember. *(Opening his paper)* Pendeja!

GLORIA: *(Checking the mail)* What?

FRANK: I said . . . Qué pareja!

GLORIA: Oh . . . I thought you said something else . . . Cabronsito! *(She opens a letter)* You know, if you really wanted to talk to your father that bad, you should have gone to see him in the hospital.

FRANK: I didn't go cause I was mad at him. He used to beat me.

GLORIA: Come on, Frank! You make it sound like he beat you with a whip or something. All he ever did was hit you with the newspaper.

FRANK: Yeah, like I was some kind of dog. I hated that.

GLORIA: He only hit you with the paper when you was acting stupid. He didn't like you gambling, that's all.

FRANK: He used to gamble too!

GLORIA: Frank, he won. You always lose.

FRANK: That's because his mother's spirit gave him the numbers. Told me so himself. Why can't he do that for me? I was his favorite.

GLORIA: Yeah, but you didn't go to his funeral.

FRANK: So! He was dead. I didn't want to see him like that.

GLORIA: Well, maybe his ghost is mad at you for that. *(She opens another letter)* Frank, why are we getting bills for the taxes on the house? I thought we paid this.

FRANK: What?

GLORIA: It says right here, see? Mr. Pérez, you didn't pay your taxes.

FRANK: What taxes are they talking about exactly?

GLORIA: THE TAXES! You know! The real estate taxes. Didn't you pay them?

FRANK: Of course I paid them. Don't pay no attention to that bill. The check is in the mail.

GLORIA: Tú te crees que yo soy una pendeja!

FRANK: Weeeeeelll.

GLORIA: It says here if we don't pay five thousand dollars by the end of the month, they're taking the house!

FRANK: Let me see that. They can't take this house. It must be some kind of computer mistake.

GLORIA: Mistake is right! And you made it! This hasn't been paid for two years!

FRANK: Calm down, honey. *(Backing up)* Ayuda me, Papi!

(A figure dressed all in black emerges from the corner of the stage.)

GLORIA: Your father can't help you now! *(Pause, she feels a presence)* Oye, talking about your father, what about the money he left you? Your emergency money. We could use that. This is certainly an emergency. We can go to the bank right now.

FRANK: Gloria! *(Pause)* My father didn't leave me any money.

GLORIA: What! I remember you showed me four thousand dollars. You told me your father left it to you. If he didn't leave it to you.... Frank! Was that *gambling* money?

FRANK: *(Smiling lamely)* Well . . . errr . . . well . . .

(The GHOST *is upset)*

GLORIA: Uh-huh! I knew it. I knew you couldn't stop!

FRANK: But honey.

GLORIA: Don't give me that honey crap! How could I be so stupid? I know this man . . . why do I always end up listening to his mierda?

FRANK: But honey, it was a sure thing. I won. I hit. You can't be mad cause I won four thousand dollars . . . can you?

GLORIA: *(Tapping her foot)* Where is it? Show it to me. Put it in my hand so I can pay the taxes.

FRANK: I . . . errr . . . errrr . . . I don't have it. *(He sits at the table)*

GLORIA: You lost it, right? No, you don't have to say a thing. *(She sits next to him in frustration)* Oh, God, what are we going to do? Where are we going to get five thousand dollars from, Frank? We're gonna lose the house.

*(*GHOST *puts his arm around them.* FRANK *pats his hand thinking it's* GLORIA. GLORIA *pushes his hand away thinking it's* FRANK.*)*

FRANK: Don't worry, honey. We'll get the money.

GLORIA: How? Betting on a horse? Maybe we'll hit the number! Or . . . or . . . maybe your father will give you the numbers for the Lotto! *(*GHOST *says "no." She feels his* *presence again)* He left everybody in the family four thousand dollars. Even your slutty sister and your no-good brother, Louie. What happened to you?

FRANK: I didn't get anything. *(He goes over to the hat)*

GLORIA: I can't believe he liked Louie Palangana better than you.

FRANK: I guess so. *(Pause)* Maybe Louie needed Papi more than me. I don't know. I didn't want anything from him. Really. Not that way, anyway. I loved my father. I wanted him to spend his money on himself for once. Take a trip. Buy a new suit. Go to Florida with a wicked young woman or something. Louie and Carmen just pissed his money away. Shoot, he could have done that himself. I didn't want his money. I wanted him. I don't want to be alone.

(GHOST is touched by this speech. He wipes his eyes with a large handkerchief.)

GLORIA: You're not alone, honey. I'm here.

FRANK: Yeah, but for how long? We're broke.

GLORIA: Don't blame me, Frank. You know how I am.

TOGETHER: No money, no honey.

GLORIA: Oh, God, I can't take this. We're gonna be homeless. Living on the street like animals. Digging for food in garbage cans. Begging for change on the subway. I won't be poor again, Frank. Either you come up with this money or I'm leaving you.

(GHOST is moved by this speech. He wipes his eyes again. Then as he sees them argue, he claps his hands at them loudly.)

FRANK: Don't do this, honey. I'm sorry. Don't leave. What the hell was that?

GLORIA: You heard it too. Frank . . . there's something here.

FRANK: It's rats, we've got big rats in here.

GLORIA: Mira no me huege. Aquí hay un ghost!

FRANK: There's no such thing.

(The GHOST picks up the hat and floats it across the room. He puts it on the table.)

GLORIA: Did you see that? I'm telling you—Aquí hay un ghost!

FRANK: I didn't see nothin'.

GLORIA: Frank, don't play with me. Your father's hat just floated across the room. It wasn't no wind. Y yo no soy loca. It's him!

FRANK: Who?????

GLORIA: Your father. He's here.

FRANK: You're crazy, Gloria. My father is dead and gone. *(Ghost kicks him in the ass)* Hey! Gloria, please tell me you kicked me?

GLORIA: How could I kick. . . . Did somebody kick you???

FRANK: I . . . I . . . I . . . think so.

GLORIA: See, see. I told you. It is him. I know about these things. Yo no soy una pendeja. I know when there's an espíritu around.

FRANK: Calm down, Gloria. There's a perfectly logical explana . . . (GHOST *picks up the hat and puts it on his head*) Okay, ask him what he wants.

GLORIA: No, you ask him.

FRANK: You ask him.

GLORIA: He was your father. Go ahead, ask him what he wants. (GHOST *shakes the table*)

FRANK: Did . . . did . . . did you see that???

GLORIA: He wants you to go over to the table.

(*She pushes him. He won't go. She pushes him harder. He goes crossing himself.*)

FRANK: Okay, Papi . . . I believe . . . believe me, I believe. What is it . . . what? (GHOST *picks up the paper and puts it in front of him*) What is it?

GLORIA: He wants you to read the paper.

FRANK: I read the paper already.

GLORIA: Read it again. You must have missed something.

FRANK: I read everything important.

(GHOST *forces him to sit at the table and pops him on the head with his paper.*)

FRANK: Owwww! I hate that!

GLORIA: Stop acting stupid.

FRANK: Hey, I'm never stupid! (GHOST *hits him again*) Okay! Okay, I'm stupid. Show me already!

(GHOST *puts the paper on the table, turns the pages, stops and smacks the table. They both jump.*)

GLORIA: Look, Papi. It's one of those unclaimed accounts pages.

FRANK: Check . . . check for Papi's name.

GLORIA: (*After she looks*) It's here!

(GHOST *brings over the phone and holds it for her in the air.* GHOST *dials the number.*)

FRANK: Call . . . call the bank. (GLORIA *dials*)

GLORIA: Hello? I would like to inquire about the Pérez account in today's news. Really! And . . . and who gets the account? What???? How much???

FRANK: What'd they say? What'd they say?

GLORIA: Five . . . five . . . five . . .

FRANK: Five what? Carajo!

GLORIA: He left you $5,555.55 *(FRANK and GHOST cheer together. Then FRANK is depressed. He takes the hat back to where it was)* What's the matter, honey?

FRANK: I don't want it. *(GHOST is disappointed)*

GLORIA: What do you mean you don't want it?

FRANK: I . . . I can't take it.

GLORIA: No sea cabeza dura. We need it.

FRANK: I don't care. I won't accept no blood money. I can't. I just . . . *(GHOST hits him with the paper)* Okay, okay, I take the money.

GLORIA: Good. Let's go to the bank before you change your mind.

(She leaves to get her stuff.)

FRANK: Pa . . . Pa . . . Papi . . . are you there? *(GHOST touches his hair)* You're really there, huh? Papi . . . I . . . I . . . miss . . . you . . . I . . . . really . . . miss you. . . . I don't have nobody to go to the ball game with. And . . . and nobody knows the fight game like you. You told me that Buster kid was going to beat Iron Mike. I shoulda bet it. *(Pause)* Papi, I didn't get a chance to say good-bye to you. I'm sorry I wasn't there, Papi. Can you forgive me? *(Pause)* I still love you, Papi. *(GHOST hugs him, then kisses him. GHOST exits)* Oh wow! *(GLORIA returns)*

GLORIA: What! What happened?

FRANK: He . . . he kissed me. Kissed me good-bye. He didn't kiss Louie Palangana good-bye. *(Pause)* Damn, he's gone.

GLORIA: He's not gone, Papi. He'll always be alive in your heart.

FRANK: Yeah. Yeah, that's right. *(They go to exit. He stops and returns)* Pa . . . Papi . . . thank you for everything, Papi. And thank you for being my father. *(Pause)* Errr. Papi, do you think you could give me the numbers for the Lotto? *(Paper hits him from offstage)*

(Blackout.)

Estorias del Barrio: Special People of International Character

Frank Pérez

CHARACTERS

Casting Agent   *Male in his thirties opening a talent agency*

Tomás   *Latino cab driver and part-time actor*

Sara   *Latina actress in her late twenties*

John   *Latino actor in his thirties*

Sylvia   *Black Latina actress in her twenties*

Act I: Scene 1

(The scene opens with the CASTING AGENT *on the phone at his desk. The desk is filled with the usual things an agent would have on their desk: a copy of* Variety, Backstage, *video-tapes, pictures, résumés, and a phone. The agent is talking with a client about a project they're auditioning for today.)*

AGENT: Don't worry! I'll get you the best Hispanic talent available. Of course not! Look, the script is not a hard sell. Trust me! Hold on, I have another call. Hello? Special People. Who? Oh, yeah, the letterheads and my sign! Where are they? What do you mean there's a problem? Look, Carlos or José. Juan? Fine. Look, Juan, if I don't get my sign and my letterheads here by five P.M., I don't want them! Comprende? Yes, of course I want them the way they're printed! That's the way I ordered them! You guys better get your act together and have my sign and letterhead here pronto! No buts—bye! *(Soothing voice)* So, babe, don't worry about a thing. I'll let you know how things are going. You'll be by later, right? Fine. Listen, I have to go. Some calls are coming in and I have to get ready for these actors. I'll call you. Hello, Special People, can I help you? Yes, auditions start at ten o'clock. . . .

(As the AGENT *continues talking on the phone, a man enters past a row of folding chairs, stage left. He has a short jacket, cab driver's cap, manila envelope, and a pencil he keeps behind his ear. He walks toward the* AGENT's *office.)*

TOMÁS: Excuse me, is this the place for the auditions?

(The AGENT *motions for him to sit down in the waiting room.* TOMÁS *looks at his watch, sighs and goes toward the chairs and notices a mirror at the end of the row of chairs. He looks at the mirror, grins, fixes his hair and jacket, then sits.)*

AGENT: *(Enters waiting room with sign-in sheet and tray)* Hi!

TOMÁS: Hi. I'm Tomás. I'm here for the auditions. Is this the right place? 'Cause I didn't see no sign or nothing on the door.

AGENT: Yes, this is the right place. I'm expecting that sign today. Can I have your picture and résumé please?

TOMÁS: Sure, here you go.

AGENT: Thanks. *(Looking over résumé)* You're here early.

TOMÁS: Well, I'm double-parked downstairs. I just wanted to give you my résumé and sign in as soon as possible. I don't have a lot of work on there, but it's quality work and I'm a really good actor. *(He grins)*

AGENT: I'm sure you are but we don't start till nine o'clock. Here's the sign-in sheet and I'll see you in a few minutes. If anyone asks for me, tell them I'll be right back.

TOMÁS: Nature calls, huh?

AGENT: Excuse me?

TOMÁS: Nothing . . . heh, heh. *(When* AGENT *leaves,* TOMÁS *shakes his head and rolls his eyes)* Stupid! How could I say that?

(He signs the sheet and begins to leave as a pregnant woman enters. She is in pain and upon seeing the chairs begins trying to sit. TOMÁS *looks at her with concern.)*

TOMÁS: Are you all right?

SARA: *(Fanning herself)* Yes, I'll be all right in a minute. *(*TOMÁS *turns to leave. When he nears exit, she grabs her side in pain)* Owwwww!

TOMÁS: *(He moves toward her)* Lady, do you need a doctor or something?

SARA: No, no. I'll be okay . . . I think. *(Looking around room)* What kind of place is this?

TOMÁS: It's a talent agency . . . you know, for auditions and casting. You okay?

SARA: Yes . . . thank you. *(She smiles,* TOMÁS *turns toward the exit. As soon as he reaches it, she yells)* Ayyyyy dios mío!!!!

TOMÁS: *(*TOMÁS *runs back to her)* Lady, por favor! I think you need a doctor or something!

SARA: *(Fanning herself)* I need . . . I need . . . water!

TOMÁS: I think there's a watercooler in the hall. I'll get you some! *(He runs toward exit. As soon as he reaches it, she yells)*

SARA: Don't leave me! *(He runs back to her)* Talk to me! Keep my mind off the pain. So . . . are you a talent agent?

TOMÁS: No, I'm here for an audition.

SARA: *(Slightly disappointed)* Oh . . . it doesn't seem to be very crowded for a talent agency. It's getting warm in here again.

TOMÁS: Can I get you that water?

SARA: That would be great! *(He heads for the door and reaches exit)* Ayyy!!

TOMÁS: *(He runs back to her)* Lady, I'm taking you to the hospital. I'm double-parked.

SARA: No, no, it's all right. So what . . . you're auditioning?

TOMÁS: Yeah.

SARA: And you're the only one here?

TOMÁS: Well, for now.

SARA: *(Holding belly)* That's good.

TOMÁS: Lady, are you sure I can't call you an ambulance?

SARA: Don't worry, I know how to take care of this. *(She starts to punch her stomach)* Damn baby! Damn baby!

TOMÁS: Mira está loca!!! Lady, what are you doing?!!

SARA: That's okay. *(She removes a fake belly)* I feel much better. Where's the sign-in sheet? I'm after you. (TOMÁS *in shock, just points)* Not bad, huh? I had you going pretty good.

TOMÁS: *(Defensively)* What?! . . . No, I knew you were an actress!

SARA: Yeah, right. I had you running back and forth *(she laughs and imitates an old lady's voice)* "Can I get you that water?" Sangano! I'm sorry if I totally humiliated you.

TOMÁS: But you didn't!

SARA: Fine then. I'm Sara.

TOMÁS: I'm Tomás.

SARA: Tomás? Not too neutral, but it might work for you. What part are you auditioning for?

TOMÁS: Well . . . I don't know.

SARA: No! Don't tell me. Let me guess, I'm good at this. Let's see *(she looks him over)* I would say you're auditioning for . . . the part of a cab driver!

TOMÁS: I am a cab driver.

SARA: What?

TOMÁS: I am a cab driver!

SARA: *(She pauses, looks at him and thinks)* Wow! That's really great! You're already in character for your cab driver audition! I have to try that . . . does it work for you every time?

TOMÁS: I drive a cab for a living! I'm just here for these auditions!

SARA: Fine. Anything you say.

TOMÁS: Thank you! *(He looks at his watch)* I hope my cab is okay.

SARA: In midtown? Forget it! It probably got towed away by now.

TOMÁS: No way! I got some tourists in the cab soaking up the New York atmosphere.

SARA: So what's the story with this audition? What are they looking for? *(She looks in her oversized bag)* Cause I got it all here.

TOMÁS: I don't know. The agent took my résumé and said: "I'll be back."

SARA: Good. . . . *(She removes from her bag a wig and puts it on)* Isn't it great? I bought it for a Cher look-alike audition.

TOMÁS: But you don't look like Cher!

SARA: I know . . . but I played her from the inside and the wig helped a lot.

TOMÁS: Did you get the part?

SARA: No, but I did get a callback. Plus I use the wig for other auditions, so it's an investment. *(She puts the wig back)* I hope it's some good work. Sometimes you go to an audition and it's really "bad" work.

TOMÁS: Bad work? What do you mean bad work?

SARA: You know . . . "bad work" . . . negative image stuff.

TOMÁS: If it's work, how can it be bad? You're getting paid, right?

SARA: It's not as simple as that. You see, I'm able to get commercial work or voice-over work in Spanish or English. That's if the only work around is bad. Some people can't do that . . . I only want that one juicy part that can get me noticed. *(She looks at him)* Haven't I seen you in something?

TOMÁS: Well, I haven't done a lot of work, but I did do some work on TV.

SARA: *(She goes into her bag and removes a pair of fake breasts)* These I used for a sexy receptionist part. *(She puts them on with a sexy voice)* Hi, my name is Tess, and these . . . are my breasts! *(As she is saying this, another actor enters. He stops when he sees her with breasts on)* Hi! *(She realizes she has them on and takes them off quickly)*

JOHN: Is this the place for the auditions?

TOMÁS: This is it. Look, Sara, watch my spot. I have to go check on my fares. I'll be right back.

SARA: No problem. *(TOMÁS exits,* JOHN *signs in and sits)* Hi! . . . god, I hope they start seeing people soon.

JOHN: Have you been waiting long?

SARA: No . . . but I have another audition in about an hour and I have to absolutely positively make that one.

JOHN: It looks like we're both early for this one *(he laughs nervously)*. I'm John Rivera.

SARA: Sara Silva.

JOHN: Great name.

SARA: Thank you. I thought of it myself. You look a little nervous. Are you?

JOHN: Yeah, a little. But I don't know why. I've done this a lot of times.

SARA: I know what you mean. It never gets easy. Have we worked together before?

JOHN: I don't know . . . maybe . . . I've done all of the work around. Were you in . . .

SARA: No, no, don't tell me, I'll get it. I'm good at this. Let's see . . . I got it! Shakespeare in the Park! Right?!

JOHN: *(Sarcastically)* Well, I have done it. Were you in the Hispanic version?

SARA: I was in that one! I mean I had two lines. I remember you, though. You're very good. What have you been doing? That was a while back.

JOHN: *(Frustrated)* I haven't done as much as I'd like, but it's my fault, I guess. I've just been so busy doing real acting work, you know like . . . waiting tables, bartending, sales.

SARA: You have to survive somehow and this is the life we've chosen.

JOHN: Same way we can get into it, we can get out of it.

(The AGENT *enters the office.)*

AGENT: Good morning.

SARA: Good morning!

JOHN: Hi!

AGENT: Ah, you both signed in. Great! Where's Mr. . .

SARA: He went to check on his car. He'll be right back. That's a great suit!

AGENT: Thank you.

SARA: Mano a Mano?

AGENT: Excuse me? Oh . . . no, I didn't get it there.

SARA: This is a very nice office, but I've never heard of this agency before.

AGENT: This is a new agency. As a matter of fact, you're my first clients to come to audition. Can I have your résumés, please? Thank you. I guess we're all lucky today. *(Looking at résumés)* I have an excellent project for you all to audition for, and you're the first ones here. I'll be starting in a few minutes. Oh, and if you see someone come in with a sign for my office, send them in. Thanks. (AGENT *exits to office*)

SARA: *(SARA watches the* AGENT *leave)* Sure! No problem! A rookie! I knew it! I hope this is not a waste of time.

JOHN: He did say it's an excellent project to audition for.

SARA: *(Thinking almost to herself)* Yeah, but so many times you go to an audition and it's . . . just bad work. You know? Not at all what you want or trained for. But it's work. I'm lucky in a way, but sometimes . . . *(she looks at her watch)* Where is this guy? I should have taken his turn.

(SYLVIA, a black latina actress, enters.)

SYLVIA: *(She reacts upon seeing SARA)* Ave Maria! And my day was going so good! I knew it! I got up too early, too!

SARA: *(Antagonistic)* Here we go again . . . Hello, Sylvia.

SYLVIA: Hello nothing, Sara. Who told you about this audition?

JOHN: *(To SARA)* What's the problem?

SARA: This is Sylvia. She swears that any audition we're both on for she doesn't get because she's a black latina actress and I'm not . . . fortunately . . . just kidding, Sylvia.

SYLVIA: *(To JOHN)* What! You see! This is what I'm talking about! Look, I'm sorry. This is a waste of time. Now I have two hours to kill. John?

JOHN: Yes?

SYLVIA: Don't you remember me? We did that sixteenth-century revival? Remember the tragic-comedy musical?

JOHN: Yeah . . . Sylvia. How you doing?

SYLVIA: So, so. What's up with you?

JOHN: Not too much. Haven't done that much acting work. I've been too busy with my forty-seven part-time jobs. I've been thinking of quitting, though. I just get to a certain level and that's it. Maybe it's me. I shouldn't be so choosey with parts.

(TOMÁS enters, counting some money.)

SARA: Finally! The agent was looking for you. He'll be out in a minute.

TOMÁS: Tell him I'm ready and I got my tip.

SARA: Tip?! You mean those people you left waiting in the cab gave you a tip? Ave Maria!

TOMÁS: Only in New York.

SARA: Only tourists in New York!

TOMÁS: *(Looking around office)* Man, it got crowded in here fast.

SARA: *(To* SYLVIA *and* JOHN*)* Guys, this is Tomás. He's auditioning too. He's in character already.

JOHN: Hi.

SYLVIA: Hi! . . . are you auditioning for a cab driver?

TOMÁS: Ay dios mío! How you doing? *(Shaking his head)*

(The AGENT *returns to the waiting room.)*

AGENT: Ah . . . Mr. . . . Thomas, are you ready? *(The agent notices* SYLVIA*)* Oh, Hello! Can I help you?

SYLVIA: *(Very defensive)* Yes! I'm here to audition. *(To* JOHN*)* Watch.

AGENT: Oh . . . well . . . we're auditioning Hispanic talent only today.

SYLVIA: *(Trying to remain calm)* I know that. I'm a latina actress of color . . . we do exist.

AGENT: Oh, I beg your pardon. Can I have your résumé? Thanks and again, it's just that you're all so . . . different. Anyway *(to* TOMÁS*)* follow me, please. *(*AGENT *and* TOMÁS *enter* AGENT's *office)* Welcome, Tomás. I'm Mr. Warren. Tell me about yourself and the work you've done.

TOMÁS: Well, I'm not a trained actor. I'm what you call a natural talent. But I've done work on TV. I played a rapist on *Americas Unwanted.* I also played a crooked super, an illegal alien assassin, and I also played a good guy once. But I was killed in the end by police—mistaken identity. But if I can I'd like to show you some of my . . . ah . . . characters! Yeah!

AGENT: Fine. Go ahead. But keep it short. *(He begins to take notes)*

TOMÁS: First, this is a heroin addict *(he slowly nods to the left).* This is a methadone addict *(he slowly nods to the right).* This is a heroin addict on methadone *(he slowly begins to nod forward).*

AGENT: Okay! Tomás, I've seen enough. You're obviously, ah . . . a very animated personality and from your résumé I can see that you have worked, although not a lot. I think we can possibly work something out. Why don't you take these sides, read them over, and I'll call you back to video your reading.

TOMÁS: Great! *(*TOMÁS *exits)* All right, I got it!

SARA: What happened?

TOMÁS: I got a callback!

SYLVIA: Did you read any of the script?

TOMÁS: No, but he gave me some sides *and* he said he'd *call* me *back*. Callback!

SARA: That's not a callback! You just had an interview. *(JOHN laughs at TOMÁS)*

TOMÁS: What are you laughing at? Don't you be laughing at me cause I get work, my friend. *(AGENT enters with sides for actors)*

AGENT: In order to speed things up so it won't get too crowded, I'm giving you all sides to read now. So you can look them over.

SARA: *(Looks at watch)* Great! I think I'll make that appointment.

AGENT: Also, before I meet with you individually I want to tell you about the project. The director is a well-known one, but unfortunately I can't mention his name right now. We do need Hispanics for certain parts in this project, but we're not looking for just anybody. While the script is a bit raw right now there will be plenty of changes. But believe me, it's a great opportunity for the right person. So I want you to keep this in mind when you read over these sides.

SARA: Don't worry. We're all aware of the changes a script goes through.

AGENT: Good! Now let's see . . . police sergeant. *(He gives side to JOHN)* Woman *(he gives sides to both ladies)*. Okay! I'll give you all a couple of minutes, then we'll start.

(AGENT exits. The actors are all reading the sides. TOMÁS starts laughing, enjoying what he's reading, while others are shaking their heads in disgust. SARA reads quietly. When she is finished, she looks out and lets out a sigh.)

TOMÁS: Hey! This stuff is funny. It's the same as the work I did on *Americas Unwanted.*

SYLVIA: You see! I knew it! I've been around long enough to know when I hear that phrase: "The script is a little raw," I know what's coming—a bad script.

TOMÁS: Mira, please! It's not that bad. Besides, I think the guy really likes us.

JOHN: When you've been around long enough, you develop a sense of pride and integrity.

TOMÁS: Pride and integrity don't pay the rent, and they didn't help me get these: *(He pulls from his wallet two cards and talks like an announcer)* My AFTRA and SAG cards for the TV and film unions. *(Gloating)* I don't leave home without it. *(He laughs)*

JOHN: How did you get those cards? You know how long it took me to get those?

TOMÁS: Two for one deal, bro'! *Americas Unwanted* got me the TV union card and the TV union got me the film union card.

JOHN: You know how hard some people have to work to get those cards and you play some thief and get them just like that! Damn, that's what's wrong with this business.

TOMÁS: Excuse me! I did not play a thief! My friend . . . I was a rapist!

JOHN: *(Shakes his head in disgust)* Sylvia, do you want to help me run through these lines so I can get this over with?

SYLVIA: I might as well, cause I'm not auditioning. I don't want to read this stuff. *(JOHN and SYLVIA step to center stage, spotlights come up on both of them)*

SYLVIA: Sarge, you have to give me a break! I need more time. I'm close on this one, I can feel it.

JOHN: More time! You know how much property damage you've caused looking for this phantom killer . . . and so far no leads. Not even a suspect!

SYLVIA: I know, I know, but I feel a break coming soon!

JOHN: Let me guess—you have a gut feeling, right?

SYLVIA: Of course, Sarge.

JOHN: Look. I'm not a hard guy, but you have to understand. The captain has a special interest in this case. My butt is on the line on this one!

SYLVIA: Just twenty-four hours, Sarge.

JOHN: *(He sighs and rubs his stomach)* They don't pay me enough for this. . . . All right. . . . I'll cover you for twenty-four hours, but that's it! After that you're on your own. And if I get any more reports of property damage, you're on suspension! Now get the hell out of here! *(Lights up)*

SYLVIA: Not bad, John.

JOHN: Yeah, right! Now I'm an under four lines actor.

TOMÁS: That was okay, but let me show you how it's done, son. Sara, can you read with me?

SARA: *(She sighs)* Oh well, let's give it a shot.

(Lights come down on them. A spotlight comes up on both. TOMÁS *looks around and looks out to audience.)*

TOMÁS: Ah . . . the magic of theater.

SARA: Hi, papi, what can I do to you or for you?

TOMÁS: You can start by telling me your name.

SARA: Maria.

TOMÁS: *(Like a psycho)* Beautiful name *(looking her over)* Beautiful body . . . beautiful neck.

SARA: Jew want me baby? Jew have to pay dee money and I'm all yours.

TOMAS: Pay? Pay? Oh my chiquita you don't understand . . . crime does not pay! *(He fakes stabbing her and lights come up)*

SYLVIA: That's it! I've seen enough! This is bullshit!

SARA: Hey! I didn't get to my good lines yet . . . why jew do this to me!

SYLVIA: Sara, what's wrong with you? You're more talented than this!

SARA: This is work, Sylvia. You're gonna get me better work?

JOHN: Sylvia's right. This is the type of work that's making me think of leaving the business.

TOMÁS: If you want to give up, then do it. But don't get on her case for wanting to work *(looks at watch)*. Coño, I hope I didn't get a ticket. *(Looks at office)*

JOHN: *(Angry)* Look, I'm not quitting because I'm giving up. You just have no idea what it's like to go on countless auditions and because I don't look Hispanic, people tell me I'm not "Hispanic enough." Then they try to tell me: "You should change your name" all the time.

TOMÁS: So?! Change your name! What's the big deal? I mean if someone came up to me and told me I could get more work by changing my name, man, I would have changed it to . . . Sol Solberg even!

JOHN: That's not me. That's not what I'm about. I'm a professional.

TOMAS: *(Applauds)* Very nice. *(John frustrated with him, sits)* You know, you talk about names? I was the only Puerto Rican in my neighborhood. When I would pick up my mother from shopping, we'd walk home and I'd hear some people say things under their breath. They didn't think I heard them, but I did and I know my mother did too. But she never flinched. She would say: "Ignore the ignorant." I did and it worked for me.

JOHN: Your mother . . .

TOMÁS: Yo! Cuidao!

JOHN: Relax, you mother was right. Ignore the ignorant, which is exactly what I'm going to do. *(He turns to his sides and starts reading)*

TOMÁS: If they're gonna offer me good money to play a bad guy. Hey, there's no choice. (SYLVIA *gets ready to leave)*

JOHN: Sylvia, aren't you auditioning?

SYLVIA: Nah, there's nothing for me here. It was nice seeing you again.

JOHN: You should at least read for this guy.

SARA: *(Antagonistic)* What's wrong, Sylvia? Leaving so soon?

SYLVIA: *(Angrily moves toward* SARA*)* Don't you start with me, Sara, cause I'll kick your . . . (JOHN *moves to hold back* SYLVIA*)*

TOMÁS: All right, a fight! Dalé! Arráñala! Come on, man! Don't hold them back!

JOHN: Come on, Sylvia! Forget it! It's not worth it.

SYLVIA: No, I'm tired of this shit! And I'm definitely not going to take anything from her! Everywhere it's the same thing! Black theaters say I'm not black. Latino theaters say I'm black. Where the hell am I supposed to go?

SARA: I'll tell you where to go.

(SYLVIA lunges at SARA while JOHN is holding SYLVIA back.)

TOMÁS: Let her go, man! Ahora sí!

(The AGENT walks in to see all this commotion.)

AGENT: What's going on here? *(They all stop and look at the* AGENT*)*

TOMÁS: Oh . . . we're all getting into character. *(*SYLVIA *and* SARA *fix themselves)*

AGENT: Oh . . . I see, you actors! First of all I'd like to say that in looking over your résumés I'm quite impressed with the caliber of talent we have here. I spoke to the director and he'll be here this afternoon to look at videotapes of your auditions. And judging from your résumés, you'll all get serious consideration for these parts. *(The actors all look at each other. A knock is heard on the door and the* AGENT *moves toward the exit)* Yes? Finally! My sign! Great. Thanks. Well, today you can all take part in the unveiling of my new office sign. *(He leans sign on chairs and removes cover from sign. The sign reads: "Special People of International Character" with the initials S.P.I.C. underneath)* Isn't it great? I thought of it myself! *(The actors stare in disbelief)*

JOHN: Do you know what those initials of your sign stand for?

AGENT: What? S.P.I.C. Spic? Spic!!! Oh no! It was purely unintentional! I'll change it! I'll change it to . . . Exotic! How's that?

JOHN: *(He hands the* AGENT *his sides)* I don't think I'll be auditioning for this part. You ready, Sylvia?

SYLVIA: Sorry, nothing personal. But I have another appointment.

AGENT: But I'll change the sign! What's the problem?

JOHN: So, Sara! It was nice seeing you again.

SARA: Yeah . . . but I think I can find some other work. Sylvia, where's that audition you're going to?

SYLVIA: Oh no you don't. *(The actors start to leave)*

TOMÁS: You guys are crazy. This is money you're blowing!

SYLVIA: Tomás, you mean after all we've said, you still don't get it?

TOMÁS: Look, I know I'm going to make some money.

SYLVIA: I feel sorry for you. Come on, Sara. Let's see if we can find a meter maid downstairs.

TOMÁS: Meter maid? *(He looks at the actors, then at* AGENT*)* You know, this is bad work, negative image stuff. *(He runs offstage after actors)* Come on. Don't call the meter maids. It's gonna cost me money! Coño man!

(Lights fade.)

II

Gender Plays

Just the Boys

Dennis Moritz, with concepts and interludes by Michael Le Land II, and additional dialogue by Shelita Birchett

CHARACTERS

Gerry

Dave

Walt

Ralf

Evelyn

Cathy

Linda

Jody

Frank

Act I: Scene 1

(Main stage area is garage, professional space with tools, dark major lighting, cars, and dense cluttered spaces. Various places to perch or lean: crates, jacks, swivel chairs, intense local lights focus on work, characters in garage wander with purpose in search of tools, parts or subject. This area is middle of actions, but not precise middle of acting area. Should be on a shift to stage right. Hazy, moody light as if humid. Brown, black, and gray colors.

Away from center are various staging areas with minimal or no props, used when action takes place outside the garage. Feel should be realistic with sharp edge . . . pushed.

In garage, GERRY, WALT, RALF *working, initially take no notice of* DAVE. DAVE *addresses audience.)*

DAVE: *(To audience)* Men don't talk about anything. Objects. Mechanisms. Theories. Cryptic. Difficult for me. Cryptic. Men put this tense encasement around what's said. Cryptic. For instance, I knew a sixtyish circle-track rider, Lucky Strikes folded into the sleeve of his white T-shirt. Met him at a suburban gas station, under a tarp at the back, the car he drove round and round for years. "Ran that. Some surface rust on her now. She could run. Put her in the corner and hung there. Fight all the way. Grab the wheel all the way. Surface rust on her now. She could run. Want some whisky?" Like that pressed out phrase.

My friend Gerry builds race cars. I have hung for years in the garage and taken in the look of cars. We go over topics, do technical things, make up theories about events, assess hidden motives, play the game, make the deal, speak with fondness and fear about the obstacle.

GERRY: Rat motor.

WALT: Mouse motor.

RALF: Mopar.

ALL THE BOYS: Corvette.

WALT: Vette.

RALF: GTO.

WALT: Allard.

RALF: Cunningham.

GERRY: Devin.

ALL: Cars.

DAVE: Metal and plastic fabrications that move. Functional art. We do the deal. The personal is a slant and not specific, falling under returns to topics.

(As DAVE *does the following,* GERRY *looks up and responds in dialogue.)*

DAVE: Nervous about things?

GERRY: Why should I be nervous about things?

DAVE: Nervous about things?

GERRY: Why should I be nervous about things?

DAVE: Nervous about things?

GERRY: Why should I be nervous about things?

*(*GERRY *continues work.)*

DAVE: Then tirade on money. Those who fail to pay, the intricate and talented work that goes unacknowledged and uncompensated: Art. Right. Art.

Emotion means esthetics. That curve and slope. That grill, the sideview and overall view, structures with no excess or dazzle. Fit and fabrications. Under the hood, for instance, where each hose or harness is routed simply. Or the '50's and '60's esthetics of dazzle and gaudy fullness. Function. Or the excess that means an esthetic expression. I go on. Feelings mean . . . feel is a twist of the wheel and a corner taken well as we drive, each wheel planted and screeching, emotion is a race done strategically. Emotion is a sign-off statement and a beer. "Glad you stopped by." This is a little bit about how man don't say anything.

Act I: Scene 2

(Lights up showing GERRY *wearing a suit jacket over mechanics outfit and glasses. The rest of the boys sit on chairs in the audience as though in a classroom.* JODY, CATHY *and* LINDA *are frozen in very dynamic positions. They become animated and physically interact with* GERRY *when he comes near them).*

GERRY: *(To the boys)* Casanova 71. Marcello Mastroianni. See the picture? It's the game, nothing easy. Harder ones make for attraction. Oh, I had a lot of easy. *(Moves toward* CATHY*)* Some have loved me to the extent that it appalled me. *(Moves toward* LINDA*)* I like the ones who are emotional and erratic. It's the challenge. Figure them out better than they know themselves. Get on them about their own approach and feelings before they even know their own pattern. *(*GERRY *goes to phone)* What's life, anyway? Tell me life is not about challenge . . . *(*GERRY *goes: "Ring, ring."* CATHY *answers her cellular phone as though she has been waiting for his call and says: "Gerry, Gerry."* GERRY *hangs up the phone without speaking).* And recreation? Turn the magic key. Figure out the mythic puzzle. I would not be satisfied with a straight-ahead relationship that was strictly lovey-dovey sitting in front of the TV, summer vacations in a trailer home. The Bickerstaffs. The Smithonians. You have to watch it, man. It's easy to regard loving relationships like a plaque on the side of a recreational vehicle, old and done with. It's a mental thing *(moves toward* JODY*)* as much as a physical thing. I want to be on my toes. Let the bitch rip.

(Lights dim.)

Act I: Scene 3

(Lights up in garage. GERRY *sleeping on stage.* EVELYN *enters in a stocking mask. She locates a wrench and makes as if to attack. Suddenly screams.* GERRY *wakes up as if under attack and screams. She removes the stocking mask. They embrace. The boys enter. At first,* GERRY *and* EVELYN *continue. When they see boys, they are embarrassed, stop.)*

GERRY: Well, Evelyn's the one, man, Evelyn. The rest do not matter. I'm clearing them out, Evelyn.

Act I: Scene 4

(We hear GERRY's *answering machine on the loudspeakers.)*

GERRY: *(His voice on the machine)* You know what this is, you know what it does. *(Answering machine beep)*

(Lights up on LINDA *visible on telephone.)*

LINDA: *(On telephone to the answering machine)* Gerry, ce soire, Linda. Chez le mouse, besoine mon amour, call me. *(*LINDA *hangs up the phone and goes straight to* GERRY. *When* LINDA *enters the garage space, the boys snap out a doo-wop cadence and make a high-hat cymbal noise)*

BOYS: *(Simultaneously)* Tche, che, tche, che, tche, che, tche, che, tche, Linda!

LINDA: *(Addresses each line to different boy. To* GERRY*)* You don't understand my limits or how I love you.

BOYS: *(Simultaneously)* Tche, che, tche, che, tche, che, tche, che, tche, Linda!

LINDA: *(Gasping to* RALF*)* I am sick now. Please stop off at the pharmacist and get some medicine. Of course, I'll pay.

BOYS: *(Simultaneously)* Tche, che, tche, che, tche, che, tche, che, tche, Linda!

LINDA: *(Sternly to* WALT*)* Why did you walk into my room? Do you think you can walk anywhere you want? Are you from New York?

BOYS: *(Simultaneously)* Tche, che, tche, che, tche, che, tche, che, tche, Linda!

LINDA: *(Matter of factly to* GERRY*)* You wish to control me with love, but I prefer to be controlled by money.

BOYS: *(Simultaneously)* Tche, che, tche, che, tche, che, tche, che, tche, Linda!

LINDA: *(Plaintively to* DAVE*)* I need ten thousand dollars to cover the expenses of this house or else I loose everything. I am in this situation because my father reneged on our agreement and he stole money from a bank account in trust for me.

BOYS: *(Simultaneously)* Tche, che, tche, che, tche, che, tche, che, tche, Linda!

LINDA: *(Alluringly to* RALF*)* If you pay me a hundred dollars, I'll let you fuck.

BOYS: *(Simultaneously)* Tche, che, tche, che, tche, che, tche, che, tche, Linda!

LINDA: *(Passionately to* GERRY*)* Not that way, touch me like this, from this angle. Slower. Point up, let me turn around. Tell me how you like the look of my breasts. Say beautiful. Stroke. Easy. Pinch a little. Harder. Easy.

BOYS: *(Simultaneously)* Tche, che, tche, che, tche, che, tche, che, tche, Linda!

LINDA: *(Plaintive to* DAVE*)* Don't talk about going out now.

BOYS: *(Simultaneously)* Tche, che, tche, che, tche, che, tche, che, tche, Linda!

LINDA: *(Imperiously to* WALT*)* Why should I go out with you?

(Lights dim. Boys exit except for GERRY. LINDA *and* GERRY *stay.)*

GERRY: Here's a hundred dollars. Take off your clothes. *(He puts money down)*

LINDA: Thanks. We'll fuck. *(She begins to take off clothes and prepare)*

GERRY: *(Sits, watches. When* LINDA *is nearly finished and ready,* GERRY *jumps up)* Sorry, I can't do it for money. Don't call me anymore. Stop ringing the phone. I mean it, goddamn it.

(He leaves money. Lights down.)

Act I: Scene 5

(GERRY on phone in garage, as if in midconversation. CATHY talks on phone in her satellite area.)

GERRY: Don't call me anymore. I'm finished. I mean it.

CATHY: That's right.

GERRY: It'll really mess things up if you call, so don't.

CATHY: Don't call me anymore. Fuck off!

(Lights dim on GERRY. Lights stay up on CATHY who dials phone. We hear phone ring and pick-up by answering machine and JODY's voice.)

JODY: *(JODY's voice on her answering machine)* You have reached 976-mojo, to put the roots on someone, press one.

("Black Magic Woman," the song, plays. The scene is set for a seance/spell-casting. CATHY sits at conjuring table. JODY brings in lava lamp, sets it on table to begin ceremony. JODY wears black glasses, jewelry, and other artifacts that signify her supernatural connection.)

JODY: Gerry's psychic aura compelled you. The blues and yellows that surround his body are vital, lively, but scattered and unfocused. His psychic aura is pushed out and immature. His undeveloped state attracts your deep, healing spirit.

CATHY: Gerry had so much talent. Those cars *are* artworks. Brilliant. Brilliant hands, and all that energy! *(CATHY taps her fingers, convulses legs once or twice)*

JODY: A man possessed, demonized by his erratic gifts.

CATHY: I felt that.

JODY: You tried to open up Gerry's eyes to some obvious principles. His life is difficult, economically precarious, virtually hand to mouth. You laid out principles of investment, image, marketing. He could have been an important player in the mainstream influential world.

CATHY: A media darling. Television spots.

JODY: But a dark, erratic spirit. A man-child. Well.

CATHY: Doesn't that new young bird, Evelyn, sum up all the points about Gerry. Just a young vulnerable bird, really. Evelyn adds nothing to Gerry's life. She teaches him nothing.

JODY: Evelyn is destined to be exploited by his hungry, restless soul.

CATHY: Really?

JODY: Here. Follow the written instructions. This will straighten Gerry's aura out. *(She blows out candles, snaps one, viciously)* These instruments will help him to . . . mature. Growth hurts, but is good for karma.

*(*JODY *and* CATHY *engage in bad African dancing, music.* JODY *watches* CATHY *perform the following ritual. She stands in the background and gives supportive signals.)*

CATHY: *(Wears boxer shorts under her skirt. She takes them off as she begins her speech)* You left these big-sized drawers, washed so many times they're soft.

(Examines them) These have been used already. Even the way they are. I sprinkled a special white powder I bought. Lit black candles. Said this weird language. The weird language was in the instructions given to me by a very effective lady. The powder dried them out. What awful smells there. At first I could barely go near them. However, it settles in a few days. The smell seeps in deep. The smell stops, disappears, dissipates.

(Puts pants to her cheek) The powder spreads out and takes its course. Whoever wore them before, softens up. Don't expect what was in them to be as hard now as it was. Here's a note just to let you know. I also include a few reminders left around my house from when you were here a few weeks ago. It's part of the process.

(Digs into her pants and pulls out pubic hair. Winces, then puts it in the envelope. After a pause, she puts pants on under her skirt) They're on their way. Surprise!

(Lights dim on CATHY).

JODY: Occult. Voodoo. Intellectual concepts. Just belief systems. Powerful. Voodoo. Occult. People come clean and show themselves right away. Go right there. My spells and chants. Need that. Need me. Booga, wooga, cooga, booga, cooga, googa. Puts them straight. I put them straight. Straighten out their karma. Aligned with their stars . . . that personal melodrama just swirls around otherwise. They need control! My job is control.

Act I: Scene 6

(Lights up on kitchen in GERRY's *house.* EVELYN *and* GERRY *making love on floor. The following passage is a simultaneous internal monologue. Characters do not hear each other until after sex.)*

EVELYN: Why do you want me?

GERRY: You're the one, Evelyn.

EVELYN: You have so much more experience.

GERRY: I mean it.

EVELYN: You're the one been everywhere with the race cars . . .

GERRY: You're absolutely beautiful.

EVELYN: Earlier on the road as a musician.

GERRY: I like your looks.

EVELYN: I don't know anything. Haven't been anywhere.

GERRY: Intelligence.

EVELYN: All those friends and women around.

GERRY: Talent.

EVELYN: I don't measure up to them . . .

GERRY: You're the most talented person I ever met.

EVELYN: They're attractive and know what they're about.

GERRY: You're beautiful, Evelyn.

EVELYN: I don't know about anything.

GERRY: Right.

EVELYN: I'm confused.

GERRY: You're in incredible shape.

EVELYN: What can I do?

GERRY: I mean it.

EVELYN: My face is full of zits today. Please don't look at my face that is full of zits, pimples.

GERRY: You work out all the time.

EVELYN: People always call you on the telephone, no one calls me.

GERRY: You're an athlete.

EVELYN: I don't have any money. I owe the college and the hospital money. I can't pay. I only jogged three times last week. I think I'm getting fat. I know how excess weight turns you off. Sometimes I eat a half-gallon of ice cream in one sitting. What will you do then? When you see me do that?

GERRY: When you see me do that. When you see me do that. When you see me do that.

EVELYN: I want to jump out the window. Run out in front of a car. Tear my clothes off and jump off a bridge.

(EVELYN *climaxes. They dress after sex. In the following dialogue, characters talk to each other*).

EVELYN: You'll hate me if I stay. I won't have any money. What if I want to lock myself in a room and paint day after day?

GERRY: You're a brilliant painter, Evelyn. That's fine with me. Do anything you want. Anything that makes you happy. Just stay here in this house. Don't worry about the money.

EVELYN: How can I believe you? All those girlfriends who keep calling up?

GERRY: I was always up front and honest with you, Evelyn. I told you about everything. You know that. Those are people I was involved with before we met. I told them I'm finished with them. I had to finish up my involvements, like I said. Now it's done. I'm doing things just the way I told you I would.

EVELYN: What if my face turns into one big zit? Then what? And if I eat cookies and ice cream anyway?

GERRY: I don't care. You're beautiful.

EVELYN: What if I only jog three times a week from now on?

GERRY: Two times is okay.

EVELYN: What about how I can't keep my hands off you and what if I make you satisfy me whenever you walk in?

GERRY: I'll deal with that.

EVELYN: Promise?

GERRY: Here are the keys to a car I put together for you. I want you to have it. Just stay here. Come over to the garage. If you need money for groceries later today, or need money for anything, ask for whatever you want. You're the one, Evelyn. I mean it.

(EVELYN *takes the keys and holds onto them tightly. Lights dim in kitchen space.* GERRY *passes directly to garage.* GERRY *begins work with the boys.*)

Act I: Scene 7

(EVELYN *enters garage and throws driveshaft at* GERRY, *goes out and gets fender and flings that. Exits. Returns and throws car trunk.*)

EVELYN: Cathy told me everything. Damn you. You are a deceiver. I won't be misled anymore. How could I believe you? I should have known by how you give things to me, want me to live in your house. I won't be caught in that locked house. My ideas will not be dominated by yours. (*She throws car keys at him. Runs out*)

GERRY: Now I know why people buy guns.

DAVE: Who?

GERRY: Evelyn won, so she runs out. I said how she won and I finished with the rest, finished with them in my system, never said that to anyone. If it had been normal, all this would have happened in a period of transition. First Evelyn, then me finishing off. Certainly finishing off what goes on in the head. But she lived in this house when things developed. No neat way to tie up ends. Phone calls. Visitors in front of her open to misinterpretation and confusion. Under the same roof with no privacy.

DAVE: Oh.

GERRY: I couldn't hide anything. It was all open to misinterpretation. Of course she jumped at that. If I could talk to her for five minutes.

DAVE: Is that a tune from the radio?

GERRY: *(Sings)* If I could talk to her for five minutes. *(Boys take up tune and sing a riff on it. Phone rings in garage.* DAVE *picks it up.* DAVE *speaks in phone. We hear* CHARLES *over sound system)*

CHARLES: Woof.

DAVE: Charles?

CHARLES: Woof.

DAVE: Yeah, Charles?

CHARLES: Woof.

DAVE: What's going on, Charles?

CHARLES: Hammer fight. I want to get into a hammer fight.

DAVE: What?

CHARLES: I want to get into a hammer fight!

DAVE: Have you ever been in a hammer fight?

Act I: Scene 8

Cathy Interlude

(CATHY enters with a gun behind her back.)

CATHY: I need closure.

GERRY: Well, why don't you close the door on your way out?

CATHY: I don't think so. *(She pulls out gun)* I've had time to think.

GERRY: Thinking's good.

CATHY: Your ancestors treated my ancestors real bad. I thought my love for you could overcome four hundred years of pain, but I will not be treated this way! Because I am black woman, black woman I am. I will not be your Naomi Campbell, your Halle Berry, your Robin Givens. What? Do you think that because your dick is white it should be bronzed? Because that would make it brown . . . maybe black. *(She pretends to shoot the boys. They react as if shot)*

CATHY: Ha!

(Blackout.)

Act I: Scene 9

Evelyn and Jody

EVELYN: I paint evenly all over the canvas, directly from objects I arrange out there, they are there in front of me, as I see them, vases, glasses, chairs, tables . . . arrangements I like. When I enter the paint, then it's all right. The gap between myself and out there closes up, pressed tight, I am inside the paint, okay? That doesn't make me comfortable, stable or happy, but it's okay. I'm inside the paint.

JODY: Messy work.

EVELYN: See . . . truth. You have to be inside the truth in order to talk about it. If you are outside and looking in . . . if you are outside the painting and looking in . . . you're just lying . . . I can't tolerate lying.

JODY: Gerry uses you. Sorry. I had to say that. When I found that Gerry had a place for you to live in his house, well, I didn't think he'd seduce and use you. I mean, I knew you needed a place to stay. I figured he'd be your landlord, not your lover and exploiter.

EVELYN: Cathy told me everything.

JODY: How well do you really know Gerry?

EVELYN: See, I know a truth test I can use. *(Holds up her hands)* See the little nicks and scratches? Red gouges on my arm? When I was in high school I did that and let the blood drip down. No one lies when I drip blood.

JODY: Gerry was after me. Asked me in on drinking bouts, obvious what he wanted. He tried it out on me.

Act I: Scene 10

(DAVE, RALF, and WALT are playing with a Ouija board. GERRY comes in, ranting.)

GERRY: I don't believe how Cathy comes over like that on Saturday morning. Finished two years ago between us. No physical contact whatsoever.

RALF: The voodoo lady. Didn't you sleep with her two weeks ago?

GERRY: I have not slept with her for two years, sober. Two weeks before on the phone, Cathy says how we will never talk again, never say anything to each other again. I say you are right. So Saturday she's at the door saying how the car broke down, screaming how the car I gave her two years ago doesn't work. In a minute she's talkin' to Evelyn, whispering. In a minute Evelyn is out the door. Later I hear how Cathy whispered fantastic stuff to Evelyn, invited her over so I couldn't hear. Made up some fantasy, nothing true. Not limited by anything true. Cathy says how I am fucking Linda on Tuesday and Thursday, fucking this other one on Wednesday and Friday. Saying how I made wonderful love to her all the time. I haven't fucked Linda for at least a year. What the hell was she talking about? So Evelyn believes my ex-ex-ex girlfriend and takes off.

DAVE: You're Satan. Beelzebub.

GERRY: At least . . . she should have said: "Yeah, I was sucking his dick ten minutes ago . . ."

DAVE: What are we doing?

GERRY: She didn't figure out the simple message. The woman who talked to her was an ex-girlfriend who wanted to get me back.

DAVE: Did the *s* tattoo wear off your chest yet?

GERRY: Never figured on Cathy saying things, making up things like that. Never figured anyone to do that, laughing about it on the phone. I can't believe these things Cathy says, then laughs about taking my underwear to a spiritualist and occultist. Laughing saying how my young chick is a sicky and unstable, better watch Evelyn, that chick will go nuts. Cathy laughs, saying how everyone knew I was fuckin' Linda. Any thoughts that came to her head. Right out with it. Fantasies, lies, vicious made-up stuff.

DAVE: *(Sings)* Everyone she meets reminds her of you.

GERRY: *(Sings)* No one I see reminds me of me. I'm going to have to give her a lot of space.

DAVE: Don't forget to give yourself a lot of rope.

Act I: Scene 11

DAVE: *(DAVE steps out of action and addresses the audience)* I stopped crying for good in seventh grade. Still crying about lateness then. I ate lunch too long and so arrived late. All class lines made up in the yard. No place for me, late. Therefore, a demerit. So, in public, I cried. A physical thing. I shook and had to cry. Could not hold back. Oh, I was just late for school. Crying was a problem for me. Second grade Mrs. Low talked to me, so I cried. Kindergarten, shoe untied, no pencil, forgotten milk money, a harsh look. I cried. The last time I cried it was seventh grade. My math teacher kept me there, in the yard, after the rest funneled out. He said: "You don't have to cry." Delivered in kindness. You don't have to cry. Said to me by a kind man: "You don't have to cry." A mustache on his lip, such as my father's. Suddenly it stopped. No longer happened. When I gained mastery of the cry it was with relief and nervousness. It was only a conscious loss, or it was not a conscious loss. See? The next moment I no longer could cry. Gone. Men don't talk about anything. Therefore, I do not know if it was a mental or emotional loss. I really don't cry.

Act I: Scene 12

(CATHY, LINDA, JODY, FRANK, *and* EVELYN *are all on stage frozen. Boys in audience as if in classroom.* GERRY *wears sport jacket and glasses like a teacher.*)

GERRY: Evelyn talks to all these people who never even met me. Lesbians and bisexuals. Women who had men just run out on them. This artist she rents from, he wants to control her. Tells her about me. Never even met me. These bitter women who make a point of dating guys tied up with someone else. Yeah, ask them for advice and opinions.

Act I: Scene 13

GERRY: (*On the phone*) Uh-huh. Whatever, Cathy. Whatever. Look, I am black woman, black woman I am. Sam I am. Whatever the hell your name is. All right, Cathy. Remember, I'm a mechanic. Your brakes. Your brakes. Your brakes. You just stay away from Evelyn.

(*All the boys pretend to be* CATHY *and attack* GERRY.)

GERRY: I'm gonna kill Ralf, you, and Walt.

DAVE: Now I know why people buy guns.

GERRY: Well they all come back, even Maralyn asked back two months after we split. She saw some other guys for a month or two. In the middle of fucking Maralyn, I was in the middle of fuckin' Maralyn, she says how she wants back with this new guy she knew for a week. Fine, I say. See yah. She goes. Two months later she wanted to know if I had a girlfriend yet. Did I want to get together. Well, I did have a girlfriend and no, I didn't want to get together. This chick will never find someone like me. I hope she does go out, it'll speed things along.

DAVE: Put your thing in the vise over there. Clamp it on good. Therapy.

GERRY: My big mistake was to talk to Cathy at all. How about that? Just fixed her car for nothin'. . . .

DAVE: Get drunk. It's easier to cut.

GERRY: Cut what?

DAVE: Get drunk, cut something off and send it to Evelyn.

GERRY: That artist.

DAVE: Van Gogh did his ear.

GERRY: Evelyn'd get a laugh out of that. Maybe they sell ears in Woolworth's?

DAVE: Noses anyway. Some dildos look convincing. Touch up the color and make sure it's long enough and thick enough to be convincing.

GERRY: Soft and limp.

(Lights dim.)

Act I: Scene 14

Party Interlude

(Free jazz music plays. GERRY *and* EVELYN *are having a heated argument with* JODY *present. There's a knock at the door,* JODY *breaks up argument.* EVELYN *goes to answer the door. The boys come in.* RALF *enters last carrying a case of beer.* DAVE *shakes hands with* GERRY, *all freeze.* LINDA *enters.* EVELYN *trips her as she enters. All freeze.* CATHY *enters carrying a small container of cream cheese as party favor. All the boys see her and look horrified as everyone freezes. All the girls congregate together. Look over at* GERRY. *Freeze.)*

RALF: You've got to keep control.

(All look at RALF, *as if he's crazy.)*

GERRY: Control.

*(*CATHY, *overt and hostile, makes her way to* GERRY. DAVE *intercepts her, poses like Heisman Trophy, holds* CATHY *back. Freeze.* DAVE *dances away with* CATHY. EVELYN *goes to* GERRY. GERRY *motions to console her. She turns her back and screams. Freeze.* WALT, *who has been getting high with* LINDA, *goes to* GERRY. *Freeze.)*

WALT: He's hurtin'. The eyes bloodshot. The man's hurtin'. Nothin's right around here. Don't know about takin' this. Hey man, your car's on fire outside. Why don't you take a look. I said your car's burnin' out there and take a look at it for let's say a day or two?

*(*WALT *crosses away.* LINDA *pinches* GERRY *on the butt.* RALF *tries to pick up* CATHY. JODY *and* DAVE *try to pick each other up. Freeze.* EVELYN *tries to hit* GERRY. WALT *physically blocks and picks her up.* JODY *crosses to* GERRY. *Freeze.)*

JODY: When did you fuck her last?

GERRY: Two days ago.

JODY: Good, that gives you a lot of leverage.

*(*EVELYN *and* GERRY *find each other. Everyone dances. Fade to black.* EVELYN *and* GERRY *exit kissing.)*

Act I: Scene 15

JODY, CATHY, LINDA: *(Say lines together.* EVELYN *eats ice cream on stage. The voices of the chorus go in and out as if a speech/choir)* He fucked around frequently on Deborah. Never took her anywhere. How much older is he then you? He was always after Geraldine. Eduardo is looking for a date. Black men can really fuck. Better find out about that before you make any long-term decisions. You have time. Anything worth keeping stands up to time. Try something else. After all, a strong interest should survive. Time never wrecks an arrangement. It serves to clarify, provide insight and perspective when you're in a thing, it's all dash, dash, nonstop or a dead end. You don't see. So much misery around when inexperience and rashness takes over. How is it possible to be sure unless you wait? I hope you're not set on pain. You're not alone if you are set on pain. Pain is hard. We all can stand only so much. Now, relying on oneself, that's the first and most important. Make sure of your own income, attitude, wisdom, point of view. An older person fights better. The see-saw flips up and down so fast. Be sure. Firm. If not Eduardo, well, you haven't known the pleasures of Renaldo. No one has to rush into a long-term arrangement. Renaldo is another great fuck.

(Lights down.)

Act I: Scene 16

"I'm in Love With My Car"

(Song by Queen "I'm in Love With My Car," played over sound system. The boys' names are called on stage as if performing at a stadium rock concert. RALF *is called first and appears in a huge Afro wig. He is the drummer.* DAVE *appears next. Throws his shirt to the audience, like the "Red Hot Chili Peppers."* DAVE *plays bass guitar.* WALT *next. Plays lead guitar. A rhythmic clapping from the audience.* GERRY *comes out as the lead singer.* GERRY *lip syncs. The boys play "air" instruments. Everyone turns around one by one, back to the audience, run offstage. Get toy cars and play with them as lights fade to black.)*

Act I: Scene 17

(Lights up on JODY. *Yell cross stage to* DAVE.)

JODY: You're dressed well, except for the socks, white socks.

DAVE: Tryin'.

(DAVE writes on a pad as WALT speaks. This speech can appear as DAVE's imaginative projection. Live music plays during the speech.)

WALT:

Did you see those black guys in here the other day?
Dancin', dancin'
Did you see those black guys in here?

Dancin' dancin'
Dancin' to the corner
Had the white mouse in their sights
Dancin' and dancin' toward his place
Under the girder, between the cars, by the wall
Two black guys dancin' to the mouse
Had him in their sights
Never saw a mouse smart as that
Turned on them, out from under them,
Fast and past them
Givin' them the finger as he run out
Never saw a mouse so hard to get
Two black guys dancin' and dancin'
No black mouse ever did that
White mouse got cleanly away
Strange and unnatural to see a white mouse in here

*(*GERRY *comes in. He and* DAVE *watch.)*

WALT: Took a cab downtown and got away.

(Lights down.)

Act I: Scene 18

Women's Interlude: "You Could Drive a Person Crazy"

("You Could Drive a Person Crazy," from the musical Company *is on speakers. Women are discovered as lights come up.* LINDA *calmly drinks from a bottle of tequila.* EVELYN *is eating a piece of fruit.* JODY *is meditating.* CATHY *is walking with a very small shopping bag. Blackout. Lights up.* LINDA *is smoking a joint and drinks tequila.* EVELYN *is eating a big pretzel.* JODY *is reading a self-help book.* CATHY *is walking with more shopping bags. Blackout. Lights up.* LINDA *is taking pills, smoking a joint and drinking.* JODY *is tearing out pages of the self-help book.* CATHY *has a tremendous number of shopping bags.* EVELYN *is eating an enormous candy bar. Blackout. Lights up.* LINDA *ties a belt around her arm, ready to shoot up, drops her pills and staggers on stage, trying to pick them up.* CATHY *has so many boxes, has one on her head.* JODY *has a voodoo doll out.* EVELYN *eats frantically, runs around bumping into everybody. Bit should be timed so that it ends on the button of the song. At the end of the button,* JODY *kicks voodoo doll across the stage. Blackout.)*

Act I: Scene 19

*(*WALT, GERRY, RALF *and* DAVE *in garage.)*

WALT: Ever see a white mouse? Saw one in here. Did you ever see the white mouse in here? I think that is startling and abnormal. A white mouse in here, the dog, Gasoline, why does he do that? Did the dog Izzy do that with the cat, since it is Gasoline's space and only place to have fun, upset and making out something, the dog named Gasoline.

(LINDA *enters holding an envelope with papers and a hundred dollars rolled up in her hand.*)

LINDA: Gerry, I need to speak to you. Okay, boys. Play with your cars or your balls or something. (*She shoos boys offstage. A violent argument in French erupts.* WALT *and* DAVE *exit.*)

RALF: You know something? Your French really sucks. (RALF *exits*)

LINDA: I have taken my temperature. I am ovulating now. It is my time of the month. I want to have a child with you or Bob. I have been graphing my temperature changes for months. Today is a best bet for having a child. Bob's genes are okay, I've found out about them. It'll be better with you because I am not attracted to Bob. You turn me on and your genes are equivalent to Bob's. Here is a hundred dollars so you can fuck me and I can have a child. I am getting there, older. My mother, who committed suicide, said wife mottoes about age. You probably can guess why she killed herself. My mother committed suicide because of my father's impossible behavior. For the duration of the pregnancy I will take no Valium, poppers, nor will I sniff, smoke or inject any drug. This is a legal agreement I've brought with me for you to sign. This way you give up the rights of paternity. Of course, you cannot expect any paternity rights. So sign. Here's a hundred dollars to fuck me so I can have a child.

GERRY: Where does that leave me?

LINDA: Bye. (*She throws the legal papers at him*)

GERRY: What are you saying about me?

LINDA: Bye. (*She throws the money at him and leaves*)

Act I: Scene 20

Garage

GERRY: In such pain. Never thought that would happen. Like the man says: "The whoremaster pays his dues." It's tearing me up.

DAVE: Do you have *any* work to do?

GERRY: I know, you're tired of hearing me.

WALT: I have no interest in talkin' about what or how I do. I will try never to say how or how well. I have no intention to talk myself up, old guy. Diesel mechanic. Expected to have this date with a young chick. Prepared himself. Told us elaborately what he would do. All day he says how and what. Been hard all day, he says, hard and ready. Goes home early to prepare. Afraid to blow it all out without enjoying himself. Afraid of blowing it all out too fast so she would fail to enjoy herself. Old man. Goes home. Showers. Jerks it off. Cleans and dresses. Now what do you think? What do you think happened? I would not talk about all that or think about that. I prepare by thinking about something else. What happens? Let it happen then, when I'm there, in the middle of whatever.

GERRY: Expert.

WALT: You're the expert man. Whoremaster.

GERRY: Gettin' whupped. (GERRY *takes out a sandwich, inspects it and pulls out a dead mouse*) Dead mouse, see that?

WALT: (*Kicks at mouse*) I do not eat what women make for me. Who knows the white powder could be sprinkled. The spirits and the occult. She really steals your underwear, man. She laughs and does something with that and you're fucked up. Or it is a risk not necessary to take? Do you or anyone know when and if it gets hard? I won't say how big or effective my method. Not for me. Think about something else. Rather weld up this piece of shit. Try thinking about something else. Mine ain't that big. I am not overpowering or skilled. I don't talk about five times a session. But it is hard as glass and stays that way. My woman's sick. Broke. Broken. Broken down. But I'll be all right.

GERRY: I got enough work to make three thousand a week. If only I could get my head straight. I'm just hurtin', man.

Act I: Scene 21

(*Lights up on* FRANK *talking to* EVELYN. EVELYN *paints elaborately*).

FRANK: I know guys like that. You cannot believe them. Ruled by fantasy. Dreamers. Better put rules on the fantasy. Better be the master of the dream. Otherwise . . . blame everything on voodoo. Do you want to hurt yourself? Wonderful and convincing actors, since they believe what they say. People who dream, unfortunately, are very convincing. You meet that type. Bigger than life. They throw everything out in the end. Let them admit just one mistake. Never. How they patch up disappointments. Building more dreams on what? You put your hand out. Get into an over-emotional state when it's life or death and it often is life or death. Not always springtime or summer. Not an easy popping out of flowers. Not always sweet smell and color. Someone like you has work and commitment. Can you afford to sidetrack? Deflect? Invest in quicksilver when you've got purpose and application and creative work that pays money? A person who sniffs after every opened up slit, excuse the expression. Let me tell you it's different for men, though today it is not fashionable to say that. Today, people pretend toughness and calluses. Can you stand to be walled off and numbed? Scars? Thick skin. Mind locked. Hope, joy leaking from wounds? Thick makeup, extreme emotions in whirling knots. Now you feel like you can handle anything. Well.

(*Lights dim out.*)

Act I: Scene 22

(EVELYN in house space with pills. GERRY *tries to talk to her.)*

EVELYN: Why did you see friends like her? Why did you repair her car? Why were you so cruel to me that day when you were in the garage talking? Why were you so abrupt to me? Friends do not make for obstacles like that. I am very upset. I am taking a trip away from here. I want to take off my clothes and jump off a bridge. I want to take pills and leave. I want to spiral out into another place.

(EVELYN and GERRY freeze. DAVE *enters).*

DAVE: Later that night Gerry called me. He was drunk and difficult to understand. He said that I had to go over and save him. He said he didn't think he could handle what was going on. When I got there, Evelyn had a knife in her hand and was yelling in a little girl voice. She had lined up the kitchen knives neatly in a row. Gerry had trouble getting up. He said: "Dave, I can't handle this." When Evelyn saw me, she backed up against the wall and dropped her knife. She squatted on the floor, closed her eyes, and fell asleep. I heard her snore. I picked her knife up, looked through all the drawers, put the knives in a bag, and took them to my house.

(Blackout.)

Act I: Scene 23

(EVELYN in classroom space. Boys frozen stage left. GERRY *frozen stage right. Women sitting in the audience taking notes).*

EVELYN: My heart is a black pit. I am a monster. I am not by nature paranoid or suspicious. I have no choice. I will not be hurt like this. I appreciate how I have grown since I met him and the long way I came and the interesting people I met because of him. I miss you, also. But my feelings often got hurt and I did not know things until much later. He insisted that I keep our relationship secret. Incidents with other women did not come out until later. Then all these details became clear from shear weight of detail, I must assume. Anyway, he spoke to her, after things were supposed to be finished with them. But this is not a factual decision alone. What am I to make of the way he's so nice all the time now when he was not that way before?

(Blackout.)

Act I: Scene 24

DAVE: I told my friend Dave Davis I'm tired of women. How they interest me. The cut doo-dad, the eyes and lips that scrunch up and glitter. I know it's me. Wait. The attraction to how they look and say things. Please! I mean, I'm saying please to myself. Speaking to myself. So much time has been spent in love with women. My attentions on pout, smile, giggle, their delight in seeing me. "Talk, please talk." I look away. Turn my ear to the side so as not to impede a flow. "Yes . . . yes . . . yes . . ." And I do mean specific women. I love to look and listen to women. Hear women out. I have entered how women feel. I have entered the world through how women feel. Many characters in things I've written are figments of women talking, of course much of me gets said that way. Through women figments. I told Dave I'm tired of that. Women. Women characters. He said: "I know what you mean, and yes, many of my characters are women. My poems even come out of women's mouths." I'm tired of saying it through women characters. Just the boys.

Between Blessings

Gloria Feliciano

CHARACTERS

Father David   *A priest, thirty-eight years old, homosexual. Teller of Diego's story. Repressively angry and somewhat haunting.*

Diego   *Subject character, twenty-eight years old, homosexual. Balanced and down-to-earth.*

Papi   *Diego's father, fifty-eight years old, homophobic. Very Puerto Rican and macho. A rager.*

Tito   *Diego's younger brother, twenty-five years old, homophobic. Macho, upbeat and funny.*

Act I: Scene 1

Reminiscences

(Lighting: mood lighting. Religious music is playing in background . . . maybe "Enigma" or "Mea Culpa"; monks chanting.

One narrow board against background on which a light reflecting a confessional booth window is reflected and one crucifix on far right stage. There is a travel bag open on a chair on the left side of the room and a larger bag on a table center stage. On the far left is a lounge chair.

FATHER DAVID *removes the rosary from around his neck, puts it down on the table, and stares at it. He then starts to pick up things around the room when he comes across a güiro. He picks it up and stares at it pensively. He is surprised when he looks up and notices that he has an audience. He proceeds to reminisce and talk to the audience as if they are one person sitting in front of him. To audience.)*

FATHER DAVID: Oh, hi! Didn't hear you come in. It's kinda noisy here with confessions going on. *(Chuckles)* More guilt than sins—but a lotta traffic! Know what this is? It's a güiro. Musical instrument. My friend Diego's dad made it for me. It's made from pepino. That's a fruit. Yeah, he would gut the fruit and put it out to dry for a couple a days. Then he'd cut grooves into it. See here. *(Demonstrates grooves)* Then with a fork he'd scratch it and it would make a unique scratchy sound.

(Demonstrates sound) Quite the craftsman—his dad. *(Pensive)* We were from the same town in Puerto Rico—Mayagüez! He and his family had moved to New York a couple of years before me. Actually they became like my family after my parents sent me to the seminary here in New York. Oh I'm sorry—*(smiles, somewhat embarrassed for his neglect)* My name is René David. Father David that is! Well, I guess you figured that out by now.

(Resumes his story) Yep, sent me away to pasture. Like sheep in a herd. Nah, not even. More like a misfit boarding the last ship to salvation. *(Sarcastically)* Hey! Guess they had to do what they had to do. *(Dramatically with arms out and shoulders up as he proceeds to pace around)* What were they to do? We were devout Catholics. I was an altar boy. Attended mass every Sunday, participated in family rosaries every evening. But they had a big problem obviously—I was gay.

(Pause, then looks down on his robe) These? Oh, don't worry about them. I'm not sexually active. No, no I take this robe and my commitment to its merits very seriously. Homosexuality is a sin. No getting around that. Yes, sir! An unyielding position of the Church.

(Shrugging his shoulders as he continues to pace) A position it cannot change. If it did it would no longer be Catholicism. It would be kinda like rewriting the scriptures. And the consequences of such a change? Could be devastating! *(Sits and starts picking on some grapes)*. Lots of homosexuals going to heaven. It would be an abomination. No, absolutely not! This is not negotiable. *(Returns to his story)* Well, anyway, that's what they did. They sent me away. Bottom line is: I was sick. Needed to be ridded of my demons.

(Gets up and goes back to his piles and continues to sort through things as he packs. He comes across a letter and becomes distracted as he skims through it, then looks up at the audience) Diego's letter. *(Holds up letter)* Been over a year now since this letter. Nice guy. My closest friend, actually. Have nice memories of him and the family. Yep, became like my little brother during my seminary years. Let's see. There was his dad and mom, his brother Tito and of course, Diego. Oh, and Gigi. Let's not forget Gigi, their poodle. Chased around her tail a lot. Very moody. She just showed up at their door once. No owner.

(Pauses, then smiles) Crazy, too. Only ate when you put a broom next to her plate. It made her furious to see the broom, so she'd jump to her plate and gobble down the food before the broom did. I think she must have been hit with a broom where she came from. The anger just stays there, you know? Anyway, most Sunday's after saying mass, I'd go over and spend the day with them. Watch his dad sand down his instruments. Then, when he got through working, we'd sit in the backyard and try to outdrink each other. His ma would always make me drink olive oil with milk. Yuch! Says it would make the alcohol float in my stomach and protect it. Also keep me from getting drunk.

(Smiles) Fun, those days. I guess eventually we kinda went our separate ways. I became more and more committed to the Church and Diego moved to the West Coast to pursue his dream—the theater. He felt getting as far away as possible from the family would allow him to be more himself. Seemed to be doing okay, except for his haunting respect for Papi.

(Shaking his head fondly). Papi! *(Smiles)* Oh, that was his dad. I called him Papi also. Papi was like a father to me, too. He was a real character. Very strong-willed and opinionated. Diego seemed almost afraid of him. Papi seemed to have his domineering presence about him. I guess feeling dominated can be scary. I was lucky. My parents were more the analytical and reserved type. When they didn't like what they saw, they just quietly got rid of it.

(Speaking as if audience is disputing him) They sent me away to the "religious sanitarium," didn't they? After all, for my problem, isolation was the only answer. *(Sarcastically smiling)* For all they knew, it might have been contagious! *(Pause)* With Diego, well, it was a little different. Papi was a good man. A very proud father. But only willing to see what he wanted to. And it didn't matter how far Diego went. Papi had dug a hole in Diego's conscience that seemed to have devoured his individuality. He tried to get me to help him with this. *(Puts his head down)* I guess I let him down. He called me one day from the West Coast and asked me to make time to meet with him. Said he had a problem he needed help with. He wanted to communicate with his father and clarify some things. I tried to get him to talk on the phone that day but he refused. He insisted we talk in person. Then his letter arrived about a week later. Pretty heavy stuff. What was I to do?

(Looking down thoughtfully as if thinking it through for the first time, then proceeding as if giving a discourse) As a representative of the Church, I had a job to do, and could only speak on behalf of the Church. *(Looks back up to audience)* At least that's how Father Pasqual saw it. My pastor, that is. *(Sarcastically)* I was asked to—"steer him in the right direction."

Diego had two very powerful demons in his head. "Talk to Papi?" "Don't talk to Papi?" He was petrified to face him. Actually, that's the reason he had moved away in the first place. When he first moved away, Papi was beside himself. For the first few weeks he would come and visit me every day just to talk about him. That's all he ever talked about, constantly, to anyone who would listen. . . .

(Lights fade.)

Act I: Scene 2

A Visit from El Compai

(Lighting: regular white lighting. Jíbaro music is playing in the background. A kitchen table where PAPI *chats with his compai.* PAPI *is busy working on a guitar. The doorbell rings and his compai enters.)*

PAPI: Compai, estaba perdío? Qué pasa? *(Hugs him, yells out to his wife)* Pura, el compai is here! How's la comai these days? Good. Good. Glad to hear that. How are the girls? Sit, sit down. *(To his wife)* Pura, why don't you get el compai something to drink? *(To el compai)* How about a shot? Here, I got some *(searches through his collection of booze)* . . . Palo Viejo. Huh? Can't turn that down! Okay—tell you what. How about some *(plants a bottle of Añejo and two shot glasses on the table)* . . . Añejo! Una fría? You got it. *(Yells out to his wife)* Mujer trame una Bohwayser. Qué caray—I'll have the same, too. Make that two, Negra! *(Notices beer in an ice bucket and yells back out to* PURA*)* Never mind, Negra, they're over here!

(To el compai) I'm okay. Awaiting a letter from Diego. He told his mother he wrote me a couple a days ago, but I still haven't received it. Well, you know, he always worries me. No, no, he's fine. I just wish that he were living closer so we could see him more often. No, he moved from here. He's in a bigger apartment now. Says

the other place was too small. Yeah, he's still writing and acting. Well, he says he's doing well.

(Shrugging his shoulders defensively) I know what the hell that means. But he says he's doing well. Yeah, well at least he's in entertainment, you know? I think he's got the right idea, but he really needs to get into music—instrumental kind of stuff. Why not! You know how many years that boy spent listening to me play my guitar and singing aguinaldos. In fact, in Puerto Rico, you know who used to live the our carretera and sit him on his lap to sing to him? Ramito. That's right! Qué va compai, don't forget my sons were brought up in a musical environment. Yeah, well— first few years of their lives they practically lived in that shop I had in Puerto Rico—remember? Then when we moved to New York they would spend all their time in the shop here.

(Impatiently) Okay—so it's a garage and not a shop. The point is that they always watched me at my craft and some of it was bound to rub off. No, no, no. Tito was always the observer, the listener. You know to this day how the kid loves to play conga. He still has an incredible ear for music. *(Getting increasingly excited)* And Diego—don't you remember how he was always glued to me fidgeting quietly with the instruments? Which reminds me—*(yells to* PURA)

Pura, did you get the mail? All right, Negra, don't forget to check it on your way back! *(To el compai)* This distance thing—*(impatiently)*. You know Diego moving away like he did—it wasn't always like that, you know? I don't know what happened to that boy. It's funny. I still remember how around eleven he started to behave a little strange toward me. I know, but it's like he started to become detached. Like he lost himself. I don't know—I guess they just grow up. But you know the one thing that has always stuck in my mind? One day—out of the blue—he just stopped saying "bendición" to me.

(Baffled) Yeah. No, he still said it to his mother, but not to me. No, I never questioned it. It's like some manly thing was going on with him, you know, and I guess he just felt too grown up to say it. But it has always stayed with me. *(Pause)* You know, inside.

(Grabs the bottle, pours himself a drink, and gulps it down) I don't know, maybe one day he'll feel comfortable about saying "bendición" again and go back to it. To me, that'll be the sign that he has become a grown man. *(Pensively smiling)* He was a good kid, you know? I mean there was one time when he surprised me by making a güiro all on his own. You know, he kept it a secret until it was finished, so he could surprise me. I was so proud of him! Mira, let me show you.

(Papi goes to the closet and pulls out an old sad-looking güiro shaped more like a deformed cucumber than a güiro . . . penis.)

Diego did this. Yeah, well maybe a little deformed. But the point is he was seven years old at the time. *(Offended)* What's the matter? Don't you see the resemblance? Well, you just gotta have an eye for these things. Only a craftsman can appreciate its potential. Bah! Your eye is just not trained to appreciate these things. *(PAPI turns to the door. His wife enters and hands him a letter)* Oh, you got the mail? Anything come in?

(To el compai) Talk about the devil. It's the letter from Diego!

(PAPI *opens the letter eagerly and starts to read outloud. As he is reading he sits back in his chair.*)

Dear Papi:

Cómo estás? Bien, I hope. Cómo está Mami? Sorry you haven't heard from me lately. Been real busy. You know how it is in the theater. Kinda like getting sucked into a black hole. Have some really exciting stuff coming up if I can get it produced. But—that's the world of the arts for you.

Hope you are still making those cuatros. One day real soon I hope to be working side-by-side with you.

(*To make his point, he excitedly points to the letter to his compai*) Keep those güiros, you know they're my favorite. Tell Mami I miss her bacalaitos. Can't wait to eat them again. Well, anyway, gotta go, Papi. Hope to see you guys real soon. Take care of Mami. Tell her to heat up the oil for my bacalaitos 'cause I plan to be out there soon.

(*Waives the letter around in testimony of his point. Puts the letter down as he shakes his head and grabs the bottle of booze*) Qué muchacho! Let's have a real drink. (*Pours two shots*) C'mon, we're celebrating! What are we celebrating? Diego, what else? Well, he says he's coming home soon. Weren't you listening?

(*Pushes one glass toward el compai*) Tenga! Beba hombre! When my son comes home we are going to have the biggest party you ever seen in this house. It'll be not just his coming home but the beginning of our new business. And then—I'm gonna find him a wife!

You watch—I'm gonna turn his life around. My son and I are going to become real partners in developing a lost craft—handmade musical instruments! What are you talking about—nobody makes these things by hand anymore! This, you don't learn in school! This has been passed down from generation to generation in my family. My father taught me this. And my grandfather taught my father. It's a gift.

Yeah, well take el cuatro for example: Did you know that right now there are only about five cuatro makers and they are all back home on the island? You know what that means? We'll be the only authentic handmade cuatro makers in the United States! We'll make a killing, man. I'll make them and he'll market them, you know?

(*Lifts his shot glass.*)

Here, let's toast. You didn't have a drink. That was a beer. Ah, you're getting old, chico. (*Grabs el compai's shot and the bottle of booze*) Here, I'll have a double. One for you and one for me. (*Phone rings. Talks into phone*) Hello? Tito! Dios te bendiga. Cómo estás, mijo?

(*Compai gets up to leave.* PAPI *tries to stop him*) Wait, no se vaya compai—it's Tito! (*Motioning him to stay*) No, no, espere! Ah! Está bien, está bien. How about a hand of dominos later? (*The door closes. He speaks into phone*) No, no, it was el Compai. No, no it's all right, he was just leaving. You know him, un mamao, one drink and he's wiped out!

So when you comin' over? Well, you still gotta come up for air, my boy. What's her name? Margarita. She Puerto Rican? Muchacho que lio te has buscao. No, no, no. That's not my business. You know me. I mind my own business. Just be careful. Don't forget you learned from the best! Well, you know—your wife. She should not suspect—she's a good woman. Just remember how the old man did it and you'll be fine.

Yeah, well *that* was just one time and it was an unfortunate mistake. They happen, you know? Oh yeah, well there *was* that other time, but that was different. That was because Chavela had to go and open her big mouth to your mother. All right, all right, never mind! Look, take this advice—think about how I would have handled it and do the opposite, okay?

Yeah! Yeah! Yeah! Your mother? She's in the kitchen. All right, I'll put her on—wait. Sí que Dios me lo bendiga, mijo! *(Yells out to his wife)* Pura—telefono! *(Chuckles and talks to himself as he sits back at the table)* Jodios muchachos salieron a su pai, cagao! Con cojones! Big cojones! *(Looks up at* PURA *who was on the phone for only a brief period)* What happend? Why you hung up so soon? Comin' over? When?

Yeah, yeah. He told me he wanted to come over this weekend, but he's been having car trouble. Hey, maybe we can get them both to come for Father's Day. I'm sure if we planned it early enough. We would just have to give Diego enough time to arrange a flight and stuff. *(Irritated)* Listen, I know Diego. He's not gonna let some stupid job stop him from coming if he wants to. So, if he can get out here, he will.

Cloud? You think I'm living in a cloud? Yeah, well maybe that's because you don't know them the way I do. It's a man thing. Diego takes after me. *(Agitatedly to himself)* How the hell he got caught up in that theater garbage is beyond me. That's sissy shit.

(Grabs the bottle of booze and pours himself another drink and gulps it down) For maricones, that's who that's for. I'm gonna get him out of that shit, too. Ain't seen one thing he's done yet! It's just a phase. I know my son. Just a phase. Don't start your shit, all right? I'm just having a drink. Can't I have a drink in my own house? Yeah, well, why don't you make yourself useful and go make me something to eat. In fact, I'm not even hungry. Why don't you just go do your grocery shopping and leave me alone.

(You hear the door as PURA *slams it on her way out)* Váyase al carajo y déjeme quieto! *(Grabs the bottle of booze and proceeds to take the cap off as he talks to himself)* Stupid bitch! *(Is interrupted from pouring his drink when the phone rings. Talks into phone changing his tone)*

Father. How the hell are you? No, no, we're fine. Just finished having a talk here with Pura about the boys. No, no, we weren't arguing, just kinda disagreeing. What else? Diego and his job. No, no, I know. Yeah. No, no. I know the theater is his life, but I keep telling Pura how he and I got plans for the future and she just makes me lose it with her hardheadedness.

Yeah, but you know how she can be when it comes to our views on the boys. Well, yeah, I know, I know. But to me they'll always be my boys. Yeah, I just spoke to Tito. He may be coming over this weekend. Diego? No, he's still tied up with his work. Why, did you talk to him? No, I just got the letter he sent me last week. Yeah, he sounded fine.

Well, Pura and I were trying to figure out how to get the two of them to come over for Father's Day. You know? Kinda like an old family get together. Yeah, Father's Day. Hey, maybe you'd like to join us? We can sit down and have a couple of glasses of wine and just like in the old days, it'll be our secret. Yeah, you know how it was always a riot? You and I trying to outdrink each other? You with your red wine and me with my pitorro?

Yeah, well, let's see if I can get the boys—er guys—to come over. Well, you still got about a month to plan it, so think about it. No, no. She's not here—she had some shopping to do. All right, I'll tell her. Amen.

(Hangs up the phone and proceeds to talk to himself) Talk about clouds. There goes one motherfuckin' drunk living in the clouds. He needs to quit hiding behind that collar. Ah fuck it! I got my own shit to worry about.

(Pours himself another drink. Blackout.)

Act I: Scene 3

A Bundle of Sticks

(Music: Danny Rivera "Mi Viejo." Lighting: regular white lighting. A couch and a side table in center stage. On the left is a chair with a small table and a telephone. On the right is a wall by the door with a woman's dress and wig hanging from a nail. A pair of large-sized high heel shoes are on the floor just beneath the dress. DIEGO *is laying on the couch writing a letter when he hears the door.)*

DIEGO: Who is it? You got the key—use it. *(To his lover,* KEVIN, *who has just walked in)* What's up? Writing to Papi. He wants me to go out there for Father's Day. No, he just wants me to spend some time with the family. No, of course I'm not going. I'm telling him my work schedule won't allow it. Read it? What you wanna read it for? I know what I said, Kevin. I don't need you to remind me. Yeah, well I guess I'm just not ready, all right?

*(*DIEGO *gets up from the couch)* Look, I know you're trying to help. But you can't cause you don't understand, okay? It's a cultural thing. You ain't Puerto Rican. You can't understand. It's hard to explain. It's just gonna crush him. I know it's up to me, but you don't know Papi. He's a very proud man. The way he sees it, his boys are real men and real men don't "fuck" other men.

No, I'm not saying that's all you are. I'm saying that's how Papi thinks. This would be like a personal defeat—an embarrassment for him! No, of course you're not an embarrassment to me. *(Pauses, then glances over to the dress on the wall)* I mean, sometimes, I wish you would give up that dressing up shit. Well, yeah, that cross-dressing shit that you love embarrasses me, okay! Cause why the hell you gotta go around trying to look like a goddamn woman? No, I don't. Explain it to me cause I sure as hell don't feel like I have to walk around looking like a loca just cause I'm gay.

I'm a goddamn man. That's it. Plain and simple. A man whose physical attraction is toward a man, not a woman. Well "your royal locaness" is what makes that world out there look at us and say we're "patos." And I'm sick of that shit. I just want to continue to be a man. Period. No stereotypes. No nothin'. Just a man!

No, you're wrong. It's not the closet rationale again. You know, it's said that we are not only misunderstood by the straight world—but sometimes we don't even understand our own behavior. What do I mean? You have to ask? Look at us. I don't have a clue as to why you have to wear this shit.

(Grabs the wig hanging on the wall and throws it on the floor) And you don't have a clue as to why I'm embarrassed by it. Yeah, but you're not a woman! You're a fuckin' man! You know how I feel? I feel like I've had it. I'm just tired, man, of people treating gays like they are mutants. We're not bad people. I feel like I'm living under this constant suffocation. Oh, it's just me, huh? Do you ever ask yourself why we are ridiculed? Oh, you're not ridiculed? Why don't you come back home with me. Let me take you to my neighborhood. Come let me introduce you to some friends of my family. You know why you're not ridiculed? Because you function within an environment that's safe for you.

I've never seen you venture out to a nongay community in your drag.

No, you're wrong about me. It is not about acceptance or fitting in. It's about being able to be yourself anywhere you chose. Without being censured. I got an even better one for you. Faggot! Yes, faggot! Go ahead, tell me where the word came from?

Yeah, Kevin. That's the dictionary definition—a bundle of sticks. Do you know why we are called that? In the sixteenth century, homosexuals were prosecuted by the Catholic church and thrown in jail for being gay. No, let me finish. In those days they would execute serious criminals by burning them and used faggots to keep the fire going. However, there were times during these executions when they would run out of faggots and throw in homosexuals to keep the fire going. That's right. And so homosexuals became faggots!

Yeah, well, I can't. You think you got all the answers. You're out of the closet. You're liberated. You're free of these hang-ups. You know what else you are? You're dead wrong! No, you think you got it all figured out. In your little world it's supposed to go something like this: You realize you're gay—you accept it—you tell your family and then you're free and can behave accordingly. Well, you know something? It ain't that easy.

Why? Because I, for one, have no need to go around behaving like a loca. And I, unlike you, have loving and caring family members that are living straight lives and don't understand me—and I can't change that!

Because this lifestyle is not normal to them. They are old-fashioned and Latinos. They cannot accept it. And to tell them is going to destroy them. Yeah, well, why does it have to be a destroy them or destroy me situation? I don't get it.

No, I'm telling you, they can't. I've heard the conversations that go on in my house. I've heard my brother and Papi talk. We're not people to them, Kevin, we're subhuman. We're "maricones."

(The argument suddenly stops. DIEGO *puts his head down)* Maricones? It's like faggot but ten times worse. *(There is a pause of dead silence. Then he sighs as he tilts his head up trying to hold back the tears)* Yeah. I am sorry, too, for some of those things

I said. It's just that I look at myself, a healthy guy, just as human as the next guy and yet I have to live in exile from my own family just so that I can be myself. I love my parents. I miss them. I am still that same person that they brought into this world. I just have different preferences. Why can't they accept that?

Look I can't talk about this anymore. I think I really need to be alone. Yeah, of course I still wanna go out tonight. No, I'll be okay. Love you too!

(DIEGO*'s lover leaves and he lays on the couch thinking. He is in a very pensive mood. He gets up, picks up the phone, and proceeds to dial. Talks into phone)* Yes, may I speak with Father David? Yes, tell him it's Diego Martínez. Yes, I can hold. Hi, René. I need to talk to you. Yeah, something is the matter. But I need to speak with you in person. I'm thinking of going to New York for Father's Day weekend. But I was wondering if there was a possibility of my seeing you before I see my family? Sure. No, I really don't want to discuss this over the phone. Look, I'll tell you what I'm gonna write you to fill you in on what this is about. I'm too emotional right now to talk about it.

I can't. I really can't. No, I'll be okay. I just need to see you in person, okay? Yeah. No, the Thursday before Father's Day is perfect. That's four weeks from now. Yeah, that's good. Okay, good. Listen, it's real important that you not tell Papi that I am meeting with you. I'd like this to be only between you and me. All right. Thanks. Look forward to seeing you again. Oh, by the way, don't even tell the family we spoke, okay? Take care. Amen.

(DIEGO *goes back to the couch and reads the letter he was writing. He crumples up the letter, then gets up and throws it to the side of the room. Then he sits up on the couch with his head down staring at the floor and nested in his hands.)*

Fuckin' lies. My life is one big pathetic lie!

(*Blackout.*)

Act I: Scene 4

Tito's World

(*Music: conga music—Rubén Blades, "Pedro Navaja" is playing in the background. Lighting: regular white lighting. Brick building tenement with garbage cans, bags, and two milk crates in the background. Tito, wearing a white hat with a dark ribbon and a dark suit and white unbuttoned shirt, makes his entrance dancing to the music in the background.*

TITO *turns on the stage to the salsa music in the background. Dances a few steps, then stops and tips his hat to a woman walking past him. Then turns and talks to his friend.)*

TITO: Yo, brother, what's up? Where you going? No, just stay here and chill with me, bro'. Yeah, I'm on my lunch hour—but I'm Tito—I can get back whenever I want. Relax. It's not like you got something important to do. Yeah, well I still got forty-five minutes. No, I stopped by the record shop. Picked up some CD's. No, it's not a party. Just the family. Yeah, celebrate Father's Day with the old man. Yeah, Diego arrives next week. You should see, boy, Papi and Mami are totally into it. Making preparations and shit. Yeah, even Father David is going. You should stop by the house Sunday. It should be cool.

Nah, Mami wants to cook and Papi wants to barbeque. Personally, I don't care, I just want . . . (*Stops midsentence as a passerby approaches*) Check this out. . . . (TITO *directs his attention to a gay man walking by*) Mira mami—estás buena! Ay cuidao que te partes! (*Watches the gay guy as we walks away*) Fuckin' faggots! Yeah, right. But let me tell you, I've seen some fine bodies on some of them. Yeah, man, just like women. You be all cool and shit thinking what a fine looking mami. Then boom— "hi!" That deep voice from hell scares the shit out of you.

(*Repeats himself mimicking a deep voice*) "Hi!" Get the fuck out a here. I tell you one thing. They pull that shit on me and I'll bust their face in. What'd you mean, that's what I deserve. You just jealous, bro'. Yeah, that's right jealous cause you can't get no fine mami's like I do. I can't help it if they want me and not you.

No brother, I'm not even trying. I could be minding my own business and there it is—some fine-looking mami just throwing herself at me. What about my wife? I'm not really cheating on her. Because cheating on her would be like having a longterm affair. These are just casual acquaintances. Yeah, well, that's what I call 'em! Papi taught me the difference. He has always taught us to be men of integrity.

He says you should always show respect for your wife. She should never know you cheat on her. And should she ever find out—lie like a mother! He says it's a man's God-given right to have more than one woman. It makes life more exciting and keeps the Mrs. on her toes! And you know what? He's right!

He says you just gotta look out for the pitfalls. Well, like for example, if the mamis start to call you "Chulo." "Chulo?" I don't know, it's like a term of endearment in Spanish. Kinda like "real lover." And sometimes if the passion gets heated enough they may even call you "Papi Chulo." Well, that's kinda like real "lover daddy." You know what he says? If that happens run in the opposite direction!

Why bro'? Cause you're in deep shit if she calls you that. (*Emphatically*) The minute they put that "DADDY" shit in there, they are claiming ownership of you. They have now made plans for you. Your individuality as you know it is history. Yeah man. See, they'll start to be nice. They'll want to iron your shirts and cook for you. But don't fall for it. It's a trap, brother! Yes! They are methodically laying out the bait. If you are not on your toes, you could get confused and maybe even think you're in love.

Papi always says that's the time to go back to the Mrs. Cause no man can eat that much food or own that many shirts that he's gonna need two women to do it. Papi's a smart dude, man. Let me tell you, he used to have 'em lined up when he was younger. (*Proud*) Yeah, man, the man was a lover. Un puto! I love my ol' man. Sometimes I worry cause I see him gettin' old n' shit. Yeah, I know. I try not to.

(*Distracts from conversation*) Check out this one coming. See it! Yes, "it"! The similarity between her and her dog. Yeah, man. Just watch as she gets closer. Saw it? It's the truth, bro. That bitch is so ugly. I can tell you that she's had that dog at least seven years. Cause. Every two to three years that subtle transformation takes place. You know (*pause*) the transformation that brings them closer to the dog's appearance. Man I know.

I'll tell you. I went out with this chick once. She was crazy about her dog. I only saw her for like a couple of months. But one day she came and told me it was her dog's birthday. So I says: "How old?" And she says: "Three." I said to myself: "Yep, I'm atta here."

Why? Bro', it was just a matter of time. The chick had one of those Chinese dogs. You know, the kinds with the rolls of thick skin on the face? Right, a shih tzu! And she was turning forty, too! You know what was gonna happen to her. I loved her too much, man. I didn't have the heart to stick around and watch the inevitable.

A forty-year-old shih tzu for a lover? No, brother, I was out a there. Yeah, I like older women. They're kinda cool. It's kinda like they got it all under control, you know? They can mother you and take care of you. You don't gotta worry about anything. Unless they're married. You can forget that shit. I ain't running down no fire escape in my underwear.

(Switches his attention to a man with a food cart) Oh, there goes Don Cholo. I'm hungry, man. *(Whistles)* Don Cholo! Espere! You want one, bro'? *(Reprimandingly)* Knishes? *(Lying and mockingly)* Yeah, knishes. What, you never seen a knish cart with a Puerto Rican flag before? *(Yells to Don Cholo again)* Don Cholo, deme cuatro!

*(*TITO *walks over to cart and comes back with four fritters)* I just told you—it is a knish! Well, it's a Puerto Rican knish!

(He proceeds to unwrap his fritter from the napkin and looks over at his friend defensively) Yeah, they're a little skinnier and. . . ? *(Somewhat concerned)* Well, no, not exactly potato—it's flour. In it? Bacalao. *(Annoyed at him)* Bacalao is codfish, asshole! Yeah, just eat the shit, all right? It's good!

(Smiles as he remembers) Mami makes these at home. When she makes them people can smell them throughout the whole building. All of a sudden neighbors stop by to return things they have borrowed just to have an excuse to be in the house. Good, right? *(Insulted)* They're not salty. Gimme that jíbaro. You need to sophisticate that palate of yours.

(Goes back to fritter and becomes engulfed in savoring it) Can't wait to see my brother, man. No, man. He got some fancy producer job. Hey, man. The guy's moving up in the world. No, just for the weekend. He's leaving Monday night. No, just to spend Father's Day with Papi. Family get-together, you know. Come on, bro'—join us. It'll be cool! All right, well if you change your mind, let me know. Take care, brother.

(Turns to passerby) Mami. *(Kisses as if calling a dog. Blackout.)*

Act II: Scene 1

The Retreat

(Regular white lighting. Religious music, same as Act I: Scene I, playing in the background. One narrow board against background on which is reflected the light of a confessional booth window and one crucifix on far right of stage. There is a table center stage. On the far left is a lounge chair. DIEGO *enters the confessional area.)*

DIEGO: René? Father David? *(Talks to himself)* Not here. Guess I'm early!

    (DIEGO *sits on the edge of table with his back toward the entrance and waits.* FATHER PASQUAL *walks up behind him).*

    Oh, hi Father Pasqual. No, no, I'm a, waiting for Father David. What do you mean not here? He said he would be here. He was expecting me. Away on a retreat? Will I be able to see him? Oh, so you are here to take his place? Father David told you about my dilemma, huh? With all due respect, I'm afraid it's Father David I need to talk to.

    (Long pause) Conflicted? Yeah, I guess that's the word—conflicted. But let me re-phrase that. It's not my homosexuality that's a problem. It's my father's inability to accept it. Ah, you don't think my father is the issue here.

    (Frustrated) Yeah, but my problem is my father! No, I'm afraid I have to disagree. Oh, so then, you think the problem is my perception of the situation? Heh! You know, you sound like Kevin. Yes, my lover. What's the matter, Father? Did I say something wrong? No, it's just that you seem offended by my statement.

    (Long pause) Wait, wait—you're hurt because I love someone? Pardon me, Father, but isn't Christianity about love? Oh, I see. So you would have preferred that I lie than refer to him as my lover? *(Pause hearing* FATHER PASQUAL*'s voice)* No, to have to act upon our feelings. Celibacy until marriage, huh? Will you marry us, Father?

    It's not sarcasm. I think's it's a legitimate question, don't you? Spiritual fortification? Aha, and that is going to salvage the situation with my father? You know, Father, this kind of thinking is why I felt I had to part ways with the Church—and my problem now is I'm afraid I am going to have to part ways with my family.

    Because Papi is a very proud man. This would undoubtably be a shameful thing for him. Resist temptation. That way there is nothing to tell. That simple, huh? So, you're saying I should just deny my feelings and there will be nothing to tell? But it is not quite that simple, Father. How do you intend to help me if this is not a two-way conversation, Father?

    No, it's not! You are preaching to me about the Church's position on homosexuality—but that's not what I am here for. No, you are telling me that I cannot love another human being. Forget the Church for a minute. How can you believe in your own heart that love, of any kind, is wrong?

    Sin? No, to me, Father. It is merely an expression of our love. No, Father, absolution has no place in this conversation. I'm afraid you can't help me. No, it's not resistance. It's your insistence on changing in my head what the problem is. Of course that's the problem. I know, I am the one living it.

    (Pauses) Look, as I said, I didn't think you could help me and I was right. No, I don't think that you knowing Papi is changing anything. Well, Father, with all due respect I think that when you allow yourself to see beyond Church doctrines, you might be able to see that we are human beings with feelings just like everyone else. No, I think there's nothing further to discuss. When is Father David due back?

    (Sounding a little cynical) Three months? Seems like an awfully long time. No, I'm just surprised that he didn't remember this trip when we spoke. *(Half smiling)* Oh, so it was one of those last minute things, hum? Tell me, did this have anything

to do with me? His own issues, huh? You know, Father, I gotta go. No, no, I don't think talking again tomorrow will be of any help.

No, it's not cynicism. I think that perhaps you did help. I think your denial of all of this just prepared me for Papi. Thanks. No, no, I don't think so. Yeah, okay. Thanks for your time. Yeah, I'm fine, Father. Amen!

(DIEGO *pauses and stares at the audience as if wanting to say more, but doesn't. He gets up, turns toward the cross and makes the sign of the cross. Blackout.*)

Act II: Scene 2

Bendición Papi

(*Regular white light. Jíbaro Music. Kitchen table with a refrigerator in the background.*)

DIEGO: Me huele pero no me sabe! (*Toward* MAMI *with arms open wide*). Bendición Mami, cómo estás? (*Switching attention*) What do I smell? (*Leaning over looking to the pot*) Ummmm! I'll take them. (*Teasingly*) All right, all right, but if I'm not un "e-x-e-r-a-o" then who are you gonna fight with?

(*Stepping back one step as he looks at her up and down*) Let me look at you. I've missed you so much. You look good, Ma. Where's Papi? (*Opens refrigerator*) Taking a bath? (*Yelling out toward* PAPI *in the bathroom*) It's about time, Papi! (*Picking at food from refrigerator. Coming out of the fridge licking his fingers*) So tell me. Where's Tito? Oh, yeah? What time does he get out of work? Oh, so he should be here shortly?

(*Back to the refrigerator and takes a beer*) It's about time that bum started working. (*Opens beer can*) Yeah, I know, the layoff wasn't his fault. But Ma, it's been almost a year. He's a bright guy. He shoulda found a job sooner. No, I think it's called milking the unemployment. Well, what the hell, I guess if he's entitled to it, why not?

(*Makes a face at the "hot" beer*) Ugh! It's hot! (*Throws out beer*) How's the compai? And his girls, they okay? Nineteen. Goddamn! When did that happen? Yeah? You crazy, Ma—those girls are like my sisters! I know there's no blood relation, but you know I saw them grow up, Ma! Nah! Nah! Forget that. No. No girl! No, I'm not waiting on anything. Ma, I don't want kids. Yeah, well we can talk about that later.

(*Pulls a chair and sits*) Listen, I heard that René, or should I say, Father David, was transferred away somewhere. No, I just happened to have stopped on my way here. Yeah, Father Pasqual told me. Didn't you know? That's strange? No, I'm just surprised he didn't stop by to say good-bye to you guys. Had you spoken to him lately?

(*Apprehensive*) Papi? What he talk to him about? No, no, just curious. No—ah—I haven't spoken to him. I was looking forward to seeing him, though. (*Doorbell rings. To* TITO) Tito—Little brother. (*Hugs* TITO) What's going on, man? Yeah. Yeah, you too? How's it going? How's Myra. Yeah? (*Totally surprised*) Baby? (*Half-smiling*) Get atta here. Serious? (*Happy*) Ma, why didn't you tell me? Holy shit! I'm gonna be an uncle. Goddamn bro'!

When is she due? Oh, man, I gotta go see her. You behaving yourself? Yeah, I bet you are.

(PAPI enters. To PAPI*)* Papi! What's up, viejo? *(Hugs* PAPI*)* You look good, Papi. Let me see, where's that beer belly of yours? Diet? You serious? Shit, well, it's working. Look at you? Yeah, I'm good. No, just working hard, you know. What new place? Papi, it's been almost two years since I moved there. I know, it sure does fly. Back to New York? Nah, I don't think so. I love it out there. Married? Nah, don't you start, too. Don't worry about it. You got one already coming. *(Teasingly)* Grandpa! Yeah, I think a drink is in order, why not? Besides, your beer is too hot. Papi, you been replacing that fridge for the last eight years!

(Waving his arms up in innocence) Sorry, sorry! I won't get her started. *(To* MAMI*)* Ma, Ma, it's okay. I'll buy you a new fridge, okay? *(Sits at table savoring the food aroma)* Uuuuuu, Ma, that food smells good!

(To PAPI*)* Yeah, Ma was just telling me that you guys had invited René, excuse me, Father David *(making the sign of the cross in jest)* over on Sunday. Well, I don't think you should expect him. I heard he was sent away somewhere. Yeah, I'm surprised he didn't stop to see you guys, either. Oh, no. I found out cause I stopped by to say hi before I came here. You know, it's on the way so I thought I let me stop by and say hi and they told me he was away.

I saw Father Pasqual. Seen him lately? Oh, yeah, I forgot, you're allergic to the church. I talked to him briefly. He wasn't very informative about René. So I said my hellos and left. *(To* MAMI*)* When do we eat, man, I'm starving?

(Grabs a chair and sits at the table) Yeah, well don't worry about it. I'm sure I can eat some more—that was just an appetizer. No, don't worry about it. Just pile those beans right on top. *(To all)* What? I'm gonna sit by myself?

(To TITO*)* Tito, isn't Myra coming over? Oh, she is? Well, tell her I'm gonna go see her tomorrow evening. You guys gonna be home? Why not, where you gonna be? Who's Margarita? Your wife is pregnant, bro'. What are you crazy? Yeah, Tito, but that shit isn't right. The woman is having your child. You're screwed up, bro'?

(To PAPI*)* Of course I don't approve, Papi. You don't do shit like that, especially when your wife is expecting. *(Surprised)* Don't tell me you think it's okay? Well, then, tell him. *(To* MAMI*)* No, ma, don't touch upon that subject. I didn't come here to hear fights about Papi's Don René escapades, all right? Papi's cool now, look at him. A changed man.

(To PAPI*)* Right, Papi? No, no. I ain't getting married. And don't try to change the subject. This is about you. Why? Cause it ain't for me. Yeah, well, we'll talk about that later. Just some things. Yeah, well we'll talk later. No, I didn't go and father illegitimate kids. What kinda joke is that? *(To all)* You know, you guys just gotta stop this marriage shit with me cause it ain't gonna happen.

(To PAPI*)* I know, Tito is younger, but he's he and I'm me. Well, some people are just not cut out for that. Just that . . . that some people are not cut out to be married. No, I got friends. Well, some of them are girls, but no "girlfriends."

(To TITO*)* He got married? Oh, yeah? Well good for him! *(Looking up at* MAMI*)* Get atta here, Ma—Cheo got married, too? They got any kids yet? Yeah? Good for him!

(To TITO*)* No, I already told you no way I'm getting married. No, I ain't holding out on you, Tito. Believe me! *(*DIEGO *pauses, looks around the table and takes a deep*

breath as he becomes more serious) On second thought, you know what, this is part of what I came down here to talk to you about. No, no, Papi, wait, no toast, please. Let me finish.

(Long pause) Look, you guys need to know something about me. Uhm. This is really hard for me to say—*(pause)*. There is a person I'm seeing—but it's not a girl. It's a guy! His name is Kevin.

(Bows his head, then lifts his head and stares into space) I don't like women, okay? No, Papi, don't joke. You know exactly what I mean. *(Defiantly looking at* PAPI, *raising his voice)* You heard me, Papi. Don't make me repeat it. *(Looking away to his side)* I'm sorry! I just don't know how else to put this. There is just no easy way. *(Dead silence at the table. He stares back into space)* Somebody wanna say something?

(To TITO*)* Where you going to, Tito? *(*TITO *exits. Again there is dead silence)* Mami, where you going? You okay? *(To* PAPI*)* Look, Papi, I can understand if you don't want to talk to me. Believe me, I do. But I really could not hold this in any longer. I'm hurting, Papi—real bad. I'm hurting for you and I'm hurting for Ma and I'm hurting for Tito. Yes, I know that you're hurting, too. But this had to be said. It didn't just happen, Papi. This is who I have been for many years. I don't know. I guess I must have been around ten or eleven.

(Pacing the stage) Nothing. What could I do? I would hold in my feelings and feel like there was something drastically wrong with me. Walking around like a time bomb. Always feeling ashamed of myself. Feeling like I was some kind of pervert who was unworthy of his family.

(Turning to PAPI *in a pleading tone)* Nobody knows, Papi. That's why I moved away. To save you the embarrassment of having to explain to people. Trying to save Mami the pain. It's been really hard for me, Papi. You have no idea. I didn't ask for these feelings, they were just there and I didn't know what to do with myself. I knew that getting away from the family was the only way that I could face myself and my feelings. I thought that maybe going away and learning more about it would make me stronger and I could overcome it. But it doesn't work that way, Papi. This is not something you overcome. I don't know how to explain it.

No, I don't know what it's going to do to us. I don't. And I guess I'm scared to know. But you know what I think? It's time that it all be out in the open because I can't bear keeping this a secret anymore. Nothing's changed. Look at me—I'm still the same person!

Well, maybe so, but you're going to have to tell me what those changes are? *(There is silence)* Tell me, Papi. *(There is a long silence)* Papi, please say something. Papi? Yeah, I wrote him a letter telling him. That's why I stopped by to talk to him. Yeah, Father Pasqual knows. He's the only other person. Papi, this is not a first for him. He's not gonna tell anyone. He's a priest.

(Pause) Do you want me to go walk with you? Listen, how about if I stay up so we can talk when you come back? Well, then, do you prefer I leave? Papi, wait.

*(*DIEGO *gets up and looks at* PAPI *as he goes out the door.)*

Bendición, Papi!

(Blackout.)

Act II: Scene 3

Papi Unleashed

(Lighting very dark with light shining from behind the stage producing an almost silhouette-type effect on half of the stage. The remaining half is not lit. Danny Rivera's "Mi Viejo" plays. Setting is a bar, interior and exterior. Stage is divided by a wall that separates the outside and the inside of the bar. There is a crate against the exterior wall.

PAPI *is seated on a milk crate outside the bar with his side to the audience, head down, sobbing uncontrollably like a child. His head is facing the floor, nested in his hands and his elbows rest on his knees. There is a bottle of booze by his feet. As his crying subsides, he puts his hand in his pocket and pulls out his wallet.*

He flips through some pictures and stops at one in particular. He pulls it out of the slot and stares at it for a minute. Proceeds to sing, hugging picture as song plays in the background. Music stops.

PAPI *stares again at the picture, then tears it up. He tosses the picture pieces on the floor and kicks them with his feet. He grabs the bottle and takes a big drink. Head angled up, he puts the bottle down.*

He gets up, places his wallet back in his pocket, and digs into his other rear pocket and pulls out a handkerchief. He wipes his face and tucks it back in his pocket. Then takes another sip from his bottle. He places the bottle back down and proceeds to walk into the bar.

Lights fade out on the exterior scene and interior of the bar is faded in slowly as he proceeds to walk into the bar.

PAPI *walks over to a stool and sits down.*

PAPI: Let me get a shot of the usual. *(*PAPI *grabs the shot and gulps it down immediately)* Let me have another one. *(He grabs the shot and gulps it down again and slides the glass out for another refill)* Things? Things could be better, I'm afraid. You know when life kicks you in the ass? No, yeah, yeah, Pura is fine. Nah, it's not something you'd understand, Ricardo. Tito is fine. Diego? I don't know, I haven't seen him. He was supposed to come this weekend, but he called and said he couldn't make it. You know, work. Yeah, yeah.

(Sarcastically) Sunday? That's the big day. Papi and the family. Angry? Why, I look angry to you? Talk about what? You got no kids, right? Then what would you know? You ain't even been married. So what if I had one too many! I got money! You sell—I buy! Yeah, I know it's late. See? I got a watch. I can tell time. So, go ahead. Take care of business—close! Who's stopping you? Go ahead! Go ahead! Just gimme a double before you go.

Yeah, I'm driving but I ain't drunk. *(Gulps his drink)* No, I can get home okay. Yeah, yeah. Just go—go! *(As he watches the bartender walk away he mumbles in a low voice)* Fuckin' faggot. *(Spins around his stool to face the audience)* Fuckers are all over the place. Tan como el arroz blanco. *(To audience)* What the hell you looking at? Your son ever tell you he's slept with a man, huh? Hey, don't feel sorry for me, okay? 'Cause I don't need your sympathy. Yo soy un hombre! I can handle this. I got cojones. That's right—big balls! Maybe my son doesn't, but I do. I got enough for the both of us, all right!

(Bows his head and becomes pensive. Then becomes amused as he chuckles and looks up at the audience) There is a bright side, you know—

(Pointing his finger in a drunken fashion) I always wanted a girl. So there you go! I got one! Betcha you couldn't do that? But I can. That's right, I can because "I" am Arsenio Martínez. And I am a man! And I can make anything happen.

(Proceeds to mimic a dialogue, talking to an imaginary nurse) Nurse, tell the Martínezes they have a nine-pound boy—I mean girl. *(To audience)* No, no better yet, a M-A-R-I-C-O-N! And congratulations to them—they are in style now!

(Lashes out at the audience) Oh, what the hell do you know? You ain't got one of those. You don't know what I feel. *(In a challenging tone)* Go ahead, intellectualize it! Tell me I'm wrong! You're probably all maricones for all I know!

(Mumbling to himself with hate and disgust) Fuckin' d-i-s-e-a-s-e-d motherfuck-ers. *(To audience)* You know what I think? I think this world has gone crazy. Yeah, crazy! In my days if I told my dad something like this, I'd be banned from the house. I'd be disowned. You know why? Cause my papi didn't raise patos, that's why. We have real men in my family. That's right—we are Martínezes. We work. We raise families. And we are in charge. We are real machos. Okay?

(Looking almost crazy and obsessed) I don't know where that boy came from. He was probably switched in the hospital. *(As if having a revelation. Totally drunk)* Well, I'll be a son of a bitch! All these years I been raising someone else's kid. Goddamn it—I been cheated! That's not my kid! I'll sue them! Yeah, that's what I'll do. I'll get them for every penny. Tomorrow I get me a good lawyer. I'm gonna get to the bot-tom of this. You watch.

Ricardo, gimme another drink. I'm dry. *(Spins around on the stool almost falling)* What you mean you're closed? I want another drink. Ah, to hell with you. You ain't no good, anyway!

(Stumbles off the stool and proceeds to walk out. Acting dainty and effeminate with hand up and wrist folded) No, I can drive myself home *(effeminately folding his wrist)*—thank you!

(Stumbles out the door. Lights fade on exterior as he proceeds to walk out. He spots the bottle by the crate and takes a big gulp. He tucks the bottle under his arm as he walks wobbling off stage. Blackout.)

Act II: Scene 4

Conclusion

(Lighting: fade in mood lighting. Religious music as in Act I: Scene 1. One large board on which is reflected the light of a confessional booth window and one crucifix on far left stage. There is a travel bag open on a chair on the left side of the room and a larger bag on a table center stage. On the right is a lounge chair. FATHER DAVID *is seated.)*

FATHER DAVID: Oh, you're back. Well, as you know by now, I was not allowed to meet with Diego. But here it is a year later. I finally caught up with him. He's now living back in New York with Mami. I visit them regularly. Unfortunately, Kevin and he split up after he decided to move back to New York. Left his job and relocated so he could be near Papi.

Papi? Papi is at St. Joseph's hospital—comatose. Car accident the night he walked out on Diego. Too much to drink. Lost control of the car—*(cynically)* or so they say! *(Saddened)* Things are totally different without Papi. I wish I had been with the family that evening. Don't know that I could have changed anything, but just wish I hadn't been denied the opportunity to share the blame.

Instead, what do I have? Just this feeling of guilt that is constantly gnawing at me for really believing I had no choice. I had rules to obey. *(Angrily)* Rules. *(Chuckles in cynical disbelief)* I don't know why this story comes to mind right now but . . .

(Pulls out a cigarette) I had a friend who told me once that her aunt, a faithful devout Catholic and active member of her former Church where she continued to attend even after she had moved away—*(proceeds to light the cigarette)* was dying of cancer.

One day, when her aunt made a turn for the worse, she went to the priest at this Church and asked if he would come and pray for her aunt at her deathbed. The priest asked her for her aunt's name and address, then looked at her and said, regretfully, that he could not go because it was not within his parish's district. *(Smiles and shakes his head)* She, of course, was totally disheartened by the fact that despite all her aunt's devotion to this church, he did not even know who she was.

(Puts out his cigarette harshly, then gets up slowly) Look, let's face it. There are just too many churchgoers to keep track of. And priests are busy people who, though devoted to their followers, sometimes can be distracted and make mistakes. So maybe he didn't remember her.

But you know what really frightens me is that this man could so blindly obey these rules that clearly made no sense given the reality—a distraught person pleading for a final blessing!

My friend has never again visited the Church. Yet she says that to this day she says she still misses it. Something is very wrong. And I'm afraid it goes beyond homosexuality.

(Counting with his fingers to make his point) Women cannot be admitted into the clergy. Priests are not allowed to marry? *(Chuckles)* God forbid that a man of the cloth who preaches procreation and family values lower himself to such a mundane thing as raising his own family.

(Faint and subtle background noise begins. Sarcastically) Makes sense, doesn't it? But look at me. What am I if not a hypocrite? Yes, a hypocrite to my own kind if I wish to be in the priesthood.

(Chuckles) It's a prerequisite—hypocrisy, that is! *(Pauses and looks toward the confessional)* Pardon me a minute. Let me close this door. I'm afraid these confessionals seem to be getting noisier and noisier these days.

(Reflection of confession booth disappears as he closes the door and subtle background noise stops) There, we can hear better already. The world has changed and the Church, my friends, it seems to me, is unable to change, irrespective of the consequences. And believe me, they are big! Big enough to make one question oneself.

The way I see it, no institution should have the power to rule over one's spirit. Especially if it seems to have disconnected from reality.

(Intercom rings. To intercom) Be right down. *(To audience)* Well, I've gotta run. My cab is here. *(He gets up and starts to gather his luggage by the door. He stops and takes a look in the mirror and stares at himself)* Oh, I almost forgot—I guess I won't be needing this anymore.

(Puts the collar on the table. Turns back to the audience, pauses and stares at them lovingly for a minute, then makes the sign of the cross.)

God Bless!

(Walks to the light switch, turns off lights, and exits. Lights fade.)

III

Hip Hop and Rap

The Preacher and the Rapper

The Crime

The Preacher and the Rapper

Ishmael Reed

Prologue:

RAPPER:

Ladies and Gentlemen, we're turning down the lights
to show you a rap about a cultural fight—
about Three Strikes, a rapper, and Jack Legge
a preacher
I'll vie you some background till I hear
from my beeper
The country's turned right and the
politicians have found
that the sure way to election
is by dissing black sound
the preachers and the journalists
are not far behind
Using columns and pulpits to
hasten rap's decline.

CHORUS:

The preacher and the rapper
One's dreadlocked, and one's dapper
A man of the cloth
and a man of the streets
The issues are old
and the passions run deep
and try as they might
will their minds ever meet?

They're blaming hip-hoppers
for all that's gone wrong
that the source of all misery
can be found in its songs
that the children tune in
and get carried away
and pick up an Uzi
the very same day
that the women are bitched

and the women are ho'ed
and the mind of a rapper
is the mind of a toad

CHORUS:

The preacher and the rapper
One's dreadlocked, and one's dapper
A man of the cloth
and a man of the streets
They're on opposite sides
will their minds ever meet?

Now Congress is preparing
to put Rap on trial
claiming words on
these records
are nasty and foul
and the volume they're played at
is enormously loud
and that nudity and profanity
should be banished from sight
as a surefire way to end
this terrible blight.

CHORUS:

The preacher and the rapper
One's dreadlocked, and one's dapper
A man of the cloth
and a man of the streets
A man with a beat and a
sailor in God's fleet
They're on opposite sides
will their minds ever meet?

(Beeper sounds. He exits.)

Act I: Scene 1

(St. John's Church. REV. JACK LEGGE is about fifty-five years old, prosperously robust with gold teeth. He wears an expensive black clergyman's outfit. Kunte cloth draped over his shoulder. His black shoes are fastidiously shined and he wears rings on three of his fingers. REV. JACK LEGGE is praying. He has one follower. Sitting in a chair, her back to the audience, she is dressed in Olosun cult clothes. White gown, turban, etc. On the wall is a poster of Charlton Heston dressed as Moses in the Ten Commandments. The REV. is on his knees, praying.)

REV. JACK LEGGE: . . . and Lord, we pray to you to end this drought. Replenish our congregation so that we may fight the evil of this time, Heavenly Father. Save St. John's Baptist Church. Fertilize our garden. Make up a well-spring of Christian hope. We call upon you, Heavenly Father.

You know our situation. You know that your membership has dwindled. That your children are being persecuted like never before. That thine enemies now rule this country. That our great and beloved United States of America has been taken over by worshipers of alien gods. Of strange and exotic idols. Serpent cults. Bizarre chants are being uttered in the streets of our capital and we are like Paul, a stranger in a strange land when he tried to spread the Gospel but finding opposition at every turn. They have driven your children into the corners of America. They have reduced our once powerful Church to a congregation trembling with fear as our rights are trampled by worshipers of the Mother Goddess. You must help up, O God! Restore us to the pinnacle as you did for Daniel, and Joseph, preparest a table for us in the presence of our enemies and have our cup runneth over. I implore you, O Lord! *(Rises from his knees. He begins to sing and clap his hands)* This little light of mine, I'm gonna let it shine. This little light of mine, I'm gonna let it shine. This little light of mine, I'm gonna let it shine. Let it shine, let it . . . sister? Why ain't you singing along?

SISTER: I didn't come here to worship this morning, Rev. I came to say good-bye.

REV. JACK LEGGE: Good-bye. Good-bye. But you, the last faithful follower? At one time, St. John's Church had ten thousand members. Look at us now *(frowns)*. People have abandoned Jesus for sin and fornication, and are living loose in a variety of new familial relationships. Sister, you give me strength. Because I know that if I just have one faithful follower, I can rebuild. Slowly build up a congregation so that we will be ten thousand strong as we were in the beginning. With far-flung missionary posts, Bible sales, and our television ministry theme parks, and the Rev. Jack Legge Bible College. Why, we built a replica of the Wall of Jericho, which is still the major tourist attraction for the state of South Carolina until this woman Barbara Sung and the Wicca Party began running things.

SISTER: I'm sorry. I've made up my mind.

(Places his arm around her shoulder. She removes it)

REV. JACK LEGGE: What's the matter?

SISTER: I've joined the Yemaja Temple.

REV. JACK LEGGE: The Yemaja what?

SISTER: O da bo, Rev.

REV. JACK LEGGE: Ya-what? A-what? But, but you have been a member for twenty years. You're going to give up the Lord, just like that? You mean you're not going to worship in your home church no more? Sister, what's come over you?

SISTER: I'm sorry Rev. Legge, but according to our teachings, Christianity and Islam are invader religions. They are not indigenous to West Africa, the ancestral home of most African-American people.

REV. JACK LEGGE: Sister, who be putting these wicked ideas in your head? You know, you'd better be careful. God don't like one to put no strange idols before him. Jesus said: "He who is not with me is against me. You'd better not mess with the Lord!"

SISTER: I'm sorry Rev., but we've been taught that Jesus is not our problem. *(REV. expresses shock)* Africans didn't kill Jesus, the Romans did. So why could we share the guilt for an offense that we had nothing to do with? Good luck, Rev. And may Olodumare be with you. *(Exits)*

REV. JACK LEGGE: *(Sits down, wipes his face with a handkerchief)* Another one gone over to the forces of Satan. What am I going to do? I'm six months behind in my Cadillac notes. Lost that TV hour, got evicted from my fifteen-room rectory. *(Pause)* That sexual harassment suit caused me a lot of damage. A lot of damage. But I weathered that storm. I had to pay one third of the Church's coffers to settle out of court. That greedy Jezebel. It was worth it, though. She had a butt that you could grow tomatoes on and a pussy as tight as a bulldog's grip. Still, things have changed since the 1990s. Boy, I was steppin' high then. The delectable juices of filet mignon dripping from my lips, banquets honoring me. Plenty of parish sisters in case I need to relieve the tension—that's an occupational hazard for a public man like me. The finest Scotch from Ireland and three kinds of wine. Hanging out with high-class folks. Statesmen, clergymen, and the most powerful business leaders in America. Invited to do op-eds in the *Wall Street Journal* in which I traced the problems of the black community to their forgetting to honor Jeeeeesssusss. I called for the politics of conversion. Congressional committees calling upon me to testify about the moral evil that was vanquishing America.

(Stage goes dark.)

Act I: Scene 2

(Lights up on a table topped with microphones with the call letters of different stations on them. A TV cameraman is photographing the scene. A black congressperson, MABEL JOHNSON *with wide hat, fur collar, gaudy tasteless dress, wearing high heels and a blonde wig, is chairing a committee.* THREE STRIKES, *a rap star, is seated next to* REV. JACK LEGGE. *He wears dark glasses. Baseball cap and other hip-hop attire.)*

CHAIRPERSON: And Rev. Legge, tell the committee the threat that these nasty rap records are to the minds of the youth of today.

REV. JACK LEGGE: What effect do they have? They do have plenty of effect, sister. Plenty of effect. They have made them into licentious slaves to the passions of the flesh. They have turned them into violent predators. Why, when I look over my shoulder on a dark street and see that it's a white person walking behind me and not a black, I am relieved. They put evil thoughts in the mind of the young men. Get them to disrespecting they women. Using filthy words to express theyselves. Cussing out and issuing threats against our fine gentlemen in blue who provide a thin line between the jungle and we law-abiding citizens. I have a lyric right here that illustrates the viciousness of this nasty music. It's called: "Put It In the Butt," by Luther Campbell.

THREE STRIKES: That's not the title. It's "Put It In The Buck."

CHAIRPERSON: *(To* THREE STRIKES*)* Shut up, you!

THREE STRIKES: I've been sitting here for an hour listening to this ignorant rant.

CHAIRPERSON: *(Banging the gavel)* Three Strikes, if you don't shut your mouth, I'm going to have the Sergeant at Arms! . . .

THREE STRIKES: This insane ignorant attack on rap by this—

REV. JACK LEGGE: Watch what you say, sonny. I'm a man of the Lord!

THREE STRIKES: Charlatan!

REV. JACK LEGGE: Charlatan? *(Rising in a threatening manner)* You call me, a man who walked with Martin Luther King, Jr., who was with the leader in Selma, Montgomery, and Birmingham—*(preaches)* whose clothes were soiled with the blood of the prophet as his life ebbed away on the balcony of the Lorraine Motel—you call me, a charlatan. Young man, you owe me an apology *(catches the eye of* CHAIRPERSON *who nods in agreement)*

CHAIRPERSON: I'm going to hold you in contempt of Congress, Three Strikes, if you don't let the Rev. continue. You young people have no breeding. Your parents don't care anything about you. No wonder you're producing this pornographic smut.

REV. JACK LEGGE: As I was saying, Madame Chairperson, I think that it is time for the Congress to step in and stamp out this as though it were the evil serpent underneath one's foot. These vile records ain't doin' nothin' but putting people up to violence and misogyny. *(Applause)* They are causing the country to be threatened with a tidal wave of carnality *(applause)*.

CHAIRPERSON: Now do you have something to say, Three Strikes? Make it brief. The committee has to take a lunch break. By the way, where did you get such a ridiculous name as Three Strikes?

THREE STRIKES: The way I look at it, Madame Chairperson and Rev. Legge, the black man has three strikes against him. He is born black, a man, and poor.

REV. JACK LEGGE: *(Laughing)* Ain't he crazy?

CHAIRPERSON: I sure do get tired of you young punks wallowing in your misery. You ought to go out and get a real job instead of disrespecting our women with these seedy songs of yours. Now proceed.

THREE STRIKES: Madame Chairperson, Rev. Legge, both of you are wrong about rap. What we do is merely reflect the attitudes of the community. We didn't invent the social conditions that led to the breakdown of social values. We're merely the messengers.

REV. JACK LEGGE: That ain't no excuse.

THREE STRIKES: You can slay the messenger, but you can't slay the message. Besides, if you black leaders were more accessible to the needs of young ghetto people, maybe we wouldn't have a generation that's gone buck wild. It seems that you're using rap as a scapegoat for your inability to reach young people. Every time I see you in the papers, Madame Chairperson *(sarcastically)* you're playing golf or at some posh resort or on a vacation in Bermuda paid for by your big business sponsors who are doing more to pollute the country than all of the music ever written.

CHAIRPERSON: You're out of order, sonny boy.

THREE STRIKES: And you, Rev. Legge, the only reason that you're in on this is because of your insatiable need for publicity. Why, with all of the money that you raked in from your TV ministry, why haven't you built a recreation center for the youth? Or a senior citizen's home?

CHAIRPERSON: How dare you insult Rev. Legge. He is the kind of role model that our community needs instead of you rappers with your half-dressed nasty girls, your swimming pools full of Budweisers, and your gold teeth and chains. Look at some of these awful lyrics. *(Puts on glasses and reads from paper)* S my D, from New 2 Live Crew: "And won't you lick my clit, bitch." Such foul words, I have to gargle with mouthwash after uttering them *(pulls out a bottle of mouthwash, gargles, spits in a cup)*. I've never had an occasion to use such words as shit, bitch, fuck, and dick *(said lustfully)* until I began this investigation. It makes me feel . . . dirty all over. Needless to say, the experience has been trying.

THREE STRIKES: You artless tasteless boogee negroes. You tried to stop ragtime and you failed, you tried to stop the blues, you failed. You tried to stop gospel and you failed, you tried to stop rhythm and blues and rock and roll and you failed, you tried to stop the rhumba, the samba, and the salsa and you failed.

CHAIRPERSON: *(Banging gavel, furiously)* Mr. Sergeant at Arms!

THREE STRIKES: You tried to stop be-bop and Charlie Parker—

CHAIRPERSON: Mr. Sergeant at Arms!

THREE STRIKES: . . . lives! (SERGEANT AT ARMS *grabs* THREE STRIKES *and begins to escort him from the hearing room)* When you stop rap here where do you go next? There's Hawaiian Rap, Japanese Rap, Togoland Rap, Italian Rap—

REV. JACK LEGGE: The boy don't respect nobody.

THREE STRIKES: People are rapping in Russia, Afghanistan, Madagascar. They're rapping in Beijing and Paris, Amsterdam and Hamburg, Singapore, Lagos and Tokyo,

Kinshasa, you'll never stop it. Never, never. Vive la Rap! Rap libre! *(Exit with* SERGEANT AT ARMS.*)*

CHAIRPERSON: Rev. Jack Legge, I'm sorry for his outbursts. We have the votes. The votes that will outlaw this filthy music once and for all. Let me read the newest song by Three Strikes: *(Passionately)*

Ream my dick, my buttercup
Lick it till it shrivels
up
Make me come all
in your mouth
Suck me, love me
Sex me, south

Let me tickle
your warm wet cunt
stroke your bush
with my hard thick runt
you give me a pull
and I'll give you a push
and then I'll play with
your cute little tush

(She stops, gazes into the distance, longingly.)

REV. JACK LEGGE: You needn't read further, Madame Chairperson. *(She recovers)* Having to listen to these filthy CDs and watching these old MTV videos must have been trying for you. These wicked videos show half-clothed women, gyrating like savages in the darkest Africa. A . . . er . . . so I've heard. Every Christian in the country is grateful to you, Madame Chairperson, for coming down hard on this generation of youth who are a shiftless evil bunch. And I pledge my support and all of the resources at my disposal to fight to the end. We can win. With the help of the virtuous and moral individuals of this great nation, we will defeat rap. This ugly monster, this fiend from the bottomless pit who has put our Christian values at risk.

(Dark. Lights go up. Spotlight on NEWSPERSON.*)*

NEWSPERSON: Ladies and gentlemen, here is a late-breaking story. The Senate has followed an earlier House vote in banning Rap music from the airwaves. The President says that he will sign the bill that will make it a federal crime to record, disseminate, purchase or even hum a Rap tune, or even to imagine the lyrics of a Rap tune. Those convicted of breaking this law can be subject to a mandatory sentence of life imprisonment. So jubilant was a public weary of this filthy uncivilized music invading the sanctity of our alabaster land—America—that Monday has been declared a national holiday. Church bells will ring. The horns of ships will blast. Rev. Jack Legge, the sensible black leader who led the drive to ban Rap music, will receive the Medal of Freedom during ceremonies that will be held in the White House next week.

(Stage goes dark. Then lights.)

Act I: Scene 3

(St. John's Church.)

REV. JACK LEGGE: Boy, those were the days. *Meet the Press. Face the Nation. People Magazine. The Times. Newsweek. Time.* My face was everywhere. *(Reveals empty pockets)* Now my bank account is about the size of a mosquito's peter. All these people are into this old Africa mess. Little do they know that lions and tigers are still walking through towns over there. Santería. Yoruba, and this strange heathen belief that the chinaman's smuggled into the country. Goes by the name of Buddhism. What nonsense. God must be mad. A woman sitting in the White House. A follower of Sophia. S'pozed to be some kind of woman Earth Goddess. Saint John said that at the end of time women would be going with women and men would be lying with men. People don't seem to have the time for Jesus no more. They better get right or something terrible is going to happen to this nation. If the people and their leaders don't shape up, praying to false idols and . . . and . . . and worshiping a woman. Speaking of women *(pulls out small black book)*, this stress is getting too much for me. I need a date *(soldiers arrive)*.

1ST SOLDIER: Rev. Jack Legge?

REV. JACK LEGGE: That's me.

2ND SOLDIER: You're under arrest.

REV. JACK LEGGE: For what? *(They carry him off kicking and protesting.)* I know my rights. What is the meaning of this? Why, I marched with Martin Luther King, Jr. He wouldn't make a speech without having me okay it. I kept the shirt that bears the prophet's blood. Hey, not so rough. I'm a man who demands respect. You better not mess with a servant of the Lord. Hey, hold it, stop. Stop it.

Act I: Scene 4

(The Oval Office. THE PRESIDENT OF THE UNITED STATES, *an Asian-American woman. She is seated on the floor in a lotus position. Her eyes are closed. New Age music in the background. Incense floating up.* THREE STRIKES *enters now, older, grayer. He is the Attorney General. He is dressed in white, traditional sokoto and a fila.)*

ATTORNEY GENERAL: *(To audience).* She's in the Oval Office all day. Into her meditations she says. Not a single piece of legislation has been passed. The government is at a standstill. Mail hasn't been delivered in months. All of the postal employees are meditating. The Wicca members of Congress haven't returned from their retreat in Arizona. They're attending some spiritual edification conference. Our people can't do business for lack of a quorum. I don't know how long the Santería party will be able to maintain an alliance with these people. Before the Chinese entered Tibet, a sizeable part of the adult male population was freeloading off of the working people. They justified this on the grounds that they were receiving wisdom and that this was work. With the Wicca people in power, this religion, a mishmash of Orientalism, self-improvement philosophy, California mysticism, and purist ecology, a similar kind of parasitism is happening here.

(PRESIDENT *blinks her eyes until these are fully open. She sees the* ATTORNEY GENERAL *and smiles. He smiles back.*)

PRESIDENT: *(To audience)* Him again. I made him Attorney General as a conciliatory gesture to the Santería after the last election. I wonder, do they really sacrifice people? That's the rumor. All of the animals they sacrifice to spirits. And then that drumming. There are drums all over. The whole city sounds like Prospect Park. They're such a noisy people. When they call their members for a vote in the House of Representatives, they insist upon using a conch horn instead of the electronic system. I hope that they won't gain more seats in the House. It's a good thing that we Wicca people run the Senate. They talk a good game about their devotion to women's rights, but women priests or what they call "Babalawo" are very rare. Also, how can they revere such demanding egotistical and authoritarian gods? Gods who drink rum. Eat meat. And have sex with people.

ATTORNEY GENERAL: Ms. President, I consulted with members of the department. We've decided to arrest the Christian leaders and reprocess them. Close down the remaining churches. Of course, there will be those who will complain about the infringement upon First Amendment rights, but it'll blow over. The public has lost its patience with these Christians. The violence. The misogyny.

PRESIDENT: I think this is the best course of action.

ATTORNEY GENERAL: Outside of the mayhem and the grisly murders still taking place in the Christian sections, the country is at peace. The temples are filled with people. Crimes of violence are way down. People are not shouting at each other anymore. Everybody goes around talking like Avery Brooks in *Star Trek: Deep Space Nine.* But in the Christian corridors, crime, violence, child and spousal abuse are still taking place. People in these areas lose their tempers with the slightest provocation. Everybody is armed.

PRESIDENT: They're nothing but trouble. They have these shoot-outs in their places of worship. On the day they celebrate their so-called savior, even. Some of the bloodiest battles occur on Christmas and Easter. Crazed disciples enter temples, mosques, and synagogues and engage in shoot-outs. Seems that religions that originated in the Middle East are hotheads. Nothing but Jihads, Crusades. Witch hunts. Maybe it has something to do with their all worshiping a volcano god.

ATTORNEY GENERAL: The public is through with the behavior of these Christians. Nothing but homicide and genocide wherever they go.

PRESIDENT: What do you propose, Mr. Attorney General?

ATTORNEY GENERAL: We're going to ban the Bible, the Koran, and the Torah. These books, as you know, Ms. President, are full of sexist comments and instructions. Hostility toward women is the hallmark of these religions.

PRESIDENT: Do you suppose their unruliness had something to do with their diet? Their breathing methods? Maybe a crackdown is in order. *(To audience)* This is an election year, right? If I can get rid of these people I will win reelection with no problem. The Wicca Party will come in with another landslide.

ATTORNEY GENERAL: *(To audience)* Fat chance. I sense a growing disillusionment with this regime. Everything is so cool and calm. People miss the excitement of former times. The Wiccas have declared a curfew all over the country—from ten P.M. to eight A.M. is the national quiet hour. There's no fun in Wicca, unless you're on the inside. People want to party. To let the good times roll again. Carnivals. Mardi Gras. We'll go through the motions of cracking down on these Christians. Get rid of their leaders. Then their followers will be up for grabs. They will have no choice but to side with us. With their support we will have a new religious majority in the country. After all, we use Christian saints as ways. Ways to get to our loas. The Christians have nowhere to go. They will have to join us. They hate the Wiccas. Christians used to burn people like her at the stake.

PRESIDENT: *(Starry-eyed)* Just think. Twenty years ago I was a minor poet and then I won a fellowship from the Only Oil Foundation to spend three weeks in residence at a country estate.

ATTORNEY GENERAL: That was the beginning of a notable career. *(To the audience)* She tells this goofy story at every occasion.

PRESIDENT: And one day while strolling through the meadow, a beautiful white horse galloped up from nowhere and spoke to me. Told me that destiny had great plans for me. That I would bring peace to a country nearly destroyed by random mayhem and violence. It was then that I swore off porterhouse steaks forever. Much later Sophia came to me in a dream and revealed to me that yes, indeed, she was that horse. The rest, as they say, is history. I defeated an obese freak who was addicted to country hams. So grossed out on hydrogenated oils he was until he couldn't go two minutes without fatigue. This glutton was a symbol of the Age of Greed. For breakfast he ate steak and eggs. Those awful calorie-laden western omelets. After I was elected, meditation centers were established in every neighborhood. Compulsory low-fat diets were forced upon the public. Fruit, natural grains, cereals, beans. A big market emerged for Psyllium Hydrophilic Mucillod.

ATTORNEY GENERAL: *(To audience)* There have been riots all over the country protesting this bland diet. We'll promise to restore Barbeque. French fries. Hi-fat ice cream. Steak. There are so many sacred cows wandering around that traffic is tied up from Pittsburgh to Riverside, California. The black market in steaks is making millions in profit. The compulsory diet issue alone should gain us seven states.

PRESIDENT: The first thing I did after the election was to declare war on meat eaters. I banned the marketing of steaks. But now some person is involved in a hot black market in steaks. Oh, I wish that I could get my hands on that person. I'll put him under the jail. Why haven't you caught him?

ATTORNEY GENERAL: We're doing all that we can. *(Hands her a document)*

PRESIDENT: What's this?

ATTORNEY GENERAL: It's the executive order that will allow our soldiers to raid the mosques, churches, and synagogues. Drastic steps must be taken to end the Judeo-Christian threat to civilization once and for all.

PRESIDENT: You have my unequivocal support. And once again we show the country that the Santería and the Wicca, regardless of their differences, are capable of working in harmony for the common good. *(They eye each other suspiciously for a moment)*

ATTORNEY GENERAL: Thank you, Ms. President. *(He exits)*

PRESIDENT: One thing about them. They certainly wear beautiful clothes. I wonder who his designer is? *(Female* AIDE *enters)*

AIDE: Your Excellency, we have the final draft of the official prayer in school that all school children will be required to recite before the beginning of classes.

PRESIDENT: Read it to me.

AIDE: "Our maker Sophia. We are women in your image. With the old blood of our wombs we give form to new life. With nectar between our thighs we invite a lover. We birth a child. With our warm body fluids we remind the world of its pleasures and sensations."

PRESIDENT: Wonderful. Simply marvelous.

AIDE: I have a question, though.

PRESIDENT: What?

AIDE: Won't the boys be upset having to recite this prayer?

PRESIDENT: Women have had to recite creeds for thousands of years that addressed a god of the male gender. It's time for payback. *(Snaps fingers, vogue-like gesture made popular in the film* Paris Is Burning*)*

AIDE: And the Santerías?

PRESIDENT: Don't worry about them. They're very adaptable. You see how quickly they incorporated Sophia and Gaia into their pantheon? They're just two more spirits to them. I think they feed Sophia macrobiotic food. Those people have so many spirits to obey that they spend all of their time in ritual. No wonder they were the runners-up in the last election. They didn't have enough time to campaign. And listen, I'll tell you something. If we win the House in the next election, we may have to crack down on the Santería. I don't trust them. We can run ads accusing them of Satanism and cannibalism. They're meat eaters like the rest. Only they have an exemption from the Supreme Court. They say it's part of their religion. After the next election, we'll see about that.

Act II: Scene 1

RAPPER:

What you visit upon others
can happen to you
Now Jack Legge the preacher
is in a hell of a stew.

In the 1990s
He was riding a wave
Now it's twenty years later
and he's considered a knave
A different regime
Is running things now
And they and the Christians
don't see eye to eye.

The prisoners in jail
include eaters of steak
And that's not all strange
in this off-the-wall state.

So sit back and chill out
and hear this weird tale
about Three Strikes and Jack Legge
and a Pope making bail.

CHORUS:

The preacher and the rapper
One's dreadlocked, and one's dapper
A man of the cloth
and a man of the streets
The issues are old
and the passions run deep
and try as they might
will their minds ever meet?

(Jail cell. Pope is being interviewed by the newscaster. He's playing solitaire and isn't looking at her.)

NEWSCASTER: The world press is focused upon this federal prison today. Inside this jail cell is a man who used to be one of the world's most powerful men. But now, as a sign of the declining power of the Christian church, the Pope has been thrown in jail after being seized on the eve of his American tour. Your Holiness, how are you holding up?

POPE: I've had better days.

NEWSCASTER: The Sung government has said that because of your stand on abortion and women priests they couldn't guarantee your safety. That they have placed you in protective custody. But insiders say it's because of a complaint made by a young boy.

POPE: A baseless lie. I am not guilty.

NEWSCASTER: It's going to be hard to prove it, Holy Father. After the scandal of the last three decades and the cash the Church has paid out to quash suits made in connection with these complaints, people are wondering whether the charges are true?

POPE: Let them believe what they want to believe.

NEWSCASTER: How do you feel when you see your photo on the cover of all the magazines? The lurid copy. The press being almost obsessed with every development, every detail about your private life on display in supermarkets?

POPE: I don't feel a thing to tell you the truth. I just want to get the whole thing over. Clear my name.

NEWSCASTER: Thank you for giving us this exclusive interview, your Excellency.

POPE: My pleasure.

NEWSCASTER: This has been an exclusive interview with the Pope, who had been held in an American prison for six months. The government says it's because there have been threats against his life as a result of the Church's stand on abortion and women priests. But few believe the official story.

(She writes a check and hands it to him.)

POPE: Thank you.

NEWSCASTER: Don't you think it's degrading for a man of your stature to benefit from checkbook journalism?

POPE: Hey, I'm just trying to make bail.

NEWSCASTER: Thanks for the interview, anyway. *(She exits)*

POPE: A thousand bucks more and I'll have my bail money. *(Goes over to his tape recorder and puts in a tape. Some music by Giovanni Gabrielli. Begins to do push-ups. Momentarily* REV. JACK LEGGE *is roughly shoved into the cell that holds the Pope. Brushes off his clothes.)*

REV. JACK LEGGE: *(To guards who are leaving)* You'll pay for this! You'll pay. Why, I marched with Martin Luther King, Jr. It was I whom he asked for advice when he was composing his famous "March on Washington" speech. I was with him in the

Birmingham jail. I wear his blood on my clothes. I have proof. *(Turns around and notices the other jail occupant. To himself)* Well, at least they put me in a cell with a white man. I'm afraid of these young brothers. When I walk down the street and someone is following me, I'm relieved when I discover that it is a white person behind me.

Aren't you—why yes, your Excellency *(kneels and kisses his ring)*. It's an honor. I'm sharing my cell with you . . . I read about your . . . er . . . troubles—they're persecuting us Christians all over the globe, it seems. Look at me. Why, I was one of the top strategists for the Southern Christian Leadership Conference—thrown in jail like a common tramp.

POPE: Take it as a learning experience. I've learned a lot in these past six months of incarceration. I've read much of the opposition's work. Marx. The Protestants. Buddhism. Santería. I've even delved into this Sophia business that's been sweeping the West, posing the greatest threat to the Christian Church since the cult of Isis.

REV. JACK LEGGE: A woman god, ha! That'll be the day.

POPE: I wouldn't be so sure. As I said, I've had a lot of time to think. This isn't the same as viewing the world from my Vatican apartment of plush red carpets and pre-Raphaelite paintings. This is real. This is, what my fellow inmates would call, the nitty-gritty. You know what I'm saying? What are you in for?

REV. JACK LEGGE: They won't say. Came to my church. Hauled me away.

VOICE: Help me! Please, somebody help me!

REV. JACK LEGGE: What's that?

POPE: It's a young *Village Voice* reporter. He was always praising prisoners as the true voice of the disenfranchised masses. Said that they are the vanguard of the revolution. Said he read it in a book. He got himself arrested so that he could write a book from the inside. Poor fellow. The Ass Bandits got hold of him. They're passing him around and trading him for cigarettes and candy.

REV. JACK LEGGE: That's not going to happen to me. I'll be out of here as soon as my lawyer hears about this.

(Television comes on. New Age spacey music.)

NEWSCASTER: This is Violet Ray with the main points of the news. Thousands of people from all over America converged upon Florida today for the annual Odun rites. Master priest drummer Babatu Olatunji, his dancers and chorus excited Miami's largest stadium, which was filled to capacity. Many African deities came down and joined in the celebration. Shango, Oshun, Oya, Orungan, Dada, Babalu, Ifa and many others. Unlike the old Christian days, not a single episode of violence was reported. President Barbara Sung congratulated the worshipers for being so well-behaved. Though she disapproves of animal sacrifice and meat eating, she said that she would continue to observe the religious freedom of the Santería, guaranteed by the Supreme Court. In other news, President Barbara Sung has declared the January Holiday of Martin Luther King, Jr., the prophet of nonviolence, to be a day of national celebration. If the celebration is not observed in New Hampshire, President Sung has promised to send in troops. As you know, the observances for George Washington, Abraham Lincoln, and Columbus have been eliminated from the calendar due to President Sung's having declared it inappropriate to celebrate the births of men associated with violence. And finally a repeat of the lead story. Troops are beginning to withdraw from occupying the Christian zones where they were sent after the Christmas riots. Each year during Christmas the Christians get drunk and begin to engage in a rampage of violence. The 9-1-1 calls increase beyond the capacity of our law enforcement agencies to handle them. On Easter, as you know, many of the more fanatical devotees of the Christian cult drive nails through their hands in imitation of their Lord about whom the preposterous claim was made that he rose from the dead. Experts say that one of the reasons that followers of desert religions are so violent is that their core belief is based upon mutilation and blood sacrifice.

(Newscaster shivers with disgust.)

Ms. Sung has decided to take stern measures against the Christians who are still engaged in misogyny and are promoting violence and racism, all of which are against the law. Millions of Bibles have been confiscated and burned. As part of the new crackdown, several prominent ministers have been arrested and will be re-processed (REV. JACK LEGGE *is stunned*) as a way of cleansing society of Christianity and its cousin religions, which have led to the deaths of millions over the centuries. The charlatan and imposter Reverend Jack Legge has been seized and now share's a cell with the criminal Roman Pope who was arrested on the eve of the Pope's tour of America after a youngster came forth and identified the Pope as the man who molested him in a fantasy.

REV. JACK LEGGE: Re-processed. What is that? I ain't done nothing wrong. Why, that's crazy! *(Goes to bars)* Guard. Guard. There has been a mistake. I was with Martin Luther King, Jr., from his early days. Why, I used to write his term papers in college. It was me who researched his Ph.D. dissertation.

(ATTORNEY GENERAL *approaches the cell.*)

REV. JACK LEGGE: Who are you?

ATTORNEY GENERAL: I'm the Attorney General.

REV. JACK LEGGE: Well, that's more like it. The government has realized its mistake and sent you to apologize, right?

ATTORNEY GENERAL: *(Ignores* REVEREND*)* Pope, you're free to go. The child has changed his testimony. He says that it wasn't you who seduced him in his fantasy. It was Elvis. There's an all-states bulletin out on the King of Rock and Roll and he's been sited in a number of places. We believe an arrest is imminent.

POPE: *(Rising, exiting from the cell, shaking his head)* You Americans are crazier than anybody would have ever believed. You arrest me as soon as I land in New York on the first leg of my American tour. You throw me in jail and won't allow me to consult a lawyer. All because of some kids' fantasy.

ATTORNEY GENERAL: A fantasy, huh? What would you call the notion of virgin birth, or the Ascension?

REV. JACK LEGGE: Look, you. Me and the Holy Father ain't going to stand for none of your blasphemy. *(POPE and* ATTORNEY GENERAL *ignore him)*

POPE: Young man, you have a lot to learn. *(REVEREND nods in agreement)* And even you would admit that those truths that were revealed by faith are much stronger than some emotionally disturbed youngster, bringing charges of such a bizarre nature against me.

REV. JACK LEGGE: You tell him, Pope.

ATTORNEY GENERAL: Half the graves in Europe are filled with heretics whom your church put to death for denying those revealed truths as you call them. Fantasies as I call them.

POPE: How did a fantasy become the same thing as reality in American law?

REV. JACK LEGGE: Good question, Pope. Answer the man. How did it? *(Challenging, gets into the* ATTORNEY GENERAL*'s face)*

ATTORNEY GENERAL: *(Ignores him)* You know as well as I, Pope, that in the West it begins with Plato's cave allegory and continues through Immanuel Kant's *Critique of Pure Reason.* Both argue that objective reality can never be known, right?

POPE: God knows objective reality. Besides, Plato was a pagan and Kant couldn't make up his mind about whether to be a pagan or a Christian.

REV. JACK LEGGE: You're right, Pope. God knows everything. *(To* ATTORNEY GENERAL*)* I guess he told you, chump!

ATTORNEY GENERAL: You don't know whether God knows objective reality because you cannot know God.

POPE: His being is manifest.

REV. JACK LEGGE: I know Him in my heart.

ATTORNEY GENERAL: Max Weber's comment that the objective interpretation of human meaning necessarily involved the subjective viewpoint of the observer is echoed in Heisenberg's principle of indeterminacy. The Japanese have a concept known as Shin-nyo, which closely means "suchness," the true nature of things that eludes all description for which the word "fu-ka-shi-gi" is used.

REV. JACK LEGGE: What's the Japs got to do with it? Stick to the subject. You're changing the subject because the Pope is beating your argument.

ATTORNEY GENERAL: *(Ignores* REVEREND*)* Of course, the Yoruba were into indeterminacy thousands of years before Plato. They even have a god Eshu, who is a god of indeterminacy, of chance and uncertainty, just as the Haitians reaffirm Plato's theory of knowledge, with their belief that the real world is alive beneath the sea, and that the world perceived through the senses is a pale reflection of this world. For the Akan people of Ghana, dream life is just as true as real life.

REV. JACK LEGGE: There you go with that old heathen Africa mess again. You embarrassing me. You make the Pope think that we still savages. In the jungle. There ain't nothin' in Africa but reptiles and drums.

POPE: He's a real *fregniacciaro.*

ATTORNEY GENERAL: *Fregniacciaro.* That's bullshitter, right? *(*POPE *nods)* We're just amateur bullshitters next to you fellows. You invented the cosmological and teleological and ontological proofs for the existence of God. This real con-job in which the proof for the existence of God was rigged in the premise. Something like God exists because God exists.

POPE: Those proofs lasted for seven hundred years. You should be so lucky. *(Pause)* Besides, what about your god, Olodumare?

REV. JACK LEGGE: He got you now, infidel.

ATTORNEY GENERAL: Olodumare is rarely mentioned in Santería. We respect his intermediaries who provide us with services. Unlike your God who allegedly interferes in the affairs of men, Olodumare is sort of like a C.E.O. who presides over a large staff of messengers. Also, unlike your God who has sent armies into the field for centuries, sometimes backing both sides, there is seldom an army that can claim its mandate from Olodumare. Olodumare never punished children who mocked a prophet. Olodumare never turned cities to sand simply because the inhabitants within engaged in unorthodox sexual practices. We even have a hermaphrodite god—Olokan. She/he lives on the ocean floor. Other Santería gods are also gender neutral. Christianity condemns gays and lesbians to death. Leviticus says: "They shall surely be put to death." 20:13.

POPE: *(Pause)* You have a strange country here. You can be sure that when my lawyers sue you for false imprisonment, that it won't be a fantasy. It will be real. Am I free to go? *(*ATTORNEY GENERAL *nods.* POPE *gathers the Bible and rosary, puts on his skullcap. Begins to lift suitcase).*

REV. JACK LEGGE: Can I give you a hand, Pope? *(Reaches for suitcase).*

POPE: No, that won't be necessary.

REV. JACK LEGGE: I insist. *(They begin to struggle with the suitcase)*

POPE: *(Annoyed)* I said I'd handle it.

REV. JACK LEGGE: I know that we have had fallings out, your Excellency, but maybe now that the Church is under attack, we Protestants and Catholics ought to make up. Bury the hatchet.

POPE: Maybe so. *(POPE begins to exit)*

REV. JACK LEGGE: As for you *(to* ATTORNEY GENERAL*)* you should be ashamed of yourself, humiliating the Pope. Putting a Pope in jail for the first time in history.

POPE: Not true.

REV. JACK LEGGE: What?

POPE: Pius VII was detained by Napoleon. The Church survived Napoleon. In the 1840s, Pius IX was imprisoned by a revolutionary Committee of Public Safety. The Church survived that challenge, too. *(POPE and* ATTORNEY GENERAL *are studying each other as he delivers these lines)* We'll survive you, too.

ATTORNEY GENERAL: Pope?

POPE: Yes?

ATTORNEY GENERAL: Didn't you wonder why there was no outcry against your arrest?

POPE: That didn't bother me. How do you explain it?

ATTORNEY GENERAL: The Church is dead in this country. The Mother Goddess, which your early Church supplanted, has made a strong comeback. Maybe back there in the nineties when you had a chance, you should have ordained women priests.

REV. JACK LEGGE: Ha! Ha! That's crazy. Don't listen to him, Pope.

POPE: He has a point.

ATTORNEY GENERAL: And your stubbornness at the Cairo conference, refusing to make even the slightest concession to the Pro-Choice movement didn't help.

POPE: You're right, we didn't budge. Maybe we'll change. This time in jail has given me time to think. When do you have time to think? To sort of kick back and mull things over?

ATTORNEY GENERAL: I don't follow.

POPE: You and the New Agers are in charge now, but the same crowds who are applauding you today may be shouting for your crucifixion tomorrow. History always seems to be eager to get on to the next act. Good day, Attorney General. And Rev. Legge, keep carrying the cross. The forces of the Lord are down but not out. Maybe all of what is happening is merely a wake-up call. *(He exits)*

REV. JACK LEGGE: Good-bye, Pope. Have a good trip back to Italy and I'm sure that the rest of America's dwindling Christian band apologize for the awful treatment you've suffered at the hands of these heathens and idol worshipers. A wake-up call from the Lord. Yes indeed. *(To* ATTORNEY GENERAL*) Y*ou are on top now, but we are united. Catholics and Protestants. Why, even though we may have disagreements, me and the Pope believe in the same thing.

ATTORNEY GENERAL: How about celibacy?

REV. JACK LEGGE: *(Pause)* Well . . . I . . . a *(removes a handkerchief and begins to wipe his brow).*

ATTORNEY GENERAL: Do you recognize me?

REV. JACK LEGGE: *(Stares for a moment)* Can't say that I do.

ATTORNEY GENERAL: You don't remember the Congressional hearings in the 1990s. The hearings that led to the criminalization of Rap music?

REV. JACK LEGGE: Oh yes! Mabel Johnson and I were successful in our attempt to get rid of that nasty music. Made it a federal crime to create, manufacture, disseminate, and listen to Rap music. That hothead Three Strikes desisted, though. Made a bootleg version of the music, was arrested, and got a long . . . *(recognizes the* ATTORNEY GENERAL *as* THREE STRIKES) . . . sentence—hey! It's you. Three Strikes!

ATTORNEY GENERAL: That was my name before my transformation. My new name is Ogun Jagun Jagun. *(*REVEREND *bursts out laughing.* ATTORNEY GENERAL *ignores it)* That long prison sentence gave me a chance to think. I decided that you were right, Reverend. That violence and sexist attitudes toward women should be curbed. The way they're smacked around, humiliated, bruised, beaten, raped, murdered. I read a lot of books in prison and decided that of all of the books that I read, the most influential was the Bible.

REV. JACK LEGGE: I'm glad to hear that, son. Glad you see it my way.

ATTORNEY GENERAL: Not exactly. The Bible, as you know, is the paradigm, the frame of reference of the Judeo-Christian religion and it was after a close line-by-line reading of the scriptures that I decided that it was the Bible that created the basis of our culture's attitudes toward women and violence. From the beginning of the Bible, the book of Genesis, when women are made from the rib of a man and one woman is blamed for the introduction of sin into the world to the end when women are called whores. The Bible is a manual for women haters. Not only that, but there are constant instructions to commit violence against women—"thou shalt not suffer a witch to live" Exodus 22:17—which led to the extermination of women during the Middle Ages or women's holocaust, to the reference to Babylon the great, the Mother of harlots and abominations of the earth in Revelations 17:5. There are constant admonitions in this Bible of yours to fight against the enemies of this psychotic god that your people worship. A god who receives fiendish pleasure from the sufferings of his followers and even his own son. A god who unlike our Orishas can't eat and can't dance, won't make love to a woman—a brooding, dangerous and melancholy god who dwells alone. The greatest taboo in Yoruba is to dwell alone. I regret the songs that I recorded back there in the nineties which disrespected women and were filled with scatology.

I joined the Santería temple and became a follower of the Orishas. I dedicated my life to eliminating violence and misogyny from American life. And Reverend, you gave me the idea by leading the fight to banish Rap from the airwaves. You struck a blow for women's rights. I am to blame for making those underground recordings that got me arrested. But it was during that time in jail that I learned the truth. *(Slowly, deliberately)* That if criminalizing Rap was a good way of ridding the world of the misogynist culture, then criminalizing Christianity and its associate religions—Islam and Judaism—would help to end misogyny and violence once and for all.

REV. JACK LEGGE: Look here, buddy. You'd better not fool around with God—God don't like ugly.

ATTORNEY GENERAL: Your God is a racist, sexist, homophobic, and a misogynist. Throughout your Bible there are demands that women be subservient to men. "Wives submit yourselves unto your own husband, as unto the Lord," says Ephesians 5:22. "The husband is the head of the wife," again, Ephesians 5:23. ". . . the head of the woman is the man," says Corinthians 11:3. Your God doesn't like women talking back or challenging men; for doing so, they get labeled "contentious" as in ". . . a continual dropping in a very rainy day and a contentious woman are alike," Proverbs 27:15. For your Bible, women are evil: "Keep them from the evil woman, . . ." Proverbs 6:24, and are seen as causing the downfall of men: "She hath cast down many wounded; yes, many strong men have been slain by her." How can we tolerate a religion that condemns nonconformist women and homosexuals to death? Your God? Your God is a cruel god. What does he do to Hagar, concubine of the patriarch, Abraham? Sends her and her son into the wilderness without any means of providing for herself. I can't think of anything so cruel.

REV. JACK LEGGE: It's not for us to judge the ways of the Lord. We are just supposed to have faith and to obey like sheep.

ATTORNEY GENERAL: Think of the wars, the genocide. The hate crimes. The persecution of blacks, women, and homosexuals as a result of these ugly Biblical instructions. The massacres. The show trials. The lynching. Mass suicides at Jonestown and the Order of the Solar Temple. And you had the nerve back there in the 1990s to accuse rappers of misogyny? No rapper ever stoned a woman to death because he read it in some crazy patriarchal book

REV. JACK LEGGE: You ought not to be saying these things. God will punish you.

ATTORNEY GENERAL: I'll take my chances. Your God versus mine.

REV. JACK LEGGE: *(Mutters)* Pagan savages. Look, I'm about fed up with this conversation. I demand that I be released. I'm not as influential as I once was, I admit, but I still have some powerful friends. When Mabel Johnson hears about this, you will have some explaining to do. She is one of the three Christians who still have a seat in Congress. (MABEL *is led into the cell, she has aged like all of the other characters who appeared in Act I. She wears a leopard-skin coat.)*

MABEL: *(To guard)* Get your hands off me. I have congressional immunity. You can't do this to me.

REV. JACK LEGGE: Mabel, what you doing here?

MABEL: Some of these crazy Wicca police came to my house in the middle of the night. Turned the place upside down. Said they were looking for evidence.

REV. JACK LEGGE: Evidence. Evidence for what?

ATTORNEY GENERAL: She's been making a profit from illegal steak sales. She's raked in millions (PRESIDENT SUNG *enters with* AIDE).

PRESIDENT: I just wanted to see for myself the face of a person so vile as to sell steaks when I personally prohibited the marketing of such poison.

MABEL: You can't prove a doggone thing.

PRESIDENT: Oh! We can't, can we? All of your cohorts have confessed. They're making deals with the prosecutors. They said that you are the mastermind behind the whole scheme.

MABEL: They what? Those dirty low-down sneaks! *(Mutters)* Those disloyal mother-fuckers.

REV. JACK LEGGE: That ain't the reason they're persecuting you, Mabel. Don't you recognize this man? It's Three Strikes.

MABEL: *(Shocked)* Three Strikes! That filthy-mouthed Rap singer?

ATTORNEY GENERAL: We're looking at some serious time here. And to think, you hauled me before a Congressional committee for singing Rap songs.

PRESIDENT: As much as I detest Rap music, no Rap music ever gave anybody a heart attack.

MABEL: Selling bad meat was the only way that I could stay in office. It takes a fortune to be a candidate these days.

PRESIDENT: You won't have to worry about running for office anymore.

ATTORNEY GENERAL: You can get ten years for raising the cholesterol level of the population.

MABEL: Ten years? That's ridiculous.

PRESIDENT: Ten years, my foot. I'm going to have to re-process these two. We must rid the nation's gene pool of characters like these.

ATTORNEY GENERAL: Re-processing. But, Ms. President, isn't that extreme?

PRESIDENT: You keep out of this. Oh! Now I get it. You're in cahoots with your fellow meat eaters. I knew it. You barbarian. Guard! Take these people to the re-processing center.

ATTORNEY GENERAL: What? You would . . . me? You're asking for it. The Santería party will have you impeached.

PRESIDENT: Let them.

REV. JACK LEGGE: Now wait a minute. Re-processing. Isn't that a little extreme? What is it, anyway?

ATTORNEY GENERAL: If you are such a loyal follower of your God, then maybe He will save you from the fate that awaits you.

MABEL: Re-processing. It's probably unconstitutional. I know my rights.

REV. JACK LEGGE: Yes. Good question.

ATTORNEY GENERAL: They're going to make us an example the way I was made an example by those Congressional hearings that took place in the 1990s.

PRESIDENT: Don't worry. You won't feel a thing. It's painless. We take you into a little room and—the Wicca way of execution is much more civilized than the crude and barbaric gas chamber, the electric chair. You'll die smiling with enlightenment.

REV. JACK LEGGE: Now hold on a minute. Ain't nobody said nothing about no execution. Let me out this place. Help! Help! *(Guard restrains him)*

MABEL: You won't get away with it. I knew I should have voted for the immigration bill barring these people from coming over here. These chinks have taken over the country. They are worse than white people.

PRESIDENT: Now look here, dearie. Don't try guilt tripping me. The Chinese never owned black slaves.

ATTORNEY GENERAL: Only yellow slaves. I suspect that this meat business is just a cover. She wants to use us to gain re-election. She wants to distract attention from her failed policies. The meat prohibition. The national quiet hour. Compulsory aerobics.

PRESIDENT: Nobody cares anything about you. Who would protest? A lowly high-fat peddler, wearer of animal skins and carnivorous steak thief, a has-been broken down colored preacher and a follower of *(contemptuously)* voodoo. The public will thank me. They're tired of your cult and its disgusting practices.

MABEL: You're just persecuting us because we're black.

PRESIDENT: Race. Race. Race. That's all you people think about. You can't tell us about oppression. We lived under the hated Japanese occupation. Your so-called servitude was a picnic in comparison to that. The slave master took care of all your needs. That's why you people developed a welfare mentality. You people are loafers.

MABEL: *(Lunges for* PRESIDENT, *stopped by guards)* Why you yellow slut. I'll wrap your sorry ass around my fist you motherfuckin' slope. *(*REVEREND *is shocked)* Excuse my French, Reverend *(sheepishly)*.

PRESIDENT: That's it. That's it. Resort to violence. You people are the most violent in the world.

ATTORNEY GENERAL: When the Santería hear about this, there will be a civil war that will make the one of the 1860s seem like a playground spat. I would advise you against proceeding with this madness. *(Guards begins to remove the* ATTORNEY GENERAL, MABEL, *and* REVEREND).

PRESIDENT: Let the Santería try. I'm way ahead of you, my friend. I ordered raids on Santería party headquarters on my way over here. Tonight I will make a speech to the nation. Tell the public what was going on inside those places. After that, whatever public support that you had will plummet.

REV. JACK LEGGE: Can't we talk this over? Please?

MABEL: *(To guards)* Get away from me. Let me go. Take your hands off me. *(Kicks one in the shins)*

REV. JACK LEGGE: Help me, Jesus! Please help me! I don't want to be re-processed. I want to live. Have mercy. Somebody help me.

(We still hear the REVEREND'*s screams for help from offstage.* PRESIDENT *checks to see if coast is clear. Sits down. Puts on Yankee's baseball cap. Removes a hamburger from a McDonald's bag. Begins to eat. Really enjoys it.)*

Act II: Scene 2

(St. John's Church. SECRETARY *hears* REVEREND *screaming. Rushes in. She is played by the same actress who plays* MABEL. *He is seated at a desk. The TV is turned on to the* Oprah Winfrey Show, *no sound.)*

REV. JACK LEGGE: Help me. Please. Somebody. *(He's breathing heavily and sweating profusely. She wakes him)* Mabel—you're all right!

SECRETARY: Mabel? What's wrong with you? My name is Jacqueline. I'm your secretary, Reverend. You been hittin' the Scotch again?

REV. JACK LEGGE: Oh, yes! Of course...I...I...had a bad dream *(calmly, thoughtfully)* "Thou scarest me with dreams and terrifiest me through visions." Job 7:14

SECRETARY: What did you say, Reverend?

REV. JACK LEGGE: Forget it. Look, what is my sermon for Sunday?

SECRETARY: "Her Abominations Spilleth Over."

REV. JACK LEGGE: Change that. Make it something like: "Mary Magdalene: Holy Witness."

SECRETARY: But Mary Magdalene was a prostitute. Why preach a sermon about her?

REV. JACK LEGGE: There's not a scintilla of proof in the Bible that the Divine Person was a prostitute. For too long the role of women in the Bible has been denied. It's time to give them their due. After all, had there been no Magdalene, we would never have had a witness to the Resurrection, and without Mary, Christ's mother, there would have been no Christ. While the men betrayed our Lord, these women stood by him to the end and beyond. And daughter—

SECRETARY: Yes, Reverend?

REV. JACK LEGGE: I want you to put an ad in the *Amsterdam News* and the *City Sun.* We could use a new assistant pastor, a woman. All of the ones under me are men. I want you to get me a qualified woman who can handle pastoral duties. People get tired of looking at the same old hardheads every Sunday. We need some innovative approaches.

SECRETARY: Reverend, what's come over you? You once said that you'd die and go to hell before you'd share the pulpit with a woman.

REV. JACK LEGGE: *(Ignores this remark)* I want you to sell the two Cadillacs. We could use the money to set up a soup kitchen in the church here. Take . . . take these rings *(removes them)* and cash them in. We could start a youth program. Keep kids off the street. And sister, call my maid. Tell her to give my three hundred suits and ninety shoes to the Goodwill. Don't look right. Our basking in luxuries while our people go hungry. As for my twenty-room mansion in Brooklyn, I want you to see about converting the place into a home for senior citizens. I'll move into an apartment. Hell, Jesus didn't live in no palace. He moved from town to town, living in different people's houses. Another thing. That greedy Jezebel—I mean the daughter with whom I was supposed to have a private prayer in the home? Cancel that engagement indefinitely. Now what you got for me today?

SECRETARY: Connie Chung's show. You're supposed to debate Ice T, Dr. Dre, and this new Rap star Three Strikes.

REV. JACK LEGGE: Call it off.

SECRETARY: What?

REV. JACK LEGGE: I said call it off.

SECRETARY: But Reverend, this will give you an opportunity to harangue against this music that encourages violence and degrades our women. Besides, you know how you love photo opportunities. You've become the lightning rod for those who want to banish this music from the airwaves.

(Messenger enters. Dressed in suit. Same actor who played the POPE).

MESSENGER: Reverend Jack Legge—

REV. JACK LEGGE: That's me *(hands him an envelope)*. Haven't I seen you somewhere before? *(Opening the envelope)*

MESSENGER: I don't think so. *(Exits)*

SECRETARY: What is it, Reverend?

REV. JACK LEGGE: It's a subpoena from Congress asking me to appear before some committee that's out to do away with Rap music.

SECRETARY: That's a wonderful opportunity, Reverend. It'll probably be broadcast on all the networks. (REVEREND *rips up the subpoena*)

REV. JACK LEGGE: I'm not participating in no drive that would criminalize the free expressions of hip-hoppers, be-boppers, hard-rockers or anybody else. I may disagree with the music and the lyrics, but I can't subscribe to any proposition that would smack of censorship. Do you think that Martin Luther King, Jr., and I made all of those sacrifices so that words and music would be censored? That artistic expression would be criminalized? I doubt it. What would have happened had Jessssussss, the greatest rapper of them all, been reluctant to propose such radical ideas in his time had he lacked the nerve to speak out, to address taboos, to hold his tongue. The world would be quite different. I mean if we began outlawing groups whose expression we object to where would it end? *(Pause)* Who would be next? These kids are sending out a wounded shrill cry from those shut up in these festering inner cities. Police brutality, media harassment, unemployment, malnutrition, low birth weight, landlord exploitation. They didn't create these conditions, they are merely exhibiting them for us.

As for sexism and misogyny, the Church has plenty enough of its own to take care of without worrying about others. And if we can't straighten out the Lord's house, how are we going to straighten out the house of popular music? We would be hypocrites. Jesus Christ hated hypocrisy. Some of his strongest statements are against hypocrisy. "Ye also outwardly appear righteous unto men, but within ye are full of hypocrisy and iniquity." Mathew 23:28 or "What is the hope of the hypocrite, though he hath gained, when God taketh away his soul?" We don't want to be hypocrites like the Pharisees whom Jesus condemned to woe. Now daughter, I want you to take a letter. Address it to the Pope at the Vatican. *(She begins to take dictation)*

Dear Pope:

As a fellow Christian, I was ashamed of the way your organization clowned and carried on at the recent Cairo conference. Where do you get off telling a woman when she can and when she can't have a baby? You ain't no woman. Have you ever been pregnant? No, you haven't. Have you ever suffered morning sickness? No, you haven't. Have you ever had an accidental pregnancy and didn't know how you were going to feed the child? Or been raped by some man or by your own father, the height of iniquity? The answer is no. Until you have done these things, you should keep your mouth shut. And one more thing. I'd be real careful about trying to rule other people's morality. I read the newspaper. *(Lights begin to dim)* And it seems to me that you have plenty of problems yourself without going around condemning others. The Vatican debt is about $56 Million, ain't it? *(Dimmer)* You remember what Jesus said about the Pharisees in Matthew 23:27: "Woe to you, scribes and Pharisees, hypocrites! For you are like whitewashed tombs, which, outwardly, appear beautiful, but within are full of dead men's bones and all uncleanliness." Seems to me *(Rap music begins to come up)* this pretty much describes the condition of the Church, Pope. We put up a good front—with our swell edifices and rich congregations—but inside . . . inside . . . deep in the soul of the Church, there is rot and disease and the bones of dead men. Before we pretend to cleanse others, we should root out the evil in us. *(Lights down, music up, spotlight on Rapper)*

RAPPER:

And so we conclude
the preacher and the rapper
our queer story and rhyme
about the hazards and drawbacks
of making art into a crime
you have your tastes and I
have mine and that's just fine
So give me one good reason
why we should fight all the time?

Some like Bach and others Mozart
the Count, the Duke, and the
venerable Earl Hines
Some like Cecilia Cruz
Willi Bobo and others, my man
Dr. Funkenstein
There's only good music
and bad music
Lenny Bernstein
was heard to say
That's a pretty good point
Why don't we keep it that way?
That's a pretty good point
Let's keep it that way

CHORUS:

The preacher and the rapper
One's dreadlocked, and one's dapper
A man of the cloth
and a man of the streets
The issues are old
and the passions run deep
and try as they might
will their minds ever meet?

The Crime

Glenn Wright and Raúl Santiago Sebazco

Act I: Scene 1

(In the darkness of the theater we hear a disco cut "Funky Town" come up. In syncopation to the beat of the music, we see flashing neon signs such as Eat At Joe's and Pink Flamingo Bar and Grill. We see a man crouching in the darkness of an alley and leaning up against a wall. He peeps out from behind the wall and looks up and down the street. He wears a small little burglar mask and a striped T-shirt. He carries a small gun in his hand. He looks like the classic image of the mugger.

He begins to talk to himself and then turns to the audience.)

MUGGER: Yeah . . . aggravation . . . humiliation . . . being treated like an idiot . . . being looked upon like some fool . . . even though you've been through fourteen years of school. Go look for a job . . . and then you'll see . . . there's no possible opening no matter what you want to be . . . pushed and shoved up and down . . . made to look like a lowdown clown . . . I'm sick and tired of all this sweat and grime . . . I'm going to make me some money like the politicians do . . . by committing a crime . . . I'm going to show how I will deal . . . that's why I am out here on this foggy night . . . to steal.

(The MUGGER *listens to the clicking footsteps of his approaching* VICTIM. *As soon as the* VICTIM *appears, the* MUGGER *steps behind him and locks his arms around his neck and drags him into the alleyway.)*

VICTIM: Hey, what's going on? Get your arm off my neck!

MUGGER: No way, motherfucker, cause I need your check!

VICTIM: *(Struggling)* Help! Police! Robbery!

MUGGER: Be cool, fool. Or I'll blow off your face!

VICTIM: All right . . . all right . . . relax. You're the main man in this place!

MUGGER: Now listen good, punk! *(Puts gun to face)* Give me your money . . . or your life.

VICTIM: Okay, don't shoot. Relax, please, I have a child and a wife!

MUGGER: Look, I don't want to hear that! I don't give a fuck about your child or wife, all I want is your check. Now give it up . . . or I'll break your neck. Don't you know my life's been a total wreck!

VICTIM: Your life's been a total wreck? And because of that you grab me by the neck and throw me on the floor. And on top of that you want my check. What I broke my back for?

MUGGER: Hey, man. Leave your Rap session for later. Because during this session I'm the annihilator. *(Grabs him by the shirt)* You better give me your money or else beware. For the wounds you'd bleed no doctor can repair!

VICTIM: *(Defiantly)* You . . . you . . . you . . . mugger! You filth! You slime! Profound scum. Why don't you go out and lay on a railroad track, you bum! Robbing people like me who work and push, and try to deal with reality.

MUGGER: Hey, mister! Don't try to be a hero. Because if you do, in a very short while your life may just be worth zero!

VICTIM: You . . . you think you can get away with . . .

MUGGER: *(Interrupting)* Hey, I said this ain't no Rap session. Shit! Now what I am about to teach you is an ass-whipping lesson.

(The MUGGER *beats up his* VICTIM *and leaves him on the floor gasping for air. The* MUGGER *stands over him.)*

MUGGER: Look motherfucker, there is no sense in crying cause I'll whip you some more. Your best bet is to keep shut . . . or else . . . I'll really whip your butt!!

VICTIM: *(In pain)* Take my money . . . but spare my life. Don't kill me, please. I have a child and a wife!

MUGGER: Like I said, man. I'll kill you . . . and I'll leave you on that floor!

VICTIM: All right! All right! I'll give you all my money. *(Takes off shoe and pulls out wad of money)* But please remember, I'm a family man.

MUGGER: Look, man, fuck you! And your clan! All I want is your money in my hand. *(The* VICTIM *moaning in pain gives the rest of the money to the* MUGGER. *Trying to excuse himself for this)* Look man, compared to you, my lifestyle may seem strange because well you see, my life at one time had a change. Now everything has been rearranged. I can't no longer deal with reality. Neither with all the ass-up changes of time. This is the cause, you see of my committing . . . the crime.

VICTIM: You commit crimes. You say you can't deal with time. You know you are driving ME out of my fuckin' mind. Let's forget my money. Take it. And just you go and be on your way!

MUGGER: *(Angry)* What! Be on my way! Be on my way! Look man, I am tired. I don't want to be humiliated anymore today. How dare you say this? When it's on your back you lay! *(He throws the* VICTIM *on the floor and pulls rope out of his back pocket and begins tying the* VICTIM *up)* You dare tell me be on my way? After all the shit I've been through in my time and day. Do you know! I was born and raised on the

Lower East Side where the cops used to take me and kick my hide. They whipped my ass and broke my neck and left my motherfuckin' body in a hell of a wreck. And now you tell me be on my way? Man. Do you think I am going to take what you said *(pulls his gun out)* I am going to put a bullet through your fuckin' head.

VICTIM: *(Looking up nervously through the barrel of the gun)* Hey, wait! You say you're from the Lower East Side?

MUGGER: *(Cocking the gun)* That's what I said.

VICTIM: Wait! Well . . . ah, if you really don't mind me saying . . . I grew up on the Lower East Side, too!

MUGGER: *(His gun trembling as he aims it at the* VICTIM's *head)* Look man, I don't want to hear it!

VICTIM: But, hey please! Understand. We are from the same place.

MUGGER: Yeah, but to my kind you're a total disgrace, man. Compared to you things we do are ultimately different and easier, too. You see? We don't just rob, we don't just steal. We take it upon ourselves, brother, to kill.

VICTIM: Oh, wait! Just what part are you from?

MUGGER: I'm from the section called Monster Hill. I never ran and I never will. You know, motherfuckers there are always aware that there's nothing in the air but merciless fear.

VICTIM: Monster Hill? What part of Monster Hill?

MUGGER: FDR . . . also known as the Drive. Motherfuckers there never take any jive. And to be specific . . . 555.

VICTIM: 555? . . . 555? . . . 555! You mean that part of the Drive! Shit! Man! That's where my family lived and I grew up . . . 555!

MUGGER: Oh yeah! Why, I ain't never seen you around, fool. Did you ever go to school?

VICTIM: Y-Yes, yes I went to school. That's how I learned that working hard is the rule. And if you don't mind me saying, maybe if you listen you can be taught the rule.

MUGGER: You show me the rule, man you better be cool. Like I've said, I'm the one who's making the rules around here. If anything you better lay back and fear to say your last prayer.

VICTIM: Fear? What is there to fear? We both come from the same atmosphere.

MUGGER: Oh, no, we ain't. I went to Junior High School 22. Also known as the double deuce. Where crime and grime is always loose.

VICTIM: Me too! Man, I went there. There is something to you, I swear.

MUGGER: What was the principal's name?

VICTIM: The principal, his name was . . . oh, Jerry Zame.

MUGGER: Yeah . . . well, you still might be lyin'.

VICTIM: Well, don't stop there . . . keep on tryin'.

MUGGER: What was the teacher's name, man?

VICTIM: The teacher, the teacher? His name was Gicy Dan!

MUGGER: Gicy Dan! What's your name?

VICTIM: Hondo! Man! My name is Hon . . . remember the dude who's word you considered bond?

MUGGER: No way!

VICTIM: I remember you. Your name is Bob. You was the dude who helped me get my first job.

MUGGER: How do you know my name?

VICTIM: I told you. You started me off toward my fame.

MUGGER: What! Man! Are you really Hon? Or are you layin' a sucker rap on me? The one who's in control of this so-called reality?

VICTIM: Hey, Bob. Listen, man. We've been through times together . . . don't you remember?

MUGGER: Remember what?

VICTIM: Remember that very month of September . . . you and me. Jane and Dee, screwing our asses off in the house on the tree?

MUGGER: Hey, wait a minute! How do you . . .

VICTIM: No, you wait a minute. Now think back to that month of October when you and me broke night just to get sober.

MUGGER: Hey!

VICTIM: We went all over, we even stole a Chevy Nova . . . remember we picked up Nathan and Willie and went to that dance? The one where you split your yellow pants?

MUGGER: Yeah, yeah . . . now I remember. That was the month after September. Now I can really see, you was the nigger who tried to hip me to reality. . . . God . . . Hon my old friend. *(Begins to untie him)* Damn, it's been a while since I seen your smile. Well, hey, Hon . . . I still can't see that ultimate difference between fantasy and reality.

VICTIM: I can't believe what you sayin', Bob. You were never a slob, you always kept a job. What's the matter, Bob? Have things been that bad?

MUGGER: Yeah, man. Times have been really bad. It seems compared to fantasy, reality's been bad.

VICTIM: Hey, Bob! Do you remember that day on the fifth of December you sat me down and took my frown and made it ultimately turn around?

MUGGER: Hey, Hon! You know, in a way I'm sad. And then again glad. Glad because I have been woken up. Sad because I waited till it was too late. I am a total failure.

VICTIM: Look, Bob, maybe you can still be someone after all.

MUGGER: What on earth makes you say that? Here I am in a convict's condition, with no thoughts, with no feat, and with no ambition.

VICTIM: Don't you know that can all be changed? I felt that way before, but now I've rearranged.

MUGGER: Yeah, in what way?

VICTIM: Well, as you see, I'm doin' pretty good. Working hard like I should.

MUGGER: Hey, Hon, just what is your occupation?

VICTIM: I am a social worker, a creator, a guidance educator. In essence, a mind stimulator.

MUGGER: How did you get that job?

VICTIM: Well . . . hey, I had help from a friend who stuck by me to the very end.

MUGGER: A Hon . . . maybe that's what I need. A friend. Yeah, a friend indeed. To stick by me to the very end and help me make my dead-end mind pattern end.

VICTIM: Well, you can come down and see me any day. That is when it's not on my back, mugged, out in an alleyway I lay.

MUGGER: *(Laughs and feels happier)* Well, Hon, I'm really sorry this happened. Especially to an old friend. Hmmm, my word, I'll never do this again.

VICTIM: Well, look, Bob. Remember we have a date. And till that time comes, don't just hang around and wait.

MUGGER: Okay, Hon. I think I see what you mean . . . and from this day on, I'll remain clean.

VICTIM: In fact, I just remembered. I know about this job opening!

MUGGER: Yeah? What kind of job?

VICTIM: Don't worry, Bob. It's not one made for a slob. *(Both* MUGGER *and* VICTIM *laugh and really begin to enjoy the time that was)* Look, you give me a call tomorrow around noon.

MUGGER: Hey, I don't want to put you out of your way. You're sure that isn't too soon?

VICTIM: Look, don't worry about the time. Just remember this, my friend, and forget about the crime.

MUGGER: Damn, Hon. It's sure been a long—Oh, by the way, don't forget your money.

VICTIM: Oh, right! I got a lot of family bills to pay.

(The MUGGER *and* VICTIM *start slowly to walk out together from the alleyway.)*

MUGGER: *(Thinking)* Hey . . . whatever happened to Jane?

VICTIM: Jane?

MUGGER: Yeah . . . you know . . . the girl that was sweet as candy cane?

VICTIM: Oh, her. I know now who you're talking about.

MUGGER: Who?

VICTIM: *(Proud of his conquest)* My wife.

MUGGER: Ha, ha! No shit! Congratulations. You got married to Jane . . . ahhh . . . whatever happened to Mike?

VICTIM: Oh, well, he had a terrible accident on a motorbike.

MUGGER: Yeah? Too bad. *(Shaking his head)* Well, what about Judy Mar?

VICTIM: Who?

MUGGER: You remember Judy Mar? The girl you introduced me to at Raymond's Casbard on a Christmas Eve . . . she was with this guy named . . . Steve.

(Lights begins to fade.)

VICTIM: *(Excited)* Hey, wait! Remember that time when you and I played hookey from school?

MUGGER: *(Laughing . . . they slap five)* Hahahahahahah! How can I forget!

(They disappear into the street behind the alley wall.)

VICTIM: We were with, ah, Bugaloo, ah, who else?

MUGGER: Ah . . . Choco and . . .

(They begin to sound distant.)

VICTIM: Hector!

MUGGER: And . . . Cool!

(Lights blacked out.)

MUGGER: . . . and we went up by the rocks to hang out and swim. Weren't those great days? I remember Slim brought a six-pack and we got so wacked that . . .

(They fade out laughing.)

THE END

IV

Monologues and Performance Pieces

WHITE SIRENS

Lois Elaine Griffith

(EUPHEMIA HOLDIP *speaks in the beginning.*)

Damn (zumzum things)
give me a headache.
Tourists all over the place.
What they coming here for
Barbados ain't no new frontier.

Wear these one time
sell them in the shop.

Let them laugh at me.
Grandmum knew to die just in time
leaving it all to me.
It ain't all that much
but it belongs to me.

Let's see what the seawater wash up today.

These are good too.

I see how she wear them
turning lobster red.
She ain't got no tropic sun where she come from.
Hummmph
peeping at beach boys behind shades.

I'll keep this and sell it back to one of them for a pound sterling.
Mavis said she looking for something like this.
Tuppence for that.
Hold the cap like so for piss potting.

Twilight
signal duppy coming out
down yonder way.
Smell rising up from the sands.

Shed me blood in the sands.
Dropped me half-formed child.
Tore out me wee-wee bugaboo/wiggling and squirming alive.
Laid to rest just one backra seed.

Who going patter-patter.
Hear a baby crying in the grasses outside.

No.
Jumbees in me house
watching as I be at me
bug-eyed astaring out
ain't see nothing yet.
Casting obeah net for walkers in dreams
making dreams after they be cut off
ain't got nothing else to do.
You see them sometimes in corners stealing
shadows moving
searching and peeping
away out lost
and still be keeping noise.
Baddarax.
Bruggadung
kiss ma ass
all them busylickums.
Who me
I ain't afraid of ghosts you know.
Hadja-bucks scrunch up they face
not a damned thing they can do to me.

Conjure me
I conjure back.
Conjure me
I conjure back.

*(A Clinical Approach/*FRÍA TUDOR*)*

When they said
Rapunzel, Rapunzel
let down your golden hair
they were calling to me
to come down under
the drums called through the earth
the drums of Africa.
My great-great grandfather heard the call
from the other side of the earth
the drums called him and he went off
to fight in the Boer Wars
to enter the cradle of the earth
to expose the germ of civilization.
Landed gentry
that's all they said I was.
They laughed at a woman pioneer
I come from Anglo-Nordic stock

fire and strength
forging off into the African bush country
a novelty among the gorillas and homo cannibalis.
I am daring
knowledge for its own sake.
I studied many years to understand the species
the indigenous life-forms of the territories.
It's a slow methodical process
collecting data on the fauna
recording it accurately
consolidating it
researching the mores,
the ritualistic behavior,
kinship, the basic structure of social relationships.

My studies of certain groups
certain homo primitivus
have unearthed certain behavioral characteristics
tendencies of exaggerated development in certain areas
to which I draw cross-cultural parallels
significant in the diverse assumptions
made by both male and female members of the species
in areas of individual pursuits
role playing
role playing
role playing
playing the divine miss
I have observed
there is a woman
they have created her out of a man's body
and pumped sand into the tits
This makes them swell.
They cut off the cock
to trench out a hole.
They lit it with neon lights
and offered it for sale
to the leather studs
who otherwise would fuck in the closet.

Role playing in the early menopausal cycle
the liberated liberal female
playing at the dynamic of privilege
and dealing with the consequences of power reduction
when sectors of the male population of the species
gratify themselves sexually with robots and clones.
There are definite patterns of outrage in her behavior

aggressive toward herself
a vacuum is created by a lack of attentive touching and caressing.
She is empty-handed.
Rapunzel, Rapunzel
let down your golden hair.
I do so for my own masturbatory enjoyment.

The effervescence of posteditorial pleasure
is most definitely a lingering and refreshing phenomenon
facing the nation with the sparkle of self-induced appeasement.
Could there possibly be queries into the guarantees of such freedom?

(EUPHEMIA HOLDIP *speaks after* FRÍA TUDOR *[Clinical Woman] and before* PAMELA SIDNEY-WRECK *[Daddy's Girl]*)

You hear the drum sounding
calling to the dancers.
Smell the air
mango fruit and papaya
all that sweetness in the air.
I looked to trust her.
I taught her to use the dictionary
when Miss Gladstone say
look up "phenomenon"
and with all that tutoring
she didn't know "f" from "ph."
Meshing
webbing
treating mean to storm eye.
She and I best friends
Sidney
gave her all my Indian heads
then she telling me
her mummy didn't want no colored girls
sitting up at the birthday table.
All in front of Mavis and Enid
real light, light-skinned girls.
She telling them they could come.
They could pass.
Mind you now
she and I
we best friends
and mummy pissy drunk.
I got a nest
outway
I got a stove and cooking pot.

I fired up
seeing her face again
over at the Holiday Inn.
Rains coming
season harvest moon.
I spitting silver seeds
sowing seeds of me own spitting.
I be rotted deep.
Mark a vévé here.
Standing in circle
ringing around me conjure juice
singing tunes
singing winds
to conjure she.

(Slightly intoxicated woman talking in a bedroom to herself and a lover. [Daddy's Girl]
PAMELA SIDNEY-WRECK.*)*

When I played the holy Virgin Mary
mother of God
the Christmas pageant director
Mr. Tweedy had a fit
he caught me with Brandy/Brandy was a boy
Brandy played Jesus
the young man who did all those miracles.
We were making out behind the altar
I mean we were going together
I mean I wouldn't let him go all the way
but I guess Mr. Tweedy didn't know that
I made him touch my tits
just suck on them a little/baby Brandy
Jesus at my breast.
When Sidney, my adorable mother,
took me to Mexico City for her second divorce
I met chico
a wetback
a real live Jesus
so hot
to run his fingers through this little girl's hair
white blond hair
over my ass
I was as beautiful as a holy virgin.
Then there was that sulky little bitch Maria
she would come in the morning
make up the beds

just when I was doing my toilette.
Sidney always liked to refer,
that time in the morning
when she would throw chico out of her room
or take him out on his leash
to bronze some more in the sunshine
her toilette.
Sometimes he'd sneak by
run his fingers through my hair
tickle my mouth with his mustache
my mouth
you know I could actually
fold these lips between my legs
over his mouth
I can do tricks like that for all sweet daddies' lips.
Yes, I was daddy's favorite girl.

Yes I was daddy's favorite girl.
Sometimes I'd stay away from school a whole six months
I mean I had a tutor wherever I went
but I lived with my daddy for six months once.
Sidney was on her honeymoon
Barbados this time.
Mother always used her family name.
So I parked my ass on daddy's lap
while he tickled at me
But he could reach out
and touch tits
while bouncing on his knee.
I got used to feeling safe with money
I picked his pockets
I'd sneak out at night for cigarettes
and daddy tumbling with tits on his brown satin sheets.
He'd say stains dry clear on chocolate brown
blood doesn't show as much on chocolate
white satin
white satin will pick up anything
a water drop will leave a mark
on white satin.
You see me I am white satin
Stains
I put them away on my chocolate part
I hide them between my legs
where the hair is unbleached

you can't see them
just the glow of white satin
and syrup of my daddy's drool.

What I am talking about
the old man
who has a seat on the Street
and loves to drool over me.
I mean the old man on the Exchange
he loves to drool over me.
His daughter and I are cousins
we resemble each other
slightly
she's one of the daughters of the American Revolution.
As a father
he never quite learned
how to give his baby girl a bath.
Poor daddy
poor, poor daddy.
Al Jolson made up for it
he had a Mammy who'd scrub him all clean and white
Al Jolson
that boy had a lot of heart.

You know I used to model.
I've got the shape for it wouldn't you say
when America sees it on me
it's for sale
they have white sales all the time
you can read about them in the papers
everybody's all ready to buy.
They paid me by the hour
to use my white front
I made them pay
extra work meant
overtime making money selling appearances
how I appear.
I accept gifts
I got these diamond earrings from a prince
O he was a charmer!

He never laid a hand on me that prince
he used to love to run his fingers
through my white blond hair.
You know it was short
and my prince

he bought me a three-piece suit just like his
and an old hat
and a cane
and these white satin hot pants
and we'd go out and jam.
We jammed it up
O we were a sight
he and I'd go out to clubs
and tear it up dancing in hot pants.

(EUPHEMIA HOLDIP *speaks after* PAMELA SIDNEY-WRECK *[Daddy's Girl] and before*
KARENA PILL *[Simple Woman.])*

Tsk-tsk-tsk
per-johnny
per-johnny
get a grief lump caught all up in she throat.
But looka out
see them molly-boobies flying round back
no counting for stupidness in a torch light.
They better stay out the crochet lacing.
I going set it out for sale tomorrow.

Macou
long time lost at sea
in a damn dinghy.
Whistling frogs talking all night
about hurricane traveling northward
on to Guadaloup.
Alligator in Cayman bays
know a brew under sunbeams.
He say we making a pretty baby.
That white thing between he legs
always searching out his own.
O but he could be sweet.
Husha up
keep the sound under.
Mark the music of the dancing
summer nights be cooling
hollow space where the wind be speaking to me between the trees
and sky be full of whispering.
I catch a wing-fly.
Pstt, pstt
put a nigger-ten where it drop.
Per-wing-fly
per-wing-fly.

I making nigger-ten where it drop.

*(Simple Woman/*KARENA PILL—*in Beauty Parlor.)*

No one really talks about me that way.
Life is quite simple
I don't hate Jews
I drink wine occasionally
I keep a good house
my two children go to private school
my husband has a good job
I go shopping twice a week
I have a good marriage.
I live for my home, I really do.
I'm not clear on the issues in the feminist press
I mean this revolution against men
it seems so extreme,
but when homosexuals come to power
they want everything their way.
I have to tell you this:
Last evening my husband and I went to the house of
an artist associate of his from the office.
Well, there were some impromptu theatrics
and one of the negro women there recited a poem.
She honestly was sure all the women present could identify.
I mean I'm a woman
but there is a certain brutality.
I would never submit my body to sexual decadence and call it love.
Love is just a way of ordering things
and I have everything around me well ordered.

(There is a glass of water on the vanity. She takes out several vials of pills. She lines them up in order by color. As she speaks, she lines one pill from each vial in order.)

Ordering time
being active
you know that old saying "Idle hands?"
Yes, the devil will take his due.
I keep busy though
I take a tennis lesson every week—
confidentially, I have to watch my shape.
I also work with the P.T. A.

I keep busy
but no matter how much I do
I save a little time for me.
I'll have my hair done

I'll have a manicure
I'll have my brows plucked
or maybe I'll just be going out for the evening with my husband.
I'll want the makeup done well.

(A roll of white toilet tissue is on the vanity. She uses it in her toilette.)

This is the best thing for makeup.
I can just grab a handful of it
actually this kind is more squeezably soft.
Very absorbent, too!
White fluff toilet tissue.
I always say if a man cares to notice
how soft and fluffy it is
mmmmmmm soft
I'll give it to him
if he wants it soft
I can give it to him soft,
all he has to do is ask.
I'll get him some soft white fluff.

Keeping busy
keeping things in order
but sometimes those kids drive me up a wall.
I have a woman who comes in to help
with the cleaning and with the kids.
It's funny, I mean no offense
but Theodora is as she would say about herself:
Yes'm, I'm sure enough an old-time country Mammy
and when she goes through her routine
I just burst out laughing.
O Theodora's a dear, that one.
But sometimes
I get
so angry
I just
clean up
everything all by myself
from top to bottom
everything all by myself.
I put it in order
the order of things
these things
in their place.
I keep busy
that's what I do

I put things in order.
I can only cry when I'm alone
so I keep busy.
I've always been an active person.
That's what it's all about.
It's simple.
I'm a very simple woman.
Ultimately I think back to nature
keeping busy
even as a young lady
I was active in all kinds of ways.

(EUPHEMIA HOLDIP *speaks after* KARENA PILL *[Simple Woman] and before* DANIELLE *[Danny]* DART *[Hippy Dippy].)*

All these botherations.
Get off.
Hold strain.
Hushaback.
Crackling and popping
skinning and grinning
the white baby sucking on the Mammy boobie.
Them American folk up there
they love that sort of thing you know
eating it up like some piece of sweetie.
Hmmmmmmmmmm.
No come at me with your fire-rage
steel toys.
What you going buy
you come just for a look-see
I ain't no mannequin.
No vex me so
a make of me frazma.
Drag your own damn skin
all clatter-clatter
red legs bassa-bassa fête-ing at midnight.

(DANIELLE DART *[Miss Hippy-Dippy]*

At Rice and Beans Party.)

Look
I've been involved in struggles for the past fifteen years.
Not just black rights.
All power to the people.
But dig it sister

under the guise of the liberal democratic system
Capitalism ain't nothing but white faggot boys in the conference room
who cannot account for the rape of the poor.
The silent majority will awaken to thunder on its doorstep.
You and I bring the get-down-thunder music
into their Sears & Roebuck living rooms.
Mine is a small part.
I was not born black in the vanguard of the struggle.
Yes, I'm a honky
but I do my part for the revolution.
There is a very dear man in my life
his name is Maynard
and I love him in a way I've never loved another person
after I broke off with Bubba.
Both outstanding black men
Maynard is so aware of the intricacies of the damned system
the hypnotic force of the fucking dollar
he can screw it with his fly closed.
A fantastic mind.
He absolutely astounded his professors in London.
He presented his final paper:
Psycho-sexual implications of modern finance—
the old farts sat there with their mouths hanging.
The struggle is not an economic one.
I can ask my father for a hundred thousand dollars in credit
to travel around the world for a couple of years
but the age of the Grand Tour is passé.
It's time these old ballbreakers assume a definite responsibility.
The need is not so far away as Zimbawe or Angola
but right here in our own urban ghettos.
Dig it—
Maynard is a whip
rapping with Dad under my grandfather's portrait
sipping White Russians and running it down.
He asked Dad if he held me hostage for the revolution
how much would he pay?
I thought the old man would shit oil.
Rhetoric on the value of life
that's all he could offer
a million dollars wouldn't be too much.
Feminism is part of the racial struggle.
I as a white sister feel the same oppression you feel
the negation of personhood.
We niggers of the system must unite in this revolution.

(EUPHEMIA HOLDIP *speaks after* DANIELLE DART *[Hippy-Dippy] and before* CON-
STANCE WHITING *[The Swimmer].*)

> *Duppies dancing when the moon is full.*
> *You see*
> *you see them*
> *yonder so in that corner.*
> *Sleepwalkers at low tide*
> *traipsing around*
> *chasse-ing*
> *with the arse all stuck up and butting.*
> *Macou saying I good to look at*
> *not all painted up.*
> *Mumbo jumbo talk*
> *duppie talk.*
> *I saw he first at government house*
> *looking me up and down.*
> *I give him something to look at.*
> *Ha-ha-ha-ha-ha*
> *I can't trust you, Macou*
> *I can't walk a dinghy in high heels.*
> *Coming back all wizzy-wizzy*
> *splashing up*
> *asounding gurgling, gurgling.*

(*The* SWIMMER/CONSTANCE *[Connie]* WHITING

Press Conference at Pool Side.)

> *The resistance was strong at first.*
> *I used to struggle and fight it.*
> *It was a hassle just to stay afloat.*
> *I couldn't let it beat me.*
> *Can you imagine being beaten by water?*
> *It was a challenge*
> *then, too, it was good exercise*
> *and the men I would meet at the health spa!*
> *I had junior membership privileges*
> *cause I loved a good massage every once in a while.*
> *Well, they all had such fantastic physiques—*
> *I was just a little water baby when I joined up*
> *a cute kid.*
> *It really did wonders*
> *strengthening my thigh muscles.*
> *Then I got serious about it*
> *and it became easy*

and for some strange reason
I was really good at the butterfly stroke.
I was really good at it.
So I entered the local meets
and I always seemed to win at the butterfly.
My strength wasn't in distance.
I think it's the form.
I'm very form conscious
there's something about making a clean line—
it's exhilarating.
The guys at the spa
they started teasing me
calling me mermaid.
I mean I never thought to make a profession of it;
although Esther Williams
sure enough swam her way to Hollywood.
There are certain advantages to being a champion,
especially when I entered the Miss Georgia beauty pageant.
I was the first runner-up in my state finals.
I was more than just a beauty queen in a bathing suit.
I was Champion Butterfly
that was my nickname.
I did some commercials.
That tuna company
used my solid, packed shape on their label
till feminists
started picketing the plant
raising a whole hullabaloo
(misleading advertising
the soft sexy sell).
Doesn't everyone go for the pretty white package?
The one with the smiling mermaid?
Isn't it really the psychology of instant identification?

And it wasn't false advertising.
I am Champion Butterfly
and I wish to god Busby Berkeley were still alive.
But the point is not about glamour,
it's about good clean competition,
philosophies that our American way of life are based on:
Good clean competition—
I learned that one in college.
I was captain of the women's varsity swim team
(that was before I was Champion Butterfly).
I've made a few marks for myself in this world

and people still remember
my face from the can,
this solid form
can cut through water.

It's just not about getting over with sex.
You know when I started out
I used to think that Tab, Chet, Tick, and Wade,
college romances all,
I used to think they would resent
my broad shoulders.
But actually, swimming does wonders
for a woman's pectoral muscles
I mean the bustline really develops.

(EUPHEMIA HOLDIP SPEAKS AFTER CONSTANCE *[Connie]* WHITING *[The Swimmer]*
and before SISTER MERIDITH KAY *[The Nun].*)

Frupse a worth ain't it
blossom fallen fretting.
Arise
kamerlock ash star
backar fain
homumbay homumbay
dreepos anung
rockeration
homumbay homumbay
treedispersal oblung see time
crayloo agatus
seen bloodless
homumbay homumbay
crealatall betankum
charget velionis dock
warm sangre
homumbay homumbay.

(SISTER MERIDITH KAY *[The Nun].*)

Underneath this habit
my body remains unpierced by the sun
clean and pure
unblemished, unsoiled, pristine,
devout as the first day I took my vows
devout I became a servant of Mary.
I entered the order.
I took on the habit.
I became a slave of love

divine love
holy rocking and rolling
bumping and grinding
caught in the immaculate conception of a wet dream
heaven on earth.
Take me, Holy Mother, take me
claim me with that love thing uniquely ours
femina misteriosa
rip into me with the potency of that tool
love power
love wonder in the depths of night.
O yes, temptation stalks my footsteps.
My sisters are so gentle in their ways.
We indulge in ecstasies of love
the gay life.
Yes, for this love I have renounced evil
for the sublimity of this love
and the transcendent movement
clitoris erectus, alleluia,
I can feel it moving inside me
searing my weak flesh
ebbing and flowing
then reaching a climax
flooding me with the joy of life.
This gay life
this marvelous promise of my vows
chastity, obedience
alleluia.
I remain clean
unpierced by the reckless pursuits of men after the flesh,
untouched by their lust.

Carnal desire
the quicksand on which I stand under this habit.
Sister Mary Monica is leaving the order.
Must be the devil in her soul
tempting her to destroy us.
Sister Mary Monica
the bitch couldn't stand to see me
spreading my arms and legs
spreading the message of this gay life
the message of purity in ecstasy
being a slave to love
divine love.

Flower of Nubia
strayed from thy nest
I fear for thy need
now in the hour of thy longing.
O sweet mysteries
banquets at midnight
rose without thorns—
   optas
   mamman firmam et maturam
wanting
the firm ripeness of breast
   tanges
   cum digito titillatio mani
touching
the tickle finger of hand
   sciis
   osculum linguae fervidae
knowing
the hot kiss of tongue
   sentis
   tactum humidum vulvae
feeling
the wet touch of cunt.
   Flos adorandus vesperorum nigerorum et velvetorum es
adorable flower of black velvet evenings
   desiderabamus
   consolatiam nostrum amplexi taciti
yearning
the comfort of our silent embrace
   cantabamus
   in profundo spiriti ardentis
singing
together in the depths of passion's breath
   sentiebamus
   gaudium violetae apertae
sensing
the joy of the opening violet.
   Flos adorandus vesperorum nigerorum et velvetorum es
adorable flow of black velvet evenings
   alleluia
alleluia
   alleluia
alleluia
   alleluia
alleluia

(EUPHEMIA HOLDIP *speaks after* SISTER MARY DEKAY *[The Nun] and before* DIXIE PEARL RAUNCH *[White Rot].)*

Size up,
size up and give way.
Lick mouth jibber-jabber.
Them no-account downalong frumpsies
come along all swishy-swishy and airified.
Wash back the tide on the dead sand.
Bajam beach under hideaway moon
drum sounding
mauby setting night.
I shake a switch.
Come ballahoo mark a vévé
Old ballahoo dragging a red leg.
Razzy-looking
must be some person outside child.
Size up, size up
ain't no place for hags here.

(DIXIE PEARL RAUNCH *Greasy Spoon Diner.)*

About the fragrance of the magnolia
and the honeysuckle rose
and sipping mint juleps on the porch
they just be pussyfooting around honey
the South ain't hardly like that I know of.
I ain't finished high school.
They say I come from the wrong side of the tracks.
But let me tell you
tracks go two ways
and I'm free white and over twenty-one.

I used to live in a trailer camp outside Baltimore
the southeastern route crossing on the highway.
I worked in this place,
a lot of truckers always passing through.
See this here ankle bracelet?
A guy from Wisconsin gave it to me one time.
Of course after a few drinks
I could give it right back to him
if you know what I mean.

Sometimes I even used to hang out in nigger town.
I had some real good friends over in nigger town
Couple of real nice gals,
used to work with me,

back in the Dixie.
O those were the days.
I had this fancy dress
well
it was sort of fancy.
It was cut low
and had a flower here
and some ruffles around here.
It was my hot stepping dress.
There was this guy over in nigger town.
I used to run into him sometimes
when it was the gals' night out.
Zanzibar was the spot we'd hit
and sometimes I'd be the only white face in the place.
It was around the time niggers were just starting out
being allowed to use the bathrooms.
I know it used to bug the hell out of Alley Mae,
especially when I'd be flirting around with Butch.
He was one fine-looking black buck.
And he was black all over—
I mean all over.
I know that little bitch was jealous
but like I said
sometimes I'd be the only white face in the place.

There was this queen who'd work the bar.
In those days, let me tell you,
queens were an exotic breed.
Not that it's changed all that much,
but this one over at the Zanzibar was a roar!
A red wig,
diamond earrings,
the whole number.
Zambezi used to say
the only woman he could relate to was Rita Hayworth
and if he could take Butch,
he'd feel like a real white woman.
O child he'd have me cracking up!
The way he'd talk
with all that honey and darling dribble.
Honey, I told you
all that sipping mint juleps on the porch
is just pussyfooting around
and a black pussy that can't get no play is a dried prune.

It was written all over Alley Mae's face:
dried pussy, dried pussy.

I tell you again
I'm free, white and over twenty-one
and I got to keep the juices flowing strong.
I'm about getting what I want when I want it
so if you want something I got
we can negotiate on these circumstances.
I mean, that's what I keep trying to teach my kid,
and now that she's got a kid—
you know looking at me
you couldn't tell I'm a grandmother.
I keep myself up.
And along comes that brat
with another brat
and trying to move in on me yet.
I've had enough of dirty diapers for a lifetime.
Hmmmmmm
said she wanted someone to love all her own.
I said, "Look girl, you got yourself."
What did I know at seventeen with a brat
and a bunch of dirty diapers
with all my friends running around
having a good old time
and me sitting around
with a brat and a bunch of dirty diapers.
But she knows how to take care of herself, she's tough.
I taught her real good like my mother taught me.

She is one down out lazy ho'.
I ain't doing my job and hers too.
Cara Lee, you got the graveyard shift, girl.
You better get your ass out here.
I ain't touching the floors.
I'm telling you again now—
just keep you hands off my boa.
And don't be putting your old stink shoes next to my new gators.

(EUPHEMIA HOLDIP *speaks after* DIXIE PEARL RAUNCH *and before* BANCA RAMÉE.)

Wet tangle weed smoking
garden once between me legs
tore out me baby-bed
scorched up
cinder stone for goat feet

ashen seed
me boy-child in a bandage bag.
Bechrist lord
I ask for a sign
you sending rancid meat
don't set right in me belly.
Castoffs from the States
fitting tight on a broad bean
hmmmm
miss lady's used-to-be softie
to wipe she botsy clean.
I ain't going be propping sorrows in hand-me-downs
had enough of that sort of thing.
Midwife rags
I burned the whole damned stinking mess.
Cut from mooring
adrift you hear a siren wailing
Macou
you hear me bleeding for you touching
how you do me so
Macou
you hear me
I standing spitting flame
you hear me.

*(*BLANCA RAMÉE *into* EUPHEMIA *frenzy.)*

You'll give me what.
Confetti
ticker tape
O the key to the city
I haven't won the World Series
j'ai fait une petite voyage chez moi
and returned unscathed.
You knew I'd be back.
You bought me a return ticket.
I wasn't about cashing it in.   *Traveling out to a rendez-vous*
I detest provincial onion soup.
Tu me connais bien, chèri
ha-ha-ha-ha   *manqué crossed missing*
how very well you know me.
I look the same
you call me crystal don't you   *meeting place*
                                                        mind you ways girl

What, you like it that way.

Je suis sans couleur
une vagabonde
sans souci
sans pays
a carefree gypsy.
Do you keep an account
with Fredericks of Hollywood
ha-ha-ha-ha

Maintenant—
just entertaining a few friends.
It's an insomniac's night
and we're playing charades
you know
how much I love party games.
Thunder, lightning
if I can endure
saison du mistral
I can endure anything, chéri.
Not at all
I have no desire to go home again
to be a peasant.
Je suis très fatiguée.
Why don't you
stay with your wife.
Going away on business
Why don't you come to Barbados
it's fabulously exotic
c'est merveilleux.
We'll talk tomorrow
now be sweet
I'll get back to you
I'll keep you on hold

I'll keep you on hold

I'll keep you on hold

be about sipping tea
  with the pinky out like so.

Bien élèvée
  colonial rearing
done lost a taste for sea eggs
still moving
and squirming alive
sans cesse.

Budding nipped
source of storm cloud
  coming on
stubby leavings
Macou gleaned me out
set to wind
cut off.

  With me pinky out like so
like so
see me here naked, Macou
standing under thunder.
See she all pretensive
brazen bleach head
sunburnt siren
Where you be Caymen bay
Where the pointsettas be blooming
Long time gone way
she siren calling you
home
Barbados
barbaric Bajans
calling it Bimshire
so refined
coming in the furty's way.
Me aching for you sea wind
kissing me cheek (in an over-shower).
Storm flowering

I'll keep you on hold

I'll keep you on hold

I'll keep you on hold

strange fruit.
Hanging seed
breeding hunger.
Barbaric torrent.
Barbaric lodger
cunning glamour for a tongue-lashing
you caulking island backside
you saw face stingaree
you festering sea wort.

Amor de Mis Amores

Eva Gasteazoro

Introduction

(Amor de Mis Amores   Melodrama a Ritmo de Danzón *is a one-woman performance work in two acts with a video preset. It is a series of stories or "cuentos," allowing the audience to be a voyeur into the private lives and thoughts of the two principal characters,* MOTHER *and* DAUGHTER. *Ms. Gasteazoro plays both characters, switching back and forth as their stories unfold.*

The MOTHER *represents a rapidly disappearing way of life and point of view. She is an upper-class Nicaraguan beauty of the fifties, born to be a queen and to act like one. Her children, her clothes, her house, her husband, are there only to adorn her existence. Life is a dream until her husband is killed and she is forced to face reality.*

The DAUGHTER *is a young, independent woman who chooses to leave tradition behind. From this vantage point, she opens up a Pandora's box of memories, which are funny, sad, grotesque, tragic, and real. She sees herself as her mother, her mother as herself, and finds that what she loves most deeply and hates most violently are one and the same.*

Spanish is interspersed, used to portray aspects of the cultural context of the piece, along with movement/dance sequences utilizing the boleros *and* danzones *of the period.*

The video, Cuna *("Crib"), is a collage created from childhood family footage by Mary Ellen Strom and Ms. Gasteazoro. The performance preset consists of a five-minute videotape loop, accompanied by Cuban instrumental* boleros, *that repeats itself for the twenty to thirty minutes between audience arrival and the start of the show. The size and number of monitors used depend on the nature and character of the performance space.*

Ms. Gasteazoro uses a number of props and a variety of costumes during the progression of the piece: a sturdy yellow wooden armchair; a black lectern; a clothesrack with a full-length mirror hanging on one end; glamorous, Chanel-like clothes from the '50s; patent leather high heels, a white broad-brimmed hat, white gloves, and cat-like dark glasses.

Preset: video tape with Cuban boleros.)

Act I
Mis tías

(*The first act is performed as a straightforward reading using a lectern. The daughter is the narrator, becoming the various women as she evokes their stories.*

She is dressed as a contemporary woman wearing black slacks, a white shirt, and dark glasses.

Lectern, up, center-right; armchair, center-left facing diagonal right.

The performer walks on stage as the last image on the videotape, the mother, is brought to a still. The mother and she wear the same type of glasses. She carries the story in hard copy, and places it on the lectern. She stands at the lectern. Pause. Mother and daughter look at the audience. Video image is gone. Daughter begins to tell the story.)

NARRATOR: Good evening, ladies and gentlemen. Let me tell you a story. A story about some women in Nicaragua. The other women, so many, the ones who didn't count, who didn't have children. Spinsters. Innocents at the end of the line. Testigos de pueblo. Beatas en igelsias vacías/blessed among the blessed in empty churches. Old maids bathing in chastity. The ones without a man, who didn't count, because they didn't have a husband. The many, many aunts.

    (Pause) My aunts, mis tías, they aged alone, wasting away in their old clothes. Their dresses growing larger day by day, hanging on brittle bones, blown by the wind, silent through pale, pale rooms.

    (Moves away from lectern) Mamalola. She was eight-four years old. She never moved from her hammock. She never learned how to use her dentures. They would fall out of her mouth and, clenc, clenc! . . . on the china.

    La Fulgencia would bring Mamalola her soup in a bowl, *(impersonating a very old, heavy woman dragging her feet)* slowly dragging, her legs bursting with varicose veins packed in thick stockings. One day, it took Fulgencia so long that Mamalola died waiting for her soup. So then, La Mimi, who could hardly see, decided to sit in a rocking chair *(going to chair)* by the door and stop everyone . . . coming in or leaving the house. *(Sits down)*

LA MIMI: *(Very old and almost blind, talking to imaginary person walking in the door; she's loud and cranky)* A ver niño, vení para acá, who are you? Let me see you in the light. Did you eat? I haven't had anything since yesterday morning. I know there is food because I can smell it. Look, look at my flesh, look how it hangs. I'm only telling you this so that everybody here *(indicating the audience)* knows that Fulgencia is starving me to death, too.

NARRATOR: *(Gets up; to audience)* She would only eat what she bought from the street vendors. She thought all the other tías were out to poison her. *(Pause)* La Totito *(as if she were talking about an angel; her favorite aunt)* devoted herself to care for the birds and very soon she started to look like a bird. *(Returning to lectern; she grabs the top of it as a bird would grab its perch)* She would look at you from one side *(moves head sideways, like a bird)*, with eyes like the eyes of the lora; and she would make cooing sounds, like mourning doves; or sing *(walks diagonal left, singing the words— bird chatter—absent-mindedly, as Totito wandering through the dark empty house)*, dichoso fui! *(Pause)* Dichoso fui! *(Pause)* Dichoso fui! *(Pause)* Her doves would fly freely throughout the dark house, shitting on the wooden floors, nesting in the balconies among the piles of dusty magazines, and on the very high rafters, overgrown with spiderwebs. *(To audience)* Sometimes you couldn't tell who was passing through the rooms, la Totito o las palomas.

LA CHITA: sitting all day at her desk, doing the accounts for the farm *(at lectern; reads from hard copy, as Chita. Chita is loud and authoritative)*: Forty-five tons of cotton per acre; seven hundred pounds of insecticide for the plague; one thousand two hundred córdobas in fertilizante; already, more than fifty workers; and now they want to eat cheese. I'm going to take fifty cents off their salary, per meal. *(As NAR-RATOR):* She would spend hours calling imaginary workers by name *(As Chita):* Isabel Galea! Braulio Castillo! Pedro Altamirano! Petrona Dávila! *(As Narrator):* And she would pay them with coffee beans. All day long, la Chita adding numbers aloud, with números y números y números.

Next to her, la Susanita, at the sewing machine, *(exaggerating the caricature)* incessantly pedaling, day in and day out; mending everything in sight; ripping out; and mending again. *(Pause)* La Chepita broke her hip when he was eighty-nine years old. One day she slipped on bird's shit and she never got up again from her bed. The sweat. The urine. The electric fan clenc, clenc, clenc, clenc, clenc, clenc. *(Pause)*

Mis tías. They all died. One by one. Mamalola, la Mimi, la Chita, la Chepita, la Susanita. La Totito was the last one. Mis tías never left their house. They buried them all in the walls of one of the rooms. They remained there. Se quedaron ahí *(pause)* para siempre.

(Lights fade out.)

(The performer takes the lectern off stage, and brings in the clothesrack with all the props and costumes hanging on it. Hat is left behind curtains. Places it diagonally, with mirror facing down-left. She starts changing into new costume.

Nicaraguan radio—switching stations—is heard throughout the entire transition.

The performer looks at herself in mirror as she gets into new clothes. She transforms into a glamorous, Hollywood-style woman of the '50s. Finally she dabs perfume behind her ear. She takes the rack offstage.)

Act II
Amor de mis amores

(Danzón starts. After the introductory notes, she appears—wearing hat—as if under camera lights, dancing to the rhythm of the danzón; freezing for seconds in Vogue-like poses. A minute into the music, she angrily demands to stop the music.)

MOTHER: ¡No más música! *(Impatiently clapping to technician)* ¡No más música! por favor! *(Pause. Smiles at the audience, showing her costume with self-consciously theatrical, feminine gestures)* White hat, white organza blouse, ruffles, deep V-neck, patent leather belt, four big black buttons, wide satin skirt, high heels, gloves—white gloves, dark eyebrows, green eye shadow, red lipstick . . . *(opens skirt),* red petticoat!

(To audience) Ladies and gentlemen, what do you think? *(Addressing imaginary husband on stage)* Y a usted, mi amor, ¿qué le parece? *(She walks to where the husband is; and becoming him, answers the diva admiringly)* ¡Divina! Es usted una reina. La amo. ¿Qué quiere? ¿Joyas? ¿Perlas, esmeraldas zafiros, rubíes, diamantes? *(He covers entire stage, surrounding her)* . . . Christian Dior, Coco Chanel, Balenciaga? Buenos Aires? ¡Madrid! La pasión de los toros de Madrid. *(Enticing her)* ¡La Habana! Los

cabarets de la Habana. Vamos a la Habana. *(Pause)* The Waldorf Astoria! Let's go to New York! *(Pause)* Ma cherie, venez avec moi à Paris. Les Folies Bergeres, le George V, ou bien, le Ritz. *(To audience)* I want to take her to the very best places. I want everyone to see her . . . with me. I want everyone to admire her, I want everyone to envy me. *(Back to her)* You're a queen, my queen, my woman.

(To audience) ¡Señoras y señores, *(showing her as trophy)* mi mujer! Mine! All mine! *(Singing)* Te vas porque yo quiero que te va. *(Speaking to audience)* Ladies, if you ever feel lonely *(pause)*, smoke a cigarette. Gentlemen, five hundred córdobas in your pocket can get you anything you want.

MOTHER: *(Applauding the winner)* ¡Fantástico, divino, encantador!

DAUGHTER: *(As a contemporary woman; to the audience)* I don't wanna know anything about her. I don't wanna see her. I don't wanna hear her. I don't wanna be near her. I don't wanna touch her. I don't want her to touch me. *(Pause)* Her perfume! *(Pause)* I don't want any phone calls telling me she's out of it again. Why me? Where is the rest of the family? If she wants to drink herself to death, let her do it. I've got my own life to live. Right?

MOTHER: *(Sitting on the chair, she recalls imaginary servant, stretching out her arms for acceptance or refusal)* Tráiganme a la niña. *(Pause)* Llévense a la niña. *(Pause)* Tráiganme a la niña. *(Pause)* Llévense a la niña. Tráiganme a la niña. Llévense a la niña. . . . *(Repeats gestures in silence. Changes gestures: to many small children; as if to mice)* Vengan mis amores lindos, mis corazones, mis muñecos lindos de vida. Vengan con mami, aquí está mami para ustedes, con ustedes, aquí. . . . *(Begins to get hysterical)* Un momentito, no corran, no, no, no, son muchos, no, así no, despacito, por favor, la falda, el vestido, no, que ando de blanco. *(More hysterical)* Ay no, por favor, que me van a volver loca. Cálmense, no peleen, carajitos, pórtense bien o se van de aquí. *(Totally paranoid, starts climbing on the chair)* Aaay! Vénganse a llevar a estos niños, aaay, aaaaay, aaaaaay, *(reaching climax on chair)* aaaaaaayyy, aaaaaaaaayyyyyyyyyyyyy!

(Immediately, we hear the first notes of "Amor de mis amores" by Agustín Lara. She regains composure little by little; sits down; takes off hat in grand gesture; touches up makeup; relaxes. She indulges completely in the music and in herself, until nervously removing her gloves, she realizes that the chair is not in exactly the right place. She angrily throws gloves on floor. She calls the maid.)

MOTHER: ¡Juanita! *(Music stops)* ¡Juanita! *(To imaginary maid)* ¿Qué significa esto? *(Pointing to chair)* ¿Cuántas veces te tengo que decir que esta silla . . . en su lugar? No, no es así. *(Moving chair an inch)* ¡Es así . . . !, el ángulo perfecto. Además . . . *(emits guttural, uneven, high-pitched sounds; gesturing wildly and babbling to the maid that she hasn't done her work. Suddenly very calm, and controlling a sweet voice)* Juanita . . . , un café . . . hirviendo por favor. Juanita . . . ¿dónde está María Eva? *(Pissed off)* Juanita, . . . los niños . . . siempre . . . bajo tu vigilancia. ¡María Eva! ¡Juanita! ¡María Eva! *(Hysterical)* ¡Juanita! ¡La silla! ¡María Eva! ¡Juanita! ¡La silla!

¡Mar . . . ! *(Looking down menacingly at a little girl)* ¡Ajá! ¿En tu cuarto? ¿Sooooola? *(To the maid)* Juanita, que sea la última vez que yo encuentro . . . a esta niña . . . jugando . . . *(to the little girl)* sooooola! *(She crouches and becomes the little girl)*

DAUGHTER: *(As little girl; to audience)* It's time to escape. Mis tías? They live just one block away. *(Calling out)* Mamalooooola! Bendición, Mamalola. Bendición, Mamalola. Bendición, Mamalola. *(To the audience.)* Her bedroom is so dark. She never moves from her bed, shrouded in mosquito netting. She's so scary *(as if telling a ghost story)*, so skinny, so skinny . . . , not a single tooth in her head and she never knows who we are. We call her la muerta. Uuuuuuyyyy! La muerta, la muerta! *(Becomes Chita, the aunt, scolding the children)* Fuera de aquí . . . estos muchachitos! ¡Juera, fuera! Dejen de molestar a Mamalola. Mamalola, no es juguete.

(Little girl; to the audience) So we ran up to the second floor, like horses on the wooden staircase. *(Chita again)* ¡No corran, muchachitos! Se van a matar. Parecen caballos, . . . caballos, *(voice fading out as if in a dream)* . . . caball . . . ! *(Little girl; entering a huge attic in an old house, and finding all kinds of treasures)* Old uniforms from the war . . . , trunks filled with broken rifles . . . , military hats and boots . . . faded banners and battle flags on the walls. . . . *(To audience)* All things belonging to our great-grandfather, the Minister of War. *(Standing next to chair as in an old portrait)* Don Ricardo Alfonso López Callejas, Ministro de la Guerra, in command during the Civil War, when the liberals burned down the city, 1927. *(Playing war with other kids)* Este rifle es mío. Yo quiero las botas. No, ese bastón es mío. A mí me toca llevar la bandera. Aquí . . . metámonos . . . este ropero es la trinchera. Corran . . . ahí vienen. Piñano, piñao! Aaayyy! Punk! ¡Estás muerto! ¡Muerto, muerto, muerto! *(As Chita again)* A jugar al patio. Al patio, al patio, al patio!

(Little girl; to the audience) The patio . . . three times the size of the house. A jungle, banana trees, platanillos, flowers, giant ferns, avocado, guava, coconut, mango trees. We get wet in the fountain. The geese chase us. We bury ourselves in mounds of coffee beans, screaming, yelling, fighting . . . teasing the lora . . . a huge green parrot with a sharp beak and ugly black claws . . . really mean bird! This one . . . , she hates me. We never know where she is. She flies out of nowhere and . . . fump! . . . in my hair. We tease her with a long stick, 'til she screams at the top of her lungs. *(Becoming the lora)* Aaaaagh! Aaaaaagh! Aaaaagghhhhh!!!!!

(In place, she turns to the other side. She knocks at the mother's bedroom) Toc, toc, toc! Mamá, ¿se puede? Toc, toc, toc. Mamá, ¿se puede? *(Mother opens door)* Ja, ja, ja, ja, ja. *(She can't suppress laughter. Explains to audience)* She's wearing . . . her wedding gown. *(She becomes the mother)*

MOTHER: *(Movement section: trying but failing to speak; showing full range of emotions—arrogance, rage, breaking down, arrogance again. She moves very slowly, carrying the wedding dress with its long, heavy train. Long pause, until she stands in front of chair)* Súbite en esa silla, *(pointing to the chair)* María Eva. Ayúdame con los botones. *(Imaginary girl stands on chair helping mother with the buttons. Mother, facing imaginary mirror, sucks in her stomach; trying to fit into gown)*

(Becoming GIRL*)* No se puede, Mamá . . . están muy lejos. No se puede. . . .

(As MOTHER*)* Sigue tratando, María Eva. . . .

(As GIRL*)* No se puede, Mamita, no se puede. *(Gestures and lines are repeated convulsively several times)* No se puede, no se puede. *(Girl crying)*

DAUGHTER: *(As contemporary woman, to audience)* I had to be like her. I had to look like her. I had to do like her. I should have a husband. I should have children. I should have a house. I should be beautiful, and if not, I should make myself beautiful. Put makeup on and change my looks, change the shape of my eyebrows, change the shape of my mouth, *(in crescendo)* shave my legs, shave my armpits, do my lips, change the color of my skin, and one day, when I'm eighteen years old, it would be time to parade *(parading)* in my white gown, in front of the adult world, in front of the men, in front of the fathers, so that they, the men, could choose, would choose for their young, little men . . . para sus machitos! *(She spits)*

MOTHER: *(As in front of mirror; walking straight back, straightening hair and mumbling to herself. Begins to speak softly, her words unintelligible)* A María Eva, me le ponen el pelo pegado, se lo agarran y se lo alizan . . . ese pelo rebelde, esa niña rebelde, imposible, *(nervous)* insoportable, insolente, arréglenla bien, manténganla en orden. ¡Tienen que ser perfectos! Tienen que ser como yo, andar nítidos, *(more nervous; undoing hair)* siempre en su lugar, y esta niña insolente, insoportable, *(screaming hysterically)* que no la aguanto. . . . *(Freezes looking at audience; hair is completely disheveled. Turns back and arranges hair)*

   *(*GIRL *is left sitting on chair.* MOTHER *now turns to her very sweetly. Words are inaudible. She gestures everything)* Qué linda, mi amor, sentadita como una princesa, con su vestidito abierto para que no se aje, su collarcito de perlas, y sus piernitas juntas—una princesa—un día, vas a ser tan grande y tan linda como mami. *(Begins to speak)* No, no puedes salir a la calle sola, sólo los hombres andan en la calle, *(going around the chair)* sólo los hombres salen solos, sólo los hombres son hombres, *(rasiing voice)* solo los hombres van a la finca, sólo los hombres saben tirar, sólo los hombres saben boxear, solo los hombres juegan beisbol, *(screaming)* solo los hombres, solo los hombres, solo los hom . . . ! *(She freezes)*

DAUGHTER: *(As a contemporary woman. Positions chair facing straight right. To audience)* One day she decides she's going to learn how to drive. That means, HE *(Pointing to imaginary father)* is going to buy her a brand new car, because the family car is a shift, and that's too complicated for her: *(Mimicking mother)* The clutch, the accelerator, the rearview mirror, the directionals, the gear shift, no, no, no, no, no, the new car has to be an automatic. *(To audience)* The following day, at the sacred hour of the aperitif at noon, because every single day of the world, when *(pointing at him)* HE comes home from the office, she's *(mimicking mother's pose)* at the bar, waiting . . .

FAHTER: *(Moving to where "father" was)* Tesoro mío, I have a surprise for you.

DAUGHTER: *(Pointing at chair)* A used car, badly needing a paint job, bent fenders, holes, in the seats! And . . . *(mimicking Mother)* what did HE think, that *(arrogantly; pointing to herself)* SHE . . . *(Dignified. Hurt)* ¡Nunca!

DAUGHTER: Two days later *(pointing to chair)* un *impala,* último modelo, silver green, parked in front of the house.

MOTHER: *(Excitedly)* Ay, amor, qué carro más lindo. Everybody, let's go for a ride!

CHILDREN: Sí, Mami, sí, Mami!

DAUGHTER: *(To audience; telling story as she mimics mother)* She goes into her bedroom *(picking up gloves from floor)* for her gloves . . . so the sun won't burn her white hands . . . we get in the back seat, father is in front and she . . . *(sitting on chair)* at the wheel! She wanted to use one foot for the accelerator and the other one for the brakes, one hand on the steering wheel, and the other arm like this.

MOTHER: *(Waving out the car window)* Ja, ja, ja, ja, ja adiós Olguita, cuánto tiempo, adiós Don Mariano, tanto gusto, Ana María, te llamo más tarde.

FATHER: *(Giving instructions to mother)* Fíjese en el retrovisor. *(A little impatient)* Enrolle más que le va a dar a ese carro. Ponga el pidevía antes de doblar.

MOTHER: *(Waving again)* Adiós, Doña Licha, gusto de verla. Mariita linda, sí, gracias. *(Pointing to children in back)* Sí, aquí van, ja, ja.

FATHER: *(More impatient)* ¡Cuidado con la bicicleta! ¡Párese que ahí hay un alto! ¡Vaya más despacio, que no ve que va con los niños! *(To the children in back)* ¡Silencio, ahí atrás! *(Hysterically)* ¡Cuidado la señora! ¡La va a matar! ¡Deténgase! ¡Ya no más!

DAUGHTER: *(Getting up from chair; placing heels neatly next to driver. To audience)* She never learned how to drive. *(Moves chair to face opposite direction)* One night, he's driving, all of us in the car . . . *(Sits down; becoming the child)*

(Blackout.)
Singing
Fast!
Faster!
Headlights!
aaaaaaayyyyyy!
No. No.
No more man
No more husband
No more father
(Leaving the chair; facing father's death)
                              . . . Papá

(Takes off gloves and puts them down as if on the tomb. Tchaikovsky's Swan Lake fades in. Girl starts dancing ballet for the father, which turns into playing baseball, boxing; music ends; finally, she hits the imaginary father several times in the stomach.)

MOTHER: *(As in the beginning, showing off her elegance; this time, a mature, sexy widow)* Black decolletée, below the shoulders; black sapphires; tight, tight, black nylons; Cuban heels; long, red fingernails, red mouth.

DAUGHTER: *(Announcing to the audience; showing trophy)* The most beautiful widow . . . ever seen . . . in Managua. Entertaining her many admirers . . . *(Using distinctive masculine gestures for each one of them)* The first category is: Don Arnulfo García Breally, general manager of Taca International; Don Carlos Menéndez Chávez, his government's ambassador to France; Don Alfredo Fernández, owner of Monsac, a textile factory; Don Miguel González Herrera, the biggest ranch in Guanacaste; Don Ruperto Inturay, a prominent politician . . . *(delivering speech)* ¡Porque así . . . pensamos . . . los nicaragüenses!; Don Porfirio Toledo, former boyfriend and now . . . a respected . . . gynecologist.

The second category is: Armando Suarez, entomologist—that was a trip to Mexico; Manolo Piñero, a pianist accompanying Joselito—same trip to Mexico; Hans Lubasch, telephone repairman; Gerardo Tapia, salesman in a furniture store, *(pointing to someone in audience)* you sold us the stereo, remember? And in Miami Beach, at the Columbus hotel, Pepe Rivera, alias "El Curro," a matador from Morocco.

MOTHER: *(Mother is alone, tired, older; she wanders around the house singing and humming to herself)* Sin ti, no podré vivir jamás, tararitarirarán . . . y pensar que nunca más tararirarán. *(Sits down)* Sin ti, tararirariraran es inútil vivir. *(Becomes uncomfortable)* Es inútil vivir. *(Shows signs of aging in front of mirror)* Como inútil será ja-ja-ja-ja . . . buscando que te perdone . . . *(disturbed)* que me puede ya importar si lo que me hace llorar . . . ja-ja-ja-ja-ja-ja-ja, *(very disturbed, talking to imaginary children)* váyanse a la mierda, hijoeputitas, váyanse a la mierda . . . ja-ja-ja-ja-ja . . . *(sings again; drunk; beginning to break down)* sin ti, es inútil ya vivir . . . voy a hacer lo que me dé mi gana, a meterme lo que se antoje, de ahora en adelante ésta es mi vida. *(Starts undressing: throws away belt, skirt and, finally, shoes)* Four big black buttons . . . ja-ja-ja-ja-ja, aaaaaghhhhh!!!! *(Regains composure; gets up from chair as contemporary woman)*

DAUGHTER: *(Gazing lovingly at mother)* My mother.

(As a GIRL, *sometimes as a* WOMAN; *to audience)*

Shhhhhhh!
She just turned off the
*   air-conditioning.*
I know she'll be gone
*   for at least two hours.*
I can go in now.
The sheets are still cool.
*   Five, six, seven dresses*
*   all over,*
The ones she decided not to wear.
Her perfume is still here.

If I close the door
   quickly
I'll be able to keep it
   for as long as I like.
I'll go under the sheets
   and pretend
      I'm sleeping with her.
My cheek resting on the
sweet smell of her white skin.
Nobody in the world.
   knows where I am.
Perhaps
I can stay here.
   forever.

(*Danzón starts very faintly.* GIRL *stars playing dress-up with* MOTHER'*s clothes, puts on skirt, shoes, gloves, and finally, the hat. She poses as for a photograph. Lights fade. Music fades.*)

CHAPTER & VERSE
(A Poem in Progress)

Carl Hancock Rux

CHARACTERS

Prophet Poet: *Pageantry and tinkling symbols*

Yo Mama Arsula: *Weary blues and vail tradition*

Our Nig Brother man: *All anger and negritude*

Daddy Boy: *All forgiveness and longing*

Fallen Diva: *Lasciviousness and Drama*

Blues Singer: *Traveling light*

Broken Doll: *Holy Virgin*

The Voices: *Spirit Barometers*

(Authors Note: This is not a play within the linear confines of traditional theater. It was written as an exercise in movement, language, and a capella vocalizations exploring faith and the deviation from tradition. Redemption is the quest of each character. Some of the poems are sung, or have lyrical structures that can be improvised by the performers. In some cases, sounds and breath technique should underscore monologues. The Voices should sing in harmony like a fiery gospel choir, a blues chorale, and West African griots. Movement is integral to the progression of each moment.)

Chapter 1, Verse 1: Ritual and Procession

THE SPACE: *A Black church Sunday Morning Service. A family gathering. A holy place in the middle of a wilderness.*

THE SONG: *Sounds hurl through the dark. Alto blues. Jazz whispers. Soprano cry and percussive breath. Some lights fade in. The community huddles on a large wooden block, moaning in broken tongues. Wailing. Faces are to the ground. An orchestra of screams. This is a plaintive cry. It builds, then subsides as the lights come up on the Voices in the Wilderness who begin to chant softly. The Voices are elevated above the stage on high holy chairs, surrounded by copper bells, tambourines, rain sticks, etc. They are the musicians as well as the chorus.*

THE DANCE: *Huddled bodies relax and fall into each other, resting heads on stomachs, arms entwined with legs. Lights come up on* PROPHET POET, *who stands upstage left. His robes are all colors and torn. His symbols are tickling and weighing him down. He listens and responds in his body. He removes his shoes and covers his head. He is near a podium that is draped in fabric. Florida water, olive oil, beads and other objects are at the foot of the unused podium creating an altar space. He anoints himself with three gestures (Prayer, Exile, Carnality) and the Voices repeat these gestures. He holds a large book with torn pages.*

As he speaks, the community leaves the wooden block, one by one, on individual journeys, traveling throughout the space eventually finding their different environments, where they reside.)

PROPHET POET: *(Opening the book, and reading in monotone-repeating three gestures)* All they that were numbered in the camp of Dan, and those that encamp by him shall be the tribe of Asher, but the Levites were not numbered among the tribe of those from the Philadelphian nation . . . were not numbered . . . as the Lord commanded . . . so they pitched their tents . . . so they pitched their standards . . . so they set forward . . . every one after their families . . . according to the house of their father. . . . So they come from a north country. They that were not numbered . . . tribal. Come gathered from some captive coast. . . . All those from the place of the Carribe and the hills of the poplar and blood . . . with them blind and lame, come loud, come silent. Madonna and child, mourning together. They were not numbered so they pitched their tents . . . all those from industrial green housing and the place of excrement and the well of deep sorrow. . . . A great remnant. They come weeping and wailing by rivers and waters. These are the names of the sons of Aaron and the sons of James and the daughters of naked women wandering . . . when they offered strange fire before the Lord . . . they shall keep his charge and they shall keep his instruments and they shall keep his commandment. . . . all these . . . they come to bleed, then heal. To sing, then dance. A final time. In spirit. To sing. Then dance. To weep and wail, by rivers and waters. Tribal. To bleed. A final time. In spit and in spirit. All they that were not numbered . . .

(The community is in place. There should be lights or slides that bleed throughout the space, creating the illusion of fire escapes and stained glass storefront windows at different times. There are pews, one altar space, and one large wooden block downstage center. The characters move throughout the space freely and the wooden block is always lit, taking focus. DADDY BOY *and* OUR NIG BROTHER MAN *are together.* YO-MAMA ARSULA *sits in a comfortable chair near a window. Above, a small table is covered with communion cups and many bottles of wine.* BROKEN DOLL *is surrounded by the limbs and heads of various dolls.* THE FALLEN DIVA *is entangled in flowers; she walks between sheer drapes that hang from the rafters and spill onto the floor.* THE BLUES SINGER *is the only one laughing. She visits each environment, offering an internal song, and finds herself residing in the various spaces for a while, before leaving one to go to another.* THE VOICES *are always together, in their choir robes, playing their instruments. They stand to sing the opening hymn. During the hymn, the community mutters.)*

Verse 2

Voices: (Traditional)
Did anybody see who came and took their lives?
Anybody see who came and took their lives?
I was high
High

High in the hills
trying to hide.

Did anybody see?

Were you there when they spilled the blood?
Were you there when they spilled the blood?
It came down
down
down to the valley like a flood.
Were you there when they spilled . . .

There's no room to dig another grave
There's no room to dig another grave
Where we stand
Stand
Stand will be our final resting place
No . . . there's no room to dig another
grave.

(*The Blues Singer wails.*)

PROPHET POET: (*In grandiloquent Preacher's cadence*) There is a time to live! And uh—a time to die! A time for peace! Uh-huh—a time to fight! A time to kill! A time to wish! A time to forget! And uh—a time to question! A time to accept! A time to be quiet! A time to fall! And uh-huh.

(ARSULA *catches the spirit silently. The community catches the spirit silently.*)

ARSULA: Remember the dances. Ghost dances. David did it, naked. Miriam waited till she crossed over. Persistent prayer—have to pray till change comes. Repetition. Same dance. Over and over again. Remember that. Same songs. Same words. Don't go changin'. And never speak to the prophets directly. Never. Herodia's daughter danced . . . till she heard from Gawd! Faded into the margins dancin'! Mama Lily danced . . . till her toe got caught on a nail. Died of gangrene, dancin'! O yes! Yes she did . . . ghost dances. And a little wine is good for the stomach. Remember that! Yes . . . I remember that . . .

PROPHET POET: (*Invocation*)

All are reverent . . .
Harlem tenement, storefront and sign
hang from tinted glass.
Last hope for last tribes, asking why
to the ceiling . . . a peeling sky
of glory. Hear the story of redeemed man
and anointed womb.
Who shall ask for peace?
Who shall ask for pardon?

Salvation is in a name.
The shame of plain-faced women
is turned to pride, like
water into wine.
A penny is our last hope for
eternity.

And who shall ask for
peace?

Who shall ask for peace?
Who shall ask?

Glory! Glory!
Heads wrapped in white sheets—
to bury the dead.
Fresh young bodies in fresh white sheets.
The beat of hope is driving,
the beat of redemption is driving,
the beat of anointed womb—
for whom shall we pour this
anointed wine and break this bread—
for whom shall we break this bread?

The dead shall bury themselves
in white sheets.
The beat of glory, thumping.
The beat of the story, thumping.
The beat of hope, thumping.

I see tilting trees and wilting flowers,
I hear children crying and mothers singing
I feel the lost pages of lost books
beneath my feet . . .
and white sheets blowing from naked bodies . . .

Our grief is but a moment!

FALLEN DIVA: *(mockingly)* The preacher says!

PROPHET POET: *(Arsula repeats under)*

Our grief is but a moment . . .
Our fading pain sustains itself only in the mind,
and a kind breeze blows by,
Holy Ghost and power . . .
Our spines have been staked into the
ground.
The sound of truth

is like a gospel song on a blue note . . .
for whom shall we pour this wine?
For whom shall we break this bread?
For whom?

(BROTHER MAN *screams out, percussion builds—the dance changes.*)

BROTHER MAN: SCREAM! SCREAM! SCREAM! Hands. Caging. Us. In. Ceiling. To floor. Holding. Back. Trapped. Locked. Spirits.

BROKEN DOLL: *(She joins him, ripping out the hairs of the doll's heads)* SCREAM! Smell. Blood. Excrement. Smell. Urine. Tight. Hair. Matted . . .

FALLEN DIVA: No heads to glorify God, no God to glorify in.

PROPHET POET: Our pain is only for a moment . . .

BROTHER MAN: SCREAM!

ARSULA: Pentecostals. Ties strangle. Wool suits are as binding armor. Nickel. Dime. Nickel. Dime.

DADDY BOY: Time. SCREAM! Buried fists. Fists in face. Face of fists. Fathers. Fists. Father's face. Fist in face. Escape. Welfare check. Wedding ring. Handbags. Memories. Heart. Dream. Full. Us. Dreamful us.

FALLEN DIVA: SCREAM! Little Girl, Scream! Raped. Beaten. Image. Rod. Nappy. Nigger. Girl. Spoiled. Themes. Dark. Light. Spit. Mirrors. Blond. Blue. Insults. Insults. Insulting. Ruined. Insulting blues and blondes! Little girl. Little girl blues.

ALL: SCREAM! Fathers. Strangers. Cordless. Climb. Climb. Climb. Wind push you back. Walk. Ground swallow your steps. Swim. Waves paralyze your strokes. Pray. Don't know the name. Don't know the name. The name? The name! The name of our who's? God. The name of God? Don't know the name of God. Of our God. Sing. Notes all flat and sharp. All flat. All sharp. God. The name. Who's name? Who's God? Our God. All flat and sharp. All flat and sharp.

BROTHER MAN: SCREAM! SCREAM! SCREAM! SCREAM! SCREAM! SCREAM! SCREAM!

FALLEN DIVA: *(Laughing at him, speaking softly)* No voice. No voice. No voice to be heard . . .

ALL: *(Whispering)* No voice. No voice. No voice.

(Pause. Percussion ceases. They rest.)

PROPHET POET: *(Continuing his sermon)*

All are reverent . . .
In a storefront church somewhere,

tired people cast their cares,
and dance about the room,
cause the
joy replaced the gloom.
On the altar prays the mothers,
on the
pulpit preach the brothers,
askin'
God to pay the rent,
cause the welfare check was spent,
and the
winter wind is kind,
and the
truth is on our minds,
the sisters bend their spines,
the deacons moan and whine,
Oh!
The Old Promised land,
will be mine! Will be mine!
Death don't worry me,
it's the
thing that makes us free!
Life on earth is but a day,
before we find another way!
Anutha
door to pass thru . . .
Anutha
work
to do . . .
Anutha creed to write in blood . . .
as we journey thru the mud . . .
Ya'll don't hear me. . . . Can I get a witness? . . .
I feel like preachin'. . . . Wish I had some
help this evenin'. . . . Ya'll don't hear me.
Somebody help me . . . wish I had some help
Can I get a witness. . . .

(There is no response.)

PROPHET POET: *(Facing the wooden block)* Testify! Tell what and why . . . in this hallowed space. Thread together you elegies, weave the poems of lamentations. . . . *(Reading from the book)* "Soon your souls will be as dry soil beneath the rain. Your seeds will root down and spring up and your sorrows will be no more!" . . . and your sorrows will be no more. . . . Voices In The Wilderness! Testify! Lost tribes come from some other place. . . . Testify! Tell what and why . . . bring it! . . . Bring it! . . . And your souls . . . as dry soil . . . beneath the rain.

(THE DANCE: PROPHET *motions to the block. The community hesitates. A few attempt to move toward it but retreat. The* VOICES *sing out.*)

Chapter 2/Verse 1: Voices in the Wilderness

(*A Spiritual*)

> Lord, how come me here?
> Lord, how come me here?
> I wish I never was born . . .
>
> There ain't no freedom here, Lord
> there ain't no freedom here, Lord.
> I wish I never was born . . .

(*Humming continues under* BROTHER MAN *as he moves downstage and testifies on the block.*)

BROTHER MAN:
The call is tribal. The march is angry. The faces—
sharp. When my eyes opened this morning,
they did not greet the sun
no. They looked out into the blinding dark.
The night's fierce blade. What place is this?
And darkness cut, deep into my sight/split
the canvas coat of my protection shield.
Vision stabbed, I spilled my . . . blood and water
across the floor, like rushing waves, opened by
mouth and screamed,
echo canyon high, mountain cry:
WHAT PLACE IS THIS?

The abyss of silent nuthin's happiness . . .
Wait to hear your soul drop to the bottom,
falls for a lifetime/
My silhouette is cut on the bias . . .
Appliqué to an evil white night moon grin . . .
An evil white night moon grins . . .
LORD? HOW COME ME HERE?
I'm askin' you
cuz
I heard your name from the pew
when somebody said, believe, receive, relieve
my sins at your throne. . . . Is this true?
What chariot picked me up from heaven's side

and let me slide into this strange land,
where my feet sink, fall fast into the muck mud mire of things?

(ARSULA *weeps and the* BLUES SINGER *hums.*)

BROTHER MAN: Can you hear my mother praying? How come the veil is draped across her looking glass? Dare she ask why there's trouble in this land? I can't stand to see her tears no more. Valleys gash like tribal marks down her cobalt cheeks. Valleys gash like tribal marks down her cobalt cheeks. . . .

(DADDY BOY *moves frantically.*)

And my brother my brother he runs runs from
my brother my brother he runs runs from
his own tribe
asking why his own people use his blood
for ink black to maul his name
callin' him

NIGGER SHAME ON YOURSELF!

as he drops lifeless in concrete fields.
No one halts or yields to wash his feet . . .
Concrete fields grow lifeless men, scattered like seeds . . .
tangled weeds of the sidewalk, and no one halts
or yields to wash his feet?
What place is this ? Why? We here?
Our spirit is gone.
The sacred song
look like the sacred song was snatched from our mouths
before we hit the high note.
Look like we snatched it from each other's mouths.
When will that holy time come when our people gather
sipping merry wine from the drinking gourds?
I'm still here, waiting for the day. Looking for the harvest.
Still asking the question.
How come me here?
How come me here?
How come she here?
I wish I . . . I . . . wish I never . . . I wish I never was . . .
ALL VOICES: I wish I was never born.

(*The* BLUES SINGER *hums a slow blues.* BROTHER MAN *rests on the block.* ARSULA *gets up and looks out her window. She pours herself a drink, and lights a cigarette.*)

ARSULA: I looked around the room I was in . . . into the faces of all the men in my room. Into the deep molded carved faces . . . had to get out, out of my room. I did. I left my room. Spilled out the window, poured myself down down down the fire escape, escaped up up up the boulevard, away from my room, and all the men, and all the faces, deep carved faces in my room. To the street. Looked for new faces. I looked about the street I walked down, saw the mangled dry hair dying on tilting scalps, tilting scalps resting on slanting pavement. They called out, all these faces. "Hey! Heey!" They bargained with the motion of my ass. Propositioned by face. These faces I saw. I saw them. I saw it. I wept. I stood there. Among the sick and dying faces. The faces. The feces. Feces faces. Rotten wind-painted faces. Wept within myself. Within myself. Wept. Wept myself within their world. Cried with. With all the faces. Turning narrow faces. Fast and still. Still. Cried with/till we all became one sadness. . . . Came back to my room . . . looked around . . . locked the door . . .

FALLEN DIVA: *(Sarcastically)* So testify . . . tell the what and why.

PROPHET POET: *(Agreeing)* And soon your soul will . . .

(DIVA *turns away from him.*)

DADDY BOY: *(To* BROTHER MAN*)* Make room for me . . .

ARSULA: *(Stepping down to the block with her drink. She stands to the side of it. She sits on it. She gives* BROTHER MAN *a drink)* You better remember the ghost dances. What? You angry Brother Man! Hey! Brother Maaaan! *(Laughs to herself)* Our nig' . . . hmmhmmmmm. Our angry nig' . . . .Useta be that way myself . . . and then I saw myself thru smoked glass. A flame flickering, illuminating something of nothing. *(Singing)* "This little light of mine." *(Laughs)* Shine. Too much shine. Too much light. Flushed away the shapes and shadows. I wanted to believe myself to be . . . so I became something of vines and trees dancing on walls, drapes, water falls over edges, shiny eye brass glittering and angels, twirling, twirling, twirling.

(BROTHER MAN *goes back to his open space.* ARSULA *joins* FALLEN DIVA. *Offers her a drink.* DIVA *is too busy bowing.*)

ARSULA: I saw a grain in the clay. A smudge in the mirror. You ever see a little bit o' grit in your cream? I did, I erased myself. Erased myself to recreate myself in colors. In theory. In prose. Colors hanging and dangling and dragging from me, wrapped high on my head, towering to babel. High! High! High! High! on my head. Oh, yes . . . oh, yes . . .

(ARSULA *returns to her room*)

ARSULA: *(Taking a large swig)* Some dirty blood spilled. I signed my name with it, indifferently saw myself, and plucked the eyes out of the woman who stared back at me. I ran my hand along the rough spots of my life, till red bled into blue and purple mixed with orange; colors dangling and dragging from me, and no images could exist except I made them . . . myself was a recreation of creation. Somebody make a big mistake in me . . . so I smashed the mold. And started me over again . . . and again . . . and again . . . *(Pours herself another drink).*

BROTHER MAN: *(To* BROKEN DOLL*)* Make room for me.

FALLEN DIVA: A suicide poem. . . . Shall I perform a final note on all of this . . . on all of that . . . an after thought. Yes? Lights? Music, please *(Clears her throat)* Here goes. On bruised days I wrestle with an army of self destruction, hurling bullets of self-pity at myself, plunging knives of insecurities deep into my chest . . . and I die . . . passionately . . . release the tension in my neck, curl my body down and under to the slow backward fall of my head.

(ARSULA and BROKEN DOLL *dance to* DIVA's *monologue.)*

FALLEN DIVA: My body is limp and liquid. A dancer's flower withers interpretation. . . . Dew tears drip from my lids. Water seeps from the corners of my petal lips . . . a silent scream begins as a percussion in my stomach. A single drumbeat turns into an orchestra of rhythms! Kidskin! Copper bells! Cymbals! Bells! Volcanoes up through my throat and vomits forth! Ahh.aaahhh . . . yes . . . release . . . releeeease . . . white drapes hover over me for a moment, suspended by the wind . . . fly down and cover me . . . this room is so silent . . . silent in mourning this room respects my death. . . .

(Untangling herself from the drapes, she turns to BROKEN DOLL *who has stopped dancing.)*

FALLEN DIVA: Die now little girl . . . won't have to die no more . . . die now . . . won't have to die no more.

ALL: Little Girl. Die now. Won't Have To Die No More. Little Girl.

FALLEN DIVA: *(Poking fun at* BROKEN DOLL*)*: She? The winter melting.

ARSULA: She is?

BROKEN MAN: Springtime moistened lips on the backs of young men rising.

FALLEN DIVA: She *was* summertime. She was summertime bright. Her braids traveling behind her as she carried herself to fall.

ALL: Carried herself to fall. Carried herself to fall. Carried herself to fall.

BROTHER MAN: *(To* BROKEN DOLL*)*: Make room for me. . . .

BROKEN DOLL: Where?

BROTHER MAN: That space.

BROKEN DOLL: Where?

BROTHER MAN: In your jazz. Your cantor call. Let me ride.

FALLEN DIVA: *(To both of them)* Grow up. Grow down. Men. Atrocities!

BROTHER MAN: Make room. . . .

FALLEN DIVA: Grow down.

BROKEN DOLL: No vacancies. No room.

BROTHER MAN: That space, nestled deep . . . in sight and sound . . . like flower heads on water . . . room.

BROKEN DOLL: No vacancies.

Chapter 3/Verse 1

(Lights fade up on DADDY BOY. *Environment of memory. He paces in his wide-open space.* ARSULA *paces with him and lights a cigarette. They pace together. All watch. The* VOICES *play tinkling sounds.* BROTHER MAN *joins the pacing.)*

PROPHET POET: Yes. That'll do. Bring it. Recall it. Bring it. Remember it. Yes. That'll do.

ARSULA: *(Calling out to a room beyond her window)* Man? Man you all right? What you doin' in there so long?

DADDY BOY: *(To* BROTHER MAN*)* Make room for me.

PROPHET POET: Now don't be afra- . . . recall it . . . bring it . . . bring it . . .

ARSULA: Man? Man, you all right? Watchoo doin' in there so looooong?

DADDY BOY: *(On the block)* The last drop of ice cooled my mouth, the rest of me was aflame and wet. Fire on water. Water on fire.

ARSULA: He say he all right. Boy . . . maybe you should wait till he come out before you go. . . . Man? The boy is gettin' ready to go, wanna see you before he go!

DADDY BOY: He wore it well, well-carved man in uniform and pencil line mustache, who smiled mischievously with marble eyes from a gray and white World War II photograph. The slightly overweight towering man in the album posing beside a Christmas tree, laughing even then at how time could not distort his beauty. Glimpses of yesterday revealed laughter in his eyes, though all of my childhood revealed somber anger from cemented stares. Beautiful still . . . still beauty.

ARSULA: Man whatchoo doin' in there so long—the Boy is here to see you!

DADDY BOY: Milky complexion, hallowed face. Fainting lids. Drooling lips ajar.

ALL: Purple veins winding up trembling legs.

FALLEN DIVA: Frailty.

ARSULA: Baldness.

PROPHET POET: Age.

DADDY BOY: Death. He wore it well. Time could not distort the beauty.

ARSULA: Man, you all right? Well, open the damn door, then!

DADDY BOY: The carelessness of life's everyday existence—

BROTHER MAN: Things are as they should be.

DADDY BOY: The mapped-out-scripted-no-surprises-please-television-sitcom era called out to me to leave. Go to commercial. Stay tuned.

BROTHER MAN: Next week!

FALLEN DIVA: Script in the works.

DADDY BOY: But here's a preview so you can recline and relax and expect what you get, get what you expect.

ARSULA: Boy, come on over here and help me open this damn bathroom door! I think he fell.

DADDY BOY: *(Carrying* BROTHER MAN *in his arms):* Blood memories. Limp man in arms. Familiar stale stench. Dying flesh. The mission call that enlists us all to hug and hold. The able. Carry him in calm peacefulness.

ARSULA: Careful, now. Careful.

DADDY BOY: Sometimes death requires welcome when feat locks the door.

ARSULA: Gruntin' from the floor. On his stomach. Shorts wet and tangled. Musta been there twenty minutes. Naked.

DADDY BOY: Mother's frantic cry and disjointed concern dances question marks around our heads . . . but he was calm . . . and I was calm. . . . He was still and I was still.

BROTHER MAN: Wobbly hand. Shaking body. Marble eyes, that laugh and ask for assistance. Stammering tongue. Muted voice.

DADDY BOY: Vodka spittle. Hold onto me daddy, cuz I gotcha. Don't let go. . . . Milky skin. Hallow face. Fainting lids. Drooling lips ajar. Purple veins winding up trembling legs. Fathers and sons who want to love. Hate the thought. Too familiar. Vodka spittle. Callous hands. Mama's nursing her eye and cursing the wind.

ARSULA: Naked.

DADDY BOY: Naked and vulnerable . . . in my father, my arms reach for some piece of this vulnerability, to take as souvenir . . . to appreciate . . . share that with me . . . don't only use it with wife and women in protected solitude . . . with son . . . who comes to you already naked and exposed and asks for some compassion because of it.

BROTHER MAN: Can't talk, see him later.

ARSULA: You all right?

DADDY BOY: Years go by like people . . . they say the world is mine if I take it. Years go by like people on a summer street. Maybe next time we'll . . . Your dreams are in a broken bottle, in a can, in some shattered dream of what's supposed to be, not what is. . . . Broken black glass . . . brass frame . . . shattered . . .

ARSULA: You all right? Careful.

DADDY BOY: You fell, Daddy. That's all. Like some men do. But I gotcha. Hold right now, cause I gotcha.

ALL: Water on fire. Burning. Vodka spittle. Mama in the kitchen, nursing her eye. Milky skin. Hallow face. Fainting lids. Drooling lips ajar. Purple veins. Trembling legs. Broken black glass. Brass frames. Naked. Years go by. Years go by.

DADDY BOY: I gotcha.

ALL: Years go by. Years go by.

DADDY BOY: Hold on . . . hold out to me . . . I gotcha.

ALL: Black glass, shattered.

ALL: I remember that . . . yes . . . I remember that. . . .

(The VOICES *play a second chorus of tinkling.* BROKEN DOLL *moves toward the block as* BROTHER MAN *is carried off by the group.)*

BROKEN DOLL: *(Heads toward the block with her doll's head. She returns to her space and rakes through the doll's hair with a comb. She also tugs and pulls and braids the locks as well)* A patch of leaves played merry-go-round at her feet, little girl pulled her clear glass-eyed lace-and-ruffle doll with her to worship service, faithfully, every morning and said: "Dis here's my baby!" Raised brows in opposition . . . crowds of subdued husband jurors and supreme court sisters widened their eyes . . . at her ringless finger . . . her youth . . . her—

FALLEN DIVA   and ARSULA: Same Sunday service no shame slip she call a dress!

BROKEN DOLL: And she rocked her baby to "Victory in Jesus! My Savior Forever!"

ALL: Child never be nuthin'. Child never be nuthin'. Child never be nuthin'. I remember that . . . yes . . . I remember that . . . .

BROKEN DOLL: Sundays look like Mondays. . . . Prayer felt like pain . . . sayin' God same as sayin' goddamn . . . worship begins and ends in the sanctuary of my room, on the mercy seat, weary worn and sad, listenin' to a music . . . lascivious and vile . . . a dance of lamenting . . . aging . . . of spendthrift yesterdays and bankrupt tomorrows . . . the rhythms of emptiness inside . . . left a broken doll behind. . . .

FALLEN DIVA: *(To the* PROPHET*)* Will you perform or shall I? *(No response)* Do you know how?

ARSULA: You're not to speak to him, directly. Never do that.

FALLEN DIVA: Will you perform?

ARSULA: Blaspheme!

*(*FALLEN DIVA *clears her throat, sets her stage. She clears her throat again. Contorts her body. Attempts a few dance movements. Makes faces of agony and ecstasy. Dies violently. Throws her hands up and bows. Applauds herself. Lights fade.)*

(Drums and bells, disjointed. BLUES SINGER *sings on the block.)*

BLUES SINGER:

Nobody's fault but mine
Nobody's fault but mine
If I should die
and my soul be lost
Nobody's fault but mine.

I had another who could pray
I had another who could pray
If I should die
and my soul be lost
Nobody's fault but mine.

I had a mother who could sing
I had a mother who could sing
If I should die
and my soul be lost
Nobody's fault but mine.

(BROTHER MAN *takes* BROKEN DOLL *in his arms during the song. He moves her to the block. They dance.* DADDY BOY *joins them and takes* BROTHER MAN *in his arms. They dance. The three take each other and dance, speaking.*)

BROTHER MAN, BROKEN DOLL, DADDY BOY: Make room. Somewhere. In. The soft space. Between your thighs. Where honey drips. Walls. Sugar-frosted. Can I just lie there? No vacancies. Can I die there? Walking on water. No fear. No fear of drowning. Make room for me. Someplace. In the riff. Your canter call. Jazzing its way. Above the room. Can I ride? Swing low. Let me ride. Snake Dance. Smoke swirls. Tearing. Breath. Can't thick skin of ghetto children. Vacant halls. Make room for me there. Where? The ditch wedged into your thinking. I want. I. I grew up. I grew down. I grew up with ashy knees. I grew up and the world grew down. Me. Vanished. You. So did I. Die. Grow. Down.

BLUES SINGER:
If I should die
and my soul be lost
Nobody's fault but mine.

Chapter 4/Verse 7

(BROKEN DOLL *weaves herself out of the trilogy and brings her mutilated dolls to the block.*)

BROKEN DOLL: When I wuz a child, I painted purple finger pictures of myself against a forever orange sky, wid God's great big eyes smilin' at me through a magenta sun. But den somebody took my picture, throwed it away and sed—

ARSULA: Child! Stop all that paintin'!

BROKEN DOLL: When I wuz a child, I useta make up songs. Rhythm in my head, music in my feet and I danced to songs about me. But den somebody covered my mouth and sed—

ARSULA: Child! Stop all that singin' and dancin'!

BROKEN DOLL: When I wuz a child, my best friend wuz imagination, and we useta play for centuries in utha worlds, wif our dreams and our hopes all day long, but den somebody sed (ARSULA *and* BROKEN DOLL *together*) "Come inside, and leave imagination alone. . . ." When I wuz a child, I did as a child. But when I became grown, I put away all of my childish things. Took all the colors and the music I'd made within myself and hid them under the bed of my new self-concept. Took all of the dreams and locked them in a shelf so high above my head, I couldn't reach them anymore. . . . Put away all of my childish things. . . .

(THE DANCE: *The Community is silent.* DADDY BOY *wails.* BROTHER MAN *cries.* BROKEN DOLL *weeps.* FALLEN DIVA *screams.* ARSULA *howls. The* VOICES *join them. All are on the block, rising, falling, huddled, wailing.* FALLEN DIVA *does not leave her space. She tries to mimic the screams but cannot find it. The* PROPHET *sprinkles water around the huddled mass, chants feverishly, attempts to heal. The* DIVA *interrupts the anointing with a final scream above all of the* VOICES. *There is silence.*)

FALLEN DIVA: And our sorrows will be no more. . . . and our sorrows will be no more . . . Prophet? Poet! Where is the testimony of the priest? (*He does not respond.*)

ARSULA: You're not to speak to him.

BROKEN DOLL: You're not to speak to him directly.

ALL: You're not supposed to. The law. We were told. It's in the book. The book says. You don't ask—Never—

ARSULA: He's praying for us all. Soon he will have a word.

ALL: Yes. A word.

FALLEN DIVA: A word? A word? (*Laughing*) Here's a word. "There will be a day when the watchman on the mount will say arise! Arise!

ARSULA: Blaspheme.

FALLEN DIVA: Let us go up to the high place of our . . . God. Is this the place of our God? Ask! Ask him. Maybe the gods are hard of hearing! Ask the poet if the gods are deaf!

DADDY BOY: The law!

FALLEN DIVA: The what? (*To the* PROPHET) Save your people! Fat with vain prayer and hollow remembrance. Save the remnant. The rejected. The refuse. The refused. This last migration in the wilderness beneath a makeshift tent of holiness. Me . . . it's better we had all died than live in this . . . place . . . this way. . . . (*Standing at the podium*) "And the souls of priests, satisfied with goodness, will be made fat!" Are the gods too fat to come down and join us?

PROPHET POET: It's not the law.

ARSULA: Blaspheme.

FALLEN DIVA: *(Preaching from the podium, disrupting the altar)* We were wet and wounded, with only the vain traditions the elders taught us ... inherited ignorance.

BROTHER MAN: We were wounded.

BROKEN DOLL: ... And the children.

FALLEN DIVA: The children suffered! In need of meat we fed them grain ... and though the skill of our mothers taught us to make bread and call it meat, was it?

BROTHER MAN: In need of substance ...

FALLEN DIVA: In need of substance we gave them air, breathed by a people continuing a shallow existence!

ARSULA: Kneeling. Praying, singing all the while.

BLUES SINGER: Our voices sore.

DADDY BOY: A simple song. A simple theory.

FALLEN DIVA: Still, each morning—

ARSULA: No mercy.

FALLEN DIVA: Each noonday.

BROTHER MAN: No sun ... each evening.

BROKEN DOLL: No cool to calm the village fear.

ARSULA: The trees grew tall, though bare. Rivers deep, though empty.

BROTHER MAN: In secret places of wood and stone, we asked for strength and youth.

FALLEN DIVA: In exchange for truth! But we ate grain and called it meat because prophets, priests, and kings called it first "Propheting" from all we should *not* know! Bring it! Bring it! Tell the what and why! Where is the testimony of the elder? Bring it!

(All lights fade except the light on the block. The people angrily command the PROPHET *to testify. He twirls. He sings this poem like a lullaby).*

PROPHET POET: First he was a boy ... and then he was a man ... and ... mispronounced profanities of little football-head boys knocked him down and scarred him for life, because he played with little Barbie Dolls; girls ... combed their hair and played in a gentle world of painlessness ... he allowed them to baptize him with faggot and sissy and names of ridicule ... branding him with words of mockery, and he kept them as his own ... hid them secretly between his first and his last name ... between his pride and his ... shame ... Marilyn Monroe spoke to him from the pages of old magazines and the frames of old films, she said: "Laugh at yourself boy! Before the world laughs at you!" And so he slipped his feet into his mother's heels . . . stared at the distortion of his face in her vanity mirror . . . lips painted *Crimson Rose No. 32* . . . and he prayed to be blond and beautiful and glorified when he opened his eyes . . . prayed to laugh at his own reflection . . . every now and then someone would notice the rhythm . . . the rhythm . . . in his voice and the dance in his . . . walk . . . and call him by his middle name . . . shame . . . so he lay his head before the world and said: "CRUCIFY ME! It's all right. It's . . ." He closes his eyes . . . and he can remember the first time . . . someone ever . . . touched him. . . . It was a man of thirty-four he was just a boy of . . . four . . . he remembers the little red dress the man made him wear, it was a little red velvet dress that came from his sister's doll and socialized him into self-hatred. He remembers . . . spinning and twirling . . . and twirling and spinning . . . hands on him . . . handling him . . . and even though he promised not to tell . . . oh yes . . . he promised not to tell . . . oh my I . . . promise . . . still, every time he feels shame . . . every time he's called a name . . . he's just twirling in that little red velvet dress . . . just twirling and twirling . . . first he was a boy and then I was a man . . . no . . . first he was I was a man and then he was . . . he was a man and I was a boy. First I . . . mispronounced . . . hands on me handling me . . . thirty-four . . . four . . . four . . . Marilyn . . . blond and beautiful and glorified . . . spinning and twirling and twirling and spinning . . . and I twirl . . . and I twirl . . . and I . . .

(Beat.)

FALLEN DIVA: Our grief is but a moment . . .

(Clearing her throat and performing for the people.)

Requiem for a poet . . .
His words flew over and plunged under,
wind of words/storm of ideas—
whistling freely thru the heads
a nodding,
thru the minds
a pondering,
the meaning of the "the"
and hermeneutical patterns,
quilts of thinking
in abstract structure—
hammering down
the frame of some tradition,
dug into the soul with the simple tool
of crumpled verse and handwritten lyric
The next relevant idea!
Flung into the sky, where words and air
have each other,

hypothesis and prose come pouring down
  come pouring down

"One more please."
Minds of tender soil
moist,
dried, hard, cemented in the sun—
in the harsh light of information,
blinded inquisitive natures . . .

There were those waiting to be born!
To be creative, to be inconsiderate of time!
To force themselves and make themselves and show themselves—
there were those waiting, also, to cut themselves
and bleed
before the heads a nodding
waiting to die young too soon

. . . In the middle of a sonnet
on the last line of his haiku
for the Mother Earth and the Father Warrior Elders

words were cut off and pushed

beyond existence . . .

Did you write this one from the room of your dreams?

Make room for the next Prophet please!
Make room for the next Poet . . .

ARSULA: *(Climbing on top of the altar with her drink)*
Rhythm and Blues
and measure—
Glory hallelujah, anyhow!
Praise God, Praise God

From my seat
I see so much
so much more
than before . . .
This sweet hour of prayer
of thee O Lord I sing
yeah . . . yeah . . .
yeah . . . yeah . . .

BROTHER MAN: *(Climbing on top of the altar)*
Hey Jesus!
Down on my knees

I prayed
Help me please!

BROKEN DOLL: *(Climbing under the altar)*
I cried with blood
and sweat
from a river—

FALLEN DIVA: *(Destroying the altar)* Of sadness . . .

ARSULA:
Oooh
flood my soul.

BROTHER MAN:
My tongues were dry
from asking why
this burden fell on me.

FALLEN DIVA: And my eyes . . .

BROTHER MAN:
sought light
in the dark

DADDY BOY: *(Anointing himself with oil)*
Though while I
bent down—

ARSULA: In humble submission!

BROTHER MAN:
The anointed one
fucked me!

DADDY BOY: HEY JESUS!

BROTHER MAN:
I stretched out
without one doubt
that you were God!

ARSULA: Power in your name.

FALLEN DIVA: Just the same . . .

BROTHER MAN:
There's a hush over Jerusalem,
and there's no one who can tell
me why.

The Orishas are fire
on our tongues
but named as other gods
of other souls . . .

ARSULA: *(Singing)* One! One! One way to God . . . yeah . . . yeah . . .

BROKEN DOLL: Hey Jesus!

BROTHER MAN:
Who's gonna follow my
commandments
in these hazy times?
Drink our bread
and eat our wine?

Hey Jesus!

ARSULA:
Thou shalt serve thy people
all the day long.

FALLEN DIVA:
Thou shall not be
a false god!

BROKEN DOLL: Nor a multitude of gods!

FALLEN DIVA:
Or tolerate the
blindness of
preachers
and poets!

DADDY BOY:
Thou shall supply
the needs of thy people.

ARSULA: And supply the tithe . . .

FALLEN DIVA: And supply the air!

ARSULA: And supply the air!

BROKEN DOLL: The air.

BROTHER MAN: . . . The air, suffocates. The air.

ALL: Hey Jesus! . . . The air . . . yes . . . the air . . . the air . . . the air suffocates.

ARSULA: *(There is no response from God.* ARSULA *breaks down in laughter on the block, her dress up all around her head. Holy communion spilled all over her body)* Remember the dances? . . . The ghost dances? . . . David did it . . . Miriam waited till she'd crossed over . . . Mama Lily died o-gangrene, dancin' . . . melon rine wine time Chinese takeout tonite:

> *Nat King Cole songs of old*
> *Bessie Billie Aretha Blues King Pleasure Chimes*
> *Smokin Dancin Drinkin on the Roof Times*
> *Better than hotter than sex over an open flame.*

> *Arsula can't hear the phone*
> *Arsula moves her hips in circles*
> *Arsula spews prophetic vodka spittle.*

ALL: Dance!

ARSULA:

> *On rusty nails of bitter present days*
> *Under pealing cracked sky, I whine—*
> *"No heat in the winter*
> *no air-conditioner*
> *keep the damn window open!*
> *While I*

ALL: Dance!

ARSULA:

> *To the salsa the Ricans blast outside*
> *Lindy tonight, without Jimmy's arms around your waist*
> *Without him sipping the sweet sweat from*
> *'Tween your spongecake thighs*
> *Without staring into the square bronze face*
> *he used to have.*
> *Call you husband DAMNED! Now*
> *staring out the window, glued to the stool*
> *Bald and gray*
> *Limp dick old foot! Son of Perdition!*
> *Can't even hear the music!*

ALL: Dance!

ARSULA: Nuthin' old about you this evenin'!
> *Not the arthritic hand, or the swollen gland,*
> *not the missing teeth, or the thin hair*
> *swept behind your ears.*
> *Nuthin' stale about your tropical couhlotts*
> *or your tanktop rising above your navel.*

Don't play no "Stormy Weather" for me on a clear day!
Don't wanna hear Lena sing it no way!
Lemme hear Ethel Waters—the only member of
the wedding I'm invitin' tonight! The last Negro Mama to sing a hymn in somebody's
kitchen with fire and spit! All alone, in somebody's kitchen, callin' on the sparrow-sweat
soaked armpits and flowered hat—the last to leave the party—lemme hear Ethel
tonight, goddamn!

ALL: Dance

ARSULA:

Jimmy Ray thought he was Sugar Ray one night in the '50s
cracked his fist across your eye,
took off his belt and whipped your thighs,
cause the music was too loud three o'clock in the morning.
Minnie Gentries nursed the swell, and the pain you wouldn't show,
said, "Sula, cray, Sula why won't you cry?" I say let me die, Minnie, my head between
your knees like Dian Sands, a hymn for the Lord combing through my hair—let me die
like that! In the kitchen of Ethel Waters, on the couch of Claudia McNeil—oh yes! And
please, Lord God almighty! Somebody ask Jimmy Garrison to play the bass for me—go
get Eric Dolphy and Elvin Jones to play "Alabama"—cause I'm gonna die dancin' be-
tween Minnie Gentrie's knees in a bombed church readin' the scripture out loud—oh yes!
It's a party! He cracked his fists cross my eye, took off his belt cause the music was too
loud—tell Coltrane to turn it up! Ethel, sing louder, if you please!

ALL: Dance!

ARSULA:

Claudia McNeil say—Girl, I can rock you and sing you to rest,
I can let you suck the life from my tit,
and feed you my soul, what's left of it,
OOOH! MILES DAVIS! Tell death to kiss my ass!

ALL: Dance!

ARSULA: C'mere, girl, lemme show you—show you how—

ALL: Dance!

ARSULA:

Now move it all the way out,
let your body scream and shout . . . for you!
Let Ms. Arsula show you how . . .
not to show the pain
not to see the age,
not to live the lie
or hear the truth
not to feel the heat of hell,

or the hope of heaven.
Give it your all, girl, and—

ALL: Dance!

ARSULA:

Now move it all the way out,
let your body scream and shout . . . for you!
Let Ms. Arsula show you how . . .
not to show the pain
not to see the age,
not to live the lie
or hear the truth
not to feel the heat of hell,
or the hope of heaven.
Give it your all, give it your all and
Dance
Sula, why? Sula, why won't you cry?
What the hell do you think I'm doin'?

FALLEN DIVA: *(Pulling a lipstick from her bosom)* A final monologue . . . dedicated to
the ladies? To the women . . . shall I perform . . . an elegy? . . . a dirge? . . . requests? . . . All are reverent . . . *(She pours herself a drink with Arsula's wine and
makes a toast)* To all the sister's who know the glamour of a good demise! Who know
the passion of tragedy, the beauty of a slow fade to black . . . come, let us sing our
final song, a gospel/blues of Mama's tattered evening prayer, and ashen knees,
nappy tresses and mended dresses beneath our father's fists screaming: "PLEASE!"
Mmmmmm. . . . The scent of Clorox and poverty in the cold-water flat where she
bled to death. . . . Let's perfume ourselves in the blood, sweat, and tears of naked
women in middle passage slitting the throats of their newborn. . . . Place fruits and
flowers in your hair, the juice of fresh berries on your lips, the salt of tears behind
your ears and the round of your hips, and dance . . . to the rhapsody of the man
who was our father, who was our brother, who was our lover . . . pinching our nipples in the cool dark as we became petrified forests of wood and stone, lying there,
wanting to cry, as he traveled through our thighs and made himself at home . . .
sipped our nectar wine . . . sucked the last drop of sugar from the cane . . . to him
who came uninvited as we screamed and streamed all that was left inside us down
an unknown river . . . don't call this home! Don't call this home!

(The Community applauds.)

FALLEN DIVA: Oh . . . the ovation stands. The hungry hands of people yell for
more . . . for more . . . more more! As we fall thin and frail and dry, with nothing
left inside but a voice calling from a hollow space begging to be free . . . and still,
they ask for more! For more! For more! We shrill our voices, scratch our throats, riff
and drain the monologue . . . sing the aria of the butterfly, and die . . . and die . . .
and die. . . . In chiffon, beads and bracelets . . . hair wild as the wind, where rhine-

stone pins weep and mourn for a Fallen Diva. . . . Hear them applaud? Oh . . . they'll carry our bodies to the high place and embalm us in tragic tears . . . immortalized forever! . . . The people . . . they'll place gardenias at our feet, burn incense at our shrines, and recall the ravenous beauty of our demise. . . . For now we call this life . . . but don't call this home . . . don't call this home.

(Lights fade on the wilted FALLEN DIVA, *who has draped herself across the block. The* BLUES SINGER'*s humming is heard above the dirge of* THE VOICES *In The Wilderness. She sings and speaks to the* DIVA.*)*

BLUES SINGER: I know what you feel when you look into her eyes and you see yourself. Keep looking and you'll see yourself strong and respected. Look closer and you'll see the women triumph in her pores, the regality of their souls in her melanin. Touch her mouth with yours, and open yourselves up to information. I know what you feel, sister, when you dare to touch her hand in the jungle of social phobias, and you dare to harden your gate in the neighborhood of gender prejudice. Just keep the dance in your stride, and laugh at their disjointed rhythms. Return their stares with your steady eye, and see past their fragile facades to the land of their self-hatred! Go on girl, walk that walk! Go on girl, talk that talk! And love her, woman to woman to woman. Undertstand that you understand better than any man how to understand her, because you know that vulnerable place, there's no self-indulgence in your touch. I know what you mean when you say you love being you, in all of your glory, and question their need to see you trade your grace for the awkward machismo of ignorant man. Why spell woman any other way? Why deepen the high sing-song voice that sang sweet mellow lyrics of someone else's strength, any one else's power, but your own. Go on girl, sing that song of yourself . . . I understand it . . . and I know what you mean.

(Upbeat blues rhythm. DIVA *is resurrected. The community is engaged.)*

BLUES SINGER:
Last night I thought about yesterday
then I cried all day today
Last night I thought about yesterday
then cried all day today
But if you catch me tonight
I won't be the same old way.

This morning I bathed in oils
Perfumed my bed this afternoon
This morning I bathed in oils
Perfumed my bed this afternoon
This morning I bathed in oils
Perfumed my bed this afternoon
Kissed the sun good-bye!
And welcomed in the moon.

I'll be ready 'bout the twelfth hour
Ring my bell 'bout quarter past
I'll be ready about the twelfth hour
you can ring my bell 'bout quarter past
'Cause I don't wanna rush this thing
sweet baby
Gonna make the good times last!

They say my song is called the blues
I really don't see how, when I'm singin' 'bout you!
Looks red to me, darlin'
right now my song looks real red.
I don't see no other colors in my head.

They say my song
is called the blues
If they only knew
I see yellows—
yellows like the honey bee.
I don't see no other colors
when I'm makin' love to me.
They call my song,
call it the blues—
That was the old song,
this is the new!
I feel orange, honey!
Like the purple-orange dusk sky!
They wanna call my song the blues
I sho' don't know why!

Finai Chapter: The Anointing

(The song ends in laughter. Lights fade. Blue light comes up on the block. The music and the light washes over the Community. ARSULA *heads toward the light, the Community follows. The* VOICES *blow a hollow wooden horn instrument.)*

ÐADDY BOY:
Do you hear it?
The righteous chant
of muted voices . . .
Choir of a blood song.
The sun died and the moon
passed on—
stone night stands still—

There's a
High
Hear me Lord
I'm comin' cry—
arms stretched wide
folding into themselves
like
crumpled paper pushed by the wind . . .
Do you see it?
Our days cook and simmer
on the flame,
Days gone by . . .
we sip the air and harmonize
a prayer
for those who remain . . .
Drag on in pride,
ride this merry-go-round
can't
hold us down—
I feel it,
in us like a Man,
around us,
the light
on us
like April's first sunshine.
Sister strides
across the sky
Glass slide
Goin'

Ha'nah
Ha'nah
Ha'nah

ain't far now . . .
Just an arm's reach away
across the distance
of yesterday's pain. . . .
See the march?
Arabesque to the city—
Sister strides
Brother glides
Daddy moves
Yo' Mama
grooves

Goin',
Ha'nah
Ha'nah
Ha'nah

(THE DANCE: *The Community moves in emanipated agreement. The* POET *tries to move with them, but is unable. He covers himself with the cloth from the altar and sifts through the holy objects, scattered.*)

PROPHET POET: Speaking to the prayer, to the poem, to the spirit in me, to be birthed, may canal, damned, I hear tell of angels come this way, angels that ride the heads of those who call themselves prophets, I hear tell, too, of hell hounds barking at the thing, I carry, ready to snatch it out, consume it, speaking to the dark I know, holding all the sacred secrets untold, no answers coming, spinning, spinning, and the thing keeps knocking at the walls, begging, but my legs are shut, tight, so tight, mouth closed, no words, no voices, closed . . .

FALLEN DIVA: No one way . . . no face to God . . . no Bitter song . . . no rescued soul . . . and still a dance and still a song. . . .

PROPHET POET: *(On his knees)* They that were not numbered . . . tribal. Come gathered from some captive coasts. All those form the place of the Carribe and the hills of the poplar and blood . . . with them blind and lame, come loud, come silent. Madonna and child, mourning together. They were not numbered so they pitched their tents . . . all those from industrial green housing and the place of excrement and the well of deep sorrow . . . a great remnant. They come weeping and wailing by rivers and waters. These are the names of the sons of Aaron and the sons of James and the daughters of naked women wandering . . . when they offered strange fire before the Lord . . . they shall keep his charge and they shall keep his instruments and they shall keep his commandment. All these . . . they come to bleed, then heal. To sing, then dance. A final time. In spirit. Speaking to the prayer, to the poem, to the spirit in me, to be birthed, my canal, damned, I hear tell of angels come this way, angels that ride the heads of those who call themselves prophets. I hear tell, too, of hell hounds barking at the thing, I carry, ready to snatch it out, consume it, speaking to the dark I know, holding all the sacred secrets untold, no answers coming, spinning, spinning, and the thing keeps knocking at the walls, begging, but my legs are shut, tight, mouth closed, no words, no voices, closed.

(*The Community invites a poet from the audience to read. When the poem is finished, they embrace each other, as well as the* POET PROPHET, *and chant, engaging each other in a ballet of hands.*)

ALL VOICES:
Heal Thyself Nation
Heal Thyself Nation
Heal Thyself Nation
The Power is in your hands.

(The Community is one body, dancing. When the chant is finished, everyone removes their shoes and covers their heads. They anoint themselves with three gestures, and THE VOICES *repeat these gestures. They all stand on the block together and a member of the Community must stand in the center of the group and dance furiously to vocal percussion, completely possessed, and offering high praises to the spirit. There is a blackout on the final exhilarated breath.)*

I Live In Music (A Work in Progress)

Ntozake Shange

COLLABORATING ARTISTS:

1–4 **Musicians**

1–6 **Dancers**

Poet

Choreographic Designer

Scene 1

(Music starts from the back of the house. The musicians have hand-held instruments, blending sound between them for a dynamic of space and air. The musicians cross along the back of the house while performing and end at opposite extremes from their starting positions. The musicians will chant and echo softly "I Live In Music" as they make their way through the audience onto the stage.

Musicians reach midway down the audience; poet enters and starts "I Live In Music".)

POET:
I live in music
is this where you live
I live in music
I live on C-sharp street
my friend lives on B-flat avenue

(Dancers enter. A blending of echoes, answers, and song underscoring the poem. Climax is reached as community is formed center stage.)

POET:
Do you live here in music?
Sound
falls round me like rain on other folks
saxophones wet my face
cold as winter in st. louis
I live in music
hot like peppers I rub on my lips
thinkin' they waz lilies
I got fifteen trumpets where other women got hips
& an upright bass for both sides of my heart
I walk round in a piano like somebody
else/be walkin' on the earth
I live in music

live in it
   wash in it
I could even smell it
wear sound on my fingers
sound falls so fulla music
ya cd make a river where yr arm is &
hold yrself . . . hold yrself in a music

(Voices become one sound in unison as they de-crescendo into a fadeout. Bodies move to instruments. POET *and* DANCERS *move into lit spaces on the stage.)*

Scene 2:

(Music starts. DANCERS *enter moving in downstage circle spotlight only.* POET *enters and circles outside dancers' circle.)*

POET:
chicago in sanfransisco & you
me
wait
love is musik
touch me
like sounds
chicago on my shoulder
yr hand
is now a kiss

I get inspired in the middle of the nite
when you make love to me

after i've held you & kissed you & felt all that
I get inspired get cherished
free of pain
not knowin' anymore what is a dream
but is love like they are singin' to me odawalla
reeese & the smooth ones
here where you kissed me
& I feel you
I cd make it up again
but we're already musik
joseph roscoe lester don & malachi
I hear em in our sweat
& nobody is speakin'
but the rhythms are chicago
melody on the loose

when you make love to me
I shout like the colors on joseph's face
am bound to air like roscoe's horn
like the "cards" are stacked in our favor
one slight brown thing bip-bloo-dah-shi-doop-bleeeha-uh
refusin' false romance
        when it wasn't what ya wanted
        or who ya thot was comin'
        but it was real tenderness
        can't lie
I remember cards always gotta have a full deck
gotta have a woman
queen of spades
like malachi slipped in wit the grace of nefertiti or eubie blake
this ain't what we expected
but it waz colored
waz truth
waz gotta rhythm
like you feel to me.

I really wanted to be a waitress to serve em in a negress way
push my waist thru a black skirt & amble like an alto in bird's mouth
a secret
too sweet to hold tears
I wanted musik
& they brought love in a million tones
& I am not the same anymore
not anymore
you wanted a sigh
I made like a flute
I pull
I ease back & splee-bah-wah-she-do-the-do-tso
ring like a new reed cant stoppa cherokee
a jackson in yr house
congliptis
all round
the art ensemble cd make ya love more
cd make you love more
chocolaté or miz t. In all her silver
don't inspire me like I get inspired when you hold me in chicago harmonies
& we waltz like vagrants
get up
signal the release of pain
scream
sing

then sigh
groan
sound
make the sound that kisses me
one note
you
make me melody
is
is musik
uh true uh
yes
musik is the least love shd bring ya
most ya'll ever have
you
yes
musik
you
let love musik you
you kiss me like the sound
we
let love
is the musik
watch us dance
& let the musik
you take it all
get the musik
let the musik love you
close
like silence.

(*Everyone leaves asking "Where do they live?" And answering themselves with "I Live In Music.*)

Scene 3:

(ARTISTS *enter from opposite sides of the stage and walk in opposite directions, making a spiral toward center stage. Walk slowly.*)

VOICE 1:   The distance is not really so great.

VOICE 2:   But that's Brooklyn.

VOICE 1:   And . . .

VOICE 2:   You think he goes there on purpose?

VOICE 1:   He lives here, you say.

VOICE 2:   Right.

VOICE 2:   Well, I guess, that's the end of that.

VOICE 1:   Yet, you have no problem going to Montreal, Paris, and you feel Brooklyn is too far away.

VOICE 2:   It's not there.

VOICE 1:   Brooklyn is not there?

VOICE 2:   No, it's just the bridge.

VOICE 1:   What bridge?

VOICE 2:   Well, how many do you know about?

VOICE 1:   The Bay Bridge, the Chesapeake Bay Bridge, the Verrazano-Narrows Bridge, le Pont-Royal . . .

VOICE 2:   So now we're . . . *(Voice 1 and 2 sing together)* "sur le pont d'Avignon".

VOICE 1:   If you gonna sing it like that won't nobody find it. Avignon'll disappear from history you sing like that.

VOICE 2:   How does it go?

VOICE 1:   What?

VOICE 2:   The bridge?

VOICE 1:   The bridge? Went somewhere with Art Blakey. You can't hear it

VOICE 2:   Not the way you do.

VOICE 1:   That's funny. Nobody hears anything like anybody else does, but we manage to talk and sing. We were singing, we were, weren't we? In the fall daddy came in one evening when the sky looked most on fire. It was World Series time. The garden lost all the sunlight every afternoon when swarms of birds black as, black as the Magi rolled up, kept the whole house in a . . . in an embrace, like we didn't belong in the rest of the world at all. And it was quiet. Mama was somewhere singing something nobody could hear. I sat by the window waiting for the shadows of the birds to float over me and the dead leaves, when this lush, wonderful warmth lifted me outta myself into the garden. I thought the sun had pushed the birds out the way, but it was daddy playin' Art Blakey and the Jazz Messengers. I thought it was illicit.

VOICE 1:   Why did you think that?

VOICE 2:   Oh my. Because, as Felipe says, "Jazz is a woman's tongue stuck, dead in your mouth."

VOICE 1:   Yes, that's what he thinks. What did you think?

VOICE 2:   Well, we awready established that you can't hear it.

VOICE 1:   What?

VOICE 2:   The bridge?

VOICE 1:   No.

VOICE 1:   But it was warm and lush.

VOICE 2:   Yes, yes it was.

VOICE 1:   You wanna know something funny? I had this dream. I was at a truly elegant party. Parquet floors, crystal octagonal chandeliers, and singing champagne glasses. Everything wonderful to taste. All the men in the world I ever dream about holding me—they were all there. I was having a wonderful time, sort of like Scarlett O'Hara at that first party at Seven Oaks. Well, I felt unbearably gorgeous, when suddenly I realized that my clit was glowing. I mean, like silver neon lights in Las Vegas, my pussy was beaming artificial light all over this very delicate and elegant fête. No matter how I held myself, what contortions I forced my body into, this glow was irrepressible. People started to stare at me. I was so embarrassed. Then, just as I was about to cry, he came in, took possession of the space, addressed the whole damn lot of them and said: "Oh, her clit's going to get brighter than that. We've been working on it."

VOICE 1:   God, that's funny.

VOICE 2:   Well, that accounts for your shoelaces.

VOICE 1:   What'd you mean?

VOICE 2:   They're silver lamé, no?

VOICE 1:   Well, yes, but I bought these the day after . . . oh, I get it, I'm wearin' my clit on my shoes.

VOICE 2:   No, more like the glow. The unbearably gorgeous glow you're wearing and getting around fairly well, I might add.

VOICE 1:   Yes, right.

VOICE 1:   Did you ever hear that tune "Moanin'," by Bobby Timmons?

VOICE 2:   I think I can vaguely recall something like that.

VOICE 1:   I finally met him when he was playing in the cocktail lounge part of this jazz joint. What the fuck was he doin' there? I mean, Jesus, he was frail and so modest. I kept hearing him playin' and looking at him. It doesn't match.

VOICE 1:   The music and the man.

VOICE 2:   Not at all like your clit and your shoes.

VOICE 1:   I'm not kiddin'. It disturbed me. I kept hearin' those chords in the fall, when the birds go south, and daddy comes home, and, then, this great, oooh, this great rush of sound takes over. It was Art Blakey.

VOICE 2:   You said it was illicit?

VOICE 1:   It was dark. It was quiet.

VOICE 1:   You should talk. You live with your goddamned mother.

VOICE 2:   How do you know I live with my mother?

VOICE 1:   You called me from her house last night in my dream. You said it wasn't safe to do our work today. Communication lines were down. All the bridges were out.

(End facing each other center stage. Lights fade to black.)

Scene 4:

*(*POET *moves out in space dancing Latin dances in silence.* POET *starts to speak. The rhythm of the words bring the* MUSICIANS *in.* DANCERS *join* POET. POET *fades out, settles and continues as if story-telling in front of a party.)*

> **POET:**
> *if hector lavoe is not jackie wilson*
> *who sings you to sleep at night?*
> *in whose arms did you sleep well or not?*
> *cuz i've raced thru streets and dreams kept*
> *undercover*
> *by interpol*
> *and the state police*
> *folks swear never existed. why i've been held in a*
> *coro as far as the archipelago and toda la gente conocí*
> *el señor hector lavoe*
> *mira*
> *tu puede ir conmigo*
> *hasta managua &*
> *the earthquake was no more a surprise*
> *than you*
> *con su voz*
> *que viene de los dioses*
> *and the swivel of the hips de su flaca*
> *as you dance or*
> *when she sucks the hearts*
> *out of the eggs of*
> *tortugas*
> *anglos die to see float*
> *while all the time we dance around them split up*
> *change partners*
> *and fall madly in love*
> *all this time compañero*
> *when they come for you*

becuz an inhospitable world
es incomprensible
don't you know
that jackie wilson took up the flack that su flaca couldn't handle
escúchame
criollo
hay personas en detroit
on your side & they don't care
how the syllables fall
or the linguistic nitch
they create for market identifications
what we are dealin with here is an inexcusable disruption of a way of life
thousands upon thousands
whose every move
is determined by the sound of your voice,
does it matter
you seek out women other men wish they'd had the nerve to want for their own? does it
  matter you don't always show up
or you attend and your
voice could not make it? no, negro, no en mi vida
porque
nobody put a tec-nine to your head
tied you up like philip wilson
or prostrated themselves
como machito
si nada es real
nuestra vida es permanente
si ellos vienen con todos los armas, n'importa porque nosotros somos an army of
  marathon dancers
lovers
seekers
and collectors
we have never met an enemy we can't outlive
querido, I can assure you myself
that nobody's gonna take you away,
mangle
deform
the sound of you
in our lives no guns
no napalm
no dirges
no marshal law
and U.N. condoned invasions
of our actualities can take you from me

oh sparrow oh ismäel,
oh the closest I ever got to beñe moré in my lifetime,
do you really believe
that I would let you cease to be
carnal
I asked jackie wilson
and he said "we can't do without him
he's just like me."

(After speaking, POET *joins the group. As music fades, performers make shapes for group picture as last note ends.)*

Scene 5:

(Music starts—blues. Frozen DANCERS *start to move off as they watch transformation of the* POET *into "Crack Annie." Annie is complete as she steps onto box or table, lights close in on her. She leaves her inner focus and addresses the audience. Music softly underscores and fades out as Annie leaves the stage.)*

POET:
I caint say how it come to me
shit somehow
it just come over me
& I heard the Lord sayin' how beautiful
& pure waz this child of mine
& when I looked at her I knew the Lord waz right
& she waz innocent
ya know
free of sin
& that's how come I gave her up to cadillac lee
well
how else can I explain it?

who do ya love I wanna know I wanna know
who do ya love I wanna know I wanna know

what mo could I say?

who do ya love I wanna know I wanna know
who do ya love I wanna know I wanna know

it's not like she had hair round her pussy or nothin'
she ain't old enough anyway for that
& we sho know
she ain't on the rag or nothin'
but a real good friend of mine from round twenty-eighth street
he told me point-blank

ain't nothin in the whole world smell
like virgin pussy
& wazn't nothin' in the universe
taste like new pussy
now this is my friend talkin'
& ya know how hard it is to keep a good man fo yo self these days
even though I know I got somethin sweet & hot to offer
even then
I wanted to give my man cadillac lee
somethin I just don't have no mo
new pussy
I mean it ain't dried up or nothin'
& I still know what muscles I got to work in my pussy
this a-way
that but what I really wanted
my man
cadillac to have for his self
waz some new pussy
& berneatha waz so pretty & sweet smellin'
even after she be out there runnin' with the boys
my berneatha vida
waz sweet & fine remember that song "So Fine."

so fine my baby's so doggone fine
sends them thrills up & down my spine
whoah-oh-oh-yeah-yeaeaeah-so-fine.

well
that's my child
fine
& well cadillac always come thru for me
ya know wit my crack
oh honey
lemme tell you how close to jesus I could get thanks to my cadillac
lemme say now
witout that man i'd been gone onto
worms & my grave
but see I had me some new pussy
waz my daughter
lemme take that back
I didn't have none
any new pussy
so I took me some
& it just happened to be berneatha
my daughter
& he swore he'd give me twenty-five dollars & a whole fifty cent of crack

whenever
I wanted
but you know
i'm on the pipe
&
I don't have no new pussy
& what difference
could it make
I mean shit
she caint get pregnant
shit
she only seven years old & these scratches
heah
by my fingers that's
where my child held onto me
when the bastard
cadillac
took her like she wazn't even new pussy at all
she kept lookin at me & screamin'
"mommy,
mommy help me
help me"
& all I did waz hold her tighter
like if I could stop her blood from circulation
if I could stop her from hurtin'
but no
that ain't how it went down at all
nothin' like that
trust me
I got scars where my daughter's fingernails broke my skin & then
when he waz finished with my child
cadillac
he jump up & tell me to cover my child's pussy
with some cocaine
so she wdn't feel nothin
no mo
I say
why ya aint done that befo?
why ya wait till ya done
to protect her
he say
befo I lay you down & give ya some of the same
dontcha know
ya haveta hear em scream befo ya give em any candy
& my lil' girl heard all this

my child bled alla this
& all I could do waz to look for some more crack with the fifty cadillac done give me
but
I wazn't lookin for it for me
jesus knows
I wanted it for berneatha
so she wouldn't haveta remember
she wouldn't have to remember
nothin' at all
but I saw dark purple colored marks by her shoulder
where I held her down for cadillac
i'm her mother & I held her & if ya kill me
i'll always know
i'm gonna roam round hell talkin' 'bout new pussy
& see my child's blood caked bout her thighs
my child's shoulders purple wit her mother's love
jesus save me
come get me jesus
now
lord take my soul & do with it what ya will
lord have mercy
I thought bearneatha waz like me
that she could take anythin'
ya know
caint nothin' kill the will of the colored folks
but lord I waz wrong
them marks on my child
no
not the marks
from cadillac
the scars from my fingers
purple & blue blotches
midnight all ruby on lenox avenue at 7:30 on sundays
that heavy quiet
that cruelty
I caint take no mo
so lord throw me into hell befo berneatha is so growed
she do it herself
all by herself
laughin & shovin' me
& prowlin' & teasin'
sayin'
you a mother
what kinda mother are you
bitch

> tell me
> now
> mommy what kinda mother
> are you
> mommy
> mommy
>
> I say
> I heard etta james in her eyes
> I know
> I heard the blues in her eyes
> an unknown
> virulent blues
> a stalkin' takin' no answer but yes to me blues
> a song of etta james
> a cantankerous blues
> a blues born of wantin' & longin'
> wantin' & longin' for you
> mama
> or etta mae
> song of a ol hand-me-down blues hangin' by its breath
> alone a fragile new blues hardly close to nowhere
> cept them eyes & I say
> I heard a heap of etta james in them eyes
> all over them eyes
> so come on Annie
>
> so tell mama all about it
>
> tell mama all about it
> all about it
> all about it
>
> tell mama.

Scene 6:

(Walk out and tell the audience a story with musical accents.)

POET: And like Pete "El Conde" Rodríguez, smelling like warm cognac, pure and sweet sweat *que toca* the sidewalk like Pacheco, I saw her, *la gringa negra* and her body was singing to me. No, really. Listen, listen to her stroll Avenue C. "*Canta, canta, canta mi canción, querida. Canta, canta, mi querida, canta mi canción.*" I admit there's every possibility that Liliane, I always call her "*mi luchadora,*" she had no image of me before I took her, captured her, however you want to say it in English. I'm in charge of *visiones del sur,* south of Sixth Street and anything between First Avenue and the East River *está mi corazón, está mi tierra.* I'll fight for it and I'll love it, *mira.* I make it black and white, two-dimensional, *con claridad* once I get *una cosa* that no one else seems to be able to see; once I get la cosita in a photograph: There's no gettin' away. So I mambo with long legs. Challenge telephone poles, carnal. That's chicano talk. I'm telling you I whipped around *la gringa negra* like all of El Gran Combo on New Year's Eve. She startled, stepped back and ba-tum, I took her picture.

I smiled, relaxed, moved out of her way, but she was mine. *Tu m'en tiende, yo tengo su cara* and when she walks her limbs cry out like a *mulatta* who never tasted fresh coconut milk, at least not from Puerto Rico.

But that's a lie, just like the camera lies. When I catch what nobody wants anybody to know just wafting across their cheeks, trickling out the side of their eyes, a shallowness or a hurt allegedly disguised. I lied about meeting Liliane, myself, the pace of it. I wished I coulda been alla that for her, *mi luchadora negra,* but like Felipe said years ago: "I'm nothin' but a Spanish-speaking colored kid." So what would Liliane want with me? I asked her once, but her English was not only syncopated, it was multisyllabic, but I ain't really no different than her in the gut. I could see things, even invisible things. Anyway, one time I said to her black ass: "*Negra,* what do you want with me?" And she said something about a "man" and language. That was a bit much, you know. Just bopping over my head. So I 'plained: "Listen, *querida, cojones* is the problem on the Lower East Side, the Loaisida.

First, take a look down any of those mean streets, baby, and you can line up the "able-bodied:" able to shoot smack, able to fuck kids, able to make a home outta a tumblin' down assortment of rooms with no heat, no runnin' water, and a broken-down toilet. Look down the street, man, and see the fierce some beauty of the young girls' bows, their mother's fingernails, and immaculate kitchens. Watch the lost Ricans find themselves homes, building after building, brick by brick, learning plumbin' and electricity like that, see the junkies rip it out later on tonight like tearing their grandma's, *su abuela's,* heart right out. Raunchy *corazón,* is what I call it. The hip boys wishing for more evidence of their masculinity lie up by our window blarin' the latest *merengue* from Santo Domingo. Askin' em to quiet down is takin' yourself for an Anglo, some fool imaginin' he could put a halt to *la fuerza* of our presence. Can you get to that? Cause you can't play radios on the trains, white folks believe we done lost our music. Ain't that a gas? Like what they can't hear just don't exist, man. But at night the Caribbean oozes out of the streets, *negra,* like how I'm gonna do you, right? Tell me, I'm lyin', *querida,* can you tell me I'm lying, Liliane. C'mon.

We laughed and fucked some more. We don't seem to have no bilingual or multicultural dilemma gettin' to some primeval state of being. Actually, I always thought it was funny that this little bitch talkin' all the time using English vocabulary, this sassy-assed gal could hardly say hello in Spanish, but could talk her way all over Fort-de-France, she didn't do nothin' but scream when we did what it was we did. Now, this is East Sixth Street and ain't a lot gone down anywhere that ain't gone down here but I always gave my baby, *mi luchadora,* a pillow she could bite on. Then I'd turn up Willie Colon's anything real loud. She like Colon. Knew all the brass choruses, every trombone solo by heart. Between him and his mouthpiece and her body and my tongue, she was speakin' all kinds of languages. Sometimes, she'd admit that she saw the same things I saw in the faces of our people, but that took time and careful questioning to get her to say yes she saw what I saw, how I saw it and when I saw it. She'd swear to me that our visions were the same. But she was so hardheaded, I couldn't possibly take her word for it the first time she figured out how to say something to me that might make me stop. I mean to leave her talking whatever tongue those groans that creep from her thighs to her mouth might be speaking. Now I'm a nice fella but I had to get her to where she spoke my language; I had to get her to where she knew wasn't nobody could understand her but me. Nobody could insist that particular tongue but me. Ever. Not a soul.

Liliane insisted, as she had to; she was an intellectual. The girl truly believed certain thoughts, even certain gestures, were impossible in certain languages. She was driven by some power I never understood, to learn every language, slave language, any black person in the Western Hemisphere ever spoke. She felt incomplete in English, a little better in Spanish, totally joyous in French, and pious in Portuguese. When she discovered Gullah and papiamento, she was beside herself. I kept tellin' her wasn't no protection from folks hatin' the way we looked in any slave owner's language, but she had to believe there was a way to talk herself outta five hundred years of disdain, five hundred years of dying cause there is no word in any one of those damn languages where we are simply alive and not enveloped by scorn, contempt, or pity. There's no word for us. I kept tellin' her. No words, but what we say to each other that nobody can interpret.

And when she'd get quiet and her legs sorta swayed by my shoulders like palm leaves, then, I'd start to sing to her thighs again, her navel, the sides of her pussy would glow, be soakin'. She'd speak my language to me again. I'd give her back the pillow and turn Cortigo up high. She'd make like she didn't understand a lot of what I'd say to her, but if she got on my nerves, I'd put on Ismael Quintano. *Mua.* She'd either start taking off her clothes or talkin' to me like she knew I had some goddamn sense. I hadda great sense of her, but that's not enough to keep her. Not the way I used to have her, regular, wild, relentless and soft as a tropical surf. My Liliane, she said she can't keep giving in like that. That's how she put it, being taken to some other tongue. She called it giving in. I called it being mine. She said that was ontologically impossible. Of course, I threw her the pillow again.

But she's gone—

She-ee-ee's—go-oh-oh-oh-ne,
My baaa-be lef' me,
Be-lieeh-eh-eh-ve me,
She's gone, gone, gooooooohne.

Left me at her opening, I guess, *La Lucha Continua* applied to me as well as to South Africa. Anyways, there was this story I toldt her one night after she was sighin'—humming the way I could make her talk, that tongue, *mi lengua negra.* I toldt her this story I wanted to make a photographic novel, à la Duane Michaels, I wanted her for it. Now, I know I want more than that, but some ideas done bode well *con una mujer, come me comba tiente morena, mi dulce negrita, mi negra mohada.*

The apartment wasn't much, wasn't nothin' really. There was the proverbial tub in the kitchen and real live closet for a W.C. More overwhelming was the insecticide from the bodega downstairs. I kept tastin' plantains, yellow and green ones, cassava, yuca, all kindsa greens, apples, oranges, everything, tastin' like dead mice or barely crawlin' cucarachas. Everythin' for us to eat, poisoned long "fore smack was runnin'" through our veins, "fore grass smoke rings swirled through the stairway, way "fore coke had us all thinkin'" we was the genius of Velazquez, Picasso, Rivera by a multiple of Einsteins. Just the small *y el ritmo* held my photographs round my baby, kept her protected from the elements, left her in my hands for my eyes.

That's why I'd always tell Señor Medina to pick me an avocado that *mujer,* Liliane, would pick up. He ran the bodega with his wife who was simply the make-believe eyebrow woman to me. She plucked out all her eyebrows and assiduously drew her new daring black ones on her face like every hour and a half. Her name was Soledad, but I just called her *"ojos."* She liked that, bet that crotch even tingled thinkin' I was swayed by her looks. Anyway, I could just see Liliane, pissed as hell, askin' for this avocado that she knew I could a gotten myself, but I convinced her I didn't ask her for much, not like a real Latina, I mean. And I knew the Medinas wouldn't speak English to her cause it was beyond their version of the world that *mi negra linda* wasn't a *morena* at all, but a regular niggah. And I could see Liliane embarrassed when the gringo blacks listened to her speak Spanish and subtly disown her. I figured she needed that every once in a while. *Y,* if she's not gonna give me any babies, the least she could do is bring me an avocado, *sí?*

Gotta keep her on her toes, ya know, a bit off balance, outta focus. It's not like we lived in some sorta black-and-white frame. Well, that'd be pretty difficult considering the way Liliane looked at things. She saw the most pristine forms, dazzling color in anythin'. She felt the texture of stuff: rice, skin, water, the ringlets of black naps on my chest. I couldn't have forced her vision to be any less, but I tried 'til it was no more use. We didn't really go out 'cept round the neighborhood. How many social clubs with little red lights, a ghetto box, a pool table and Budweiser beer can you go to? How many Nuyorican poets can ya listen to shout about the righteousness of the FALN and a free Puerto Rico?

Once Liliane tried to get me to go to Casa de Nuestro Mundo for Borinquen extravaganza: poets and performance artists from the island and all us Nuyoricans. I told her I wasn't going cause I wasn't into being snubbed by white Latinas from Ponce or San Juan whose legitimacy was founded on how well they spoke Spanish and how uncolored they were. Like most descendants of slaves from any place, Liliane was committed to the notion that slavery some other where in some other tongue was less pernicious than what she knew. I read Guillién to her, Luis Palos Matos, Pedro Albiza Campos, José Luis González. I read to her in Spanish all about the scum, the vicious degradation of our people by Spaniards, *criollos,* and their precious mulattos. But like a child who's gotta have her hands held in the fire to know it burns, off she went. And the Spanish-speakin' white boys went crazy, when the

spanglesh-speakin', maybe only English-speakin', maybe not white enough mainland Ricans performed. She had to get out of the way of flying chairs and fists 'cause
the white boys, *los blancos,* felt their true heritage violated by the hybrid: by the colored hue of the language we created and our skins as telling and African as the *bata.*
One more illusion lost. I just asked her why she thought I callt her *mi negra.* Why
from me the word would never leave her: *negra, mi negra,* Liliane. Don't you understand bringin' one bloody colored Rican in the house, bathing him, nursing
him, giving him money to get out of town is not gonna free Puerto Rico. Gettin'
bullets taken outta the limbs of *independista's* women, that ain't gonna free Puerto
Rico. It ain't gonna free you neither, *negra, mi negra bella,* when they land on your
bell in the middle of the night or an O.D. or with the hell beat out of em by some
more radical *independistas* or *anti-independistas.* They was too out of it to know
more than somethin' happened, man. Can you and Lili help me out? This once,
man, okay? Liliane'd always go to some corner and begin some ritual or other with
candles and fruit, pictures of the Virgin Mary, Santa Barbara, Santa Cecila, San
Raphael. She'd hum her rosary and look at me 'til I felt my bones ache from the hurt
welling from her eyes, or her mouth. Her mouth hadda way of curlin' round itself,
like when ya eatin' pomegranates. I'd see her like that with her lips, makin' shapes
like she was tryin' to drink me, all my juices, and I'd forget whoever was round and
I'd have to have her talk, just for me, just the way our language is, and sometimes
she'd curse me, push or throw one of her sacred objects, but she would talk and she
would go get the cassette for me. Then her face was calm. Then I knew, she'd let go
of everythin' but me. I'm smilin' now, cuz once the music was on, her eyes closed
and I told her what she'd see and she answered me, in my tongue. Sometimes, she
almost prayed in my tongue and then I'd tell her a story. I'd hold her and tell her,
keep your eyes closed and listen, *Escúchame. Escúchame, cariña.*

Liliane's favorite story, when she was dripping and naked, especially if she was
tremblin' and holdin' me so she wouldn't leap off the bed, her favorite story was
about a young girl at the Corso for the first time. This is how it goes. Once upon a
time a young girl, a pretty young girl, *una morena,* bronze like you with the pi-
quancy of a ginger flower, adorned herself in organdy and silk. She tugged at a very
loud garter belt and slowly wound brand-new stockings up her long legs. She
stuffed taffeta slip upon taffeta slip neath the swing of her skirts and giggled at herself in the mirror, dabbing rose lipstick from one end of her smile to the other. She
put her lovely feet, toes wigglin' to dance, she put them toes in a pair of fancy cloth
shoes with rhinestone butterflies twirlin' about her heels. Yes, she did. Then she
tossed a velvet shawl round her shoulders and was off to the Corso.

The East Side train was not quite an appropriate carriage for such a *flaca tan
linda,* but she rode the ske-dat-tlin' bobbin' train as if it were the QE2. At Eighty-
sixth Street she ran into a mess of young brothahs who callt to her, whispered, whis-
tled, circled her, ran up behind her, got close enough to smell her, made her change
her direction once or twice, 'til they realized she was determined to walk up the
steps to the Corso and they couldn't cause they had rubber-soled shoes. We all knew
you can't wear rubber-soled shoes on the glorious floor of the Corso. So, *cariña,* the
young girl who looked so beautiful, she looked almost as lovely as you do now,

chica. She sashayed by the bar, through the tables crowded with every kinda Latin ever heard of, and stationed herself immediately in front of *el maraquero* in the aqua lamé suit. *Oígame, negrita.* His skin was smooth as a star-strewn *portegría* night, see, like me, *negra.* Put your hand right there by my chin. Now, his bones jut through this face with the grace of Arawak deities. Like that, see. Now, run your fingers through my mustache *porque* his lips blessed the universe with a hallowed, taunting voice; high, high, *como* a cherub, yes, a Bronx boy on a rooftop serenading his *amante, sí.* The way I speak to you, now, *sí.* This young girl was mesmerized. She was how you say when you bein' *bourgesa,* "smitten," right? No, don't move your fingers from my lips, not yet. But the most remarkable feature of *el maraquero,* what did her in, as we say, had the young pussy twitchin', ha, was *el ritmo* of the maracas in his hands. Ba-ba-ba/baba . . . Ba-ba-ba/baba. Oh, she could barely stand the tingling sounds so exact every beat, like an unremitted, *mira,* an unremitted waterfall, Ba-ba-ba/baba . . . Ba-ba-ba/baba . . . Ba-ba-ba/baba. Oh, she started to dance all by herself. It was as if your folks said the Holy Ghost done got holdt to her. She was flyin' round them bambos, introducing steps the Yorubans had forgotten about. She conjured the elegance of the first *danzón* and mixed it with twenty-first century Avenue D salsa. The girl was gone. No, *dulce,* don't move your fingers. Here, let me kiss them. One by one. Cause that's what happened to the beautiful mad dancin' girl and our *maraquero.* For she was so happy movin' to the music he was makin' and she imagined he meant for this joy to overwhelm her. She started to cry ever so slightly. Let me kiss the other one. No not that one, the littlest one. With all her soul she thought he was tossin' those maracas through the air for her. So naturally her tears fell on the beat. No, don't laugh. Listen. Listen. The tears fell from her cheeks slowly and left aqua lamé streaks on her cheeks. Really. Then once they hit the floor, it was like a bolt of lightning hit *el maraquero,* who jumped into an improvisation whenever one of them tears let go of that girl's body. Soon it was she who was keepin' *el ritmo* and he was out there on some *maraquero's sueño* of a solo. Now you know, *el maraquero* has to be disciplined. He's gotta control, oh, the intricacies of Iberian and West African polyrhythms as they now exist in salsa music, right? Okay, let me have the other hand. No, I want to lick the palm of your other hand or I can't finish the story. You want me to finish the story, don't you? Well, good. Now I'll have kissed all your fingers and your palms and the bend in your arm. So *el maraquero* became agitated. He wanted to know where his sound had gone, and to be honest, so did the rest of the orchestra. Well, he hadn't noticed our beautiful young girl in her slips and organdy, her shoes with twirlin' butterflies. He wasn't like me, huh, he didn't see the surrender in her dancin' to his music. So he was astonished when he went to play and no sound came from the maracas. Our young girl, Liliane, who was so much like you, saw what he felt and she knew as he did not know that you do not own the beauty you create. Right, hear me. You don't own the beauty. Oh, I wanta kiss one of those rose tits of yours. No, I'm not finished with the story. Yes, let me nearer. No, don't move your fingers. *El maraquero* is fuming. The young girl who's been dancin' and crying all filled up with something she can't call by name 'cept to say that she likes it. She starts cryin' inconsolably cuz *el maraquero* has lost his music and she doesn't know where it is 'cept that not owning beauty doesn't mean you lose it. Well, let's see that finger again. No, I want the next one. No don't rush me. The young girl runs toward him and he's really pissed. I mean, no, I'm not pissed, I'm lickin' you, *pendeja*. He doesn't understand that he'll be playing no more music, no nothin' 'til he accepts that this young girl in her frilly dress and *mariposa* slippers has got holdt to his music. She's so upset about him not tink-tink-tink-tinktinkin' for her. Out of *desesperación* she starts to sing to him and one by one the seeds that had been her tears that had been her legs and hips dancin' to his *ritmo* all returned to the maracas and *el maraquero* never lost sight of her again. Turn over. From then on, *negrita*, he played for his life every *canción, cada coro,* cause his *chabala* would dance and cry his *ritmo* for him and then give it all back with her tears, her tears from feelin' what she had no name for, had never felt before, and couldn't do without. Right? Liliane, isn't that how it is for you?

Oh, she'd jump up and call me every lowdown exploitative muthafuckah in the world. It was *"chinga-this"* and *"chinga-that."* "I'll be damned if it ain't some sick-assed voyeuristic photographer thinks his art is nurtured by a woman's tears." "Suck it, niggah," she'd scream, or sometimes she said, "Suck it, spic," if she was really mad. Then she'd turn around, tryin' to dress herself in this state. Something was always on backward or she put on mismatched shoes, threw my hat on her head steada hers. She'd go stormin' out saying, "My art is not dependent on fuckin' you or hurtin' you. Niggah, my art ain't gotta damn thing to do with your Puerto Rican behind. Besides you can't take pictures, anyway. Go study with Adal Maldanado, you black muthafuckah."

That's when I could watch her go down the avenue, wet and smellin' exactly how I left her. Then I watched all the other muthafuckahs just feel how she walked, talkin' under her breath in that butchered Spanish she talks when she's mad at me. I watch them watchin' her, and I know if I strolled down the street within the next hour I might as well be who I said I was in the beginning: Pete "El Conde" Rodríguez *que toca la música.* Only the instrument I played is named Liliane.

Musta worked her too hard. She don't come round anymore. Well, not for a while. *Canta, mi canción, cariña, canta, canta.* "Speak my tongue, *negra,* it's good for ya. Liliane, I know I was good to you. Good to you. Hasn't Victor-Jesús María always bathed you in kisses, *con besos líderes?* Didn't I, *negra,* didn't I . . ."

(Music starts, performer walks off during light cross-fade.)

Scene 7:

(Music starts—smooth, airy, light and free. POET *comes in listening and settles into the lit area.)*

POET:
you fill me up so much
when you touch me

I cant stay here
I haveta go to my space

people talk to me
try to sell me cocaine
play me a tune
somebody wanted to give me a massage
but I waz thinkin 'bout you
so I waz in my space

i'm so into it
I cant even take you

tho I ran there with you
tho you appear to me by the riverbed
I cant take you
it's my space
a land lovin' you gives me

shall I tell you how my country looks
my soil & rains
there's a point where the amazon meets the mississippi
a bodega squats on the eiffel tower
toward mont-saint-michel

i'm so into it
I cant even take you

it's my space
a land lovin' you gives me

there's a bistro there near the pacific
& the pyramid of the moon is under my bed
I can see the ferry from trois islets to río
from my window
yr eyes caress my shoulders
my space is a realm of monuments & water
language & the ambiance of senegalese cafes

I can't take you tho
you send me packin'
for anywhere
i've never known
where we never not exist
in my country we are
always
you know how you kiss me
just like that

where the nile flows into the ganges
how the arc de triomphe is next to penn station
where stevie wonder sleeps in d-sharp whole note
& albert ayler is not in the east river

my space
where I sip chablis from yr mouth
& grow roses in my womb
where the mississippi meets the amazon
neruda still tangos in santiago at dawn
where I live

(Performers softly enter and echo "I Live In Music" with silent movement in between.
All voices join, slowly fade, create last group picture as lights fade out by the final words:
". . . touch me".)

ALL VOICES:
jean-jacques dessalines is continually re-elected
the moon sometimes scarlet

I can't take you
but i'll tell you
all I can remember
when you touch me.

Transplantations: Straight and Other Jackets Para Mí

Janis Astor del Valle

Act I: Scene 1

(Stage is dark. MI *stands wearing a straightjacket, with her back to the audience. Lights come up slowly on her. Music cue: Kabuki. Strobe light on.)*

MI: I am so tired that I don't remember the exact moment I got IN—it's all a blur. One moment I was chopping sofrito for my girlfriend's omelette—one moment I was loving her, one moment I was loving myself, and the next, I was OUT. I was OUT, but not really OUT. I mean I was OUT, like a light. OUT like a light on the deconstructed Bruckner Expressway.

(Fade out Kabuki music. Strobe light off. Music cue: "Son Con Son" by Millie Puente. Lights up full. Music fades out as MI *starts to speak.)*

MI: *(Turning to audience)* I thrived, the first seven years of my life, in the Bronx. And though I spent the next decade and a half transplanting my little Puerto Rican self into the rural countryside of northwestern Connecticut, I've always considered myself to be a city kid at heart. Those early days, Mami and me buying plantanos and ajo at Hunts Point (it used to smell so good then, as pure and gentle and strong as Mami's kitchen), Christmas shopping at Alexander's or Macy's in Parkchester—all of Parkchester was decked out for Christmas—or Korvette's on White Plains Road, meeting Papi for real pizza on Westchester Square, bein' babysat by my big brother Linky who got me hooked on the four-thirty movie and Frank Sinatra and Humphrey Bogart and Edward G. Robinson and James Cagney . . . those early days. Thunderous colors and vibrant rhythms keep my heart beating and my head revering. I don't remember the exact moment I got IN—it's all a blur. One moment I was chopping sofrito for my girlfriend's omelette and the next, I was OUT. I was OUT, but not really OUT. I mean I was OUT, like a light. OUT like a light on the deconstructed Bruckner Expressway . . . and then I woke up, and suddenly found myself strapped IN . . . but, you see, it wasn't sudden at all . . . no, no, no—this was thirty years in the making . . . *(struggling to take off straightjacket)*. Childhood was handing on catch phrases like a fish out of water—

No digo yo!
Poca vergüenza!
Par carajo,
Coño!
Estás emborrachado—

mami and papi
will start speaking
Perfect English when they think
i'm listening
but I want to hear more
catch phrases thrown
around our New England
house like my brother's handball
on our old schoolyard wall
to wall
P.S. 93
oh, say can you see me
here, beneath the corn
stalks, I'm trying to get off
this farm but these weeds
are too high
we used to live in the Bronx (takes off straightjacket), *in a high rise,*
fifth floor, 5-A, 955
Evergreen and Story Ave
we had a terrace and I could wave
to Maria, Joaquin, and Eddie D.
I used to see my people for miles
oye, can you hear me?
I'm comin' down!
can't see nothin' now
but land and noisy quiet
ain't no stickball
no amarillos
no coquito
no rice and beans
only in my mami's kitchen
once a week
'cause IGA don't have no
Spanish food, mami says
we have to stock up
on our monthly trip
to the Bronx
to my tita's kitchen
and in my Puerto Rican dreams . . .

(Lights fade.)

Act I: Scene 2

(Music cue: "Yemaya Ochun Prelude," la India. Lights come up, music fades out as MI *begins to speak.)*

MI: I was in the middle of second grade when we left the Bronx—population infinity—and moved to New Milford, Connecticut, population five. Suddenly, we were the only Puerto Ricans for miles; a quarter of a century ago, New Milford was nothing but hills of trees and whiskey wheat, valleys of banks and churches. 20/20 voted it the typical New England town back in the '80s. "Poor little New Milford!" my mother would sing from time to time—and I never really could understand what she found so poor about a town that was run by bankers and clergymen. "Poor, little New Milford," she would almost chant, while washing dishes, or shoveling a path for us through six foot snow drifts. Three days after moving to Connecticut, Mami planned our first trip back to the Bronx, to Co-op City, my Tito's—that's what we called my grandfather, Mami's father. It was New Year's Eve and Tito's birthday. Mami had made a gigantic pot of arroz con habichuelas, and a jumbo tupperware full of potato salad—Tito's favorite—for the occasion. We had gotten hit with two snowstorms in as many days, totaling five and a half feet, plus high water, so what was a few feet of snow? Mami dispatched the troops: Her and my father on the driveway, me and my brother Jeff at the car. But, instead of a driveway, Mami and Papi uncovered a one-hundred-foot sheet of ice. That shit was hard as a motherfuckin' rock! Mami wasn't singing: "Poor little New Milford" this time. In fact, she wasn't singin', period. She was only chopping, chopping away at that ice as if it were a garden of wayward garlic. Boy, could that woman chop ice—almost as fast as she chopped sofrito. Three hours later, we were all ready to pile in our '62 Rambler—except Papi, who was carefully descending the stairs to the walkway outside our house, carrying, like the Holy Grail, the potato salad, which Mami had transferred from the tupperware to a huge glass bowl for decorative purposes. Suddenly a thunderous thump, a clanging of flesh against wrought iron and concrete, and the tumultuous whir of the potato salad zooming from my father's hands like a flying saucer, crashing and cracking into a bundle of ruins amongst the stairs. My father lay dazed. The first words out of Mami's mouth were: "Ay, Dios mío, my potato salad!"

(Blackout.)

Act I: Scene 3

(Lights up on MI *at stool.)*

MI:

She
Taught Me
Not to shave

She . . .
The vivacious cadence of her alto voice makes everyone stop
To look.

Puerto Rican womanhood donning the body of a German commandant;
Shoulders flung back in exuberant pride,
Thick, strong arms
Coupled with long, slender hands that refuse to salute,
Eyes and chin tilted ever so skyward,
Heart and bosom up and out—
Is she really only five foot six?
Feisty spirit of enlightenment carried out,
Up and over the trenches
Of a sexist society
By an Olympic runner's legs;

yet, she disdains
Movements.

Her fears tiptoe extra slowly around what she perceived to be land
Mines, and she sometimes retreats—

Her husband didn't want her to work outside of the home,
So she waited twenty-two years before taking a part-time position
At the local department store—

But her cheers quickly paved the way to my front line:
"Don't EVER let a man
Make mincemeat out of you!"

She gives advice, I take commands. (Salutes)
Governed by tradition,
Half-teasing, half-jealous,
She labels me,
"Daddy's girl."

"No!" I insist, I love and respect my father, but he will always
Have the home team advantage—I am
My mother's daughter.

Still, she doesn't want to believe
That she could be my hero; in her world,
Heroes are men
And women are women
Shaving and not shaving and not speaking Spanish
And still.

Still

Fighting losing battles.

My paradoxical hero,

My Mami.

(Lights fade out.)

Act I: Scene 4

(Music cue: Kabuki. Strobe light comes on, but slower than before.)

MI: *(Arms folded)* I am so tired that I don't remember the exact moment I got IN—it's all a blur. One moment I was chopping sofrito for my girlfriend's omelette—one moment I was loving her, one moment I was loving myself, and the next, I was OUT. I was OUT, but not really OUT. I mean I was OUT, like a light. OUT like a light on the deconstructed Bruckner Expressway.

(Fade out Kabuki music. Strobe light off. Blackout.)

Act I: Scene 5

MI: How is it that all the Puerto Rican weddings I've been to, the women were always dancing—with each other—I mean, they would carry on! And nobody ever said nothin'. In fact, the men cheered them on! Mami was one of those women; when she got on the floor with her amigas and her sisters, you couldn't stop them . . . yet Mami, who left the Jehovah's Witnesses because they were too restrictive, tells me that homosexuality is a sin . . . *(pause, folds arms)*. Am I my mother's daughter?

(Lights fade out.)

Act I: Scene 6

(Music cue: Jíbara music. Lights come up.)

MI: I was five the first time I went to Puerto Rico.

(Jíbara music fades out.)

MI: Mami and me were going to visit her family in Ponce, on the southern part of the island. We flew on a jumbo jet to San Juan, then had to switch to a rickety commuter plane for Ponce. Man, that thing looked like a leftover from the Wright Brothers. I thought it was nerves until I saw everybody else in the plane shakin' too. I had two handfuls of Hershey's Kisses—I squeezed them into fists, shut my eyes, echoed Mami's "Ay, Dios mío," and was ready for takeoff.

MAMI: Mira, Mija, qué linda las montañas . . .

MI: I opened my eyes to Mami pointing out the window—I expect to see water, I mean we were on an island, right? But only miles and miles of majestic mountains—deep, verdant green stood below, rose up and down and all around us. The beauty made me instantly dizzy with excitement and fear. I had to shut my eyes again. Meanwhile, Mami was singing.

MAMI: Yo soy jíbara, yo soy jíbaro.

MI: I didn't know what that meant, but it sounded nice, so I started singing too.

MI: *(Age five)* Yo soy jíbaro . . . Mami, que es jíbaro?

MAMI: Como mi familia . . . porque me familia vive en el campo—

MI: Like my family . . . because my family lives in the country—no, not country houses, those were their only houses—

MAMI: Son jíbaros.

MI: They're country people. Years later I found out the more common meaning for jíbara was "peasant." The plane finally landed, rumbling to a halt. I opened my eyes, and unclenched my fists, which were bathed in melted kisses. The ride from Ponce airport to Titi Cadén's *(Mami's aunt)* house was endless—I thought we were traveling to another country. The roads twisted and turned from pavement to dirt, with fewer houses and more trees. After nearly an hour, we were there. Titi Cadén was waiting for us outside. She swept us up in her arms, covering us with " Bienvenidos, la bendición, mi familia!" It was almost like being at home. Titi Cadén didn't have hot water or a telephone, but she did have plenty of love, and a beautiful little next-door neighbor, Marisol, my first crush . . . I don't remember much more about that first trip to Puerto Rico, except Titi Cadén's delicious bacalao frito and Marisol . . . Marisol and me hit the beach everyday, buildin' sand castles, playin' water tag, holdin' hands . . . she was so beautiful—a little darker than me, jet black curly long hair, big round eyes and a smile that made my heart giggle . . .

(Covering one eye.)

In a King-
Sized Bed
We were Queens—Reinas—
Together, letting our Hearts
Rule our Heads
With golden-clad wrists
Of Afro-Latino ancestry
The Warriorness in You
Merengued with the Warriorness
In Me
For one weekend
We were finally freed
In the New England hills of my girl
Hood—(covering right, then left eye, crosses right)
What paradox for a backdrop!
Nevertheless, we were blessed
By Some

One, by Autumnal
Colors, by Love, by Peace, by Full
Moon
Light,
By Ourselves
In a King-
Sized Bed
We Queens—Nosotras Reinas—
Together, letting our Hearts
Rule our Heads
One weekend finally freed—
Isn't that
The Way
We should always
Feel?

(Blackout.)

Act I: Scene 7

(Music cue: Carousel. Lights up. Music plays softly in the background.)

MAMI: Mija, Linky gave me five dollars to spend for your birthday—that's a dollar for every year! He said: "Mami, take her to Korvette's and buy her anything she wants—anything." So, now, Mija, pick out whatever you want.

MI: I headed straight for the toy section. I had dreamed of this moment for weeks, maybe even months; I knew exactly what I wanted. But just when my happy little hands reached OUT, Mami stepped IN.

MAMI: *(Looking around nervously)* Mija, these are boys' toys . . .

MI: I looked from my beloved prize and back to Mami's nervous eyes . . .

MAMI: Mija, you can have anything you want—*(pointing)* mira, hay Barbie, allí!

MI: But in those days, my fingers still had a mind and a heart of their own, so they clutched the beautiful bag of one hundred multicolored plastic cowboys and indians and wouldn't let go.

MAMI: Are you sure?

MI: I hugged my big brother's best birthday present closer to my chest, knowing and loving that Linky's gift would enable me to play soldiers with my other brother *(nodding as a child)*. "I'm sure! I'm ready to go home!"

MAMI: *(Shaking her head sadly)* Ay, Mija . . .

(Music stops suddenly. Sound cue: phones ringing. Lights on stool.)

MI: Word spreads like a California wildfire in my family, courtesy of my titi's—not titties—titi is Puerto Rican for aunt; within two days I had a reputation.

(Sound cue: phone rings once.)

TITI MAGDALENA: Iris, don't buy her a doll for Christmas unless it's GI Joe—the mother says she's playing with the boys' toys, tu sabes?

TITI IRIS: Ay, no! Qué pobrecita, la mama! *(Phoning Maria)* Maria, Magdalena me dijo!

TITI MARIA: Ay, bendito, qué pasó? She was such a beautiful little girl!

TITI IRIS: Yo sé, and the way she always had her dressed to the nines! Pero, tu sabes, she has too many sons que her little girl don't know how to be a little girl!

TITI MARIA: *(Phoning Christina)* Sí, sí, Christina, I'm telling you, Iris me dijo! She won't even look at a dress, goes into a tantrum every time when the mother shows her a skirt! Sí, sí, the mother's in tears! Y only plays with boys' toys!

TITI CHRISTINA: Pues, if she was my daughter, I'da slapped the shit outta her!

MI: I don't know where they got their information about the dresses—I didn't stop wearin' those 'til I was at least ten or eleven . . . as for the doll situation, that I just couldn't get into playin' babies—walkin' around with a doll, pretendin' it's your baby, feedin' it, burpin' it, changin' it; I mean, where's the entertainment value in that? Now, Action Jackson and Big Jim—they were fun! Do you remember Big Jim, with the button you press in his back to make his arm do karate chops? Man, that was exciting! Or, how about Evel Kneivel with his battery operated motorcycle, doin' wheelies and jumpin' ramps. . . . .I used to love buildin' ramps just to see how high he could go before he fell off the bike . . . yeah, those were dolls I could get into . . . Mami took it in stride; or at least she tried to hide when she cried, but I spied and so I collected Malibu Barbie and Skipper, too . . . *(they looked Puerto Rican)*. They went campin' with the guys and they would all climb mountains. But since Malibu Barbie and Skipper only had their bathing suits, I let them wear GI Joe and Big Jim's clothes—I mean, you can't climb mountains in bikinis, can you?

(Blackout.)

Act I: Scene 8

(Music cue: "Son Con Son" by Millie Puente. MI *begins a mock tango, holding the strait-jacket as her partner, to the music.)*

MI: *(Arms folded)* No armarillos, no coquito . . . no rice and beans . . . only in my mami's kitchen once a week . . . no matter how often and how long we visited New York, it was always a day too short. I missed the Bronx and my oldest brother, Linky, who stayed there. Pues, he was nineteen and he had a good job with Manny Hanny; I was seven and I had no voice, no choice, but I also had no idea how much I really missed my native New York. I mean, it was a slow kind of missing—in

Spanish, we say: "She stayed con la gana," with the yearning. It's the kind of missing that never dies; not even the act of forgetting can kill that type of yearning. Because you can forget a memory, but not a feeling, not a sense, not a smell. I mean, in New York, we didn't go to church, we went to Yankee Stadium! And Orchard Beach—a day at Orchard Beach was a day in heaven! The juicy scents of mami's pollo frito and coconut lotion, the majestic sounds of a thousand portable radios blastin' Tito Puente. And my Uncle Raymond takin' me to the Bronx Zoo or White Castle's or just hangin' out with me and turnin' me on to the latest Jackson Five hit. Tu sabes, the kids in Connecticut didn't even know who Michael Jackson was—they were into Donny Osmond. I've never thought of my family as middle class, although to our old friends in the Bronx, it seemed that moving to Connecticut automatically meant we had "made it." What I wanna know is what exactly did we make? And where did we make it to? What I wanna know is what exactly did we make? And where did we make it to? We may have made it out of the Bronx, but we were still working-class folks, just relocated to another state is all. Shit, in Connecticut we still didn't have a garage or a dishwasher! Middle class? The kids I went to school with in Connecticut, they complained that they were only middle class—coño, if having a two-car garage, two-story house, five acres of land and a closet full of L. L. Bean was middle class, we must have been poverty-stricken!

(Blackout.)

Act I: Scene 9

(Music cue: Donny Osmond's "Go Away Little Girl".)

MI: My first friend and my first crush in Connecticut was Jeanette DiPatria. Not Spanish, Italiana. She was a year older than me and born in the Bronx, too, but her family had moved to Connecticut before mine so she had already lost her Bronx accent. Actually, I didn't even know I had an accent, but I caught on pretty quick when Jeanette and her brother, Joey, kept laughing at me every time I said "soder." After several weeks of intense drilling by Jeanette and Joey, I soon learned to say "soda" and other words just like them. *Mami and Papi will start speaking perfect English when they think I'm listening* . . . the little Spanish I knew, I didn't know what to do with. It's not that it wasn't allowed in the house, it just wasn't encouraged. So, in seventh grade, I took Spanish, bringing in all my catch phrases that I had picked up at home, only, I didn't realize there's a big difference between Castilian—what we learned in school—and Puerto Rican Spanish. I flunked the first couple of vocabulary tests, mostly cause I couldn't spell, and frequently argued with my teacher about the existence of nonexistent words and phrases like: "perate, a 'mimir o pow-pow, and coñocarajo." I hated school.

(Lights out.)

Act I: Scene 10

(Stage is still dark.)

MI:

> They didn't teach
> Angela Davis
> Or
> Maria Irene Fornes
> Or
> Tillie Olsen
> Or
> Sonia Sanchez
>
> *(Lights come up.)*
>
> In my Connecticut
> Public High School
> (We were lucky enough
> To get a taste of
> Lorraine Hansberry and Lillian Hellman)
>
> And they didn't teach
> Me
> What to do
> With my Latina lesbian hands
> Holding an American pen
> At that New
> England
> School
>
> 1979 and I had cried
> Myself to sleep
> At least one hundred eighty-five nights
> that sophomore year
> Never knowing why
>
> no amarillos
> no coquito
> no rice and beans
> only in my mami's kitchen
> once a week
>
> So I wrote
> With a secret pen
> Closet writer
> Closet case
> Closet Puerto Rican

And hated Monday mornings
And dated
Boys
and loved
Girls—
But only in my journal.

And learning how to paint
my straight girl face
was as easy as learning how to paint
the Sistine Chapel
without a palette

I dated boys.
I loved women,
But only in my journal.

1980, and I, half-waiting
For Mr. Right,
Wondered what it would be like
To salsa with Elena or Kate
Instead of José or Bill.

Junior prom came
And went
Without Mi—
I was home,
In my closet,
Writing and
Dreaming of Elena and Kate and Marisol and Grace—
I dreamed I was their date
Merengue, cha-cha, hustle, salsa, bump
And grind . . .
Lips to lips,
Breasts to breasts,
Eye to eye . . .
I didn't really know how
to dance, but in my mind,
in my closet,
in my spaghetti straps—
forget that prairie dress shit—
in my mind, I wore
stiletto heels,
it was so fly
I didn't even feel
the sting of the WASPs

in my mind,
I did not hide . . .

The idea of Queen and Queen
Of the Prom
stayed with me the rest of the year.

1981, Graduation's here

And who gives a flying fuck
When they're force-feeding us
Reagan?

I stopped dating boys
That June.

1982, and I fell in love
With you
And gave birth
To the secret thoughts
that, until then, had resigned themselves
To the permanent residence IN
side my head.
Yet someone said
IT
Was a
SIN.

So, I started dating
Boys again.

"I'm too white for the Spanish kids, and too Spanish for the white kids," my sixteen-year-old niece revealed one day. I was so relieved she was telling me this over the phone, because I didn't want her to see the pain in my face, the pain in my ears, hearing history repeat itself. But silence is painful, too, so before it got too painfully quiet, I spoke up. "Me, too, mija, me, too."

Voices in the night
Or day, my own
People sayin'
"You're so white!" or
"You're so straight"
"Gringa, Blanquita
La Niña Bonita!" they
Tuck me
In
Under a blanket of
In

Security . . .
A Puerto Rican Sister
Pushin' time
Shares, condos
On this Isla Verde beach
As fast
And slow
As dope
My Sister, lighter
Than me
Has the huevos
To speak, "You must
Have some of that pure

European blood
In you, like me!"
"I'm not like you!"
I think. I
Think, "Who would
Want more
Of her so-called
Pure, European
Blood that contaminated
History with trans
Fusions of Imperialism?

Conquistadores—Conquerors
Conquering, Raped
A People, A Land A
Culture." I think.
So disarmed by my
Thoughts and fear,
How can I
Let the words
Out? "Nenita,
Tenemos todos
Colores en mi familia!"
"We have every color

Of the rainbow and more in
My family, honey!"
I suddenly shout.
I am a
Puerto Rican Lesbian, I think.
But I'm tired.
So tired of having

To defend
My light skin
My Anglo-looking face
My New England education
My accentless accent
My Spanglish-laden Spanish
My long straight hair
And my flat, flat ass
To voices in the night
Or day, my own
People
And you,
Tired.

(Kabuki music and strobe on.)

MI: I am so tired that I don't remember the exact moment I got IN—it's all a blur. One moment I was chopping sofrito for my girlfriend's omelette—one moment I was loving her, one moment I was loving myself, and the next, I was OUT. I was OUT, but not really OUT. I mean I was OUT, like a light. OUT like a light on the deconstructed Bruckner Expressway.

(Blackout. Kabuki music off.)

Act I: Scene 11

(Music cue: Santana's "Gitana." Light up. Music fades as MI speaks.)

MI: By the time I was in my early twenties, I realized that I had stayed con la gana for New York most of my life. So, nearly ten years ago, I uprooted and transplanted my Self from Connecticut to Manhattan's Upper East Side, thinking I would finally get back to my roots . . . the Upper East Side? What the fuck was I looking for on the Upper East Side? The only Puerto Ricans in that neighborhood were nannies and doormen. There were no rice and beans at the Food Emporium—coño, you couldn't even get plantanos—plantains—for at least thirty blocks! I didn't know this then, I only knew something was out of sync with the sterile skyscrapers and sunless skies of the Upper East Side. So, I fled East Seventieth Street, moved to Carroll Gardens, and had a fling with Maya. She was the first Puerto Rican-Dominican I had ever met and couldn't resist her long-as-Crystal Gale's hair, which I later found out was a weave. A year later, I still hadn't found my roots or a steady girlfriend, so, I moved from Brooklyn to Chelsea to Staten Island and ended up in Hoboken. Funny thing was, though I found a lot of Latinos, I couldn't speak to them. I could walk into a Puerto Rican or Dominican restaurant and order carne guisa or café con leche, but I couldn't carry on a conversation beyond "cómo estás?"

All is
Not fair
In Food and Beverage

You tell me
As one of your co-workers—one
Of my Latino brothers—repeatedly
Stabs you with the butcher
Knife or ignorance
"I heard a dirty rumor, I heard a
Dirty rumor—I heard you don't like men!"
He jabs.
"Is it true, is it true, you're into
Women?" the taunting tone
Demands.
Somebody saw us kiss
Last Friday morning
When I dropped you off
At work
Somebody saw us
Somebody saw
Us some
Body saw us
Kiss
When I dropped

Your heart
Plops
To the chopping block
(The knife twists)
Prime cut
Roast rump
He craves
To slice
It up

Your mouth
Is raw
With anger
And fear
"I'll fuck anything
That walks!" is all
You can retort.
(There is safety in
Half-lies.)

He turns on
His meat
Grinder and blender
Simultaneously

"Why you like that? Why
You like that? Why, you?" he asks
Incredulously.
Licking his lips, his eyes affixed
On your breasts, he secretly
Desires to puree, strain
And taste test.

But other customers away.
Your co-worker zips up
His machismo and
Walks away.
This time.

At home
Alone,
You cry first
All the words you couldn't say to him,
Then, pick up the phone
And dial me.

In a calmer state of mind
You surmise, "It all comes down to pride—
If they can't control or fuck you, they don't
Want to deal!"
But your next breath
Remembers the fear.
"Maybe I should just get married and have kids!"

My heart
Momentarily
Plops
To the chopping block,
Then springs back
Into place.

"You could marry me
And have kids!" I boldly state.

"Really?"

"Yeah, really. But some
Homophobe
Saw us kiss
Last Friday morning,
So, I'll drop you off
At the corner,

And kiss you
At home."

Act I: Scene 12

(Music cue: José Luis Guerra's "A Pedir Su Mano." Lights up. Music fades as she begins to speak.)

MI: I lasted exactly a year in Sinatraville, then returned to New York, via Ninety-eighth and Amsterdam. Muchos Dominicanos, and I felt almost at home, but at a distance, too. I still couldn't order more than the most basic of meals—I saw a sign for Mondongo and thought they had misspelled Mofongo, mashed green plantains, but I found out too late that the tripe soup in front of me was definitely not Mofongo. One of the cooks offered to help me with my Spanish in exchange for helping him with his English, but just when we were gonna get started, I lost my job and my apartment and sought refuge in a Chelsea convent for three years—no, I didn't become a lesbian nun, that would've been redundant—besides, that's Spanish, that means star—we're still together today, nearly five years later, back on the Upper West Side in our own apartment. Estrella's not really Spanish, she's African-American, but she *feels* Spanish since her parents conceived her in Cuba. That's what she says. Our first Christmas together, I was really poor. But I saw these earrings that I knew she had to have. It was Christmas Eve and the guy sellin' em on Bleecker and Broadway was just about to close up shop. I reached into my pocket and pulled out all I had left: four tokens and a dollar . . . he let me keep the dollar.

He first mistook me for a WASP.
"They're African seeds,"
He tells me
With pride and sincerity
For a smile

"I made them myself—
You know African seed?"
He asks, gently holding

A pair
Near, still
Smiling
Through the windchill
factor, twenty below
And counting

Africa flows
In my Puerto Rican
Blood, *I think while*
Returning the smile
And almost whispering

My reply, "Yes, I
Know African seeds."

But on the verge
Of my quivering lips
Lives
Another Truth—
Words that can
Not escape
The Prison of Fear—

In
Com
Plete
Sen
Ten
Ces
Born from
Over-zealous thoughts—
Once fallen on deaf ears—
Delivered C-Section—
I had to cut, I had
To cut, I had to
Censor Myself

Although I know
Self-imposed silence
Is the worst kind
Of noise

I had to shut, I had
To shut, I had to
Lock the gate
To my cell, to my
Self, just
In case he also mis
Took me
For something else
When all I really wanted
To do
Was tell the brother
How
I know
African seeds
How
I have felt
Africa beating

In my lover's heart
How
My lover
Is
A Woman
An African-American
Woman

Woman
Of color
Of Soweto
Of Sahara
Of Kalahari
Of Kwanza

Of Fulani
Of Mandela
Of Malcolm
Of King
Of Niger
Of Savannah
Of Green
And Red
And Yellow
And Gold . . .

Beyond this pale
Olive skin, behind
These horn-
Rimmed
Spectacles
Lives a Puerto Rican
Sister
Loving your earrings,
Brother,

Loving your African seeds
Loving them so much
But not loving my

Self enough
To tell you
They're not for me,
They're for my lover.

(Music cue: "A Pedir Su Mano" plays. Lights fade out.)

Act I: Scene 13

MI: I was wearin' men's boxer shorts way before they became fashionable and long before Hanes started makin' em for women! Flannel pajamas, too. I wore my dad's hand-me-downs. Nah, I wasn't into cross-dressing, I just thought his clothes felt more comfortable, so soft and natural; they were made better and lasted longer, too. Papi didn't seem to mind until I came out . . . I didn't even come out to him—I came out to my mother, but she told him I was a lesbian and she told me that he cried and it was right about then that he stopped wearin' boxers. And he stopped givin' me his hand-me-downs. He never really said anything, but he didn't really have to. I knew. And it's funny, tu sabes, about a year ago, I was writing a play and all of a sudden I got writer's block—just at the point when the Latina lesbian daughter is confronting the homophobic father. And I haven't been able to write another word since. And that's really weird for me, cause I've been writing plays since I was about nine, and I never suffered writer's block like that. Only I didn't know they were plays when I was a kid. I called them stories and me and cousins would perform them at our Tita's *(grandmother's)* house in the Bronx. She lived in Castle Hill, between the projects and the river, with a great view of the Whitestone Bridge, especially at night. Her neighborhood became the backdrop for many of my stories. I always cast my cousin Val and myself as the dope addicts; the rest of the cousins played neighborhood big shots like cops, parents, principals, and fellow drug dealers. Oh, and sometimes we'd let Val's little sister be our seven-year-old al-coholic sidekick, Chicky. I don't know why I was writing about those types of char-acters. Maybe I had some sick fascination with their desperation. Or maybe I was just so used to being fed those images. Anyway, I'm happy to say that through the years my writing has evolved and I'm now writing about more realistic people—like me and my friends: Latina lesbians with happy endings. And I've done pretty well for myself. Although, sometimes, I look at Rosie Pérez and I think maybe I haven't done well enough. Maybe I haven't suffered enough. If only I had bad hair, if only I had been a shade darker. Or, if only I had stayed in the Bronx, kept my accent, permed my hair, and joined a gang. I could've passed for a light-skinned Puerto Ri-can and been a star! I'm sure I would've had a feature film or two under my belt by now—probably co-starring Jessica Lange as the adoptive mother of my illegitimate child or Michelle Pfeiffer as my sympathetic but tough-as-nails high school teacher . . . or, Al Pacino as my drug-dealing big brother . . . or, Miriam Colon as my maid! I coulda been a contender, but I guess I'm just not marketable enough. . . .

I don't remember
the exact moment
I got IN
it
could have been
the moment
Mami scolded me,
Pulling her hands

through my man-
tailored buzz
cut

it could have been
the moment
Jesse Helms
tried to shut
my lesbian fingers
up

or, maybe it
was when
the nation deemed
immigration its curse,
bilingual, an official dirty word—

it could have been
the moment
my girl
friend
told me
I danced
like a
white chick—

Or maybe it was when
A New York City critic
said I was miscast
in my autobiography—

I don't remember
the exact moment
I got IN
but it
could have been
it could have been
when
I started
buyin' in
to this shit!

I don't remember the exact moment I got IN—it's all a blur. One moment I was chopping sofrito for my girlfriend's omelette—one moment I was loving her, one moment I was loving myself, and the next, I was OUT. I was OUT, really OUT. I mean I was OUT.

(Blackout.)

V

Comedy
and Satire

Savage Wilds

El Cabrón

Savage Wilds

Ishmael Reed

CHARACTERS

Dr. Marlin: *Host of wild game show,* Savage Wilds

Sheena Queene: *Co-producer*

Vanessa Bare: *Co-producer*

Jackson: *Prop man*

Mr. Greenbelt: *Owner of Greenbelt TV Network*

Uncle Sanford: *Comedian, star of* The Uncle Sanford Show

Matron

U.S. Attorney Richard Head

Ralph Kincaid: *White agent*

Juan Paige: *Black agent*

Mayor B. V. Dongson

Mrs. Dongson

Cookie Boggs: *Reporter, National Feminist Radio*

Act I: Scene 1

(Office. Desk and chairs. Blowup of TV Guide *cover with* VANESSA *and* SHEENA *in Safari outfits. Khaki shorts, shirt. Helmets. They are posing, holding guns.* SHEENA *is on the phone pacing up and down.* VANESSA *is listening with anticipation.* VANESSA *is black. A wide-eyed bimbo type. Very attractive, about thirty.* SHEENA *is white, about the same age. Also attractive, but hard and bitter. A feminist. Nouveau white trash.)*

SHEENA: But how could that be? We pulled out all of the stops. All of the publicity and advertis—you're sorry? You can imagine how we feel? We might lose our jobs. *(Hangs up phone)*

VANESSA: Sheena, how'd we do?

SHEENA: *(Dejectedly)* You can't do any worse. We came in twenty-fifth, behind re-runs of the *Mr. Peepers Show.*

VANESSA: *(Tearfully)* We're going to be fired. Oh, I knew it wasn't going to work. You and your bright ideas. Having Dr. Marlin bitten by a Gabon viper! He could have been killed. The ambulance attendants said that in five more minutes he would have been dead. The Gabon viper is one of the deadliest snakes in the world.

SHEENA: I was trying to save our jobs. You know that Mr. Greenbelt is upset that the show hasn't taken off. It's had to compete with wars, genocide, disasters, massacres, serial murders, riots, and all of the other stuff people are watching while eating dinner. I don't know about you, but I am heavily in debt. You have to be a millionaire to live in New York these days. I still haven't recovered from the crash of '87.

VANESSA: *(Pouting)* You think that you have problems? I just bought a 1955 fully restored red hard- and soft-top Ford Thunderbird with an 8-cylinder engine and telephone. It cost thirty-five thousand dollars. I'm living in this exclusive East Side condominium that's taking fifty percent of what I earn.

SHEENA: You can kiss that good-bye if this show doesn't start to move. You'll have to get rid of your wardrobe, too. You have more clothes than Jackie Kennedy.

VANESSA: *(Huffy)* There's nothing wrong with looking neat. Presentable. I have a reputation to uphold. I was voted Miss Virginia in 1983. (SHEENA *eyes her contemptuously; pause)* I just called the hospital. Dr. Marlin has been taken off the critical list. The swelling in his arm has gone down. You have to admit that he is a real company man. Allowing himself to be bitten like that so's to improve the ratings.

SHEENA: There you go sympathizing with some guy.

(Door opens. Jackson, the black prop man. White shirt, tie, pants, shined shoes. A clean-cut type. He carries a yellow legal pad clamped to a clipboard.)

SHEENA: *(Rudely)* What do you want? (VANESSA *glares at him, folds her arms, and sighs impatiently)*

JACKSON: I have the prop list. (SHEENA *snatches it from him and examines it, while glaring at him, hostilely)*

SHEENA: Cut out the bookshelves. They look too PBS. And get rid of that pipe rack. It looks too . . . too oral. I hate it when he's waving that pipe about. Have him sit in a red lounge chair. You'll also need some colorful bandages. Something that will look good on TV. The hospital bandages won't look right in color. *(She hands the clipboard back to him; he examines it)*

JACKSON: You forgot to initial it, sweetheart. *(The two glare at him intensely)*

VANESSA: *(Mean)* Who you callin' sweetheart?

SHEENA: Yeah? What do we look like? A couple of whores to you?

VANESSA: You're always making some flirtatious remark when you come in here.

SHEENA: Next time you do it, we're going to kick your ass. *(He smiles sheepishly)*

VANESSA: So apologize.

JACKSON: *(Swallowing his pride)* I didn't mean to offend you, Vanessa, Sheena.

VANESSA: *(Mimics)* I didn't mean to offend you Vanessa, Sheena. Ms. Bare and Ms. Queene to you. *(They glare at him)* Sheena, do we have to continue using him? I know a sister who can do his job.

JACKSON: *(Humiliated)* Ms. Bare, Ms. Queene.

SHEENA: Now get lost. *(He exits)*

VANESSA: The soul brothers are never going to change. I'm thinkin' about buying me a pistol. *(Phone rings,* SHEENA *picks it up)*

SHEENA: *(Excitedly)* It's Mr. Greenbelt. He's coming downstairs. *(They hurriedly exit)*

Act I: Scene 2

*(*GREENBELT *enters. Yuppie type. In powersuit. Looks at his watch.* VANESSA *and* SHEENA *enter. They've discarded their safari outfits and wear the San Francisco night-on-the-town outfits of* Savage Wilds, II *They're heavily made up. They approach* GREENBELT *and begin to cling to him.)*

SHEENA: *(Exaggeratedly)* Ohhhhhh! Mr. Greenbelt.

VANESSA: Daddy, oh! Daddy!

GREENBELT: Cut it out you whores. I don't want no ass. Oh, I knew I shouldnta hired you broads. I shoulda hired a man. One man could do the job of twenty of you cunts. What was the meaning of the stupid stunt that you pulled on *Savage Wilds?* It was boring. Not only did you come in behind the *Mr. Peepers Show,* but you got these animal rights people callin' up here protestin' about the way you treated the snake. The sponsor, Polyester Potato Chips, is threatnin' to drop the show. Oh, Jesus, I got to sit down. *(They almost collide with each other, trying to provide him with a chair. He sits down, gulps some pills. They unbutton his shirt and begin to massage his chest, panting as they do so. Vanessa begins to remove his shoes. He slaps her hand)*

GREENBELT: Will you two cut it out?

SHEENA: But Mr. Greenbelt. It was a critical success. The newspapers said that it set a new high for live television.

VANESSA: The way we kept our cool as Dr. Marlin was writhing in pain.

SHEENA: We might get a Grammy, an Emmy. *(*VANESSA *nods)*

GREENBELT: Who cares about statues? I can't put no fuckin' statue in the bank. I need people glued to the set when my shit is on. And that Dr. Marlin? Where'd you get that asshole? Fire his ass!

VANESSA: But Dr. Marlin has been here twenty years. He's an institution.

GREENBELT: The only institution that I know about is Greenbelt Television Network and how I can make a buck or two or the shareholders. They're puttin' pressure on me so I have to put pressure on you. Now I'm going to give you one more shot. If next week's show doesn't come in within the top ten, you broads are out on your fannies.

VANESSA AND SHEENA: *(Together. On their knees)* Please, Mr. Greenbelt. Don't fire us. *(*VANESSA *tugs at his pant leg. He shakes his foot away)*

SHEENA: *(Suggestively)* Daddy, can't we talk about this in private? I'll make it worth your while.

VANESSA: I'll pose for those art pictures you wanted, Mr. Greenbelt, honey.

GREENBELT: You women and minorities are always making lewd proposals to me. It's final. If you don't make this show climb by next week *(he makes a throat-cutting gesture with his finger)*. Anyway, you're the creative people, so create.

(He starts for the exit, laughing at his latest remark. UNCLE SANFORD *enters. He is an elderly, gray-haired, black man who walks bow-legged—a la Redd Foxx—and wears a plaid sports jacket, rust brown pants, white shoes, and a checkered cap. He wears dark glasses with loud pink or green frames.)*

GREENBELT: *(Angrily)* You still here? I told you to pack your stuff and get out in an hour. If you don't get out, I'm going to call security and have them throw you out.

SANFORD: *(Pitiful)* Mr. Greenbelt, have a heart. Please. *(Begs with hands clasped)* I just came by to say good-bye to the girls. You'll let me do that, won't you?

GREENBELT: Make it quick. *(Turns to girls)* So, create . . . *(laughing, he exits).*

VANESSA: *(To* SANFORD*)* Good-bye? Good-bye for what?

SANFORD: I got fired.

SHEENA: Fired? But you came in number one last week. You've been number one for ten years.

SANFORD: But I came in number two last night. *(Sobbing)* What did they expect? The World Series was on another channel. That Greenbelt has no mercy. He has the heart of the Internal Revenue Department. Look girls, you wouldn't be able to lend me a subway token so that I can get down to the blood bank before it closes? I don't have nothin' to eat.

VANESSA: But what happened to the three homes in Bel Air, Miami, and Lake Tahoe?

SHEENA: The pied-à-terre on Central Park West?

VANESSA: The cash, securities, and diamonds?

SHEENA: *(Sarcastically)* Waddaya do? Toot it up your nose?

SANFORD: *(Squeezing his nose)* What nose? *(Squeezing his nose)* This thing is plastic. I had a Beverly Hills physician fix it. As for my wealth, I lost it because of the different races.

VANESSA: Discrimination?

SANFORD: No. Churchill Downs. Belmont. Golden Gate Fields. I don't have nowhere to go. I called about my last job. You remember, the one I had where the customers would drink whiskey and get into fights and where I had to do my makeup in the toilet and when it was time to get paid, the club owner would skip town. They said that they don't want me either.

VANESSA: You poor dear. Here, I'll lend you a subway token *(goes into her purse)*.

SHEENA: *(To* VANESSA*)* What's the matter with you? Helping some guy.

VANESSA: He reminds me of my father . . . a . . . I . . . can't even remember his name. *(She hands* SANFORD *the subway token)*

SANFORD: Oh, thank you, Ms. Vanessa. You know, Ms. Vanessa, this is the first time I've seen you with some clothes on. *(*VANESSA *glares at him. He realizes that he has blundered. Nervous. Exiting, a shit-faced grin)* Well, I'd better get going. Look, if you two hear of anything, let me know. I'll do anything. Sweep. Buff. *(He exits)*

VANESSA: *(Reflectively, nostalgically)* He'll make a comeback. His jokes are old, but he's been down and out before and managed to make a comeback. All of those years he spent in obscurity, working one-night stands. He had to work around so much cigarette smoke that one of his lungs had to be removed. Probably gave a lot of his money to his friends. He was always a soft touch. The kind of gentle, sweet man who would give you the shirt off his back. A man like that is hard to find these days. Most of them just want to fuck and doze off.

SHEENA: How can you say that about a pig—hey wait! What did you say?

VANESSA: Most of them just want to fuck and doze off.

SHEENA: No, before that?

VANESSA: *(Puzzled)* A man like that is hard to find these days?

SHEENA: Sister . . . you've just given me a great idea. We can make the ratings shoot right through the roof.

VANESSA: Sheena. I knew that you'd come up with something. I hope it won't get anybody hurt.

SHEENA: Don't worry. It'll be as safe as a girl scout cookie. *(*JACKSON *enters. Has a bouquet of roses. Begins to read the card.* SHEENA *is puzzled.* VANESSA *seems embarrassed)*

JACKSON: *(Reads from card accompanying the roses. Teasing)* "None of these roses is as beautiful as you *(makes melodramatic gestures)* . . . my sweet. My heart aches for you. Every particle of my being shakes for you. My every pore yearns for your divine love. My heart takes flight like an eagle when I think of you. You are the honey that oozes into my passion. I'd climb the highest mountain for you, swim the deepest ocean, have pain in the warm September rain over you, my heart is burning and churning for you . . . .*(*VANESSA *snatches the flowers and the note from him.* JACKSON *is cracking up)*.

VANESSA: You fresh thing. How dare you read my mail.

SHEENA: *(Laughing)* Who on earth is that from?

VANESSA: *(Embarrassed)* Just a fan.

JACKSON: The guy really has it for Vanessa. He's been sending flowers from Washington all week. You got these guys falling head over heels in love with you, huh babes? *(They both turn on him)*

SHEENA: Who you calling babes?

VANESSA: You may call your mama babes, but you don't be callin' us feminists no babes. Ain't that right, Sheena?

SHEENA: We warned you.

(They rush him and begin to pummel him. We hear his screams as the lights go down.)

Act I: Scene 3

(Prop room. UNCLE SANFORD is sitting in the red lounge chair. He is snorting from a coke spoon. He drops the spoon. He gets on his hands and knees and starts to sniff the spilled coke from the floor. JACKSON comes on, halts before SANFORD, surprised. SANFORD looks up at JACKSON with dog-like pitiful eyes.)

JACKSON: Uncle Sanford! What are you doing here?

SANFORD: *(Slowly gets to his feet)* I thought that I could live down here in the prop room for a while until my luck changes. I mean, Jackson, be a brother. You won't tell will you?

JACKSON: Yeah, I heard that they fired you from your show. Too bad. Didn't you save anything?

SANFORD: I never thought about it. I mean, the show was number one for two years. I thought that it would always be number one. I don't have no insurance, and I owe the government five million dollars in back taxes. My creditors are auctioning off all of my things tomorrow. This Las Vegas chorus girl that I married—you know, the one who is thirty years younger than me—she sold a story about me to the *National Enquirer.* You know, about my habits and problems, and those nasty parties we used to throw. I'm the laughingstock of the nation. I'm afraid to show my face in public after what she wrote. Last night I thought about committing suicide.

JACKSON: *(Disgusted)* There's nothing like always being on top in this business. Look at you! Just think. Last week you still had your own parking space and dressing room. This week you're down here in the prop room, asking me if it's okay if you can sleep here. With the little money I have I've invested in bonds. My wife and I are saving money for college so that our son will have it better than we had it. That's the way you build an aristocracy. Each generation looking out for the succeeding generation. Who knows? Maybe my kid will end up being head of the Federal Reserve, or running some Wall Street brokerage house, play polo. Join the Republican Party. You had your chance, and you squandered it. Guys like you only live for the day. I don't plan to work in the prop room all of my life. As for you, you're better off dead.

SANFORD: *(Pulls wine bottle from coat and takes a swig)* Look youngblood, have a little respect. I was the first black man to fly coast-to-coast first class. I owned fourteen cashmere sport coats and thirty Chinese servants. I had a bigger dressing room than Clark Gable. I played golf with General Eisenhower. But then I had a joke crisis. No matter how hard I'd try, the jokes wouldn't come. *(Takes another swig)* These hip comedians came on the scene, like Dick Gregory, and comics like me were discarded like old phonograph records. But now, my kind of humor is in again. People got tired of Gregory, Mort Sahl, and people like that who worried them and made them think. They wanted somebody like me. Somebody who would just entertain them. Somebody who wouldn't hassle them with a lot of social issues. I worked hard to get where I am. For twenty years, when I couldn't get into my makeup in the toilet and the people would get into fights—

JACKSON: Jesus. Don't you get sick of that story? I know I do. *(UNCLE SANFORD offers him a taste from a bottle of Wild Irish Rose)*

SANFORD: Have a swig. I bought it with the money I got from the blood bank.

JACKSON: Don't bother me with that. I have to get this lounge chair ready for the next show. I have to keep my head clear. The future doesn't belong to cloudy heads.

SANFORD: You don't drink no wine. You don't snort no coke. Man, what kind of blood are you?

JACKSON: *(Pauses. Then proudly)* A twenty-first century blood. Your generation had your chance and you blew it. Now it's our turn. We're going to build dynasties like the Kennedys and the Rockefellers.

SANFORD: Well if it weren't for the sacrifices we made *(takes a swig and makes an ugly face)* you wouldn't have had your chance. Malcolm X.

JACKSON: Malcolm X. Who is that?

SANFORD: That's what's wrong with you, youngblood. You don't read no history. I'll bet that you don't even read books.

JACKSON: I have a book right here. *(Holds up book)* "How to Survive The Crash of Ninety-Nine."

SANFORD: All you think about is money, youngblood. Don't you ever think about soul?

JACKSON: Soul. You can't buy no groceries or put a down payment on a house with soul. That's what's wrong with the black people of today. Too much soul. Too much love. Trying to be the nation's conscience. Fuck being the nation's conscience. It's time for us to start acting like, like Americans. Making money for ourselves and to hell with the next fellow *(UNCLE SANFORD shakes his head)* Yeah, Ms. Sheena *(sarcastically)* he's right here. It's for you. *(Hands the phone to SANFORD)*

SANFORD: What . . . that *is* good news. You can use me? Oh, Sheena, that's so kind of you to help out an old man like me. How can I ever make it up to you? Glory be.

(JACKSON *looks at him with disgust*) Yes. This will be the first step in my comeback. Before long, I'll be number one again. Hotdog. One thing, Ms. Sheena. How did you know that I was in the prop room? Security told you? But how did they know? A camera. *(Looks around)* But I don't see no camera. Okay, Ms. Sheena, I'll be right up. Oh, thank you, Ms. Sheena.

JACKSON: What are you so happy about?

SANFORD: Ms. Sheena says that they have a job for me. A walk-on. *The Savage Wilds Show.* I'm on the comeback trail. I just keep coming back. Here, she wants to talk to you. (JACKSON *snatches the phone from him.* SANFORD *exits hopping and skipping.* JACKSON *looks at him disgustedly*)

JACKSON: *(Sarcastically)* Yes, Ms. Sheena. What do you want? I'm preparing the lounge chair that you said you wanted. *(Pause)* Dummy bullets. How am I going to find dummy bullets this time of night? *(She hangs up hard. He holds the phone from his ear. Hangs up. Mimics)* That's my problem. Where the hell am I going to get dummy bullets? *(Thinks for a few seconds, then indicates to the audience that he's gotten a bright idea, snaps his fingers. Smiles)*

GREENBELT: How's that youngster of yours, Jackson? He must be ten years old about now.

JACKSON: *(Flattered and surprised)* He just turned ten, Mr. Greenbelt. What a great memory you have. (GREENBELT *presses two tickets into* JACKSON*'s hand. Examines tickets*) Two tickets to the World Series. Gee, thanks, Mr. Greenbelt.

GREENBELT: Don't mention it. You and your boy go out and have a good time on me, and you know, Jackson, I like your moves. You keep going and you might end up with your own show.

JACKSON: Thanks, Mr. Greenbelt. Wow! My own show. You know, Mr. Greenbelt, Dr. Marlin. . . .

MARLIN/GREENBELT: What is it Jackson?

JACKSON: I'm glad that you men are back in charge! *(He puts his arm around their shoulders. They all smile)*

Act II: Scene 1

(MATRON, *a stout black woman at her desk, talking on the phone. She wears a house dress, slippers, and a policeman's hat.* VANESSA *lying on a cot, sobbing softly.* SHEENA *is comforting her. They're wearing prison outfits, or dresses of the same drab color.*)

MATRON: They put up a little commotion when we brought them in here, Warden, but they have cooled down. We had to segregate them from the rest of the prison population. Uncle Sanford was popular around here. The white girl—she give me some lip. I had to bust her one. (SHEENA *pauses. Glares at* MATRON. MATRON *catches her eyes and glares back.* SHEENA *averts her eyes from* MATRON*'s and continues to comfort* VANESSA. MATRON *continues to glare)* They complaining about the prison food. Think that this is the Hilton. This ain't no damn hotel . . . the newspapers. They callin' up. But I told them what you said, Warden. They ain't allowed to give no interviews. They trial ain't gonna be nuthin' but a damned circus. Killing that po man because the people who watched the show was tired of them hunting animals. *(Glares at the two angrily)* Had him shot dead right on that wild game show, *Savage Wilds* just so's the ratings would go up and they could keep they producin' jobs. I don't know what's wrong with these wimmin of today. Cold-blooded if you ask me, Warden. Thank you, Warden. Okay, Warden. *(Hangs up. To audience)* Always want some excitement. Too much excitement in the world if you ask me. The way they tricked that po Uncle Sanford. The man was already down on his luck after he lost his show, *The Uncle Sanford Show* because he came in third in the ratings for one week. How was that man supposed to compete with the World Series that was on the other channel? Now these two ho's told him that he could get a little work on they show. The people they work for said that they show need some excitement. They wanted human meat. Now these two lyin' heifers told Uncle Sanford that he would be the game, and that they were going to use dummy bullets and that he should just play dead when he was captured. They put real bullets in there. They were so hard up for ratings and trying to keep their jobs.

Everybody in Harlem was at Uncle Sanford's funeral. There was so many flowers there, the people couldn't even get into church. There was all these black limousines from downtown. The rich white people were paying their respects. Well, these two *(pointing her head in the direction of* VANESSA *and* SHEENA*)* swore up and down that they didn't put real bullets in the gun, but don't nobody believe them. *(*VANESSA *begins to sob loudly)*

SHEENA: Will you cut that out? I'm trying to think. *(*MATRON *rises, stares at them contemptuously and exits)*

VANESSA: *(To* SHEENA, *delicately)* You should have seen the look on my mother's face at the arraignment. She was so ashamed. I wanted to make her so proud. Be somebody. Now I'm in jail for murder and it's all your fault. Poor Uncle Sanford. You and your big ideas. We might get life imprisonment.

SHEENA: We'll get out of this. They'll find out who did it.

*(*MATRON *comes in and sets down a tray. Beans on paper plates.* SHEENA *and* VANESSA *glare at her.)*

VANESSA: *(Pretentious)* Beans, again? I refuse to eat them *(haughtily)*. They give me flatulence.

MATRON: *(Puts her hands on her hips and momentarily stares at her)* Flatulence. Well, whatever this flatulence is, it's damned better than a bad case of the farts. *(*MATRON *laughs loudly.* SHEENA *and* VANESSA *look at her, disgustedly)*

SHEENA: Why can't we eat with the rest of the prisoners?

MATRON: It's for your own good. Uncle Sanford was real popular around here. Real popular. Every week when his show come on, all the girls would watch it. Why would you go and have him killed? Just to get to the top of the ratings? Did it for money, if you ask me. You some greedy nice whores if you ask me.

VANESSA: *(Pleading)* We're innocent. We didn't do it. We just wanted him to be shot with dummy bullets. Somebody put real ones in. Why doesn't anybody believe us? We were just trying to keep our jobs.

SHEENA: Who cares about Uncle Sanford? He used to come on the set with cocaine all over his face and . . . and you remember all of those paternity suits by those young women? Women who could have been his daughters? Just another dead pig. A womanizer and a drunk.

MATRON: You not going to last long around here talkin' that way, dearie.

SHEENA: *(Angry)* I'm not your dearie. *(The* MATRON *grabs her by the wrist and brings it behind her back.* VANESSA *jumps up, comes to* SHEENA's *defense; the* MATRON *knocks her down)*

MATRON: *(Releases her grip)* We all have to respect each other around here. That way there will be no confusion. *(*SHEENA *has a pained look, wrings her hand)*

*(*U.S. ATTORNEY RICHARD HEAD *enters. He and* SHEENA *have eye contact. She looks at him as if annoyed. He is a round white man. About forty. He is wearing a suit and striped tie. Cordovan shoes. Natty hat.* MATRON *stares at him angrily.)*

MATRON: Who let you in?

HEAD: *(To* MATRON*)* You can go. I want to be alone with the girls.

MATRON: I'm not goin' nowhere until you show me some ID.

(He flashes his badge).

HEAD: United States Attorney for the District of Columbia, Richard Head at your service. *(*MATRON *glares at him. Looks him up and down for a moment.* MATRON *exits mumbling)*

SHEENA: *(Rubs her shoulder)* She's got a grip like Mike Tyson.

VANESSA: What do you want?

HEAD: The black prop man confessed. He said that you daily humiliated him and that if it weren't for you he would have been the director of *Savage Wilds.* He blamed all of his problems on the women's movement.

VANESSA: That's a paranoid.

SHEENA: These black guys are always imagining that people are ganging up on them. Blaming everything on the system or the women's movement. What a bunch of crybabies. Always pretending to be the victim.

VANESSA: Does it mean that we're free to go?

HEAD: Yes.

VANESSA: We're free. I can't believe it. *(Jumps up and embraces* SHEENA*)* Oh Sheena, we're free. Let's go and order the biggest steak we can find. I hated this prison food. Let's go to the Plaza. Let's see *(Dreamy-eyed . . . recites slowly with relish)* I'll start off with a cocktail, then I want a steak, potatoes, green peas, salad with a Thousand Islands dressing, custard, and Cuban coffee—

SHEENA: Not a chance of our getting back on TV though. I'll have to declare chapter eleven.

VANESSA: *(Weakly)* Me, too.

HEAD: I'm in a position to get you back on the air. You can do something for your country as well. *(*VANESSA *looks puzzled)*

SHEENA: What do you mean?

HEAD: You've heard of the Mayor's problem? Mayor B. V. Dongson of Washington D.C. *(*VANESSA *looks shocked)*

SHEENA: Who hasn't? There's a guy who can't seem to keep his pecker in his pants. Boy, do I feel sorry for his wife. Smokes crack, too.

HEAD: We don't have any evidence. We've been trying to get the guy for ten years, with no success. That's where you come in.

VANESSA: What do you mean?

HEAD: We got the idea from your show. We're going to bag the son of a bitch. Stop his swagger.

SHEENA: Not me. I'm not gettin' mixed up in no murder.

VANESSA: Me neither.

HEAD: Who said anything about murder? *(Pause)*

SHEENA: What do you want us to do?

HEAD: We need you two to be lovebait.

VANESSA: Lovebait?

HEAD: You know, a honey trap. We want you to lure the guy into a compromising situation. We'll do the rest.

VANESSA: I'm not going to be your whore!

*(*SHEENA *nudges her)*

SHEENA: *(To* HEAD*)* Do you mind if we have a little confab?

HEAD: Go ahead.

SHEENA: *(They caucus)* Let's hear what he has to say, first.

VANESSA: I don't think it's right.

SHEENA: Since when have you gotten so high and mighty? I know all about how you used to entertain Mr. Greenbelt and his television executive friends at those broadcast conventions. (VANESSA *looks down. Embarrassed. To* HEAD) What do we get out of it?

HEAD: We're looking for someone to produce our new show: *The Founding Fathers.* All about the Contras, the freedom fighters who tried to bring democracy to Nicaragua.

SHEENA: I'm not participating in a show that glorifies male violence.

VANESSA: You tell him, Sheena.

HEAD: We're going to have the script written so that the leader of the Contras is a woman. If you like, we can change the title to *The Founding Mothers.*

SHEENA: A woman, I don't believe it.

HEAD: She'll be the commander. A white. Vanessa, you may be interested that her assistant will be a black woman, and she will have a love interest, even.

VANESSA: Oh, Sheena, this is a real opportunity.

SHEENA: How much?

HEAD: Double what you made on the last show.

SHEENA: (*Looks to* VANESSA *who nods her head wide-eyed*) You got a deal, pal. (*They shake hands*)

HEAD: I'm glad that you guys decided to come aboard. Especially you, Vanessa.

SHEENA: What does he mean? (VANESSA *looks as though a secret that she's kept is about to be revealed*)

HEAD: Tell her, Vanessa. Vanessa has been the Mayor's mistress for three years.

SHEENA: What?

VANESSA: It's not true, Sheena, don't believe him. (U.S. ATTORNEY *provides photos.* SHEENA *inspects them. Recoils*) He victimized me, Sheena, he made me do it. He asserted his male dominance over me. I didn't want to. I was unwilling, Sheena. I was duped. He . . . he . . . seduced me. He victimized me. You've heard of the Stockholm syndrome. He treated me like a slave on the plantation.

SHEENA: But in this picture, you're on the top.

HEAD: He was screwing your friends, too.

VANESSA: (*Suddenly, angry*) Let me see those pictures! (*Snatches the pictures with each one. Pauses on one*) Why that son of a bitch. He said that he only did that with me and his wife. Before I met him, I thought that Crisco was something that you cooked with.

SHEENA: You sure are a sucker for men. You'll never be a feminist. They mold you in their hands like putty. Don't you have any self-control?

VANESSA: *(To* HEAD*)* What do you want me to do? I'll do anything to get him. He can't treat me as if I were some kind of streetwalker.

SHEENA: That's the spirit, sister.

HEAD: Right on, Vanessa. Get your things together. We have to catch the shuttle to Washington, but not before I buy you two a dinner at the Plaza. *(*VANESSA *and* SHEENA *beam. They exit.* HEAD *has his arms around their shoulders)*

Act II: Scene 2

*(*U.S. ATTORNEY*'s makeshift secret office. A desk and a couple of chairs. Photo of Bush on the wall.* WHITE AGENT, *in shirtsleeves, loosened tie. Both* BLACK *and* WHITE AGENTS *are clean-cut all-American types. He's reading a skin flick magazine. Radio is on.)*

RADIO: This is Cookie Boggs, National Feminist Radio. People have just about had it with the black mayor of this town. Swaggering around Washington as though he owned the place. Giving his black buddies the high five and saying 'hey bro, hey man.' And things like that. And generally behaving like a coon with his genitals wrapped around his neck. Rumors of his cocaine-smoking persists, though U.S. Attorney Richard Head hasn't been able to get a grand jury to indict or uncover any evidence. Everybody knows that Mr. Head is bucking for Attorney General of the United States, but he'll not even be considered if he doesn't stop this big black buck from waving his fanny in his face. He must find some way to gain the respect of Washington's white people who are tired of the daily minstrel show that passes for government here in the nation's capitol, a black jungle. This is Cookie Boggs from National Feminist Radio.

*(*BLACK AGENT *enters)*

BLACK AGENT: Sure wish I could be transferred. What's wrong with this joker, Head? You've worked under him for three years.

WHITE AGENT: I don't know. The guy's into a fantasy number about the Mayor. It's obvious. He's been unable to get a grand jury indictment. He's losing face.

BLACK AGENT: He's losing ass, too. Why doesn't he get these generals and senators who be attending these freak parties?

WHITE AGENT: If you got everybody who was doing drugs and partying with drag queens, there'd be nobody to run the government. You heard about the President and that young girl who freaked out on acid?

BLACK AGENT: Then why are they doing the Mayor? I think they're racists. What about these guys in the Secret Service and the National Security Council who are doing coke? And what about the Coast Guard? They're supposed to be fighting drug smuggling and it turns out that they're not only doing coke, but taking bribes and telling the smugglers the best times to bring in their cargo.

WHITE AGENT: There you go with that racist shit, again. Seeing conspiracies that aren't there.

BLACK AGENT: Well, why do you think that Head is so antsy about this guy? Look at all these prescription drugs he's gulping down all day.

WHITE AGENT: Maybe he just wants to make the Mayor an example for the rest of them. The Mayor just happens to be black. Look what they did to Gary Hart and Senator Towers. They were white.

BLACK AGENT: Yeah, but that was the press who caught them. The government didn't have those guys under surveillance twenty-four hours a day. Cameras, bugs, and everything else. They even put a microphone on Mrs. Dongson's cat. The Mayor does something to this guy's innards and it's because he's black, that's why. *(Pause)* Any luck on the honey-trap bait?

WHITE AGENT: Nothing. I even tried one of those high-class call-girl agencies.

BLACK AGENT: Maybe we'll hire one of those sexual surrogates.

WHITE AGENT: What?

BLACK AGENT: Well, they're not exactly whores, Ralph. They help guys who can't, well, you know, perform.

WHITE AGENT: You sure that's legal?

BLACK AGENT: Since when have we been concerned about legalities? Besides if we get caught we can probably make more money than we're making now.

WHITE AGENT: Explain.

BLACK AGENT: Well, look at North. Haldeman. Erlichman. Nixon and Reagan. They made more money at breaking the law than at abiding by it. Lecture fees, books, TV appearances. *(They laugh. Pause)*

WHITE AGENT: Hey, I got the new Digital Underground rap.

BLACK AGENT: Oh, yeah? Where did you get it?

WHITE AGENT: Over at the FBI.

BLACK AGENT: What was it doing over there?

WHITE AGENT: I guess they're keeping an eye on these rappers. They say that this song encourages anarchy.

(WHITE AGENT puts a cassette in the tape recorder. HEAD enters. They don't see him. He stands there glaring at them. WHITE AGENT sees him and stops and tries to warn BLACK AGENT, who is dancing, by pointing at HEAD standing in the doorway. Finally, BLACK AGENT turns around and sees HEAD. He is embarrassed. He stands frozen. WHITE AGENT turns off the recorder.)

HEAD: I warned you guys about playing those rap records. I hate that shit. It brings on my migraines. *(Gulps down a pill)*

WHITE AGENT: Yessir.

HEAD: Barbaric ape people's music.

BLACK AGENT: *(Angry, but controlled)* What the fuck do you mean by that, sir?

HEAD: This stuff is eroding the moral fiber of our society. It's leading to illegitimate babies and crack smoking. *(Pause)* Where are those photos I asked you to get? (BLACK AGENT *removes photos from envelope.* HEAD *examines the photos. Says to himself)* Yellow toilet paper. Wonder what that means?

BLACK AGENT: *(Indignant, angry)* Sir, do I have to photograph the guy in the toilet? Suppose he discovers our stake out? Shouldn't we permit him to have at least some privacy? You got pictures of him and his wife in intimate positions.

HEAD: YOU DO WHAT I TELL YOU TO DO. THIS BUCK IS NOT GOING TO MAKE A FOOL OUT OF ME! *(Both the* WHITE AGENT *and the* BLACK AGENT *stare at him. He notices)* What are you two staring at? And you *(to* BLACK AGENT*)* . . . you sound like you're on his side. You know, I was against the department hiring your kind. You lack control. Objectivity.

BLACK AGENT: I don't like the guy, sir. But the Washington establishment is full of freaks. Why him?

HEAD: *(Weakly)* He's a poor role model. *(They both crack up.* HEAD *gives them a stern look. They stop)*

BLACK AGENT: A lot of people are saying you're on the guy because he's black. Forty million dollars just to get him on a misdemeanor charge. You could have built four neighborhood treatment centers for that kind of money.

HEAD: You're just like all of the other blacks. Seeing conspiracies and plots that don't exist. You're paranoid. *(Continues to study photos)*

WHITE AGENT: Sir, I wasn't able to find anybody cheap enough for the honey trap.

HEAD: I took care of it.

BLACK AGENT: Who are they, sir?

HEAD: Sheena and Vanessa from *The Savage Wilds Show.*

WHITE AGENT: But I thought they were in jail for the murder of Uncle Sanford? Man, that was my favorite show. *The Uncle Sanford Show.* Every Thursday night we'd send out for pizza and the whole family would sit around the tube and watch Uncle Sanford.

BLACK AGENT: Mine too. Those broads killed the man in order to boost the ratings for their wild ass game show. How low can you go?

HEAD: They're innocent, you idiots. The prop man did it. He replaced the dummy bullets with real ones. He had it in for the girls. Accused them of hindering his career. *(Shouts into the next room)* Girls! Come in here. I want to introduce you to the fellows. *(*VANESSA *and* SHEENA *enter. Introduced all around)*

HEAD: What do you say we get over to the hotel? The mobile unit has just informed me that the mayor has left his favorite topless place for home. *(They exit)*

Act II: Scene 3

(The living room of the MAYOR'*s house. The* MAYOR'*s* WIFE *is seated at the table with plates laid out and a candle burning. A bottle of moderately expensive wine is on the table. His* WIFE *is walking up and down, looking at her watch. A very attractive woman of about thirty-five. She is dressed as if she's going out on the town.)*

WIFE: Where is that fool? Two hours late. I've called all over town and to his limousine. No answer. What could be taking him so long? I'll bet he's drunk again. He comes home drunk and immediately wants to have sex. He makes love with that beeper on the night table. Gets up and rushes out of the house when it goes on. Hasn't eaten dinner here in four months. My father told me not to marry this fool. A graduate of Spellman like me. I could have done much better. Much better. All of the men who used to ask me out. One of them is now a member of the President's cabinet. Doctors, lawyers, educators. No, I was in love. Feel for his sweet talking jive. He used to be so tender. So loving. Those days when we were organizing for SNNC, defying the Klan. Registering voters in Mississippi. He was right there with Martin and Stokley. There was something pure and clean about being on the outside. Now we're on the inside. Big house. A long way from sleeping in tents and freedom marches. Children in private school. Mayor of the most powerful city in the West. The FBI and that nutty U.S. Attorney Richard Head are after him. All of these people saying that they've smoked crack with him. I hope it's not true. And even if it were, he wouldn't be the only politician in town who does coke. Why won't this Richard Head leave us alone? What is he after? That's all B. V. talks about. Richard Head. How he's outfoxing this fool. I know they're tapping the phone. God knows what else they're doing. I feel eyes watching me when I'm out on errands. Vultures' eyes. Waiting for me to drop. Vultures' eyes crawling up and down my spine. *(Shivers and holds her arms as though she has goose pimples)* Waiting for me to show any sign of weakness. Even when we're making love I feel as if I'm being spied upon. Still, he won't be cool. I know he has these women. He comes in with their musk all over him. Strands of hair all over his shirt. I can tell. Any woman can tell another woman's smell. They flirt with him in public. Right in front of me. He thinks they're enjoying him. They're screwing what he stands for. Power. There are people all over this town trying to get in bed with power. They even have these hideaways in the capitol where these politicians go and meet men or women, whatever their predilection. I know. I wasn't born yesterday. He says it's because of the pressures of the office. I'm tired of these black men who blame all of their failures on the system. On racism. I'm tired of politics. He told me to stick with him until after the next election and he'd enter the Betty Ford clinic. I'm not sure I can wait that long. Trying to put up a good front. Well, I'm tired of playing the loyal devoted wife and smiling before the camera when there ain't nothing funny. I don't know why I've stayed with him so long. I try to tell myself it's for the children. But when he looks at me with those dark snake eyes, and tells me those loving lies, I forget about my anger. And that walk of his. It's more of a dance than a walk. The man's walk could have been choreographed by Katherine Dunham. It's like enchantment what he does to me. Something comes over me. He turns me on and off as though I were a spigot. *(Pause)* It's our anniversary and he's late. Probably forgot. He should go to a clinic. Maybe a counselor. The children. They have to go to school. Take the ridicule of their classmates who call their father a crackhead. They get into fights with the other children. And the newspapers. And the talk shows. We had to chase away a TV crew the other night. They were using telephoto lenses to spy into the kitchen. (MAYOR *enters. Has a bobbing street walk*)

MAYOR: Hi, babe. *(Goes over and kisses her. She recoils from his affectionate gesture, folds her arms. Glares at him)*

WIFE: Don't give me that hi babe shit.

MAYOR: What's the matter, hon?

WIFE: This is our anniversary and you come stepping in here at two A.M. in the morning.

MAYOR: *(Slaps his hand against forehead)* Aw, damn, I knew that there was something I forgot. Look baby. I'll make it up to you. We'll go to Bermuda after I announce re-election. I was busy downtown, making the rounds. You know how I like to get out with the people. Go to the bars. Talks to my constituency. That way I keep on top of the pulse of the community.

WIFE: Keeping on top of your whores.

MAYOR: There you go getting paranoid again.

WIFE: *(Shows him a tiny cellophane bag)* B.V., I found this in the bathroom. B.V., this isn't one of those crack bags, is it?

MAYOR: *(Reaches for the bag innocently)* Let me see. *(He examines, continuing to feign innocence)*

WIFE: Look, if you don't respect me and respect yourself you could at least respect your children.

MAYOR: *(Innocent)* I don't know how it got there. *(She rises. Angry)*

WIFE: You don't know how it got there? You need some help. Everybody knows about it and even though they can't get a grand jury to indict you, they'll get you sooner or later. *(Sympathetic)* Why don't you go to a clinic? Get help?

MAYOR: Clinics are for sick people. I don't need any help. Can't nobody beat me. I'm invincible. I'm announcing for re-election next week. There's nobody in the polls who can touch me. You read too many newspapers. You know that the media and the white boys in the U.S. Attorneys office are against me. They hate a black man who . . . who dresses well. Talks good and is a great lover. I don't hear no complaints from you in the bedroom department. You was screaming so loud the other night that one of my bodyguards had to bust down the door. He thought that somebody was robbing us. *(Starts to mimic)* Let me have it. OOOOOooooo! Let me have it. Yes. Yesssssss! *(He laughs, nastily. She slaps him and hurries, crying from the room)*

   *(*MAYOR *puts his hand against his cheek. Pauses for a moment. Sits down and pours himself a glass of wine)* Just like a black woman. Try to get in the way of my career. If it wasn't for them, we'd be ruling the world. We'd be African kings, striding the world like Atlas. Heroes and champions. Golden, bronze and ebony gods. Hot damn. *(Laughs, then serious)* They're in cahoots with the white power structure to keep the brothers down. Always accusing me of drinking too much. Smoking crack. Hell, I can quit anytime I want. They can't catch me. They can't prove that I'm smoking crack. Richard Head. Ha. Ha. A simple, corny white boy. Can't get nothing on me. The newspapers. A white racist cabal. Trying to catch me because I'm so great. Hell, as long as I keep the fat cats downtown happy, they can't touch me. The members are crazy about me. Naming they babies after me. Everywhere I go they almost create a mob scene trying to shake my hand. To get a glimpse of me. And the women! Every woman in town is trying to get in bed with me, and the only regret I have is that I can't satisfy them all. How did that singer put it? *(Sings)* "I Got Ladies By the Dozen. And Money By the Ton." *(Phone rings. Picks it up. Grins)* Hey, baby, what is it? Look, I meant to visit you in jail but I figured you'd be out. I know you're ambitious, but I figured you weren't that ambitious to have a man murdered on television . . . a party to celebrate? Well alllrighgghghghgt. Just you and me and . . . oh yeah! The one who is on the show with you? I always did know that she was a freak. She got a nice behind. *(Puts on coat. Starts out. Yells off stage)* Hey, baby, I got to run downtown to take care of a little business. I'll be back in about an hour.

Act II: Scene 4

(Hotel Room. A crummy dive. VANESSA, SHEENA *are present.)*

HEAD: *(On phone. Offstage we hear the beginning of the* MRS. DONGSTON'*s monologue from scene 3, being replayed.* HEAD *hangs up)* Okay? The mobile unit says that the Mayor has left the house. Now let's have one more run through before he gets here. I'll play the Mayor. *(Referring to the tape of* MRS. DONGSON'*s, which is still running, he says)* Turn that thing off!!!

VANESSA: *(Tired)* Again?

SHEENA: I'm exhausted.

HEAD: You guys ready back there?

AGENTS: *(From offstage)* Ready. *(SHEENA goes into the other room. VANESSA sits on the couch. HEAD sits offstage. Bell rings. VANESSA answers. HEAD taking the role of MAYOR DONGSTON)*

VANESSA: Oh, Mr. Mayor. *(Enters room with her. Walks the way he thinks black men walk)* Come here, pretty mama. *(He turns her around and kisses her for a long time. Puts his hand on her behind. She knocks it away)* Baby we have plenty of time for that. Come, let's sit down for a minute. *(They sit down on a shabby dirty couch)*

HEAD: Where's your friend?

VANESSA: She's in the bedroom getting comfortable.

HEAD: I'm sorry I didn't visit you in jail. I missed you. Whenever I make love to my wife, I'd imagine that it was you.

VANESSA: *(Playing along)* That's so sweet of you, baby!

HEAD: You're more important to me than the stars. The moon. The sun and the mountains. You my love nourishment.

VANESSA: You talk so nice

HEAD: You know that these white boys are trying to bust me. They can't stand a black man being all fine, and . . . and invincible. I'm invincible. They can't stand a black man talkin' that talk. And walkin that walk. A noble and bold brother man. A super cool dude.

VANESSA: I got the new Digital Underground record. Would you like to hear?

HEAD: Oh, yes. Digital Underground are my main brother men. I love them dudes. *(She puts on the rap record. The ATTORNEY starts to dance. Awkward. Silly. Snapping his fingers)* Funky down! Funky down! *(SHEENA enters)*

SHEENA: Vanessa. So this is the foxy dude you been tellin' me about? Hey, baby. What's the happenins?

HEAD: I can dig it. Yes, indeed. I can dig it.

VANESSA: Mr. Mayor, this is Sheena. She's my partner.

HEAD: Yawl got some blow?

SHEENA: Do we have some blow? Come on into the bedroom. We got that. And we got some other things that you might want to indulge. *(Does a mock bump and grind. Winks)*

HEAD: Well alllriiiiiiiiiiiiiiiiiiiighghghghght. Okay! *(Changes to natural voice)* Now, at this point you all disappear into the bedroom and we make the snatch. Do anything you have to do to get him to smoke the crack pipe. *(Bell rings. HEAD, excited)* There he is now.

(Disappears into the other room where agents have set up video equipment. VANESSA, *smoothing her clothes, goes to the door.* MAYOR *enters.)*

VANESSA: Oh, your honor, how nice of you to come.

MAYOR: *(Walks in. Looks around, Grins)* It's been a long time, baby, we have lots of catching up to do. *(He tries to kiss her, she resists)*

VANESSA: We have plenty of time for that. Let me take your coat. Why don't you make yourself comfortable? *(She takes the coat into offstage. He rubs his hands together and looks around the apartment)*

MAYOR: How was your trip down from New York?

VANESSA: It seemed to take forever. I was so eager to see you.

MAYOR: I knew that you'd get off. The idea of you killing Uncle Sanford was absurd. I knew that they'd made some kind of mistake. *(VANESSA returns to the room. He tries to pull her toward him)*

VANESSA: Why don't I put on some music? How about some rap music?

MAYOR: I hate that shit. Put on something grown-up. Some Barry White. *(She puts on Barry White's "Ecstasy")*

VANESSA: Would you like something to drink?

MAYOR: Yes! Get me a Scotch. *(She goes over to the bar, and prepares a glass of Scotch. She brings the bottle and the glass to him. She puts them on a broken-down coffee table situated in the front of the couch. He drinks some. She sits on his lap. They kiss briefly)* You know I missed you, baby. Plenty of nights I'd be lonesome by the moon, longing for your warm embrace. Dying for a plunge between your gentle thighs. These other women—they mean nothing to me. My wife, she doesn't satisfy me the way you do. *(Pause)* She's an Episcopalian, you know. . . . Come here. I want to caress your voluptuous breasts and lay my head in your nurturing lap.

(SHEENA enters.)

VANESSA: This is my friend, Sheena.

MAYOR: *(Looks her up and down. Enthusiastic)* Are we going to have funnnnnnn tonight!

(Away from his vision, VANESSA glares at him, evilly.)

MAYOR: How are you, Ms. Queene? I'm a fan of yours. I used to watch that show of yours and Vanessa's every week. It was great. The way you had the host Dr. Marlin bitten by a Gabon viper so's to improve the ratings and the most daring hunt of all. The way you bagged Uncle Sanford. Of course, the way I look at it, he was a fool for volunteering for a stunt like that in the first place. You could say that he staged his own entrapment and was responsible for the tragic consequences. *(SHEENA and*

VANESSA *stare at each other. He doesn't see)* It almost worked except for the prop man having to go and put the real bullets in the gun. You know, some of the brothers are real reactionary when it comes to women. Anyway, Vanessa here tells me that you like to party?

SHEENA: I love to party, Mr. Mayor. But not with something as lame as Scotch.

MAYOR: What did you have in mind?

SHEENA: I have some glory nose. You know about that?

MAYOR: I'm willing to try anything.

VANESSA: Why don't we go into the bedroom. Make ourselves comfortable? *(They rise and go into the other room. Momentarily we hear voices from the bedroom)*

VANESSA: Mr. Mayor, slip into this. Relax. Lay back. *(Pause)*

SHEENA: What am I going to do with all that? *(Giggles. Laughter. Pause. Moans and little cries)*

VANESSA: *(Husky passionate voice)* I love it. Godddd . . . do I love it. Mayor let me put some more Crisco on.

MAYOR: Do me. Awww do me. Right there. Easy now. Right there. Go on, girl. *(Moans, sighs)* Damn, girl, what are you doing? Where did you learn that? Vanessa, your friend is a pure freak.

VANESSA: I told you she was.

SHEENA: Save some for me, don't hog it all. Andrew Dice Clay was right! It's as huge as an oak tree! *(Pause)*

MAYOR: Don't be selfish, Vanessa. There's enough to go around. *(Giggles; nasty laughter. Pause)*

SHEENA: This is so goooooodddddddd. Yummie. Are you trying to drive me out of my mind? No? Oh, God. No. Stop it. Stop. I mean. I mean keep going. Keep going. *(Moans and cries rise. Get louder. Then cease altogether. Pause)*

VANESSA: *(Weak, tired)* Let me have some more . . . *(Pause)*.

SHEENA: Naw. Let's light up first. You want some, Mr. Mayor?

MAYOR: Don't be so formal. Call me B.V. That's what my intimates call me. Listen I haven't done this before. You have to show me.

VANESSA: You're a liar. You've done it plenty of times. Do you hear that? Plenty.

SHEENA: *(Laughter)* You've got the thing upside down, Mr. Mayor. Let me show you how. *(Pause)* There. Now you've got it.

HEAD: *(Commotion begins. Screams)* Okay, Mayor admit that you have a problem. This is the end of your playing the cool dude. Read him his rights, guys. Get your pants on. *(Two* AGENTS *begin to read and continue to read)* Nice work, girls.

(Commotion tumbles out into the living room. The MAYOR *is struggling with the* AGENTS *and* HEAD. *He is naked from the waist up. No shoes.* HEAD *follows, rubbing his hands, gleefully. A triumphant fiendish look. The men sit him on the sofa.* WHITE AGENT *still reading him his rights. The* MAYOR *puts up a fight. Surrenders.)*

HEAD: Strip him! And I'll frisk him personally. He may be hiding something up his cavity. *(Both of the* AGENTS *are shocked. The two women nod and smile)*

WHITE AGENT: *(Shocked)* But . . . what? Are you out of your mind, sir?

BLACK AGENT: You're not going to strip nobody, Head. This is not some kind of street criminal. This is the Mayor of Washington. *(*HEAD *and* BLACK AGENT *glare at each other intensely for a moment)*

HEAD: *(Glaring at the* BLACK AGENT *who has deprived him of an attempt to probe the* MAYOR *rectally)* Okay, pad him down.

BLACK AGENT: *(Sadly)* Put your hands up against the wall, Mayor. *(He rises, the* BLACK AGENT *frisks him.* VANESSA *and* SHEENA *look to each other, smiling, obviously enjoying themselves)* Okay, Mayor. You can sit back down.

MAYOR: *(To* VANESSA*)* You set me up. You tricked me. You goddamn bitch. You. You dirty . . . you lowdown . . . why? *(He tries to get at* VANESSA *and has to be restrained. He shakes himself loose. Sits down on couch. The* AGENTS *go after him, but* HEAD *nods and they leave him alone. The* MAYOR *puts his head on his fists. He finally begins to laugh . . . a long sinister laugh. He laughs until he cries. The two* AGENTS *laugh, nervously.* HEAD *manages a weak smile. To* VANESSA*)* How much they pay you? Or did you do it on the cheap, as usual?

VANESSA: *(Screams)* You were screwing all of my girlfriends. I hope they give you the electric chair.

MAYOR: And you, Richard. One of your traps finally worked. Congratulations! I had you all wrong. I underestimated you. All of those winters your people spent in Europe taught you patience. Persistence.

HEAD: Why thank you, Mr. Mayor. And look, it may not turn out so bad. You can resign and seek treatment.

MAYOR: *(Angrily)* I ain't resigning from a motherfucking thing. And yeah, I'll probably get treatment, but who's going to treat you? *(Pause. They glare at each other like bucks pawing the ground before battle)* Who's going to treat the people you work for? *(He rises from the couch.* BLACK AGENT *drapes his coat over him. He glares at* BLACK AGENT. *Throws the coat on the floor)*

HEAD: What do you mean by that? I don't need any treatment.

MAYOR: I can clean myself up but how is a government that lies and sets up people with crack and whores going to clean itself?

SHEENA: Now wait a minute, buster.

VANESSA: What whores? I don't see no whores.

MAYOR: I can get rid of my stains, but how is your government going to get rid of its? One of the most powerful governments in the world reduced to pandering? *(Laughter).* Reminds me of the old African proverb. No matter how high the vulture flies it can't get rid of its stink. *(To* BLACK AGENT, *a look of disgust)* What kind of home are you? Sucker!

BLACK AGENT: *(Pauses before answering)* You made your bed, now you have to lie in it, Mayor. I'm sorry. *(The* MAYOR *looks to* VANESSA, *who stares back, defiantly, to the* AGENTS, *who lower their heads, and to* HEAD, *who manages a smirk. He straightens out his back. Holds his head high, musters considerable dignity)*

MAYOR: Yeah, well maybe I have been a bad husband. A substance abuser. A liar. And maybe even a dickhead. But who expects any more from a politician? There are politicians all over town who've done worse than I have done. Why do you think I'm the one they used the tricks on? Besides, all I did was smoke from a crack pipe. At least I'm not flying it in or bringing it in by ship, like your people are. I get set up while they go to college campuses on speaking tours. *(He laughs. The others in the room don't know what to make of this recital)*

HEAD: That's enough of our paranoid speeches, Mayor. *(To* AGENTS*)* Take him downtown.

MAYOR: Okay, let's go. *(*The two AGENTS *grab his elbows. He shakes them off. They look to* HEAD. *He nods. They permit the* MAYOR *to exit without holding his elbows. He exits, head high, walking his arrogant street walk.* VANESSA *and* SHEENA *follow the two* AGENTS *and the* MAYOR*)*

HEAD: *(*HEAD *sits down. A look of satisfaction and peace. He sits there for a moment)* I wonder whether I should supervise the urine test. Look over the Mayor's shoulder. See to it that the Mayor wee wees into the paper cup. Guess the boys will take care of it. But then the black agent may substitute the Mayor's sample. Switch cups so that the Mayor won't be trapped. Imagine him, standing in the way of the strip search. *(Eyes light up. Snaps his fingers as if to say "I got it")* The hair samples. I'd love that. Maybe I can be the one who clips off strands of his hair for the lab. *(Pause)* Naw. It'll be okay. Finally caught the son of a bitch. Tried to make a fool of me. *(Stretches and yawns)* Haven't been able to sleep for ten years. Gonna go home. Kick off my shoes. Watch some tapes of *My Little Margie*. That show always relaxes my nerves. Going to stay in bed for two weeks. *(Gulps down some pills. Rises)* How does he walk like that? *(Imitates* MAYOR*'s walk. Phone rings.)* Hello? *(Perks up, immediately. Stands to attention)* Why President Skippy . . . I . . . it's an honor. You cancelled your trip to the summit so's you could hear the outcome of the sting? Why, Mr. President . . . I didn't know it was that important. The highest priority, huh? The honey trap worked like clockwork, Mr. President . . . he was really mad, tried to harm that black gal, but she was cool. No, sir. You have complete plausible deniability. Nobody can trace it to you.

Mr. President? May I make a suggestion? I think, sir, that we ought to put the net on some of these black agents. The one we have told the Mayor that he was sorry. . . . These homes stick together. Yessir . . . Yessir . . . the Attorney General is resigning and you want me . . . Mr. President you can count on me! What's that, Mr. President? You want the bedsheets? Deliver them to the White House through the back entrance? But, Mr. President, I'm sure that the hotel has plenty of clean sheets if the White House wants to borrow them. You want the ones in this suite? But they were all laying on . . . whatever you say, Mr. President. And the video tapes. But we can edit them for you, Mr. President. The raw footage. Okay, what else, Mr. President? The Martin Luther King, Jr., sex tapes. No inconvenience, sir. We'll get them from the boys at the FBI. You're having a private party tonight. Coming right over, Mr. President. No, I won't tell anybody. Yesssir . . . yessir . . . good-bye sir . . . strange request. I guess the deficit must be pretty high. They can't afford to buy sheets for the White House . . . cities are going to look like *Planet of the Apes*. Degenerate apes. Not if I can help it. Those Martin Luther King, Jr., sex tapes are in real demand around town. Say that the old preacher had the stamina of a bull. Insiders say that LBJ listened to them so much he couldn't concentrate on anything else. That's why we lost the war in Vietnam. (SHEENA *enters. He rises. He tries to kiss her. She resists*)

HEAD: What the hell's wrong with you?

SHEENA: Why did it take so long to spring us?

HEAD: We had to persuade the prop man to confess. It took three days. He'll be in the prison hospital for a long time. He was pretty busted up when we finished with him.

SHEENA: And the Contras show? Why didn't you let me know? You took me by surprise. Why don't you talk to me sometimes? I'll bet you discuss things with your wife *(pouting)*.

HEAD: I haven't been home more than three weeks in the past ten years. This case has taken all of my time. You know that? Look, I don't feel like arguing. You know, I don't know what I see in you, that thing about opposites attracting. I mean here I am with you, a raving feminist. I hate feminists. Maybe people are right when they say that I should have my head examined. *(Pause)* Do you think that Vanessa knows about us? *(He sits down. Pours himself a drink from the bottle of Scotch that's been left behind)*

SHEENA: Not a thing. I put her in a cab and sent her home. She asked me why I wasn't coming. I told her that it was because it was a nice night and I wanted to walk. She had second thoughts about bagging the Mayor. I think that she's still in love with him. She's always falling in love with these pigs.

HEAD: You're attracted to her.

SHEENA: *(Pause. Longing look of desire)* She reminds me of a black woman I once knew. I had a nurturing experience with this woman.

HEAD: *(Pause. Stares at her puzzled)* You mean that you had a maid? *(She nods)* My folks had one too. She took care of us more than she took care of her own children. Good nigger.

SHEENA: I wish you wouldn't use that word. I'm telling you, Head. You're such a pig. I must be crazy to be with you.

HEAD: Look, I don't want to get into some political argument tonight. Besides, Eddie Murphy and Richard Pryor say it. Why can't I? Everybody's saying it nowadays. *(Pause)* You really got carried away there in the bedroom. *(She looks at him angrily)* You went way beyond instructions. Putting that nasty thing in your mouth like that! You didn't know where that thing had been last. Then you let him penetrate you. He was only supposed to do that with Vanessa.

SHEENA: I was just trying to do a convincing job. You know I'm a professional. I was giving it my all. *(He stares at her, nastily)*

HEAD: Did you enjoy it?

SHEENA: Enjoy it! With him!! I don't know about you, Dick. *(She thinks for a moment, then with nasty sarcastic laughter)* I have an idea. Why don't you get Dongson to get a divorce from his wife so's you can marry him? You're just like your old boss J. Edgar Hoover. You know what they said about him.

HEAD: *(Withdraws a gun. Points it at her)* What do you mean by that? TAKE THAT BACK. TAKE WHAT YOU SAID BACK, GODDAMMIT. *(Begins to cry)* Don't you ever say that about Mr. Hoover. Do you understand? Mr. J. Edgar Hoover. What did you mean by that?

SHEENA: *(Frightened)* Nothing, Dick. Just a joke, Dick. *(Keeps the gun pointed at her. Then slowly lowers it. Puts a hand to his head in a gesture of fatigue)*

HEAD: I'm sorry, Sheena. I got carried away. I been working ten years to put the guy away. I thought that I would be at peace once I trapped him. But his arrest merely raises more questions. Doubts. I hate doubts. These doubts are giving me insomnia. *(He puts his head in her lap and begins to sob. She comforts him and strokes his hair)* I mean we broke the guy and he still walked out with his head high. Did you see the way he walked, Sheena? Were you watching? Doesn't he have a cool walk?

SHEENA: *(Puzzled look)* Yeah, sure Dick. I saw the way he walked. Dick, speaking of divorce. You've been promising that you were going to divorce your wife for years now.

HEAD: *(Lifts his head from her lap and sits upright. Pours two more large glasses of Scotch.* SHEENA *glares at the glass and then at him)* Let's make a toast. *(His speech is slurred. He offers the glass to her)*

SHEENA: *(She refuses)* I wish you wouldn't.

HEAD: *(Gulps down the glass and starts on the one he has poured for her)* Don't worry, I can handle it.

SHEENA: That's what you always say. You know that stuff makes you crazy. I'm not gettin' in no car with you. You know how you drive when you're drinking.

HEAD: This stuff makes me relax.

RADIO: *(Hostile, sarcastic)* This is Cookie Boggs of National Feminist Radio. Well, the women of Washington D.C. can rest safe tonight in the knowledge that Mayor B. V. Dongson has been put into federal prison where he belongs. *(*HEAD *pours another glass.* SHEENA *gets up and angrily exits.* HEAD *looks at the door for a moment)* Just a few minutes ago, we received a bulletin that the Mayor was caught in the act of smoking a crack pipe. *(*HEAD *lifts the entire bottle to his lips and slowly begins to drink the remaining Scotch)* . . . in an elaborate sting that was set up by U.S. Attorney Richard Head. Apparently the Mayor was lured into the trap by Vanessa Bare and Sheena Queene, the former hosts of the wild game show *Savage Wilds*. Just a few days ago, the sisters were cleared of all charges in connection with the murder of comedian Uncle Sanford, another one of the brothers who had trouble keeping his britches up and his zipper zipped. Congratulations, my sisters! A prop man who worked on the show has been charged with the murder. Reached at the White House, a spokesperson said that the President had no comment on the arrest that followed years of rumors in Washington that the Mayor had smoked crack on many occasions. Predictably, a spokesman for the NAACP blamed it on what? You guessed right if you said a conspiracy against black elected officials. So what else is new? This has been a special report from Cookie Boggs, National Feminist Radio.

*(*HEAD *turns off the radio. Picks up bottle of Scotch. Starts to exit, imitating the* MAYOR'*s walk. Stops. Snaps his fingers)*

HEAD: *(Mumbling)* Forgot the sheets. *(Exits stage left. Momentarily returns with the sheets. Places them in a bag. Exits carrying the sheets imitating the* MAYOR'*s walk.)*

El Cabrón

El Reverendo Pedro Pietri

CHARACTERS

The Boss: *A small-time businessman in his late thirties who used to be Puerto Rican and became Italian to get ahead in life. He wears his business suit, white shirt, and tie twenty-four hours a day. He is of medium build, has no sense of humor, and is constantly suspecting his wife of being an infidel. He is the President-for-Life of MacMacho's Messenger Service. He believes in giving the handicapped a break. And, according to his own account about success, he attributes it to not letting anyone take him for a sucker.*

His Wife: *An attractive official housewife in her late twenties who used to be Puerto Rican and became Irish under instructions from her husband when they moved out of the ghetto and into a non-Spanish–speaking community. She isn't allowed to work full time or part-time. Her day is spent preparing her husband's meals and improving her personal appearance with Avon products and the latest fashions from commercial magazines.*

Messenger: *A blind bachelor in his mid-forties, honorable and dignified and determined to work for his living. Also of medium build and going bald. He has a sense of humor but doesn't know any good jokes. Because he is blind he doesn't know what nationality he is.*

Bartender:: *A roly-poly jolly gentleman in his mid-fifties. He's either Italian or Irish but definitely not Puerto Rican. He wears a short white tuxedo jacket, white shirt, black pants. His humor is his appearance. He's very polite and careful not to use profane language in front of ladies.*

Act I: Scene 1

(Dining room of the President-for-Life of MacMacho's Messenger Service. THE BOSS *and* HIS WIFE *are having breakfast, facing each other from opposite ends of a square-shaped table covered by a white tablecloth. There is a wedding cake on the table that has been cut into. Each has a plate with a piece of cake, coffee cup, napkin, and silverware. He reads a newspaper while sipping his coffee. She holds a mirror in front of her face with one hand and applies lipstick with the other. She is elegantly dressed. For the first thirty seconds they neither say anything nor look in each other's direction.)*

THE BOSS: *(Speaks without taking eyes off the newspaper in an irritable tone of voice)* Will you be quiet and say something, already! It's too early in the morning to be bored stiff!

HIS WIFE: *(Speaks without looking away from the mirror)* You ARE NOT going to like what I have to tell you. So, I'd rather remain silent and avoid a violent confrontation this early in the morning, sir.

THE BOSS: That's nothing new! I never like what you have to say, anyway. Exciting or anticlimactic. You know that! So, just be quiet and say something. How am I to become infuriated with you if you keep your mouth shut, huh?

HIS WIFE: *(Admiring herself in the mirror)* I am having an affair with another man. I have been seeing him for over one year now, and you know what? I think I am madly in love with him. . . . *(sighs)* He is the most gentle and most affectionate person I have ever met in my entire life.

THE BOSS: I still don't hear anything. What's wrong, did the cat eat your tongue while you slept last night?

HIS WIFE: Oh, he is so agreeable and compassionate and extremely romantic, that I fall to pieces in his presence, and he puts me back together with his marvelous method of embracing me in a very tender and very simplistic manner.

THE BOSS: You women are all alike. When we want you to be quiet, you can't seem to keep your mouth shut. But when we want you to say something, you suddenly become speechless. That's why I told you to be quiet in the first place, so you can say something! But it looks like it didn't work . . . *(turns page of the newspaper)*

HIS WIFE: *(Adjusting her hair, looking in hand mirror)* Not once have we argued or discussed the economy since the very first day he swept me off my feet and introduced me to someone inside of me that I had been totally unfamiliar with. Making love before and after we make love is all we ever have time for. Tomorrow doesn't exist when we kiss and caress each other until we become missing persons. Oh, what incredible perseverance this precious person possesses. He is definitely an endangered species.

THE BOSS: You can hear a pin drop in this room. Break a dish on the floor so we can have some excitement around here this morning.

HIS WIFE: Don't get the wrong impression, sir. It's not that I don't love you anymore, I still do. But it's strictly Plutonic, because as a husband, you are wonderful, but as a lover, you are deplorable.

THE BOSS: *(Shouts, still reading newspaper)* I can't start an argument with you if you don't say something, goddamn it!!

HIS WIFE: Please don't get jealous and upset and violent, sir. I have no intentions of leaving you for him. Or vice versa. And you can't say I am being unfaithful to you. Prior to this secret sensational affair I am so enthusiastically having, you and I had no physical contact for eighteen frustrating months. You were always too busy or too tired or too distracted to pay any emotional attention to me. You demoted me from a human being to a housewife. You became oblivious of my desires. All that seemed to matter to you were your ambitions and not my feelings. What was I supposed to do for love and affection?

THE BOSS: What happened to all those silly questions you used to ask me every morning, before and during and after breakfast? Remember how I used to have to throw my breakfast at you so you could keep your goddamn mouth shut and let me eat in peace? What's the matter, you got tired of fried eggs and bacon on your face and your clothes?

HIS WIFE: *(Still admiring her good looks)* So I had an affair with another man because you didn't give a damn about me. And I will continue to see him until you acknowledge that there is a person inside this body and brains inside this head of mine. I am sick and tired of being your maid and cook and child psychologist every time business declines at MacMacho's Messenger Service! Why do I just have to be your wife? Why can't I also be your business partner, sir? This No-Women-Allowed policy at MacMacho's is total bullshit!

THE BOSS: The hell with you! I'll start an argument with you even if you don't say anything to provoke it. Why is there no sugar in this coffee? You know I drink my coffee without sugar, you idiot!

HIS WIFE: It has been one whole fabulous year that I have been committing adultery, and I felt it was about time that you knew the truth. Don't get the wrong impression, sir. Under no circumstances am I being unfaithful to you. I still prepare and serve you all your meals. I still do your laundry and clean up after all the messes you make around here. So you really have no reason to be upset. My life is complete, I have a good husband and a terrific lover. Who can ask for more out of life?

THE BOSS: *(Puts down the newspaper, faces HIS WIFE)* What is his name?

HIS WIFE: *(Puts down the hand mirror, faces THE BOSS)* What is who's name?

THE BOSS: The man you are seeing behind my back!

HIS WIFE: *(Startled)* What? I'm not seeing anyone behind your back, Mac.

THE BOSS: *(Shouts)* Yes you are, you unfaithful bastard!

HIS WIFE: *(Shouts back at him)* No I'm not! Whatever gave you that crazy idea?

THE BOSS: This wedding cake you served me for breakfast! For the past six weeks you have been serving me wedding cake for breakfast. Why? I'll tell you why! Because you are having a secret love affair with another man! Otherwise we wouldn't be eating this sweet shit so early in the morning!

HIS WIFE: The reason we are having wedding cake for breakfast is because you kept complaining that you were sick and tired of ham and eggs and home fries for breakfast! The last time I served you that, you threw it at me in a fit of anger. That's why we are having something different now, sir!

(There is a quick blackout.)

THE BOSS: What the hell happened to the goddamn lights, now?

HIS WIFE: It looks like a fuse blew out.

THE BOSS: Well, just don't sit there. Replace it with a new one at once so I can see what I'm doing. I have to leave for work soon!

HIS WIFE: YES SIR! *(Is heard rising and leaving the dining room)*

Act I: Scene 2

(When the lights go back on, THE BOSS *is sitting behind his desk at MacMacho's Messenger Service reading the* New York Times *Help Wanted ads. Since this is a small minority business operation, there isn't much furniture in the office, aside from* THE BOSS'*s desk and telephone situated in the middle of the office. To the left of the desk there is a chair. To the right of the desk in between desk and right exit there is a life-sized eye chart. On the wall in back of the desk there's a neon sign that blinks on and off:* MACMACHO'S MESSENGER SERVICE*).*

THE BOSS: Hmmm, I don't seem to see the damn ad printed here. Let me call them up and find out what the hell happened. . . . *(puts down newspaper)* I paid for the ad in advance, it should have been printed. *(Picks up phone receiver, dials a number)* Hello, advertisement department please . . . *(waits)* . . . Hello? This is MacMacho's Messenger Service. I placed an ad in your classified section for a full-time messenger, and it doesn't seem to have been printed. M-A-C-M-A-C-H-O. Yes. Okay, I'll hold on . . . *(waits)* . . . it was printed? I have the Classified Section right in front of me and I don't see it printed here. Are you sure? Oh, wait a minute, I think I found it. The print is so small. How do you expect anyone who is looking for a job to find this ad? I paid fifty dollars for it! The least you can do is make it readable! Let me speak to your supervisor. Well, have him call me as soon as he comes in. I don't care if it's a she or a he, just have him call me as soon as he gets in. *(Hangs up the phone)* Bastards! You pay them modestly for a decent-sized ad, and they print one that you have to use a magnifying glass to locate. How the hell is someone supposed to answer this microscopic ad?

    (Keeps reading newspaper . . . yawns) Business is awfully slow around here this morning. *(Yawns again. The phone rings, puts down newspaper to answer the phone)* Hello? *(Shouts)* How many times have I told you not to call me up at this time? I'm up to my head in work! I don't have time to bullshit with you on the phone. There is too much work to be done here! If it isn't an emergency don't be calling up at this time, ever! Good riddance!!! *(Slams down the phone)* Getting married was the biggest mistake I ever committed in my life! Jesus! Can that damn woman be a nag. She wants to know if I got here okay. Of course I got here okay! *(Picks up newspaper to read)* I'm bored stiff. *(Puts down newspaper)* I'm going to have me some fun until business picks up. *(Picks up the phone, dials a number at random. Covers phone mouthpiece with a white handkerchief to disguise his voice He waits for his call to be answered)*

    Hi, baby . . . *(breathes heavily in a vulgar manner)* . . . never mind who this is, just pretend you have my big cock in your mouth and all my ten fingers up the crack of your asshole and my kneecap forcing its way into the tunnel of your juicy wet cunt. *(Makes sound as if in a sexual frenzy)* Don't hang up you dumb bitch, start masturbating, like you are supposed to do when you receive an obscene call! Squeeze your tits until the pain becomes so unbearable you fuckin' whore . . .

ahhh . . . ahh . . . lick my asshole . . . let me urinate into your mouth so you can vomit after swallowing my piss. Let me jerk off first and then dial 911 . . . ahh aah . . . I'll close my eyes and pretend to come all over your face . . . ahh . . . ahh . . . spread your buttocks so I can penetrate with my God-sized rod . . . let me taste your twat and spit on your face you dumb broad . . . ahhh . . . let me jerk off into your ears . . . ahh. . . .

(A slightly bald middle-aged man enters the office. He wears dark glasses and uses a walking cane, which he cautiously taps on the floor. His clothes indicate hardship. Upon noticing his presence, THE BOSS *hangs up the telephone. He starts at the man who is evidently blind. As he reaches the desk and continues walking)* May I help you, sir?

MESSENGER: *(Facing in the direction he heard the voice coming from)* Yes, I am answering your ad in the newspaper for full-time messenger work.

THE BOSS: *(Surprised)* You! Are answering my ad?

MESSENGER: Yes, sir.

THE BOSS: How did you find out about my ad?

MESSENGER: From the *New York Times'* Classified Section, sir.

THE BOSS: You! Read the *New York Times?*

MESSENGER: Yes, sir. It's more informative than the *Daily News* and the *New York Post* put together.

THE BOSS: *(Says to himself)* This guy thinks I was born yesterday. *(To* MESSENGER*)* Please have a seat, and we will SEE if you qualify for the position.

(He walks in the direction of the voice he hears, reaches the front of the desk, taps his walking cane against it.)

THE BOSS: The chair is to the left side of the desk.

MESSENGER: Thank you, sir. *(Finds chair with walking cane, sits down)*

THE BOSS: Tell me, what kind of work have you previously done for a living?

MESSENGER: I used to be a cab driver.

THE BOSS: How long ago was that?

MESSENGER: Up until last week.

THE BOSS: Did you resign or were you fired?

MESSENGER: I resigned, sir. I got bored driving a taxi. Plus, it was getting too dangerous. Cab drivers aren't safe anymore with the high unemployment rates in this city.

THE BOSS: What else have you done besides driving a cab?

MESSENGER: I was an usher in a movie theater for a few years.

THE BOSS: Have you ever been arrested?

MESSENGER: No, sir. I have a clean record. Not even a traffic ticket have I received.

THE BOSS: Do you have any physical defects?

MESSENGER: None whatsoever, sir. I am in perfect health.

THE BOSS: *(Makes an UP YOURS gesture with his middle finger in front of the* MESSENGER'*s face) (Speaking to himself)* This guy must really think I'm dumb. He's as blind as a bat and says he has no physical defects. I'll show him who the real idiot around here is. *(To* MESSENGER*)* Okay, everything seems to be in order. Before we can consider you for the position, the company requires that every applicant takes an eye examination. Good vision is necessary to be a good messenger. Oh yes, before you take the eye exam, there's one more question I want to ask you: Why do you wear dark glasses and use a walking cane to get around?

MESSENGER: In my spare time I am an amateur method actor. I'll be auditioning for the role of a blind man in a play next week, and this is the way I get into character beforehand. It's the Stanislavski technique of acting. You become the character instead of just portraying the character.

THE BOSS: Really? How interesting . . . *(again makes finger gesture directly in front of* MESSENGER'*s face)* . . . very interesting. *(To himself)* Yeah, tell me anything . . . *(to* MESSENGER*)* . . . okay, let's take the eye exam no . . . *(rises, walks over to the eye chart, turns it so it faces the* MESSENGER*)* . . . will you please rise and face the eye chart over here.

MESSENGER: Yes, sir. *(Rises, faces in the direction he hears voice coming from)*

THE BOSS: *(Using a yard stick)* Cover your left eye with your left hand and read out the letters I point to on the eye chart . . . *(begins eye exam)*

MESSENGER: I-A-M-A-V-E-R-Y-S-T-U-P-I-D-P-E-R-S-O-N.

THE BOSS: *(Surprised)* Well! I'll be damned, he passed the eye exam with a perfect score!!!

(There's a quick blackout.)

Act I: Scene 3

(Same as Scene 1. The lights go on. THE BOSS'*s* WIFE *reenters the dining room. He is sitting down reading his newspaper.)*

THE BOSS: It sure took you long enough to change that fuse. Did you sneak out to see him?

HIS WIFE: Oh stop talking nonsense! It was too dark to find anything right away.

THE BOSS: You could have used a goddamn flashlight!

HIS WIFE: I couldn't find no goddamn flashlight! Listen, I'm sick, tired, and fed up with your accusations! *(Picks up mirror from the table to admire herself in it)* You have no damn reason to be suspicious of me. I have never been unfaithful to you regardless of how much you have mistreated me. *(Sits, continues looking in mirror)* So stop talking like a lunatic and finish your breakfast so you can leave and get to work on time, sir!

THE BOSS: Sure, so I can get to work on time and you can get laid on time!

HIS WIFE: Christ! I thought that by serving you something different for breakfast you would appreciate me more. But it seems to have done just the exact opposite. You are overworked, sir. I seriously think you should take a vacation so you can calm down and get this wild fantasy of me committing adultery out of your head.

THE BOSS: Yeah. Take a vacation so you and that bum can have all the time in the world to screw around.

HIS WIFE: I don't mean by yourself, I mean together, you and I.

THE BOSS: What the hell have you done to deserve a vacation?

HIS WIFE: Taken a whole lot of shit from you lately, Carajo!

THE BOSS: Goddamn it woman! I told you not to be speaking Spanish in this house. The neighbors will hear you and know that I lied about you being Irish and me being Italian. It's true what they say. You can take someone out of the ghetto, but you can't take the ghetto out of someone. *(Looks at his wristwatch)* It's almost nine. . . . *(looks at his wife)* It's time to change the subject. This argument will continue when I return from work this evening.

HIS WIFE: *(Stops looking at mirror. Faces* THE BOSS*)* What will you like me to prepare you for your supper, sir?

THE BOSS: Cook something special. We are having a dinner guest tonight. I am inviting the Messenger at MacMacho's over to celebrate his first anniversary with the company.

HIS WIFE: It has been that long, already? *(Looks into mirror, again)*

THE BOSS: Time flies. *(Drinks from his coffee cup)* What a character that guy is. I remember the first day he walked into MacMacho's Messenger Service, blind as a bat, wearing dark glasses and using a walking cane to get around. He tried to fool me into believing he had perfect vision. Imagine trying to fool me, of all people? I have to admit, he was quite clever. Would've fooled anyone but me. So determined was he to work that he passed the eye exam by guessing every one of the letters I pointed to on the eye chart. It surprised the hell out of me, but it sure didn't fool me any. What a wild imagination that blind man has. He told me he had been a taxi driver and a movie usher. Poor slob, every time I stuck my finger in his face, like this *(indicates)* he didn't notice. *(Drinks more coffee)* The wildest thing he told me was that the reason he wears dark glasses and uses a walking cane was because he is an amateur method actor preparing for the role of a blind man in an upcoming audition. *(Starts laughing)* . . . A blind cab driver . . . *(laughs louder)* . . . how will he know when to stop for a passenger or to stop, period, for a traffic light or for someone crossing against the light . . . *(hysterical)* . . . imagine being escorted to your seat in a movie theater by someone who can't see where your seat or anyone else's seat is . . . *(all of a sudden gets dead serious)* . . . how come you aren't laughing along with me? Don't you think any of this is funny?

HIS WIFE: *(Puts mirror down)* No! Being blind isn't funny, it's pathetic. It's beyond me how you can laugh at something as serious as being blind. . . . *(picks up the hand mirror)*

THE BOSS: You don't have a sense of humor. Never did and never will. Anyway, let me finish the story so I can get to work and come back to continue arguing with you later on this evening: The time had come to let it be known who the real fool was. I deliberately gave him a manila envelop with no address on it and told him to deliver it to the address indicated on the envelope. Wasn't that clever of me? *(Laughs again)* Boy, did I sure fool him. I would've loved to have seen the look on his face when he approached someone with twenty-twenty vision to have the address on the envelope read to him and . . . *(laughs louder)* . . . the person tells him there is no address written on the envelope. *(Almost falls off the chair laughing)* He finally returned a half hour later and confessed to me that he was one hundred percent blind. I was really impressed with his determination to function as a normal person. So I hired him. And he has turned out to be one of the best messengers at MacMacho's Messenger Service in terms of efficiency and punctuality. He has a remarkable memory. All I have to do is read the address of the delivery once and he gets the message across promptly and correctly. We have become the very best of friends in the year he has been working for me. *(Thinks to himself)* I wonder who referred him to MacMacho's?

HIS WIFE: It's getting late, sir. You should finish your breakfast and leave soon.

THE BOSS: Can't wait to get screwed behind my back, huh?

HIS WIFE: I'm just concerned that you will get to work late.

THE BOSS: So what if I get to work late! I'm the boss, no one can reprimand me! And take your goddamn eyes off that goddamn mirror when I speak to you, goddamn it! You can't wait until I'm gone to beautify yourself for your goddamn boyfriend?! You have to do it in front of my goddamn face, you slut? The least you can do is try to be discreet! But no, you are too dumb to be anything but obvious. Get your ass up and bring me my attaché case! And put a pillow case over your head so I won't have to see your face again this morning! Hurry up! Move! Before I get indigestion looking at you!

HIS WIFE: *(Rises)* Yes sir! *(Salutes him, leaves the dining room)*

THE BOSS: Imbecile! I'll get even with her for being unfaithful. Nobody double-crosses a MacMacho and gets away with it! As soon as business picks up OUT she goes!

HIS WIFE: *(Reenters with his attaché case)* Here you are, darling . . . *(hands it to him)*.

THE BOSS: *(Angrily takes attaché case from her)* How many times do I have to tell you that you are supposed to address me as "sir" at all times! Not Darling or Sweetheart or Angel or Pussy Cat or Flash Gordon! "Sir!" Understand? Sir! Sir! Sir! Sir! Sir! Sir! Sir! Sir!

HIS WIFE: Yes Sir! Yes Sir! Yes Sir! *(Lights begin to dim)* Yes Sir! Yes Sir! Yes Sir! Yes Sir! Yes Sir! Yes Sir! Yes Sir! Yes Sir!

(Room is completely dark. Her voice is heard in a whisper, repeating: "Yes Sir!" until it completely fades.)

Act I: Scene 4

(Same as Scene 2. When the lights go on THE BOSS is seen nervously pacing the floor of the office, talking to himself).

THE BOSS: That woman has to be crazy to do something as dumb and as stupid and idiotic and ignorant and insignificant as committing adultery on the President-for-Life of such a prestigious Messenger Service. It doesn't make any goddamn sense! I could see if she were married to some poor slob earning minimum wages—then she has every right to commit adultery! And God will probably forgive her for it. But that isn't the case here. She has never had it so good in her entire life, the ungrateful bitch! I rescued her from a fate worse than death in the ghetto, and this is how she shows her gratitude? If she hadn't met me she would have ended up as a prostitute and a drug addict. She had no future until she met me. I was the light at the end of the tunnel of her existence, because that's what that neighborhood was—a tunnel! I know. I was raised up around there among the rats and roaches and addicts and winos and pregnant garbage cans! Everyday somebody got robbed or murdered . . . *(pause)* . . . I'LL KILL HER FOR BEING UNFAITHFUL TO ME!!!

(The MESSENGER enters. THE BOSS continues talking and pacing the floor, unaware of the MESSENGER's presence. The MESSENGER cautiously walks over to THE BOSS's desk, taps his cane against it and sits down on top of the desk; his feet touch the floor.)

I should have left her in the ghetto and shared my success with someone as equally successful. But no, I had to go getting involved with someone from my old neighborhood and look how miserable it has made me? *(Pause)* Okay, I'll admit, we might not live in a mansion or have a full-time doorman, but at least they don't sell loose joints on the streets around our neighborhood and the elevator is rarely out of order. We are the only family with a Spanish name in the building. Doesn't that mean anything to her? I wonder how many of the neighbors have seen her lover entering and leaving my apartment—THE FUCKIN' SLUT!!! She won't get away with it. I'll send her back to that slum she comes from. Then she'll be sorry she was unfaithful to me. But it will be too late because I am not taking her back! I don't care how much she begs and pleads with me. My mother never approved of her in the first place. I should have listened to her, may she rest in peace. *(Makes the sign of the cross. Stops pacing, faces his desk, sees the MESSENGER sitting on top of it)* What the hell are you doing sitting on top of my desk? You know that is against company policy! Get your ass off my desk right this minute and sit on a chair like you are supposed to do when you are tired of standing up! What the hell is wrong with you? Don't you know that only the boss can sit on the boss's desk? *(MESSENGER gets off the desk and sits on the chair)* Stand up when I am reprimanding you! You have no right to make yourself comfortable when your boss is pissed off!!! Now, I'm warning you, boy, if you don't polish up your act around this office, you are going to find yourself back on the street corners beggin' the general public for spare change. Nobody will hire you if I fire you. Employers don't give a crap about the handicapped. I am an exception, but don't take me for granted because I can be as merciless as the rest of them in the business world. Understand that, boy?

MESSENGER: Yes, Mr. President. It won't happen again.

THE BOSS: It better not or you are going to regret it, and that is a promise not a threat! Is that clear, boy?

MESSENGER: Yes, Mr. President.

THE BOSS: Okay, now that we understand each other, let's get to work. The first thing I want you to do this morning is to pace the floor with me. I have something very important I want to discuss with you. Forward, march! *(BOSS and MESSENGER begin to pace the floor)* . . . and try not to tap your cane so loud on the floor, it makes me nervous.

MESSENGER: Yes, Mr. President.

THE BOSS: Before we begin this very important discussion, I want you to know that regardless of how many times I raise my voice at you on the job and absentmindedly call you boy, that I don't mean anything personal. Because we are running a business and not a social club here, arguments are unavoidable. *(Stops pacing)* You understand that?

MESSENGER: Yes, Mr. President.

THE BOSS: Personally, I consider you a real friend, not just another employee, okay? Let's continue pacing because what I have to discuss with you cannot be done standing still. *(They continue pacing)* I feel I can trust you. In the year you have been employed for me you have proven yourself to be an exceptionally honorable human being. I have all the confidence in the world that what I am about to discuss with you will not leave this office, because being the honorable person that you are means that you have the highest value for our friendship AND your job *(stops pacing)*. Am I right about that?

MESSENGER: Yes, Mr. President.

THE BOSS: To make a long story short, let's continue pacing some more. *(They continue pacing)* Have you ever been married?

MESSENGER: No, Mr. President. I'm a free spirit. I like to have many affairs and not just be confined to one person.

THE BOSS: You???

MESSENGER: Yes. My handicap doesn't interfere with my rap.

THE BOSS: I know you aren't going to believe what I'm about to tell you because of my intriguing position, but, life is unpredictable. Disappointment. Humiliation. Degradation. No discrimination against no-one . . . *(stops pacing)*. Not even your Boss! *(Resumes pacing)* Everyone, regardless of occupation can, through no fault of their own, be made a fool out of . . . *(stops pacing, faces* MESSENGER*)* My wife is cheating on me!

MESSENGER: What? I don't believe it.

THE BOSS: Neither do I, but it is true. AND I SWEAR TO YOU I'LL KILL THAT BITCH FOR CHEATING ON THE PRESIDENT-FOR-LIFE OF A PRESTIGIOUS MESSENGER SERVICE! SHE WON'T GET AWAY WITH IT!

MESSENGER: Calm down, Mr. President! You could be wrong about this whole thing.

THE BOSS: I wish I were, but I'm not.

MESSENGER: Have you apprehended her, Mr. President?

THE BOSS: No, she has apprehended herself. *(Resumes pacing)* For the past six weeks she has been serving me wedding cake for breakfast!!! And she doesn't stop combing her hair and applying makeup to her face whenever she isn't serving me my meals or cleaning up after me. How obvious can one get?

MESSENGER: Mr. President, I think you are running away with your imagination. Whenever women aren't busy doing housework they are busy combing their hair and putting on makeup.

THE BOSS: I'm well aware of that. But what about the wedding cake for breakfast? That isn't normal behavior. That indicates and implicates she fornicates behind my back!

MESSENGER: Maybe she has a sweet tooth all of a sudden. Or she could be pregnant. Women have unusual cravings when they are pregnant.

THE BOSS: *(Stops pacing)* If she is, then she has definitely been cheating because we haven't had sex in eighteen months.

MESSENGER: That explains the wedding cake. She wants you to become her husband again.

THE BOSS: I have thought about that, but I have thought about adultery much more. *(Resumes pacing)* There is no doubt in my mind she's unfaithful, or else why doesn't she argue with me anymore? How come I can shout at her all I want to and just get a dumb smile from her in return? She used to duck when I used to throw my breakfast at her for cracking the yolk, and now she doesn't blink an eyelid when I throw it at her face. The more I disrespect her and disagree with her, the more content she seems to be with me. I'll give you an example: Last Thursday just to provoke an argument with her I insisted it was Tuesday and she, well knowing that it wasn't Tuesday but really Thursday, agreed with me wholeheartedly. *(Stops pacing)* I can rant and rave and overturn the furniture and break all the dishes and windows in the house and still won't get any lip from her. Three weeks ago I went to get a six-pack of beer and returned three days later ready to tell her to mind her own business when she asked me where I had been. But all she wanted to know was if I was hungry so she could serve me something to eat. I'll tell you why she wasn't concerned that I hadn't been back for over seventy-two hours. Because while I was away, she was getting laid by that bum she screws with behind my back!

MESSENGER: Why don't you try being nice to her and see what happens, Mr. President. She will probably treat you twice as nice as she does when you are being mean to her.

THE BOSS: *(Puts his arm on the* MESSENGER's *shoulder)* You are truly a real friend. I present you all the convincing evidence and you still refuse to believe that your boss's wife is cheating on him because of the respect and gratitude you unselfishly have for me. You are really quite a guy. That is why I confided in you in the first place.

MESSENGER: I'm honored that you think so highly of me, Mr. President.

THE BOSS: I'm sure you are. Now that I poured my heart out to you, old buddy, there is a favor that I want you to do for me that concerns this predicament I find myself in.

MESSENGER: You can count on me for anything, Mr. President. That's what friends are for. To give each other unlimited moral support. You just let me know what you want me to do for you, and it will be done without any reservations or hesitation.

THE BOSS: Thanks, pal. I knew I could depend on you. Let's sit down in our designated chairs, and I'll explain to you what the nature of the favor I want you to do for me is. *(The two men sit down)* I know for a fact the man she is screwing behind my back comes around when I'm at work. I have thought about busting in on them, but I know I'll lose my self-control and kill them both. I think it will be a better idea if you were to go there instead.

MESSENGER: Me??? But I can't see anything.

THE BOSS: True. But you can sense the presence of a person or persons inside a room and distinguish how many men or women are present in the room. Blind people are gifted in that. I know, I read about it in business school. The reason for this plan is so that you can testify on my behalf in the divorce trial, and she won't be granted any alimony from me when the divorce is finalized.

MESSENGER: But why will she let me into her apartment in the first place? We don't know each other.

THE BOSS: What you do is ask for a fictitious tenant and when she informs you that you have the wrong apartment, you ask her to please let you use the toilet, and because you are blind she won't refuse your request and her lover won't run and hide in the closet. She will probably introduce you to him as her husband.

MESSENGER: I don't think that will work. Though your wife and I have never met before, she does know you have a blind messenger working for you and will get suspicious, Mr. President.

THE BOSS: I have all that figured out, pal. You will wear a disguise so she won't recognize you.

MESSENGER: A disguise? That won't conceal the fact that I'm blind.

THE BOSS: The disguise that I have in mind will eliminate any suspicion that might otherwise be aroused. You will go there disguised as a blind woman instead of a blind man.

MESSENGER: WHAT?

THE BOSS: You will put on a wig, a dress, high heel shoes, and heavy makeup on your face, especially the lipstick, and paint your nails red and use a lot of perfume. She won't notice the difference. She isn't too bright.

MESSENGER: *(Upset)* Mr. President, that is definitely out of the question. I will do any favor for you except that. Dressing in drag is against my principles.

THE BOSS: I have done many favors for you. No messenger service or any other type of business will hire a blind man. And furthermore, you won't be able to see what you look like, so it shouldn't bother you any.

MESSENGER: Mr. President I am grateful for everything you have done for me, but I am a blind heterosexual and not for one single second will I be caught dead in women's clothing, regardless of the fact that I can't see what I look like.

THE BOSS: Look at it this way, you are doing a favor for your best friend who also happens to be your employer. I know you are straight, and you know you are straight, right? Now, take for example these police decoys who dress up as broads to apprehend purse snatchers and rapists. They aren't fags, they are just doing their jobs. It's as simple as that.

MESSENGER: I am not a cop, I am a messenger.

THE BOSS: You won't be a messenger for long if you don't do me this favor.

MESSENGER: I'd rather be unemployed than to dress in drag, Mr. President. Though I can't see myself, I have to live with myself, and knowing that I wore lipstick and a dress will ruin me psychologically. I'll never be able to think straight again.

THE BOSS: You will only be dressed like that for thirty minutes. It might not even take that long. Nobody will see you. You'll get dressed here, we'll take a cab to my house, and I'll wait in the cab until you return. Then we come back here and that's that! Nobody will know anything.

MESSENGER: It still isn't going to work. Dressing like a woman isn't going to make me talk like a woman. The minute I open my mouth to say something she will get suspicious and not let me enter.

THE BOSS: Any man can speak like a woman if he really wants to, and you should really want to if you want to keep your job.

MESSENGER: If that's true then why don't you dress like a woman and apprehend her yourself, incognito.

THE BOSS: I already told you. I'll lose my self-control and kill them both if I apprehend them myself. Then you will surely be out of a job. Furthermore, I'm too tall and too masculine to look like a woman regardless of how much makeup I apply.

MESSENGER: Have you ever cheated on your wife, Mr. President?

THE BOSS: Of course. She has no business doing likewise.

MESSENGER: Isn't there another way you can go about apprehending her? Why don't you hire a private detective?

THE BOSS: They are too expensive and unreliable. *(Rises)* Now, boy, either you do me this favor or forget about working here! Messengers come a dime a dozen, especially with twenty-twenty vision.

MESSENGER: You say that nobody will find out? But what about when I have to testify at the divorce trial, and your wife swears she never saw me before? Then the truth will have to be known if you are to win the divorce case.

THE BOSS: Nobody that you know will be in court. We do come from totally different neighborhoods. I am an upper-class citizen, and you are a member of the less-advantaged class. So you really have absolutely nothing to worry about.

MESSENGER: *(Rises)* I would like to take a walk and think about it. I really can't afford to lose this job, and I know that if you fire me, nobody else will hire me . . . but man, Mr. President, dressing in drag is not only against my principles, it's also against my religion.

THE BOSS: God will understand you are doing a favor for a friend and forgive you. He knows you are straight. . . . *(rises)* Now you go take that walk and keep telling yourself that you are straight, and hopefully you will have changed your mind about doing me this favor when you return. If not, don't bother coming back.

MESSENGER: Why don't you find a real faggot to do this for you?

THE BOSS: It has to be a straight person and a personal friend for the testimony to be valid in court.

MESSENGER: *(Dejected)* I'll be back with my decision in about half an hour . . . *(starts walking out of the office)*

THE BOSS: Cheer up, pal. It will be over before you know it. *(Sits back down behind his desk.* MESSENGER *is out of the office.* THE BOSS *picks up newspaper to read. Blackout)*

Act I: Scene 5

*(*THE BOSS's WIFE *sits on a chair facing a round mirror mounted on a bureau. She brushes her hair while admiring herself in the mirror. On the desk of the bureau her makeup is spread about. A princess telephone is nearby.)*

HIS WIFE:
That husband of mine
Has to be blind
Not to see how fine
And beautiful I am.
He doesn't give a damn
About anything except his work.
Oh that man is a real jerk
Not to find me interesting.
He is always protesting
About everything I do,
We no longer even screw,
He is always too tired
To fulfill my desires
When he comes home from work.
Oh that man is a real jerk
Not to find me exciting
With a body so inviting
And a very attractive face
Full of life and grace
Admired at every place
This fine woman appears.
Compliments are always near
One has to be totally blind
Not to see how fine
Is this anatomy of mine.
Everyone else but he
Wants to have sex with me.
He doesn't treat me nice
Because I am his wife,
The only way he will care
Is if I have an affair
Behind his tired back,
He will then surely crack
And become a person again

And treat me like his friend
Instead of a maid
Who never gets laid
And cooks all his meals.
Oh darling let's make a deal
So you won't work so hard
I'll get myself a job.
Over my dead body he shouts!
He doesn't want me out
Of this household alone
Nor to use the telephone
Unless I'm calling him up
To say his coffee cup
Will be ready for him
When he comes storming in
Complaining about everything
After a hard day at work
Oh that man is a real jerk
Not to find me appealing
And ignore my feelings.
Look at how sexy I am
That fool should give a damn
And start making a pass
At these tits and this ass
That look so very fine
On this body of mine.
I thank the Lord every day
That I was born this way.
My husband is so dumb
He never made me come
But someone else did!
But someone else did!
Something that he forbids.
But that is his tough luck
For not wanting to fuck
Trying so hard to make bucks!

(The telephone is heard ringing. She picks up the receiver still facing the mirror, admiringly.)

Hello . . . *(Heavy vulgar breathing is heard on the other line)* Oh it's you again, the guy who wants me to pretend I have his cock in my mouth and all the ten fingers of his hands inside the crack of my asshole and his kneecap forcing it's way into the hairy entrance of my juicy wet cunt. Oh come on now, adolescence can be more imaginative than that. You sound as if you didn't go beyond the third grade in elementary school. Oh, go urinate in your mother's mouth. She understands your problem better than anyone else, you despicable inarticulate degenerate. *(Hangs up)* That creep calls up every day with the same uninteresting vulgarity. Of all the numbers in the telephone directory, and mine had to be the lucky one. *(Looks at her wristwatch)* Oh my God! My lover should be here any minute and I'm still not properly beautified to meet him. *(Applies lipstick, brushes her hair when she is through)* I am so lucky to have a hardworking husband and a terrific lover. Whatever my husband cannot fulfill emotionally my lover provides. And whatever my lover cannot give me financially my husband provides. Oh! Who could ask for more out of life? *(Applies mascara to her eyes)* If I were just to have a hardworking husband and not a terrific lover on the side, I doubt if I would stay married. Life would be too dull to endure. You can't persist on love alone. Sex is absolutely necessary—with or without your husband—if your marriage is to succeed. *(She brushes her hair)* There is so much romance in my lover's imagination that just thinking about him sends chills up and down my spine. Oh can that guy articulate his compliments with such profound authenticity. Jesus, why can't my husband be that romantic instead of being that successful and uninteresting? Money is wonderful, but so is compassion. I think I look lovely enough to receive him should he knock on my door right now. *(Sighs)* Oh, I'm so lucky. I'm so very, very lucky. *(Loud knocking is heard)* He's here! Oh my dear, I think I'm going to have a heart attack. Let me get hold of myself. He doesn't like me to panic, even if it's induced by him. I'm coming. I'm coming . . . *(rises)* I'm coming. . . .

(Blackout. When the lights go on THE BOSS *is seen masturbating behind his desk while speaking on the telephone. He is about to reach a climax.)*

THE BOSS: I'm coming . . . I'm coming . . . ohhhhhh . . . ahhhhh . . . I'm coming . . . oh . . . oh . . . ohhhhhhhhh . . . oooooo . . . oh baby . . . oh . . . ahhhh . . . oh baby . . . oh . . . babbbbeeeeee . . . I wish my cock was really in your mouth and my kneecap literally entering the hairy entrance of your juicy wet . . .

(Blackout. Return to Scene 5.)

HIS WIFE: *(Standing near the chair facing the mirror)* Come on in, the door is open. I knew you would be coming so I didn't bother to lock it. I'm in my bedroom beautifying myself for your presence. Come directly over, you won't be disappointed . . . *(waits with open arms for him to enter)*

(The blind MESSENGER *enters, cautiously tapping his cane on the floor.)*

HIS WIFE: Oh, my love. I thought you would never get here. *(Goes to embrace him)* Oh, I'm so overjoyed to see you . . . *(kisses him)*

MESSENGER: *(Coldly)* Your husband suspects something.

HIS WIFE: That's nothing to worry about. He has been suspecting something even before there was anything for him to suspect. *(Continues showering him with kisses)*

MESSENGER: I have to sit down. I don't feel too well.

HIS WIFE: Sure, my love. Sit down and relax, you'll feel better in no time at all. *(Helps him sit down on the chair facing the mirror)* Here, let me take your nice little walking cane from you and put it in a safe place, darling. *(Kisses his forehead)*

MESSENGER: That won't be necessary. I won't be staying long.

HIS WIFE: You look really upset. What is wrong, my lovey dovey? Does he suspect you?

MESSENGER: No, he doesn't suspect me. He's too vain to think that his wife would cheat on him with a blind man.

HIS WIFE: So then, what is this problem that seems to be bothering you so much, my love?

MESSENGER: Your husband wants me to dress up like some blind broad to inconspicuously apprehend you and the person he thinks you are screwing behind my, I mean, his back.

HIS WIFE: That is no serious problem, darling.

MESSENGER: Yes it is! I'll be damned if I'm gonna become a faggot for thirty minutes or thirty seconds to keep a job! No position is worth becoming a queer for. I'd rather beg for a living before I put on lipstick and wear a miniskirt. He can shove his goddamn job up his ass, but definitely not up mine. I'm a blind man not a blind faggot! That husband of yours is a dumb motherfucker if he thinks that I need a job that bad. I have been a man all my life, and I'm not going to stop being one now, regardless of what is at stake!

HIS WIFE: You don't really have to dress up like a woman. You can just tell him that you did and that you came up here and didn't find anyone up here with me. Furthermore, he knows you are blind and won't be able to catch anyone up here anyway, right?

MESSENGER: Wrong! He knows blind people can sense someone's presence without that person having to say anything or even move. And to make matters worse, he wants me to put the drag on in his office and then take a taxi over here while he waits for me in the cab to return to the office in drag. You and I are just going to have to stop seeing each other so he can stop being suspicious, because it seems you don't know how to be as discreet as I am about this affair.

HIS WIFE: You know something? This might work to our advantage if you can just swallow your pride and comply with his request. It isn't going to take all day. As soon as you assure him that there was nobody here, it will be one hundred percent safe for us to continue seeing each other behind his back.

MESSENGER: Listen, let's get something straight right this minute! My pride is too precious for me to swallow, not even for a solitary second! The only solution to this predicament is for us to discontinue seeing each other! There is no other way this can be done. I am not going to dress like a faggot, and I can't afford to lose my job because if he fires me, nobody will hire me! I need that job more than I need to be screwing his wife.

HIS WIFE: *(Hurt)* And all this time I thought you were in love with me and would do anything for us to continue seeing—I mean being—with each other. *(Tears fall down from her eyes)*

MESSENGER: When a man is about to come he always tells the woman he is about to come into "I Love You!" It's nothing really personal, just a traditional spontaneous brief statement at the highest point of emotional amazement.

HIS WIFE: Are you seeing—I mean screwing—another woman?

MESSENGER: I have always been screwing another woman. I'm a free spirit. I made that quite clear to you when we first became involved. You and I were just having fun, nothing else. I come and go when I please with whomever I please. I can be here today and somewhere else tonight. Because I'm blind doesn't mean I have no choice but to be a monogamist. I belong to whomever I get in bed with until it's time to climb into another bed and belong to someone else. Permanent or semi-permanent relationships are definitely not on my agenda, baby. I don't want to be attached to no one and jeopardize my independence. It was fun while it lasted but now it has gotten too precarious. We have to stop seeing each other, I mean, separate.

HIS WIFE: *(Tearfully staring into the mirror)* Then, you leave me no choice but to tell my husband everything that has been going on between you and me, in elaborate details. And hopefully he will be so humiliated that he will walk out of my life, and then you won't have to dress like a woman and we can have a normal relationship.

MESSENGER: *(Rises)* Have you lost your mind, woman? He will kill us both if he ever found out anything. It will shatter his pride and ruin his business. He won't be able to face his family or friends again, who will unmercifully ridicule him when they find out that his wife cheated on him with a blind man. And furthermore, I don't want a normal relationship with anyone if it means solitary confinement in the prison of their emotions. Unattached I don't have to answer to anyone but me.

HIS WIFE: If losing that job is what you really fear, I'll work if you move in with me. You can do the household chores. I'll also remain married to my husband, and you and I will just live together. That way you will remain unattached.

MESSENGER: I prefer to live alone. Always have and always will. Company is only temporary on my carefree schedule, baby.

HIS WIFE: What a total disappointment you turned out to be!

MESSENGER: I never promised you stability.

HIS WIFE: You can't leave me. I won't let you!!! I'll tell him everything, I swear I will!

MESSENGER: You won't tell him a goddamn thing! You don't want to die. You are too vain for rigor mortis. You won't be able to admire yourself in the mirror all day long.

HIS WIFE: You will die along with me. And if in the hereafter is the only place we can continue screwing behind my husband's back, then that's fine with me. I'm not afraid to die to continue this forbidden love affair.

MESSENGER: That isn't fair! You are blackmailing me into becoming a transvestite.

HIS WIFE: If you cannot sacrifice your blind machismo for three-quarters of an hour so that we can continue being lovers, then blackmail is the only alternative you leave me.

MESSENGER: He will never believe that it was me.

HIS WIFE: He will when I tell him that you are circumcised!

(Blackout.)

Act I: Scene 6

*(*THE BOSS *sits behind his desk. His face is concealed by a copy of* Screw Magazine, *which he reads with profound interest. The* MESSENGER *enters.)*

THE BOSS: *(Puts magazine down on hearing the sound of the walking cane)* There you are old buddy buddy of mine. I was wondering what was taking you so long, pal? *(*MESSENGER *sits on chair alongside desk)* Well now, have you decided to do your good friend the favor he has requested of you?

MESSENGER: Can I have twenty-four hours to think it over, Mr. President?

THE BOSS: Definitely not! It has to be done today so I can have peace of mine to-morrow! *(Hands him a gift-wrapped package)* Here, happy anniversary! It's a present for you. Today makes one year that you have been working here. I am also giving you a five-dollar raise, plus a twenty-five dollar bonus, which you will find inside an envelope in the gift box. I knew that when I didn't mention anything this morning you thought I had forgotten. But, as you can see—I mean feel—I didn't.

MESSENGER: Thank you very much, Mr. President. I really do appreciate this immensely. It has been a rewarding experience working for such a generous individual.

THE BOSS: Open your gift. Feel what I bought you.

MESSENGER: *(Unwraps gift. Removes the top of a box, takes out the gift)* What are these things in little plastic bags?

THE BOSS: Condoms. I remember you mentioning on various occasions what a busy sex life you have. And with all these incurable social diseases afflicting society these days, condoms make the ideal gift for any socially overactive person.

MESSENGER: Why . . . thank you very much for the condoms. They are just what I needed, Mr. President.

THE BOSS: Thank you for being such a good employee. Okay, now let's get down to some very serious business we must discuss. While you were out I went out and bought the outfit you will be wearing to impersonate a blind woman.

MESSENGER: Mr. President, at the risk of losing my job, I don't think I can go through with it. It will leave me impotent for life. I just know it will. Try to understand, Mr. President.

THE BOSS: *(Angry)* Not only will you lose your job, but I will personally see to it that you never again work as a blind messenger as long as you live. Give me back the condoms you ungrateful low-lifer! Go and beg for a living now!!!

MESSENGER: I'd rather beg than be a faggot . . . *(rises)* . . . any day!

THE BOSS: Sit the hell down, boy! *(Rises)* You know what I think? You are really a closet case, deep down inside you are that faggot that you fear so much becoming.

MESSENGER: Mr. President, I'll break this walking cane over your head if you call me a faggot again, I mean it! I might be blind but I'm not defenseless!

THE BOSS: If you weren't a faggot you wouldn't be so afraid of becoming one. Now, hit me over the head with that cane so I can shove it down your throat and bring it out your ass, you queer! *(Sits)* I'm standing up so take a swing at me, and you better connect because you won't get a second chance! Swing, faggot!

MESSENGER: Your father's the faggot! *(Swings at THE BOSS with his cane and misses him completely)*

THE BOSS: Okay, cool it. Relax. I apologize for calling you a queer. Though you didn't strike me, the attempt was bold enough to prove that you are a man and not a fag. Sit down and let's just forget the whole thing. Keep the condoms and let's continue being friends and business associates. I should have never asked you to do such a degrading favor for me. I am proud of how proud you are about yourself. You don't have to beg for a living, I want you to continue working for me *(tearfully)*. My domestic problems are not your responsibility. It was foolish of me to have expected you *(crying)* to help me solve them . . . *(cries)*

MESSENGER: Please don't cry, Mr. President. I accept your apology. And if you give me your word of honor that regardless of what bitter altercations we might have in the near future, that you will never tell anyone about this weird favor you want me to do for you. I'll go through with it, I promise. I really do appreciate everything you have done for me.

THE BOSS: Thank you very much . . . *(sniffs)* I give you my word . . . *(sniffs)* . . . of honor that nobody will ever know. . . . *(Sniffs)*

MESSENGER: *(Gives THE BOSS a white handkerchief)* Here, Mr. President.

THE BOSS: *(Takes handkerchief, blows his nose, hands it back)* Thank you. Please be seated. *(Both men sit down)* Okay, *(composed)* this is the plan: Since today is your first anniversary at MacMacho's, I told my wife I was inviting you over for supper to celebrate the occasion. Now, what I am going to do is call her up and cancel on the grounds that we have to work overtime. She will then inform that bum that he can stay a little longer, and that's when you go there dressed as a woman to get the evidence for my divorce trial. Once I win the case, you will get another raise. And don't worry about my wife defaming your character, you and her don't travel in the same social circles.

MESSENGER: I can't wait till this is over.

THE BOSS: It will be over before you know it. *(Brings out a shopping bag from behind his desk)* Everything you need to succeed as a female impersonator is inside this shopping bag. You go to the john and get dressed, then I will put the wig on your head and apply the makeup to your face when you are through. . . . *(hands him the shopping bag)* Here.

MESSENGER: *(Takes shopping bag)* Mr. President, I don't mean to be pessimistic but I don't think wearing women's clothing is going to make me talk like them.

THE BOSS: Well, let's see what happens. If your voice doesn't change, what you'll have to do is speak as little as possible when you get there.

(MESSENGER rises, exits for the john.)

THE BOSS: *(Sits down, picks up phone receiver, dials a number, uses handkerchief to disguise voice)* Hello? *(Breathes heavily)* This is the guy with the big dick again. Ready for some hot disgusting piss in your mouth, cunt? The next time I take a shit I want you to lick my asshole clean with your tongue.

(MESSENGER returns still dressed in his clothes.)

THE BOSS: *(Hangs up phone)* What seems to be the problem now? You didn't chicken out, did you?

MESSENGER: Mr. President, it's impossible. I went to put on the dress, and an image of the Creator appeared inside my head with a sour expression on his transparent face. I have no choice but to make a confession to you that will permanently end our friendship and working relationship. I'm prepared to face whatever consequence awaits me, Mr. President. I am the man who has been screwing your wife behind your back.

THE BOSS: Don't be ridiculous! My wife will never have an affair with a blind man. She's too vain and egotistical. She constantly has to be highly complimented on how beautiful she looks and how well she dresses, which will be absolutely impossible for you to do with your handicap. Now, you promised me you would go through with it. Don't disappoint me now, pal. God is a sensible supreme being. He knows you are doing this out of loyalty for a friend and not out of perversion. So you have nothing to worry about. I already called up my wife and canceled the supper engagement. The plan is ready to be put into motion, don't get cold feet now.

MESSENGER: Okay, Mr. President. I'll make a sincere effort this time. *(Exits for the john again with shopping bag)*

THE BOSS: *(Picks up receiver, dials again, waits a few seconds)* Sorry, I had to hang up on you so abruptly, whore, I had to take a mean lick in an empty soda bottle to save for you to gargle with after you lick the shit off my asshole so I won't get germs when you suck my stiff dick as I vomit in your face thinking about the disgusting thing. You just did you fuckin' pig!

*(*MESSENGER *returns wearing plain gray dress, tight at the hips, and high heel shoes.* THE BOSS *hangs up the phone.)*

MESSENGER: My voice still hasn't changed any, Mr. President.

THE BOSS: *(Rises, looks him over thoroughly)* That's because you put that dress on over the clothes you are wearing. I can see your pants rolled up to your knees. It isn't going to work if you don't do it correctly.

MESSENGER: I'm not going to be there long enough to be thoroughly observed.

THE BOSS: The minute my wife sees you she'll be able to tell you aren't a real blind woman by the unconvincing way you are dressed. You have to remove your clothes first, undergarments, also, and begin by putting on the panties first, then the bra, then the nylon stockings, then the slip—and then the dress!

MESSENGER: I'm not putting on no bra or panties. You wife doesn't have X-ray vision. She won't be able to tell if I'm wearing them or not!

THE BOSS: You won't complete the transition necessary to be convincing if you don't get completely dressed like a woman. You know about method acting. Pretending isn't sufficient. You have to become the character you are portraying to be effective. Now go back to the john and do it correctly. We are wasting precious time with your reluctancy.

MESSENGER: Goddamn it! I hate this rotten world! Why did I have to be born in the first goddamn place? I wish I was dead . . . shit!

THE BOSS: Stop talking foolish. Nobody will know but you and I. . . .

MESSENGER: Okay, okay, okay. Goddamn it! *(Exits to john, uptight)*

THE BOSS: *(Sits down)* That guy really has a problem. He must really be insecure about his manhood. I wonder if he really is a closet case? *(Picks up phone receiver, dials numbers)* Hmmmm, it seems like she disconnected the phone. . . . *(hangs up)* Well, let me find another broad's number to harass. *(Opens telephone directory. Fifteen seconds later the* MESSENGER *reenters. Whistles at him)* Ba-Ba-Ba-Boom!

MESSENGER: Stop joking with me or I'll take off these goddamn clothes!

THE BOSS: Sorry, it won't happen again. Now sit down so I can place the wig on your head and apply makeup to your face.

MESSENGER: Wouldn't the wig be convincing enough? Do I have to be further humiliated by putting on makeup?

THE BOSS: It won't work without makeup. Now sit down so we can finish. The quicker we get it done the sooner it will be over, and you can be a man again.

MESSENGER: I'm still a man! And don't you ever forget that!

THE BOSS: Sorry! I didn't mean it that way.

MESSENGER: *(Sits)* This dress is too tight on me.

THE BOSS: *(Brings out the cosmetics from his desk drawer)* Okay now, I'm going to apply the makeup.

(Blackout.)

Act I: Scene 7

(Same as Scene 5.)

HIS WIFE: *(Combing her hair, facing the mirror)* He can't do this to me. I won't let him get away with it. He can't humiliate this person and get away with it. I'm the one who's supposed to end this affair with him. Blind bastard! He doesn't even know what the hell I look like to be calling it quits on me. If only he could see how absolutely stunning I am, he'd get down on his hands and knees and beg for forgiveness for having done nothing wrong, just to keep me content. *(Stops combing her hair and begins to apply blush on her cheeks)* He thinks I won't tell my husband anything, but he's dead wrong! If he's willing to make a fool out of me then I'm willing to make a corpse out of him, because my husband will certainly kill him. He won't think twice about defending his honor. Blind or not he will get shot! I don't have to worry about anything happening to me. My husband cannot live without me regardless of what crimes I commit against his manhood. So that blind fool better reconsider dressing in drag. Nobody walks out of my life unless I personally instruct them to leave. *(Carefully begins to apply mascara)* I should have known better than to get involved with a blind man. He wouldn't be able to defend me or himself in the event of a confrontation with my husband. But, oh what a terrific lover that sightless creature is. The fact that he's blind seems to keep his rod hard all the time. It never gets soft regardless of how many times he comes. That man is absolutely amazing. I remember the first time I met him on a street corner waiting to be safely escorted crossing the street. I took his arm without decadence and assisted him across the street. When we got to the other side, I noticed he had . . . *(puts down mascara)* . . . an incredible erection. I was impressed and flattered over having giving a blind man a hard on. Even without sight he sensed how extremely attractive and beautiful I am . . . *(Applies nail polish to her finger nails)* And of course I accepted and of course we had more than one drink and of course at some point in the conversation his hand accidentally brushed my breast. And of course he apologized and of course I accepted his apology and of course we talked about the birds and the bees and the leaves of a tree outside the bedroom window of his bachelor apartment, which we entered arm-in-arm later on, slightly intoxicated but lucid enough to experience multiple orgasms on his water bed. What an enormous bicho that blind man has. Oooops! I slip. My husband doesn't want me speaking Spanish in this house. Sorry, sir, wherever you are . . . *(stares at her finger nails)* . . . not bad. I wonder what nationality my lover is . . . *(continues to polish her nails some more)* . . . he doesn't speak with an accent. He's probably a native New Yorker born in a foreign country. My old man and my old man have nothing whatsoever in common. One is always too tired to have sex, and the other one never gets tired of having sex. *(Looks at her finger nails)* He told me he wasn't always blind. Said he had perfect vision until the night he got caught with his pants down in the bedroom of another man's wife. *(Admires herself in the mirror)* The bullet entered his right eye and came out the left eye. Luckily he survived. *(Sprays perfume on herself)* He won't survive this time if he walks out on me. My husband thinks he lost his eyesight in Vietnam. If only he knew the truth. And he will if that guy tries to humiliate me. I'll tell my husband who really referred him to MacMacho's Messenger Service. And I'll tell him how he really passed that eye exam. I told him how to do it. All you have to do is spell out the words I-A-M-A-S-T-U-P-I-D-P-E-R-S-O-N! And you pass the eye exam. My husband gets his rocks off that way. It gives him pleasure to get someone to indirectly say they are stupid. When he finds out who the real dummy was this time, a crime will be committed. I wonder if he will shoot him or stab him to death?

(Blackout.)

Act I: Scene 8

(Opens on office. MESSENGER*'s makeup job has been completed.)*

THE BOSS: Repeat after me: Peter Piper Pick a Peck of Pickles A Peck of Pickles Peter Piper Picked! If Peter Piper Eats the Peck of Pickles then he Picked Another Peck of Pickles Peter Piper Picks!

MESSENGER: *(Regular voice)* Peter Piper Pick a Peck of Pickles A Peck of Pickles Peter Piper Picked! If Peter Piper Eats the Peck of Pickles then he Picked Another Peck of Pickles Peter Piper Picks, Mr. President.

THE BOSS: Something is wrong. You don't sound any different. Oh, wait a minute, I forgot the most important thing. *(Goes behind his desk, brings out a wig from the drawer)* This wig should do the trick. Since I know how crazy you are about red-heads, I bought a redhead wig for your head. *(Places the wig on the* MESSENGER*'s head)* Hmmmm . . . not bad . . . *(the wig is shoulder length)* . . . now try repeating it.

MESSENGER: *(Effeminately)* Peter Piper Pick a Peck of Pickles A Peck of Pickles Peter Piper Picked! If Peter Piper Eats the Peck of Pickles then he Picked Another Peck of Pickles . . . *(sings)* . . . Peter Piper Picks!

THE BOSS: *(Elated)* It worked! It worked! We're in business now!

(The lights of the office go off and on and continue to do so until further notice.)

MESSENGER: *(In a panic)* Something is wrong with my eyes. *(Removes shades. Rubs eyes with his hands)* I feel terrible.

THE BOSS: *(Concerned)* What seems to be the problem?

MESSENGER: *(Still speaking in a high-pitched voice)* Oh merciful lord! A volcano seems to be erupting inside my eyes. My head seems to be spinning out of control. Oh my God! I feel dizzy, I feel strange, I am about to faint!

THE BOSS: Remove your hands from your eyes so I can take a look.

MESSENGER: Nooooo, they will fall out of the socket if I do. Oh my God, this is terrible . . . call an ambulance before I die.

THE BOSS: *(Rushes to the phone, picks up receiver and dials)* Operator, get me the police, this is an emergency!

MESSENGER: Hang up that phone, I can't let anyone see me dressed like this. Let me change first before you call. Oh God! What the hell is happening to me? Mama, come back from the dead and help me, please.

(The lights remain on).

MESSENGER: *(Rises)* Take me to the john so I can change and get medical attention as soon as possible. . . . *(hand still covers eyes)*

THE BOSS: *(Goes over to him, grabs his arm)* Come on. You'll be okay. It can't be nothing too serious, I hope.

MESSENGER: *(Removes hands from eyes)* I don't believe it. . . . *(Startled)* I-I-I CAN SEEEEEEEEE! I CAN SEEEEEEEEEEE! LORD ALMIGHTY I CAN SEEEEEEEEE! *(Looks at The* BOSS*)* You are wearing a light faded gray business suit . . . HOLY SHIT I CAN SEE!!!

THE BOSS: I don't believe it! That's incredible!

MESSENGER: *(Extremely effeminate)* Oh my God! Oh Jesus and Mary and Eleanor Roosevelt, my vision has been restored . . . *(to* THE BOSS*)* . . . you are wearing a white shirt, a blue tie, and brown shoes, which, by the way, could use a good shine.

THE BOSS: *(Shakes his hand)* Congratulations. I will give you a raise and a promotion.

MESSENGER: Oh, that won't be necessary because now that I can see clearly I will find myself a decent job. Oh my God! Oh my God! My God! My God! I don't have to dress in drag after all . . . *(removes the wig, throws it on the floor)* . . . OH NO, NO, NOOOOO!

THE BOSS: What's the problem?

MESSENGER: *(In his normal voice)* Everything is getting dark again. I can't see anymore. I'm blind again!

THE BOSS: And your voice has gotten deeper. And my wife is still a no good slut, so put that wig back on and let's proceed with our plan. Now that you are blind again you have to continue working for me. . . . *(picks up wig, puts it back on the* MESSENGER*'s head . . . lights go off and on again)*

MESSENGER: *(Startled)* It's happening again, that strange feeling has returned. I feel like throwing up once more . . . *(voice changes)* oh God, why are you punishing me? *(Lights remain on)* I can see again. This is confusing.

THE BOSS: It's weird. Something strange seems to be happening to me, also. When you have the wig on I suddenly stop being suspicious of my wife. And when you remove it the suspicion automatically returns. For example, right now. You have the wig on, and I am quickly coming to the conclusion that it was foolish of me to have ever suspected my wife of cheating on me. She will never do that to me. She loves me too much to be unfaithful. There isn't a dishonest bone in her body. How foolish of me to have distrusted her!

MESSENGER: *(Removes wig)* There goes my eyesight again.

THE BOSS: My wife is a no good ungrateful motherfuckin' slut!

MESSENGER: *(Puts on wig)* Now I can see again.

THE BOSS: She is the most wonderful person in the world.

MESSENGER: Let me try this one more time. . . . *(Removes the wig)*

THE BOSS: I'll kill her. I swear I will! *(MESSENGER puts on wig)*

THE BOSS: My wife is really a wonderful human being, and when I get home this evening I am going to tell her so. You go to the john and put your clothes back on and leave the wig on to see if all you need to see is the wig and not the rest of those clothes. . . . *(MESSENGER exits for john)* I need a drink. *(Gets a pint of wine from desk drawer. Takes a long drink)* This is absolutely unbelievable. *(Takes another drink)* I'm so lucky to have such a wonderful wife . . . *(drinks again)* I'll kill her for cheating on me! He must have removed the wig just now. She'll be sorry for doing this to me. YOU FUCKIN' SLUT. . . . *(Takes another drink, puts bottle away)*

MESSENGER: *(Reenters dressed in regular clothes. Cautiously tapping his walking cane on the floor. He has removed the wig)* It didn't work. As soon as I changed back into my clothes, the lights of the air went completely out. It's not the wig. It seems I have to stay completely dressed that way to see. And I'd rather be blind than to be a fag.

THE BOSS: You still have to do me that favor. You can't back out now. Personally I think it's more important to have your sight. Regardless of the way you have to dress to see. If as a man you are totally blind and as a woman you have perfect vision, I sincerely suggest you should get used to the idea of dressing like a woman permanently. Dressing like a woman doesn't necessarily mean you are a faggot. It's just a preference of fashion. Fags dress like men and think like women. There is no reason why you can't dress like a woman and think like a man if it restores your vision. Nobody will ridicule you once you explain to them the reason behind it. Why should you be a messenger all your life when you could be a secretary with perfect sight, or a stewardess, or even a nurse. Come on, go back to the john and change again. There are so many wonderful sights for the eyes to witness in this world. *(Puts his arm on MESSENGER's shoulder)* Forget about my wife, you don't have to do me that favor if you don't want to. What matters now is that you can see if you dress like a woman. You really have nothing to be ashamed of. Tell you what I'll do for you, pal, so that you won't feel so bad about having to dress in drag. You can become my business partner. I will hire someone else to do messenger work. How about it?

MESSENGER: Why can't I become your partner without dressing in drag?

THE BOSS: Because you have to see what you are doing to be an executive in this business. Messengers can get away with poor eyesight, but executives have to have perfect vision.

MESSENGER: You will really make me your partner?

THE BOSS: Yes. And I'm not only doing this so you won't feel bad about having to dress in drag to see, but also because you are a man with a lot of determination and ambition. Your efficiency is surpassed only by your congenial personality. I trust you more than I have ever trusted any other employee that has worked for me here. You and I will make a good team.

MESSENGER: Thank you, Mr. President. I am grateful for the offer, but, uh, well, maybe I can just dress in drag during business hours?

THE BOSS: Whatever you do after working hours is strictly your business.

MESSENGER: Okay, then I'll accept the offer to become your partner.

THE BOSS: Terrific . . . *(they shake hands)* . . . this calls for a celebration. Listen, my wife will never believe what occurred here today. I am going to call her up and ask her to join us for a drink. Now, for her to believe what happened you will have to dress in drag so she can see that you can see. I won't ask you to dress like that again outside the office. Is that okay with you, partner? Nobody will recognize you.

MESSENGER: Yes, Mr. President. I guess it's okay just this one time, but never again outside the office.

THE BOSS: You have my word. And listen, you no longer have to call me Mr. President. Partner will do. We are partners now. Now you go to the john and put the dress back on. In the meantime I will call up my wife to have her meet us.

(The MESSENGER *exits for the john.* THE BOSS *sits behind his desk to call up his wife. Blackout.)*

Act I: Scene 9

(At center stage there is a circular table covered by a light-purple satin tablecloth with three chairs near it for the customers to sit. The lights are low, a spotlight shines in the immediate area of the table. This is the bar THE BOSS *selected for the celebration. The* MESSENGER *enters dressed in a tight, light-purple satin dress, matching high heel shoes, and a long hip-length flaming redhead wig. Wears heavy makeup on his face, earrings on both ears, walk-*

ing in a semiseductive manner. He is followed by THE BOSS *in his usual business attire. Loud whistling is heard as they walk over to the table.)*

1ST MALE VOICE: Wow man! Look at that gorgeous redhead!

2ND MALE VOICE: Hey baby! Come and sit at our table!

3RD MALE VOICE: What stunning red hair you have, lady. Let me buy you a Bloody Mary!

THE BOSS: You are attracting a lot of attention.

MESSENGER: *(Speaking effeminately)* Oh those guys are just drunk!

(They reach the table. THE BOSS *holds out the chair to the left side of the table for the* MESSENGER *to sit. He sits on the chair in back of the table close to both chairs.)*

THE BOSS: My wife should be here shortly. It takes her longer than other women to get dressed and beautify her beautiful face. What are you drinking?

(The BARTENDER *enters with a Bloody Mary on a tray. He's a heavyset man in his late fifties. Walks over to the table.)*

BARTENDER: *(To* MESSENGER*)* This is for you, madam, from that gentleman *(pointing) . . .* sitting in the booth at the far left. . . . *(hands him the Bloody Mary)*

MESSENGER: Tell him thank you for me, darling, I mean, sir.

THE BOSS: *(To* BARTENDER*)* I'll have a vodka martini, straight up, very dry, with an olive, please.

BARTENDER: Sure, sir. That's a mighty attractive dame you got there with you, pal. *(Exits)*

THE BOSS: You did right in changing the outfit I selected. Nobody would have believed you were an authentic lady. And you did such a convincing job with the makeup, too! You sure must get around a lot to know so much about women's tastes in clothing and cosmetics. I'd be fooled also!

MESSENGER: Darling, I mean, Mr. President! I mean Partner, the more you go out with them, the more you learn about them. Really dearie, I mean Boss, I mean Partner, no sophisticated lady in her right mind would have been caught dead in public wearing that highly tacky, tasteless, cheap, out-of-fashion, bargain-basement dress you purchased. Never! Never! Never!

*(BARTENDER *enters with martini and another Bloody Mary on the tray. Walks over to the table.)*

BARTENDER: Here's your martini, sir . . . *(hands* THE BOSS *his drink) . . .* and this is another Bloody Mary for you, madam, from another gentleman admirer who wishes to remain anonymous. *(Hands the* MESSENGER *the drink)* You sure are quite popular in this bar.

THE BOSS: Oh my dear, I haven't even touched the first drink.

BARTENDER: Take your time, we are open all night. Enjoy it. . . . *(Exits)*

*(*THE BOSS's WIFE *enters, dressed in the same identical dress as the* MESSENGER *and equally as glamorous in appearance. Nobody whistles at her as she walks toward the table.* THE BOSS *rises upon noticing her.)*

THE BOSS: Here comes my princess. Hello darling, precious companion of my existence . . . *(embraces and kisses her passionately on her lips)*

*(*MESSENGER *clears his throat as they continue kissing, oblivious of his presence.)*

THE BOSS: Oh! Excuse me . . . *(they separate)* . . . this is my wife.

HIS WIFE: Glad to meet you . . . *(shakes* MESSENGER's *hand)* . . . I have heard a great deal about you.

MESSENGER: *(Extremely effeminate)* The pleasure is mine. You are as beautiful as your husband described you to be. Please share one of these Bloody Marys with me. They were bought for me by two different customers before I had a chance to make myself comfortable here.

HIS WIFE: Why, thank you very much . . . *(*THE BOSS *holds out chair for her to sit down on)* . . . sorry I'm late, sir. *(Sits)* The taxi got stuck in a traffic jam. Traffic is unbearable in midtown at this time of day.

THE BOSS: We just shortly got here ourselves . . . *(sits down)* . . . now that we are all here, I propose we make a toast to the celebration of this very special occasion we came here to celebrate. *(They tap their drinking glasses)* To a long resourceful partnership and to your restored vision! *(They take their first drink)*

HIS WIFE: You must be thrilled to tears with this miraculous occurrence. What a wonderful feeling it must be to be able to see after so many years in the dark.

MESSENGER: It isn't as miraculous as it sounds. There seem to be strings attached to this miracle. Look at the way I have to dress AND speak. I guess it's true, deary, God does work in mysterious ways!

THE BOSS: Don't give God all the credit. I was an accomplice to his miracle. After all, it was my idea that you dress like a woman. I guess I inadvertently performed a miracle. *(To* HIS WIFE*)* Darling, the reason he dressed this way in the first place was because I was suspicious of you. I thought that you were being disloyal to me, and suggested that my good old pal over here dress up as a blind woman to apprehend you in some wild ridiculous scheme of mine to win a divorce trial without having to pay alimony to you in the court settlement on the grounds of adultery.

HIS WIFE: You thought I was cheating on you?

THE BOSS: Yes, my love. And I deeply apologize for thinking that. I was overworked and wasn't being rational in my thinking. I felt the whole world was against me. Including you. And praise the lord, because of my suspicion a miracle occurred. *(Drinks)* When because of my foolish suggestion she, I mean he, dressed up like a broad, I mean lady, I mean woman, and to my astonishment regained her, I mean his, eyesight, I felt so benevolent and worthy of myself as a human being that it no longer mattered what my inner conflicts and outer crises were. They had at that precise moment ceased to affect me negatively. I was able to understand how my suspicions were psychological and unsubstantiated. *(To* HIS WIFE*)* I had no reason to doubt you. I was just doubting myself. If I was able to perform a miracle, I can't be all that bad and certainly can be a much better husband. The real miracle was the realization of how deeply I am in love with you, my love. . . . *(*THE BOSS *and* HIS WIFE *kiss passionately)*

MESSENGER: Really, deary, public display of affection is unacceptable especially in the presence of another lady. I mean person. *(*THE BOSS *and* HIS WIFE *stop kissing)* You will just have to control your emotions until you are in the privacy of your nocturnal residence of subconscious activities and sensational emotional physical delightful discovereeeeeeese . . . oh my God! My voice seems to be completely changing!

THE BOSS: You know something? You two ladies are dressed exactly alike!

MESSENGER: *(Insulted)* I am not a lady! I am a woman. I mean a MAN who has to dress in drag, I mean in the clothes of his opposite sex to have twenty-twenty vision, and don't you forget that!

(The BARTENDER *enters with another Bloody Mary.)*

THE BOSS: Sorry, Partner. It was a slip of the tongue. . . . *(Taps him on the shoulder)*

BARTENDER: *(To the* MESSENGER*)* And here is another Bloody Mary for the gorgeous lady with the flaming red hair from that customer over there. . . . *(Points in direction of customer)* And it comes with a note . . . *(hands* MESSENGER *drink and white envelope)* . . . oh, I see someone else has joined your party? Not as lovely but very attractive, also. If I say so myself. What can I get you to drink, lady?

MESSENGER: She's sharing the Bloody Marys of my admirers. I can't possibly drink all these Bloody Marys myself.

BARTENDER: She will have to order something. There is a three-dollar minimum to sit at these tables.

THE BOSS: Bring her a glass of white wine, and I'll have another martini, please.

BARTENDER: Okay, be back shortly, folks . . . *(Exits commenting to himself about the* MESSENGER*'s physical attractiveness)* That redhead is sure quite a doll. No cover charge for her.

HIS WIFE: *(To* MESSENGER*)* You are so popular here, it's making me jealous. Aren't you going to read that note you got?

MESSENGER: Not really, deary, but then again, I'm curious myself. *(Takes note out of the envelope, reads it)* That guy must be highly intoxicated. He doesn't even know who I am and is inviting me to spend the weekend with him at the Catskills. How tacky of him to think so cheaply of me! If only he knew who was really inside these clothes and cosmetics he wouldn't be so over eager to be disrespectful, that male chauvinist pig!

HIS WIFE: *(To* MESSENGER*)* I just noticed something. You and I are wearing the same identical dress and matching shoes, too. I thought I was the only one with this outfit! *(To* THE BOSS*)* Darling, you will have to get me a new outfit that nobody else has as soon as possible. You know how I deplore being imitated. People might think I'm the imitator.

MESSENGER: I'm not imitating you. I had no idea you had a dress like this in your wardrobe, deary, really! You shouldn't get jealous. I can't help it if I'm getting all the attention instead of you. I am not doing anything to cause it. You know how I despise dressing like this. Though, I must admit all this attention I'm receiving is quite flattering.

THE BOSS: I have a gram of cocaine with me, I copped, I mean I purchased for this special occasion . . . *(to* MESSENGER*)* . . . you snort coke?

MESSENGER: Oh! As often as possible.

THE BOSS: Since you are the guest of honor, you snort first. . . . *(Discreetly puts aluminum-wrapped cocaine in* MESSENGER*'s palm)* Go to the men's room and take a three and three or more.

MESSENGER: I can't go into the men's room dressed like a woman!

THE BOSS: So go to the ladies room.

MESSENGER: I can't do that, either! I'm a man. Plus, I'll be too nervous to snort correctly knowing that I don't belong in there.

THE BOSS: I think you better start getting used to going to the ladies room. You will be dressing like a lady from nine to five and will be using the toilet more than once during that time. Always remember to sit down and urinate in the ladies toilet, and you won't run into any problems in there.

MESSENGER: But I'll be at MacMachos. I can use the men's bathroom there.

THE BOSS: Sure! But not when customers are in the office. It won't look good for business. And what about when you got out to lunch and have to use the toilet in a cafeteria? You know, we have a NO EATING ALLOWED policy at the office, which I am not going to amend because if you allow your employees to eat in the office, very little work gets done. They will be burping and farting more than they'd be working.

MESSENGER: Oh, this is going to be more difficult than I imagined.

HIS WIFE: I'll go with you so you won't be so nervous.

THE BOSS: No, let her, I mean him, go by herself. I mean himself. He has to get used to it if he is to succeed as an executive.

MESSENGER: *(Reluctantly)* Okay, I'll go. But I hope none of those horny men who can't seem to take their eyes off this table follow me in there.

THE BOSS: Don't worry. I'll keep an eye on you from here.

MESSENGER: *(Rises)* What did I ever do that was so bad to be punished so severely? Well, I hope I get back alive. . . . *(Exits)*

HIS WIFE: You should really let me accompany her, I mean him.

THE BOSS: He'll be, I mean she'll be, no, I mean he'll be okay.

(Loud whistles are heard as the MESSENGER *walks over to the ladies room.)*

1ST MALE VOICE: Shake it, but don't break it, mama.

2ND MALE VOICE: Baby, I'll leave my wife and children and house and car for you any day you say so. Just give me the word, sweetheart!

3RD MALE VOICE: Let's blow this joint and go up to my place, gorgeous.

MESSENGER: Keep your hands to yourself you fresh man . . . *(the sound of someone getting smacked across the face is heard)* . . . take that you cheap creep!

HIS WIFE: I'm seriously getting highly annoyed with all this attention she is receiving.

THE BOSS: You mean HE is receiving.

HIS WIFE: It's deflating to my ego. After all, I am the real woman, not a contrived one. Those men should be making a fuss over me, not her—I mean him. Let's go somewhere else where I can also be flattered. The men here have had too much to drink and now cannot distinguish between being attractive or looking grotesque.

THE BOSS: Don't be jealous. You have my undivided attention, dear.

HIS WIFE: You can't seem to take your eyes off of her, I mean him, also. This is humiliating. And I don't have to stand for it. I'll leave with or without you!!!

*(*MESSENGER *returns, visibly upset.)*

THE BOSS: Back so soon?

MESSENGER: I was followed into the ladies room by this very nasty man, who I had to effectively kick in the groin. Some men are such sexist bastards, it's pathetic and disgusting!

HIS WIFE: Let's go to another bar. This place is too lower class for my taste.

MESSENGER: I agree with you one hundred percent, deary. Really! The clientele is vulgar and despicable. Jesus, they see someone in a sexy outfit and go out of their minds regardless of what sex is inside the skirt.

(The BARTENDER *enters with a Bloody Mary, a martini, and a glass of white wine. Walks to the table.)*

HIS WIFE: I think we should cancel that order and leave immediately.

THE BOSS: We can't. The drinks are already served. We'll leave after we drink them.

HIS WIFE: I don't feel like drinking here, anymore.

MESSENGER: Neither do I.

BARTENDER: *(To* MESSENGER*)* This Bloody Mary is compliments of the man you smacked across the face not too long ago. . . . *(Gives him his drink, then gives the others their drinks)*

MESSENGER: Tell him to tell his mother to drink it. . . . *(Puts Bloody Mary back on bartender's tray)*

BARTENDER: I'll give him the message, mam. . . . *(Exits)*

MESSENGER: I should blow their minds and let them know they are really making passes at a man. That way they will stop harassing me with their cheap propositions.

THE BOSS: Let's drink up so we can go somewhere else. *(Lifts his glass)* Cheers!

HIS WIFE: Cheers!

MESSENGER: Cheeeeeeeeeeeeeeeeerrrrrrrrrrrrrrrrrrrrrrrrrrrrsssssssssss!

THE BOSS: I'm going to the men's room to take a few hits before we leave. *(To* MESSENGER*)* Pass me the coke. . . . *(*MESSENGER *passes him the coke)* Thank you . . . *(rises)* . . . I'll be right back. . . . *(Exits)*

MESSENGER: I can't wait till I get out of these clothes so I can speak in my natural masculine voice again.

HIS WIFE: Then you won't be able to see how beautiful I am.

MESSENGER: You can't have your cake and eat it, honey. . . . *(Drinks)*

HIS WIFE: You don't seem to be THAT highly annoyed, darling. And to be perfectly honest with you, I think you are enjoying all the attention and free drinks you are getting. You don't seem the least uncomfortable in those sexy clothes you are wearing. You have gotten so deep into that character that, under normal circumstances had my husband left us alone in a room, you would immediately grab my left tit and squeeze it gently. You don't seem interested in my anymore.

MESSENGER: If I display affection here, people will think we are dykes. I am not a faggot or a lesbian. I am straight in whatever character I happen to be portraying, lady or gentleman, honey. So don't go jumping to any incriminating . . . *(sings the word)* . . . conclusions.

HIS WIFE: Have you stopped to think about how come you can see clearly when you dress up like a woman and not at all when you dress up like a man? Don't you wonder about that?

MESSENGER: As I mentioned before, deary, God works in mysterious ways.

HIS WIFE: Sure, but don't you find it kind of weird? Is God trying to indirectly tell you something personal about yourself that you refuse to except?

MESSENGER: Honey, for your information, the real weirdo is your husband, not me! He has to see me dressed in drag to physically desire you. If I don't put on panties, he won't be able to get it hard in bed with you. I remember how he immediately started despising you when I took off the drag and refused to go along with his wild scheme, even after the revelation of being able to see dressed like a freak. I mean, that is absolutely weird as hell, deary. And before I forget to mention it, you and I are through! It's quits! I want nothing whatsoever to do with you anymore!

HIS WIFE: Why? Have you found someone in here you find more interesting than me?

MESSENGER: No! You lied to me about being a redhead. You have black hair, and I can't stand brunettes. I told you that before we got into your husband's bed for the first time. I said that if your hair isn't red I wasn't going to undress in front of you. I was just going to stick it in and take it out as soon as you reached a climax because I don't come with brunettes. I go and keep going! You exploited my handicap to seduce me! *(Tearfully)* Oh, my goodness, how can anyone be so cruel?

HIS WIFE: Don't cry. I'll dye my hair red. I'll borrow your wig when we make love.

MESSENGER: *(Crying)* It's over . . . over . . . *(sings)* . . . ohhhhhhhhhhhhhhhhhhhh-haaaaa!

HIS WIFE: I'll tell my husband everything if you leave me.

MESSENGER: *(Sings his lines)* Heeeee won't believe you. Heeee isss too arrogant and cynical and conceited and egotistical to believe that his wife cheated on him with a blind maaaaaannnnnnn! He made that quite cleaarrr to meeeeeee! When I confessed to avoid putting on a dress that I was the man who wasssss screwing his wife behind his back, so that takes care of that. . . . Tralalalalalalalalalalalalalaaaaaaaaaaaaaa!

(Customers are heard applauding and whistling. The BARTENDER *enters with three Bloody Marys on his tray. He walks to the table.)*

BARTENDER: *(To* MESSENGER*)* This drink is from . . . *(pointing)* . . . that customer over there. . . . *(Puts drink in front of him)* And this drink is from . . . *(pointing)* . . . that customer over there . . . *(puts drink in front of him)* . . . and this drink is from yours truly, me. . . . *(Puts drink in front of him)* You have a magnificent singing voice!

MESSENGER: *(Timidly)* Thank you. I was considering a singing career until I became partners with the President-for-Life of . . . *(sings)* . . . MacMacho's Messenger Servicessssss, who at this moment happens to be in the toilet doing not number one, or number two, but number threeeee!

BARTENDER: How fortunate of you. Maybe you and I can get together for dinner and drinks one of these evenings?

MESSENGER: *(Sings)* Right now I am too buseeeeeeeee to socialize with anybody-eeeeeee.

*(*THE BOSS *reenters.)*

HIS WIFE: *(To* BARTENDER*)* Can you bring us the check? We are leaving very soon, if not sooner.

BARTENDER: What's the hurry? The night is still young.

HIS WIFE: *(Sarcastically)* This place lacks the sophistication I am accustomed to.

THE BOSS: Sorry I took so long, girls!

BARTENDER: Huh! *(Exits. Commenting to himself)* That dumb broad don't look the least sophisticated to me. What the hell is she so uptight about?

THE BOSS: What is the problem?

HIS WIFE: I told him what I think about this dump.

THE BOSS: *(Noticing the drinks)* Are those more Bloody Marys from secret admirers?

MESSENGER: Yes. We should all drink one a piece so we can leave soon.

HIS WIFE: I don't want no goddamn Blood Mary. As soon as we pay the check I'm leaving. This place is the pits!

MESSENGER: Oh, she's just jealous because I'm getting all the free drinks and attention around here.

HIS WIFE: And you really seem to be enjoying it, deary.

MESSENGER: *(Rises, angry)* No, I'm not. I despise this role I am being forced to play to keep my job! So you shove your insinuations up your bloomers, bitch!

THE BOSS: Calm down. Sit! I'm still in charge around here. This small celebration is business-related. . . . *(To* HIS WIFE*)* We will leave when I say so . . . understand? *(*MESSENGER *sits)*

HIS WIFE: Yes, sir!

THE BOSS: *(To* MESSENGER*)* I don't want you to mention again that there are strings attached to the outfit you are wearing. It did restore your eyesight, didn't it? It worked to your advantage.

MESSENGER: More to my disadvantage being fanatically heterosexual in all conceivable ways possible.

(The BARTENDER *enters with the bill and a rose on the tray.)*

BARTENDER: Here is your bill. . . . *(Puts bill on the table)* And this rose *(to* MESSEN-GER*)* . . . is from me to you. . . .

MESSENGER: *(Accepts the rose. Timidly)* Why thank you, big boy.

BARTENDER: You are more than welcome, my lovely lady. Hope you drop by again very soon. You won't have any problems getting free drinks in this bar as long as I'm the bartender here. . . . *(winks at him. Speaks to* THE BOSS*)* I hear you are the President-for-Life of MacMacho's Messenger Service?

HIS WIFE: He most certainly is! And, if you redecorate this place with wall-to-wall, ceiling-to-floor shiny glass mirrors so that everywhere I look I can witness how extremely beautiful I am, it won't be such a bad spot to occasionally socialize in.

BARTENDER: If you wanted glass mirrors you should have ordered them. We have more than meets the eye in THIS BAR.

HIS WIFE: Oh, how terrific! Then we can stay here longer. Why is this bar called "This Bar" instead of a more stylish contemporary name?

BARTENDER: Because we want to keep it gay and simple for simply gay around here. We just would prefer to cater to the common working class people, like yourselves. I'll bring you a mirror right way, lady, so you can feel comfortable in this Gay and Simple or Simply Gar Bar. Be right back. *(Exits)*

HIS WIFE: I guess I will have one of your Bloody Marys now, darling. This isn't such a bad place after all. It needs work but if they serve mirrors with your drinks you can relax and feel comfortable admiring yourself in the mirror while you take a drink.

MESSENGER: And smoke a cigarette.

*(*BARTENDER *returns with large round mirror with a handle wrapped in white cloth on his tray.)*

HIS WIFE: *(Excited)* Oh great! Here he comes with the mirror.

BARTENDER: *(Reaches table)* We keep . . . *(to* HIS WIFE*)* . . . our mirrors fresh around here . . . *(begins to unwrap mirror)* . . . after a customer is through with a mirror, we do the same thing with them that we do with used drinking glasses. We wash them in detergent to be on the safe side in case someone gave it a dirty look. *(To* THE BOSS*)* Mr. President, will you happen to have any positions available at your messenger service? I have been thinking about changing jobs.

THE BOSS: Yes. We certainly do. We have a messenger position available, which my partner here . . . *(indicates* MESSENGER*)* . . . effectively and efficiently held until I promoted him—I mean her—for excellent work and impeccable conduct and punctuality. If you are interested come and see us tomorrow first thing in the morning. This is my wife . . . *(indicating)* . . . who you are unwrapping the glass mirror for. . . . *(Hands him a business card)*

BARTENDER: Glad to meet you, madam. *(Finishes unwrapping mirror)* Here you are, lady. A fresh glass mirror for you. *(Hands her the mirror. As she takes the mirror, the lights go out. The bar is left completely dark).* Holy shit! There go the lights again! That goddamn incompetent electrician was just here to repair them last week. He did a fuckin' lousy piss-poor job. Pardon the profanities, ladies.

MESSENGER: You express yourself in any way you want to, big boy. Hey, my voice seems to have gotten deeper in the dark.

BARTENDER: I'll have them back in no time, folks. The fuse box is faulty, fuses just keep blowing out all the time. They don't endure more than three days . . . *(is heard leaving)* . . . sit tight, there will be light, shortly.

HIS WIFE: What rotten luck I have!

MESSENGER: *(Speaking in his normal voice)* Some people's rotten luck are others' good fortune. With the lights out, no one can see me in drag, and I speak with my normal voice. I personally wish he doesn't repair them any time soon. Now is a good time to leave this place. Without paying also.

THE BOSS: You don't have to do that. You are no longer a messenger. You are now the partner of the President-for-Life of a Prestigious Messenger Service.

(The BARTENDER *returns with a lit birthday cake. Everybody sings: "For he's a jolly good fellow/for he's a jolly good fellow for he's a jolly good fellow that nobody can deny/That nobody can deny/That nobody can deny." . . . (Crowd applauds)* BARTENDER *puts cake in front of the* MESSENGER.*)*

MESSENGER: *(Speaking effeminately)* Oh my God! *(To* THE BOSS*)* You shouldn't have done it, Mr. President, I mean Sir, I mean Partner and good buddy.

THE BOSS: Happy Anniversary!

MESSENGER: Oh, I'm so flabbergasted I can barely express myself.

HIS WIFE: Blow out the candles so the BARTENDER can turn the lights back on and I can look in the mirror.

BARTENDER: I'll get a knife to cut the cake. . . . *(Exits)*

MESSENGER: I want to make a wish before blowing out the candles.

HIS WIFE: Be quick about it.

MESSENGER: I wish the lights will never go back on after I blow out the candles.

HIS WIFE: That's a terrible wish to make. Blow out that candle!

THE BOSS: Before you blow out the candles, I'd like to say a few words.

HIS WIFE: Oh crap!

THE BOSS: Cool it, woman!

HIS WIFE: Yes, sir!

THE BOSS: *(Rises. Holds drink)* I'd like to say it has been a rewarding experience having you get the message across for MacMacho's Messenger Service these past twelve months. As I on many occasions have mentioned to you, your efficiency is surpassed only by your congenial personality. In the darker moments of my business enterprise, you, a blind messenger, brought light into the company with your optimistic attitude toward life. When I felt friendless you reassured me that I wasn't alone in this world. That indeed I had a friend, and a very good one. That I was an accomplice to the restoration of your vision proves that if you do good unto others, others do likewise unto you. And though the Lord works in mysterious ways, I consider the miracle I assisted him in performing more of an advantage than a disadvantage. Now you can actually see how beautiful life is.

HIS WIFE: And how beautiful I am.

THE BOSS: Now you can see the sun rise in the morning and set at twilight time when crimson shadows gather the splendors of a day that has ended, creating silhouettes of the transition on the transparent walls of mid-air in unreachable horizons outside your window.

HIS WIFE: *(Rises. Holds glass)* Now you can look at my tits instead of just touching them. Now you can admire my fine ass instead of just feeling it.

MESSENGER: *(Whispering)* Will you be quiet, don't you know your husband is among us?

HIS WIFE: He will never believe I'd cheat on him with a blind man even if he hears it coming out of my own mouth.

THE BOSS: And now you can stare at the miraculous beauty of flowers on a pleasant day in a garden of your choice. Not just smell them and wonder about their beauty as you've done in the past.

HIS WIFE: And now you can stare at the mysterious beauty of my eyes without accidentally poking your fingers in them as you have done in the past and present.

THE BOSS: At last you will be able to see the birds fly in the sky!

HIS WIFE: At last you will be able to see me naked in bed!

MESSENGER: May I blow out the candles now, Partner?

THE BOSS: The leaves on trees! Eternal blades of grass everywhere the absence of cement is present! The waves of intelligent oceans! The serenity of remarkable lakes in mid-afternoons!

HIS WIFE: The traffic jams outside my bedroom window when I wake you up to leave because my husband is on his way home! The anticipation of apprehension on our worried faces!

MESSENGER: I am going to blow out the candles now.

THE BOSS: Not yet. Oh, the museums you will visit!

HIS WIFE: Oh! The different pretty dresses I will wear for your secret visits.

THE BOSS: Oh! The picture postcards of foreign countries!

HIS WIFE: Oh! The self-portrait of my wet vagina in person.

THE BOSS: Oh! Their mountains and rivers at all mystical hours!

HIS WIFE: Oh! The sight of me totally naked in the shower!

THE BOSS: Oh! The different aesthetic interpretations of life!

HIS WIFE: Oh! The visual unusual sensational expression on your face when you are on top of your best friend's wife!

MESSENGER: Let me blow out the candles, already! I want to eat some cake.

THE BOSS: The bartender hasn't returned with the knife. Oh! Christmas trees and the magic sight of children opening up gifts.

HIS WIFE: Oh! New Year's Eve and the delightful sight of me squeezing the nipples of my tight tits!

THE BOSS: All this and more you will be able to see!

HIS WIFE: And especially much more of me!

THE BOSS: Though you have to dress in drag to see the light, consider it a blessing. Sight is precious and priceless. Consider the dress a contact lens or a pair of eye glasses. You now have the option to see or not to see! Praise the lord and me!

HIS WIFE: And most important of all, now you can visually inflate my ego more accurately when you pay me the highest compliments for being so extremely beautiful in every aspect of the definition of the word!

THE BOSS: Now you can blow out the candles. But before you do, let us make a special toast to your strange good fortune and promotion.

THE BOSS: Cheers!

HIS WIFE: Cheers!

MESSENGER: *(Rises)* Cheeeeeeeeeeeeeeeeeeeeeeeeeeeeeeeeeerrssss!

(After tapping drinking glasses a few times they each take a drink. The MESSENGER *bends over to blow out the candles on the cake.)*

THE BOSS: Before you blow out the candles, I propose that because we are a team now, that we formally exchange names. Since you started working for me twelve months ago I only knew you as my Blind Messenger and you only knew me as Your Boss. *(To* HIS WIFE*)* And because of all the work that has piled up on me in the past year I have forgotten your name and have referred to you only as My Wife and you to me as Your Husband. Now that things are positively different with all of us, we should be more informal and less official with each other.

HIS WIFE: This is wonderful! Companions should know each other's names.

THE BOSS: *(To* MESSENGER*)* My name is Manuel MacMacho. You can call me Manny. . . . *(shakes his hand)* Glad to meet you . . . *(shakes* HIS WIFE*'s hand)* . . . and glad to meet you.

HIS WIFE: My name is Esposa de MacMacho. You can call me Espi. . . . *(After shaking* THE BOSS*'s hand, she shakes* MESSENGER*'s hand)*

MESSENGER: And my name is Henrietta Coloretta . . . I mean . . . *(deep voice)* Henry Coloretto. You can call me Hanky or . . . *(effeminately)* Hyyyyyyyyyyyyyyyyyyyy-ddddddddddeeeeeeeeeeee!

THE BOSS: Cheers!

HIS WIFE: Cheers!

MESSENGER: Cheers!

(A gun shot is heard. An eerie pause follows.)

HIS WIFE: *(Startled)* Why did you have to shoot him, I mean her, I mean him, forrrr?

THE BOSS: That screeching sound she was making. I mean he was making was getting on my nerves already. She, I mean he, has had too much to drink, too. Now she, I mean he, will be able to sober up and report to work on time tomorrow morning for his first day on the job as my official partner. Let's leave before the lights go back on and someone discovers the body.

HIS WIFE: Did you really believe I was having an affair with him?

THE BOSS: Don't be ridiculous, of course not. I shot him because of that screeching noise she was making. Let's get out of here!

HIS WIFE: Yes, sir!

(They are heard leaving the bar in a hurry.)

Act I: Scene 10

(The stage is completely dark. Suddenly a spotlight goes on. It shines on the eye chart. Then another spotlight goes on a few feet away to the left of the eye chart. It shines on the MES-SENGER, who is dressed like a blind messenger again, as in the beginning, with walking cane in his right hand. Another spotlight goes on at exit stage right. It shines on BAR-TENDER.)

MESSENGER: *(Speaking normally)* Hold your right hand over your left eye and read out the letters on the chart I point to with my cane.

BARTENDER: *(Puts right hand over left eye)* T-H-E-E-N-D.

(Blackout.)

END OF PLAY

VI

Musical Epics

The Goong Hay Kid

Primitive World: An Anti-Nuclear Jazz Musical

The Goong Hay Kid

Alvin Eng

CHARACTERS

Paul Mah: *A/k/a The Goong Hay Kid: Chinese American "punk-rapper" and performance artist, in his early twenties.*

Mr. Mah: *Paul's Father as seen in a flashback only. In his mid forties.*

Mrs. Mah: *Paul's Mother, also only seen in a flashback. In her early thirties.*

Sara Thomas: *Mr. Mah's paramour, Caucasian woman in her early thirties.*

Michael Mah: *Paul's dead brother, early thirties.*

Ngan-Gee: *Paul's uncle, China-born, in his mid fifties.*

Deirdre Bender: *Paul's punky ex-girlfriend and bandmate. American-born Caucasian "blondie" in her late twenties.*

Julie: *Ngan-Gee's fantasy woman, Chinese American, early thirties.*

Offstage Voice: *Nemesis/Gatekeeper of Paul's auditions and nightmares.*

The play takes place in the early 1980s in NYC's Chinatown in three primary locations: A restaurant/living room area, a nightclub stage area, and a makeshift dressing room area.

This play is dedicated to Muhammad Ali; the original rapper and "loser and still champion."

Scene 1:

(Spotlight comes up on a stage with a microphone on a stand and a stool. KID *enters carrying a big radio or boombox, which he places on the stool. He is dressed in an amalgam of punk and rap clothing—predominantly red and black.)*

OFFSTAGE VOICE: Okay, panel, this guy calls himself The Gung-Ho Kid. His sheet says he raps and does stand-up.

KID: Uh, yes and no. I consider myself more of a punk-rapper and performance artist. And I'm called The Goong Hay Kid, not gung-ho, but goong hay. Like, maybe you've heard the Chinese say: "Goong Hay Fat Choy" around Chinese New Year's? . . . You haven't? Well, just think of goong hay as the Chinese equivalent of Mazel Tov.

OFFSTAGE VOICE: That's great. Now are you gonna show us your stuff or what?

KID: Okay, it's like this. I used to think that being Chinese meant being different from everyone else. But I was wrong. Just like you all, I also so proudly hail from a traditional, all-American dysfunctional family. Yeah, us "juk-sings" or ABCs—yes,

American-Born Chinese were gently force-fed pearls of wisdom from the "juk-koks," or China-Born Chinese such as: Never trust "lo-fahns" or, ahem, white people; never trust "hok-gwais," or, black people; and only always trust your fellow "hung-ngens"—you got it! Chinese. It was like Chinese wisdom torture. But I don't think this wisdom was designed for a city like New York where you quickly learn that you can't trust anyone! I don't even trust my own judgment! I grew up thinking they were calling us unscrewable orientals, not inscrutable orientals. But, to be honest, I never thought about any of this shit until we got a television. This made me see my world very differently—particularly my parents.

(On a different part of the stage, lights come up on KID'S *mom and dad in the living room area.* DAD *is intently watching TV.* MOM *is yelling at him.* DAD *occasionally yells back, but basically tries to ignore her and watch TV.)*

KID: Yeah, they were always in those, ya know; "bang-zoom, Alice!" shouting situations like all TV families. But somehow they never made it to: "Baby, you're the greatest!" kiss and make-up stage. Well, during this period of stupefying discovery, I got my first guitar.

*(*KID *runs to parents' living room and transforms himself back into a child.)*

KID: Mama, Bop-ba, I wrote a song, look: *(strums and sings)* "I'm a Chinese Super-hero, on TV!"

*(*MOM *claps hands approvingly.* DAD *puts his hand on neck of* KID'*s guitar to stop him from playing.)*

DAD: There no Chinese hero on TV, 'cause there no Chinese hero in America!

*(*DAD *looks* KID *in the eye, then lets go of guitar neck and resumes watching TV.* MOM *motions: "Don't mind him" to* KID, *and argues with* DAD. KID *transforms himself back to present and returns to stage area.)*

KID: I could've killed him. But he was already dead. In fact, the only time I ever saw him cry wasn't with my mother or my brother and certainly not with me. It was with that goddamn television. I was about seven years old and it was Thanksgiving. He'd just finished watching *King Kong.*

*(*KID *transforms back into a child and crosses to living room.)*

KID: Bop-ba, what's wrong?

*(*DAD *is weeping, sees* KID *and shoos him away.* KID *transforms back to present, returns to stage.)*

KID: Back then I didn't know what the fuck was going on. But now I know. For my father, sitting at home in his cheap Chinatown chair while the real America—the glittering, big-titted America flickered in front of him just out of reach on TV—was torture. It was sucking the life right out of him. 'Cause he knew that no matter how many hours he worked in his laundry slaving away for a piece of the American pie, at night when he came home and turned on the TV he was just another King Kong

Chinaman on the outside looking in. But sure enough, he soon put himself in the picture. Oh yeah! "Bang-zoom, Alice!" He left us for a white woman.

(SARA *enters and ushers* MOM *out of living room and sits down next to* DAD.)

KID: Now, I won't name names, but Sara Thomas, this dry-cleaning consultant, forever changed my old man from a poor, one-laundry-in-Chinatown Chinaman to a prosperous, one-laundromat-in-every-shopping-center-in-Queens model minority immigrant. MOM just threw in the towel and went back to China, leaving me and my brother Michael with my uncle, Ngan-Gee.

(MICHAEL *enters and stands just outside the living room.*)

KID: Last time I saw my father was at this really lame truce dinner he invited us to. Big mistake.

(*All five re-arrange living room furniture to resemble a dinner table.*)

KID: At the restaurant, dad and Sara carried on like some sorry-ass rerun of "Love, American-Style" and that ain't no pretty sight.

(DAD *and* SARA *carry on all lovey-dovey for a few beats.* MICHAEL *is fuming.* KID *joins them.*)

SARA: Michael, please pass the white bread.

MICHAEL: Oh sure, pass the bread, Paulie.

DAD: No, Michael, you do it! Lazy "Kie-eye" [asshole].

(MICHAEL *angrily passes bread to* SARA.)

MICHAEL: That lo-fahn bitch is gonna suck all the blood out of him until he's finally white!

(KID *stands up and returns to performing area.*)

KID: Unfortunately, that was the only thing MICHAEL and I ever agreed on when we were growing up. All throughout that dinner I remember looking at my father and thinking: *He must finally feel like he's starring in his own TV show*—because I sure felt like I was watching one.

(*Blackout on living room area.*)

KID: Well, tonight I'd like to resurrect "The First Chinese Hero on TV" in its revised punk-rap edition. This one goes out to my father and all the television programmers of my youth.

(KID *starts rewinding his tape and raps the song "The First Chinese Hero on TV".*)

THE FIRST CHINESE HERO ON TV:
How come no one on TV looks like me?
What they got against real Chinese?

'Cause the ones you do see ain't even Chinese,
They're Midwest guys trying to look Far East!

CHORUS:
So if seeing is believing then my eyes tell lies
But lies can't disguise what will one day rise
And on that day the people will say
"This is boring, I want the real thing!"
When they cry that creed I'll heed to be
The first Chinese Hero on TV.

So I changed my name to The Goong Hay Kid
My girlfriend left, my family hid
They said you sound so dumb and look stu-pid
But what they know about becoming a hit?

(Repeat chorus)

So when the world knows my name, the world knows my face
People from my past will surely say
"He sounds so good and looks so great
we always knew he had what it takes!"

(Repeat chorus; end song)

KID: On behalf of my brethren of billions and myself, I hope I passed the audition.

OFFSTAGE VOICE: That was nice . . . uh . . . uh. . . . Gumby KID, but don't you have any material that's maybe a little more . . . ethnic? You know, we want that real Chinese thing.

KID: Well, to be honest with you, I spend an awful lot of time working the chinks OUT of my act.

OFFSTAGE VOICE: Thanks for coming down. We have your photo and phone number in case of a cancellation. NEXT!

(Crossfade to KID *entering a makeshift dressing room with a chair, bureau, and mirror. He enters and puts his boombox on the table.)*

KID: More ethnic? He'd probably ask Jesus to be "more martyr," too!

*(*KID *gets ready to go. Looks in the mirror, then a spot comes up on the ghost of* MICHAEL, *who is now covered in blood.)*

MICHAEL: So typical, Paulie. So typical. Always pipe-dreaming of being "The Man." Yellow Moses who's gonna move his people out of the wilderness of Chinatown and into the Promised Land of lo-fahn America. Well, listen up, Paulie. You ain't the real thing. You ain't even the fake thing. You're no-thing.

KID: Michael, you still hate me cause you could never get anything going outside of Chinatown. Well, you might be marooned, but not me. I can belong and get along just fine outside of Chinatown.

MICHAEL: You didn't belong to shit! They let you in 'cause you had a blond bimbo for a passport . . . just like dad.

KID: I'm not like dad!

MICHAEL: Oh yes you are, my brother. Only your bimbo comes with a beat. Remember her? Deirdre Bender, the demolished blond of Blond Faith.

(DEIRDRE BENDER *enters living room area.*)

MICHAEL: Man, when you were in Blond Faith, you were so high and mighty, thinking you're so much better than the rest of us sorry-ass Chinks down in Chinatown—

KID: I didn't think that—

MICHAEL: You probably thought you'd never have to see Chinatown again. Well, guess who's coming back for dinner?

KID: Michael, stop this.

MICHAEL: Well bro, no more hit records—

KID: We only had one.

MICHAEL: No more white chicks sucking your dick.

KID: There was really only one.

MICHAEL: Oh yeah? You never did tell me if she was a good lay?

KID: Fuck off!

(*Blackout on* DEIRDRE BENDER.)

MICHAEL: Hey, hey, Paulie! Don't get uptight with me. I didn't make *Deirdre Bender* my middle passage to the great lo-fahn frontier—you did.

KID: I did not.

MICHAEL: You didn't? Then how come when all was said and done, everyone remembers her and nobody remembers you?

KID: Lots of people know me!

MICHAEL: Nobody knows who you are because you don't know who you are . . . just like dad!

KID: Michael, what do you want from me?

MICHAEL: I want you to stop demeaning yourself in the lo-fahn fantasy world. Steer clear of these lo-fahns, Paulie. Look what happened to dad. They'll burn you just like that every time.

KID: That's not what Ngan-Gee says.

MICHAEL: Ngan-Gee. You go his way, you may survive . . . on the outside. But inside you'll die an instant death. You'll lose your Chinese soul, then you'll have no idea who you are . . . just like dad!

(KID *covers mirror with a towel. Blackout on* MICHAEL.)

KID: I know who I am. I ain't my dad. I damn well know who the fuck I am!

(KID *plays a tape on his boombox and gets down on his knees to pray. From the boombox we hear a Chinese woman singing a traditional Chinese lullaby.*)

WOMAN ON TAPE:

Ngen-sang ngooy-moong	*People's lives are like dreams . . .*
Ngen-ting om gnooy seu	*Human nature has no taste—like water . . .*
Ngen-sang sai seng	*People in this world . . .*
Tong-kee haw-see	*How long do we have. . . .*
Ngen-ting slee-gee	*People's natures are like paper . . .*
Jeng jeng buck	*Every sheet is thin . . .*
Sly-sea gneu-key	*What we know is strange . . .*
Gook gook sleng	*'Cause everything is new. . . .*

(*After tape finishes,* KID *gets up and starts to exit.*)

KID: One of these days, I'm gonna bust out. That's right. One of these days, I'm gonna bust out. BUST OUT! Bust out big time, man. BIG TIME! Then just watch out!

(KID *grabs his stuff and runs offstage. Blackout.*)

Scene 2

(*Later that afternoon. . . . Spotlight up on* KID's *uncle,* NGAN-GEE, *who is taking care of the last day's customers at his restaurant, the Pagan Pagoda Tea Parlor in Chinatown. It is raining.*)

NGAN-GEE: Just call me Ngan-Gee . . . that mean a-money in Chinese. . . .And that come-a to a-thirteen dollah even. . . . That right, you no pay me yet! . . . Oh, "shay-shay" a thank you! . . . Of course I throw in a-extra fortune cookie. No one ever leave a-my Pagan Pagoda Tea Parlor without them! (*He starts seeing tourist to the door, downstage*) Fortune Cookie likee-eee American Express of a-Chinatown! Oh, I'm glad you like a-way Chinatown look today, maybe you come back next weekend for a Chinese New Year parade and more Pagan Pagoda dim sum? . . . Oh no, that is our big holiday 'cause a-Chinese no celebrate Christmas. . . . 'Cause a-we way before B.C. Okay, all right, what that? Goong-Hay-Fat-Choy? That good! You learn from a-tape? From your cook? Very good. So maybe we see you next weekend, haveee safe-a trip back to a-why pains. . . . Of course that's whites-place! Bye-bye, we see you next time!

(As NGAN-GEE *waves good-bye to the tourists,* KID *enters and starts closing up the restaurant. Now lights up on restaurant which looks like a 1950's Malt Shoppe with Chinatown touches.* NGAN-GEE *joins* KID *in closing up.)*

NGAN-GEE: Ai-yah! [Oh God!] These damn lo-fahns don't have a clue!

KID: Ngan-Gee, you should get one of those Lifetime Achievement Oscars: Best Actor in a Chinatown Tourist Trap. Year after year, the One and Only—Ngan-Gee.

NGAN-GEE: Ha, ha. But one of these days, you learn to work lo-fahn tourists like lo-fahn charities: smile, talk-ee funny, then take 'em for all you can get.

KID: What? You really think they don't know you're making fun of them?

NGAN-GEE: I no here to make fun, just to make a-money. And at least my restaurant make money, you music make a-no sense or money.

KID: Well, at least I give 'em an honest effort—

NGAN-GEE: That you problem.

KID: . . . and don't have to act like Fred Eng in "The Year of the Dragon," and be a complete cash-kowtower to all the tourists.

*(*NGAN-GEE *stops working and glares at* KID.*)*

NGAN-GEE: Kowtowing . . . kowtowing. "Knee-ga slee juk-sing!" [Damn American Born!] What you call kowtowing I call survival! It only way for me to get around when I first come over!

KID: But that was then—

NGAN-GEE: Ai-yah, it make it easier for you kids, too!

KID: Oh, don't go on again about how you brought us to Gold Mountain—

NGAN-GEE: Just a-wake-up a-Paulie! When times get tough, you do anything to get by. At least I make-a my own way.

*(*NGAN-GEE *shakes a wad of bills at* KID.*)*

KID: Your own way? This is more like the only way Mr. Charlie let you in—through the back door. Ngan-Gee, this ain't China! You can't just shut yourself off from the rest of the world until things get better!

NGAN-GEE: And how you change a world? With your comedy "hok-gwai" music?

KID: Look, I told you. It's performance art and rap music—

NGAN-GEE: Ai-yah!

KID: But, yeah, I'd like to think that in my own small way, yeah, I can change the world.

NGAN-GEE: *(Laughing)* Ai-yah, you juk-sings have less of a clue than a-lo-fahns!

KID: No, really. When I was growing up, if I'd seen even one Chinese person in a band or on TV in some uncompromised way, it would have made all the difference in the world.

NGAN-GEE: Ai-yah! Why it always a TV, TV, TV? Why you have to always show a whole world, huh? How come you no happy just to prove things a-to yourself?

KID: Well, if you were born here like me, you'd know that people don't look out their windows for their worldview, they look at their TV sets. And when was the last time you saw any real "hung-gnens" on there?

NGAN-GEE: And what? Your Goong Hay Kid show is "real hung-gnen"?

KID: What should I do? Flit around like a butterfly, blinking fake lashes while flapping a fake fan in front of my fake-painted face? Maybe I could even bind my feet, put my hair in a bun, and book myself as a combination tourist/nostalgia/drag act! I'd be the poo poo platter of performance artists. You know, I'd probably get more gigs that way.

NGAN-GEE: Ai-yah, you know nothing but talk about everything . . . *(sighs)*. No sense trying to teach young dog old tricks.

(NGAN-GEE *comes out from behind the counter and gazes out the window.*)

NGAN-GEE: Well a-Paulie, I still look out a-window to see a-world. And with all a-rain so close to a-New Year. I always say that mean all a "hung-gnen" in heaven crying for all a-us hung-gnen still stuck down here.

(KID *joins* NGAN-GEE.)

KID: Yeah, the dirty New York rain just keeps on comin' down. It don't give anyone a break.

NGAN-GEE: But we all need a-rain, especially "hung-gnen gai" [Chinatown].

KID: Yeah, rain is just what Chinatown needs so it can mix with all the coughed up MSG to make the streets even more smelly and greasy than usual. And let me tell ya, there's nothing like coming home to that. Uh, uh. Nothing at all. Just knowing that the greasy glow of Chinatown awaits me at the end of the day makes it somehow, all worthwhile.

NGAN-GEE: I guess audition no go well today.

KID: Nah, it sucked. But what else is new?

NGAN-GEE: Nothing new. That's why people no want a Goong Hay Kid, and only want exotic oriental.

KID: Ngan-Gee, it's almost the twenty-first century—

NGAN-GEE: And you not kid no more!

KID: I know.

NGAN-GEE: A-Paulie, you be twenty-four this year! And I not getting any younger. I need some help.

KID: I know, a-Bok, I know. That's why when I bust out big time, that's gonna mean big bucks for both of us, I promise!

NGAN-GEE: Well, if that a-way you feel, then I think if you play with a-DB again, that be best chance for a-success in a-lo-fan world.

(NGAN-GEE *walks away from* KID *and resumes closing up the restaurant.* KID *catches up to him.*)

KID: That's not the point.

NGAN-GEE: Then what is a-point?

KID: Look, I'm sure you realize that next Saturday, Chinese New Year, will mark two whole years that I've been back and doing nothing but working here and getting turned away at these stupid auditions—

NGAN-GEE: And learn a-nothing from it cause you so stubborn and no want try new things. You still a-same as when you a little kid; you no happy unless everybody love you, but you no listen to nobody but a-you self.

KID: Wrong.

NGAN-GEE: Even now, I tell you what a-lo-fan want and you no listen to me.

KID: Again with the lo-fans?

NGAN-GEE: Come on. You can kid you-self, but no kid me. You entertainer. And when a-people go out, lo-fan, hung-gnen, whatever, they want to forget a-their problems and a-you do nothing but remind everybody about them.

KID: But Gnan-Gee, when I go on-stage, especially in front of a lo-fan audience, I am one of their problems . . . just like I seem to be with you "juk-koks."

NGAN-GEE: "Moe hom ngooy juk kok!" [Don't call me a juk-kok!] A-Paulie! We family and I still your boss.

KID: All right, I'm sorry Ngan-Gee, I just got a little carried away there.

NGAN-GEE: No more argue, let's just a-talk.

KID: Sure.

NGAN-GEE: Okay. You want people to see your show, right?

KID: Of course.

NGAN-GEE: My restaurant got a-big rent increase coming—

KID: This doesn't sound promising.

NGAN-GEE: Well, uh. Remember when I used to let you, a-DB and a-band use a restaurant here to play what you call a-rent parties?

KID: Oh no.

NGAN-GEE: Well, maybe you play a-rent party for me this time.

KID: Ngan-Gee, I'd like to help you out in any way I can, but I don't know about do-ing a performance down here. Shit, everybody down here still cusses me behind my back for what happened to Michael, and barely acknowledge me face-to-face when I'm working here. All they have to say is: "What? No more Blond, no more band? What happened?" As if their lives were so charmed.

NGAN-GEE: Wait. Wait. Wait. I no ask you to do rent party show here by yourself, cause a-that only help a-you. You do a-show here with a-DB. Plenty people come—and that a-help me! \

KID: Thanks a lot. Well, I said I'd do almost anything for a gig. Almost!

NGAN-GEE: So, now you a-gonna pull out on me like a-you pull out on a-Michael!

KID: What happened to Michael had nothing to do with me. He had his mind made up. No one could've stopped him.

NGAN-GEE: But you could have helped him!

KID: Hey, do I blame you for what happened to your brother?

NGAN-GEE: No talk about your father like that!

KID: No. Let's talk about it. It's about time we did.

(*A flashback:* MICHAEL *enters in clean, "non-bloodied" clothes. He is holding a suitcase.*)

MICHAEL: Lock the door, Paulie.

(KID *locks door.* MICHAEL *pours out piles of bills onto the table.*)

MICHAEL: Here, this ought to help us through.

NGAN-GEE: Ai-yah! Where you get it?

MICHAEL: Don't ask a-Bok. You too, Paulie. Anyone asks, you don't know about it, okay? Well, I gotta go.

KID: Where you going?

(MICHAEL *shows a gun.*)

MICHAEL: I'm gonna go meet dad.

KID: That won't change a damn thing.

MICHAEL: Maybe it won't, but it'll sure ease my mind. Show him that his lo-fahn cash don't make it around here. He can push mom back to hide in shame in China, but his ungrateful Number One son ain't afraid to look him in the eye and take him out! The fucking bastard!

KID: Michael, I hate him too. But I don't want to kill him.

MICHAEL: Well, you never knew what you wanted, Paulie. And you'll never have the guts to take it all the way! You too, a-Bok!

NGAN-GEE: Ai-yah, nee leng-ga. Moe nee-you nee-ga bop-ba. [You two, don't be mad at your father.] He just get a little misled here in America. Ong you ga-hing! [We still family.] In times of trouble, we have to stay together.

MICHAEL: Family? Don't give me that shit.

NGAN-GEE: Do it for your mother! Even though she back in China, her heart and soul still here with you. She just forgot how to cry or how to feel here. She go back home to try and remember.

MICHAEL: Well, I'll send her a love letter—right through dad's heart!

(MICHAEL *exits. Quick Blackout. We hear a gun shot, then lights up on* KID *and* NGAN-GEE. SARA *comes running in.*)

KID: What happened?

ARA: Call the police!

KID: Who was it?

NGAN-GEE: Sara, what happened!?

(SARA *picks up a telephone.*)

SARA: There's been a shooting on East Broadway . . . Michael Mah. . . . A scuffle . . . with his father. . . . He got shot with his own gun. . . . No! No! Michael was stealing from his father. . . . That's right, self-defense. . . . No, the father's okay.

NGAN-GEE: Yim goong! [What a shame!]

(*Quick Blackout.* SARA *exits. Lights up on* KID *and* NGAN-GEE *back in present.*)

KID: So don't blame what happened to Michael on me!

NGAN-GEE: Then don't blame a-me for what not happen for you!

(*Blackout.*)

Scene 3

(KID *is once again on stage at another audition. Set and his costume are same as in Scene One.*)

OFFSTAGE VOICE: I should tell you up front, I'm looking for ethnic acts, but I really don't book too many rap acts.

KID: Well, I see what I do as more punk-rap and performance art.

OFFSTAGE VOICE: All right, man, whatever turns you on. And if you don't mind me asking, isn't that rap stuff more for the brothers uptown?

KID: Just 'cause I wanna rap doesn't mean I want to be black.

OFFSTAGE VOICE: Just asking, just asking. . . . You know, you look familiar . . . don't I know you from someplace else?

KID: I haven't been around for a few years.

OFFSTAGE VOICE: That's it. You're Paul Wong!

KID: Paul Mah.

OFFSTAGE VOICE: Oh, Mah, sorry I blew your name, but I knew I knew your face. And I used to love that song: "Blond Faith."

KID: Thanks.

OFFSTAGE VOICE: Sorry that second album didn't pan out for you. But how's the DB?

KID: I haven't seen her in years.

OFFSTAGE VOICE: It didn't end well?

KID: No, it didn't.

OFFSTAGE VOICE: Oh. Too bad. So, whenever you're ready.

KID: Okay. Tonight I want to share with you selected passages from my personal, un-sanctified scripture: I Chink: The Book of No Change. 'Cause when I look around, that's what I see. Basically, it's like this. My people were getting fucked over in the mainland, so they came here to America thinking it was the Gold Mountain. And what did we get? A goddamn golden shower is what we got. We got pissed on, sucked off, and fucked over is what we got. Now they say it's okay to be different? We are the world? Well, to them I say this:

(KID *starts backing track on his boombox and raps the song: "I Chink".*)

I CHINK:
So you want diversity?
You want to be multi-culti?
You want to reach out to me?
First, let me tell you who I be.

Yeah, I'm the Chink who can't drive straight
The gook you love to hate
Yeah, I'm the race you saved too late
The soul you tried to cremate.

CHORUS:
So, hi! Pleased to meet you
I'm a Chink
Oh no, I've never been here before
'Cause I'm a Chink

What's that? The pleasure is yours
'Cause I'm a Chink?
Just what is this game of yours
That now includes us Chinks?

So now you like us people
You'll even treat us as equals?
No more Cold War sequels?
Well, that's unbelievable.

You treat my dad like a Viet Cong
My momma's your Suzy Wong
You bust my brother for being a Tong
So now I'm your Native Son?

(REPEAT CHORUS, END SONG)

OFFSTAGE VOICE: Well Paul, you did real well.

KID: Oh, thanks.

OFFSTAGE VOICE: But unfortunately, I think your act is a little too Chinese for my stage.

KID: What do you mean, too Chinese? Do you ever tell these white dopes on punk that they're too stupid?

OFFSTAGE VOICE: Look, Paul, since you're taking this so personally, let me give you some advice. If I were you I'd think about putting the old band back together. At least Blond Faith had a solid concept and solid songs. Now it seems like you're all over the place.

KID: But the real songs and image didn't even get out. What got out was a watered-down record company version.

OFFSTAGE VOICE: That's all that ever gets out, my friend. So if that's all, I've still got to audition a dozen more Iggy Pop clones, so I gotta send you on your way. NEXT!

(KID *enters makeshift dressing room.*)

KID: (*To himself*) Solid concept, solid songs. He's like all the record company jerks. What the fuck does he know? What do any of them know?

(*A flashback:* DB *enters restaurant section of stage.*)

DB: Hey, Paulie, what do you mean we have to get our concept down first, and our music second?

(KID *crosses to* DB.)

KID: That's right. Anyone can write songs, but why bother putting a band together unless you have a solid concept and image?

DB: So you've been developing an image for us?

KID: Yeah, and I've even been working on a sort of theme song, too.

DB: You have?

KID: Well, it's not quite finished yet. But remember I told you about my father and his King Kong complex and my whole sort of King Kong immigrant theory?

DB: How could I forget.

KID: Well, I thought we could sort of send that up—do a campy take on it.

DB: This sounds scary.

KID: Oh, it is. But rather than do the traditional King Kong and Fay Wray thing . . .

DB: Hey, Jessica Lange.

KID: All right, Fay Wray, Jessica Lange, whatever. Rather than the outsider and the damsel in distress, I thought it would be funnier to do the outsider and the femme fatale. Sort of like King Kong and Marlene Dietrich in *Blond Venus*.

DB: I'm not putting on that gorilla suit!

KID: You don't have to. Neither of us will. They'll just be props. And our centerpiece number would be kind of like this. . . . *(KID strums along on his guitar)* You'd sing: "Remember old King Kong?" And I'd answer: "He blew it all on a blonde."

(DB is very amused.)

KID: Then you'd sing: "He climbed atop the Empire State," and I'd answer: "And didn't even get to first base." And we would continue that sort of tongue-in-cheek call and response thing.

DB: Sounds great. Any thoughts on a name?

KID: Well, as long as we have an image I figured we could just go by our names. Mah-Bender . . . like Hall & Oates.

DB: Paul, they're in alphabetical order.

KID: You want to be Bender-Mah?

DB: Well, all right. I guess the other way does sound better.

KID: Good. But that's just the band name. The whole concept album would be Mah-Bender in "The Adventures of The Goong Hay Kid and The Demolished Blonde." Then, on stage, you could be like Marianne Faithful and I could be like a, a Chinese Kid *Creole*.

DB: Wait a minute. Are we talking KID Creole or King Creole?

KID: Well . . . both.

DB: I'd buy that.

KID: Great! So you like it?

DB: I think it sounds great.

(They start to make out. Then we hear . . .)

OFFSTAGE VOICE: Deirdre, Paul. I want to thank you so much for sending me your demo tape.

(KID and DB abruptly stop making out and straighten out their clothes as they respond to a record company executive.)

DB: You're welcome.

KID: Thanks for listening.

OFFSTAGE VOICE: No, thank you for letting me hear it. That "Blond Faith/King Kong" song was the most right-on take of race relations I've ever heard.

KID: You gotta be kid—

DB: No, we agree wholeheartedly. That was our intention.

OFFSTAGE VOICE: It was insightful and had a real gritty, street edge.

DB: I'm glad you picked up on that.

OFFSTAGE VOICE: Picked up on it? Deirdre, Paul, it blew right through me like a ball and chain!

KID: What did you think of that other song: "The First Chinese Hero On TV?"

OFFSTAGE VOICE: Well, that sounded a little, dare I say it, ironic. And irony, well, it may get you good, even great reviews. But irony rarely sells. But, on the other hand, that "Blond Faith" song hits a deep note in us all. Especially now!

DB: I couldn't agree more.

KID: Well, I—

DB: . . . as you were saying?

OFFSTAGE VOICE: My staff and I have been discussing it. And everyone here at MegaUnit thinks that a bi-racial band like yours is exactly what the music industry needs right now. But we would like to make some adjustments.

KID: Er, what kind of adjustments?

OFFSTAGE VOICE: Well, being that you're a new band, we wanted to make it easy for the kids in terms of product enhancement. You know, give them something familiar to focus on. So, rather than the bland: "Mah-Bender in The Adventures of The Goong Hay Kid & The Demolished Blonde," we thought we should feature Deirdre more and call the whole project "Blond Faith"—just like the song. We figure that would make the most sense to make the most dollars. What do you think?

DB: Wait a minute! This ain't right!

OFFSTAGE VOICE: Oh, please. Deirdre, Paul. Don't take this personally. It's only a business decision. Like the Beatles used to say: "We can work it out."

(Blackout on restaurant area. KID *returns to makeshift dressing room.)*

KID: No one will ever water me down again.

*(*KID *frowns and looks in mirror. Spot comes up on* MICHAEL. *He is again covered in blood.)*

MICHAEL: "I Chink." Where'd you get that? From Ngan-Gee's born-again Charlie Chan handbook?

KID: No, Michael. I wrote it all by myself!

MICHAEL: Then Paulie, don't try so hard. You may hurt yourself. And stop making fun of stuff you don't understand!

KID: What don't I understand?

MICHAEL: What you don't understand is Chinese soul . . . just like dad. . . . NEXT!

(Blackout on MICHAEL. *Spot up on* NGAN-GEE.*)*

NGAN-GEE: Wake up a-Paulie. When times get tough you do anything to get by.

KID: You're right, I'm late.

(Blackout on KID *and* NGAN-GEE, *in darkness.)*

OFFSTAGE VOICE: NEXT! SLATE IT!

(Spotlight on KID *dressed in Sumo Wrestler's robe. Standing behind a table with a wood block and a Chinese food product on it. A stagehand runs in front of* KID *and slams a film cracker.)*

KID: Paul Mah, take one.

OFFSTAGE VOICE: ACTION!

*(*KID *chops a block, then screams.)*

KID: We don't need no stinking wontons!

OFFSTAGE VOICE: CUT! Hold up the product, hold up the product! And smile please. All right. Try it one more time. Okay. Quiet on the set. We're gonna try this one again. Let's slate it again, too.

(A stagehand runs in front of KID *and slams a film cracker.)*

KID: Paul Mah, take two.

OFFSTAGE VOICE: ACTION!

*(*KID *again chops block and screams.)*

KID: We don't need no . . . goddamn racist stereotypical commercials!

OFFSTAGE VOICE: CUT! CUT! Look Kid, we'll pay you. But we gotta send you on your way. NEXT! Hey, Mel! What's going on here. You said these orientals were going to be cooperative.

(As KID *starts to leave, he turns around and grabs his crotch.*)

KID: Hey, co-op this!

OFFSTAGE VOICE: Someone get this guy out of here NOW!

(*Blackout.*)

Scene 4:

(NGAN-GEE *is in his back room/office. A desk and a bed. He pauses from doing paper work, takes a drink from his whiskey glass and pulls out a hardcore Asian pornographic magazine. As he turns the pages, he loosens his shirt and pants and starts touching himself. As he does this, he laughs and sings to himself.*)

NGAN-GEE: Gnen-sang, gnooy moong. . . . Gnen-ting, om gnooy seu. . . .

(*Across the room, in a cloud of smoke or similar fantasy effect enters* JULIE, NGAN-GEE's *dominatrix/fantasy girl. Slowly,* JULIE *enters* NGAN-GEE's *space and starts dominating/humiliating him. She brandishes a whip that she uses on* NGAN-GEE *to make her point.*)

JULIE: Stop that! Did I tell you to sing?

NGAN-GEE: Ai-yah, why not?

JULIE: Don't ask me questions! And get over there.

(*She throws* NGAN-GEE *onto the desk.*)

NGAN-GEE: Okay, a-Julie. Okay.

JULIE: What was that hideous song anyway?

NGAN-GEE: Ah, it just a-lullaby I used to sing back in my village in a-Thoisan. It reminds me of a first girl I love. . . . And a-you remind me of a-her.

JULIE: Save it, 'cause that's all I ever hear out of you, stories of the past. Well, I'm sick and tired of hearing you babble on about how that bitch broke your heart or how you've sacrificed everything and got nothing.

NGAN-GEE: Yes, yes.

JULIE: You've gotten more than you deserve!

NGAN-GEE: You're right a-Julie.

JULIE: No more of that shit—understand?

NGAN-GEE: Understand.

JULIE: Forget it! What's past is past!

NGAN-GEE: Okay, a-Julie, okay.

JULIE: So tell me something. What's my name?

NGAN-GEE: Julie.

JULIE: Excuse me, what's my name?

NGAN-GEE: Julie?

JULIE: MISS JULIE!

NGAN-GEE: Miss Julie!

JULIE: Louder!

NGAN-GEE: MISS JULIE!

JULIE: Don't you forget it, MISS JULIE!

NGAN-GEE: Miss Julie!

   (An alarm clock goes off.)

JULIE: Well, time's up.

   *(*JULIE *releases* NGAN-GEE *from her spell. He gets up and hands* JULIE *a "Hoong Bow" or good-luck red envelope with money in it.)*

NGAN-GEE: Goong Hay Fat Choy a-Julie.

JULIE: Oh, goong hay fat choy.

   *(*JULIE *gives* NGAN-GEE *a very business-like kiss, then discreetly counts the money in the "Hoong Bow" and is disappointed.)*

JULIE: You know, I really didn't want to say anything, but you been coming here for years. . . . You think maybe you could start taking a little better care of me, 'cause I always take good care of you.

NGAN-GEE: Ai-yah, you juk-sings are all a-same. Always want a-more, more, more.

JULIE: We had to learn it from somewhere. And it seems like all you old world geezers are all the same, slumming it with us and then I could just imagine how well you must take care of the girls at the white house.

NGAN-GEE: I never go to a-white house.

JULIE: Well, maybe you should consider it next time.

NGAN-GEE: Okay, then I go to a-white house. You see, I go to a-white house. I show you juk-sings. I go to a white house!

   *(*JULIE *exits in the same fantastical way she entered.* NGAN-GEE *begins to doze off on his desk, repeating . . .)*

NGAN-GEE: . . . I go to a-white house. You see, I go to a-white house.

(Lights come up on KID *in front/business area of restaurant, still wearing the Sumo wrestler's robe from a previous audition.* KID *sits at a table with a boombox on it and is working on a rap version of the lullaby he played earlier.)*

KID: Ngen-sang a ngooy moong. . . . ngen-ting, om-ngooy . . . *(repeat as needed.)*

(Ngen-Gee awakes from his stupor and is surprised to hear the KID *singing the lullaby. He quickly hides his magazine and whiskey and crosses to* KID.*)*

NGAN-GEE: Ai-yah, a-Paulie.

KID: Hi-ya, a-Bok!

*(*NGAN-GEE *examines* KID*'s outfit.)*

NGAN-GEE: You take-a this real hung-ngen stuff so serious, huh?

KID: Oh, this get-up? It was only for a regrettable audition. Hope it didn't scare you.

NGAN-GEE: It only scare me 'cause I think you mix up what's a-hung-ngen and what's a-Japanese.

KID: Oh, come on, of course I know that Sumo wrestlers are Japanese. But you think these lo-fahn casting agents know the difference?

NGAN-GEE: I still think you no know a-difference. But where you get that song?

KID: Oh, it's uh, a long story and a little embarrassing. . . . Why? You know it?

NGAN-GEE: I know it very well . . . uh, everyone back in a-Thoisan know that song. Maybe you add it to your show?

KID: And finally get a gig as exotic orientalia? Not quite. But I was actually thinking of serving it up in a new way.

NGAN-GEE: Oh yeah? Show me how you want to do it.

KID: You want to hear it?

NGAN-GEE: Yeah, sure.

KID: Right now?

NGAN-GEE: Yeah, a-why not?

KID: This is not like you, but okay, here we go. . . . Just one disclaimer though. I wouldn't be caught dead dressed like this on stage. But check this out anyway. I call it "Column Z."

*(*KID *breaks into a crass rap routine with bravura, but quickly melts into meekness in front of* NGAN-GEE*'s disapproving eyes.)*

COLUMN Z:
People know uptown, people know downtown
But it seems like nobody knows Chinatown

So there's only one way to fill that gap
I'll put my culture in my rap
Check this out:
I said a' "Ngen-sang, ngooy-moong"—WOO!
"Ngen-ting, om-gnooy-seu"—WOO!

You might miss the words
But you'll catch the drift
All new rhymes and all new riffs. . . .

(Speaking) Well, the adaptation is not quite finished, but I think you get the general idea.

NGAN-GEE: A-Paulie, can I tell you something?

KID: Please.

NGAN-GEE: No give-up a-day job. That more bad than a-way you work here.

KID: Well, most people don't know how to receive a work-in-progress. . . .

NGAN-GEE: Why don't you show some respect? For a-song, for a-hung gnens!

KID: Lighten up! I was just kidding.

NGAN-GEE: That a-problem. You always just kidding, but you not kid no more.

KID: Well, if you really want to know, I wasn't kidding, all right? If I could learn it right, I probably would add it to my act. Shit, I'd try almost anything now!

NGAN-GEE: Yeah, you try that, you try anything. A-Paulie, how come it seem like you only a-hung-gnen when it can a-help you?

KID: A-Bok, don't tell me how to be Chinese, 'cause that's all I ever hear; you're too Chinese, or you're not Chinese enough. Well, I'm sick and tired of people telling me how to be Chinese.

NGAN-GEE: A-Paulie, I no here to tell you how to be Chinese. I trying to tell you how to be a man!

KID: I am a man.

NGAN-GEE: Oh yeah. What's a man? Is it being someone who cannot face his own family? His own neighborhood? His own kind?

KID: No. Being a man is knowing who you are, knowing what you're about and then doing your thing the best you can and not getting bogged down in all that other bullshit of trying to live up to everyone else's expectations.

NGAN-GEE: Oh yeah. Then what is your "thing"? What you got to show, huh? What do you got going?

KID: All right, nothing yet.

NGAN-GEE: Nothing, period. And if I lose restaurant, you have even less!

KID: I know!

NGAN-GEE: You juk-sing always act like a-you know everything—

KID: Ngan-Gee—

NGAN-GEE: And how long you think I can keep a-running myself into a-ground while you try and play in a-clouds, huh?

KID: All right, already. Stop yelling!

NGAN-GEE: Stop dreaming!

KID: This must be about the rent increase.

NGAN-GEE: Of course it is knee-ga slee juk-sing! [Damn American-born!]

KID: Look, what do you want?

NGAN-GEE: Talk to a-DB about doing a rent party.

KID: *(Pause)* Well . . . okay. Guess it can't hurt just to talk about it.

NGAN-GEE: Good! . . . When you want talk to her?

KID: I'll call her tomorrow.

NGAN-GEE: That what I figure, so I call her yesterday.

KID: Uh, NGAN-GEE, how could you do this without even asking me?

NGAN-GEE: You too slow. If everybody take as long as-a you to a-take action, New York still be British just like a-Hong Kong!

(There is a knock at the door.)

KID: Go home! We're closed!

NGAN-GEE: Hey, hey, hey. A-Pagan Pagoda never closed. *(He goes to answer door)* What you want, order more custom fortune cookie?

*(*NGAN-GEE *opens door.* DB *enters soaking wet with rain.* KID *is stunned.)*

DB: Knee hoe mah? [How are you?]

NGAN-GEE: DB! So good to see you!

DB: You, too, Ngan-Gee!

KID: Out of all the Dim Sum joints in Chinatown she has to walk into mine.

*(*DB *and* NGAN-GEE *embrace. Then* DB *goes to embrace* KID, *but* KID *does not move.)*

DB: Don't get up.

NGAN-GEE: Oh, a-DB, so nice to see you! . . . Paulie, what a surprise, ha-ha!

KID: You're telling me.

NGAN-GEE: Come on a-DB, a-Paulie, let's just a-sit down first. I get some tea.

(NGAN-GEE *goes to get tea.* DB *sits down.*)

DB: Well, Paulie. How's the Goong Hay Kid?

KID: He's been better.

DB: I have to give you credit for sticking with it. I didn't think it would last after we broke up the band.

KID: After YOU broke up the band.

DB: Paulie, let's not go through this again.

KID: Once more without feeling.

DB: Paulie, what are you doing in rap anyway? Trying to be down with the brothers or something?

KID: Just because I'm into rap doesn't mean I want to be black. Just like playing in a band with you didn't mean I wanted to be white. I know who I am, Dee!

DB: Jeez, I was just asking.

KID: And I was just answering.

(NGAN-GEE *returns with tea.*)

NGAN-GEE: Okay, stop it! Or at least wait until a-audience is here. Now this is a-story: a-DB no do show around here for long time, a-Paulie can't find place for his new act. So I think this rent increase party good opportunity for all a-us, but if it be nothing but headache, we stop now.

(*Pause.*)

DB: Look Paulie, Ngan-Gee needs it and it ain't gonna kill anybody.

KID: Well, Chinese New Year is just a week way, I can endure.

NGAN-GEE: Okay, so we do it . . . shut up! You listen to a-Ngan-Gee now and I tell you how I gonna run a-show. But first we make a toast to it.

(NGAN-GEE *gives everyone a full cup of tea.*)

DB: To a very limited venture!

KID: With the potential for unlimited agata!

NGAN-GEE: May a-best New Year be a-next!

(*The toast.* KID *and* DB *smash their cups.*)

NGAN-GEE: Ai-yah! You two. But no worry, DB. Paulie clean it up! Come here, we gonna put a stage here like in the old days.

(NGAN-GEE *and* DB *walk around, leaving* KID *to clean up the mess.*)

KID: Same as it ever was!

(*Blackout.*)

Scene 5:

(*Showtime at the Pagan Pagoda. Chinese New Year's Eve. Restaurant looks more like a nightclub with a small stage and two mike stands in the center.* NGAN-GEE *steps into the spotlight and awkwardly checks mike by banging on it, blowing into it, etc. Then he introduces the show.*)

NGAN-GEE: Goong Hay Fat Choy! And welcome to a-first and hopefully a-last Chinese New Year's rent increase party for a-Pagan Pagoda Tea Parlour. Tonight we have a very special show for a-you all. We have a-reunion of a-DB and a-Paulie in a-Blond Faith show (*applause is heard*). And also for a-first time, a-Paulie by himself in a-Goong Hay Kid Show (*boos are heard*). My name is a-Ngan-Gee, just like a-money, so please be generous to your bartender, who is also a-me. So now, without a-further introduction, for a-first time since a-my nephew Paulie pay his rent on a-time, here Blond Faith.

(*Applause is heard.* DB *enters dressed in '70s black leather garb and stands at center mike.* KID *enters wearing a gorilla mask and black clothing.* KID *hands* DB *a rose;* DB *caresses it, then bites petals off and spits them in the air.*)

DB: Don't make me laugh—hit it!

(*They perform "Blond Faith," a punk version of an early '60's girl group song like The Ronettes or Shangri-las.*)

(DB *sings.*)

BLOND FAITH:
Remember ol' King Kong?
He blew it all on a blonde
He climbed atop the Empire State
and didn't even get to first base
Then there was Bacall
Who always made Bogey crawl
No matter how true his grit
A smokey look and that was it.

CHORUS:
Even if they plead and beg
Tell 'em "Take a hike or go buy a Deb."
'Cause this ain't no give and take
You're at the mercy of my Blond Faith—WOO!
Always say never

Never say forever
Tell 'em you don't even remember.

(The following lines are spoken over music.)

KID: Hey DB?

DB: What, Paulie? Or should I say Goong Hay?

KID: I hear you're a good dancer.

DB: What do you mean, you hear I'm a good dancer? Can't you see for yourself?

KID: No, 'cause my eyesight is close. Very, very close.

DB: Oh, I was wondering if you were squinting or just glad to see me.

KID: *(Annoyed)* Let's get back to the song.

DB:

Then there was Mae West
Who'd always top every man's best
They'd just peek at her stacking
And she knew what the fellow was packing
Now we got Debbie Harry
Who's cool, tough, and quite contrary
Although she never was woman of the year
They're still "touched by your presence dear."

(REPEAT CHORUS, END SONG)

(KID exits.)

DB: Thanks! It's nice to know that you're still out there. We'll do some more Blond Faith stuff later, but now we'd like to change the pace a little bit and bring things back to the present. Ladies and Gentlemen, making his world premiere—outside of auditions, that is, here he is—Chinatown's pre-eminent performance artist and rapper: The Goong Hay Kid!

(DB Exits. KID enters in Sumo wrestler's robe of previous scene draped over his rap stage outfit. He speaks in a sarcastic Ngan-Gee-esque accent.)

KID: It okay if you no want to applaud, it no effect me no more. When you get to be young ancient Chinese sage like a-me, it very easy to know a-difference between a-white and a-wong!

(KID mocks a "polite" Asian laugh.)

OFFSTAGE HECKLERS: Bring back the blonde. . . . Get off the stage!

KID: I hear you but a-you no bother me 'cause like-a modern-ancient Chinese proverb say: That a-effective wise guy always do battle in a-sturdy suit of irony!

(Crowd grows more impatient.)

KID: Oh, a-thank you for a-you kind-a hospitality. I now want do my first rap especially for a-you. It called: "Rock Me, Goong Hay."

(KID *starts reversing tape on his boombox and performs "Rock Me, Goong Hay." Song
starts with cliched oriental riff, after which* KID *rips off robe and goes into song.*)

ROCK ME, GOONG HAY:
Lose that shit—this ain't the mainland
I'm the Goong Hay Kid—hope you understand
Don't do no kowtowing or no rickshaw
So don't be talking no dragons or the Great Wall
I ain't good in math, don't know Kung Fu
ditto for Confucius and Fu Manchu
So don't mess with me or call me Bruce Lee
'Cause ain't no one badder than Kid Goong Hay

CHORUS:
Rock Me, Goong Hay (four times)

I only come 'round when the sun goes down
when I cruise the streets of Chinatown
where the gangs and dolls they all concede
that the baddest dude is Kid Goong Hay.
Now I'm too up on things and too down by law,
the deftest C-town B-Boy you ever saw
So don't dis me as some ping pong, ching chong,
mah jong, egg foo young, bang a gong, muh fuh huh.

(REPEAT CHORUS)

Now I'm no quick fix like MSG
Or some exotic treat from Column A or Column B
You won't find my kind on a Dim Sum tray
'Cause I'm rhymin' for tomorrow, not just today
A root-rock-rapper proud of the sound
"Break it up, break it up, break it up. Breakdown."
I'm the rappin' real deal—all brains, heart, and balls
So how inscrutable is that to you all?

(REPEAT CHORUS)

Yellow fever was our lot in this country
Now we're the so-called "model minority"
Which really don't mean shit if you think about it
'Cause plenty still despise our slanty eyes
So don't overcompensate for your sorry state
You can't keep up in the laundry or the railroad track

'CAUSE IT TAKES A NATION OF BILLIONS
TO HOLD US PEOPLE BACK!

(REPEAT CHORUS)

Goong hay fat choy!

(Song ends as it began with cliché oriental riff. Crowd resumes booing.)

OFFSTAGE HECKLERS: Rap in Chinese!

KID: Oh, why don't you shut up in English!

(Continued ad-lib heckling.)

KID: Oh, why don't you shut up in English! Yeah, go ahead and boo. But mark my words, one day you'll be saying you saw me when, so it don't bother me. Oh yeah, all great men with a higher purpose from Jesus to Bob Dylan and Muhammad Ali all got publicly humiliated, so I'll take this as a compliment.

OFFSTAGE HECKLERS: Bring back the blonde!

KID: I see that is mostly guys out there booing. Well, I bet your girlfriends are already wet from me, so stay and limp and dry behind your boos, you goddamn cowards.

OFFSTAGE HECKLERS: Where's your pride? What would your brother think?

KID: I don't care what he thinks anymore. I don't care what you think anymore. 'Cause unlike you all, I know who I am. And I like who I am. How many of you can say that? I'm not trying to hide behind my Asian Americana disguise like some lemon-coated Ken or Barbie doll who's desperately trying to fit in without rocking the boat. Well, as Putney Swope says: "Rocking the boat's a drag. You gotta sink the boat!" And you can be damn sure that boat is leaking. Shit yeah! And like Dylan says: "You better start swimming or you'll sink like a stone." Well, stones were made for casting, not people. Goong Hay Fat Choy!

(KID exits in a huff. NGAN-GEE runs to center stage.)

NGAN-GEE: Uh, we hear more from band . . . then more Blond Faith.

(Blackout.)

Scene 6:

(Pagan Pagoda after the show. The crowd has left. Only KID, DB, and NGAN-GEE remain.)

NGAN-GEE: It could be worse. I could-a get up and try to a-sing tonight too. . . . At least nobody call out request.

DB: Ngan-Gee, can you please excuse us for a moment?

NGAN-GEE: No problem. I need some air anyway. I take long walk.

(NGAN-GEE exits. After a few beats, DB speaks.)

DB: I'm so sorry for what happened tonight, you don't know. You probably won't buy it, but I didn't really want to do the show either. Of course I wanted to help out Ngan-Gee, he even called it a rent party.

KID: He's a charmer, all right.

DB: Things haven't been so hot by me lately and just hearing the words "rent party" brought back so many memories. And I know it's not all good, but we have a lot of history together. We've got a lot of history right here. Like when we used to come back here after gigs and sit for hours by that counter talking about what we were gonna name our kids: A girl would be Suzy Q; a boy, Johnny B. But both would have the middle name. . . .

KID AND DB: Dylan.

KID: I remember . . . it wasn't that long ago.

DB: I know. I think the worst part of this sort of homecoming scenario was the thought of being "DB: The Demolished Blond of Blond Faith" again—ugh! It's strange. This all started as a joke; yet it's come to define who I am in the public eye.

KID: Yeah, the joke died ugly and came back as this monster that chewed me up and spit me out.

DB: It spit us both out. Can't you see that? And I never wanted that. Like Dylan says: "I was hungry and it was your world." 'Cause that's all I was doing: playing a part that you created in your world. Then I got stuck there . . . without you. I know it was only on stage, but it felt so good to be by your side again tonight.

(DB *goes to embrace him, but* KID *just takes her hands and keeps her at arm's distance.*)

KID: All right, I wanted to do the show to see you again, too. I thought about call-ing, but I was too chicken-shit or something. And you know, everyone from Jackie Gleason to Johnny Thunders has said: "You can't put your arms around a memory." But they're wrong. 'Cause you can. It's easy. Too easy. Memories are safe. Life isn't. What's worth more—I don't know. But I do know that when your eyes are open, memories don't stand a chance. And after tonight, I just can't close my eyes like I used to.

DB: What do you mean "like you used to?"

KID: Well, after getting embarrassed like that, in my own restaurant, doing a show I knew I should've never done, I realized I've just been running back and forth like an asshole without a head, trying to live up to these stupid ideals that have been pounded into me from the juk-koks, the TV, and what not. And I've never really taken a single step for what I think or feel. Everything's been dictated by them.

DB: Everything?

KID: Everything.

DB: *(Pause)* Even me?

KID: *(Pause)* I'm sorry, Dee.

DB: *(Pause)* Paulie, we've been here before. I thought you got over worrying that you were turning into your father.

KID: It's not that.

DB: Did you ever love me?

KID: *(Pause)* No. But not because I didn't want to. Dee, I just didn't know how. And it's not just you. I've been scared to get close to anyone . . . all my life . . . cause I never knew myself.

(They stare at each other a few beats, then DB silently gathers her things. After a few beats.)

DB: You know, there were a lot of times when I really wondered if I was just your way of getting back at Michael. . . . Well, thanks for putting that memory out of its misery . . . if nothing else.

KID: There is nothing else.

DB: Well, say good-bye to Ngan-Gee for me . . . and Paulie, do you think we'll become complete strangers again?

KID: Come on, Dee, we've never completed anything.

DB: I guess so. Just like our songs . . . we just fade out.

(DB exits. KID plays tape of Chinese lullaby we heard earlier and gets down on his knees to pray. From the boombox we hear a Chinese woman singing a traditional Chinese lullaby.)

WOMAN ON TAPE:

Ngen-sang ngooy-moong	*People's lives are like dreams . . .*
Ngen-ting om gnooy seu	*Human nature has no taste—like water . . .*
Ngen-sang sai seng	*People in this world . . .*
Tong-kee haw-see	*How long do we have. . . .*
Ngen-ting slee-gee	*People's natures are like paper . . .*
Jeng jeng buck	*Every sheet is thin . . .*
Sly-sea gneu-key	*What we know is strange . . .*
Gook gook sleng	*Cause everything is new. . . .*

(After tape finishes, KID starts to exit but is blocked by MICHAEL, once again covered in blood.)

MICHAEL: So you're finished humiliating yourself in the lo-fahn fantasy world?

KID: No, I've just begun and I know who I am.

MICHAEL: Oh yeah? Then who are you . . . without me telling you?

KID: I don't need you to be me.

MICHAEL: Oh no? What are you gonna do? Keep listening to Ngan-Gee? Do another rent party? Come on. Call DB one more time!

KID: No, I'm not listening to Ngan-Gee anymore!

MICHAEL: So you finally admit he's wrong?

KID: Yeah. I know Ngan-Gee's wrong. But that doesn't make you right.

MICHAEL: Watch your mouth! Without me, you'd still be DB's whipping boy! Or should I say, pussy-whipped boy?

KID: I didn't leave her for you! No fucking way. I did that for me!

MICHAEL: You did it for you? And suppose I didn't die for you? Where would you be?

KID: Michael, you didn't die for me! But that doesn't mean I don't live for you.

MICHAEL: You don't have the soul to do it . . . so don't you dare live for me!

KID: I'll live anyway I want to!

(KID *stands up, picks up chair, and swings it at* MICHAEL, *but winds up only breaking a mirror. Quick Blackout, then lights up to reveal* KID *alone standing amidst the rubble. Blackout.*)

Scene 7:

(*Spotlight on* NGAN-GEE *on the phone in his back room office. Once again it is raining. We hear the phone ring, then* JULIE's *answering machine "answers" the call. As this happens, spotlight on* JULIE *screening her calls.*)

JULIE: (*Answering machine*) Hi, this is Miss Julie. And I know what bad boys like you want. So please leave me a message and I'll show you what pain and pleasure are all about.

(*We hear a beep.*)

NGAN-GEE: A-Julie, it's a-me, please answer . . . Julie, it's me, Ngan-Gee, please answer . . . I make a mistake. I no want go to a-white house . . . I want see you . . . I no want go to a-white house . . . I want see you. . . . Please it's me, Ngan-Gee . . . I no want to go to a-white house . . . I make mistake!

(*As* NGAN-GEE *leaves his message,* JULIE *is torn whether to answer or not, but then turns off her machine. We hear the sound of a phone off the hook.* NGAN-GEE *hangs up the phone, takes a swig from his drink, and delivers the following soliloquy.*)

NGAN-GEE: On a-night before the New Year, all a-dreams and all a-people I ever know come back. Some haunt me, some comfort me. And everybody I can no see again seem more alive than ever. Then, all a-hopes, glories, shame, and struggle I go through mean nothing. Nothing at all. Then it just me . . . and a-rain outside time, outside race, outside China, outside USA . . . but always in a-Chinatown. Even in my most happy dreams the streets are always greasy, always narrow, and always keep

me from a-looking up. Next morning I always very sad even though a new year begin. 'Cause a-funny thing is: I always wake up from dreams, but I'm not sure if I
ever wake up from this life. Maybe someday. Maybe someday.

(Blackout.)

Scene 8:

(Pagan Pagoda, first hours of Chinese New Year's day. Once again it is raining. KID *is by
himself wearing an apron over his stage outfit and cleaning up from the night before. After
a few beats* NGAN-GEE *enters and starts helping* KID. *They work in silence a few beats,
then . . .)*

KID: I know what you're thinking . . . "I told you so. Things never change and that's
why people don't want The Goong Hay Kid and only want an exotic oriental."
Well, I hope I didn't embarrass you too much tonight.

NGAN-GEE: Ah moe-sow. [Don't worry.] I'm just sorry it no work out for you. . . . I
guess a-DB go home.

KID: Yeah, she told me to tell you good-bye. And by tomorrow, you'll finally be free
of me, too, 'cause, let's face it, there's nothing left for me around here.

NGAN-GEE: A-Paulie. Why you always keep me on a-outside? Why you always keep
a-self on a-outside?

KID: I don't know. . . . Well, you saw tonight . . . I guess I'm afraid to let anyone see
what I've always known. Maybe I really am the hollow man with no Chinese soul
inside. I'm sure that's what everybody down here thinks.

NGAN-GEE: A-Paulie, it's not that you have no "hung-ngen" [Chinese] soul inside. I
think it's just that you afraid of what inside. I know, 'cause-a I just like you. Like
tonight a-when everyone boo you, it good to see you let it out and a-no keep it all
inside. That something I could never do.

KID: Ah . . . that was nothing. You should've seen me in my punk days.

NGAN-GEE: No, it something. Something a-big. I wish more of our family know how
let things out, let things go. Like me. Sometimes I feel like a-hollow man, too.

KID: Oh, come on, Ngan-Gee.

NGAN-GEE: I think that if I know how to let things go, I never make you play a-show
with a-DB tonight.

KID: How's that?

NGAN-GEE: When you no want a-restaurant, I feel like a-you no want me anymore.
And you, me, we all a-family left here in a-Chinatown, so I get a-real mad real easy.
I feel like I give everything to you and a-you give nothing to me, but I wrong. You
give me a lot. And by making you do a-show tonight, I no give something to you,
I almost take something away. I hope a-you understand.

KID: Of course I do Ngan-Gee. And you've given me something, too.

NGAN-GEE: What I give to you?

(KID *clears his throat and sings.*)

KID:
Ngen-sang ngooy-moong   *People's lives are like dreams . . .*
Ngen-ting om gnooy seu   *Human nature has no taste—like water . . .*

NGAN-GEE: Wow, I never thought I hear you sing that.

KID: I never thought I'd hear myself sing that! And uh, if you still think I shouldn't give up my day job—it's okay, 'cause I'd uh, like to keep it a while longer—if that's all right.

NGAN-GEE: Oh a-Paulie, that great.

KID: They can cuss The Goong Hay Kid offstage, but they can't cuss me out of town. I really want to help you this time, Ngan-Gee.

NGAN-GEE: Then tomorrow I tell a landlord we gonna stay.

KID: But don't get carried away and sign a ten-year lease now.

NGAN-GEE: A-Paulie, we lucky to get a two-year lease.

KID: This is true.

(NGAN-GEE *begins weeping.*)

KID: A-Bok, what's wrong?

NGAN-GEE: A-Paulie, I know that that was a-you mama singing on tape.

KID: How'd you know that?

NGAN-GEE: Please, don't hate me. But every time I hear that lullaby, I remember teaching that lullaby to her, back in a-China, in a my village in Thoisan. I meet a-you Mama in a-music school.

(MRS. MAH, *wearing traditional Chinese clothing, enters and goes to* NGAN-GEE's *side.*)

NGAN-GEE: I fall in love with her from a-start, but never tell anybody. I just a-pray that my family arrange for a-me to marry "knee-ga-Mama." We both know that never happened.

(MR. MAH, *also wearing traditional Chinese clothing, enters, walks between* NGAN-GEE *and* MRS. MAH *and takes her hand and leads her offstage. As they exit,* MRS. MAH *gives one last look of longing to* NGAN-GEE.)

NGAN-GEE: For a long time, I keep thinking that my life be so different, so much better, if only I a-marry "knee-ga Mama." I start to hate a-family. I start to hate myself. When I much older I realize that I really just waste a lot of time by not letting go of that. Then, when all a-trouble start between "knee-ga Mama and Bop-ba and a-Michael," I always feel worse for you since you a-youngest.

So I glad to see that a-you no be like me, cause a-Paulie, many more things, like a-tonight's show, no gonna go your way. But you have to learn to let it go and a-keep moving on.

KID: Ngan-Gee . . . I had no idea. I don't know what to say.

NGAN-GEE: It good to see you listen for change.

KID: Well . . . you know I did wonder why you suddenly became so interested in my act when you heard that one last week.

NGAN-GEE: Now you know. And a-Paulie, I bet she be proud to hear you sing it. But come on now, tell me a-truth; I bet you still no know what a song means.

KID: Well . . . not every word, but I'm learning.

NGAN-GEE: That good. Maybe soon you can finally put a-this song in a-your show. I mean, you still gonna do a-show, right a-Paulie?

KID: Oh, shit, yeah. But that song will never be part of it.

NGAN-GEE: Ai-yah, why not?

KID: Well, let's just say that finally being able to sing that song is something I'm happy to prove to myself.

KID:
Ngen-sang ngooy-moong   *People's lives are like dreams . . .*
Ngen-ting om gnooy seu   *Human nature has no taste—like water . . .*

(NGAN-GEE *joins* KID.)

KID AND NGAN-GEE:
Ngen-sang ngooy-moong   *People's lives are like dreams . . .*
Ngen-ting om gnooy seu   *Human nature has no taste—like water . . .*
Ngen-sang sai seng   *People in this world . . .*
Tong-kee haw-see   *How long do we have . . .*
Ngen-ting slee-gee   *People's natures are like paper . . .*
Jeng jeng buck   *Every sheet is thin . . .*
Sly-sea gneu-key   *What we know is strange . . .*
Gook gook sleng   *'Cause everything is new. . . .*

(NGAN-GEE *clasps his hands together.*)

NGAN-GEE: Goong Hay a-Paulie, goong hay.

(KID *clasps his hands together.*)

KID: Goong Hay Ngan-Gee, goong hay.

(*They look at each other awkwardly for a beat. Finally,* KID *embraces* NGAN-GEE. NGAN-GEE *returns* KID's *embrace.*)

Primitive World: An Anti-Nuclear Jazz Musical

Amiri Baraka
Music: David Murray
Arrangement: Ron McIntire

CHARACTERS

Black Musician (Man)

Black Musician (Woman)

Ham (Statesman)

Sado (Money God)

Maso (Money God)

Heart (Drummer)

Black Musician (Woman), Heart's Wife

White Musician, Latino Musician, Heart's Companions

(MAN *carrying a tenor saxophone, which is in parts, comes running into his space. A shack, a mixture of future and primitive beginnings. In the background a kind of wind music, like voices in pain, like people seeing their world blown apart. And across the back of the stage, jaded red-and-death-colored slides sweep across, sporadically—in some kind of out rhythm. Suddenly—and just swifter than clear identification—an image of horrible suffering blows by—in the rhythm of the music, the sharp broken glass shreds of sound.*

There are lights, like fires, that come up, then fade. Flicker bright.

Man has apparently been bitten by something. Blood is streaming down his arm. He is wearing some kind of metallic jump suit-like garment, and a helmet that has what looks like an oxygen mask fitted into it.

He is wrapping up his arm and placing the horn on a table where he can look at it and work on it. He works on his arm, sprinkles powder on it. He is concerned about it, but not panicky. But still he tries to fit the horn together; but some of the parts are warped and he is having some trouble making them fit. Occasionally, he picks up the mouthpiece part of the horn and makes some sounds on it. Simple sounds, then gets more ambitious. Finally, this simply drives him back to trying to fix it.)

At one point, he seems to smell something and rises quickly to go to the window and tries to seal it even more tightly. He sniffs at the bottom of the door. He goes back to the horn, and fumbling with it, sings snatches of a song.)

MAN:
in the mountains
in the valley
in the ruins
in the dead blown-up city

Poison death
fire left
Cloud of horror
Silent memory

(REPEAT FIRST STANZA)

(He stands and picks up a pile of records and weighs them in his hand. He shuffles through them. Then looks at a record player that is in parts. He shuffles them around, singing the song, a blues ballad, quiet and precise.)

Where are you
Where are me
Where are life
Where are sun

poison death
fire death
blow up death
murder death

in the mountains
in the valley
even niggers in the alley
all blown up destroyed

Poison death
Fire left
Clouds of horror
Silent tongue, silent memory

(Upstage, from the darkness a spot illuminates a STATESMAN *talking. A tall, aging man with spinning eyes. His hair plastered down like Superman. He is in a dark business suit, but has a red cape. There is a dollar sign on the cape. He is surrounded by garbage cans full of money—big bills bulge out of each can so that the tops sit slightly askew. He is making a speech, and every once in a while looking at a script he has in his inner pocket, trying to memorize. The* MAN's *dialogue must be in rhythmic, musical relationship to the song the* MUSICIAN *sings, a kind of counterpoint. But, of course, they are not in the same place— they are separated by time and understanding.)*

The MUSICIAN *is frozen, but curious. He hears, he draws closer to the door. He is still fiddling with the horn, but more quietly, obviously looking at the door, but continuing to do something as if nothing was happening. He is still singing quietly, more quietly, his song.*

Now the WOMAN *is knocking, and falling back from the door, looking around, but also checking out the shack, the windows sealed, the bottom of the door sealed, but she thinks she detects a light.)*

WOMAN:
Is anyone there?
Is anyone there?

Is anyone there?
Don't ask again
Someone waiting for you
Is anyone there?
Is anyone there?
Alone in the . . .

(Suddenly the MUSICIAN *gets up and pulls the door open.)*

MAN: Shit! Hey. Ain't nothing bad enough to put me out past whatever it is. Yeah? Who is it? A monster? Red smoke? Death on a motorcycle? Ancient shit. New horror? Hey. Dig this. *(He holds up his horn, still unable to put it together)* This is me!

*(*WOMAN, *her head around the doorway. The Brother has taken some stance like he is going to defend himself, if necessary, by blowing the horn. The* WOMAN *pokes her head around, still tentative, amazed at the stance of the Brother. He has worked himself up to where he is "going to town," squatting suddenly with the horn in some kind of karate pose extension of himself.)*

MAN: Yeh! *(Gesturing with the horn, not even seeing the* WOMAN*)* Yeh, dig this—this is me, horrible shit all together—crazy life—this is me!

WOMAN: Well.

(He looks, and finally, sees!)

WOMAN: You all right?

MAN: *(Digs himself, like someone not used to people or other eyes)* Oh? Okay, hello . . . hello and shit.

WOMAN: You all right?

(She edges forward. He is trying to welcome her, but still not certain of what and how, etc., edges backward.)

MAN: All right? What you mean? Who're you? Out there in the dark. Asking me am I okay, all right? What about you? Shit, you might be a ghost, some ambitious smoke. I might be dead. . . . *(He is admitting her to the house and retreating at the same time)* Am I all right?

WOMAN: All right?

MAN: Yeh.

WOMAN: Well, are you inviting me in?

MAN: Yeah, I opened the door. *(He is gesturing with the horn, now somewhat embarrassed at his wildness)* Am I all right?

(Sings and toots on mouthpiece)

Am I all right? Am I cool?
Am I all right? Am I well?

Am I all right? Do I have what I need?
Am I all right? Am I still breathing fine?

I'm all right, sure I'm great. It's the world
That's blown. I'm cool, It's the world
That's smashed. I'm in perfect shape.

It's just the world
It's blown apart
It's just the world
I'm doing fine.

WOMAN: *(She stands looking at the man and over her shoulder, etc.)*

He's doing great
It's just the world
He's in perfect shape
It's just the world
Wow, it's so profound
he's cool, he's hip
it's just the world
he's all right, it's just the world.

(She laughs, and the laughter while ridiculing his unrealistic stance, at the same time re-laxes him. He smiles, half-grudging.)

MAN: That does sound out, don't it? I'm all right, it's just the world that's fucked up. Wow! Wow is right! *(Then focusing on her)* Well, come on in anyway. You know so much about how we connected with the world, how come you running around in it?

WOMAN: *(Relaxing, unzippering the jump suit enough to get some air)* Hey, you don't want the whole story now, do you? *(Laughs, a mixture of lightness and bad memory)* I was part of a good thing . . . *(heavy pause)* . . . and it got . . . blown . . . wasted.

(HAM, the STATESMAN, with congealed hair, is doing his cave dance surrounded by the garbage cans overloaded with money.)

HAM: *(Sings)*

We told them you read it
We warned them, don't dread it
We were right, you knew it
We were white, we were rich.

You poor ones, don't worry
We represent your suffering too
You black and red and brown and
Yellow ones, don't worry, we are
Absolutely in touch with you.

Don't do it, we screamed, don't
Try to live. Don't try it, we sung—
We won't allow any life but ours.

Holy Mother of profit, you know
We are always true. Money Lord
we are more white, more red
more blue.

(Pause, looking around at the garbage cans as if for response.)

HAM: *(Continuing)*

And now,
what is the pleasure of the
center of the earth, what is
the will of the money gods?

(The light has been raised to show the section of the stage where the STATESMAN, *like from a past age, a fading nightmare, continues to perform a life exorcism, a death ritual to bring the dying on. The song is a poem/chant of rising death feeling. A rising struggle on light and love.*

The STATESMAN, *as he sings and dances, makes motions from time to time like he is playing a violin. He plays an imaginary violin, sometimes uses different parts of his body, arms, legs, head, as an imaginary violin, and saws away, spitting out the doomlike song.)*

HAM:

And now? And now? And now?
We've begged and pleaded
Compromised and defended
But now? But now! We'll have no more
of this. But now? But now!

We'll right the world for good.
But now! But now! But now, and now,
and now.

(His dance turns into a "blow-up" mime, his arms and body making explosion gestures, each larger and larger, and more devastating.)

So what is the word
From the Money Gods?
What is the word of Boss
Divine? Now, and now and now!!

What is the word
of the Money Gods?

*What does eternity
speak? And now and now and now!!*

*(Suddenly, the garbage cans begin to move. They wobble like they're going to fall over,
and as they tilt, the* STATESMAN *[HAM] shrieks his doom chant more intensely, like Ra and
Yma Sumac.)*

HAM: *(Continuing)*

*Begged and pleaded, pretended to
be mortal, acted humble like humans
but none of that worked, none of it
made them see who we were. And now*

*And now, Money Gods, answer. Money
Gods, speak to us, now and now the time
is now, we've acted like humans and other
passive things too long, now and now we've
Come to another time, it's passed into*

*Another clime. And now, they'll know
we'll show the depth and breadth
of our power. We wait, only for a sign
let the money gods roar out their pleasure!*

*(The cans rock, and one at a time, but rapidly, the tops of all four of them pop open—
and out of two of the cans, there are two men with top hats on who rise up, the money that
has covered them, flying everywhere.*

The STATESMAN *is ecstatic, he leaps in the air, for his prayers have been answered. The*
MONEY GODS *have appeared. He leaps and saws the imaginary violins crazily. The* MONEY
GODS *also have violins, real ones, and they play as they sing and speak and chant. One's face
is painted into a smile, the other into a frown. But they have no faces, rather they are wearing layers and layers of masks. And every so often, at indicated moments, their singing and
chants take on more significance as they discard one of the masks only to reveal the mask under it is the same as the mask the opposite one is wearing. So the Smiling God takes off a
mask to reveal a frown as the Frowning God takes off his mask to reveal a smile.*

The MONEY GODS *play the violins like telegraph messages from all over the world. The
"dit dit dit" of world news tonight. To the heightened razor craziness of their violin playing, their voices in bizarre song, which seems to combine stock exchange jargon and atmosphere and the entire range of television, radio, and billboard commercials—one after
another, and intermixed, the national anthem of commercials is their lyrics. These commercials and violin playing must be delivered in the same rhythm as the telegraph message
violins. As they emerge from the cans it is a ritualized dance, which at the same time reveals their lives as merchants and controllers of society. It is a power-mime dance they do as
they emerge, shouting the crazed commericals.*

The MUSICIAN *and the* WOMAN *are standing closer in the room, talking quietly about
each other's lives. He is still trying to fix the horn, to make it play, and still occasionally
playing the mouthpiece blues and rags, singing snatches of "Am I All Right," humming it,*

now scatting it lightly, punctuating with the mouthpiece, or the horn's keys pressed rapidly
like subtle percussion runs.)

WOMAN: You know I can fix that horn.

MAN: Well, how come you didn't fix it when you first got in here?

WOMAN: Because I was waiting for you to admit that we'd met before, that you knew
my name and that you had known me before, out there with the people of disaster!

MAN: Why would you say that? This is the first time I ever saw you.

WOMAN: The explosions took your memory.

MAN: Why are you saying this?

WOMAN: That I can fix the horn?

MAN: No. That too, but the other stuff.

WOMAN: Then who are you?

MAN: I only tell who I am to people I am in love with. *(A pause, an uneasy smile)* Who
are you?

WOMAN: You really don't know me?

MAN: Why are you talking like this?

WOMAN: *(Shrugging, like an unexpected delay)* What is that pile in the corner over
there? Extra wood for the fire?

MAN: *(Blowing into the mouthpiece)* It just might be . . . *(he goes over and pulls back
the tarpaulin)*. It's a piano . . . wasted . . . I can't do nothin' with it anyway. But it's
out past Cage right now. It's been prepared by violent reality!

*(The sound of the STATESMAN and MONEY GODS in their wild dance is heard from time
to time, like sound effects, precussive bits and pieces and a spotlight—reminds you of flashing neon signs in which flashes of the killer statesman ritual dance, with the speaker, HAM,
transfixed like a true believer and worshipper, are seen.*
*The WOMAN sits down at the piano on a box. She dusts it off, rubs at it to clean it, re-
moves boxes and bottles from around it. She pokes at it, a few smooth runs, her voice trail-
ing the notes swooning up and down the keys. She does very little, but what she does makes
the MUSICIAN stop and look at her.)*

MAN: Uhuh. *(Acknowledging)* What you gon' do? You can play that?

WOMAN: *(Nodding at the horn)* About as well as you can play that. And yours is broke!

MAN: You said you can fix it!

WOMAN: Then remember me, lover man! *(She begins to play the piano. It is a sad little
ballad, at each break of the line, she almost hums tears, tears, tears)*

MAN: You can sing too?

WOMAN: *(Extending the melodic little piece, sings)*

> As it is with the world
> so it is with love
> as it's light or dark
> so it is with love
>
> under the stars
> is more than astrology
> it has some influence
> on your psychology
>
> so let's change our lives
> for a change let's make our world
> beautiful. So let's change our world
> for a change let's make our lives
> beautiful!

(She finishes the piece with a slowing, brooding introspection, humming and slipping in and out of the lyrics, the piano poignant, but panging and banging slightly out of tune.)

MAN: Hey. *(He holds the horn up looking at it)* That was nice—some real music for a change.

WOMAN: *(She wheels around off the box)* You think I wasn't serious about fixing this horn? I can play that horn too.

(He looks at her.)

WOMAN: But that ain't my specialty. My father and grandfather could play—they built bridges and played music. They never was on television, but they swung harder than most of them that were! There was always horns and instruments, a piano around our house. Not to be looked at, like a pretty piece of furniture, but to be low-down played!

MAN: I don't know why I can't fix it myself. *(Pause)* Goddam, I can play it. And can't fix it. But where I was you could send 'em out to be fixed.

(The WOMAN *has the horn, looking at it, she pads it, pushes the keys in silent rushing scales. Looks at the mouthpiece.*
Now the "dit dit dit" madness is brought up in the lights. The MONEY GODS *are frozen in their maniacal dance posture. They are trembling and jerking like they still must play, play, but they are fixed and staring, eyes rolling around.)*

HAM: Ah, masters of reality, creators of the future, you've responded.

SADO: *(Smiling face)* Yes, of course. *(Loose sing-song, like one of Snow White's dwarfs, Dopey)* Of course, yes. We're like that. Always generous to a fault.

MASO: *(Frowning face)* We must respond. We know how absolutely powerful we are. How we run everything. *(He breaks into a song)*

If it's fun
We run it
If it's fun
We own it
If it's valuable
We define it
If it's rebellious
We confine it.

HAM: Now that you've come, to give me my words. My thoughts for the year. How to deal with weird events, invasions and such, bombings of reactors and fundings for bad actors. Overthrowing governments, assassinating patriots.

(He is taken by his speech, swaying back and forth like a drunk getting ready to have an orgasm. Suddenly Maso and Sado go into wild violin duet. Ham, picking up on it, starts to pick up his sway, the two violinists are "competing" with each other, one-upping, snarling, jumping.)

MASO: Uhh, Uhh.

SADO: Umm. Umm.

(They jump toward each other, and away like a boxing match. HAM *dances to their playing—he has a smaller violin, which he scratches at, puts in his pocket, spinning, eyes crossing.)*

HAM: *(Sings)*

Knowledge
and death
everything
and death
jungle lights itch
and death
all of it is life
all of it is death
and death.

*(*MASO *and* SADO *pick up death chant, sawing away at their axes.* HAM *now begins on flute, accompanying the* MONEY GODS, *singing and grunting and dancing.*
Every so often the two exchange masks and change the key they sing in or the tempo to show the change.)

MASO:

and death
the answer.

SADO/MASO: *(Together)*

And death
and question.

Nothing anywhere resembles
great death, nothing.

In or outside
the sun

the bloody
moon

we know, we do know
what's great

immortal
death.

SADO: *(Abruptly). What . . .*

MASO: *Do you want?*

(A stock market board bell rings and we hear ticker tape when they laugh.)

SADO: Sell!

MASO: Sell? Sell? Sell? *(Looks around wildly)*

SADO: Sell! *(The sound of chains being dragged somewhere, slave moans like the blood market of king cotton)*

HAM: *(Spinning, looking out at audience)* You hear that
        Sell, Sell, Sell!

(The three spastic madmen go through the act of selling—Freeze!)

HAM: *(Continuing)* And the prophecy, the future? Today is the day when all that is settled! When the things worldwide are set. Have they come? Will they survive? Who will wake? The powerful gods. *(Gestures at the mad* MONEY GODS *grating Sell.* HAM *goes back into dance, a trio, with two violins and a flute)*

(Lights up on the MUSICIANS—*the* WOMAN *is still bent over the horn, playing it in pantomime, checking her embouchure, etc.)*

MAN: So, what's the problem? Thought you had no trouble with such as this? You played it and repaired it and come in out the night—some black lady beautiful wizard—gonna fix my horn.

WOMAN: *(Looking up, wistfully, not saying anything at first)* It's fixed!

MAN: *(Laughing, light disbelief)* Ah, yes, fixed. Could you fix the world as easily?

WOMAN: Fix the world? *(Half-laugh, then silence)* You remember that old song, "If This World Was Mine?" *(She sings the first stanza)*

MAN: *(He is listening and not saying a word for a long time)* If This World Was Mine . . . If it was either one of ours, if it had ever been. . . .

WOMAN: But it never was . . . and if you think of times ancienter than these last few decades of destruction,. If we go back beyond the scene of this crime. If we go back to where the black nation dwelt across the seas, years and years before our slavery . . . you'd see more destruction. A nation committing suicide . . . kings and queens selling farmers to merchants. . . .

MAN: A world of destruction, now it comes round, there it goes, now it comes round again, now blood smeared on stone. Now bombs and bullets, now death flesh ripped. *(Straightens up)* But we had no say in this last million murders . . . we had no say. . . .

WOMAN: No? No way . . . *(She is looking at the horn and slowly holds it up for him)* You wanted this?

MAN: Oh, it's still fixed? *(Laughs)* You mean you can really fix.

WOMAN: Can you really play?

MAN: *(Tentatively seizing the horn)* Can I play? *(Pause)* If I can't play—the world will end now!

SADO: What . . .

MASO: Do you want? *(Staring stupidly at HAM, who, bathed in their madness, has drawn up as large as they—their stares shrink him)*

HAM: Yes. . . . Want? *(Lower key)* The future—

SADO: That's it, Bucks, that's it, of course. That's what distinguishes us, the Money Gods, *from the . . . rest!*

MASO: Our money—of course, dear Dough. . . .

SADO: Of course—but all the others . . . *want!* They're always wanting—wanting stuff. Always wanting.

MASO: Of course, yes, that's it—always wanting.

SADO: Of course, that's why this crazy path—this whining about Mars, this refusal to see our greatness—power!

HAM: *(Illuminated)* Want—of course. . . .

SADO: *(Screaming)* They want food! *(Screaming—sawing)*

MASO: *(Screams)* Why, Why, Why, they want LIFE!

SADO: SELL!

HAM: Yes, yes, that's it. They be talking 'bout . . . all these. *(At audience)*

MASO: Wanters—out there! Wanting! All the time wanting!

SADO: Crazed with Desire. While we are wholly cool, coolly whole. A buck.

MASO: Hey, wanters! *(All three take up their instruments and shoot them at the audience sawing and screaming!)*

All Three: Hey, WANTERS! WANT ALL YOU WANT! WANT. WANT. WANT. *(Crazed laughter)*

SADO: *(To* HAM*)* Now what calls us through your mouth?

MASO: Your teeth—your armpits.

SADO: SELL!

MASO: Trace the faces negative all impinge upon us as our conquests. *(Waves)* These faces! *(Violins)*

SADO: They want stuff, don't they?

HAM: Yes. *(Flutes, flutes, whistles, kazoos, etc.)*

MASO: *(Accusingly at* HAM*)* The future, you wanted.

HAM: Why—Yes—I thought—My job was to—tell these—*(harshly)* miserable wanters—what they wanted was wanting!

MASO and HAM: *(Howling)* Ha Ha Ha Ha Ha Ha.

SADO: Veddy good. What they wanted was—Ha Ha.

MASO: *(Grabs them)* But this is serious, Bread. There are evil forces everywhere. Stronger forces—than these tie-wearing weaklings who also want *(trance-like)* who at this very moment conspire to back us against the wall.

SADO: Our rocket. *(Breathy rhythm on flute underscoring)*

MASO: Their rocket.

SADO: Our triple nuke.

MASO: Their triple nuke.

SADO: Our dirt killing bleed-more.

MASO: Their dirt killing bleed-more.

SADO: LASERS.

MASO: LASERS.

SADO: A million niggers with razors. (MASO *and* HAM *look*)

MASO: What?

HAM: Not that?

SADO: Well, in a manner of speaking. *(A joke)*

HAM:

> *They're called something*
> *else in the Eastern*
> *steppes.*

MASO:

> *But they're darker*
> *and starker*
> *always wearing*
> *our parka*
> *Our enemies*
> *got niggers*
> *Too!*

> *(Amazed)*

MASO/SADO/HAM:

> *Wow!*
> *The really secret*
> *Weapon.*

> *(Song)*

> *But here with us they're*
> *wanting*
> *throughout this land*
> *like a*
> *haunting.*

MASO: Always!

SADO: Always!

(Sawing. HAM *whistles, blowing things, throwing them away.)*

MASO: Buy. *(Reverse motions, clacking of stock board).* Buy! *(Making buy motions, changing masks.)*

SADO: But they can't get nothing. All over there—depths of jungle—dying folks— you'll never—never.

HAM: They'll. You'll never! That's it—they'll never! Never! That's it, sirs. Never. *(Sawing and humping up and down.)* Uh. Uh.

(The Sister is handing the horn toward the Brother, the antics of the STATESMEN *are quiet in pantomime.)*

WOMAN: So you were saying about the world ending . . .

(The MAN *takes the horn, laughing, begins to play. A solo piece, "From the Old to the New!" Drawing closer.)*

WOMAN: So you can.

MAN: I can.

WOMAN: That was . . .

MAN: "Out of the Old into the New."

WOMAN: *(Turning toward window)* Out there, in that poison dark. Where the dead rule all that is left of a world.

(Brother plays behind her. Repeat.)

MAN:

*All that is left of
a world.*

(She plays behind him.)

*Destroyed
by idiots!*

WOMAN:

*But play some more—Hey, it's dark—
Light up the world.*

(The MAN *plays up-tempo: "The World Destroyed By Idiots Can Yet Rise Again!" Second chorus, she gets in, sharp, fertile chords. Tableau: The Madmen—The* MUSICIANs *in Flashing Lights. They take turns singing and accompanying each other.)*

MAN:

*All that I am
All that I own
Nothing it seems
Nothing but dreams.*

WOMAN:

*Dreams can be real
Make like what you feel
Be all you need
A blue spirit freed.*

MAN:

*Here in the dark
Death kills the spark
You brought light with you
You brought life with you.*

WOMAN:

*Dreams can be real
Make life what you feel.*

MAN:

> *You brought light with you*
> *You brought light with you.*

> *(Instrumental duet. Instrumental and vocal duet, saxophone piano, vocals.)*

MAN AND WOMAN:

> *But we are alive here together*
> *This is no dream, as grim as it is*
> *This is our lives, our broken world*
> *We meet tonight, like lovers in a book*
> *But this is no dream, we are alive*
> *in love, here together, to remake*
> *our world, our lives, together*
> *This is no dream, our hearts know*
> *it's real, remake our world*
> *broken hearts of dreamers*
> *the madness of screamers*
> *But this is no dream, broken*
> *world crying. This is no dream*
> *millions are dying. Remake our*
> *hearts, like lovers, together.*
> *This is no dream. Our lives*
> *reality. Let life go on*
> *Let life go on go on*
> *This is no dream!*

HAM: So today—News for the Wanters.

MASO: The Screamers.

SADO: The Pleaders.

> *(The sweep of the* MUSICIANS' *love song comes like a breath of air and the Madmen visibly shiver, pull up their coats.)*

MASO: Ah . . . what's that?

> *(Instrumental duet.)*

SADO: Crazies protesting the bomb.

MASO: Or protesting our beautiful nerve gas.

HAM: PEACE FREAKS.

SADO: Or Niggers complaining.

MASO: Women exclaiming.

SADO: But it does no good—we own the world.

MASO: Yes, Bux, you got that very right.

HAM: Right! Right!

Far Far Far Right!

MASO: WHITE ON!

HAM: The News today will be awesome. I've set up an all-Universe broadcast, a universal fact layout session.

SADO AND MASO: *(Duet)*

> *They think*
> *they can*
> *threaten us*

> *They think*
> *we can*
> *be scared*

> *They think*
> *it's flesh*
> *and blood here*

> *When it's coin,*
> *and legal tender*
> *silver certificates*

> *instead of organic*
> *parts. No feelings*

> *No Souls*
> *No memory*
> *and most of all no hearts*

> *Back us against the wall*
> *These wanters. Whole countries*
> *of them.*

(A rock thrown through the window hits HAM.*)*

HAM:

> *The News is why they*
> *Wait. The Big News*
> *The End News. Anchor*
> *of Anchors.*

MASO: Tell Them we've tried.

MASO AND SADO: *(Duet)*

> *That cannot be*
> *denied. But*

no one can
back us
against
    the wall
      no one
        not at
          all

These wanters
These taunters
These marchers
Draft Dodgers
They stomp us with their
desires.

These rioters
Cities on Fire

Fiends and criminals
Non-white idlers
Begging nations
insatiable cravings

They want
just want
and want and
want
and want

They want to rule
They want to be
They want to love

(Smirks)

Like cires in the mist
these wanters want to be
All this.

(Gestures all.)

MASO: But tonight the stand will be made.

SADO: No further steps these wanters will take

MASO AND SADO: We are the final takers!

HAM: *(Applauding)* Yes—The News! What speaks as future?

MASO AND SADO: *(Laughing maniacally)* Future?

MASO: How presumptuous of you.

SADO: How presumptuous indeed.

MASO AND SADO: We are in charge of the past.

SADO: And the future.

MASO: And as punishment for this wild wanting, this aggression all around.

SADO: We have decided no to let them *have* a future!

MASO: No future, after all . . .

HAM: *(As if he's hearing something grand and mysterious)* No . . . Future . . .

MASO AND SADO: No future at all!

HAM: And That is . . . the News.

MASO: The News.

SADO: The last News anybody will get!

(*Lights up on the two* MUSICIANS.)

WOMAN: You don't recognize me—because you don't even recognize yourself.

MAN: *(Musing)*

> *Lightning in the sky*
> *The building shaking*
> *The ground like water.*

(*Musical background: the violins, flute, etc. Piano and sax.*)

WOMAN: What do you remember?

MAN:

> *A wave of lost souls. The Blinding*
> *Light. A world full of screams*
> *Oceans of Fire.*

(*It becomes an re-enactmeent. Lights—slides.*)

WOMAN:

> *Explosions. Explosions. You were running.*
> *The sky behind you was white with Horror.*
> *A figure alone. You were running*
> *Toward me. I was fixed in the*
> *heat storm, the trashing on all sides.*
> *I had screamed myself into a silence*
> *of jagged edges.*

MAN:

> *A ring of the murdered flashing across*
> *the sky. The murderer's voices whining*
> *over radios, televisions, newspapers*
> *blown by with their lies screaming*

WOMAN:

> *I saw you race past me.*

MAN:

> *I escaped alone, the dirt on fire.*

WOMAN:

> *You carried the horn in two pieces*
> *Like I found it. The survivors had*
> *scattered. I hid in the shadows,*
> *You paused to look round. I*
> *Could barely see your face.*

MAN:

> *The world seemed midnight permanently*
> *Hell uncovered to Burn*
> *hideous like that in an eternal night.*

WOMAN:

> *You stood there staring*
> *into red darkness*
> *as if fixed*
> *already flying*

MAN:

> *It had been an evening*
> *of music, amusing*
> *conversation*
> *The Money Gods were*
>
> *Whining we*
> *tried to change*
> *the station*
>
> *They said there'd be*
> *no future*
> *That the world*
> *had been*
> *Cancelled.*

(Tableau of MONEY GODS *as they approach their last press conference. Violins and flute come in like an imminent sound of death. The* MONEY GODS' *voices: BUY, SELL are a rhythm form for the song.)*

WOMAN:

> Remember that ending
> Blind death mounts light
> Blackness and fire the
> Blown-up world weeping
> as it flies out into
> emptiness.

MAN:

> The panic, The death—Yes
> I ran ran.

(Covers eyes, then looks.)

> And where
> Were you then? When
> they blew up the world?

WOMAN:

> I was there as you came
> flying out the fire.
> I was there in the shadows
> weeping for the world.
> Too tired to run farther
> I lay there watching as you decided
> I felt your mind searching
> But I heard a music in you then
> that lifted me
> and moved me toward
> you.

MAN:

> And what did I do? Just run
> half mad, afraid . . .

WOMAN:

> And I ran
> in your direction
> I followed you
> I led you
> I advised you
> like nature.

MAN:

> And I never
> saw you.

WOMAN:

> You always
> saw me.

MAN:

> Always?
> Then what
> did
> I do?

WOMAN:

> What you're doing
> now, what
> we're doing
> now
> Reconstruct
> till fresh winds
> blow your brain
> clear again.
>
> At that moment
> you go back
> to the Fire
> The mad night
> they blew up
> the world
>
> Then you stare
> like a mad thing
> and cover your mouth
> with silence
>
> Then you wander out
> into
> the dark
> trying to
> find the old world
> like a Zombie.

MAN:

> Dreams
> Hideous Dreams

The horn
in pieces
The world
on fire
my hands
burning
the ground
screaming.

WOMAN:

Where I lived
we were close
to each other
My family and
me.

We worked
and fought
them
worked
and made
love
and picketed
worked
and sang
Made beautiful songs
out of poems
we danced
we painted
we spoke the words
of genius
we also
worked
struggled with
the Money Gods
with their stooges
and hatchet persons
Yes, the Money Gods!

I knew you then
I'd heard that sound
that beautiful horn
Carrying memories and humanity's
future
I'd heard you
You'd seen me

You'd looked in my eyes
I thought
or were you staring
past me into
this?

Like a black
crazy bird
scrambling out of
Smoke

They'd blown up
My home
my city
my family
my life . . .
all our lives

All our futures
I'd come east
toward the
water
Then you flashed
out the black fire
night

A broken horn
in your
Hands

Trying to sing.

(She comes closer.)

You were standing there
peering into the hot
dark, trying to find
a song.

MAN: *(Sings)*

Another life
like this, caught
a life looking for
your kiss

There must be
another life
somewhere

Someone take me
there.

WOMAN:

Yes, like that
A romantic thing
Why, I wandered
In this craziness . . .

You saw me then and fled
You thought I was a nightmare
An illusion. You had not
tasted me
then.

MAN:

The shadows
were
warm
Like humans
lived
there.

Now a soft face
the brown skin
lovely under
some sudden
moon

The lips there
I touched
Them.

WOMAN:

We were running
together. A wind
caressed us. I
hadn't felt a
breeze like that
so gentle
full of Music
All loveliness
seemed alien
in that
world

MAN: This world . . .

WOMAN: Except . . .

MAN: *(He reaches for her, takes her to him)* Except even without that memory you are all that loveliness means!

WOMAN: Except, remember!

MAN: I do!

WOMAN: What's my name?

MAN: Naima.

WOMAN: *(Begins to play tune on the piano)* You remember nothing. *(Lights up on the* STATESMEN*)*

HAM: *(Slowly accelerating rhythmic speech)* No future—What a coup!

MASO AND SADO: Of course—This'll teach them.

HAM: It will. It will.

MASO: And you, Ham, will go down in history.

SADO: Ha Ha. If there was any more history! We've cancelled it, remember?

MASO: Oh, Yes, Ha Ha! Cancelled History. I always wanted to do that.

HAM: I'll announce it!

SADO: Be Firm.

MASO: But Loving.

HAM: Tell Them The Buck Stops Here *(points at the Money Gods)*. Right here!

MASO: You see this little pink button I wear around my neck?

SADO: I, of course, have one too. Simultaneous Inspirational Destruct Switches. For Him and Him.

HAM: Oh, how thrilling. But, sirs, ahem, in my ignorance I thought such buttons were red!

MASO: Fiction writers' conceit. We hate anything *red!*

SADO: Better Dead! Ha Ha.

MASO: You might say it's our message to the world. Ha Ha.

SADO: But let us be serious. . . . *(both Sado and Maso pause)*

MASO: As befits world creators.

SADO: And world destroyers.

(Flashing flicks identify them seriously.)

HAM: This will be a special bulletin?

SADO: Of course. Stop all transmissions and fire away.

HAM: When?

MASO: Now—it's how the whole things goes. . . . *(Imitates studio)*

HAM: Special bulletin! We interrupt this program—all programs, all acts of any kind—with this special bulletin.

(A Rap)

The Money Gods have
decided because there's too much Wanting,
and Needing too, I might add, that
society itself has become a pest!
The MG's are sick of it. Life
with you boobs. You people You
nations You countries. So
because you continue to make your silly demands
for life, liberty, sovereignty,
independence, liberation,
heaven forbid, revolution,
and various rights of all
sorts. Because you complain
and make noise. And Strike. And Vote.
And Fight. And will not go peacefully.
Or die.
The MG's have decided to
    Cancel the world—
    Until Further Notice!

(A roar of anguish from the people heard over a TV monitor.)

MASO: *(At monitor)*

Look at them out there, scrambling
Crazy with fear!

SADO:

Turn it forward slowly
so we can see the Approach
of death to them all!

Let us watch the end—how
Thrilling.

HAM:

Awe-inspiring.

MASO:

> *Slow Forward—Look*
> *Suicides, mobs searching*
> *for us. Flags. Committees.*
> *Nasty people cursing.*
> *Look as it gets later*
> *They're trying to rush the*
> *Gray House looking for you,*
> *Ham. Ha Ha.*
> *How vulgar. They're*
> *shooting cops. Drowning*
> *politicians. They think*
> *they'll take over—but*
> *the world is done.*
>
> *We've decided*

SADO:

> *Fast forward. Let's look at*
> *the very very end. The madness*
> *and explosions.*
>
> *(A big monitor shows explosions, agony, blood, dying.)*

MASO:

> *Now! Now! Now!*

SADO:

> *Even the Gray House went up!*

HAM:

> *Wonderful! Wonderful!*
> *They thought I was still in it!*
>
> *(Maso and Sado, looking at each other meaningfully, laughing harder still.)*

HAM:

> *Is the whole world blowing up?*

MASO:

> *Of course.*

HAM:

> *Where do we hide—um retreat*
> *till the old world's blown up and*
> *a new one is created?*

SADO:

A new one?

HAM:

*Yes. Isn't that the plan, to create
a new world?*

(Sado and Maso, laughing like children.)

SADO:

*Why would we want that? A New World
Full of what? New complaints?*

MASO:

*New wants and New Wanters?
No, enough is enough.*

HAM:

*Enough—yes—of course
is enough . . . and . . .*

SADO: And . . . you mean yourself and property?

HAM: Uhuh.

SADO: Are you asking what about, Bux and I?

HAM: Uhuh.

MASO: As for you—you have ultra super bomb shelters five hundred feet under the soil. You'll survive, of course.

HAM: *(Dutifully smiling)* Yes—but . . .

SADO: If we told you you'd find it hard to believe. We're serious. We're through. The World's too old, too full of rotten wanting.

MASO: We've found a way to change into the very stuff of the universe, the very stuff of the world!

SADO: *(A blood curdling scream)* The Insect is Supreme!

MASO: *(Secret admission)* Ants are the Hippest!

MASO AND SADO: *(With violins screeching)* The Energy . . . *(Up mad screech sound! They begin to babble, like a vactic scat abstracting the facts, the reality, to a tale of their own making. Instruments used to accent their deteriorating sense of reality. A voice and violin with flute piece. The voice screamed, moaned, growled, screeched, sung, etc.).*

MASO: The ultimate energy—computer mind insects.

SADO: The Holy Scarab!

MASO: *(Clack. Clack)* Buy!

HAM: Ultimate . . . energy.

SADO: Time is energy, power, wealth, control. Nobody would ask an ant for any-thing. Ha Ha Nobody could want anything from an ant.

MASO:

Eternal Master Glorious Warrior.
Gloriously beautiful.

(SADO, *like he's been turned on by the other's rhetoric—a long song to insects.*)

MASO: *(Waving photos)*

The complex eye
ultimate historian.

SADO: Most of all, survivor! *(A sudden blow)*

MASO: *(As if praying)* Master of Creation . . . I Shall Not Want. . . .

HAM:

Freedom—The Transparent Responder. (Crawls, bumps into monitor)
Ohhh! But what's this—fast forward the world's blown up
the fire across the sky. Dead people
toe up everywhere. Skeletons and
desolation—What fire didn't
kill, radiation and disease—
But still I see—shadows—
Shadows—No, what is this?
Money Gods, what is this we see?

MASO:

Prayer to the Insect Master.

SADO:

You see only insects the holy ant
building beyond the
rationalization of broken human desire.

HAM:

I see the ants—
But the future—these shadows—
like living—humans.

MASO: What?

HAM: Look here.

MASO: *(Moving to the monitor)* There is somebody.

(The Musicians.)

MAN: I do remember . . . life. You are life to me.

WOMAN: From no knowledge to life itself.

MAN:

No, the nightmare defined it
*   What was*
*   Alive.*

(Closer to her, she is running randomly up and down the scales of the piano.)

Lost in the dark I thought
I could not grow
Now I live
among the
stars.

WOMAN:

What memory a kind of
being there when you
enter your self-
conscious
your very senses
demanding
all of what Life is
every minute.

MAN:

We're lucky to be alive
Is that a Song?

(He bends to kiss her. She plays a brief very melodic ballad.)

But we could be a Song
two poems
in search of a
home.

(Piano.)

MAN:

You smell like life! (Musing) That light beyond—(remembering) was you.
That flow of lovely words.
The tremble the air is

as it sings
to us
as quiet
as beauty
was you
I remember we lay there whispering
under the music
I said I loved you
you smiled and let me
caress you slowly—
it was like
a song.

WOMAN:

What name did you call me then?

MAN:

Naima.

WOMAN:

Then you remember.

MAN:

I always remembered.

WOMAN:

That word I tossed at you
Your eyes upon me heating
The air
through which
I returned your stare.

MAN: *(Playing lightly, the same ballad, humming the end of some phrases)*

It seemed we
were below
the surface
of the earth
A black sky with holes
Music seeping everywhere
It was Sun Ra.

WOMAN:

If there were scientists of this
life as lived
measuring that space

we came to each other
in
They'd measure the
heat
& music
Their dials would say:
MAGIC!

MAN:

All of that you said
to me
It was Africa
I said to you
Naima

WOMAN: *Yes.*

MAN:

I said, "Naima
can you
love me?"

WOMAN:

I said, "Yes," I remember
I said, "Yes,"
*   And you breathed*
*   The air into harmonies.*

MAN:

My blood the rhythm. I remember . . . I was warm and dark.

WOMAN:

We were already in each other's
Language
Passion Eyes
You said, "Come
with me."

MAN:

You smelt like
music.

WOMAN:

It was
*   Like a*
*   Song*

(Duet out, lights dim to suggest lovemaking. In the chamber, the MONEY GODS *watch ever more frantically. But they are already mad. Though the madness has been already made to seem the "norm.")*

MASO: *(Exchanging masks as rhythmic device—a bizarre game)* Hey, it's only Niggers! No people. Ha, you scared me for a second. The Ants survive. Forrrrrrrrrr-eever-rrrrrrr—Insect Deities.

HAM: Niggers? Will They not . . . reproduce?

SADO: What's your point?

MASO: You mean . . . these blobs of distorted protoplasm would have the nerve to . . . survive?

(Musicians repeat Song and Playing.)

SADO: We cannot permit it.

HAM: It seems contradictory—*(musing)*—five hundred feet below the earth!

SADO: Send heavier waves of death—

MASO: But even better, kill them before they arrive.

HAM: Death Music Future!

SADO: Of course.

(They begin to get various instruments out to wail against the living future.)

MASO:

So we prepare The Final Assault.
As Death is launched. The bombs.
The Fire.

SADO: Even beyond that!

(Song like shrieking—like a mad person humming mood music out of tune! The eerie trio gets together, the expressionist masks of face contorting, a happening of craziness attacking! We now see a music war begin. The MONEY GODS *and* HAM, *like invading monsters, blow a piece called "War of the Worlds," which sounds like laser death beams for alien maniacs!*

The MAN *and the* WOMAN *Musicans suddenly feel the presence of the* MONEY GODS *and* HAM. *They are attempting to destroy them. At first, the two stagger under the attack. It is danced by the weird trio-like ballet and burlesque; showing their ass, then leaping crude pas de trois, tour jetès, etc.)*

MAN: What's happening. Of a sudden, this air is crawling at me.

WOMAN: *(Touching her throat and eyes)* Juke Box Death Ray!

MAN: *(Closing eyes)*

In Boats. A horse.
The Whip. He's galloping
Crown Prince . . .

WOMAN: Like Bela Lugosi's theme song.

MAN: *(Shouts)* FRANKENSTEIN!

(They are making ready to play. The WOMAN—*an explosive piano run, like machine-gunning Colonialists from the high ground on a very clear day!*

The MAN—*a solo, like the horn is talking! It's trying to identify the* MONEY GODS *and attack them murderously. The* MONEY GODS *jump around, attacking, retreating. Sneak attacks, deadly rockets launched. We see a tableau of struggle. The music: an extended piece. The struggle seems a balance, back and forth—like a surreal cutting session—with death the penalty for losing!*

The three dance around to get better leverage, advantage. They try to spread out and then gang up. But it is clearly a war, all out, with exchanged solos and wincing on both sides like they're hit. But then from the dark a thumping, a deep and thunderous rumbling—the drum[s]. The MONEY GODS *notice the Brother and Sister are animated, get down harder at the sound. The drum sets the music from Africa to Latino to low-down Blues to traditional New Orleans to Big Band to Bop to Hard Bop to a rumbling dynamic solo, with the bombs rocking the* MONEY GODS!

Now a straight-ahead, impossible tempo piece, which is the beginning of a suite: 1. Tension 2. Explosion 3. Terror 4. Death 5. Silence. 6. Tone.

Silence, then weeps of violin and horn snorts—like temporary quiet on the battlefield—and suddenly a pounding on the Musicians' door.)

MAN: *(Instinctively)* The Drummer.

WOMAN: Who's that?

(The MAN *swings open the door. Violin screeching wind poison wafts in. Black jumpsuited goggles, carrying all kinds of percussion instruments, and, of course a brace of congas under wraps.)*

DRUMMER: I saw lights, I heard . . . music . . . two musics fighting back and forth.

MAN: A drummer?

WOMAN: Who are you?

DRUMMER: *(He thumps answer, the talking drum that accompanies the verse/song)*

They try to blow up
the world
Turn night
to poison
day to fire
But I am Man.

MAN:

> If the world survives
> A drummer
> must be in
> it!

WOMAN:

> Man.

MAN:

> Yes, they try
> to turn the world
> Back to animal
> rule
> Gorilla time
> Ape era
> Monkeys' business.

WOMAN:

> Even past that
> before that
> Crazier than that
> they in the past
> killing our future.

(The MONEY GODS' *laughter spits in eerily. Their faces for a second are creeping across a wall. Drum accompanying—drum popping.*)

MAN:

> And they here around us
> now. Blowing Mickey Mouse
> as vampire insect.

WOMAN:

> Yes, like they worship
> some hideous . . .
> Insects.

DRUMMER:

> Yes. I've heard
> recently the cries
> of Killer insects.

WOMAN:

> We've heard them
> praying in their

craziness—to insects
to be insects
and to kill off
human life.

DRUMMER:

No one can kill
life. It lives
Its heartbeat
is alive!

WOMAN:

Yes, you survive
the lonely darkness.

DRUMMER:

I am not alone
My name is Heart
I search for lovers—
like you

What's a drum
without a horn and
box.

(They laugh.)

I search for more life
to go with that
I've found.

MAN:

Life, out there, still?
More life?

WOMAN:

Life?

DRUMMER:

Every day, more life
We're hiding out there
Waiting for the air
to clear

A giant orchestra building
all of us, rainbow people

blowing more life in
the world.

WOMAN: *(Musing)*

Like there could be a world
after all.

MAN:

But that mad shit
we heard
that screeching
like Mickey Mouse
hatchet murder.

WOMAN:

Madness of the past
trying to kill
our future.

DRUMMER:

Yes, we know them
death figures
We heard you
Fighting them
Knew you was life
I come
You heard me
Coming.

(Drummer plays licks.)

MAN:

Life go on go on (Plays note of direction, then goes to the corner)
and look my man
Black Heart

(He uncovers yet another instrument, the bare frame of trap drums.)

Found these
Knew I'd need
some Heart music.

DRUMMER:

Heart Music!

(Rushes to set up.)

Heart here.
I need to call
some of the others
be with us
when the final
go down
go down.

WOMAN:

When the war
gon start
you need
your heart.

MAN: *(Touching her)*

Lover's music
the soul
of the
   World. . . .
      Naima, my name is . . .

(About to embrace.)

WOMAN: I know your name, Mtu. I know your name.

(They embrace. The screeching of the MONEY GODS *begins again. We see them. They look like they've been attacked, faces raw, wounded, background in shambles.)*

MAN: Get ready.

DRUMMER: *(Calls)*

Music lovers
Soul People
Heart Companions
Ready to Get Down.

WOMAN:

This the final go
Life or death.

(Kisses her partner, sitting at piano. But as MONEY GODS *begin their screech, Death Attack of the* MONEY GODS, *they look changed. Their faces are altering, changing to insects, large hideous insects, buzzing [violins], chirping, etc.* HAM *jerks around like some weird gorilla.)*

DRUMMER:

The Past versus
The Future!

WOMAN:

Yes.

DRUMMER:

Yet I am the past
that lives to be
future.

MAN:

But not
the dead past
the past of horror
terror
madness
stupidity
the past will
die and stay
dead.

WOMAN:

You are no past
man, you are
only tradition.

(MONEY GODS, *now raising their axes in combat. The Final Conflict.*)

DRUMMER: *(Calling to his Companions)*

Music Lovers
Heart Companions
Soul People!
All Who Love Life better than death!

(BLACK WOMAN, HEART'S WIFE, *a White and a Latino push warily through the door.*
They have instruments in their hands, the Life Orchestra formed meets this final challenge.
The Music War, a long final suite beginning with)

1. *Tension*
2. *Explosion*
3. *Terror*
4. *Death*
5. *Silence*
6. *Time*

But then, as a kind of Rebirth, like a history of music, the whole suite, but particularly
the Life Orchestra plays)

1. *Rebirth*
2. *New Life*
3. *Lovers*
4. *Sweet World*
5. *"Great Peace" [Reds and Blues]*

(The last music confrontation shows the insects turning in circles, made mad by the music, their monitors and machines smoking and exploding. MUSICIANs *finally are playing, embracing, and dancing life victory movement. Final chorus joins all together; they get audience to sing/chant gigantic):*

ALL:

> *YES TO LIFE!*
> *NO TO DEATH!*
> *YES TO LIFE!*
> *NO TO DEATH!*

(And at each chant, MONEY GODS *and* HAM, *dead feet straight up in air, shrink and die deader. And finally ending in unison joy laughing shouts)*

ALL: *(Continued)*

> *YES!*
> *YES!*
> *YES!*
> *YES!*

Afterword by Miguel Algarín

Part I: Theater by Poets

Allen Ginsberg wrote: "The Cafe is the most integrated place on the planet." That phenomenon, though, took some time to actualize and, initially, something of his presence. When we first started to work at the Nuyorican Poets Cafe, we were mainly serving a local community of working-class folk, mostly Puerto Rican, but it was clear from the beginning that the needs of the changing community would bring us a diverse clientele and, most important, the Cafe would become a place where everyone was welcome. It was exciting in 1974 and 1975 to serve a glass of beer or wine for fifty cents and to see the working-class factory laborer stop in because it was affordable, yet be surprised by a captivating person on stage reading poetry. It was new and the word spread throughout the Lower East Side, which we call "Loisaida."

Early on, Ginsberg caught sight of the Cafe while walking to the bank on Third Street and Avenue B. He appeared later that same night to check us out as well as the receptivity of the audience for poetry. On subsequent evenings he brought his friends William Burroughs, Gregory Corso, Lawrence Ferlinghetti, and an endless array of young protegés. We as Puerto Ricans had really not taken notice of the Beat Generation as such since our community was in the throes of both migration and survival. Soon after their appearance in the Cafe, we learned that the Beats had been challenging the citadels of mainstream literary culture.

Burroughs began to come in frequently. He read chapters from a novel he was working on at the time. I never knew what to expect except that somewhere around the seventh or eighth minute into his reading, the locals would catch on to his dry, pale-faced humor and erupt in a roar of laughter. Burroughs, who was not one for showing much external gratitude or expression of any kind, would develop a glint in his eye that made his reading even more alive. Burroughs lifted the words from the page in his voice that thoroughly enjoyed its theatrical powers. The magic enraptured the audience, and they always ended up laughing riotously. It was Burroughs who gave me the idea that the Nuyorican Poets Cafe could host a theater festival, and that poets could transfer their craft into theater.

From the same era as the Beats, Amiri Baraka, with his play *The Dutchman,* was the first of that generation of poets to put the racial crisis on stage. In preparation for the 1997 season, I asked Baraka what work he had available for theater. He said, "I've got plenty of work; what I don't get are productions." I thought it was time to stage Baraka's plays, starting with *Jackpot Melting: A Commercial,* written prophetically in 1989. Baraka positioned one actor at stage right and one at stage left with a screen drawn down. The audience was to experience the interactive moment involving television and computers, as they might in their daily lives. The couple, named Brother and Sister, have an imperfect relationship. They turn on the TV and find themselves in the altered state of "white-wash" that some African Americans undergo to make themselves network-cable ready. In *Election Machine Warehouse,* Baraka takes a scathing look at the New Deal, patriotism permeated by bigotry, and the biases that Kate Smith embodies. The play *Meeting Lillie* occurs during the 1940s with an African-American family traveling north to better themselves financially and socially. However, they discover racial tensions more demonic than the bald-face prejudice of the South. In both plays, Baraka reveals within the intimacy of a family setting the afflictions remaining from the slave era. In the play, unemployment plagues the social situation, stifling the natural human desire to pursue productive and creative endeavors. Baraka, wary of projecting political theory or using rhetoric in his plays, depends on his characters to speak directly to the audience. Every detail to the action must connect across the footlights.

The eternal problem is figuring out the potential audience. Who will come? How many? It didn't take long to face the fact that if we were to program daring theater with alternative visions, we would have to withstand playing to empty seats. Because I have read to many empty seats during my life, it really doesn't frighten me when Latino and African-American theater doesn't pull in its deserving audience. It only makes me work harder to cultivate an audience who appreciates the vision of these playwrights. The late Vivien Robinson, founder of the Audelcos, once said to me, "I don't want to be the only one sitting in the theater when this work is being performed. I have to do something about this." Vivien did. She set her mind to bringing African Americans into the theater. She felt that the plays staged by the Nuyorican Poets Cafe had to be experienced. With her presence came the audiences. She had a lot to do with defining the interactive relationship between actors and audience as it developed in our theater.

Part II: Theater Craft

There are plays not included in this anthology that were germinal to how we arrived at our aesthetic. Though we were making theater prior to 1969, it was very important when Joseph Papp gave me the use of 4 Astor Place as a studio for our theater rehearsals. At this time the theater was called El Puerto Rican Playwrights/Actors workshop. Papp saw to it that we could work undisturbed in this location away from the buzz that always surrounded his offices and the theaters across the street on Lafayette. It was during this period that Raymond Barry walked in the doors of 4 Astor Place and found us at work. By this time we had established our method. Andy and Willie, our martial arts instructors, conducted kung fu classes for two hours, in which the actors were expected to rigorously participate. The body had to be ready for the mind. If they are not in sync with each other, actors end up battering arms around or mouthing words that are disconnected from the body language. This results in futile histrionics. Raymond Barry walked in on us during these exercises. Since he had been associated with The Open Theater when it ended, he and the other actors were looking to see what they could find for work. As it turned out, he, for his part, brought us a wealth of ideas that he had developed as a member of The Open Theater, directed by Joseph Chaiken.

Chaiken's ideas about acting and the moral commitment of the actor to the audience and the self were grounded deeply in the person of Raymond Barry. With his presence, after the two hours of kung fu exercises, we'd cool down and ready ourselves for his input. Barry would sit back and begin to ask each actor to tell a story about their lives. At first a story might take fifteen, twenty, or thirty minutes to tell, but by the end of four or five workshops, the story would have been reduced to emblematic actions. The actor could now tell the story in all its complexity by going through the emblems that had surfaced by the telling and retelling of the story. This arduous process allowed for the unnecessary elements to fall away. The actors' stories underwent a miraculous condensation. This prepared them ultimately to tell the story in front of an audience, with decisive impact.

In 1973 during our martial arts exercises, an emissary from Joseph Papp brought in a handsome, fragile, yet mystically powerful man. He must have thought the El Puerto Rican Playwrights/Actors Workshop was a martial arts school. We continued our two-hour routine: we stretched, balanced, breathed, found chi, and directed the movement of it throughout the body. Actors need this capability when they project across the footlights. At the end of the exercises, Ray Barry and I moved aside as we always did to talk about the workshop. Our visitor questioned Willie and Andy about their techniques in taking amateurs through the difficult physical exercises. Then he introduced himself to Ray and me. Miguel Piñero. We knew that he had been in contractual negotiations with Joe Papp over his production of *Short Eyes*. He was being touted around town as the new word magician in theater. I was struck by the fact that I hadn't recognized him. Some years earlier Miguel had been incarcerated and I held the image of a younger carefree man. However, it soon became apparent that in prison he had developed his talent as a writer of poetry. He had turned to theater with the expert help of an enormously gifted director and actor, Marvin Felix-Camillo. Camillo was the founding director of a prison theater group called The Family. Miguel Piñero (we called him Miky) invited us out for a drink to discuss the possibilities of joining our workshop. We were anxious not to let him go, but we had only just begun our training session. Miky's eyes opened wide when we suggested he wait while we finished the workshop. Wiping his brow of sweat, he asked, "You mean it isn't done yet?" We explained our procedures for creating theater. Miky joined the circle and thus began a very important relationship with us. We ended up creating *Apartment 6D*, a combination of storytelling excerpts we had gleaned from our exercises in combination with my translations of Pablo Neruda, which were published in 1976 by William Morrow.

Miky moved into the group easily. From the start, he profoundly affected the character of our work. We strove to meld the personal and political, and this with our routine of exercises and storytelling created an aura of authority within the actors. Keeping the actors honest, open, and vulnerable was our mission. Learning words by rote from off the page would not produce live theater. The playwright, director, and poets worked with each actor individually, much like a musician tunes an instrument. People described our work as being intimate. *Apartment 6D* began a run that amazed us all with its range. When I stood back to watch this play with the Neruda poems throughout, and the force and clarity of the poet's stance vis-à-vis U.S. intervention in Central America, it occurred to me that we may have indeed learned to make a theater of ideas and political engagement intimate. If we had, it was due to the fact that the actors had completely internalized a script and integrated the dialogue with body movements.

In the early 1970s, we moved *Apartment 6D* to The Open Mind in Soho, when this area of Manhattan was still an artist haven. This was before the developers moved in to gentrify the art scene during the late 1980s and '90s. During this time, audiences cared about what they came to see. They left the theater fully engaged, having experienced a range of emotions. Ray Barry directed both the workshop and the plays with great subtlety and depth. His craft, originating as it did from Joseph Chaiken's rather elite improvisational techniques, was being tested nightly by a working-class group of actors who were savvy enough to make them their own.

We lost use of 4 Astor Place when Papp faced the first budget cuts. These were years of hardship and he could no longer afford to pay rent for this studio space, which included the use of three sub-basements. We had made the third sub-basement into a carpentry shop, the second sub-basement was for costume/wardrobe storage, and the first sub-basement stored our theater equipment.

Toward the end of our stay on Astor Place, Miguel Piñero and I felt the need to bring the work further into the streets. Somehow, all of the work so far had not touched the needs of the street. We wanted the depth of passion found among young people who were homeless, perhaps caught up by drugs or prostitution. There were plenty of runaways who might or might not find their way back home. We set out on an endeavor that still surprises me. Miky and I walked up and down Forty-second Street between Eighth and Seventh Avenues. We walked from Forty-second Street and Eighth Avenue to Fifty-seventh Street and back. We walked through the Port Authority Bus Terminal. We found children hanging out among the forgotten fire escapes of the terminal shaking with cold or sick from drugs. Some young girls were even servicing their johns for money to buy the next meal. It was a raw world that we had walked into.

We invited these young people to our workshop on Astor Place at the end of our occupancy, and then, it seems, by divine intervention, Samuel Rubin appeared. He offered us the unused theater in one of his buildings, which was on Thirty-sixth Street between Eighth and Ninth Avenues. Now, instead of worrying about whether or not the young people would bus downtown to the workshops, we were essentially taking the theater to them. A short walk and they were there. We asked them to let loose; to begin to explain their vagrancy or the abuse that had forced them into homelessness. We sought out the reasoning behind prostitution and it boiled down to drugs, food, and clothing. In short, we soon had a core of thirty-six runaways involving themselves in adult theater. As it turned out, maybe some of these teenage and preteenage youngsters just wanted a place to get out of the cold and rain, or to avoid harassment from the police. It was obvious that most of them wanted to escape the predators who wanted them for sexual pleasures.

Our first theatrical performance in Samuel Rubin's space was *Conga Mania* by Lucky Cienfuegos. The play depicted a street-hustling dice-wielding drifter poet who ends up being stabbed to death as he stacks the deck to win what was to be his last game. After *Conga Mania,* we produced *Sideshow,* which included the stories that these youngsters were eager to tell. After one of the young actors had interpreted the story improvisationally, he or she sat with Miky while he transcribed their monologues. Miky tightened the script and in turn the actors memorized their lines. When the untutored actors delivered these monologues, we were astonished with their passion.

Perhaps the audiences attending *Sideshow* expected to see a group of ghetto kids bettering themselves by way of theater. It is certain that they left reeling in these tales of street life and anger against a society that did not care about their waywardness. In this anthology, *Playland Blues* represents a play from this period. All of the characters came from this group of actors. Miky, for his part, never found an ending for the play. In a note to Joseph Papp, who wanted to stage *Playland Blues,* Miky wrote, "Joe—here it is. I can't find an ending." Piñero could not find a conclusion because in fact there would be no end to the hardships these actors faced on a daily basis.

Part III: Giving Ideas Voice

Ishmael Reed constructs metaphorical plays to depict what he observes. The audience deciphers what's going on in the performance to determine where in real life it applies. In *The Preacher and the Rapper,* we have a symposium of complex ideas played out theatrically. We are not being entertained by a slip on a banana peel or by the sudden opening of a trap door. We are made to laugh at ourselves and at the foibles abounding in government. Reed takes a futuristic look into an America driven mad by those who wield power. As a character in *The Preacher and the Rapper,* the Attorney General speaks out in an eloquent introductory monologue. The task of the performer is to absorb language and speak it out as his own in the persona of the character. A dramaturge seizes the language with the director, writer, and producer. Reed's vision is played out so that an audience member might say, "Yes, this is the potential United States twenty years in the future."

In *Savage Wilds,* Reed takes a satirical look at Washington, D.C., by focusing on its mayor, who becomes entrapped by his own weaknesses. The story is well known: the mayor is indicted and jailed for smoking crack with a woman in a motel. The Federal government pursues prosecution of the mayor as if he has no connection to the Halls of Power. Hilarious encounters occur between men with power, those who want more, and a Secret Service capable of suspending civil rights. Even though Reed's play depicts the mayor being brought to task for his wrongs, the system can't quite bury him. Would this have been believable had Ishmael Reed written about Mayor Berry's comeback before his reelection? More than likely not. But then, that is the playwright's work: to provide vision, and in this case, to satirize the conduct of the powers that be.

Reed's play *Hubba City,* in an empowering episode, depicts African-American seniors who take it upon themselves to confront the amoral dealers of contraband. The seniors create a vigilante group so they don't get run out of house and home; after all, they've labored to pay the mortgages most of their lives. In these efforts to maintain some sort of security for their old age, they discover rampant corruption from top to bottom. There's the twelve year old on the street with a 90-mm Uzi and the policeman who takes a payoff from a big-time pusher. The pusher knows the patched quilt full of holes that is the United States Customs Service, the CIA and the DEA. It is clear that no child can import Uzis or drugs and that African Americans are not the source for contraband. Again, Reed exposes the invisible structures of government and society that wield power over individuals. Most important, he suggests that people who get off their duffs to reclaim their neighborhood, if they come together, have a chance.

Performed in 1997 at the Nuyorican Poets Cafe, Reed's *The C Above C Above High C*, brings Louis Armstrong and Ike Eisenhower to the stage. The play opens with a monologue by Armstrong, who offers the reason for his perennial grin. Ultimately, the audience learns that his demeanor is a defense mechanism that disorients the powers that be, in this case, a five-star general. Over the course of the dialogue and action, the audience learns just how important jazz was in shaping the culture. Armstrong, a trumpeter, bandleader, and composer, came to be known as the ambassador of jazz while Ike was the five-star general who led the Allied forces to victory in WWII and then became president. It turns out that both Armstrong and Ike possessed the magnetism to hold their positions in the same all-encompassing society.

There were times when a play, such as *Nuyorican Nights* by Miguel Piñero, was difficult to stage, especially if the director asked for act two and Miky gave him a seven-page poem. I remember looking at Miky and saying: "This isn't a second act!" He looked back at me and said, "But it's in there." So I picked up a red pencil and reconstructed the poem as dialogue. Piñero was right! It took only fifteen minutes to make the seven-page poem into a bright, clean, clear, forceful dialogue that carried the play almost to its end. But not quite!

Those were the years of my friendship with Alvin Ailey—when it was alive and fresh. Alvin had just been moved into his swanky rehearsal spaces in Shubert Alley. He was moving about the city, more intoxicated with the promise of his new studio than he was taking care of himself. I remember how Alvin became so annoyed with the actors in rehearsal that it brought him to throwing objects from the second floor of the Cafe onto the stage. Alvin fumed, "You're not meaning what you're saying." Splat! A bottle of beer crashed. He never hit an actor; he only made them think twice about what they were mouthing. Another night Alvin was sleeping in his limo outside the Cafe when I found myself needing the ending to *Nuyorican Nights*. I had no idea how to finish it. All I knew was that Tom Waits's "Closing Time" would be the music. Alvin began to pound on the door. It was at this point that, as I told Jennifer Dunning for her biography of Alvin Ailey:

"I made a deal with Alvin that if I let him in he would move the cast around and I would send them home and we would go out and play." Algarín cued a song by Tom Waits called "Closing Time" and told Alvin to go to work. He began immediately to arrange people on the little stage and to tell them what to do. Algarín followed at his heels, pushing the dance captain to memorize every detail. Three minutes and twenty seconds later, at precisely the moment the song ended, Alvin finished putting together the dance that closed *Nuyorican Nights*. "I had tears in my eyes. I said, 'Oh Alvin, you ended the play!' He said, 'Good. Now send them home.'"*

Not all denouements arrive with such dramatic flair.

Part IV: Collaboration: Hit the Emotions!

The Nuyorican Theater Festival relies on scripts derived from writings by poets. I am not talking about "Poetic Theater" written elegantly and musically. I am talking about the plays that poets write when they are not making verse. Constructing theater from poetry demands patience, of course, and an understanding of metaphor. Such plays usually arrive at full clarity when the poets' metaphors are not only visualized by actors, but rendered as emotions for the audience to experience.

Here, the role of the director is central. It is the director who knits the production into a seamless whole. Without a director, the collaboration that is theater lacks all the necessary mechanisms of cohesion. Rome Neal is our director. His responsibility is to bond the actor to the text. First, the language of the play must flow easily from the tongue. The actor is expected to gain complete domination over the words of the script for their translation into body movement. Second, the director guarantees that whatever the tongue utters, it comes from the insights and language of the script's poet-playwright. Rome Neal is a master at enhancing all the theatrical aspects of synchrony between body and mind, actors and script.

In the past and the present, great actors practice converting what they have memorized into physical gestures with a commitment to the spiritual and intellectual content of the play. If the mind becomes illuminated in the act of speaking, the actor seizes upon a feeling that resonates throughout the body before it crosses the footlights. Hitting the feeling is as important as memorizing words or conveying the distinct meaning of the memorized word. Hitting the feeling is the moment when the fourth wall falls away and the actor walks into the three-dimensional space that the play inhabits. Rome Neal continues his relentless approach until the actors integrate the three fields of action at once: the muscular, mental, and emotional. Repetition gets the actor to that magical moment of confluence, if the theater piece is to fly off the page, strike the stage, and be of some meaning beyond the footlights.

Because we are the house of poetry in Loisaida, we recognized the theatrical advantage: poets, on a nightly basis, exercise their motor energy to ignite feelings among the listeners. Night after night, words magically arise from the pages of poets who don't profess to be actors or dancers. As wordsmiths, they facilitate cognition by creating patterns of sound from language. Their ultimate objective is to produce feeling that validates the thoughts borne from the mind. The poets, as it turns out, show little patience with actors who cannot fully realize these transitions. Ultimately, both audience and actor know when they fail to achieve the clarity they desire. At this moment, either the writer or the director steps in to refocus on the objectives of the process. A

*Jennifer Dunning, *Alvin Ailey: A Life in Dance* (New York: Addison Wesley), 1996.

great deal of trust develops as the writer, director, actors, and producer shape theater written by poets.

Sometimes it appears to be dangerous to stage a performance at the Nuyorican Poets Cafe and have an anti–Puerto Rican joke or remark stereotyping Nuyoricans as "spics." Invariably, the audience is shocked because they expect a theater free of the daily stereotypes. However, different perspectives offer insights to a community. Pete Spiro, in *How Ya Doin' Frankie Banana* presents young Italians in their ambience as they express fear and passion, and at the same time, reveal how completely encased they are by their own reality. They speak of "spics," "niggers," and "kykes" as if they know such people. They do, however, expose who they are themselves—small-time crooks or wanna-be third-rate lieutenants to a second-rate capo deep into organized crime. If the audience can withstand the initial onslaught of racial slurs peppering the dialogue, they ultimately come to an understanding of some aspects of life experienced by Italian youth of Bensonhurst. The audience witnesses the developing truism that it's wise to check out role models—in this play, the bosses of crime.

Part V: Motives: Objects in the Mirror

At the beginning, the voice of a theater piece is never apparent. It is a composite of all the elements that simultaneously work together as an audience watches. This dynamic carried Alvin Eng's *The Goong Hay Kid*. His protagonist, in efforts to become a punk rock 'n' roll rapper, is confronted by the venom of the dominant society. He doesn't fit into the box labeled "model minority." Interestingly, the actors in the auditioning process also confronted similar dilemmas that would characterize their roles. They heard voices off-stage shouting, "You're acting like a stereotype!"

The protagonist prevails upon the audience to accept his sincere desire to become a great punk-rock rapper. That's the motive. He chooses a genre of music that is indisputably a creation of African-American youth, but he doesn't want to be Black. Instead, he's at the center of a struggle that would have him wanting to assimilate, which conflicts with his effort at maintaining artistic integrity. Finally, it's apparent that the society at large offers little respect for his artistic endeavors.

Alvin Eng initially brought us the play with a cast and director. We informed him that we would consider the play but that we didn't take "packages." When the day of the play's reading arrived, Alvin brought with him his director of choice. As it turned out, this woman removed herself from consideration, creating a space for us to proceed with our in-house production. No amount of guessing can bare what is on a writer's mind. But somehow, I felt that the right decision had been made. Here, Rome Neal, an African-American director; Alvin Eng, an Asian-American writer; and I, a Puerto Rican producer, decided to begin work on preparing the play's performance. We were rewarded, especially toward the end of the run, by an audience that was increasingly more Asian. It was interesting night after night, as I introduced the director, to see this African American make his way up through the crowd to hear mutters of surprise from the audiences. Yes, once again we had angled the mirror in such a way as to reflect life in contemporary society without exploiting naïve racial categories.

In *Estorias del Barrio* we took four pieces written by Latino men and turned them over to four different Latina directors. We provided a workshop for the directors, led by Rome Neal, so that they might interpret the worlds created by men with insight and accuracy.

Conclusion: Assembling a Tradition

Is a season of plays a symposium of ideas? Can politicized drama play out against the events of the day? Can satire provide a ruthless evocation of the corruption of power in Washington, D.C.? Does looking at an Asian American evaluating assimilation into the American dream leave everyone in an audience with a little more understanding? We don't present plays about manners and gracious living. We don't assume the task, like that of religious theater in twelfth-century Spain, to convert the unbeliever. We are here dealing with the theater of the late twentieth century and the end of a millennium. In choosing these plays, the modus operandi has been to question whether the play delivers insights relevant to the current political, social, cultural, and sexual issues impacting our daily lives as this fin de siècle.

To plan a theater season takes a particular vision. The Nuyorican Poets Cafe Theater Festival has been in existence for close to thirty years and each season requires a central vision. What issue do we want to portray on stage? What motives are moving the current social tensions? And, ultimately, what intent lies behind the vision that incorporates five or six different staged plays into one season? In preparing the birth of a season, the questions continue to arise: Why, if the Nuyorican Poets Cafe is twenty blocks away from Chinatown, does it not have a regular Asian presence in the audience? What has happened to the great voices of the African-American stage? Is Baraka still writing for the theater? Why can't Ishmael Reed get produced? Is Ntozake Shange still producing her choreopoemes? And if so, does she have a choreopoem that will work with the voices of Reed, Baraka, or Pedro Petri? Do we want to stage Petri's *El Cabron,* a satirical look at the figure of "the macho" in a contemporary marriage? Answering these questions results in assembling compatible voices, the main responsibility of the producer. The plays are to recreate a social, contemporary image of ourselves that moves audiences or alerts them to the issues at hand. Plays also entertain, and no single performance satisfies all of our objectives, nor do they completely mirror the whole of our society. However, in searching for plays, we look for theatrical pieces that cleanly and clearly touch upon a major conflict without trying to size up the nation's most rampant complexities.

So much input comes together during the hour and a half from curtain up to curtain down. Costume, light, and sound designers, directors, choreographers, publicists, stage managers, technicians—they all create a part of the whole presentation that an audience experiences. It is by far the most complex art form that we produce at the Nuyorican Poets Cafe.

Another realization surfaces before each performance. We search to find what is "American" about us. Not the us as Nuyoricans, but the us as in the U.S. of A. We are constantly asking, Who is this "I" that becomes a "you" that eventually becomes an "us" and then a "we"? We consider the wonders of a national character and revelations by poets, and this collaboration might focus on domestic abuse, political aggression, economic deprivation, or sexual concerns. These are all issues that ignite many of our writers, who in turn create the narratives for our theater. Plays are stories. We don't discard traditions, but we define things according to our collective vision and integrate them into the theater that we present. We at the Nuyorican Poets Cafe enter each theater season knowing we approach the twenty-first century as Americans, all of us.

Contributors

Amiri Baraka has been a powerful force on American literature over the past forty years. He is a poet, playwright, and teacher. He emerged at a time when the Beat Poets were exerting their voice and he produced at that time such plays as *Dutchman* and *The Slave.* He has gone on to produce countless other works and an autobiography. The Nuyorican Poets Cafe has produced his: *Meeting Lillie, Jackpot Melting: A Commercial, General Hag's Skeezag.* He lives in Newark, New Jersey, with his wife, Amina Baraka, and is Professor of Africana Studies at the State University of New York at Stony Brook.

Wesley Brown is the author of one other play, *Boogie Woogie and Booker T.,* two novels, *Tragic Magic* and *Darktown Strutters,* coeditor of the multicultural anthologies, *Imagining America* (short fiction), and *Visions of America* (autobiography and essay), and the editor of *The Teachers and Writers Guide to Frederick Douglass.* He teaches literature and creative writing at Rutgers University. He would like to express his gratitude to all those who contributed to the original 1992 production of *Life During Wartime* at the Nuyorican Poets Cafe.

Janis Astor del Valle, Bronx-born, second-generation Puerto Rican lesbian, writer, performer, educator, is a member of the Primary Stages Writers and Directors Project and an actor/teacher for New York University's Creative Arts Team (CAT). Previously, Janis was a Van Lier Playwriting Fellow at Mabou Mines and a member of the Latino Writer's LAB at the Joseph Papp Public Theater. Her one-woman show, *Trans Plantations . . .* premiered at the Nuyorican Poets Cafe on May 16, 1996, under the direction and dramaturgy of Dolores Prida, with lights and sound by Pepe Burnette. Janis's other plays produced at the Nuyorican Poets Cafe include *Fuschia, I'll Be Home para la Navidad* (one-act version), and *Where the Señoritas Are,* which was co-winner of the Mixed Blood Theater's National Playwriting Contest in 1995. Excerpts of Janis's work appear in *Amazon All Stars: Thirteen Lesbian Plays* (Applause Books) and in *Torch to the Heart: Anthology of Lesbian Art and Drama* (Lavender Crystal Press).

Alvin Eng is a New York City–born and raised playwright, lyricist, and journalist. In addition to *The Goong Hay Kid,* his other works include the monologue plays *More Stories from the Pagan Pagoda* and *Over the Counter Culture,* books and lyrics for the musicals *The Last Hand Laundry in Chinatown* and *The Chinatown Bachelor Society,* and the libretto for the opera, *Mao Zedong: Jealous Son.* Eng's poetry and lyrics have been published in the anthology *Aloud: Voices from the Nuyorican Poets Cafe* and in *American*

Theatre Magazine, among others. His honors include fellowships from the New York Foundation for the Arts, the Corporation for Public Broadcasting, and The Harburg Foundation, among others. He holds an Master of Fine Arts in Musical Theater Writing from New York University and was named after the Chipmunk cartoon character.

Gloria Feliciano is the recipient of the Bronx Council on the Arts 1996 BRIO Fellowship Award for Playwriting and a poet. In addition to writing and directing *Between Blessings,* Ms. Feliciano made her directing debut in *Ricanstruction: Estorias from the Barrio,* which ran for a total of three months at the Nuyorican Poets Cafe and West End Gate. She also produced and wrote *Pittito Revolver: The Broadway 2 Mystery,* an interactive comedy show, which ran for two months at a New York nightclub. Among her other writing credits are *Zapatos Viejos,* a Spanish comedy, and various short stories. *Between Blessings* is a one-hour, forty-minute monodrama that ran for three weeks at the Nuyorican Poets Cafe in the summer of 1996 with Gilbert Arribas portraying all four characters.

Eva Gasteazoro is a Nicaraguan writer and performance artist living in New York City since 1983. Since coming to New York, Ms. Gasteazoro's work has been presented at Manhattan Theater Club, Dance Theater Workshop, Dixon Place, P.S.122, the Nuyorican Poets Cafe, the Whitney Museum at Philip Morris, the Public Theater, and numerous other venues in New York City, as well as in Puerto Rico, Mexico, Venezuela, Greece, and Nicaragua.

Lois Elaine Griffith is a writer living and working in New York City and is one of the founding directors of the Nuyorican Poets Cafe. Her plays, *Coconut Lounge, Dancehall Snapshots,* and *White Sirens* were produced by the Nuyorican Poets Cafe Theater Festival. *Hoodlum Hearts* was produced at Theater for the New City, also in New York. *White Sirens* was also produced by the late Joseph Papp at the New York Shakespeare Festival's Public Theater. She teaches English at the Borough of Manhattan Community College. Her novel, *Among Others,* is to be published by Crown Books. She is currently at work on another novel.

Dennis Moritz has written over thirty-five theater pieces, whose venues include BACA Downtown, the Joseph Papp Public Theater, St. Marks Poetry Project, Painted Bride Arts Center, Nuyorican Poets Cafe, Freedom Theater, and Movement Theater International. One of the original members of the Obie Award–winning New Works Project, he has been assisted by the NEA, NFRGP, TAPS, Pennsylvania Council on the Arts, and other granting agencies. His book *Something to Hold on to (Nine Theater Pieces)* was recently published by United Artists Books. In the past year and a half, he has collaborated with Michael LeLand, Shelita Birchett, and the Theater Double Ensemble on six projects produced in New York and Philadelphia.

Frank Perez was born in New York City of Puerto Rican parents. He has published two books for young people: a biography of the actor Raul Julia and another of the

United Farm Workers union activist Dolores Huerta. Both books are part of the series Contemporary Hispanic Americans, published by Rain Tree Stenk–Vaughn Publishers. Mr. Perez has trained with the Puerto Rican Traveling Theater's playwriting unit and was a member of the Intar Theater's Hispanic Playwrights Lab under the direction of Maria Irene Fornes. He is the cofounder of the Shaman Repertory Theater and the Puerto Rican Intercultural Drama Ensemble (PRIDE) Theater. He is also the director of the Obie-winning play, *El Cano/The Blond Man,* for the Spanish Repertory Theater. Mr. Perez's produced plays include: *Abuelita/Grandma, Next Stop: Suburbia, La Limpieza/The Spiritual Cleaning,* and *Enough Is Enough.*

Pedro Pietri is a native New Yorker born in Ponce, Puerto Rico in 1898 and 1943, who chose poetry over suicide thirty years ago. He's one of the original Nuyorican poets from Miguel Algarin's East Sixth Street poetry pad. He wrote his first play after enthusiastically watching a performance of *The Junkie Stole the Clock* by fellow insomniac Jesus Papoleto Melendez. His plays have been directed by the legendary Jose Ferrar and the notorious Juan Valenzuela.

Miguel Piñero was born in Puerto Rico and raised on the Lower East Side of Manhattan, and was cofounder, with Miguel Algarín, of the Nuyorican Poets Cafe. He was a prize-winning poet, playwright, and actor, and winner of New York Drama Critics Award for *Short Eyes.* He worked to develop TV's *Miami Vice* and appeared in countless other TV series and movies. He died in 1988.

Ishmael Reed is the author of eight novels, five books of poetry, four books of essays, two librettos, and four plays including *Mother Hubbard, Savage Wilds, The Preacher and the Rapper,* and *Hubba City.* His songs have been recorded and performed by Taj Mahal, Bobby Womack, Little Jimmy Scott, and Jack Bruce. Recent awards include: The George Kent Prize, for which Mr. Reed was nominated by Gwendolyn Brooks; The Sakai Kinu Award from the Osaka Foundation; and the 1995 Langston Hughes Poetry Award from the City College of New York. In May 1995, he was awarded an honorary Doctorate of Letters from the State University of New York.

Eugene Rodriquez is a poet, playwright, theater producer, and actor. He is a founding member of the Shaman Repertory Theater, and the executive director of the Puerto Rican Intercultural Drama Ensemble (PRIDE). As a playwright, Gene has been a member of the Puerto Rican Traveling Theater's (PRTT) Professional Playwrights Workshop for ten years. His play *Mambo Louie and the Dancing Machine* was a hit Off Broadway at the PRTT in June 1992. His short one-act play, *Un Ghost,* was produced by the Shaman Repertory Theater at the Julia De Burgos Theatro Cafe in El Barrio, and at the Henry Street Theater in Loisadia. *Un Ghost* along with *The King Is Dead* were given stage readings at the Stella Adler Theater in Hollywood as part of HBO's New Writers Workshop in July 1994. In October 1994, his one-act play *La Mariposa* was presented by PRIDE at the Nuyorican Poets Cafe as part of a one-act play festival entitled Ricanstruction: Estorias from the Barrio.

Carl Hancock Rux is a performance poet and writer. As a dramatist, his plays include, *Song of Sad Young Men, Geneva Cottrell, Waiting for the Dog to Die, Pipe: A Courtroom Drama, Singing in the Womb of Angels, Port Dream in the American House of Image,* and *Yanga (An Opera-Oratorio),* performed throughout the United States, Europe, and West Africa. Rux has also been commissioned to write poetry and text for modern dance for several contemporary companies, including The Alvin Ailey American Dance Theater, Jubilation!, The Urban Bush Women, and The Lulea Experimental Theater Festival in Sweden. Rux is the recipient of the 1994–1995 Fresh Poet Prize and the New York Dance and Performance Award (aka Bessie) for directing *Stained* by Lisa Jones and Alva Rogers.

Raúl Santiago Sebazco was born in Havana, Cuba, in May 1952 to Hilda Delgado and Raúl Sebazco. The family immigrated in 1955 to New York City. Mr. Sebazco studied filmmaking, theater, and photography and graduated in 1975 from New York University with a Bachelor of Fine Arts. He started working with the Nuyorican Poets Cafe in May of that year and directed various plays on its stage: *Gun Tower* by Miguel Piñero, *Piñones* by Tato Laviera, and *Burning* written and directed by Mr. Sebazco. He formed the Street Youth Theater in late 1979 directly out of his work in the Cafe. All the pieces featured theater kids whom he recruited from in and around the Cafe and were performed to a lively audience that came right from the community of Loisaida (the Lower East Side). Out of this effort, one acts such as *On the Corner, A Man and Wife, The World Condition, Encounters,* and *The Crime* were performed. His group of poetry-reciting and acting street kids eventually were invited to perform their works on numerous radio programs, at Princeton University and New York University, and, most important of all, on the university of the streets. Forty-second Street and Times Square was a favorite performance space for all these street plays. Mr. Sebazco later moved to Paris and directed various plays there from 1983 to 1987, where he formed the theater group Le Petit Théâtre de la Clef. Presently, Mr. Sebazco is writing a one-act musical based on the life of the Cuban poet Jose Marti and has recently signed a publishing and songwriting contract with Caliente/Warner Chappell. At the end of 1997 one of his songs will be recorded by MCA on Universal Records.

Ntozake Shange is a renowned playwright, best known for *for colored girls who have considered suicide/when the rainbow is enuf.* She is a poet (*Nappy Edges* and *The Love Space Demands*) and a novelist (*Betsy Brown, Sassafrass, Cypress and Indigo,* and, most recently, *Liliane*).

Peter Spiro. Plays produced include *The Juiceman Cometh* by Showtime Networks and *Act One* at the Met Theater in Los Angeles, California; a one-act version of *Woman in the Second Floor Window* was presented at BACA Downtown; *The Gift* was done by Theater for the Forgotten. His poetry has appeared widely in magazines and anthologies nationwide, including *Aloud: Voices from the Nuyorican Poets Cafe* and *The United States of Poetry.*

Glenn Wright was born in the Lower East Side of Manhattan in April 1960. The youngest of twelve born to the parents of Lummie May Moriss and Howard A. Wright, he attended Seward Park High School and graduated in 1979. In October of that year he met Raúl Santiago Sebazco at the Nuyorican Poets Cafe and, with Hondo Ramos and Willie Escobar under the direction of Mr. Sebazco, wrote the one-act street poetry play *On the Corner,* which was later performed at Symphony Space on Forty-second Street and Eighth Avenue to a live street audience of the famous area's underworld denizens (prostitutes, pimps, addicts, and dealers). The one-act play *The Crime,* which you find in this anthology, developed out of a story idea that Mr. Sebazco presented to Mr. Wright. A tape player recorded Mr. Wright's rhyme improvisations, which Mr. Sebazco transcribed on to the page with little rewriting. *The Crime* premiered, among other pieces of Mr. Sebazco's writing workshop, at Princeton University in May 1980 to an enthusiastic audience. It was performed by Street Youth Theater boys Mico Gonzalez, who played the mugger, and Carlos Ortiz, who played the victim. Glenn Wright, after going through a long personal nightmare of substance abuse, has through the grace of God found himself again and is presently writing a series of one-act plays based on his experiences. He wishes now to dedicate himself to writing and to the education of young people through poetry and theater as he experienced under Mr. Sebazco's direction. We wish Glenn much success.